Extraordinary Praise for Wilbur Smith

"Best historical novelist: I say Wilbur Smith, with his swashbuckling novels of Africa. The bodices rip and the blood flows. You can get lost in Wilbur Smith and misplace all of August."

—Stephen King

"Smith is at the top of his game in weaving exotic adventures."

—*Library Journal*

"Smith is a master." —*Publishers Weekly*

"Only a handful of twentieth-century writers tantalize our senses as well as Smith. A rare author who wields a razor-sharp sword of craftsmanship." —*Tulsa World*

"[Smith] paces his tale as swiftly as he can with swordplay aplenty and killing strokes that come like lightning out of a sunny blue sky."

—*Kirkus Reviews*

"Few novelists can write action scenes that all but leap off the page the way Smith can." —*The Anniston Star* (Texas)

"Each time I read a new Wilbur Smith [novel] I say it is the best book I have ever read—until the next one."

—*Times Record News* (Wichita Falls, Texas)

"Smith is a captivating storyteller." —*Orlando Sentinel*

"The world's leading adventure writer." —*Daily Express* (UK)

"Wilbur Smith rarely misses a trick." —*The Sunday Times* (UK)

"Action follows action . . . mystery is piled on mystery . . . tales to delight the millions of addicts of the gutsy adventure story."

—*Sunday Express* (UK)

THE SUNBIRD

WILD JUSTICE

Also by Wilbur Smith

THE COURTNEYS AND THE BALLANTYNES

The Triumph of the Sun

THE COURTNEYS

When the Lion Feeds

The Sound of Thunder

A Sparrow Falls

Birds of Prey

Monsoon

Blue Horizon

THE COURTNEYS OF AFRICA

The Burning Shore

Power of the Sword

Rage

A Time to Die

Golden Fox

THE BALLANTYNES

A Falcon Flies

Men of Men

The Angels Weep

The Leopard Hunts in Darkness

ALSO

The Dark of the Sun

Shout at the Devil

Gold Mine

The Diamond Hunters

Eagle in the Sky

Cry Wolf

Elephant Song

River God

The Seventh Scroll

Warlock

THE SUNBIRD

WILD JUSTICE

Wilbur Smith

THOMAS DUNNE BOOKS
ST. MARTIN'S GRIFFIN NEW YORK

THOMAS DUNNE BOOKS.
An imprint of St. Martin's Press.

www.thomasdunnebooks.com
www.stmartins.com

ISBN-13: 978-0-312-36682-7
ISBN-10: 0-312-36682-5

The Sunbird was originally published in Great Britain by Pan Books/Macmillan Publishers Ltd. in 1972.

Wild Justice was originally published in Great Britain by Pan Books/Macmillan Publishers Ltd. in 1979.

First St. Martin's Griffin Edition: September 2006

10 9 8 7 6 5 4 3 2 1

THE SUNBIRD

PART I

It cut across the darkened projection room and exploded silently against the screen – and I did not recognize it. I had waited fifteen years for it, and when it came I did not recognize it. The image was swirled and vague, and it made no sense to me for I had expected a photograph of some small object; a skull perhaps, or pottery, or an artefact, a piece of gold work, beads – certainly not this surrealistic pattern of grey and white and black.

Louren's voice, tight with excitement, gave me the clue I needed. 'Taken at thirty-six thou. at six forty-seven on the fourth of Sept,' that was eight days ago, 'exposed in a 35 mm. Leica.'

An aerial photograph then. My eyes and brain adjusted, and almost instantly I felt the first tickle of my own excitement begin as Louren went on in the same crisp tone.

'I've got a charter company running an aerial survey over all my concession areas. The idea is to pick the strike and run of geographical formations. This photograph is only one of a couple of hundred thousand of the area – the navigator did not even know what he was photographing. However, the people in analysis spotted it, and passed it on to me.'

His face turned towards me, pale and solemn in the glare of the projector.

'You can see it, can't you, Ben? Just off centre. Top right quarter.'

I opened my mouth to reply, but my voice caught in my throat and I had to turn the sound I made into a cough. With surprise I found I was trembling, and my guts seethed with an amalgam of hope and dread.

'It's classic! Acropolis, double enclosure and the "phallic towers".' He was exaggerating, they were faint outlines, indistinct and in places disappearing, but the general shape and configuration were right.

'North,' I blurted. 'Where is north?'

'Top of picture – he's right, Ben. Facing north. Could the towers be sun-orientated?'

I did not speak again. The reaction was coming swiftly now. Nothing in my life had been this easy, therefore this was suspect and I searched for the flaws.

'Stratification,' I said. 'Probably limestone in contact with the country granite. Throwing surface patterns.'

'Oh bull!' Louren cut in, the excitement still bubbling in his voice. He jumped up and strode to the screen, picked up an ebony pointer from the lectern and used it to spot the cell-like stippling around the outline of what he was pleased to presume was the main enclosure. 'You tell me where you've ever seen geographical patterns like that.'

I didn't want to accept it. I didn't want to make myself vulnerable again with hope.

'Perhaps,' I said.

'Damn you.' He laughed now, and the sound was good for he did not often laugh these days. 'I should have known you'd fight it. You are without doubt the most miserable bloody pessimist in Africa.'

'It could be anything, Lo,' I protested. 'A trick of light, of shape and shade. Even conceding that it is man-made – it could be recent gardens or agriculture—'

'A hundred miles from the nearest surface water? Forget it, Ben! You know as well as I do that this is the—'

'Don't say it,' I almost shouted, and was out of the padded leather chair, across the projection room and had hold of his arm before I realized I had moved.

'Don't say it,' I repeated. 'It's – it's bad luck.' I always stutter when I am excited, but it is the least of my physical disabilities and I have long ago ceased worrying about it.

Louren laughed again, but with the trace of uneasiness he shows whenever I move quickly or unleash the strength of my arms. He stooped over me now, and eased my fingers that were sunk into the flesh of his forearm.

'Sorry – did I hurt you?' I released the grip.

'No.' But he massaged his arm as he moved to the control panel and doused the projector, then turned the wall switch and we stood blinking at each other in the light.

'My little Yiddish leprechaun,' he smiled. 'You cannot fool me. You are wetting yourself.'

I looked up at him, ashamed of my outburst now, but still excited.

'Where is it, Lo? Where did you find it?'

'I want you to admit it first. I want you to go out on a limb for once in your life. I want you to say it – before I'll tell you another thing,' he teased.

'All right.' I looked away and picked my words. 'It looks, at first glance, quite interesting.'

And he threw back that great golden head and bellowed with bull laughter.

'You're going to have to do a lot better than that. Let's try again.'

His laughter I cannot resist, and my own followed immediately. I was aware of its birdlike quality against his.

'It looks to me,' I wheezed, 'as though you may have found – it.'

'You beauty!' he shouted. 'You little beauty.'

It was years since I had seen him like this. The solemn banker's mask stripped away, the cares of the Sturvesant financial empire forgotten in this moment of promise and achievement.

'Now tell me,' I pleaded. 'Where did you find it?'

'Come,' he said, serious again, and we went to the long table against the wall. There was a chart spread and pinned on the green baize. It was a high table, and I scrambled quickly onto a chair and leaned across it. Now I was almost on equal terms with Louren who stood beside me. We pored over the chart.

'Aeronautical Series A. Southern Africa. Chart 5. Botswana and Western Rhodesia.'

I searched it quickly, looking for some indication – a cross, or pencil mark perhaps.

'Where?' I said. 'Where?'

'You know that I've got twenty-five thousand square miles of mineral concession down here south of Maun—'

'Come *on*, Lo. Don't try and sell me shares in Sturvesant Minerals. Where the hell is it?'

'We've put a landing-strip in here that will take the Lear jet. Just finished it.'

'It can't be that far south of the gold series.'

'It isn't,' Louren reassured me. 'Throttle back, you'll rupture something.' He was enjoying himself tormenting me.

His finger moved across the chart, and stopped suddenly – my heart seemed to stop with it. It was looking better and better. The latitude was perfect, all the clues I had so painstakingly gathered over the years pointed to this general area.

'Here,' he said. 'Two hundred and twelve miles southeast of Maun, fifty-six miles from the south-western beacon of the Wankie game reserve, tucked below a curve of low hills, lost in a wilderness of rock and dry land scrub.'

'When can we leave?' I asked.

'Wow!' Louren shook his head. 'You do believe it. You really do!'

'Someone else could stumble on it.'

'It's been lying there for a thousand years – another week won't—'

'Another week!' I cried in anguish.

'Ben, I can't get away before then. I've got the Annual

General Meeting of Anglo-Sturvesant on Friday, and on Saturday I have business in Zürich – but I'll cut it short, especially for you.'

'Cut it altogether,' I begged. 'Send one of your bright young men.'

'When somebody lends you twenty-five million, it's only polite to go fetch the cheque yourself, not send the office boy.'

'Christ, Lo. It's only money – this is really important.'

For a moment Louren stared at me, the pale blue eyes bemused and reflective.

'Twenty-five million is only money?' He shook his head slowly and then wonderingly as though he had heard a new truth spoken. 'I suppose you are right.' He smiled, gently now, the smile of affection for a well-loved friend. 'Sorry, Ben. Tuesday. We'll fly at dawn, I promise you. We'll recce from the air. Then land at Maun. Peter Larkin – you know him?'

'Yes, very well.' Peter ran a big safari business out of Maun. Twice I'd used him on my Kalahari expeditions.

'Good. I've been on to him already. He will service the expedition. We will go in light and fast – one Land-Rover and a pair of three-ton Unimogs. I can only spare five days – and that's a squeeze – but I'll get a charter helicopter to fetch me out, and I'll leave you to scratch around—' As he talked Louren led me out of the projection room into the long gallery.

Sunlight spilled in through the high windows, giving good light to the paintings and sculptures that decorated the gallery. Here works of the leading South African artists mingled easily with those of the great internationals living and dead. Louren Sturvesant, and his ancestors before him, had spent money wisely. Even now in the urgency of the moment, my eyes were tugged aside by the soft fleshy glow of a Renoir nude.

Louren paced easily over the sound-deadening pile of Oriental carpets, and I matched stride for stride. My legs are as long as his and as powerful.

'If you turn up what we are both hoping for, then you can go in full-scale. A permanent camp, airstrip, assistants of your choice, a full crew, and any equipment you call for.'

'Please God, let it happen,' I said softly and at the head of the staircase we paused. Louren and I grinned at each other like conspirators.

'You know what it could cost?' I asked. 'We might be digging for five or six years.'

'I hope so,' he agreed.

'It could run into – a couple of hundred thousand.'

'It's only money, like the man said.' And again that great bull laugh started me off. We went down the staircase roaring and tittering, each in his own way. Elated and hyper-tense, we faced each other in the hall.

'I'll be back at seven-thirty Monday evening. Can you meet me at the airport, Alitalia flight 310 from Zürich? In the meantime you get your end arranged.'

'I'll need a copy of that photograph.'

'I've already had an enlargement delivered by hand to the Institute. You have got a week to gloat over it.' He glanced at the gold Piaget on his wrist. 'Damn. I'm late.'

He turned to the doorway at the moment that Hilary Sturvesant came through it from the patio. She wore a short white tennis dress, and her legs were long and achingly beautiful. A tall girl with gold-brown hair hanging shiny and soft to her shoulders.

'Darling, you aren't going?'

'I'm sorry, Hil. I meant to tell you I wouldn't be staying for lunch, but Ben will need somebody to hold him down.'

'You've shown him?' She turned and came to me, stooped to kiss me on the lips easily and naturally, with not the least sign of revulsion, and then she stepped back and smiled full into my eyes. Every time she does that she makes me her slave for another hundred years.

'What do you think of it, Ben? Is it possible?' But before I could answer Louren had slipped his arm about her waist and they both smiled down at me.

'He's doing his nut. He's frothing at the mouth and doing back flips. He wants to rush into the desert now, this minute.' Then he pulled Hilary to him and kissed her. For a long minute they were oblivious of my presence as they embraced. They are, for me, the epitome of beautiful woman and manhood, both of them tall and strong and well-favoured. Hilary is younger than he is by twelve years, his fourth wife and the mother of only the youngest of his seven children. In her middle twenties she has the maturity and poise of a much older woman.

'Give Ben some lunch, my darling. I'll be home late.' Louren pulled away from the embrace.

'I'll miss you,' Hilary said.

'And I you. I'll see you Monday, Ben. Cable Larkin if you think of anything special we will need. So long, partner.' And he was gone.

Hilary took my hand and led me out on to the wide flagged patio. Five acres of lawn and dazzling flowerbeds sloped gently down to the stream and artificial lake. Both tennis courts were occupied and a shrieking mob of small near-naked bodies thrashed the water of the swimming-pool to a sun-sparkled white. Two uniformed servants were laying out a cold buffet on the long patio trestle-table, and with a small squirming twinge of dread I saw a half-dozen young matrons in tennis dress sprawled in the lounging chairs beside the outside bar. They were flushed with exertion, perspiration dampened the crisp white dresses and they sipped at long dewy, fruit-laden glasses of Pimms No. 1.

'Come,' said Hilary, and led me towards them. I steeled

myself, trying to draw myself up to an extra inch of height as we moved towards the group.

'Girls – we've got a man to keep us company. I want you to meet Dr Benjamin Kazin, Dr Kazin is the Director of the Institute of African Anthropology and Prehistory. Ben, this is Marjory Phelps.'

I turned to each of them as she spoke their names, and I acknowledged the slightly over-effusive greetings, giving each my eyes and voice, they are my good things. It was as difficult for them as it was for me. You do not expect your hostess to spring a hunchback on you with the pre-lunch drinks.

The children rescued me. Bobby spotted me and came at a run, shrieking, 'Uncle Ben! Uncle Ben!' She flung her cold wet arms around my neck and pressed her sopping bathing-costume to my new suit, before dragging me away to become overwhelmed by the rest of the Sturvesant brood and their hordes of young friends. I find it easier with children; they either do not seem to notice or they come straight out with it. 'Why do you walk all bent over like that?'

For once I was not very good value, I was too preoccupied to give them my full attention – and soon they drifted away, all but Bobby – for she is ever loyal. Then Hilary took over from her stepdaughter and I was returned to the league of young mothers where I made a better impression. I cannot resist pretty women, once the first awkwardness wears off. It was three o'clock before I left for the Institute.

Bobby Sturvesant pours Glen Grant malt whisky with the same heavy thirteen-year-old hand she uses to pour Coca-Cola. Consequently I floated into the Institute feeling very good indeed.

The envelope was on my desk marked 'Private and Confidential' with a note pinned to one corner, 'This came for you at lunch-time. Looks exciting! Sal.'

With a quick stab of jealousy I inspected the seal of the

envelope. It was unbroken. Sally hadn't been into it – but I knew it must have taken all her self-control for she has an almost neurotic curiosity. She calls it a fine inquiring scientific mind.

I guessed she would arrive within the next five minutes so I found the packet of Three X peppermints in my top drawer and slipped one into my mouth to smother the whisky fumes before I opened the envelope and drew out the glossy twelve-by-twelve enlargement, switched on the desk light and adjusted it and the magnifying table lens over the print. Then I looked around at the hosts of the past that crowd my office. All four walls are lined with shelves, and from floor to shoulder height – my shoulder height – these are filled with books: the tools of my trade, all bound in brown and green calf-skin, and titled in gold leaf. It is a big room, and there are many thousands of volumes. The shelves above the books carry the plaster busts of all the creatures that preceded man. Head and shoulders only. Australopithecus, Proconsul, Robusta, Rhodesian Man, Peking – all of them up to Neanderthal and finally Cro-Magnon himself – *Homo sapiens sapiens* in all his glory and infamy. The shelves to the right of my desk are laden with busts of all the typical ethnic types found in Africa, Hamites, Arabs, pygmies, the negroids, Boskops, bushmen, Griqua, Hottentot and all the others. They watched me attentively with their bulging glass eyes as I addressed them.

'Gentlemen,' I said, 'I think we are on to something good.' I only speak aloud to them when I am excited or drunk, and now I was more than a little of each.

'Who are you talking to?' asked Sally from the doorway, making me leap in my seat. It was a rhetorical question, she knew damn well who I was talking to. She lounged against the jamb, her hands thrust deeply into the pockets of her grubby white dust-coat. Dark hair drawn back with a ribbon from the deep bulging forehead, large green eyes well spaced beside the pert nose. High cheekbones, wide sensual smiling mouth. A big girl with long well-muscled legs in the tight-fitting blue jeans. Why do I always like them big?

'Good lunch?' she asked, starting the slow sliding approach across the carpet towards my desk that would put her in position to check what was going on. She can read documents upside-down, as I have proved to my cost.

'Great,' I answered, deliberately covering the photograph with the envelope. 'Cold turkey, lobster salad, smoked trout, and a very good duck and truffles in aspic.'

'You bastard,' she whispered softly. She loves good food, and she had noticed my play with the envelope. I don't allow her to talk to me like that, but then I can't stop her either.

Five feet from me she sniffed, 'And peppermint-flavoured malt whisky! Yummy!'

I blushed, I can't help it. It's like my stutter – and she burst out laughing and came to perch on the edge of my desk.

'Come on, Ben.' She eyed the envelope frankly. 'I've been bursting since it arrived. I would have steamed it open – but the electric kettle is broken.'

Dr Sally Benator has been my assistant for two years, which is coincidentally the exact period of time that I have been in love with her.

I moved aside, making room for her behind the desk and uncovered the photograph. 'All right,' I agreed, 'let's see what you make of it.'

She squeezed in beside me, her upper arm touching my shoulder – a contact that shivered electrically through my whole body. In two years she had become like the children, she didn't seem to notice the hump. She was easy and natural, and I had a time-table worked out – in another two years our relationship would have ripened. I had to go slowly, very slowly, so as not to alarm her, but in that time

I would have accustomed her to the thought of me as a lover and husband. If the last two years had been long – I hated to think about the next two.

She leaned over the desk peering into the magnifying lens, and she was still and silent for a long time. Reflected light was thrown up into her face, and when she at last looked up her expression was rapt, the green eyes sparkled.

'Ben,' she said. 'Oh Ben – I'm so glad for you!' Somehow her easy acceptance and presumption annoyed me.

'You are jumping the gun,' I snapped. 'There could be a dozen natural explanations.'

'No.' She shook her head, smiling still. 'Don't try and knock it. It's true, Ben, at last. You've worked so long and believed so long, don't be afraid now. Accept it.'

She slipped out from behind the desk and crossed quickly to the shelf of books under the label 'K'. There are twelve volumes there that bear the author's name 'Benjamin Kazin'. She selected one, and opened it at the fly-leaf.

'*Ophir*,' she read, 'by Dr Benjamin Kazin. A *personal investigation of the prehistoric gold-working civilization of Central Africa, with special reference to the city of Zimbabwe and to the legend of the ancients and the lost city of the Kalahari.*'

She came to me smiling. 'Have you read it?' she asked. 'It's quite entertaining.'

'There's a chance, Sal. I agree. Just a chance, but—'

'Where does it lie?' she cut in. 'In the mineralized series, as you predicted?'

I nodded. 'Yes, it's in the gold belt. But it could, it just could, produce so much more than Langebeli and Ruwane.'

She grinned triumphantly, and bent over the lens again. With her finger she touched the indian ink arrow in the corner of the photo that gave the northerly bearing.

'The whole city—'

'If it is a city,' I cut in.

'The whole city,' she repeated with emphasis, 'faces north. Into the sun. With the acropolis behind it – sun and moon, the two gods. The phallic towers – there are four, five – six. Perhaps seven of them.'

'Sal, those aren't towers, they are just dark patches on a photograph taken from 36,000 feet.'

'Thirty-six thousand!' Sal's head jerked up. 'Then it's huge! You could fit Zimbabwe into the main enclosure half a dozen times.'

'Easy, girl. For God's sake.'

'And the lower city outside the walls. It stretches for miles. It's enormous, Ben – but I wonder why it's crescent-shaped like that?' She straightened up, and for the first time – the very first wonderful time – she spontaneously threw her arms around my neck and hugged me. 'Oh, I'm so excited, I could die. When do we leave?'

I didn't answer, I hardly heard the question, I just stood there and revelled in the feel of her big warm breasts pressing against me.

'When?' she asked again, pulling back to look into my face.

'What?' I asked. 'What did you say?' I was both blushing and stuttering – and she laughed.

'When do we leave, Ben? When are we going to find your lost city?'

'Well,' I considered how to phrase it delicately, 'Louren Sturvesant and I will go in first. We leave on Tuesday. Louren didn't mention an assistant – so I don't think you will be coming along on the recce.'

Sally stepped back and placing her clenched fists on her hips, she looked at me unkindly and asked with deceptive gentleness: 'Do you want to bet on that?'

I like reasonable odds when I do bet, so I told Sally to pack. A week was too long for the job, for she is a professional and travels light. Her personal effects filled a single small valise and a shoulder-strapped carry-all. Her sketch-books, and paints, were more bulky, but we pooled our books to avoid duplication. My photographic equipment was another big item, and then the sample bags and boxes together with my one canvas case made a formidable pile in the corner of my office. We were ready in twenty-four hours, and for the next six days we killed time by arguing, agonizing, squabbling and poring over the photograph which was starting to lose a little of its gloss. When our tensions built up to explosion point, then Sally would lock herself in her own office and try to work on the translation of the rock-engraving from Drie Koppen or the painted symbols from the Witte Berg. Rock-paintings, engravings and the translation of the ancient writings are her speciality.

I would wander fretfully around the public rooms, trying to find dust on the exhibits, dreaming up some novel way of displaying the treasures that filled our warehouse and upstairs store-rooms, counting the names in the visitors' book, playing guide to parties of schoolchildren – doing anything but work. Finally I would go upstairs to tap on Sally's door. Sometimes it was, 'Come in, Ben.' And then again it might be, 'I'm busy. What do you want?' Then I would drift through to spend an hour in the African languages section with my dour giant, Timothy Mageba.

Timothy started at the Institute as a sweeper and cleaner; that was twelve years ago. It took me six months to discover that apart from his own southern Sotho he spoke sixteen other dialects. I taught him to speak English fluently in eighteen months, to write it in two years. He matriculated two years later, graduated Bachelor of Arts in another three, Master's degree in the required further two years – and he is working on his doctorate in African languages.

He now speaks nineteen languages including English, which is one more than I do, and he is the only man I know, apart from myself – spent nine months in the desert, living with the little yellow men – who speaks the dialects of both the northern and Kalahari bushmen.

For a linguist, he is a peculiarly silent man. When he does speak it is in *basso profundo* which matches well his enormous frame. He stands six foot five inches tall and he is muscled like a professional wrestler and yet he moves with the grace of a dancer.

He fascinates me, and frightens me a little. His head is completely hairless, the rounded pate shaven and oiled to gleam like a midnight-black cannon ball. The nose broad and flat with flaring nostrils, the lips a thick purple black and behind them gleam big strong white teeth. From behind this impassive mask a chained animal ferocity glowers through the eye slits, and once in a while flashes like distant summer lightning. There is a satanical presence about him, despite the white shirt and dark business suit he wears, and though for twelve years I have spent much of my time in his presence I have never fathomed the dark depths beneath those dark eyes and darker skin.

Under my loose surveillance he runs the African languages department of the Institute. Five younger Africans, four men and a girl, work under him and, so far, they have published authoritative dictionaries of the seven main African languages spoken in southern Africa. They have also accumulated written and taped material to keep them busy for the next seven years.

On his own initiative, with just a little of my help and encouragement, he has published two volumes of African history which have raised a storm of hysterical abuse from white historians, archaeologists and reviewers. As a child Timothy was apprenticed to his grandfather, the witch-doctor and historical custodian of the tribe. As part of his initiation into the mysteries his grandfather placed Timothy under hypnosis and taped the entire tribal history on his brain. Even now, thirty years later, Timothy is able to throw himself into a trance and establish total recall of this mass of legend, folklore, unwritten history and magical doctrine. Timothy's grandfather was tried by an unsympathetic white judge and hanged for his part in a series of ritual murders the year before Timothy had completed his training and been entered into the priesthood. However, his legacy to Timothy is a formidable mountain of material – much of it palpably spurious, a great deal of it unpublishable as being either too obscene or too explosive, and the remainder fascinating, puzzling or downright scary.

I have drawn on much of Timothy's unpublished material for my own book *Ophir* – particularly those unscientific and 'popular' sections which deal with the legend of the ancients, a race of fair-skinned golden-haired warriors from across the sea, who mined the gold, enslaved the indigenous tribes, built walled cities and flourished for hundreds of years before vanishing almost without trace.

I am aware that Timothy edits the information he passes on to me – some of it is too secret, the taboos which surround it too powerful to disclose to other than an initiate of the mysteries. I am sure that much of this withheld information relates to the legend of the ancients. I, however, never abandon my attempts to milk him.

On the Monday morning of Louren's return from Switzerland, Sally was so overwrought by the possibility that Louren would veto her inclusion in the preliminary expedition that her company was unbearable. To escape her and to kill the last long waiting hours, I went down to Timothy.

He works in a tiny room – we are a little pressed for space at the Institute, which is congested with neatly stacked pamphlets, books, folders, and piles of loose paper that reach almost to the ceiling – and yet there is room for my chair. This is a long-legged affair like a bar-room stool. For although my legs and arms are regulation size, or better, my trunk is squashed and humped so that from the seat of an ordinary chair I have trouble seeing over the top of a desk.

'Machane! Blessed one!' Timothy rose with his usual

greeting as I entered. According to Bantu lore those of us with club feet, albino pigmentation, squint eyes, and humped backs are blessed by the spirits and endowed with psychic powers. I derive a sneaky sort of pleasure from this belief, and Timothy's greeting always gives me a lift.

I hopped up on my chair, and began a desultory conversation which flicked from subject to subject and changed from language to language. Timothy and I are proud of our talents – and I suppose we do show off a little. There is no other man living, of this I am convinced, who could follow one of our conversations from beginning to end.

'It will be strange,' I said at last in I forget what language, 'not to have you along on a journey. It will be the first time in ten years, Timothy.'

He was immediately silent and wary. He knew I was going to start again on the lost city. I had shown him the photograph five days before, and had been pumping him steadily ever since for some significant comment. I changed into English.

'Anyway, you are probably not missing anything. Another groping for shadows. God knows there have been many of those. If only I knew what to look for.'

I broke off and froze with expectancy. Timothy's eyes had glazed. It is a physical thing, an opaque blueish film seems to cover the eyeballs. His head sinks down on the thick corded column of the neck, his lips twitch – and the goose flesh runs up my arms and the hair on the back of my neck fans erect.

I waited. As often as I had seen it I could never shake off the supernatural thrill of watching Timothy going into trance. Sometimes it is involuntary – a word, a thought will trigger it, and the reflex is almost instantaneous. Then again it can be a deliberate act of auto-hypnosis, but this involves preparation and ritual.

This time it was spontaneous, and I waited eagerly

knowing that if the material was taboo it would be but a few seconds only before Timothy broke the spell with a deliberate effort of will.

'Evil – ' he spoke in the quavering, high-pitched voice of an old man. The voice of his grandfather. A little spittle wet the thick purple lips, ' – an evil to be cleaned from the earth and from the minds of men, for ever.'

His head jerked, the conscious mind intervening, his lips worked loosely. The brief internal struggle – and suddenly his eyes cleared. He looked at me and saw me.

'I'm sorry,' he murmured in English, turning his eyes away now. Embarrassed by the involuntary display, and the need to exclude me. 'Would you like some coffee, Doctor? They have repaired the kettle at last.'

I sighed. Timothy had switched off, there would be no more communication that day. He was closed up and defensive. To use his own expression, he had 'turned nigger' on me.

'No thanks, Timothy.' I looked at my watch and slipped off the stool. 'Still some last-minute things to do.'

'Go in peace, Machane, and the spirits guide your feet.' We shook hands.

'Stay in peace, Timothy, and if the spirits are kind I will send for you.'

Standing on the rail of the coffee bar in the main hall of Jan Smuts Airport I had a good view of the entrance to the international terminal.

'Damn it,' I swore.

'What is it?' Sal asked anxiously.

'B. Y. M. – a whole platoon of them.'

'What are B. Y. M.?'

'Bright young men. Sturvesant executives. There, you see the four of them beside the bank counter.'

'How do you know they are Sturvesant men?' she asked.

'Haircuts, short back and sides. Uniforms, dark cashmere suits and plain ties. Expressions, tense and ulcer-ridden but poised to blossom as the big man appears.' And then I added in an unaccustomed fit of honesty, 'Besides, I recognize two of them. Accountants. Friends of mine – have to prise money out of them every time I want a roll of toilet paper for the Institute.'

'Is that him?' asked Sally, and pointed.

'Yes,' I said, 'that's him.'

Louren Sturvesant came out of the doors of the international terminal, the first of the Zürich flight through customs and immigration, the airport public relations officer trotting to keep pace with him. Two other B. Y. M. a pace behind him on either side. Probably a third taking care of his luggage. The four waiting men broke into smiles that seemed to light the hall and hurried forward in order of seniority for a brief handclasp and then fell into formation around Louren. Two of them running interference ahead of him, the others closing in at either hand. The public relations officer fell back bewildered to the tail of the field, and Anglo-Sturvesant drove across the crowded floor like an advancing Panzer division.

In their midst Louren stood out by a golden curly head, his sun-bronzed features grim in contrast to the artificial smiles around him.

'Come on!' I caught Sally's hand and dove into the crowd. I am good at this. I go in at the level of their legs – and the pressure from this unexpected level cleaves them open like the waters of the Red Sea. Sally ran through behind me like the Israelites.

We intercepted Anglo-Sturvesant at the glass exit doors, and I dropped Sally's hand to crack the inner circle. I broke through at the first attempt and Louren nearly tripped over me.

'Ben.' I saw immediately how tired he was. Pale beneath

the gold skin, purply smudges under the eyes – but a warm smile cleared the fatigue for a moment. 'I'm sorry. I should have warned you not to come. Something has come up. I am on my way to a meeting now.'

He saw the expression on my face, and clasped my shoulder quickly.

'No. Don't jump to conclusions. It's still on. Be at the airfield at five o'clock tomorrow morning. I'll meet you there. I must go now. I'm sorry.'

We shook hands quickly.

'All the way, partner?' he asked.

'All the way,' I agreed, grinning at the schoolboy inanity, and then they swept on by and disappeared through the glass doors.

We were half-way back to Johannesburg before Sally spoke.

'Did you ask him about me? Is it fixed?'

'There wasn't time, Sal. You saw that. He was so rushed.'

Neither of us spoke again until I turned into the grounds of the Institute and parked the Mercedes beside her little red Alfa in the empty car park.

'Would you like a cup of coffee?' I asked.

'It's late.'

'It isn't. You won't sleep anyway – not tonight. We could have a game of chess.'

'All right.'

I let us in at the front door and we went through the public rooms, crowded with glass cases and wax figures, to the private staircase that led to my office and flat.

Sal lit the fire and set out the chessmen while I made coffee. When I came back from the kitchen she was sitting cross-legged on a tooled leather pouffe, brooding over the ivory and ebony chessboard. I caught my breath at the fresh dimension of her loveliness that the light and setting presented to me. She wore a patchwork poncho, as brilliantly coloured as the Oriental carpets strewn on the floor about her – and the gentle sidelighting glowed on the soft sun-touched olive of her skin. Watching her, I thought my heart might burst.

She looked up with those big soft eyes. 'Come,' she said, 'let's play.'

If I can weather the storm of her first lightning, volatile attacks then I can smother and wear her down with pawn play and superior development. She calls it the creeping death.

At last she toppled her king with a little groan of exasperation and stood up to pace restlessly about the room, hugging her own shoulders under the vivid poncho. I sipped coffee and watched her with covert pleasure until suddenly she swirled and faced me with long legs astride and clenched fists on her hips, her elbows tenting the poncho around her.

'I hate the bastard,' she said in a tight, strangled voice. 'A big arrogant god-man. I knew the type as soon as I saw him. Why, in the name of all that's holy, does he have to come with us? If we make any significant discovery, you can guess who will hog all the glory.'

I knew immediately she was talking of Louren – and I was startled by the acid and gall in her tone. Later I would remember it, and know the reason. But now I was stunned and then angry.

'What on earth are you talking about?' I demanded.

'The face, the walk, the flock of idolaters, the condescending air with which he dispenses favours, the immense overpowering conceit of the man—'

'Sally!'

'The casual, unthinking cruelty of his presumption—'

'Stop it, Sally.' I was on my feet now.

'Did you see those poor little men of his – shaking with fright?'

'Sally, you'll not talk of him like that – not in front of me.'

'Did you see yourself? One of the gentlest, kindest, most decent men I have ever known. One of the finest brains I have ever been privileged to work with. Did you see yourself, scampering and tail-wagging – God, you were rolling on your back at his feet – offering your belly to be tickled—' She was almost hysterical now, crying, tears of anger running down her face, shaking, white-faced. 'I hated you – and him! I hated you both. He was demeaning you, making you cheap and, and—'

I could not answer her. I stood stricken and numb – and her temper changed. She lifted her hand and pressed it to her mouth. We stared at each other.

'I must be mad,' she whispered. 'Why did I say those things? Ben, oh Ben. I'm sorry. So very sorry.'

And she came and knelt before me, her arms went around my body and she hugged me to her. I stood like a statue. I was cold with fear, dread of what was to come. For although this was what I had long prayed for, yet it had come so suddenly, without a moment's warning, and now I had been thrust far beyond the point of no return, into unknown territory. Sally lifted her head, still clinging to me, and looked up into my face.

'Forgive me, please.'

I kissed her, and her mouth was warm and salty with tears. Her lips opened under mine, and my fear was gone.

'Make love to me, Ben – please.' She knew instinctively that I must be led. She took me to the couch.

'The lights,' I whispered harshly, 'please switch off the lights.'

'If that's what you want.'

'Please, Sally.'

'I will,' she said. 'I know, my darling.' And she switched off the lights.

Twice in the darkness she cried out: 'Oh, please Ben – you're so strong. You are killing me. Your arms are – your arms.'

Then not long after, she screamed, an incoherent cry without form or meaning, and my own hoarse cry blended with it. Then there was only the ragged sound of our breathing in the darkness.

I felt as though my mind had broken free from my body and floated in warmth and darkness. For the first time in my life I was completely at rest, contented and secure. There seemed to be so many first times with this woman. When at last Sally spoke, her voice came as a small shock.

'Will you sing for me, Ben?' And she switched on the lights on the table beside the couch. We blinked at each other, owl-eyed in the muted glow. Her face was flushed rosily, and her hair a dark unruly tumble.

'Yes,' I said, 'I want to sing.' I went through into my dressing-room and took the guitar from the cupboard, and as I closed the door there was my reflection in the full-length mirror.

I looked with full attention, for a stranger stood before me. The coarse black hair framed a square face, with dark eyes and girlishly long lashes, a heavy simian jaw and a long pale forehead. The stranger was smiling at me, half shy – half proud.

I glanced down the strange, telescoped body over which I had agonized since childhood. The legs and arms were over-developed, thick and knotted with slabs of muscle, the limbs of a giant. Instinctively I glanced at the body-builder's weights in the corner of the room – and then back to the mirror. I was perfect around the edges – but in the centre was this squat, humped, toad-like torso, covered in a shaggy pelt of curly black hair. I looked at that remarkable body, and for the first time in my life, I did not hate it.

I went back to where Sally still lay on the soft monkey-skin kaross that covered the couch. I hopped up, and squatted cross-legged beside her with the guitar in my lap.

'Sing sad – please, Ben,' she whispered.

'But I'm happy, Sal.'

'Sing a sad song – one of your own sad ones,' she insisted, and as I picked out the first notes she closed her eyes. I was grateful, for I had never had a woman's body to gloat over. I leaned forward and as I touched the singing strings, I caressed the long smooth length of her with my eyes, the pale planes and rounds and secret shadows. Flesh that had cradled mine – how I loved it! I sang:

'In the lonely desert of my soul,
The nights are long,
And no other traveller journeys there.
O'er the lonely oceans of my mind
The winds blow strong—'

And in a short while a tear squeezed out behind her closed lids for there is a magic in my voice which can call up tears or laughter. I sang until my throat was rough and my picking finger tender. Then I laid the guitar aside and went on looking at her. Without opening her eyes she turned her head slightly towards me.

'Tell me about you and Louren Sturvesant,' she said. 'I would like to understand about that.'

The question took me by surprise, and I was silent for a moment. She opened her eyes.

'I'm sorry, Ben. You don't have to—'

'No,' I answered quickly. 'I'd like to talk about it. You see, I think you were wrong about him. I don't think you can apply ordinary standards to them – the Sturvesants. Louren and his father, when he was alive, that is. My own father worked for them. He died of a broken heart a year after my mother. Mr Sturvesant had heard of my academic record, and of course my father had been a loyal employee. There are a few of us, the Sturvesant orphans. We have nothing but the best. I went to Michaelhouse, the same school as Louren. A Jew at a church school, and a cripple at that – you can imagine how it was. Small boys are such utterly merciless little monsters. Louren dragged me out of the urinal where four of them were trying to drown me. He beat the daylights out of them, and after that I was his charge. I have been ever since. He finances this Institute, every penny of it. At first it was something just for me, but little by little he has become more and more involved. It's his hobby and my life – you will be surprised how knowledgeable he is. He loves this land, just as you and I do. He is caught up in its history and future more than you or I will ever be—' I broke off, for she was staring at me in a way that seemed to pierce my soul.

'You love him, Ben, don't you?'

I blushed then, and dropped my eyes. 'How do you mean that—'

'Oh, for God's sake, Ben,' she interrupted impatiently. 'I don't mean queer. You just proved the opposite. But I mean love, in the biblical sense.'

'He has been father, protector, benefactor and friend to me. The only friend I've ever had. Yes, you could say I love him.'

She reached up and touched my cheek.

'I'll try to like him. For your sake.'

It was still dark when we drove in through the gates of Grand Central Airport. Sal was huddled into her coat, silent and withdrawn. I was light-headed and brittle-feeling from a night of love and talk without sleep. There were floodlights picking out the private Sturvesant hangar at the east end of the runway, and as we approached I saw Louren's Ferrari parked in his reserved bay, and beside it another half-dozen late model saloons gleaming in the floods.

'Oh God,' I groaned. 'He's got the whole team with him.'

I parked beside the Ferrari, and Sal and I began unloading our equipment from the boot. She picked up her easel and slung it over her shoulder, then with a huge folder of parchment in one hand and a box of paints in the other she ducked through the wicket gate into the hangar. I should have gone with her, of course, but I was so absorbed in checking my luggage that it was three or four minutes before I followed her. By then it was too late.

As I stepped through the low aperture into the brightly lit hangar, my stomach churned with alarm. The gleaming sharklike silhouette of the Lear jet formed a backdrop for a tension-charged tableau. Seven of Louren's bright young men clad in the regulation casual garb – smartly cut safari suits and fleece-lined car coats – stood in a discreet circle about the two protagonists.

Louren Sturvesant very rarely loses his temper, and when he does it is only after severe and prolonged provocation. However, in less than two minutes Sally Benator had managed to achieve what many experts before her had never accomplished. Louren was in a towering, shaking, tight-lipped rage, which had his seven B.Y.M. awed and slack-mouthed.

Sally had dropped her load of equipment on the concrete floor and was standing with clenched fists on her hips and bright explosions of colour burning in her cheeks, trading Louren glare for glare.

'Dr Kazin told me I could come.'

'I don't care if the goddam King of bloody England told you that you could come. I'm telling you that the plane is full – and that I have no intention of dragging a female with me on the first break I've had in six months.'

'I didn't realize it was a pleasure jaunt—'

'Will somebody throw this bitch out of here?' shouted

Louren, and the B.Y.M. roused themselves and made a tentative advance. Sally picked up the heavy wooden easel, and held it in both hands. The advance petered out. I scuttled into the void and grabbed Louren's arm.

'Please, Lo. Can we talk?' I almost dragged him into the flight office – although I thought I detected a twinge of relief from Louren as I rescued him.

'Look I'm terribly sorry about this, Lo. I didn't have a chance to explain—'

Five minutes later Louren strode out of the office, and without a glance at either Sal or the frozen group of B.Y.M., climbed into the jet and a moment later his head appeared beside that of the pilot in the window of the cockpit as he adjusted his earphones.

I went to the junior B.Y.M. and gave him the word of the law.

'Mr Sturvesant asked me to tell you to arrange a charter to Gaberones for yourself.' Then I turned to the others. 'I wonder if you could give us a hand with the luggage.'

While a gang of the most highly paid stevedores in Africa carried Sally's luggage, she preened with shameless triumph. I managed to whisper a harsh warning.

'Back seat,' I snapped. 'And try and make yourself invisible. You will never know how close that was. Not only did you nearly miss the trip, but you almost talked yourself out of a job.'

We had been airborne for ten minutes before the pilot came back along the aisle. He stopped beside us and looked at Sal with open admiration.

'Jesus, lady.' He shook his head. 'I would have given a month's salary not to miss that! You were great.'

Sally, who had been suitably subdued since my warning, immediately perked up.

'With boys that size I don't even spit out the bones,' she declared, and a couple of B.Y.M. who heard it swivelled in their seats with startled expressions.

The pilot laughed delightedly and turned to me. 'The man wants to speak to you, Doctor. I'll change places with you.'

Louren was chit-chatting with flight control over the radio, but he waved me into the co-pilot's seat and I squeezed behind the wheel and waited. Louren ended his transmission and turned to me.

'Breakfast?'

'I've eaten.'

He ignored it and passed me a leg of cold turkey, and a huge slice of chicken and egg pie from the hamper beside him.

'Coffee in the Thermos. Help yourself.'

'Did you get your £25 million loan?' I asked with a full mouth.

'Yes – despite a last-minute panic.'

'I didn't think you needed to borrow, Lo. Have you fallen on hard times?'

'Oil prospecting.' He laughed at my suggestion. 'Risk money. I prefer to gamble with other people's money, and play the certainties with my own.' He changed the subject smoothly. 'Sorry about the detour. I am dropping the boys off at Gaberones. They've got a series of meetings with the Botswana government. Routine stuff, just settling the details of the concession. Anyway, it's not too far off our course. Then we can press on alone.' He filled his mouth with turkey and spoke around it. 'Met. report is lousy, Ben. Thick cloud down on the deck over the whole northern area. Happens about once in three years that you get low overcast in the desert – but today's the day. Anyway we'll have a stab at picking up the hills and the ruins, no harm done if we can't though. We'll not learn anything more from the air.' He was relaxed and easy, not a trace of his early rage, he could switch it on or off as he wished, and we talked and laughed together. I knew his mood, it was holiday and release. He was truly looking forward to it.

Lost city or no lost city, it was an excuse to get out into the wild country that he loved.

'This is like the old days God. Ben. how long is it since we got away together? Must be all of ten years. Remember the canoe trip down the Orange River – when was that? 1956 or '7? And the expedition to find the wild bushmen.'

'We must do it more often, Lo.'

'Yes,' he said, really meaning it: as though he had a choice. 'We must, but there is so little time. It's running out so quickly – I'll be forty years old next year.' And his voice was wistful. 'God. If only we could buy time with money!'

'We've got five days,' I said, heading the conversation away from the quicksands, and he picked it up eagerly. It was another half an hour before he mentioned Sally.

'That assistant of yours, the prize fighter. What's her name?' And I told him.

'Are you having it away with her?' he asked. It was said so naturally, so casually, that for an instant I did not realize what had been said. Then I felt my vision blur with red rage, felt the blood pound in my temples and heat my throat and face. I think I could have killed him then, but instead I lied in a thick, shaken voice.

'No,' I said.

'Just as well,' he grunted. 'She's a wild one. Well, as long as she doesn't mess up the trip.' If only I had told him then, but it was too private a thing – too precious and fragile to despoil with words, especially the words he had chosen. Then the moment was passed, and I was sitting trembling and shaky as he talked on lightly about the five days ahead.

As we flew the cloud solidified beneath us, congealing into a dirty greyish blanket that stretched away in all directions to the horizon. We crossed the border between South Africa and the independent African state of Botswana. At Gaberones the ceiling was down to a thousand feet when we landed. Despite Louren's assurance that we would be speedily airborne once more, there was a deputation of senior government officials, and an invitation to drinks and food in a private dining-room of the airport. Hot, sticky weather with intent white faces talking softly and greedily to shiny intent black faces – all of them sweating in the heat and whisky fumes, and the thick swirls of cigar and cigarette smoke.

Three hours more before the Lear jet with just four of us aboard slashed up into the cloud cover, then burst through into the high bright sunshine.

'Wow!' said Louren. 'An expensive little party. That black bastard Ngelane has just raised the price of his honour by another 20,000. I'll have to square him, of course. He could squash the whole deal. It has to go through his ministry.'

Louren flew northwards with the map on his lap and a stopwatch in his hand. His eyes darted from compass to airspeed indicator and back to the watch.

'Okay, Ben. You'd better let Roger take over the controls. We'll go down into the porridge and take a look-see.'

With Louren and the pilot, Roger van Deventer, at the controls and Sal and I braced in the doorway of the cockpit behind them, the jet slanted down towards the floor of dirty cloud. A few wisps of the stuff flickered past and then suddenly the sun was gone and we were enfolded in the dark grey mist.

Roger was flying, his attention completely on the instrument panel, and as the needle of the altimeter slowly unwound I saw his hands tightening on the wheel. We dropped steadily lower through the grey filth. Now Roger pulled on the flaps and airbrakes and throttled back. The three of us staring forward and down for the first glimpse of the earth. Down we sank, and still down. The pilot's tension turned to active fear. I could smell it, the rank greasy tang of it. It was infectious. If he, the hardened fly-bird, was afraid, then I was prepared to be terrified. I knew suddenly that rather than risk Louren's wrath he would fly us straight into the ground. I decided to intervene, and opened my mouth. It was unnecessary.

'Overflown,' grunted Louren, checking the stopwatch. 'Ease up, Rog.'

'Sorry, Mr Sturvesant, there is no bottom to this stuff.' Roger said it like a sigh, and lifted the Lear's nose. He opened the throttle and let off the airbrakes.

'No go!' I murmured with relief. 'Forget it, Lo. Let's go on to Maun.'

Louren turned to look back at me, and instead looked into Sally's face. She stood behind his shoulder. I could not see her expression, but I could guess what it was by the tone in which she asked softly, 'Chicken?'

Louren stared at her a moment longer, then he grinned. I could have turned Sally over my knee and beaten that luscious backside to a pulp. The warm active fear I had felt the minute before, turned now to cold numbing terror for I had seen Louren grin like that before.

'Okay, Roger,' he said, slipping the map and stopwatch into the pocket beside his seat. 'I've got her.' And the Lear stood on one wing as he pulled her around in a maximum-rate turn. It was so finely executed that Sally and I merely sagged a little at the knees as gravity caught us.

He levelled out and flew for three minutes on even keel, retracing our course. I stole a glance at Sally's face. It was bright-eyed, and flushed with excitement – she was staring ahead into the impenetrable murk.

Again Louren banked the aircraft steeply and came out of the turn flying the reciprocal of our previous course and eased the nose downwards. This was no cautious groping with flaps and half throttle. Louren flew us in boldly and fast. Sally's hand groped for mine and squeezed. I was afraid and angry with both of them, I was too old for these children's games, but I returned her grip. As much for my own comfort as hers.

'Christ, Lo,' I blurted. 'Take it easy, will you!' And no one took the least notice of me. Roger was frozen in his seat, hands gripping the armrests, staring ahead. Louren was deceptively relaxed behind the controls, as he hurtled us into mortal danger – and Sally, damn her, was grinning all over her face and hanging on to my icy hand like a child on a roller coaster.

Suddenly we were into rain, pearly strings and snakes of it writhing back over the rounded Perspex windscreen. I tried to protest again, but my voice stuck somewhere in my parched throat. There was wind outside now. It buffeted the sleek gleaming body of the Lear, and the wings rocked. I felt like crying. I didn't want to die now. Yesterday would have been fine, but not after last night.

Before my own reflexes had even registered, Louren had seen the ground and caught the headlong plunge of the jet. With a soft shudder that threw Sally and me gently together he pulled us up level with the earth.

This was even more terrifying than the blind fall through space. The dark hazy outlines of the low scrubby tree-tops flicked by our wingtips close enough to touch, while ahead of us through the rain-mist an occasional big baobab tree loomed and Louren eased the jet over its greedily clutching branches. Seconds that seemed like a lifetime passed, then abruptly the filthy curtains of rain and cloud were stripped aside and we burst into a freak hole in the weather.

There before us, full in our path and washed by watery sunlight, stood a rampart of red stone cliffs. It was only the merest fleeting glimpse of red rock rushing down on us, then Louren had dragged the jet up on its tail and the rock seemed almost to scrape our belly as we slid over the crest and arrowed upwards into the clouds with the force of gravity squashing me down on buckling knees.

No one spoke until we had plunged out into the sunlight high above. Sally softly disengaged her hand from mine as Louren turned in his seat to look at us. I noticed with grim satisfaction that both he and Sally were looking slightly greenish with reaction. They stared at each other for a moment. Then Louren snorted with laughter.

'Look at Ben's face!' he roared and Sally thought that was very funny. When they finished laughing, Sally asked eagerly:

'Did anyone see the ruins? I just got a glimpse of the hills, but did anyone see the ruins?'

'The only thing I saw,' muttered Roger, 'was my own hairy little ring.' And I knew how he felt.

The cloud was breaking up by the time we reached Maun. Roger took us in through a gap and put us down sedately, and Peter Larkin was waiting for us.

Peter is one of the very few left. An anachronism, complete with fat cartridges looped to the breast of his bush jacket and his trousers tucked into the tops of mosquito boots. He has a big red beefy face and huge hands, the right index finger scarred by the recoil of heavy rifles. His single level of communication is a gravelly, whisky-raddled shout. He has no feelings and very little intelligence, so consequently never experiences fear. He has lived in Africa all his life and never bothered to learn a native language. He uses the lingua franca of South Africa, the bastard Fanagalo, and emphasizes his points with boots or fist. His knowledge of the animals on which he preys is limited to how to find them and where to aim to bring them down. Yet there is something appealing about him in an elephantine oafish way.

While his gang of hunting boys loaded our gear into the trucks he shouted amiable inanities at Louren and me.

'Wish I was coming with you. Got this bunch of Yanks arriving tomorrow – with a big sack of green dollars. Short notice, you gave me, Mr Sturvesant. But I'm giving you my best boys. Good rains in the south, be plenty of game in the area. Should run into gemsbok this time of year. And jumbo, of course, shouldn't be surprised if you get a simba or two—'

The coy use of pet names for game animals sickens me, especially when the intention is to blast them with a high-velocity rifle. I went to where Sally was supervising the packing of our gear.

'It's after one o'clock already,' she protested. 'When do we get cracking?'

'We'll probably push through to the top end of the Makarikari Pan tonight. It's about 200 miles on a fair road. Tomorrow we'll bash off into the deep bush.'

'Is Ernest Hemingway coming with us?' she asked, eyeing Peter Larkin with distaste.

'No such luck,' I assured her. I was trying to form some idea of those who were accompanying us. Two drivers, their superior status evident in the white shirts, long grey slacks and shod feet, with paisley-patterned scarves knotted at the throat. One for each of the three-ton trucks. Then there was the cook, carrying a lot of weight from his sampling, skin glossy from good food. Two gnarled and grey-headed gunboys who had jealously taken out Louren's sporting rifles from the other luggage, had unpacked them from their travelling cases, and were now fondling and caressing them lovingly. These were the elite and took no part in the frenzied scurryings of the camp boys as they packed away our gear. Bamangwatos most of them, I listened briefly to their chattering. The gunboys were Matabele, as was to be expected, and the drivers were

Shangaans. Good, I would understand every word spoken on this expedition.

'By the way, Sal,' I told her quietly, 'don't let on that I speak the language.'

'Why?' She looked startled.

'I like to monitor the goings-on and if they know I understand they'll freeze.'

'Svengali!' She pulled a face at me. I don't think I'd have laughed if anyone else had called me that. It was a bit too close to the bone. We went to shake hands and say goodbye to Roger, the pilot.

'Don't frighten the lions,' Roger told Sally. Clearly she had made another conquest. He climbed into the jet and we stood in a group and watched him taxi out to the end of the runway and then take off and wing away southwards.

'What are we waiting for?' asked Louren.

'What indeed,' I agreed.

Louren took the wheel of the Land-Rover and I climbed in beside him. Sally was in the back seat with the gunbearers on the bench seats.

'With you two – I feel a damned sight safer on the ground,' I said.

The road ran through open scrubland and baobab country. Dry and sun-scorched. The Land-Rover lifted a pale bank of drifting dust, and the two trucks followed us at a distance to let it settle.

There were occasional steep, rock-strewn dry river-beds to cross, and at intervals we passed villages of mud and thatched huts where the naked pot-bellied piccaninnies lined the side of the road to wave and sing, as though we were royalty. Sally soon ran out of pennies, throwing them to watch the resulting scramble, and clapping her hands with delight. When she started tossing our lunch out of the window I pulled my guitar from its case to distract her.

'Sing happy, Ben,' Sally instructed.

'And bawdy,' added Louren, I think it was to needle her, or perhaps test her.

'Yes,' agreed Sally readily. 'Make it meaty and happy.'

And I started with the saga of the Wild, Wild Duck, with Sal and Louren shouting the chorus at the end of each verse.

We were children going on a picnic that first day out, and we made a good run of it to the pan. The sun was a big fat ball of fire amongst the tattered streamers of cloud on the horizon when we came out on the edge of the pan. Louren parked the Land-Rover and we climbed out to wait for the trucks and stared out with silent awe across that sombre, glistening salt plain that stretched away to the range of the eye.

When the trucks arrived they spilled their load of black servants before they had properly stopped, and I timed it at seventeen and a half minutes to when the tents were pitched, the camp-beds made up and the three of us sitting around the fire, drinking Glen Grant malt on the rocks of glistening ice that dewed the glasses. From the cooking fire drifted the tantalizing smell of the hunter's pot as our cook reheated it and tossed in a dash more garlic and origanum. They were a good, cheerful gang that Larkin had given us and after we had eaten they gathered around their own fire fifty yards away and sweetened the night with old hunting songs.

I sat and listened half to them, and half to the involved and heated argument between Sal and Louren. I could have warned her that he was playing the devil's advocate, needling her again, but I enjoyed the interplay of two good minds. Whenever the discussion threatened to degenerate into personal abuse and actual physical violence, I intervened reluctantly and herded them back to safety.

Sally was staunchly defending the premise of my book *Ophir* that postulated an invasion of southern central Africa by Phoenician or Carthaginian colonizers in about 200 B.C. and which flourished until about A.D. 450, before disappearing abruptly.

'They were not equipped for a major voyage of discovery as early as that,' Louren challenged. 'Let alone a colonizing . . .'

'You will find, Mr Sturvesant, that Herodotus records a circumnavigation of Africa in the reign of King Necho. It was led by six Phoenician navigators as early as 600 B.C. or thereabouts. They started at the apex of the Red Sea and in three years returned through the Pillars of Hercules.'

'A single voyage,' Louren pointed out.

'Not a single voyage, Mr Sturvesant. Hanno sailed from Gibraltar to a point south in the west coast of Africa in about 460 B.C. a voyage from which he returned with bartered ivory and gold sufficient to whet the appetites of all the merchant adventurers.'

Still Louren attacked her dates. 'How do you get a date of 200 B.C., when the very earliest carbon-datings from the foundations of Zimbabwe are mid-fifth century A.D. and most of them are later?'

'We aren't concerned with Zimbabwe, but with the culture that preceded it,' Sally came back at him. 'Zimbabwe could have been built towards the end of the ancients' reign, probably only occupied for a short time before they disappeared; that would fit neatly with your carbon-dating of around A.D. 450. Besides the carbon-dating from the ancient mines at Shala and Inswezwe show results at 250 and 300 B.C.' Then she ended it with fine feminine logic. 'Anyway, carbon-dating isn't *that* accurate. It could be out by hundreds of years.'

'The mines were worked by the Bantu,' declared Louren. 'And Caton-Thompson – and of course, more recently, Summers – said—'

Fiercely she attacked Louren. 'Did the Bantu, who only probably arrived in the area about A.D. 300, suddenly conceive of a brilliant prospecting talent which enabled them to locate the metal lodes where not a scrap of it showed in the ore as visible gold or copper? Did they at the same time develop engineering know-how that enabled them to remove 250,000,000 tons of ore from rock at depth – remember they had never demonstrated these talents before – and did they abruptly forget or cease to use them for another thousand years?'

'Well, the Arab traders – they may have—' Louren began but Sally rode over him without a check.

'Why did they mine it at such risk and expenditure of energy? Gold has no value to the Bantu – cattle are their standard of wealth. Where did they learn how to dress and use rock for building? The Bantu had never done it before. Suddenly the art was fully fledged and highly skilled, and then instead of becoming more refined, the art *deteriorated* rapidly and then died out.'

With assumed reluctance Louren retreated steadily before her onslaughts, but he made his final stand when my own theory of incursion from the west instead of the east came under discussion. Louren had read the views and arguments of all my many detractors and critics and he repeated them now.

The accepted theory was that the point of entry was from the Sofala coast, or the mouth of the Zambezi. I had put forward the theory, based on the evidence of early texts and extensive excavations of my own, that a Mediterranean people left that sea through the Pillars of Hercules, and voyaged steadily down the western coast of Africa, probably establishing trading stations on the Gold, Ivory and Nigerian coasts, until their southward explorations led them into an unpeopled vacuum. I guessed at a river mouth long since dried and silted or altered in its course and depth in the present day. A river that drained what then would have been the huge lakes of Makarikari, Ngami, and others long since disappeared, shrivelled by the progressive desiccation of southern Africa. They entered the river, possibly the Cunene or the Orange, journeyed up it to the source, and from there sent their metallurgists overland to discover the ancient mines of Manica – and who knows but they discovered the diamonds in the gravel of the lakes and rivers, and certainly they would have hunted the vast herds of elephant that roamed the land. Sufficient wealth to justify the establishment of a city, a great walled fortress and trading station. Where would they site this city? Clearly at the limit of water-borne travel. On the shores of the furthest lake. Makarikari, perhaps? Or the lake that overflowed the present boundaries of the great salt pan.

Sally and Louren argued with increasing acrimony and bitterness. Sally called him 'an impossible man', and he countered with 'madam know-it-all'. Then suddenly Louren capitulated and the next minute all three of us were joyously anticipating the discovery of the lost city of Makarikari.

'The lake would have spread at least fifty miles beyond the boundaries of the present pan,' Louren pointed out. 'Only a hundred years ago Burchell describes Lake Ngami as an inland sea, and nowadays it's a puddle you can jump across without straining yourself. It's altogether probable that the ancient lake extended to the foot of the hills on which our ruins are placed. We have plenty of evidence of the gradual desiccation and drying up of southern Africa, read Cornwallis Harris' description of the forests and rivers which no longer exist.'

'Ben.' Sally grabbed my arm with excitement. 'The crescent-shape of the city, do you remember me puzzling on it? It could be the shape of the ancient harbour with the town following the shoreline!'

'God,' Louren whispered. 'I can hardly wait for tomorrow.'

It was after midnight, and the whisky bottles had taken a terrible beating before Louren and Sally went off to their tents. I knew I could not sleep so I left the camp, passing the fire around which lay the blanket-cocooned bodies of our servants, and I walked out onto the surface of the pan. The stars lit the salt a ghastly grey, and it crunched crisply with each pace I took. I walked for a long time, stopping once to listen to the distant roaring of a lion, from the edge of the bush. When I returned to the camp a lantern still burned in Sally's tent, and her silhouette was magnified against the pale canvas, a huge, dark portrait of my love. She was reading, sitting cross-legged upon her camp-bed, but as I watched she reached across and extinguished the lantern.

I waited a while, gathering my courage, then I went to her tent, and my heart threatened to hammer its way out of its malformed rib-cage.

'Sal?'

'Ben?' she answered my whisper softly.

'May I come in?' She hesitated before she replied.

'All right – just for a minute.'

I went into the tent, and in the gloom her nightdress was a pale blur. I groped for her face, and touched her cheek.

'I came to tell you that I love you,' I said softly, and I heard her little catch of breath in the dark. When she answered her voice was gentle.

'Ben,' she whispered. 'Dear, sweet Ben.'

'I would like to be with you tonight.'

And it seemed to me there was regret in her voice as she replied, 'No, Ben. Everyone would know about it. I don't want that.'

The morning started off as the previous day had ended. Everybody was in high spirits, laughing at the breakfast table. The servants sky-larked as they broke camp and repacked the trucks – and by seven o'clock we had left the road and were following the edge of the pan. The Land-Rover leading and the trucks following our tracks through scrub and rank grass, and across the dry ravines which meandered down to the pan.

We had been going for an hour when I saw a flash of pale movement among the trees ahead of us, and three stately gemsbok broke out onto the open pan and trotted in single file away from us. They moved heavily, like fat ponies, the pale mulberry of their coats and the elaborate black and white face masks standing out clearly against the grey of the pan surface.

Louren slammed the brakes on the Land-Rover, and with the smoothly executed timing of the professional the old Matabele gunbearer put the big .375 Magnum Holland Holland into Louren's hand and he was gone, running doubled-up behind the fringe of grass that lined the edge of the pan.

'Is he going to kill them?' asked Sally in her little girl voice. I nodded and she went on, 'Why – but why?'

'It's one of the things he likes doing.'

'But they are so beautiful,' she protested.

'Yes,' I agreed. Out on the pan, about six hundred yards from the Land-Rover, the gemsbok had stopped. They were standing broadside to us. Staring at us intently with heads held high, and long slender horns erect.

'What's he doing?' Sal pointed at Louren who was still running along the edge of the pan.

'He's playing by the rules,' I explained. 'It's an offence to fire within 500 yards of a vehicle.'

'Jolly sporting,' she muttered, biting her lip and glancing from Louren to the distant gemsbok. Then suddenly she had jumped from the Land-Rover and clambered up onto the engine bonnet. She cupped her hands around her mouth and yelled.

'Run you fools. Run, damn you!'

She snatched her hat and waved it over her head, jumping up and down on the bonnet and howling like a banshee. Out on the pan the gemsbok erupted into startled flight, galloping diagonally away from us in a bunch. I glanced at Louren's small figure, and saw him drop into a sitting position with elbows braced on his knees, head cocked over the telescopic sight. The rifle jerked, and smoke spurted from the muzzle – but it was a second or two before the flat report of the shot reached us. Out on the pan the leading gemsbok slid over his nose and rolled in a drift of white dust. Louren fired again, and the second animal tumbled with legs kicking to the sky. The last gemsbok ran on alone.

Behind me the old gunbearer spoke to the other in Sindebele. 'Hou! This is much man.'

Sally climbed down off the bonnet, and sat silently while I drove to where Louren waited. He handed the rifle to the gunbearer, and as I relinquished the wheel to him the bitter tang of burnt cordite filled the cab of the Land-Rover. He glanced at Sally. 'Thanks,' he said, 'I prefer a running shot.'

'Why didn't you kill all three of them?' Her tone was neutral, without rancour.

'You are only allowed two on a licence.'

'Christ,' said Sally in a voice that now reeked of anger and outrage, 'how bloody touching. It's not often you meet a true gentleman.'

And Louren drove us out to where the dead animals lay. While the servants skinned and butchered the carcasses, Sally remained in the back seat with her face averted, her hat pulled down low over her forehead, and her eyes glued to a book.

I stood beside Louren in the bright sunlight that was

intensified by the glare of the white salt surface, and watched the gunboys cut the incisions in the skin and flay the gemsbok with the skill of a pair of Harley Street surgeons.

'You might have warned me we had one of *them* on this trip,' Louren told me bitterly. 'Am I ever regretting having given in to you and letting her come along!'

I didn't reply and he went on, 'I've a bloody good mind to send her back to Maun on one of the trucks.' The suggestion was so unworkable that it didn't give me even a twinge, and Louren went on immediately, 'She's your assistant – try and keep her under control, will you!'

I moved away, giving him time to recover his temper, and took the map-case from the seat beside Sally. She didn't look up from her book. I walked around the vehicle and spread the aeronautical large-scale map on the bonnet of the Land-Rover, and within two minutes Louren was with me. Navigation is one of his big things, and he fancies himself no end.

'We'll leave the pan here,' he pointed to where a dry river-bed joined the eastern extremity of the pan, 'and strike in on a compass-bearing.'

'What kind of going will we meet, I wonder.'

'Sand veld, like as not. I've never been in there before.'

'Let's ask the drivers,' I suggested.

'Good idea.' Louren called the two of them across and the gunboys, who had by now finished the skilled work and were leaving the rest to the camp boys, joined us as was their right.

'This is where we want to go to.' Louren pointed it out on the map. 'These hills here. They haven't got a name marked, but they run in line with the edge of the pan, like this.'

It took a moment or two for the drivers to figure out their bearings on the chart, and then a remarkable change came over both of them. Their features dissolved into blank masks of incomprehension.

'What kind of country is it between the pan and the hills?' Louren asked. He had not sensed the change in them. The drivers exchanged furtive glances.

'Well?' asked Louren.

'I do not know that country. I have never heard of these hills,' Joseph, the elder driver, muttered, and then went on to give himself the lie. 'Besides there is much sand, and there are river-beds which one cannot cross.'

'There is no water,' agreed David, the second driver. 'I have never been there. I have never heard of these hills either.'

'What do the white men seek?' asked the old gunboy in Sindebele. It was obvious that maps meant nothing to him.

'They want to go to Katuba Ngazi,' the driver explained quickly. They were all convinced by now that neither Louren nor I had mastery of the language, and that they could speak freely in front of us. This then was the first time I heard the name spoken. Katuba Ngazi – the Hills of Blood.

'What have you told them?' demanded the gunbearer.

'That we do not know the place.'

'Good,' the gunbearer agreed. 'Tell them that there are no elephant there, that the wild animals are south of the pan.' The driver dutifully relayed this intelligence, and was disappointed in our obvious lack of dismay.

'Well,' Louren told them pleasantly, 'you will learn something today. For the first time you will see these hills.' He rolled up the map. 'Now get the meat loaded and let us go on.'

In five minutes the whole tone of the expedition had changed. Sally and the entire staff were all in the deepest depression. The smiles and horse-play were gone, there were sulky faces and meetings in muttering groups. The tempo of work dropped to almost zero, and it took almost half an hour to load the butchered gemsbok. While this was happening I led Louren away from the cluster of vehicles out of earshot and quickly told him of the exchange between the African servants.

'Hills of Blood! Wonderful!' Louren enthused. 'It means that almost certainly they know about the ruins – there is probably a taboo on them.'

'Yes,' I agreed. 'But now we are going to have to watch for attempts to sabotage the trip. Look at them.' We turned to watch the slow-motion, almost somnambulistic movements of our staff. 'My guess is that it's going to take longer to reach the Hills of Blood than we allowed for.'

We got off the pan once more, for the going is suspect with soft places beneath the crust that will bog a vehicle, and we followed the firm but sandy ground along the edge. We crossed another of the steep ravines, after having scouted for a place where the banks were flattened, and drove on for twenty minutes before we realized that neither of the trucks was following us. After waiting ten minutes, with both Louren and I fuming impatiently, we turned back and retraced our course to the dry river-bed.

One truck was hanging half over the edge of the ravine, one front wheel and one rear wheel not touching earth, but its belly heavily grounded. The other truck was parked nearby, and fourteen grown men were sitting or standing around in various attitudes of relaxation without making the least attempt to free the stranded truck.

'Joseph,' Louren called the driver. 'How did this happen?'

Joseph shrugged his shoulders disinterestedly, but he was having difficulty hiding his satisfaction.

'All right, gentlemen, let's get it out,' Louren suggested with heavy irony. Half an hour later, despite the ladylike efforts of all fourteen of them, and despite Joseph's hearty clashing of gears and desperate engine racing and stalling, the truck still hung over the edge of the ravine. Finally they all climbed out of the ravine and looked at Louren and me with interest.

'Okay, Ben?' Louren turned to me as he began to strip his bush jacket.

'All right, Lo,' I agreed. I was delighted to see how well Louren had taken care of himself. His body looked rock-hard, and denuded of fatty tissue. At six foot two, he carried a mass of muscle whose outlines beneath the skin were unblurred.

I kept my shirt on. My body, although it has the same utility as Louren's, is not so good to look at.

'Front end first,' Louren suggested.

The truck had been unloaded, petrol tank about half filled, I estimated the front end weight at a little over two thousand pounds. I windmilled my arms as I looked at the problem, loosening up cold muscles. The servants looked puzzled, and one of them giggled. Even Sally put aside her book and climbed out of the Land-Rover to watch.

Louren and I went to the front of the truck and stooped to it, placing our hands carefully, bending at the knee, spreading our legs a little.

'All the way, partner?'

'All the way, Lo.' I grinned back at him, and we began the lift. I started slow, just taking up the slack in my muscles, bringing on the strain evenly and letting it build up in shoulders, thighs and belly. It was a dead unmoving mass and I started to burn the reserves, feeling the tension turn to pain and my breathing start to scald my throat.

'Now,' grunted Louren beside me, and I let it all come, rearing back against it with my vision starting to star and pinwheel. It came away smoothly in our hands, and I heard the gasps and startled explanations from the watchers.

We lifted the front of the truck clear of the ravine, went around to the back and did the same there. Then we started to laugh, a little shakily at first, but building up to a full gale. Louren put his arm around my shoulder and led me back to face our retinue of retainers who were looking discomfited and uneasy.

'You are – ' Louren told them, still laughing, ' – a bunch of frail old women and giggling virgins. Translate that for them, Joseph.'

I noticed that Joseph gave them a correct rendition of this pleasantry.

'And as for you, Joseph, you are a fool.' Louren stepped away from me towards Joseph, one quick dancing step, and hit him with an open hand across the side of the head. The sound of it was shockingly loud, and the force of it spun Joseph fully around in a tight circle before throwing him to the ground. He sat up groggily, with a thin trickle of blood running out of the corner of his mouth where teeth had cut into the thick under lip.

'You see that I am still laughing,' Louren pointed out to his startled audience. 'I am not even angry yet. Think a while on what may happen to anyone who makes me really angry.'

The truck was reloaded with alacrity and we went on.

'Well,' said Sally, 'we can be sure of full co-operation for the rest of this trip. Why didn't the big white bwana use a sjambok, rather than soiling his hands?'

'Tell her, Ben.' Louren did not look around at either of us, while I told Sally quickly about the campaign of deliberate obstruction that we had run into.

'I'm sure Louren didn't enjoy hitting the man, Sal. But he ditched the truck deliberately. We've got three and a half days left to get to these Hills of Blood, and we can't afford any more tricks.'

Sally immediately forgot her concern for Joseph. 'Hills of Blood,' she gloated. 'My God, it conjures up visions of human sacrifice and—'

'More likely it's merely the red colour of the cliffs,' I suggested.

'And this taboo thing.' She ignored me. 'It must be because of the ruins! Oh God, I can feel it in my blood – temples stuffed with treasures, relics and written records of a whole civilization, tombs, weapons—'

'You will notice my assistant's unbiased, unromantic and thoroughly scientific approach,' I pointed out to Louren, and he grinned.

'It irks me like hell, but for once I feel the way she does,' Louren admitted.

'For once that makes you smart, dearie,' Sally told him tartly.

It was two in the afternoon before we reached the point on the eastern extremity of the pan where we were to cut off on compass for the hills, and almost immediately it became apparent that we would not reach them that day. The going was heavy, sand-veld clutched at the wheels of the vehicles and reduced our rate of progress to a low-gear slog. Half a dozen times the trucks bogged in the thick sand, and had to be dragged out by the four-wheel transmission of the Land-Rover. Each time this happened there was a profuse offering of apologies from the driver and crew concerned.

The sand had absorbed all traces of the recent rains, but they showed in the new growth of green that decked the thorn and acacia trees – and more dramatically in the display of wild flowers that were spread everywhere in carpets and thick banks.

Their seeds and bulbs had lain dormant for three long years of drought, waiting for this time of plenty – and now the bright crimson of King Chaka's fire burned brilliantly among the fields of Namaqua daisies. Star lilies, Ericas, golden Gazanias and twenty other varieties made a royal show, and helped to lessen the frustrations of our snail's progress.

At every enforced halt, I left the cursing and hustling to Louren, and wandered away from the vehicles with my camera.

Sunset found us still fifteen miles from the hills, and when I climbed into the top branches of the flat-topped acacia under which we camped, I could see their low outlines on the eastern horizon. The cliffs caught the last slanted rays of the sun, and glowed orange-red. I sat in the fork of the main trunk and watched them until the sun was gone and the hills melted into the dark sky.

A strange mood gripped me as I watched the far hills. A mystic sense of pre-destiny filled me with a languid melancholy – a sense of unease and disquiet.

When I climbed down into the camp, Louren sat alone by the fire, staring into the flames and drinking whisky.

'Where's Sally?' I asked.

'Gone to bed. In a sulk. We got into a discussion about blood sports and beating up blacks.' Louren glanced at her tent which glowed with internal lantern light. There was no singing from the servants' fire as Louren and I ate grilled gemsbok liver and bacon, washed down with warm red Cape wine. We sat in silence for a while after we had eaten, and finished the wine.

'I'm bushed,' Louren said at last, and stood up. 'I'll just call Larkin. I promised to check in every second night. See you in the morning, Ben.'

I watched him cross to the Land-Rover and switch on the two-way radio set. I heard Larkin's boozy voice through the buzz and crackle of static. I listened for a few minutes, while Louren made his report. Then I stood up also and moved away from the campfire.

Restless, and still under the spell of my mood of disquiet,

I wandered into the dark again. The gemsbok carcasses had attracted a pack of hyena to the camp, and they giggled and screeched out among the thorn trees. So I kept close to camp, passing Sally's tent and pausing for a while to draw comfort from her nearness, then walked on towards the servants' fire. My feet made no sound in the soft sand, and one of the old gunbearers was speaking as I approached. He had the attention of all the others who squatted in a circle about the low fire. His words came to me clearly, and stirred my memory. I felt the tingle of them run along my spine, and the ghost fingers stroked my arms and neck bringing the hair erect.

'This evil to be cleaned from the earth and from the minds of men, for ever.'

The words were exactly those that Timothy Mageba had spoken – the same words, but in a different language. I stared fascinated at the lined and time-quarried features of the old Matabele. It was as though he sensed my scrutiny for he looked up and saw me standing in the shadows.

He spoke again, warning them. 'Be careful, the spider is here,' he said. They had named me for my small body and long limbs. His words released them from the spell that held them, they shuffled their feet and coughed, glancing at me. I turned and moved away, but the old Matabele's words stayed with me. They troubled me, increasing my restless mood.

Sally's tent was dark now, and Louren's also. I went to my own bed and lay awake far into the night, listening to the hyenas and pondering what tomorrow would bring. One thing was certain, by noon we would know if the patterns on the photograph were natural or man-made, and with that thought I at last fell asleep.

We could see the hills from the front seat of the Land-Rover by ten the following morning. They showed orange-red beyond the tops of the taller acacias, stretching across our front, higher at the centre of our horizon then dwindling in size as they strung out on either hand.

I took over the driving from Louren while he pored over map and photograph, directing me in towards the highest point of the cliffs. There was a distinctive clump of giant candelabra euphorbia trees on the skyline of the cliff – and these showed up clearly in the photograph. Louren was using them to orientate our approach.

The cliffs were between two and three hundred feet high, their exposed fronts furrowed and weather-worn, rising almost sheer to the crests. Later I was to find that they were a form of hardened sandstone heavily pigmented with mineral oxides. Below the cliffs grew a small grove of big trees, and it was clear that there was underground water trapped there to nourish these giants. Their exposed roots twisted and writhed up the face of the cliff like frenzied pythons, and their dense, dark green foliage was a welcome relief from the drab greenish grey of the thorn and acacia. In a strip about half a mile wide, the ground before the cliffs was open and sparsely covered with a low growth of scrub and pale grass.

I threaded the Land-Rover through the scrub towards the cliffs in a silence which momentarily grew more strained. Closer we crawled towards the towering red cliffs, until we had to crane our necks to look up at them.

Sally broke the silence at last, voicing our disappointment and chagrin. 'Well, we should be within the great walls of the main enclosure now – if there was one.'

We parked at the foot of the cliff and climbed out stiffly to look around us, subdued and reluctant to meet each other's eyes. There was no trace of a city, not a single dressed block of stone, not a raised mound of earth nor the faintest outline of wall or keep. This was virgin African bush and kopje, untouched and unmarked by man.

'You're sure this is the right place?' Sally asked miserably, and we did not answer her. The trucks came up and parked. The servants climbed down in small groups, peering up at the cliffs and talking in hushed tones.

'All right,' said Louren. 'While they set up the camp we will scout the area. I will go along the cliff that way. You two go the other way – and, Ben, take my shotgun with you.'

We picked our way along the base of the cliff, through the grove of silent trees. Once we startled a small troop of vervet monkeys in the high branches and they fled through the tree-tops in shrieking consternation. Their antics couldn't raise a smile from either Sally or me. We paused to examine the cliff at intervals, but there was little enthusiasm or hope in our efforts. Three or four miles from camp we stopped to rest, sitting on a block of sandstone that had fallen out from the cliff face.

'I could cry,' said Sal. 'I really could.'

'I know. I feel the same way.'

'But the photograph. Damn it, there was definitely *something* showing. You don't think it's his idea of a joke, do you?'

'No.' I shook my head. 'Lo wouldn't do that. He was just as keen as we were.'

'Then what about the photograph?'

'I don't know. It was clearly some sort of optical illusion. The shadow from the cliff, and cloud perhaps.'

'But those patterns!' she protested. 'They are geometrical and symmetrical.'

'Light can play funny tricks, Sal,' I said. 'Remember that photograph was taken at six o'clock in the evening – almost sunset. Low sun throwing shadows, you could get almost any effect.'

'I think this is the most disappointing thing that has

ever happened to me.' She really did look as though she might burst into tears, and I went to her shyly and put one long arm around her.

'I'm sorry,' I said, and she pulled a face and offered her lips to be kissed.

'Wow!' she said at last. 'Dr Kazin, you do carry on!'

'You ain't seen nothing yet.'

'I've seen too much.' She broke away gently. 'Come on, Ben. Let's circle back to camp, away from the cliff. There may be something out there.'

We tramped slowly through the heat. The flowers were out here also, and I noticed the bees crawling busily into the blossoms, their back legs thick with yellow pollen. We found where the recent rains had scoured a shallow ravine, although there was no remaining trace of moisture. I climbed down into the ravine and examined the exposed layers of stone and earth. Three feet from the surface the pebbles were rounded and water-worn.

'Good guess, Sal,' I told her as I picked out a few pebbles and found the shell of a bivalve encrusted in the half-formed sandstone. 'That proves at least a little of our theory. At one time this was the bed of a lake – look.'

Eagerly Sal clambered down beside me. 'What is it?'

'A type of *unionidae*, fresh-water African mussel.'

'I wish,' said Sally, 'that it were something a little more exciting.' She dropped the ancient shell in the sand.

'Yes,' I agreed, and climbed out of the ravine.

My only excuse is that my reasoning was clouded by intense disappointment and my recent physical excitement with Sally. I do not usually behave in such a cavalier fashion with scientific clues. Nor do I usually miss as many as four hints in the space of an hour. We walked away without a backward glance.

The camp was fully set up and functioning smoothly when Sal and I trailed in, sweaty and dusty, and sat down to lunch of tinned ham and Windhoek beer.

'Anything?' asked Louren, and we shook our heads in unison and lifted our beer glasses.

'Warm!' Sally spoke with disgust at her first taste of the beer.

'Cook has got the refrigerator going. It'll be cold by tonight.'

We ate in silence until Louren spoke. 'I raised Larkin on the radio while you were away. He will send in a helicopter tomorrow. We'll have a last search from the air. That will settle it once and for all. If there's nothing doing, I will fly out. Some things are brewing back in Johannesburg, and there is only one passenger seat, I'm afraid. You two will have to bus out the hard way.'

It was at that moment that a deputation arrived, headed by Joseph, to tell us that some unknown and foolish person had left the taps open on four of the water tanks. We had thirty-five gallons of water between seventeen people to last the rest of the trip.

'Therefore,' added Joseph, with evident relish, 'we will have to leave this place tomorrow, and return to the nearest water on the Maun road.'

There were a few expressions of disgust at this latest, clearly deliberate setback, but none of us could work up any real anger.

'All right, Joseph,' Louren agreed with resignation. 'Break camp tomorrow morning. We will leave before lunch.' There was an immediate improvement in employer-employee relations. I even noticed a few smiles, and heard a little laughter from the cooking fire.

'I don't know what you two intend doing this afternoon,' Louren lit a cigar as he spoke, 'but I noticed elephant spoor when I did my little recce this morning. I'm taking the Land-Rover and the gunbearers. Don't worry if I don't arrive back tonight, we may get hung up on the spoor.'

Sally looked up quickly; for a moment I thought she was going to start her anti-blood sport campaign again, but instead she merely frowned and went back to her ham. I watched the Land-Rover drive off along the base of the cliff before I suggested to Sally:

'I'm going to try and find a path up to the top – do you want to come along?'

'Deal me out, Ben,' she answered. 'I think I'll do some sketching this afternoon.'

Hiding my disappointment as best I could, I set off along the base of the cliff, and within half a mile I had found a game trail leading into one of the bush-choked gullies that furrowed the face of red rock.

It was a steep climb and I toiled up with the sun burning onto my back and bouncing off the rock into my face. From cracks and crannies in the cliff-face an army of furry little rock rabbits watched my endeavours with avid interest. It was forty minutes before I came out on the top, my arms scratched by the thorny undergrowth of the gully and sweat soaking my shirt.

I found a good vantage point on the front edge of the cliff under the spreading shade of a giant euphorbia, and my first concern was to sweep with the binoculars for any trace of ruins. The thorn bush at the base of the cliff below me was fairly open and scantily grassed, and immediately it was obvious that there was no trace of any human habitation or cultivation. I shouldn't really have hoped for more, but disappointment gave a sickening little lurch in my guts. Then I dismissed it, and turned the glasses towards the camp far below. A Bantu was cutting firewood, and for a while I amused myself by watching the axe-stroke, then listening for the sound of the blow seconds later. I searched further from the camp and picked up Sally's rose-coloured blouse at the edge of the grove. She had obviously given up all hope of a major discovery and, sensible girl, was deriving what other enjoyment she could from the expedition. I watched her for a long time, trying to decide how exactly to proceed with my campaign to make her my own. I had spent one night with her, but I was not so naïve as to believe that this proved a breathless and undying passion on behalf of a sophisticated highly intelligent and extravagantly educated modern Miss. Angel that she was, yet I was pretty damned certain that my Sally had played the game with other men before Dr Ben stumbled starry-eyed into her bed. The odds were extremely high she had been motivated by respect for my mind rather than my body, pity, and possibly a little perverse curiosity. However, I was almost certain she had not found the experience too repulsive, and I had only to keep working on her to change respect and pity into something a little deeper and more permanent.

A good quiet sense of peace came over me as I sat there in the high kranz; slowly I realized that this whole journey had been worthwhile and I found myself wishing that I could stay longer at these haunting Hills of Blood, with their mystery and silent beauty. Sally and I together here in the wilderness where I could teach her to love me.

A flicker of movement in the corner of my eye made me turn my head slowly, and within six feet of where I sat a marico sunbird was sucking the nectar from the blossoms of a wild aloe, its metallic green head shimmering as it dipped the long curved bill into the fiery red blossoms. I watched it with an intense pleasure, and when it was gone on quick darting wings I felt as though I had missed something. The feeling became stronger, making me restless; there was a message somewhere that was trying to come through to me but it was being blocked. I let my brain relax, and had the feeling that it was just there at the very fringe of my conscious mind. Another second and I would have it.

Dull on the hot breathless hush of afternoon the double boom-boom of distant heavy gunfire jerked my attention away. I sat up and listened for another thirty seconds – then it came again, boom, and again. Louren had found his elephant.

I picked Sally up in the field of the binoculars. She had heard it also, and was standing away from her easel staring out into the bush. I stood up also, my sudden restlessness still persisting, and started down the cliff path again. I could not shake off the mood, and it grew stronger. There is *something* here, I thought, something strange and inexplicable.

'You and I are lucky, my friend,' Timothy Mageba had told me once. 'We are marked by the spirits and we have the eye within that can see beyond, and the ear that can catch the sounds of silence.'

It was cool now in the heavily shaded gully and my shirt was still damp with sweat. I felt the goose pimples rising on my skin but not entirely from the chill. I began to hurry, I wanted to get back to the camp and Sally.

For dinner that night we ate grilled elephant heart sliced thin and covered with a biting pepper sauce, served with potatoes roasted in their jackets. The beer was icy-cold as Louren had promised, and he was in an expansive mood. It had been a good day's hunt, fully compensating him for the other disappointments. Lying in the lantern light beyond the fire were four long, curved yellow tusks of ivory.

When Louren sets out to be charming, he is irresistible. Although Sally tried to maintain a disapproving attitude at first, she soon succumbed to his charisma and she laughed with us when Louren gave us the toast, 'To the city that never was, and the treasure we didn't find.'

I went to bed a little drunk, and I dreamed strange dreams – but I woke in the morning clear-headed and with an unformed sense of excitement buoying me, as though today something good was going to happen.

The helicopter came out of the south an hour before noon, drawn to us by the smudge fires of oil-soaked rag; it sank noisily down towards the camp on its glistening silver rotor, and raised a whirlwind of dust and debris.

There was a brief conference with the dark-haired young pilot, then Louren climbed into the seat beside him and the ungainly craft lifted into the air once more and began a series of sweeps along the cliffs, rising higher with each pass until it was a dark insect speck in the aching blue of that hot high sky. Its manoeuvres were so clearly indicative of failure that Sally and I soon lost interest and went to sit in the shade of the dining tent.

'Well,' she said, 'that is that, I guess.'

I didn't answer her, but went to the refrigerator and brought us each a can of Windhoek. For the first time in days the fabled Kazin brain began running on all cylinders. Thirty gallons of water shared between two persons meant a gallon a day for two weeks. Water? There was something else about water in the back of my mind. Sally and water.

The helicopter landed once more on the outskirts of the camp, and Louren and the pilot came to the tent. Louren shook his head.

'No go. Nothing. We'll have a bite of lunch and be on our way. Leave you to make the best of it home.'

I nodded agreement, not telling him my plans to forestall any argument.

'Well, Ben, I'm sorry about this. I just can't understand it.' Louren began building himself a sandwich of bread and cold slices of roast gemsbok fillet, smearing it with mustard. 'Anyway, it won't be the last disappointment we will ever have in our lives.'

Twenty minutes later Louren's essential luggage was packed in the helicopter and while the pilot started the motor we said our farewells.

'See you back in jolly Jo'burg. Look after those tusks for me.'

'Good trip, Lo.'

'All the way, partner?'

'All the way, Lo.'

Then he was ducking under the spinning rotor and climbing into the passenger's seat of the helicopter. It rose in the air like a fat bumble-bee and clattered away over the tree-tops. Bumblebee? Bee! Bee! My God, that was what had been niggling me.

Bees, birds and monkeys!

I grabbed Sally's arm, my excitement startling her.

'Sally, we're staying.'

'What?' She gaped at me.

'There are things here we've overlooked.'

'Like what?'

'The birds and the bees,' I told her.

'Why, you randy old thing,' she said.

We split the water fifteen to twenty gallons. That would give the servants a little over half a gallon a day each for two days, sufficient to get them out safely. Sally and I would have a full gallon a day for ten days. I kept the Land-Rover, making sure the petrol tanks were full, and there were twenty-five gallons in the emergency cans. I kept also the radio, one tent, bedding; a selection of tools including spade, axe and pick, rope, gas lanterns and spare cylinders, torches and spare batteries, tinned food, Louren's shotgun and half a dozen packets of shells, together with all of Sally's and my personal gear. All the rest of the equipment was loaded onto the two trucks and when the servants were all on board I took the old Matabele gunbearer aside.

'My old and respected father,' I spoke in Sindebele, 'I

have heard you speak of a great mystery that lives in this place. I ask you now as a son, and a friend, to speak to me of these things.'

It took him a few seconds to get over his astonishment. Then I went on to speak a sentence that Timothy Mageba had given me. It is a secret code, a recognition signal used at a high level among the initiates to the mysteries. The old man gasped. He could not question me now, nor ignore my appeal.

'My son,' he spoke softly. 'If you know those words then you should know of the legend. At a time when the rocks were soft and the air was misty,' an expression of the uttermost antiquity, 'there was an abomination and an evil in this place which was put down by our ancestors. They placed a death curse upon these hills and commanded that this evil be cleaned from the earth and from the minds of men, for ever.'

Again those fateful words, repeated exactly.

'That is the whole legend?' I asked. 'There is nothing else?'

'There is nothing else,' the old man told me, and I knew it was the truth. We went back to the waiting lorries and I spoke to Joseph first in Shangaan.

'Go in peace, my friend. Drive carefully and care well for those who ride with you – for they are precious to me.' Joseph gaped at me, his wits scattered. I turned to the camp boys and changed to Sechuana.

'The Spider gives you greetings and wishes you peace.' There was consternation amongst them as I used my nickname, but when they drove away they had recovered from the shock and were laughing delightedly at the joke. The trucks disappeared amongst the thorn trees, and the sound of their motors dwindled into the eternal silence of the deep bush.

'You know,' Sally murmured reflectively, 'I think I've been took! Here I am stranded 200 miles from anywhere with a man whose morals are definitely suspect.' Then she giggled. 'And isn't it lovely?' she asked.

I had found the spot on the top of the cliff where I could lean out over the drop, supported by a hefty young baboon apple tree, and obtain a good view of the rock screen on either side, as well as over the open plain below. Sally was down beyond the silent grove, and I could see her clearly.

The sun seemed at the right angle for her, although it was shining directly into my eyes. It was only ten or fifteen degrees above the horizon now and the golden rays brought out new soft colours from rock and foliage.

'Yoo hoo!' Sally's shout carried faintly up to me, and she held both hands straight up towards the sky. It was the signal we had evolved to mean, 'Come back towards me.'

'Good,' I grunted. She must have picked them up. I had explained to her carefully how to shade her eyes against the slant of the sun's rays and to watch for the arrow-straight flight of the tiny golden motes of light. It was an old trick used by bee hunters to find the hive, a bushman had taught it to me.

I pulled back from the cliff, and began working my way through the thorns and thick bush that clogged the crest. I had guessed where to begin the search, for the chances were enormously in favour of the hive being located in this tall wall of red rock with its many gullies and crevices, and now with Sally calling the range for me from below, it was only a matter of fifteen minutes before she windmilled her arms and I heard her call.

'That's it! Right under you.' Again I leaned out over the edge, and now I picked up the swift sunlit flight of the returning bees as they homed in on the cliff below me.

Leaning far out I could make out the entrance to the

hive; a long diagonal crack the edges of which were discoloured by old wax. It must have been an enormous hive, judging by the number of workers coming in, and by the extent of the waxing around the entrance. In such an inaccessible position it had probably remained undisturbed by man or beast for hundreds of years. A rarity in this land where honey is so highly prized.

I tied my white handkerchief to an overhanging branch to mark the spot and in the swiftly falling dark I went down to Sally on the plain. She was very excited by our small success, and we discussed the implications of it over our dinner.

'You are really quite clever, Doc Ben.'

'On the contrary, I was as slow as doomsday. I had to beat my head against all the signs for two whole days before I tumbled to it,' I told her smugly. 'The place is thick with birds, animals and bees, all of which must have a good permanent supply of surface water. There is supposed to be no permanent water for two hundred miles – well, that's wrong for sure.'

'Where will we find it, I wonder?' She was all big-eyed and enthusiastic again.

'I can't even guess, but when we do I promise you something interesting.'

That night when I came into the tent in my pyjamas, having modestly changed outside, she was already in her bed with the sheets up under her chin. I hesitated in the space between the two camp-beds, until with a mischievous grin she took pity on me and lifted the blankets beside her in invitation.

'Come to Mama,' she said.

In the chilly darkness before dawn I huddled in my leather jacket on the cliff above the hive, and waited for the sun. I was a very happy man again, some of my doubt dispelled during the night.

Down on the dark plain there was a flash of light. Sally

at her place beyond the grove again, probably lonely and a little scared in the African darkness with its night rustlings and animal cries. I flashed my torch down at her to reassure her, and the dawn started coming on quickly.

Dawn was a thing of soft pinks and roses, misty mauves and mulberry – then the sun burst up above the horizon and the bees began to fly. For twenty minutes I watched them to decide the pattern and purpose of their flight. There was a fan of workers winging wide out over the plain. These were the pollen-gatherers. I established this by leaning out and watching their return, through the binoculars, checking the bunches of yellow pollen on their hind legs as they alighted on the protruding bulge of the crack.

In so doing I discovered another pattern of flight that I might have missed. A steady stream of workers was dropping almost vertically down towards the dark foliage of the silent grove below me – and on their return there was no pollen on their legs. Water-carriers then! I signalled Sally in towards the base of the cliff; this morning our roles were reversed by the slant and angle of the sun's rays. After a while she waved to let me know she had spotted them, and I began the laborious climb down to the plain.

She had to point out to me the indistinct flight of bees down the cliff towards the grove, but even then the shadow cast by the cliff caused them to vanish before we could establish their exact destination within the grove. We watched them for thirty minutes, then gave it up and went into the trees to search at random.

By noon I could swear that there was no sign of surface water within the environs of the grove. Sally and I flopped down side by side with our backs to the sturdy trunk of one of the mhoba-hoba trees, the wild loquat tree that legend states the ancients brought with them from their homeland, and we looked at each other in despair.

'Another blank!' She was perspiring in a light dew across her forehead and temples and a dark curl was plastered to the skin. With one finger I pushed it gently back and tucked it behind her ear.

'It's here, somewhere. We'll find it,' I told her with the confidence I did not feel. 'It's got to be here. It just has to be.'

She was about to answer me, when I pressed my fingers to her lips to silence her. I had seen movement beyond the last trees of the grove. We watched the troop of vervet monkeys crossing the open plain at a gallop with their tails in the air. As they reached the grove they shot up the trunk of the nearest tree with comical relief. Their little black faces peered down anxiously from the massed green foliage, but they did not notice us sitting quietly at the base of the mhoba-hoba.

Confidently now they moved across the tree-tops towards the cliff, the big males leading with the mothers, with infants slung beneath their bodies, and the rabble of half-grown youngsters followed them.

They reached the top branches of a gargantuan wild fig tree, one of those whose roots and trunk were embedded in the vertical cliff wall of red rock, and whose branches spread wide and green fifty feet above the earth – and they began to disappear.

It was an astonishing phenomenon, sixty monkeys went into the tree and dwindled swiftly until the branches were deserted. Not a single monkey was left.

'What happened to them?' whispered Sally. 'Did they go up the cliff?'

'No, I don't think so.' I turned to her grinning happily. 'I think we've found it, Sal. I think this is it, but let's just wait for the monkeys to come back.'

Twenty minutes later the monkeys suddenly began reappearing in the branches of the wild fig again. The troop moved off in a leisurely fashion along the cliff, and we waited until they were all out of sight before we went forward.

The convoluted and massed roots of the wild fig formed a flight of irregular steps up towards the point where the trunk emerged from the cliff. We climbed up and began examining the trunk, working our way around it, peering up into the branches high overhead. The trunk was gigantic, fully thirty feet around, deformed and flattened by its contact with the uneven wall of red rock. Even then we might have missed it, had there not been a smoothly polished footpath leading into the living rock – a path worn by the passage of feet and paws and hooves over the course of thousands of years. The path squeezed between the gross yellow trunk of the wild fig, and the wall of rock. In the same manner as there is often a cave behind a waterfall hidden by the falling water so our wild fig screened the entrance.

Sally and I peered into the darkened recess behind the trunk, and then we looked at each other. Her eyes were sparkling bright and her cheeks flushed a dull rose.

'Yes!' she whispered, and I nodded, unable to speak.

'Come on!' She took my hand and we went in.

The opening was a long vertical crack in the cliff and good light came in from high above. Looking up I saw how the rock was polished by the paws of the monkeys who came in that way.

We moved on down the passage, the wall rising twenty feet on each side of us to a narrow vee of a roof. Immediately it was clear that we were not the first human beings that had entered here. The smooth red walls were covered with a profusion of magnificent bushman rock paintings. The most beautiful and well preserved that I had ever seen.

'Ben! Oh Ben! Just look at them!' One of Sally's specialities is bushman art. 'It's a treasure house. Oh, you wonderful clever man!' Her eyes shone in the gloom like lamps.

'Come on!' I tugged at her hand. 'There will be plenty of time for that later.'

We moved slowly along the narrow passage as it slanted steadily downwards for another hundred feet. The roof above us climbed progressively higher, until it was lost in the gloom above. We heard the squeak of bats from the dark recesses of the passage.

'There is light ahead,' I said, and we went on into an open chamber, rounded, perhaps 300 feet across with sheer walls which rose 200 feet upwards. Like the interior walls of a cone, they narrowed into a small aperture high above which gave a view of cloudless blue sky beyond.

I saw immediately that this was an intrusion of limestone into the red sandstone, and that it was a typical sink-hole formation, very similar to the Sleeping Pool at Sinoia in Rhodesia.

Here also the floor of the cavern was a basin which led down to a pool of water. The water was crystal clear, obviously very deep as the pale greenish colour showed, perhaps 150 feet across, the surface mirror-smooth and still.

Sally and I stood and stared at it. The beauty of this great cavern had paralysed us. Through the tiny aperture 200 feet above us the sun's rays poured in like the beam of a searchlight, striking the walls of shimmering limestone and lighting the entire cavern with an eerie reflected glow. From the arched roof and walls hung great butterfly wings and stalactites of sparkling white.

The walls of the main chamber were also decorated to a height of fifteen feet or more with the lovely bushman art. In places water seeping from the rock had destroyed the graceful figures and designs, but mostly it was well preserved. I guessed there was two years' work for Sally and me in this wondrous place.

Slowly she disengaged her hand from mine and walked

down to the edge of the emerald pool. I stayed where I was in the mouth of the tunnel, watching her with rapt attention as she stood at the edge of the pool and leaned forward to peer down into the still water.

Then she straightened and slowly, with deliberate movements, began to strip off her clothing. She stood naked at the edge of the pool and her skin was as pale and translucent as the limestone cliffs. Her body, for all its size and strength, had a delicacy of line and texture to it that reminded me of the Chinese carvings in old ivory.

Like a priestess of some old pagan religion, she stood beside the pool and lifted her arms. With a strange atavistic thrill this gesture brought to my mind an ancient forgotten ritual. There was something deep in me that I wanted to cry out, a blessing perhaps, or an invocation.

Then she dived, a long graceful curve of white body and flowing dark hair. She struck the water and went on down, deep. The sweet clean shape of her showed clearly through the crystal water, then she came up slowly from the depths and broke the surface. Her long dark hair was slicked down over her neck and shoulders, she lifted one slender arm and waved at me.

I felt like crying out aloud with relief. I realized then that I had not expected her to come up again from those mysterious green depths. I went down to the edge of the pool to help her out of the water.

Presently we moved slowly around the walls of the cavern and passage, awed by the profusion of paintings and engravings, Sally with her damp hair hanging to her shoulders and her face shining with wonder.

'There is work here spread over 2,000 years, Ben. This must have been a very holy place to the little yellow men.' The light failed before we had completed half the tour of the cavern, and it was chilly and scary in the passage as we groped our way out. It was only then that I realized we had not eaten that day.

While Sally warmed up a hash of bully beef and onions, I raised Peter Larkin on the radio and was relieved to hear that the two trucks had returned safely to Maun. I ended the transmission by asking Larkin to get a message through to Louren. 'Tell him we have found some very interesting rock paintings and will be staying on here indefinitely.'

'How are you for water?' bellowed Larkin, his voice distorted by static and Scotch whisky.

'Fine. We managed to find an adequate supply here.'

'You found water?' roared Larkin. 'There isn't any water there!'

'A small catchment in a rock basin from the last rain.'

'Oh, I see. Okay then. Keep in touch. Over and out.'

'Thanks, Peter. Over and out.'

'You are a fibber.' Sally grinned at me as I switched off the set.

'All in a good cause,' I agreed, and we began to prepare lanterns, and cameras, and sketching equipment for the following day.

The old bull elephant was mortally wounded. Blood, slick and shiny, poured from the wounds in throat and shoulder and the shafts of fifty arrows pincushioned his massive frame. He stood at bay, with his back humped in agony, while around him swarmed the brave little yellow hunters with drawn bows, and pelting arrows. A dozen of their number were strewn back along the path of the hunt, their frail bodies crushed and broken beneath the great round pads and cruel ivory shafts – but the others were closing in for the kill.

The ancient artist had filled his canvas of red rock with such movement and drama that I felt myself a witness to the actual hunt. However, the light was tricky and the best reading I could get was F.11. at 1/10th of a second.

Reluctantly I decided to use flash. I try to avoid it where possible for it tends to distort colour and throw in false highlights. I began setting up tripod and camera when Sally called.

'Ben! Come here, please!'

The echo effect and distortion caused by the lofty cavern could not disguise the urgency and excitement in her voice, and I went quickly.

She was in the main cavern beyond the emerald pool, where the rear wall cut back steeply to form a low recess. It was gloomy in there and Sally's torch beam jumped quickly over the smooth rock surface.

'What is it, Sal?' I asked as I came up beside her.

'Look.' She moved the torch beam down and I stared at the representation of a massive human figure before me.

'Good God!' I gasped. 'The White Lady of the Brandberg!* It's the same!'

Sally played the beam of the torch down across the figure until it spotlighted the vaunting erection that thrust from its thighs.

'That *lady* is beautifully hung,' she murmured, 'if you get the point.'

The figure was six feet tall, dressed in yellow breastplate and ornate helmet with a high arched crest. On his left shoulder he carried a rounded shield on which yellow ornamental rosettes were set in a circle about the central

* The White Lady of the Brandberg is one of the most celebrated and controversial rock paintings yet discovered in Africa. Its date is agreed at about A.D. 0–200, but its interpretation is the subject of much dispute. One source claims it is a Xhosa circumcision candidate daubed with white clay (one thousand miles from the territory of the Xhosa). The famous Abbé Breuil named it a lady, and Credo Mutwa in his recent book *Idaba My Children* gives an intriguing interpretation in which he concludes ' – It is not a Lady, but a strikingly handsome young white man, one of the great emperors who ruled the African Empire of the Ma-iti (Phoenicians) for nearly two centuries.'

boss. In his other hand he carried a bow and sheaf of arrows, and from his waist hung sword and battle-axe. His shins were protected by greaves of the same yellow metal and on his feet were light open sandals.

The figure's skin was depicted as deathly white, but a fiery bush of red hair hung onto his chest. The display of his sexual parts was clearly a stylized indication of his dominant and lofty status. The effect was in no way obscene but gave to the figure a masculine pride and arrogance.

'A white man,' I whispered. 'Armour and rounded shield, bow and battle-axe. Could it be—'

'A Phoenician king,' Sally finished for me.

'But the Phoenician type is more likely to have been dark-haired, hook-nosed. This man would have been an unusual figure among the ancients, to say the least. A throw-back, perhaps, to some north Mediterranean ancestor. How old is it, Sal?'

'I can't be sure yet, but I'd say 2,000 years. This wall of paintings is the most ancient in the whole cavern.'

'Look, Sal.' I pointed eagerly.

Beyond the central figure was an army of stick figures that followed the king. They were not executed in such detail, but the swords and helmets were unmistakable.

'And look there.' Sally directed the beam of the torch onto a row of white-robed figures that stood at the king's feet. Tiny figures, perhaps nine inches tall.

'Priests, perhaps – and, oh Ben! Look! Look!'

She played the beam across the stone canvas, and for a moment I did not recognize it – then my heart jumped. Like a huge frieze, that was obliterated in places by moisture, moss and lichens, or that was obscured by the myriad figures of men and animals drawn over it, and that yet managed to maintain its imposing majesty and power, swept the drawing of a stone fortress wall. It was built in blocks with the joints clearly shown, and along its summit was the decorative pattern of chevrons, identical to the one that graces the main temple wall at the ruins of Zimbabwe. Beyond the wall rose outlines of the phallic towers we had expected to find.

'It's our city, Ben. Our lost city.'

'And our lost king, Sally, and his priests, and warriors and – oh, my God! Sally, look at that!'

'Elephants!' she squealed. 'War elephants with archers on their backs, just like Hannibal used against the Romans. Carthaginian – Phoenician!'

There was so much of it, a curved wall 100 feet long and ten to fifteen feet high and every square inch of it thick with bushman paintings. The figures and forms were interwoven, some of the earlier pictures overlaid and smothered; others, like our white king, standing proudly untouched and unspoiled. It would be a major undertaking to unravel those portraits which related to our lost civilization, from the great mass of traditional cave art. This was Sally's special skill, my camera could only capture the whole confused scene, while she would patiently and painstakingly pick out a figure or group of particular interest that was almost entirely obliterated and recreate and restore it on her rolls of wax paper.

However, there was no suggestion of such work beginning now. Sally and I spent what was left of the day climbing and crawling along the back wall, peering and probing and exclaiming with wonder and delight.

When we got into camp that night we were physically and emotionally exhausted. Peter Larkin had a message for us from Louren:

'He says to wish you good luck, and that one of the oil helicopters will be in your area within the next few days. Is there anything you need, and if so give me a list. They will drop it to you.'

The next ten days were the happiest of my entire life. The helicopter came as Louren had promised with the name 'Sturvesant Oil' blazoned across its fuselage. It carried a full load of necessities and luxuries for us, another tent, folding chairs, a surveyor's theodolite, gas for the lamps, food, extra clothing for both of us, more paper and paints for Sally, film for me, and even a few bottles of Glen Grant malt whisky, that sovereign specific for all the ills of man. A note from Louren enjoined me to carry on with what I was doing as long as it looked promising. He would give me his full support, but I was not to keep him in the dark too long as he was 'dying of curiosity'.

I sent him my thanks, a roll of film showing the paintings which had no ancients in them, and a batch of polythene bags containing samples of pigments from the cavern for carbon-14 dating. Then the helicopter flew away and left us to our idyll.

We worked from early each morning until dark each evening, mapping the cavern in plan and elevation, and photographing an overlapping run of the walls and relating this to our map. Sally alternated between assisting me and continuing with her own task of isolating our ancient figures. We worked in complete harmony and understanding, breaking off now and then to eat our lunch beside the emerald pool, or to swim naked together in its cool limpid water, or at times just to lie idly on the rocks and talk.

At first our occupation of the cavern seriously affected the ecology of the local fauna, but as we hoped would happen, they soon adapted. Within days the birds were dropping down through the hole in the cavern roof to drink and bathe at the edge of the pool. Soon they ignored us as they went about their noisy and vigorous ablutions, shrieking and chattering and spraying water, while we paused in our labours to watch them.

Even the monkeys, driven by thirst, at last crept in through the rock passage to snatch a mouthful of water before darting away again. Rapidly these timid forays became bolder, until at last they were a positive nuisance, stealing our lunch, or any loose equipment that was left unguarded. We forgave them, for their antics were always appealing and entertaining.

They were wonderful days of satisfying work, good loving companionship, and the deep peace of that beautiful place. There was only one day on which anything happened to ruffle the surface of my happiness. As Sally and I were sitting below the portrait of our wonderful white king, I said: 'They won't be able to deny this, Sal. The bastards are going to have to change their narrow little minds now!'

She knew I was talking about the debunkers, the special pleaders, the politico-archaeologists, who could twist any evidence to fill the needs of their own beliefs, the ones who had castigated me and my books.

'Don't be so certain of that, Ben,' Sally warned. 'They will not accept this. I can hear their carping little voices now. It's second-hand observation by bushmen, open to different interpretations – don't you remember, Ben, how they accused the Abbé Breuil of retouching the paintings in the Brandberg?'

'Yes. That's the great pity of it – it *is* second-hand. When we show them the paintings of the fortified walls, they will say, "Yes, but where are the walls themselves?"'

'And our king, our beautiful virile warrior king,' she looked up at him, 'they'll emasculate him. He will become another "White Lady". His war shield will become a bouquet of flowers, his milky white skin will change to ceremonial clay, his fiery red beard will suddenly turn into a scarf or a necklace, and when they reproduce his portrait it will be subtly altered in all those ways. The *Encyclopaedia Britannica* will still read,' she changed her voice, mimicking a pedantic and pompous lecturer, '"modern scientific opinion is that the ruins are the work of some Bantu group, possibly the Shona or Makalang."'

'I wish – oh, how I wish we had found some definite proof,' I said miserably. I was facing for the first time the prospect of delivering our discovery to my learned brothers in science, and the idea was as appealing as climbing into a pit full of black mambas. I stood up. 'Let's have a swim, Sal.'

We swam side by side, an easy breaststroke, back and forth across the pool. When we climbed out to sit in the spot of bright sunlight that fell from the roof above, I tried to alleviate my unhappiness by changing the subject. I touched Sally's arm and with all the finesse of a wounded rhinoceros, I blurted out, 'Will you marry me, Sally?'

She turned a startled face to me, her cheeks and eyelashes still bejewelled with water droplets, and she stared at me for fully ten seconds before she began to laugh.

'Oh, Ben, you funny old-fashioned thing! This is the twentieth century. Just because you done me wrong – doesn't mean you have to marry me!' And before I could protest or explain she had stood up and dived once again into the emerald pool.

For the rest of that day she was completely occupied with her paints and brushes, and she had no time to even look in my direction, let alone talk to me. The message was received my end loud and clear – there were some areas of discussion that Sally had put the death curse on. Matrimony was one of them.

It was a very bad day, but I learned the lesson well, and decided to clutch at what happiness I now had without pressing for more.

That evening Larkin had another message from Louren:

'Your samples 1–16 give C.14 average result of 1620 years ± 100. Congratulations. Looks good. When do I get in on the secret? Louren.'

I perked up at this news. Assuming our old bushman artist had been an eye-witness of the subjects he had drawn, then somewhere between A.D. 200 and A.D. 400 an armed Phoenician warrior had led his armies and war-elephants across this beloved land of mine. I felt guilty about excluding Louren from the secrets of our cavern, but it was still too soon. I wanted to have it to myself a little longer – to gloat upon it, to have its peace and beauty to myself, unsullied by other eyes. More than that, it had become the temple of my love for Sally. Like the old bushmen, it had become a very holy place to me.

On the following day, it was as though Sally was determined to make up for the unhappiness she had caused me. She was teasing, and loving, and mischievous all at once. At noon with the beam of sunlight burning down on us, we made love on the rocks beside the pool, Sally skilfully and gently taking the initiative once again. It was a shattering and mystic experience that scoured the sadness from the cup of my soul and filled it to the brim with happiness and peace.

We lay together softly entwined, murmuring sleepily, when suddenly I was aware of another presence in the cavern. Alarm flared through me, and I struggled up on one elbow and looked to the entrance tunnel.

A golden-brown human figure stood in the gloomy mouth of the tunnel. He was dressed in a short leather loin-cloth, a quiver and short bow stood up behind his shoulder, and around his neck hung a necklace of ostrich egg-shell beads and black monkey beans. The figure was tiny, the size of a ten-year-old child, but the face was that of a mature man. Slanted eyes, and high flat cheekbones gave it an Asiatic appearance, but the nose was flattened and the lips were full and voluptuously chiselled. The small domed skull was covered by a pelt of tight black curls.

For an instant we looked into each other's eyes and then, like the flash of a bird's wing, the little manikin was gone, vanished into the dark passage in the rock.

'What is it?' Sally stirred against me.

'Bushman,' I said. 'Here in the cavern. Watching us.'

She sat up quickly, and peered fearfully about her.

'Where?'

'He's gone now. Get dressed – quickly!'

'Is he dangerous, Ben?' Her voice was husky.

'Yes. Very!' I was pulling on my clothes quickly, trying to decide on our best course of action, running over in my mind the words I would speak. Although it was a little rusty I found the language was still on my tongue, thanks to sessions of practice with Timothy Mageba. They would be northern bushmen here, not Kalahari; the languages were similar but distinctly different.

'They wouldn't attack us, would they, Ben?' Sally was dressed.

'If we do the wrong thing now, they will. We don't know how holy this place is to them. We mustn't frighten them, they have been persecuted and hunted for 2,000 years.'

'Oh, Ben.' She moved closer to me, and even in my own alarm I enjoyed her reliance upon me.

'They wouldn't – kill us, would they?'

'They are wild bushmen, Sally. If you threaten or molest a wild thing it will attack you. I've got to get an opportunity to talk to them.' I looked around for something to use as a shield, something strong enough to turn a reed arrow with a poisoned tip. Poison that would inflict a lingering but certain death of the most unspeakable agony.

I selected the leather theodolite case, and tore it open along the seams with my hands, flattening it out to give it maximum area.

'Follow me down the passage, Sal. Keep close.'

Her hand was on my shoulder as I led her slowly along the rock passage, using the four-cell torch to search every dark corner and recess before moving on. The light alarmed the bats and they fluttered and squeaked about our heads. The grip of Sally's hand on my shoulder became painfully tight, but we reached the tree-trunk that guarded the entrance to the cavern.

We crouched by the narrow slit between rock and tree-trunk, and the bright sunlight beyond was painful to my eyes. Minutely I examined each tree-trunk in the grove, each tuft of grass, each hollow or irregularity of earth – and there was nothing. But they were there, I knew, hidden waiting with the patience and concentration of the earth's most skilful hunters.

We were prey, there was no escaping this fact. The accepted laws of behaviour did not apply out here on the fringe of the Kalahari. I remembered the fate of the crew of a South African Air Force Dakota that force-landed in the desert ten years before. They hunted down the family of bushmen that did it, and I flew to Gaberones to interpret at the trial. In the dock they wore the parachute silk as clothing, and their faces were childlike, trusting, without guilt or guile as they answered my question.

'Yes. We killed them,' they said. Locked in a modern goal, like caged wild birds, they were dead within twelve months – all of them. The memory was chilling now and I thrust it aside.

'Now listen to me carefully, Sally. You must stay here. No matter what happens. I will go out to them. Talk to them. If,' I choked on the words, and cleared my throat, 'if they hit me with an arrow I'll have half an hour or so before – ' I rephrased the sentence, ' – I'll have plenty of time to get the Land-Rover and come back for you. You can drive. You'll have no trouble following the tracks we made back to the Makarikari Pan.'

'Ben – don't go. Oh God, Ben – please.'

'They'll wait, Sal – until dark. I have to go now, in the daylight.'

'Ben—'

'Wait here. Whatever happens, wait here.' I shrugged off her hands and stepped to the opening.

'Peace,' I called to them in their own tongue. 'There is no fight between us.'

I took a step out into the sunlight.

'I am a friend.'

Another slow step, down over the twisted roots of the wild fig, holding the flattened leather case low against my hip.

'Friend!' I called again. 'I am of your people. I am of your clan.'

I went slowly down into the silent hostile grove. There was no response to my words, no sound or movement. Ahead of me lay a fallen tree. I began sidling towards it, my guts a hard tight ball of tension and fear.

'I carry no weapon,' I called, and the grove was quiet and sinister in the hush of afternoon.

I had almost reached the fallen tree, when I heard the twang of the bow string and I dived for the shelter of the dead trunk. Close beside my head the arrow fluted, humming in the silence, and I went down. My face was pressed into the dry earth, my heart frozen with fear at the close passage of such hideous death.

I heard footsteps, running from behind me and I rolled over on my side ready to defend myself.

Sally was running down the wild fig roots towards me, ignoring my instructions, her face a pale mask of deathly terror, her mouth open in a silent scream. She had seen me fall and lie still, and the thought of me dead had triggered her panic. Now as I moved she realized her mistake and she faltered in her run, suddenly aware of her own vulnerability.

'Get back, Sal,' I yelled. 'Get back!' Her uncertainty turned to dismay and she stopped, stranded half-way between the cavern entrance and my dead tree-trunk, undecided on which way to move.

In the edge of my vision I saw the little yellow bushman rise from a patch of pale grass. There was an arrow notched to his bow and the feathered flights were drawn back to his cheek as he aimed. He was fifty paces from where Sally hovered, and he held his aim for a second.

I dived forward across the space that separated Sally from me at the instant the bushman released the arrow. The arrow and I flew on an interception course, two sides of a triangle with Sally at the apex.

I saw the humming blur of the arrow flash in belly-high at Sally and I knew I could not reach her before it struck. I threw the flattened leather case with a despairing underhand flick of my wrist as I dived towards her. It cartwheeled lazily, spinning in the air – and the arrow slapped into it. The deadly iron tip, with the poison-smeared barbs, bit into the tough leather of the case. Arrow and case fell harmlessly at Sally's feet, and I picked her up in my arms and spinning on my heels, doubled up under her weight, I raced back towards the cover of the dead tree-trunk.

The bushman was still on his knees in the grass ahead of me. He reached over his shoulder and pulled another arrow from his quiver; in one smoothly practised movement he had notched and drawn.

This time there was no hope of dodging, and I ran on grimly. The bow-string sang, the arrow flew, and instantly I felt a violent jerk at my neck. I knew I was hit, and with Sally still in my arms we fell behind the dead tree-trunk.

'I think I'm hit, Sal.' I could feel the arrow dangling against my chest as I rolled away from her. 'Break off the shaft – don't try and pull it out against the barbs.'

We lay facing each other, our eyes only a few inches apart. Strangely, now that I was a dead man I felt no fear. The thing was done, even if I was hit a dozen more times, my fate would be unaltered. It remained only to get Sally safely away before the poison did its work.

She reached out with shaking hands and took the frail reed arrow, lifting it gingerly – and then her face cleared.

'Your collar, Ben, it's lodged in the collar of your jacket. It hasn't touched you.'

Relief washed through me as I ran my hands up the shaft of the arrow, and found that I was not dead. Carefully lying on my side while Sally held the tip of the arrow from my flesh, I shrugged off my light khaki jacket. For a moment I stared in revulsion at the hand-forged iron arrow-head with the sticky toffee-coloured material clogging the wicked barbs, then I threw jacket and arrow aside.

'God, that was close,' I whispered. 'Listen, Sal, I think there is only one of them here. He's a young man, panicky, probably as afraid as we are. I will try to talk to him again.'

I wriggled forward against the reassuring solidity of the dead tree, and raised my voice in the most persuasive tones that would pass my parched throat.

'I am your friend. Though you fly your arrows at me, I will not war with you. I have lived with your people, I am one with you. How else do I speak your language?'

A deathly, impenetrable silence.

'How else do I speak the tongue of the people?' I asked again, and strained my ears for a sound.

Then the bushman spoke, his voice a high-pitched fluting, broken up with soft clucking and clicking sounds.

'The devils of the forest speak in many tongues. I close my ears to your deceits.'

'I am no devil. I have lived as one of yours. Did you never hear of the one named the Sunbird,' I used my bushman name, 'who stayed with the people of Xhai and became their brother?'

Another long silence followed, but now I sensed that the little bushman was undecided, puzzled, no longer afraid and deadly.

'Do you know of the old man named Xhai?'

'I know of him,' admitted the bushman, and I breathed a little easier.

'Did you hear of the one they called the Sunbird?'

Another long pause, then reluctantly, 'I have heard men speak of it.'

'I am that one.'

Now the silence went on for ten minutes or more. I

knew the bushman was considering my claim from every possible angle. At last he spoke again.

'Xhai and I hunt together this season. Even now he comes, before darkness he will be here. We will wait for him.'

'We will wait for him,' I agreed.

'But if you move I will kill you,' warned the bushman, and I took him at his word.

Xhai the old bushman came to my shoulder, and heaven knows I am no giant. He had the characteristically flattened features, with high cheekbones and oriental eyes, but his skin was dry and wrinkled, like an old yellow raisin. The wrinkling extended over his entire body as though he were covered with brittle parchment. The little peppercorns of hair on his scalp were smoky-grey with age, but his teeth were startling white and perfect, and his eyes were black and sparkling. I had often thought that they were pixie eyes, alive with mischief and intelligent curiosity.

When I told him how his friend had tried to kill us, he thought it an excellent joke and went off into little grunting explosions of laughter, at the same time shyly covering his mouth with one hand. The younger bushman's name was Ghal, and he was married to one of Xhai's daughters, so Xhai felt free to josh him mercilessly.

'Sunbird is a white ghost!' he wheezed. 'Shoot him, Ghal, quickly! Before he flies away.' Overwhelmed by his own humour, Xhai staggered in mirth-racked circles, giving an imitation of how he thought a ghost would look as it flew away. Ghal was very embarrassed and looked down at his feet as he shuffled them in the dust. I chuckled weakly, the sound of flighted arrows very fresh in my memory.

Xhai stopped laughing abruptly, and demanded anxiously, 'Sunbird, have you got tobacco?'

'Oh, my God!' I said in English.

'What is it?' Sally was alarmed by my tone, expecting that something else horrifying had happened.

'Tobacco,' I said. 'We haven't any.' Neither Sally nor I used the stuff, but it is very precious to a bushman.

'Louren left a box of cigars in the Land-Rover,' Sally reminded me. 'Is that any use?'

Both Ghal and Xhai were intrigued with the aluminium cylinders in which the Romeo and Julieta cigars were packed. After I showed them how to open them and remove the tobacco, they cooed and chattered with delight. Then Xhai sniffed the cigar like the true connoisseur he was, nodded approvingly and took a big bite. He chewed a while and then tucked the wad of sodden cigar up under his top lip. He passed the stub to Ghal who bit into it and followed Xhai's example. The two of them squatted on their haunches, positively glowing with contentment, and my heart went out to them. It took so little to make them happy.

They stayed with us that night, cooking on our fire a meal of bush-rats threaded on a stick like kebabs, and grilled over the open coals without gutting or removal of the skin. The hair frizzled off in the fire and stank like burning rags.

'I think I'm going to throw up,' murmured Sally palely as she watched the relish with which our two friends ate, but she didn't.

'Why do they call you Sunbird?' she asked later, and I repeated her question to Xhai.

He jumped up and did his celebrated imitation of a sunbird, darting his head and fluttering his hands. It was convincingly done, for bushmen are wonderful observers of nature.

'They say that's how I act when I get excited,' I explained.

'Yes!' Sally exclaimed, clapping her hands with delight as she recognized me, and then they were all laughing.

In the morning we went to the cave together, all four of us, and in that setting the little men were completely at home. I photographed them, and Sally sketched them as they sat on the rocks by the pool. She was fascinated by their delicate little hands and feet, and their enlarged buttocks, a recognized anatomical peculiarity named steatopygia, which enabled them to store food, like a camel stores water, against the contingencies of the wilderness. Ghal remarked to Xhai on the activity in which Sally and I had been engaged beside the pool when he discovered us the previous day, and this led to much earthy comment and laughter. Sally wanted to know the source of it, and when I told her she blushed like a sunset, which was a pleasant change, for I am usually the blusher.

The bushmen were enthusiastic over Sally's sketches, and this enabled me to lead them naturally to the rock paintings.

'They are the paintings of our people,' Xhai boasted. 'This has been our place from the beginning.'

I pointed out the portrait of the white king and Xhai explained frankly, without any of the reserve or secrecy I had expected.

'He is the king of the white ghosts.'

'Where did he live?'

'He lives with his army of ghosts on the moon,' Xhai explained – and my critics accuse *me* of being a romantic!

We discussed this at some length, and I learned how the ghosts fly between moon and earth, how they are well disposed towards the bushmen, but care should be taken as the common forest devils will sometimes masquerade as white ghosts. Ghal had mistaken me for one of these.

'Have the white ghosts ever been men?' I asked.

'No, certainly not.' Xhai was a little put out by the question. 'They were always ghosts, and they have always lived on the moon and these hills.'

'Have you ever seen them, Xhai?'

'My grandfather saw the ghost king.' Xhai avoided the question with dignity.

'And this, Xhai,' I pointed out the drawing of the stone wall with its chevrons and towers, 'what is this?'

'That is the Moon City,' Xhai answered readily.

'Where is it – on the moon?'

'No. It is here.'

'Here?' I demanded, my blood starting to race. 'You mean on these hills?'

'Yes.' Xhai nodded, and took another bite of his five-dollar cigar.

'Where, Xhai? Where? Can you show it to me?'

'No.' Xhai shook his head regretfully.

'Why not, Xhai? I am your brother. I am of your clan,' I pleaded. 'Your secrets are my secrets.'

'You are my brother,' Xhai agreed, 'but I cannot show you the City of the Moon. It is a ghost city. Only when the moon is full and the white ghosts come down, then the city stands upon the plain below the hills – but in the morning it is gone.'

My blood no longer raced, and my excitement cooled.

'Have you seen the Moon City, Xhai?'

'My grandfather saw it, once long ago.'

'Grandpa was a big mover,' I remarked bitterly in English.

'What is it?' Sally wanted to know.

'I'll explain later, Sal,' I said, and turned back to the old bushman. 'Xhai, in all your life have you ever seen such a city as this? A place of tall stone walls, of round stone towers? I don't mean here at these hills, but anywhere. In the north, by the great river, in the desert of the west – anywhere?'

'No,' said Xhai, 'I have never seen such a place.' And I knew that there was no lost city north of the great Pan or south of the Zambezi, for if there were, Xhai would have come across it in seventy years of ceaseless wandering.

'It was probably some old bushman who wandered 270 miles east of here and saw the temple at Zimbabwe,' I suggested to Sally that night as we sat around the fire and discussed the old bushman's story. 'He was so impressed that on his return he painted it.'

'Then how do you explain your white king?'

'I don't know, Sal,' I told her honestly. 'Perhaps it *is* a white lady with a bouquet of flowers.'

It seems that whenever I receive a serious disappointment – Sally's rejection of my proposal, and the story of the Moon City were both serious – my brain ceases to function for a period. I missed the clue completely, and the link-up was so obvious. I mean, for God's sake, I have a tested I.Q. of 156 – I'm a god-damned genius!

In the morning the two bushmen went, back to the families they had left by the Pan. They took with them the treasures we lavished upon them. A hatchet, Sally's make-up mirror, two knives and half a box of Romeo and Julieta cigars. They trotted away into the vastness of the Kalahari, without a backward glance, and left us poorer for their going.

The helicopter came the following week, bringing in a full load of supplies and the special equipment I had asked Louren to send us.

Sally and I carried the rubber dinghy up to the cavern and inflated it beside the pool, taking it in turns to blow until we felt dizzy.

Sally launched it and paddled happily around the pool while I assembled the rest of the equipment. There was a short glass-fibre fishing-rod, a heavy one, twenty-five ounces, and in the case which held a 12/0 Penn Senator fishing-reel was a note from Louren: 'What are you after, for crying out aloud? Sand fish, or desert trout? "L"'

I fitted the reel to rod, threaded the line through the runners, and attached the five-pound lead weight to the end of it. Sally paddled us out into the centre of the pool. I dropped the lead weight over the side, disengaged the clutch on the reel, and let the line start running out.

As I had requested, the plaited Dacron line was marked at intervals of fifty feet, and as each marker of coloured cotton disappeared into the luminous green water, we counted aloud.

'Five, six, seven – my God, Ben. It's bottomless.'

'These limestone sink-holes can go down to tremendous depths.'

'Eleven, twelve, thirteen.'

'I hope we've got enough line.' Sally eyed what remained on the spool dubiously.

'We have got 800 yards here,' I told her. 'It will be more than enough.'

'Sixteen, seventeen.' Even I was impressed, I had guessed at a depth of around 400 feet, the same as the Sleeping Pool at Sinoia, but still the line unwound steadily from the big-game fishing-reel.

At last I felt the weight bump on the bottom, and the line went slack. We looked at each other with awe.

'A little over 850 feet,' I said.

'It makes me feel scary, hanging over a hole in the earth that deep.'

'Well,' I said with finality, 'I had plans to explore the bottom with a Scuba, but that's out now. Whatever is down there will stay there for ever. Nobody can dive that deep.'

Sally looked down into the green depths, and the dappled, moving, reflected light illuminated her face weirdly. There were shadows in her eyes, and her expression was dazed. Suddenly she shook herself violently, a shudder that went through her whole body, and she tore her eyes away from the green surface.

'Oh! I felt funny then. A really creepy sensation, as though something walked over my grave.'

I began to wind in the fishing-line, and Sally lay back flat on the floor of the dinghy staring up at the rock roof high above. It was a laborious task to recover all that line, but I worked away steadily.

'Ben.' Sally spoke suddenly. 'Look up there.' I stopped winding and looked up. We had never looked up at the opening in the roof from this angle. The shape of the opening was different.

'There, Ben. On the side,' Sally pointed. 'That piece of rock sticking out. It's square, too regular to be natural, surely?'

I studied it for a while.

'Perhaps.' I was dubious.

'You know we have never tried to find where the cavern opens out onto the top of the hills, Ben.' Sally sat up excitedly. 'Can't we do that? Let's go up and look at that piece of square stone. Can we, Ben?'

'Of course,' I agreed readily.

'Today. Now! Can we go now?'

'Hell, Sal. It's after two o'clock already. We will be out after dark.'

'Oh, come on! We can take torches with us.'

The growth of vegetation at the crest of the hills was dense and spiny. I was glad of the machete I had with me, and I hacked a path for us through it. We had marked the approximate position of the hole from the plain below, but even then we blundered about in the undergrowth for two hours before I nearly walked into it.

Suddenly the earth opened at my feet in that frightening black shaft, and I threw myself backwards, nearly knocking Sally down.

'That was a near one.' I was shaken, and I kept a respectful distance from the edge as we worked our way around to where a slab of stone jutted squarely out into the void.

I knelt on the lip to examine the stone. Far below, the surface of the emerald pool glowed in the gloomy depths. I do not like exposed heights, and I felt distinctly queasy as I leaned out to touch the flat surface of the stone.

'It is certainly regular, Sal.' I ran my hands over it. 'But I can't feel any chisel marks. It's been badly weathered though, perhaps—'

I looked up and froze with horror. Sally had walked out onto the stone platform as though it were a diving-board. She stood now with her toes over the edge, and as I watched in horror she lifted her hands above her head. She pointed them straight at the sky with all her fingers and both thumbs extended stiffly in that same gesture she had used when first she saw the emerald pool.

'Sally!' I screamed, and her head jerked. She swayed slightly. I scrambled to my knees.

'Don't, Sally, don't!' I screamed again, for I knew she was about to plunge into the hungry stone mouth. Slowly she leaned out over the gap. I ran out onto the stone platform and as she went forward beyond the point of balance my hand closed on her upper arm. For brief unholy seconds we teetered and struggled together on the lip of stone, then I dragged her back, and pulled her to safety.

Suddenly she was shaking and weeping hysterically, and I clung to her, for I also was badly scared. Something had happened that was beyond my understanding, something mystical and deeply disturbing.

When Sally's sobs had abated, I asked her gently, 'What happened, Sal? Why did you do it?'

'I don't know. I just felt dizzy, and there was a black roaring in my head, and – oh, I don't know, Ben. I just don't know.'

It was another twenty minutes before Sally seemed sufficiently recovered to begin the journey back to camp, and by then the sun was setting. Before we reached the path down the cliff face it was completely dark.

'The moon will be up in a few minutes, Sal. I don't fancy going down the cliff in the dark. Let's wait for it.'

We sat on the edge of the cliff huddled together, not for warmth, for the air was still hot and the rocks were sunbaked, but because both of us were still a little shaken from the experience we had just come through. The moon was a big silver glow beneath the horizon, then it pushed up fat and yellow and round above the trees, and washed the land with a soft pale light.

I looked at Sally. Her face was silver-grey in the moonlight with dark bruised eyes, and her expression was remote and infinitely sad.

'Shall we go, Sal?' I hugged her lightly.

'In a minute. It's so beautiful.' I turned to stare out over the moon-silver plain. Africa has many moods, many faces, and I love them all. Here, before us, she put on one of her more enchanting displays. We were silent and engrossed for a long time.

Suddenly I felt Sally stir against me, half rising.

'Ready?' I asked her, rising with her.

'Ben!' Her hand closed on my wrist with surprising strength, she was shaking my arm.

'Ben! Ben!'

'What is it, Sal?' I was seized with dread that her earlier mood had returned.

'Look, Ben. Look!' Her voice was choked with emotion.

'What is it, Sal? Are you all right?'

With one hand she was shaking my arm, with the other she was pointing down at the plain below us.

'Look, Ben, there it is!'

'Sally!' I put both arms around her to restrain her. 'Easy, my dear. Just sit down quietly.'

'Don't be a fool, Ben. I'm perfectly all right. Just look down there.'

Still holding her securely, I did as she asked. I stared and saw nothing.

'Do you see it, Ben?'

'No.' And then, like the face in the picture-puzzle, it was there. It was there, as it should have been from the beginning.

'Can you see it?' Sally was trembling. 'Tell me you can see it too, Ben. Tell me I'm not imagining it.'

'Yes,' I mumbled, still not certain, 'yes, I think—'

'It's the City of the Moon, Ben. The ghost city of the bushmen – it's our lost city, Ben. It is – it must be!'

It was vague, hazy. I shut my eyes tightly and opened them again. It was still there.

The double enclosure around the silent grove, vast symmetrical tracings on the silver plain, dark shadowy lines. There were the dark circles that marked the spots on which the phallic towers had stood, some of them obscured by the trees of the grove. Beyond the walls were the honeycomb cells of the lower city, crescent-shaped and spread around the shores of the ancient, vanished lake.

'The moon,' I whispered. 'Low angle. Picking up the

outline of the foundations. They must be so flattened that we have walked over them, lived on top of them for a month! The light of the full moon is just the right strength to cast shadows where the remains stand slightly proud.'

'The photograph!'

'Yes. From 36,000 feet, the light low enough and soft enough to give the same effect,' I agreed.

'We probably wouldn't have seen it from such a low altitude, the helicopter didn't go high enough,' Sally suggested.

'And it was noon,' I agreed. 'High-angle sun, no shadows. That is why Louren didn't see it from the helicopter.' It was so simple, and I had missed it. Some bloody genius – they must have botched the tests.

'But there are no walls, Ben, no towers, nothing. Only the foundations. What happened to it? What happened to our city?'

'We will find it, Sal,' I promised. 'But now let's mark it, before it disappears again.'

I handed her the one torch from the knapsack, 'One flash means "come towards me"; two flashes, "move away from me"; three, "move left"; four, "move right"; and a windmill means "you're on it".' Quickly we agreed a simple code. 'I'll go down onto the plain and you signal me. Put me on top of the large tower first, then guide me around the perimeter of the outer walls. We had better work fast – we don't know how long the effect will last. Give me a flat cut-out sign when it goes.'

It lasted a little over an hour with me scampering about on the plain in obedience to Sally's signals, and then the city faded, and slowly vanished as the moon rose towards its zenith. I went up to fetch Sally down from the cliff. I was bare to the waist, having ripped my shirt to shreds and tied strips of it onto clumps of grass and shrubs as markers.

Back in camp we built a huge fire and I got out the Glen Grant to celebrate. We were so elated, and there was so much to discuss and marvel over, that sleep was long delayed.

We went over the lighting phenomenon again in greater detail, agreeing how it worked and ruefully remembering how close we had come to the truth when we discussed the low sun effect on our very first day, the day we discovered the fresh-water mussel shells. We discussed the shells and their new significance.

'I swear here and now, with all the gods as my witness, that I will never again toss a piece of vital scientific evidence over my shoulder.' I made oath and testament.

'Let's drink to that,' suggested Sal.

'What a wonderful idea,' I agreed, and refilled the glasses.

Then we went on to the old bushman's story.

'It just goes to show you that every piece of legend, every piece of folklore is based on some fact, however garbled.' Sally becomes all philosophical after one shot of Glen Grant.

'And let's face facts, my blood brother Xhai is a champion garbler of facts from way back – the City of the Moon, forsooth.'

'It's a lovely name. Let's keep it,' Sally suggested. 'And what do you think about Xhai's grandfather actually meeting one of the white ghosts?'

'He probably saw one of the old hunters or prospectors, remember, we nearly had ghost status awarded us.'

'Literally and figuratively,' Sally reminded me.

The talk went on and on while the moon made its splendid transit of the sky above us. Every now and then serious discussion degenerated into effusive outbursts of, 'Oh, Ben. Isn't it wonderful. We've got a whole Phoenician city to excavate. All to ourselves.' Or, 'My God, Sal. All my life I've dreamed of something like this happening to me.'

It was long past midnight before we got our feet back on

the earth, and Sally brought up the subject of practical procedure.

'What do we do, Ben? Do we tell Louren Sturvesant now?'

I poured another drink slowly, while I considered this.

'Don't you think, Sal, we should sink a pothole, a small one, of course, on the foundations. Just to be certain we're not making fools of ourselves?'

'Ben, you know that's the first rule. Don't go scratching around haphazardly. You might destroy something valuable. We should wait until we go in on an orderly, organized basis.'

'I know, Sal. But I just can't help myself. Just one tiny little hole?'

'Okay,' she grinned. 'Just one tiny little hole.'

'I suppose we'd better try and get some sleep now, it's past two o'clock.'

Just before we finally drifted off, Sally murmured against my chest, 'I still wonder what happened to our city. If the bushman picture was correct then huge walls and towers of masonry have vanished into thin air.'

'Yes. It's going to be exciting to find out.'

With that strength of character which I am able occasionally to conjure up, I firmly thrust aside the temptation to open a trench within the temple enclosure, and instead I chose a spot upon the foundations of the outer wall where I hoped I would do minimum damage.

With Sally watching avidly, and volunteering more than her share of advice, I marked out with tapes torn from my sheets the outline of the intended excavation. A narrow trench three foot wide and twenty foot long, set at a right-angle to the run of the foundations so as to open a cross-section of the horizon.

We numbered the tapes at intervals of one foot, and Sally cross-referenced her notebook to the markings on the tapes. I fetched the cameras, tools and tarpaulin from the Land-Rover. Our trench was only thirty yards from the tents. We had camped almost on top of the ancient wall.

I spread the tarpaulin ready to receive the earth removed from the trench, and then I pulled off my shirt and threw it aside. I was no longer ashamed to expose my body in front of Sally. I spat on the palms of my hands, straddled the tapes, hefted the pick, and glanced at Sally, sitting attentively on the tarpaulin with a big floppy-brimmed hat on her head.

'Okay?' I grinned at her.

'All the way, partner!' she said, and I was startled. The words jarred, they were Louren's and mine. We didn't say them to other people. Then suddenly I thought, what the hell! I love her also.

'All the way, girl!' I agreed and swung the pick. It was good to feel the pick feather-light in my hands, and the head clunking deep into the sandy earth. I worked steadily, swinging pick and shovel easily, but soon the sweat was running in rivulets down my body and soaking my breeches. As I shovelled the earth from the trench and piled it on the tarpaulin, Sally began sifting it carefully. She chattered away happily as she worked, but my only reply was the grunt at each swing of pick.

By noon I had opened the trench along its full length to a depth of three feet. The sandy soil gave way at a depth of eighteen inches to a dark reddish loam which still held the damp of the recent rains. We rested and I ate a mess of canned food and drank a bottle of Windhoek to replace some of my lost moisture.

'You know,' Sally looked me over thoughtfully, 'once

you get used to it, your body has a strange sort of beauty,' she said, and I blushed until my eyes watered.

I worked for another hour, and then suddenly the bite of the pick turned up black. I swung again – still black. I dropped the pick, and knelt in the trench.

'What is it?' Sally was there immediately.

'Ash!' I said. 'Charcoal!'

'An ancient hearth,' she guessed.

'Perhaps.' I didn't commit myself, luckily, so that later I could chide her for her presumption. 'Let's take some samples for dating.'

I worked more carefully now, trying to expose the layer of ash without disturbing it. We sampled it and found that it varied between a quarter of an inch and two inches deep across the full horizon of the trench. Sally noted the depth from the surface, and the position of each of the carbon samples we took, while I photographed the trench and tapes.

Then we straightened up and looked at each other.

'Too big for a hearth,' she said, and I nodded. 'We shouldn't go deeper, Ben. Not like this, crashing in with pick and shovel.'

'I know,' I said. 'We will stop on half the trench, leave the layer of ash undisturbed – I'll make that concession to the rules – but I am sure as hell going down on the rest of it, to bedrock, if I can!'

'I'm glad you said that,' Sally applauded my decision. 'It's exactly what I feel as well.'

'You begin at the far end, I'll start here and we will work towards each other,' I instructed, and we began lifting the layer of ash from half the trench. I found that immediately below it was a floor of hard clay and, though I didn't say so, I guessed it was a building filler. A transported layer, not occurring naturally.

'Go carefully,' I cautioned Sally.

'Quoth the pick-and-shovel man,' she muttered sarcastically without looking up, and almost immediately she made the first discovery from the ruins of the City of the Moon.

As I write I have her notebook in front of me, with her grubby, earthy fingerprints upon the pages and her big school-girlish handwriting filling it.

Trench 1.	Reference AC. 6.II.4. Depth 4'2½".
Item:	One glass bead. Oval. Blue. Circum. 2½ mm. Pierced. Slightly heat-distorted.
Remarks:	Found in layer of ash at Level I.
Index No.	CM. I.

This laconic notation can give no idea of our jubilation, the way we hugged each other and laughed in the sun. It was a typical blue Phoenician trade bead, and I cupped the tiny pellet of glass in my one hand.

'I'm going to take it and stick it up their backsides,' I threatened, referring of course to my critics.

'If that end is as narrow as their minds, Ben dear, then it will be a pretty tight fit.'

I started using a small pick and fifteen minutes later I made the next discovery. A charred fragment of bone.

'Human?' Sally asked.

'Possibly,' I said. 'Head of a human femur – the shaft has been burned away.'

'Cannibalism? Cremation?' Sally hazarded.

'You do run on,' I said.

'What do you think then?' she challenged. I was silent for a long time, then I made up my mind, and came out with it.

'I think at this level the City of the Moon was sacked and burned, its inhabitants were slaughtered, the walls thrown down and its buildings obliterated.'

Sally whistled softly, staring at me in mock amazement.

'On the evidence of one bead, and a piece of bone – that has to be the greatest flyer of all time!'

That evening, in reply to Larkin's bellowed queries, I replied, 'Thanks, Peter. We are fine. No, we don't need anything. Yes. Good. Please tell Mr Sturvesant there is no change here, nothing to report.'

I switched off the set, and avoided Sally's eyes.

'Yes,' she told me sternly. 'After a stinking one like that, you should look guilty!'

'Well, you said yourself it's only one bead and a piece of bone.'

But by the evening two days later, I had no such excuse, for I had sunk my trench seven feet five inches and there I uncovered the first of four courses of dry packed masonry. The stones were skilfully dressed, and squared. The joints between each block were so tight that a knife-blade would not go between them. The stones were bigger than those of Zimbabwe, clearly intended to support the weight of a substantial edifice; the average size was approximately four feet, by two, by two. They were cut from red sandstone similar to that of the cliffs and as I examined the workmanship I knew beyond any doubt that they were the work of artisans from a powerful and wealthy civilization.

That night I spoke to Larkin again.

'How soon can you get a message through to Mr Sturvesant, Peter?'

'He should have got back from New York today. I can put a phone call through this evening.'

'Please ask him to come right away.'

'You mean you want him to drop everything and come running – that's a laugh.'

'Just do it, please.'

The helicopter arrived at three o'clock the following afternoon, and I ran to meet it, pulling on my shirt.

'What have you got for me, Ben?' Louren demanded as he climbed, big and blond, out of the cabin.

'I think you are going to like it,' I told him, as we shook hands.

Five hours later we sat around the fire and Louren smiled over the rim of his glass at me.

'You were right, lad. I do like it!' This was the first opinion he had expressed since his arrival. He had followed Sal and me from excavation to cavern to cliff-top, listening attentively to our explanations, shaking his head with a rueful grin when I explained our theory of low-angle light on the ruins, firing a question occasionally in the same tone I had heard him use in a directors' meeting. Each time the question was relevant, incisive and searching, as though he were evaluating a business deal.

When Sally spoke he stood close to her, looking frankly into her face, those marvellous classical features of his rapt and still. Once she touched his arm to enforce a point and they smiled at each other. I was happy to see them so friendly at last, for they were the two people in the world I loved.

He knelt with me in the bottom of the trench and caressed the worked stone with his hands, he held the charred bone and melted glass bead in his palm and frowned at them as though trying to draw their secrets from them by sheer force of concentration.

Just before sunset, at Louren's insistence, we returned to the cavern and went to the rear wall. I lit one of the glass lanterns and placed it so that its light fell full on the painting of the white king. Then the three of us sat around it in a semi-circle and studied it in every detail. The king's head was in profile and Sally pointed out the features, the long straight nose and high forehead.

'A face like that never came out of Africa,' she said, and as a contrast she picked out the painting of another figure further down the wall. 'Look at that. It's a Bantu and no mistaking it. The artist was skilled enough to differentiate between the features of each type.'

However, Louren's attention never wavered from his scrutiny of the king. Again he seemed to be trying to wrest its secrets from it, but the king was regally aloof and at last Louren sighed and stood up. He was about to turn away when his glance dropped to the white-robed priest figures below the king.

'What are those?' he asked.

'We have named them the priests,' I told him, 'but Sally feels they could be Arab traders or—'

'The figure in the centre—' he pointed out the central priest figure, and his voice was sharp, almost alarmed, 'what is he doing?'

'Bowing to the king,' Sally suggested.

'Even though he is bowing, he stands taller than the others?' Louren protested.

'Size was the bushman artist's way of showing importance. See the relative size of the king – although they are pygmies they always show themselves as giants – the size of the central priest would signify that he was the High Priest, or the leader of the Arabs, if Sally is right.'

'If he is bowing, it's with the top third of his body only and he is the only one doing it. The others are erect.' Louren was still not convinced. 'It's almost as though—' his voice trailed away, and he shook his head. Then suddenly he shivered briefly, and I saw the goose-flesh appear on the smooth tanned skin of his upper arms.

'It's become cold in here,' he said, folding his arms across his chest. I had not noticed any drop in temperature, but I stood up also.

'Let's get back to camp,' Louren said, and it was only

after I had built up the fire to a cheerfully crackling, spark-flying blaze that he spoke again.

'You are right, lad. I do like it!' And he took a swallow of the malt whisky. 'Now let's start talking prices,' he suggested.

'Set it out for us, Lo,' I agreed.

'I will negotiate with the Botswana Government. I can put a little leverage on them. We'll have to have a formal agreement drawn up, probably split any finds fifty-fifty, they'll have to guarantee us access and exclusive rights. That sort of thing.'

'Good. That's certainly your bag of tricks, Lo.'

'Knowing you, Benjamin, you have a list of your requirements, the men you want, equipment – am I right?'

I laughed and unbuttoned my top pocket. 'As a matter of fact—' I admitted as I handed him three foolscap sheets. He glanced over them quickly.

'Very Spartan, Ben,' he congratulated me. 'But I think we can go in a bit bigger than this. I'll want at least a rough landing-strip here to start with, something to handle a Dakota. The hot weather is coming. You'll die living out under canvas. We'll need solid accommodation, also office and storage space with air-conditioning. That means a generator for lighting and to pump water down from the pool.'

'No one can ever accuse you of being half-arsed, Lo,' I told him, and we all laughed. Sally refilled my glass. I was jubilant and mightily pleased with myself that evening. I had much to be proud of, ferreting out a secret so well hidden for millennia, and Louren was going to back me all the way, partner. The whisky went down my throat like water.

I used to drink a lot of whisky. It was a way of forgetting certain things and making others easier to accept. Then about six years ago I found I hadn't worked on a book for a year, that my memory and intellect were blurry and unreliable, and my hands shook in the morning. I still drink a tot or two of an evening, and occasionally I take on a full blast of the stuff. But now I drink because I am happy not because I am sad.

'Come on, Ben. Tonight we've got something to celebrate.' Sally laughed and poured me another heavy portion.

'Wow! Gently, Doctor,' I protested weakly, but that night I got drunk, pleasantly, contentedly, floating drunk. With dignity I refused Louren's offer of assistance and made my own way to the tent wherein Sally had discreetly segregated me since Louren's arrival. I fell on top of my bed fully clothed and went to sleep. I half awoke when Louren came in and climbed into his bed across the tent: I remember opening one eye and seeing the glow of the waning moon through the fly of the tent – or was it the first glow of dawn? It didn't seem important then.

The personnel for the project was the most important consideration, and here I was lucky. Peter Willcox was due for his sabbatical leave from Cape Town University. I flew down to see him, and in six hours convinced him that he wouldn't enjoy the fleshpots of Europe at all. Heather, his wife, was a little harder to sway, until I showed her the photographs of the white king. Like Sally, rock art is one of her big things.

They were good people to have on a dig. We had been together on the excavation of the Slangkop caves. They were both in their thirties; he a little paunchy and balding with steel-rimmed spectacles and trousers always on the point of falling down. He had to keep tugging at the waistband. She was thin and angular, with a wide laughing mouth and a snub, heavily freckled nose. They were childless, cheerful, knowledgeable and hard-working. Peter plays a very jazzy accordion and Heather has a voice that harmonizes well with mine.

Peter introduced me to two of his post-graduate students whom he recommended without reservation. I was startled at my first meeting with them. Ral Davidson was a young man of twenty-one – although the fact that he was a man was not immediately obvious. However, Peter assured me that beneath all the untidy hair lurked a promising young archaeologist. His fiancée was an intense bespectacled young woman, who had graduated at the head of her year. Although she was depressingly plain and I prefer my women beautiful, Leslie Johns endeared herself to me immediately by whispering breathlessly, 'Dr Kazin, I think your book, *Ancient Africa*, is the most exciting thing I've ever read.'

This display of good taste secured the job for them.

Peter Larkin found me forty-six African labourers from the southern territories of Botswana, who had never heard of the Hills of Blood nor of any curse upon them.

My only disappointment was with Timothy Mageba. I spent five days at the Institute in Johannesburg on my way back from Cape Town, mostly trying to convince Timothy that I needed him at the Hills of Blood.

'Machane,' he said, 'there is work here that no one else can do.' I was to remember those words later. 'Where you are going there is work that many men are capable of. You have these men and women already, specialists all of them. You do not need me.'

'Please, Timothy. It would be for six months or so. Your work here can wait.'

He shook his head vehemently, but I hurried on.

'I really want you, and need you. There are things that you alone can explain. Timothy, there are over fifteen thousand square feet of paintings on the rocks. Much of it is symbol, stylized emblems which only you—'

'Dr Kazin, you could send me copies of them. I can still give you my interpretation.' Timothy switched to English, which with him was always a discouraging sign. 'I hope you don't insist that I leave the Institute now. My assistants cannot work without my direction.'

We stared at each other for a few seconds. It was a deadlock. I could order him to come, but an unwilling helper is worse than none at all. There was a rebellious, independent spirit smouldering in Timothy's dark eyes and I knew that there was some deeper reason why he refused to accompany me.

'Is it—' I hesitated. I was about to ask him if the ancient curse was the reason for his refusal. It was always disquieting to find superstition influencing an intelligent and well-educated man. I was reluctant to come straight out with it, for even with an African like Timothy the direct question is considered gauche and discourteous.

'There are always reasons within reasons, Doctor. Please believe me when I tell you it would be better if I did not accompany you this time.'

'All right, Timothy,' I agreed with resignation, and stood up. Again we locked glances, and it seemed to me that he was different. The flickering fires burned brighter, and again I felt the stirring of unease, of fear even, deep within me.

'I promise you, Doctor, that my work here is at a critical stage.'

'I will be very interested to see it when you are ready, Timothy.'

My four new assistants arrived on the commercial flight from Cape Town the following morning and we drove directly to the Sturvesant hangar where the Dakota transport was waiting for us.

The flight in was noisy and gay. Peter had his accordion along, and I never travel without my old guitar. We hit a couple of easy ones like 'Abdul Abulbul Emir', and 'Green grow the rushes, oh!', and I discovered with delight that

Ral Davidson whistled with a clarity and purity that was truly beautiful, and that Leslie had a sweet little soprano.

'When we've finished this dig, I'm going to take you lot on tour,' I told them, and began teaching them some of my own compositions.

It was three weeks since I had left the Hills of Blood, and as we circled it I could see that changes had taken place in my absence. The landing-strip, complete with wind-sock, had been gouged out of the dusty plain. Near it stood a cluster of prefabricated buildings. One long central bungalow with the residential quarters grouped around it. A skeletal metal tower supported a 2,000-gallon galvanized iron water-tank, and beyond that was the encampment which housed the African labour force.

Sally was waiting for us at the landing-strip, and we piled our luggage into the Land-Rover and went to look at our new home. I expected Louren to be there but Sally told me he had gone the previous day after a stay of a few days.

Proudly Sally showed us over the camp. The central air-conditioned bungalow was divided into a small common room and lounge at the one end, in the centre was a large office and beyond that a storage warehouse. There were four residential huts, air-conditioned, but sparsely furnished. Sally had allotted one to the Willcoxes, one for Leslie and herself, one for Ral and me, and the fourth for Louren or other visitors, pilots, and overnight guests.

'I could think of a few improvements in the sleeping arrangements,' I muttered bitterly.

'Poor Ben.' Sally smiled cruelly. 'Civilization has caught up with you. By the way, I hope you remembered to bring your bathing costume, no skinny dips in the pool any more.'

And perversely I regretted all that Louren had done for me. The Hills of Blood were no longer a lonely, mysterious place in the wilderness, but a bustling little community, with aircraft landing regularly, Land-Rovers kicking up the dust and even the clatter of an electric water-pump shattering the dreaming silence of the cavern and disturbing the still green waters of the emerald pool.

Quickly my group settled into their allotted tasks. Sally worked on at the cavern, with a single young African assistant. Each of the other four was placed in charge of a team of ten labourers and assigned an area in which to work.

Peter and Heather shrewdly elected to work outside the main walls, in the ruins of the lower city. It was here that the ancients would have disposed of their rubbish, broken pottery, old weapons, discarded beads and the fascinating debris of a vanished civilization.

Ral and Leslie with dreams of gold and treasure jumped at the chance of excavating within the enclosure, an area which the ancients would have kept swept and scrupulously clean, and therefore much less likely to yield finds of interest. That is the difference between experience and inexperience, between the impetuosity of youth and the cool calculations of an older head.

I kept myself free, in a supervisory and advisory capacity. Spending my time at those places where it could do the most good. Anxiously I watched Ral and Leslie to assure myself that their approach and technique were satisfactory, then I relaxed as Peter Willcox's recommendation proved correct. They were clever, enthusiastic youngsters and, more important, they knew their way around an archaeological dig.

The four teams shook themselves out as the dullards amongst the African labourers were sorted from the bright ones. In a shorter time than I had hoped for, the firm of Kazin and Company was breaking ground and doing good business.

It was slow, painstaking and thoroughly satisfying work. Each evening, before the nightly singsong in the common room, the day's work was discussed and any discoveries evaluated and related to their place in the general picture of the site.

The first conclusive discovery we made was that the ash layer at Level I persisted throughout the site, even in the lower city. It was by no means evenly distributed, but showed up in patches of varying thickness. Carbon-dating, however, gave a fairly constant result, and we settled at a date of A.D.450. This date seemed to be concurrent or to slightly pre-date the oldest bushman paintings in the cavern.

We were agreed that bushman occupation of the cavern would have followed immediately after the departure or disappearance of the ancients from the city. Scrupulously we referred to the first occupations as 'ancients', considering the term 'Phoenician' as yet unproven. A condition which it was my most dearly-held hope would soon be altered.

Associated with the ash layer were haunting scraps of human remains. Ral uncovered an incisor in the ash against the base of the main tower, Peter a complete humerus together with many other unidentifiable bone fragments. These unburied human remains went a long way to ensuring a general acceptance of my theory of a violent end to the City of the Moon.

This was reinforced by the baffling disappearance of walls and towers, which we could reasonably accept once stood on these bases of clay, with their vestigial stone foundations which occurred spasmodically along the outline of the temple enclosure.

Ral hesitantly suggested an enemy so crazed with hatred, that he had set out to obliterate all trace of the ancients from the earth. We could all accept this.

'Fair enough. But what happened to thousands of tons of massive masonry?' Sally spoke for all of us.

'They scattered it out across the plain,' Ral hazarded.

'A Herculean task, besides the plain was a lake in those days. To get rid of it they would have scattered it along the area between cliff and lake. There is no sign of it.'

Apologetically Peter Willcox reminded us of the account in Credo Mutwa's book *Indaba My Children* of how an ancient city was carried by its people, block by block, out of the west, and how the city was rebuilt at Zimbabwe.

'This is red sandstone,' Sally cut in brusquely. 'Zimbabwe is granite, quarried from the rock on which it stands. Zimbabwe is 275 miles east of here. The labour involved is unthinkable. I will accept that the building skills and techniques were transported, but not the material itself.'

There were no more ideas forthcoming and we could turn from theories to facts. At the end of six weeks Louren Sturvesant visited us for the first time. All digging and other work was suspended as for two days we held a seminar, with myself as Chairman, in which we presented Louren with all our accomplishments and conclusions to date.

These were very impressive. To begin with, the list of artefacts, pottery sherds, and other relics filled 127 typewritten foolscap pages. Peter and Heather were responsible for most of these and they opened the seminar.

'So far all excavation without the enclosure has been confined to the area north of it, and lying within 1,000 feet of the outer perimeter. In the main it seems to have been a complex of small rooms and buildings built from adobe clay and roofed with poles and thatch—'

Peter described the area in detail, giving the average size of the rooms and the exact position of each object discovered. Louren started thrashing around in his chair, and fiddling with his cigar. Peter is meticulous, almost old-maidish, in his approach to his work. Finally he reached his conclusions. 'It seems, therefore, that this area was an extensive bazaar and market.' And he led us through into the warehouse to examine the finds from this area. There were fragments of badly rusted iron, a bronze comb, the handle of a knife fashioned in the shape of a woman's body, fourteen rosettes of bronze that we guessed had embossed a leather shield, twenty-five pounds' weight of bronze discs, and stars and sun objects which were clearly ornaments, sixteen shaped and beaten bronze plates that we hoped might comprise part of a suit of body armour, a magnificent bronze dish twenty-four inches in diameter chased with a sun image and set around with an intricate border pattern, and another forty pounds' weight of bronze scraps and fragments so badly battered and damaged as to be unidentifiable.

'These are all the bronze objects so far discovered,' Peter told Louren. 'The workmanship is crude, but not recognizably Bantu in conception and execution. It would relate more closely to what we know of Phoenician craftsmanship. Unlike the Romans and Greeks, they placed little value on the arts. Their artefacts, like their buildings, were massive and roughly executed. One other fact that emerges is the veneration of the sun. It was clearly a generally polytheistic community but one in which sun-worship predominated. In this settlement, it appears that Baal, the Phoenician male deity, was personified by the sun.'

I thought Peter was verging on the mistake of special pleading but I let him continue without interruption. After discussing each item separately, Peter led us to the next row of tables that carried all the glass and pottery.

'One hundred and twenty-five pounds' weight of glass beads – the colours are predominantly blue and red. Phoenician colours, with greens and whites and yellows recovered only in Levels I and II. In other words, later than A.D. 50 which coincides approximately with the final phase of absorption of Phoenician civilization by the Romans in the Mediterranean area, and its gradual disappearance.'

I interrupted. 'The Romans were so thorough in their absorption of Phoenicia and all her works, that we know very little of them . . . .'

My attention wandered to Sally. She was in a sparkling mood, a complete change from the previous six weeks when she had been moody and withdrawn. She had washed her hair and it was shiny and springing with soft lights. Her skin also shone with golden hues where the sun had touched it, and she had coloured her lips and dramatized her eyes. Her beauty squeezed my heart. I forced my mind back to the row of tables.

'. . . A case in point is this recovery of pottery,' Peter was saying. He indicated the huge display of fragments, portions, and a very few complete pieces. 'On all of this, with one exception, there is not a single inscription. This is the exception.' He picked up a sherd which was set out in a place of honour, and passed it to Louren. Although we had all gloated over it before, we crowded around Louren as he examined it. There was a symbol cut into the baked clay.

'A chip from the lip of a cup, or vase. The symbol could conceivably be a Punic T.'

Louren burst in impulsively, turning to me and laying a hand on my shoulder, 'Conclusive, Ben. They must accept that, surely?'

'By no means, Lo.' I shook my head regretfully. 'They will cry, "Imported." The old trick of discrediting anything you can't explain, or which doesn't support your theories, by saying that it was brought in during the course of trade.'

'Looks as though you can't win, Ben,' Louren sympathized, and I grinned.

'At least we haven't uncovered any fourteenth-century Nanking pottery – or a chamber pot with Queen Victoria's portrait on it!'

Laughing we moved on to the next display of copper

and copperware. There were bangles and brooches, green-encrusted and eaten away. Bales of copper wire and, significantly, ingots cast into the shape of a St Andrew's Cross each weighing twelve pounds.

'Those aren't something new,' Louren remarked.

'No,' I agreed. 'They turn up all over central and southern Africa. And yet the shape is exactly that of the ingots taken from the tin mines of Cornwall by the Phoenicians – or the copper ingots from the ancient mines on Cyprus.'

'Still not conclusive?' Louren looked at me and I shook my head, leading him on to see the iron work we had recovered. All of it was so badly rusted and damaged that the original shape was a matter of conjecture and guess-work. There were hundreds of arrow-heads, mostly associated with Levels I and II, spear-heads and sword-blades, axe-heads and knives.

'Judging by the quantities of weapons, or what we take to be weapons, the ancients were a warlike people. Alternatively they were a people fearful of attack and well armed against it,' I suggested, and there was a general murmur of agreement. From the iron section we went on to a display of my photographs, showing each stage of the excavations, views of the lower city, the temple, the acropolis and the cavern.

'Pretty good, Ben,' Louren admitted. 'Is that all you have for me?'

'The best comes last.' I couldn't help a little showmanship in my presentation, and I had screened off the end of the warehouse. I led him beyond the first screen with all my team hovering anxiously to judge his reaction. It was gratifying.

'Good God!' Louren stopped short and stared at the phallic columns with their ornamental tops. 'Zimbabwe birds!'

There were three of them. Although incomplete, they

stood about five foot high, and were thirty inches in circumference. Only one of them was relatively undamaged, the other two had been mutilated so as to be hardly recognizable. The carving on top of each pillar had obviously originally depicted a vulturine bird shape with heavy beak, hunched shoulders, and predatory claws. They were similar in design and execution to those recovered from Zimbabwe by Hall, MacIver, and others.

'Not Zimbabwe birds,' I corrected Louren.

'No,' Sally affirmed. 'These are the ones from which the Zimbabwe birds were copied.'

'Where did you find them?' Louren asked as he moved in for a closer scrutiny of the green soapstone figures.

'In the temple,' I smiled at Ral and Leslie, who looked suitably modest, 'within the inner enclosure. They are probably religious objects – you see the sun symbols around the collar of the column – clearly they are associated with the worship of Baal as the sun god.'

'We have named them the sunbirds,' Sally explained, 'as Ben felt a name like the birds of Ophir was a bit too pretentious.'

'Why have they been damaged like this?' Louren indicated where deliberate blows had shattered the brittle green stone.

'That's anybody's guess.' I shrugged away the question. 'But we know that they had been toppled and were lying without design or direction in the layer of ash at Level I.'

'That's very interesting, Ben.' Louren's eyes were drawn to the final screen at the end of the warehouse. 'Now come on, you secretive old bastard, what have you got behind there?'

'What the whole city and colonization was based on – ' I opened the screen, ' – gold!'

There is something about that beautiful buttery metal that holds the imagination captive. A hush came over the party as we stared at it. The objects had been carefully cleaned, and the surfaces shone with the special soft radiance which is unmistakably gold.

To coldly itemize the collection detracts in some way from its excitement and mystery. The gross weight of the pieces was 683 fine ounces. There were fifteen rods of native gold as thick and as long as a man's finger. There were forty-eight pieces of crudely wrought jewellery, pins, brooches and combs. There was a statuette of a female figure four and a half inches tall –

'Astarte – Tanith,' Sally whispered as she stroked it, 'Goddess of the moon and the earth.'

In addition there were a handful of gold beads with the string long ago disintegrated, dozens of sun discs and many chips, tacks and flakes and buttons of no definite shape or discernible purpose.

'And then,' I said, 'there is this,' picking up the heavy chalice of solid gold. It had been crushed and flattened, but the base was undamaged. 'Look,' I said, pointing to the design worked into it with uncommon delicacy of line.

'Ankh? The Egyptian sign of eternal life?' Louren looked to me for confirmation, and I nodded.

'For the Christians and heathens amongst you. We know that the Pharaohs on occasions used the Phoenicians to supply treasure for their empire. Was this,' and I turned the chalice in my hands, 'a gift from a Pharaoh to the King of Ophir?'

'And do you remember the cup in the right hand of the White Lady of the Brandberg?' Sally asked.

It was enough to keep us arguing and locked in discussion into the early hours, and the next day Sally, helped by Heather Willcox, presented her drawings and paintings from the cavern. When she showed the tracing of the white king, that frown of concentration again creased Louren's brow, and he stood up and went to examine it more closely. We waited for a long time in silence, before he looked up at Sally.

'I would like you to make a copy of this, for my own personal collection. Would you mind?'

'With the greatest of pleasure.' Sally smiled happily at him. The mood of sparkle and smile was still strong upon her and she was enjoying the sensation that the display of her work was causing. Sally, like most beautiful women, is not completely averse to standing in the limelight. She knew her work was damned good, and she liked the plaudits.

'Now I haven't been able to decide what these are.' Sally smiled as she hung a new sheet on the common-room board. 'There are seventeen symbols similar to this which I have so far isolated. Heather calls them the walking cucumbers, or the double walking cucumbers. Have you any ideas?'

'Tadpoles?' Ral tried.

'Centipedes?' Leslie was a bit more feasible.

That was the end of our imagination, and we were silent.

'No more offers?' Sally asked. 'I thought that with the formidable collection of academic qualification and worldly wisdom we have assembled here we could do better—'

'A bireme!' Louren said softly. 'And a trireme.'

'By Jove.' I saw it immediately. 'You're right!'

' "Quinquereme of Nineveh, from distant Ophir," ' Peter quoted joyously.

'The shape of a ship's hull, and the banks of oars,' I enlarged upon it. 'Of course – if we are right then vessels like that must have plied regularly across the lakes.'

We could accept it, but others certainly would not.

After lunch we went for a tour of the excavations, and Louren again distinguished himself with an inspired guess. A series of large regular cell-like rooms had been uncovered by Peter's team in the angle formed by the cliff and the enclosure wall. They were joined by a long corridor, and there was evidence of paved floors and a system of drainage.

Each room was approximately twenty-five feet square, and it seemed that these were the only buildings outside the enclosure which had been made of stone blocks and not adobe clay.

The closest we could come to a purpose for these cells was to call them 'the prison'.

'Do I have to do all the work around here?' Louren sighed. 'When you've just shown me pictures of the war elephants?'

'Elephant stables?' I asked.

'Very quick, lad!' Louren clapped me on the shoulder and I blushed. 'But I believe they are called elephant lines in India.'

After dinner I worked for an hour in my dark room, developing three rolls of film, and when I was finished I went to look for Louren. He was leaving again early the following morning and there was much for us to discuss.

He wasn't in the guest room, nor in the lounge, and when I asked for him, Ral told me, 'I think he has gone up to the cavern, Doctor. He borrowed a torch from me.'

Leslie looked at him in a way which was clearly meant to be highly significant, a frown and a quick little shake of the head, but it meant as much to him as it did to me. I went to fetch my own torch, and set off through the silent grove, picking my way carefully around the open excavations. No light showed from the entrance of the tunnel beyond the great wild fig tree.

'Louren!' I called. 'Are you there?' And my voice bounced hollowly from cliff and rock. There was silence once the echoes died, and I went forward into the tunnel. Flashing my torch into the darkness ahead, ducking my head under the zooming flight of the bats, and hearing my own footsteps magnified in the silence.

I could see no light, and I stopped and called again.

'Louren!' My voice boomed around the cavern. There was no reply, and I went on down the passage.

As I stepped out from the mouth of the tunnel, suddenly the beam of a powerful torch flashed from across the cavern shining full in my eyes.

'Louren?' I asked. 'Is that you?'

'What do you want, Ben?' he demanded from the darkness behind the torch. He sounded irritable, angry even.

'I want to talk to you about the plans for the next step.' I shielded my eyes from the beam.

'It can wait until tomorrow.'

'You are leaving early – let's talk now.'

I started to cross the cavern towards him, averting my eyes from the dazzling beam.

'Point that light somewhere else, won't you,' I protested mildly.

'Are you deaf!' Louren's voice rasped, the voice of a man used to being obeyed. 'I said tomorrow, damn you.'

I stopped dead, stunned, confused. He had never spoken to me like that in my life before.

'Lo, are you all right?' I asked anxiously. There was something wrong here in the cavern. I could sense it.

'Ben,' his voice crackled, 'just turn around and walk out of here, will you. I'll see you tomorrow morning.'

I hesitated a moment longer. Then I turned and walked back down the passage. I hadn't even had a glimpse of Louren in the darkness beyond the torch.

In the morning Louren was as charming as only he can be. He apologized handsomely for the previous evening. 'I just wanted to be alone, Ben. I'm sorry. I get like that sometimes.'

'I know, Lo. I am the same.'

In ten minutes we had agreed that although the circumstantial evidence of a Phoenician occupation of the city was most encouraging, it was not conclusive. We would not make any public announcement yet, but in the meantime Louren gave me complete *carte blanche* to proceed with a full-scale excavation and investigation.

He flew out with the dawn, and I knew he would be in London for breakfast the following morning.

The weeks that followed Louren's departure were dissatisfying for me. Although the work on the ruins went forward steadily, and my assistants never faltered in their enthusiasm and industry – yet the results were uniformly disappointing.

There were other finds, many of them, but they were repetitive. Pottery, beads, even the occasional gold fragment or ornament no longer thrilled me as it had before. There was nothing that added a scrap of knowledge to the store we had accumulated already. I roved the site restlessly, anxiously hovering over a new trench or exposed level, praying that the next spadeful of earth turned would expose an inscribed pallet or the headstone to a burial vault. Somewhere here was the key to the ancient mystery but it was well hidden.

Apart from the lack of progress on the excavation, my relationship with Sally had deteriorated in some subtle fashion which I was at a loss to explain. Naturally there had been no opportunity for any physical intimacy since the arrival of the others at the City of the Moon. Sally was adamant in her determination not to allow our affair to become common knowledge. My amateurish manoeuvrings to get her alone were deftly countered. The nearest I came to success was when I visited her at the cavern during the day. Even here she had her assistant with her, and often Heather Willcox as well.

She seemed withdrawn, taciturn, even surly. She worked over her easel with a fierce concentration during the day, and she usually slipped away to her hut immediately after dinner. Once I followed her, knocking softly on the door of her hut, then hesitantly pushing the door open when there was no reply. She was not there. I waited in the shadows, feeling like a peeping Tom, and it was after midnight before she returned, slipping out of the silent grove like a ghost and going directly to her room where Leslie had long ago switched out the light.

It was distressing for me to see my laughing Sally so withdrawn, and finally I visited her at the cavern.

'I want to talk to you, Sal.'

'What about?' She looked at me with mild surprise, as though it were the first time in days that she had noticed me. I sent the young African assistant away and prevailed on Sally to join me on the rocks beside the emerald pool, hoping that its beauty and associations would soften her mood.

'Is something wrong, Sal?'

'Good Lord, should there be?' It was an awkward unsatisfying conversation. Sally seemed to feel I was prying into affairs that did not concern me. I felt my anger rising, and I wanted to shout at her:

'I am your lover, damn you, and everything you do concerns me!'

But good sense prevailed, for I am sure presumption of that magnitude from me would have severed the last tenuous threads of our relationship. Instead I took her hand and, hating myself for the blush that burned my cheeks, I told her softly, 'I love you, Sally. Just remember that – if there is ever anything I can do—'

I think it was probably the best thing I could have said, for immediately her hand tightened on mine and her face softened, her eyes went slightly misty.

'Ben, you are a sweet dear person. Don't take any notice of me for a while. I've just got the blues, there is nothing anybody can do about it. They will go on their own, if you don't fuss.'

For a moment she was my old girl again, a smile quivering precariously on the corners of her mouth, and in those great green eyes.

'Let me know when it's over, won't you?' I stood up.

'That I will, Doctor. You'll be the first to know.'

The following week I flew back to Johannesburg. There was the Annual General Meeting of the trustees of the Institute which I could not avoid, and I was committed to a series of lectures for the Faculty of Archaeology at the University of Witwatersrand.

I was scheduled to be away from the site for eleven days. I left it all in Peter Willcox's safe hands, after extracting from him a promise that he would cable me immediately if any new development broke.

The three girls fussed around me, packing my case, making a picnic lunch for me to eat on the plane, and lining up to kiss me goodbye at the airstrip. I must admit that I rather enjoyed all the attention.

I have often found that living too close to any problem narrows one's view of the whole. Three hours after leaving the City of the Moon, I made a minor breakthrough. If there had been walls and towers standing on the ruined foundations, then the rock must have been brought from nearby. The obvious place was from the cliffs themselves. Somewhere in those cliffs, close to the city, there was a quarry.

I would find it, and from its extent I would calculate the actual size of the city.

For the first time in weeks I felt good, and the days that followed were gratifying and solidly enjoyable. The meeting of the trustees was the type of festive affair which can be expected when funds are unlimited and prospects are favourable. From the Chair Louren was most complimentary when he renewed my contract as Director of the Institute for a further twelve months. To celebrate the thirty per cent rise in my remuneration, he invited me to a dinner at his home where forty people sat down at the yellow wood table in the huge dining-room, and I was the guest of honour.

Hilary Sturvesant, in a gown of yellow brocade silk and wearing the fabled Sturvesant diamonds, gave me her almost undivided attention during the meal. I have a weakness for beautiful things, particularly if they are women. There were twenty of them there that night, and in the drawing-room afterwards I held court like royalty. The wine had loosened my tongue, and washed away my confounded shyness. No matter that Hilary and Louren had probably primed the other guests to make a fuss of me, for when at two o'clock in the morning I went down to the Mercedes with Hilary and Louren escorting me I swaggered along seven feet tall.

This new-found confidence carried me through the series of four lectures at the University of the Witwatersrand. The first of which was attended by twenty-five students and faculty members, the latter outnumbering the former two to one. The word got out, however, and my final venue was changed to one of the main lecture theatres to handle the audience of 600 that turned up. I was an unqualified success. I was prevailed upon to return at an early date – and there was an unsubtle hint from the Vice-Chancellor of the University that the Archaeology Chair would be vacant the following year.

For the last three days of my visit I spent every minute at the Institute. With relief I found that not much had suffered in my absence, and my multitudinous staff had kept things running smoothly.

The bushman exhibition in the Kalahari Room was completed, and open to the public. It was magnificently executed, and the central figure of the main group reminded me sharply of my little friend Xhai. The model was depicted in the act of painting on the stone wall of a cave abode. With his stoppered buck-horn paint pots, and reed pipes and brushes, I imagined that this was how the artist who had painted my white king had worked. It gave me an odd sensation, as though two millennia had rolled away, as though I could send my mind back along the years. I spoke of it to Timothy Mageba.

'Yes, Machane. I have told you before that you and I are marked. We have the sign of the spirits on us, and we have the sight.'

I smiled and shook my head. 'I don't know about you, Timothy, but I've never been able to pick a winner—'

'I am serious, Doctor,' Timothy rebuked me. 'You have the gift. It is merely that you have not been taught to develop it.'

I will accept hypnotism, but talk of clairvoyance, necromancy, mantology and the like leaves me feeling embarrassed. To divert the conversation from me and my gifts, I asked, 'You have told me before that you are also marked by the spirits . . .'

Timothy looked at me steadily from out of those disturbing black eyes. At first I thought I had insulted him by my thinly disguised question, but suddenly he nodded that cannon-ball head. He stood up, closed and locked the door of his office before returning to his seat. Quickly he stripped shoe and sock from his right foot, and showed it to me.

The deformity was shocking, although I had seen photographs of it before. It was of fairly common occurrence among the Batonga tribe of the Zambezi Valley. There had been a paper on it published in the *British Medical Journal* during 1969. The condition was known as 'ostrich-footed', and consisted of a massive division between the metatarsus of the big toe and the second toe. The effect was to make the foot resemble the claw of an ostrich or predatory bird. Timothy was obviously very sensitive about this deformity, and almost immediately replaced his sock and shoe. I realized later that he had shown it to me in a deliberate attempt to enlist my sympathy, to create a bond between us.

'Both feet?' I asked, and he nodded. 'There are many people in the Zambezi Valley with feet like that,' I told him.

'My mother was a Batonga woman,' he answered. 'It was this mark that qualified me for training in the mysteries.'

'Does it hinder you at all?' I asked.

'No,' he answered brusquely, and then went on almost defiantly in Batonga. 'We men of the cloven feet outrun the fleetest antelope.'

It was a beneficial mutation then, and I would have enjoyed discussing it further but I was warned by Timothy's expression. I realized the effort it had taken him to show me.

'Will you have some tea, Doctor?' He reverted to English, closing the subject. When one of his young African assistants had poured cups of strong black tea for us, Timothy asked, 'Please tell me how the work at the City of the Moon is progressing, Doctor.'

We chatted for another half hour, then I left him.

'You must excuse me now, Timothy. I am flying back tomorrow morning early and there is still much to do.'

I was awakened by a soft but insistent knocking on the door of my suite in the Institute. I switched on the bedside light and saw that the time was three o'clock in the morning.

'Who is there?' I called and the knocking stopped. I slipped out of bed, shrugged into a dressing-gown and slippers, and started for the front door, when I realized the risk I was taking. I went back to my bedroom and took the big ugly automatic .45 from the drawer. Feeling a little melodramatic, I pumped a round into the chamber and went back to the front door.

'Who is it?' I repeated.

'It's me, Doctor, Timothy!'

I hesitated a moment longer – anybody could call themselves Timothy.

'Are you alone?' I asked in Kalahari bushman.

'I am alone, Sunbird,' he answered in the same language, and I slipped the pistol into my pocket and opened the door.

Timothy was dressed in dark blue slacks and a white shirt with a windcheater thrown over his shoulders and I noticed immediately that there were spots of fresh blood on the shirt and that there was a rather grubby cloth wrapped around his left forearm. He was clearly much agitated, his eyes wide and staring in the light, and his movements jerky and nervous.

'Good God, Timothy, are you all right?'

'I've had a terrible night, Doctor. I had to see you right away.'

'What have you done to your arm?'

'I cut it on the window pane of my front door, I fell in the dark,' he explained.

'You'd better let me have a look at it.' I went towards him.

'No, Doctor. It's only a scratch. What I have come to tell you is more important.'

'Sit down at least,' I told him. 'Can I get you a drink?'

'A drink, thank you, Machane, as you can see I am upset and nervous. That is how I came to injure my arm.'

I poured both of us whisky, and he took his glass in his right hand and continued moving nervously around my sitting-room while I sat in one of the big leather armchairs.

'What is it, Timothy?' I prompted him.

'It is difficult to begin, Machane, for you are not a believer. But I must convince you.'

He broke off and drank whisky, before turning to face me.

'Yesterday evening we spoke at length about the City of the Moon, Doctor, you told me how there are mysteries there that still baffle you.'

'Yes.' I nodded encouragement.

'The burial grounds of the ancients,' Timothy went on. 'You cannot find them.'

'That is true, Timothy.'

'Since then I have thought heavily on this matter.' He changed into Venda, a language better suited for the discussion of the occult. 'I went back in my memory over all the legends of our people.' I imagined vividly how he must have thrown himself into hypnotic trance to search. 'And there was something there, like a shadow beyond the firelight, a dark memory that eluded me.' He shook his head and turned away, pacing restlessly, sipping at his drink, muttering softly to himself as though he still searched in the dark archives of his mind.

'It was no use, Doctor. I knew it was there, but I could not grasp it. I despaired of it, and at last I slept. But it was a sleep greatly troubled by the dream demons – until at last . . .' he hesitated, '. . . my grandfather came to me.'

I stirred uneasily in my chair. Timothy's grandfather had lain twenty-five years in a murderer's grave.

'All right, Doctor.' Timothy saw my small movement of disbelief, and changed smoothly to English. 'I know you do not believe such things can happen. Let me explain it in terms you can accept. My imagination, heated by my search for a long-forgotten fragment of knowledge, threw up a dream image of my grandfather. The one from whom the knowledge was learned in the first place.'

I smiled to cover my spooky feelings; at this time of night with this half-demented black man talking of dark things, I felt myself falling under his spell.

'Go on, Timothy.' I tried to say it lightly, but my voice croaked a little.

'My grandfather came to me, and he touched my shoulder and he said, "Go with the blessed one, to the Hills of Blood and there I will make the mysteries known to you and open up the secret places." '

I felt my skin prickle. Timothy had said 'The Hills of Blood', and nobody had told him that name.

'The Hills of Blood,' I repeated.

'That is the name he used,' Timothy agreed. 'I can only believe he meant your City of the Moon.'

I was silent; reasonable man at war with primitive superstitious man within me.

'You want to come with me tomorrow, Timothy?' I asked.

'I will go with you,' Timothy agreed. 'And perhaps I will be able to show you something for which you search – then again I may not be able to.'

There was certainly nothing to lose. Timothy was obviously sincere, he was still tense and nervously aware.

'I have already invited you to join me, Timothy, and I was very disappointed when you refused. Of course you may come with me – we can certainly see if the sight of the ruins stirs something in your memory.'

'Thank you, Doctor. What time will you leave?'

I glanced at my watch.

'Good Lord, it's four o'clock already. We will leave at six.'

'Then I must hurry home and pack.' Timothy replaced his glass on my cabinet, then he turned to me. 'There is a small snag, Doctor. My travel papers have expired and we will have to cross an international border into Botswana.'

'Oh, damn it,' I muttered, deeply disappointed. 'You will have to get them renewed and come up with me on the next trip.'

'As you wish, Doctor,' he agreed readily. 'Of course, it will take two or three weeks – and by then the whole thing might have faded from my memory.'

'Yes.' I nodded, but I felt a prick of temptation. I am usually a law-abiding person, but now as I thought about it I saw that no harm could come from what I intended. The chance that Timothy might lead me to the burial grounds of the ancients was worth any risk.

'Would you like to take a chance, Timothy?' I asked. Formalities concerned with the coming and going of Sturvesant aircraft had been reduced to a minimum. There were daily arrivals and departures, and a phone call to the airport authorities was all that was necessary before departure. The Sturvesant name carried such weight that there was never a head count on arrival or departure. At the City of the Moon Louren had arranged special status with the Botswana Government, and we were virtually free from bothersome red tape.

I could have Timothy in and out within three days with nobody the wiser and no damage done. Roger van Deventer would accept my word that Louren had sanctioned the flight. I could see no problems.

'Very well, Doctor, if you think it's safe.' Timothy agreed to my proposal.

'Be at the Sturvesant hangar before six.' I sat down to scribble a note. 'If you are questioned at the airport gate, which I doubt, show them this. It's a note authorizing you to deliver goods to the Sturvesant hangar. Park your car behind the flight office, and wait for me in the office.'

Quickly we made our arrangements, and when I stood at the window of my bedroom and watched Timothy's old blue Chevy pull out of the Institute car park I felt a mixture of elation and apprehension. Idly I wondered what the penalty was for aiding illegal exit and entry, then dismissed the thought and went to make myself some coffee.

Timothy's Chevy was in one of the parking bays when Roger van Deventer and I drove up in the Mercedes. We went through into the hangar. The big sliding doors were open and the ground crew was readying the Dakota for the flight, and through the glass doors of the flight office I saw Timothy sitting hunched at the desk. He looked up and smiled at me.

'I'll get the clearance, Roger,' I suggested smoothly. 'You go and start the engines.'

'Okay, Doctor.' He handed me the flight dossier. We had done this before, and I had banked on the same procedure. Roger climbed up through the door of the fuselage, while I went quickly into the office.

'Hello, Timothy.' I looked at him and felt a twinge of concern. He was huddled into his blue windcheater, and there were lines of pain cut into his forehead and the corners of his nostrils. His skin was grey and his lips pale purplish blue. 'Are you all right?'

'My arm is a little painful, Doctor.' He opened the front of his jacket. The arm was in a sling, freshly bandaged. 'But it will be all right. I've had it attended to.'

'Do you feel up to this trip?'

'I'll be all right, Doctor.'

'Are you sure?'

'Yes, I'm sure.'

'All right, then.' I sat down at the desk and picked up the phone. It was answered at the first ring.

'Airport police!'

'This is Dr Kazin – from Sturvesant, Africa.'

'Oh, good morning, Doctor. How are you this morning?'

'Fine, thank you. I want to clear a flight to Botswana on ZA-CEE.'

'Hold on, Doctor. Let me get the particulars. Who are the passengers?'

'One passenger, myself – and the pilot is Roger van Deventer as usual.'

I dictated while the constable on the other end took it down in laborious shorthand. Until finally he said: 'That's okay, Doctor. Have a good flight. I'll give your clearance to control.'

I hung up and smiled at Timothy.

'All clear.' I stood up. 'Let's go.' And I led the way out of the office. The engines of the Dakota were ticking over. The three black ground crew inexplicably left their positions beside the landing gear and began walking rapidly towards me.

'Doctor!' Timothy's voice behind me, and I turned back towards him. It took me four or five seconds to realize that he had a short-barrelled Chinese model machine-pistol in his uninjured hand and the muzzle was pointing into my belly. I gaped at him.

'I am sorry, Doctor,' he said softly, 'but it is necessary.'

The ground crew closed in on each side of me, they gripped my arms.

'Please believe me, Doctor, when I tell you that I will not hesitate to kill you if you do not co-operate.' He raised his voice without taking his eyes off me. 'Come,' he called in Venda.

Five others came through the outer door of the hangar. I immediately recognized two of the young Bantu assistants from the Institute, and one of the girls. All of them carried those stubby, lethal-looking machine-pistols and between them they supported a badly wounded stranger. His feet dangled loosely, and blood-soaked bandages covered his chest and neck.

'Get him into the plane,' Timothy ordered crisply.

All this time I had stood dumbly, paralysed with shock, but now the party carrying the wounded man squeezed past between my captors and the side wall. They were blanketing each others' line of fire, the whole group was off balance and at that moment I regained my wits. I braced my legs, leaned forward slightly and heaved. The men on my arms shot forward like thrown darts, crashing headlong into Timothy and knocking him down in a floundering heap.

'Roger!' I shouted. 'Radio! Get help!' Hoping my voice would carry over the sound of the aircraft engines. The third ground crew leaped on my back, one arm locking around my throat. I reached up, took him at wrist and elbow and wrenched against the joint. His elbow went with a rubbery popping sound and he screamed like a girl, his arm loose and flabby in my grip.

'Don't shoot,' shouted Timothy. 'No noise.'

'Help!' I screamed, the engines drowning my cry. They dropped the wounded man and came at me. I ducked and went in low. I kicked for the groin of the leader, and felt my boot sock into him, fleshy and soft. He doubled over and I swung my other knee up into his face. It crunched as the gristle of his nose collapsed.

Timothy and the ground crew were scrambling to their feet.

'No shooting.' Timothy's voice was desperate. 'No noise.' I went for him. Leopard-mad with rage, hating him for this betrayal with the full strength of my being, wanting to see his blood splash and feel his bones break in my hands.

One of the girls hit me with the steel butt of the machine-pistol, as I brushed past her. I felt the sharp edge of it cut into the flesh of my scalp, it threw me off balance. One of the ground crew grappled with me, and I took him to my chest and hugged him. He screamed, and I felt his ribs buckling in my grip.

They hit me again, steel biting into the bone of my skull. Blood poured warmly down my face, blinding me. My arms went soft, I dropped the man I was crushing and turned to charge into the others. Blinded with my own blood, my maniacal roars deafening me, they hit me again, crowding around me as I flailed and groped for them. The blows rained on my head and my shoulders. My knees collapsed, and I went down. I was still conscious, hot waves of anger buoying me. The boots started then, crashing into my chest and belly. I doubled up, blind, rolled into a ball on the cold oily concrete, trying to ride that storm of booted feet.

'Enough, leave him.' Timothy's voice. 'Get him to the aircraft.'

'My arm. I'll kill him.' The voice pig-squealing with agony.

'Stop that.' Timothy again, and the sound of a palm slapping against a face. 'We need hostages. Get him into the plane.'

They dragged me across the floor, many hands. I was lifted and thrown heavily onto the metal floor of the fuselage. The door slammed closed, muting the engine noise.

'Tell the pilot to take off,' Timothy ordered. 'Get the Doctor into the radio compartment.'

I was hustled down the length of the aisle. Blinking the blood out of my eyes, I saw the white ground engineer and his black ground crew lying bound and gagged against the wall of the fuselage. They were stripped of their overalls, which the gang had used to impersonate them.

Rough hands forced me into the steel chair in the radio compartment, and they tied me so tightly that the ropes bit painfully into my flesh. My face felt swollen and numb, and the taste of my own blood was thick and metallic in my mouth.

I turned my head, looking into the cockpit. Roger van Deventer was at the controls. There was a livid red swelling under his eye, and his grey hair was rumpled, his face pale and terrified. One of them stood over him with the muzzle of a machine-pistol pressed firmly against the back of his head.

'Take off,' instructed Timothy. 'Observe all routine procedures. Do you understand?'

Roger nodded jerkily. I felt sorry for him, I had guessed he was not cast in the heroic mould.

'Sorry, Doctor,' he tried to explain. 'They jumped me the moment I stepped aboard.' His full attention was on the job of taxiing the big aircraft out onto the still dark airfield. He did not look at me. 'I didn't have a chance.'

'That's all right, Roger. I didn't do so good either,' I replied thickly. 'I only got in two good licks.'

'That is enough talking for now, please, Doctor. Mr van Deventer must attend to the business of take-off,' Timothy admonished me, and I turned to give him the most expressive glare of hatred that I could force from my numbed features.

Roger asked for and received control clearance, and the take-off was routine and uneventful. The tense, anxious black faces relaxed and there were a few nervous laughs.

'You will fly on course for Botswana,' Timothy instructed Roger. 'Once you are over the border I will give you a new course.'

Roger nodded stiffly, the machine-pistol still held at his head. I was assessing the strength of the gang, I had already formed a working idea of their motives. Apart from Timothy and the eight who had overwhelmed me, there were five others. These were the ones who had captured and guarded Roger and the ground crew. The wounded man and the two I had damaged were laid out on the floor of the cargo hold. The two girls were working over them, both girls from the Institute, they were fitting a splint and changing bloody bandages.

As I watched, the gang members began changing from civilian clothing into camouflage paratrooper battle-dress. I saw the red star shoulder flashes, and my last doubts were dispelled. I turned my head and found Timothy was watching me.

'Yes, Doctor.' He nodded. 'Soldiers of freedom.'

'Or the bringers of darkness, depending how you look at it.'

Timothy frowned at my retort. 'I had always believed you to be a man of humanity, Doctor. You, I would have expected, could understand and sympathize with our aspirations.'

'I find it hard to sympathize with gangsters carrying guns in their hands.'

We stared at each other for a few moments. Then abruptly he stood up and came to the radio equipment beside my chair. He switched on the set, glanced at his watch, and began sweeping the bands. The station came on loudly, and immediately all movement in the aircraft arrested, all attention fixed on the announcer's voice:

'This is the South African Broadcasting Corporation. The time is seven o'clock and here is the news. A spokesman for the South African Police states that at 2.15 a.m. this morning a detachment of the Security Police, acting on information received, raided a farm house on the outskirts of Randburg, a suburb of Johannesburg. A pitched battle between police and a large gang of unidentified persons armed with automatic weapons ensued. Elements of the gang escaped in four motor-cars, and after a chase by the police, two vehicles managed to evade pursuit. Initial reports are that eight of the gang were shot dead, and four were captured wounded or unhurt. It is anticipated that many of those escaping were also wounded. A full-scale police hunt is now in progress, and all roads out of the Witwatersrand area are under surveillance, together with all airports. It is with deep regret that we announce the death of three members of the South African Police Force, and the critical wounding of two—'

A ragged cheer rang out through the aircraft, and one or two of the gang clenched their fists over their heads in the Communist salute.

'Congratulations,' I murmured sarcastically to Timothy and he looked down at me.

'Death is ugly, slavery is worse,' he said evenly. 'Doctor, there is a bond between us.'

'My head is sore, my face is too painful to listen to your Communistic cant,' I told him, 'don't give me fancy words, you bastard. You want to burn my land and soak it in blood. You want to tear down everything I hold dear and sacred. It is my country and with all its faults I love it. You are my enemy. There is no bond between us – except that of the knife.'

Again we held each other's eyes for a long moment, then he nodded. 'To the knife then,' he agreed and turned away. The Dakota bore on steadily into the north, and my injuries began to ache. I closed my eyes, and rode the long dizzy swells of pain that rose up out of my guts and exploded in my head.

The Mirage jet came up out of the east and flashed silvery sleek across our nose, and as it passed with incredible speed I saw the Air Force roundels and the goggled face of the pilot staring at us. Then it was gone, but immediately the Tannoy crackled into life.

'ZA-CEE. This is Air Force Red Striker Two. Do you read me?' I stared out of the window beside my head, and saw the Mirage turn sparkling in the sunlight high above us. Timothy came running forward to the set beside me and stared at it for a moment. The atmosphere was hushed and tense. Timothy could not reply, his Bantu accent was too thick for deception.

Again the jet howled across our front. The gunman crouched low behind Roger's seat hidden from view.

'ZA-CEE.' Again the call was repeated. Timothy was sweating lightly, his face blue-grey with strain and the pain of the arm-wound. He turned from the set and motioned to two of his men.

'Bring him,' he pointed to the white ground engineer. They dragged him into the radio compartment and held him in front of me. His face was pale and shiny with sweat, his terrified eyes held mine in pitiful appeal, the gag cut into his mouth. One of them stood behind him and pulled his head back, exposing his throat and stretching the pale skin so that the arteries showed blue and pulsing. He reached around in front of the man, and laid the glistening blade of a trench knife against his throat.

'I am serious, Doctor,' Timothy assured me as he freed the rope from my arms and put the microphone of the radio transmitter into my hand. 'Reassure them. Tell them there are only two aboard, and that you are bound for the City of the Moon on a routine flight.' He placed his finger on the transmit switch of the set ready to cut if off.

The terrified engineer moaned into his gag, the knife pressed to the softly throbbing skin of his throat. They pushed him towards me, closer so that I could see his face clearly.

'Air Force Striker Two this is ZA-CEE standing by.' I croaked into the mike, staring fascinated into the engineer's terrified face.

'Report your complement and destination.'

'This is Dr Kazin of Sturvesant, Africa on a routine flight from—' As I spoke I saw them relax, the tension eased and Timothy's hand moved from the transmit switch of the set. The engineer's eyes held mine and I wanted to tell him that I was sorry, that I wished I could save him. I wanted to explain that I was trading his life for those of fourteen of my country's most dangerous enemies, that the sacrifice was worthwhile, and that I would willingly add my own life to the price. Instead I shouted into the handset:

'Hi-jacked by terrorists! Fire into us! Disregard our safety.' Timothy's hand darted to the transmit switch, and at the same moment he turned towards the hostage. I think he was going to intervene, to try and stop it. He was too late.

The knife slashed across the tensed throat, slitting it deeply beneath the line of the jaw. The blood burst forth like a ruptured garden hose, it sprayed out in a red fountain that drenched both Timothy and me. It pumped in great liquid jets that splashed against the roof of the cabin, then dribbled in thick cords and strings to the floor. The engineer was keening a high wailing sound like steam from a kettle, and the air from his lungs burst from the severed windpipe in a pink froth that spattered the radio set.

The Tannoy was squawking, 'Reverse your course! Conform to me! Conform to me immediately, or I will fire into you.'

Timothy was cursing as he wrestled the microphone out of my hand: I was screaming and fighting against the ropes.

'You animals! You filthy murdering bloody animals.'

One of the gang lifted his machine-pistol to hit me in the face, but Timothy knocked his arm away.

'Get him out of here!' He jerked his head towards the still twitching, kicking corpse of the engineer – and they dragged him out into the cargo hold.

'Mirage is attacking!' shouted Roger, from the cockpit, and we saw it coming from ahead of us, a silvery flash as it bore in on a head-on interception course.

Timothy snatched the microphone to his mouth. I saw

that his face was speckled with the engineer's blood. 'Hold your fire!' he shouted. 'We have hostages aboard.'

'Attack!' I screamed, tearing and jerking at my bonds. 'They'll murder us anyway! Open fire!'

The Mirage jet pulled up steeply ahead of us, without opening fire, and howled a few feet over our heads. The Dakota rocked violently in the slipstream. I was still screaming and struggling to tear myself loose. I wanted to get at them. The steel chair was rocking from side to side. I got to my feet against the side of the fuselage and heaved with all my strength. The seat buckled a little, and again the guard lifted his machine-pistol.

'No,' shouted Timothy. 'We need him alive. Tell Mary to bring the morphine.'

The Mirage sheered off, then circled in to take up station a hundred feet off our starboard wingtip, I could see the pilot staring helplessly across the gap at us.

'You have spoken to Dr Kazin,' Timothy warned the pilot of the jet. 'And we have four other hostages. We have already executed one white hostage and we will not hesitate to execute another if you take any further hostile action.'

'They're going to kill us anyway,' I shouted, but Timothy broke the contact.

It took five of them to hold me still for the hypodermic, but at last they got it into my arm, and though I tried to resist the drug, I felt myself going muzzy and misty. I tried to maintain my struggles, but my movements became lethargic and uncoordinated and slowly I drifted off into unconsciousness. My last waking memory was hearing Timothy giving Roger a new course to fly.

Pain and thirst woke me. My mouth was thick and scummy and my head was a mass of solid blinding agony. I tried to sit up and cried out aloud.

'Are you all right, Doctor? Take it easy.' Roger van Deventer's voice, and I focused my eyes on him.

'Water?' I asked.

'Sorry, Doc.' He shook his head, and I looked around the bare white-washed room. Four wooden bunks and a lavatory bucket were all the furnishings, and the door was barred and grilled. The three Bantu ground crew sat on one of the bunks across the room, looking lost and unhappy.

'Where are we?' I whispered.

'Zambia. Some sort of military camp. We landed an hour ago.'

'What happened to the Air Force jet?'

'It turned back when we crossed the Zambezi. Nothing they could do.'

And there was nothing we could do, either. For five days we sat in the airless, oven-like room with its stinking bucket, until on the fifth day our guards came to fetch me. With much shouting and many unnecessary shoves and blows I was marched down a corridor and into a sparsely furnished office whose main furnishing was a portrait of Chairman Mao. Timothy Mageba rose from behind the desk and motioned my guards to leave.

'Sit down, Doctor, please.' He wore paratrooper camouflage, and the bars and stars of a Colonel in the Chinese People's Army.

I sat on the wooden bench, and my eyes fastened on the half-dozen bottles of Tusker beer that stood on a tray. The bottles were bedewed with cold, and I felt my throat contracting.

'I know how fond you are of a bottle of cold beer, Doctor.' Timothy opened one of the bottles, and offered it to me. I shook my head.

'No, thank you. I don't drink with murderers.'

'I see.' He nodded, and I saw the little shadows of regret in those dark brooding eyes. He lifted the bottle to his own lips and drank a mouthful. I watched him thirstily.

'The engineer,' he said, 'the execution, it was not intended. I did not mean it to happen. Please understand that, Doctor.'

'Yes. I understand. And when the smoke of our burning land blackens the skies, and the stink of our dead sickens even your dark spirits, will you cry out, *I did not mean it to happen?*'

Timothy turned away and went to stand at the window, looking out over a parade ground where squads of uniformed Bantu drilled under a dazzling sun.

'I have been able to arrange for your release, Doctor. You will be allowed to return in the Dakota.' He came back to stand before me, and then he changed from English into Venda. 'My heart cries out to see you go, Machane, for you are a man of gentleness, and strength, and great courage. Once I hoped that you might join us.'

In Venda I answered, 'My heart weeps also, for a man who was a friend, one I trusted, one who I believed was a man of goodwill, but he is gone now into the half-world of the criminals and the destroyers. He is dead to me, and my heart weeps.'

It was true, I realized. It was not just an attempt to shame him. Beneath my hatred and anger, there was a sense of sorrow, of loss. I had believed in him. I had seen in a man such as he was, a hope for the future of this poor tormented continent of ours. We looked at each other wistfully, regretfully across a space of four feet that was as wide as the span of the heavens and as deep as the chasms of Hell.

'Goodbye, Doctor,' he said softly. 'Go in peace, Machane.'

They took us in the covered back of a three-ton truck to the airstrip, bare-footed and stripped to our underclothes.

They formed a double line from the truck to the Dakota. There were perhaps 200 of them in paratrooper uniform, and we were forced to walk down the narrow aisle with jeering black faces on each side of us. There were Chinese instructors with them, their lank black hair flopping out from under the cloth uniform caps, grinning hugely as we passed. I was bitterly aware of the mocking eyes and jibes aimed at my crooked exposed back, and I hurried towards the refuge of the Dakota. Suddenly one of them stepped out of the ranks in front of me. Deliberately he spat at me, and a storm of laughter went up from them. With a thick gob of yellow phlegm plastered in my hair, I scrambled up into the cabin of the aircraft.

The Air Force Mirages picked us up an hour after we crossed the Zambezi river and they escorted us to the military airfield at Voortrekker Hoogte. However, my almost hysterical relief at our safe home-coming was shortlived. Once a doctor had cleaned and dressed the clotted and suppurating gashes in my head, I was hustled away in a closed car to a meeting with four unsmiling, grimly polite, officers of the police and military intelligence.

'Dr Kazin, is this your signature?'

It was my recommendation for the issue of Timothy Mageba's passport.

'Dr Kazin, do you remember this man?'

A Chinaman I had met when I visited Timothy at London University.

'Are you aware that he is an agent of the Communist Chinese government, Doctor?'

There was a photograph of the three of us drinking beer on the tow-path beside the Thames.

'Can you tell us what you spoke about, please, Doctor?'

Timothy had told me that the Chinaman was an anthropology major, and we had discussed Leakey's discoveries at Olduvai Gorge.

'Did you recommend Mageba for the Sturvesant travel scholarship, Doctor?'

'Did you know that he went to China and received training as a guerrilla leader?'

'Did you sign these order forms for twenty-seven drums of fuller's earth from Hong Kong, Doctor – and these customs declarations?'

They were standard Institute forms, I could recognize my signature on the customs form across the desk. I did not remember the shipment.

'Were you aware that this shipment contained 150 lb. of plastique explosives, Doctor?'

'Do you recognize these, Doctor?'

Pamphlets in a dozen African languages. I read the first line of one of them. Terrorist propaganda. Exhortations to kill, burn and destroy.

'Were you aware that these were printed on your press at the Institute, Doctor?'

The questions went on endlessly, I was tired, confused, and began contradicting myself. I pointed out the wounds on my head, the rope burns at my wrists and ankles, and the questions went on. My head throbbed, my brain felt like a battered jelly.

'Do you recognize these, Doctor?'

Machine-pistols, ammunition.

'Yes!' I shouted at them. 'I had pistols like that against my head, in my belly!'

'Did you know that these were imported in cases of books addressed to your Institute?'

'When you obtained police clearance for the Dakota flight, Doctor, you stated—'

'They jumped me after the phone call. I've explained that a dozen times, damn you!'

'You've known Mageba for twelve years. He was a protégé of yours, Doctor.'

'Do you mean to tell us that you were never approached by Mageba? Never discussed politics with him?'

'I'm not one of them! I swear it—' I remembered the blood spraying against the cabin roof, the crunch of steel biting into the bone of my skull, the spittle clinging in my hair. 'You've got to believe me, please! Oh God, please!' And I think I must have fainted, it went all dark and warm in my head and I slumped sideways off the chair onto the floor.

I woke in a hospital room, between clean crisp sheets – and Louren Sturvesant sat beside the bed.

'Lo, oh thank God.' I felt all choked up with relief. Louren was here, and it would be all right now.

He leaned forward, unsmiling, that marvellous face cold and hard as though it had been cast in bronze. 'They think you were one of the gang. That you set it up, that you were using the Institute as the headquarters for a terrorist organization.'

I stared at him, and he went on remorselessly, 'If you have betrayed me and your country, if you have gone over to our enemies, then you can expect no mercy from me.'

'Not you also, Lo. I don't think I can stand that.'

'Is it true?' he demanded.

'No!' I shook my head. 'No! No!' And suddenly there were tears streaming down my face and I was shaking and blubbering like a baby. Louren leaned forward and gripped my shoulder hard.

'Okay, Ben.' He spoke with infinite gentleness and pity. 'It's okay, partner. I'll fix it. It's all over now, Ben.'

Louren would not let me go back to my bachelor quarters at the Institute, and I was installed in a guest suite at Kleine Schuur, the Sturvesant residence.

The first night Louren woke me from a screaming nightmare of blood and mocking black faces. He was in a dressing-gown, with his golden curls disordered from sleep. He sat on the side of my bed, and we talked of the good, sane things we had done together and the things we would do together in the future, until at last I slipped off into untroubled sleep.

For ten lazy, idyllic days I stayed at Kleine Schuur, spoiled by Hilary and fussed by the children, protected from the news-hungry Press, and sheltered from the realities and alarums of the outside world. The bruises faded, the scabs dried and fell away, and I found it more and more difficult to respond to the children's cry of 'Story' with something new. They shouted the punch-lines in chorus, and corrected me on the details. It was time to go back into the stream.

In one unpleasant day-long session I told the story of the hi-jacking at the public inquiry, and afterwards faced the Press of the world. Then Louren flew me north in the Lear jet, back to the City of the Moon.

On the way I told him how I intended to find the stone quarries – and then the tombs of the ancients.

When he grinned and told me, 'That's the tiger – get in there, boy, and tear the bottom out of it!' I realized that I had been enthusing and emoting a little. I remembered Old Xhai's imitation of the Sunbird, and put my fluttering hand firmly back in my lap.

A hero's welcome was waiting for me at the City of the Moon, they had followed my adventures on the radio. But now they opened a case of Windhoek beer and sat round me in a circle while I told the whole story again.

'That Timothy, he always gave me a funny feeling.'

Solemnly Sally demonstrated her amazing gift of hind-sight. 'I could have told you there was something fishy about him.' Then she stood up and came to kiss me on the forehead in front of them all, while I blushed crimson. 'Anyway, we are glad you're safe, Ben. We were so worried about you.'

The next morning, after I had driven Louren to the airstrip and watched him take off, I went looking for Ral Davidson. I found him in the bottom of a trench measuring a slab of sandstone. He was covered by a skimpy pair of shorts and a mass of hair that almost completely obscured his features, but he was burned a deep mahogany brown by the sun and was lean and fit. I had become very fond of him. We sat on the edge of the trench dangling our feet over the side, and I explained to him about the quarry.

'Gee, Doc! Why didn't we think of that before?' he enthused. That evening we drew up an elaborate search pattern, with a schedule to enlarge the area of search in expanding spirals each day. Ral's gang was temporarily withdrawn from the excavations within the temple, and armed with machetes for the assault on the thick, spiny vegetation on top of the cliffs.

The whole search was planned like a military operation. I had been dying to find an opportunity to use the walkie-talkie radio sets with which Louren had, unbidden, supplied us. This was it. Ral and I checked the radios, shouting things like, 'Over to you' and 'Roger!' and 'Read you five five!' at each other.

Peter Willcox muttered something about 'boy scouts', but I think he was a little jealous that he hadn't been invited to join the search. Leslie and Sally, however, were infected by our enthusiasm and they victualled the expedition with sufficient food and drink to keep an army bloated and drunk for a week. They turned out in a pink dawn, still in their pyjamas and dressing-gowns, Leslie with her hair in curlers, to wave us off and wish us luck. At the head of my gang of stalwarts, laden with food and equipment, feeling a little like Scott or bold Cortez, I led them towards the gap in the cliffs which had become our regular route to the top – and ten hours later, sweaty, bedraggled, scratched by thorns, stung by hippo fly and other insects, broiled by the sun and in a filthy temper, I led them down again.

We repeated this routine daily for the next ten days, and on the tenth evening when we paused half-way down the gap in the cliff to rest, Ral suddenly looked at the steep sides of the gap and said in a voice of wonder:

'Gee, Doc! This is it!'

For ten days we had been using the steps cut by the ancients into their quarry. Thick growth had covered the neat terraces from which they had sawn the red stone. We found some of the half-formed blocks of masonry still *in situ*, only a little undercut and almost unweathered in this protected gully. The marks of the saws were fresh upon them as though the workmen had laid down their tools the day before, instead of 2,000 years ago. Then there were blocks, cut in the rough, and abandoned half-way through the process of dressing. Others were completed, ready for transporting – yet others were in transit, discarded haphazard along the floor of the gully.

We cleared the undergrowth from around them and were then able to follow each fascinating step of the process of manufacture. The whole team came up to assist. They were jubilant with this new success, for we had all been a little put down with the recent total lack of progress. We sketched and mapped, measured and photographed, argued and theorized, and there was an evident renaissance of enthusiasm in all of us. The feeling that we had reached a dead end in the investigations was dispelled. I have a photograph, taken by one of the Bantu foremen who thought us all mad. We are clowning it up, posing on one of the bigger blocks of masonry. Peter strikes a Napoleonic attitude, hand in the breast of his jacket. Ral's hairy visage is adorned with a ferocious squint, and he poises a pick-axe murderously above Peter's head. Leslie is coyly showing a little cheesecake, and that is almost as bad as Ral's squint, with those legs she could kick elephants to death. I am sitting on Heather's lap, sucking my thumb. Sally has Peter's glasses on her nose and my hat pulled down over her ears; she is trying to look hideous, but failing resoundingly. This photograph illustrates the mood of those days.

After their assistance was no longer needed, the others went back to their separate tasks with renewed energy. Ral and I stayed on in the quarry. I brought up my theodolite and we set about calculating its extent and the amount of masonry removed from it. It was impossible to measure accurately the irregular excavation, but we decided that approximately a million and a half cubic yards of rock had been removed.

Then by a study of the method of quarrying and using the volume of abandoned blocks as a very rough guide, we guessed that the ratio of dressed finished blocks to waste material would be about 40:60. Finally we arrived at a figure of 600,000 cubic yards.

Up to this point we had been working with fairly factual figures, but now we pushed off into an ocean of conjecture.

'At least it's not as bad as drawing a dinosaur from its footprints,' Ral defended us, as we used the map of the foundations of the temple together with our calculation of rock volumes to reconstruct a complete elevation of the vanished City of the Moon.

'Here, let me do that!' Irritably Sally took the paintbrush out of my hand on the first evening, after she had watched my efforts for ten minutes.

'I think the batter of the main walls is a little excessive,' Peter murmured critically, watching her, 'if you compare the walls of the elliptical building at Zimbabwe—'

'Yes, but take the temple of Tarxien at Malta,' Heather

interceded. 'Or the main walls of Knossos.' And before Ral and I could do a thing to prevent it, the project had become a group effort that replaced the nightly song-fest in the common room.

With everybody contributing from their own particular area of the dig, and from their own specialized talents and interests, we built up a series of pictures of our city.

Massive red walls, ornamented with the chevron patterns of the waves that made Phoenicia great. Red walls that caught the rays of the setting sun, the evening blessing of the great sun god Baal. The tall towers, symbols of fertility and prosperity, rising from the dark green foliage of the silent grove. Beyond it, the vertical gash in the cliffs that led through a secret passage into the mysterious cavern. Again a symbol of the organs of reproduction. Surely this must have been sacred to Astarte – more commonly worshipped by the Carthaginians as Tanith – goddess of earth and moon, and so ranks of white-clad priests wound in procession through the grove, past the towers and into the secret cavern.

We knew that the Phoenicians made human sacrifice to their gods and goddesses. The Old Testament described the infants delivered to the flaming belly of Baal, and we wondered what dreadful ritual our peaceful emerald pool had seen, depicting the victim dressed in gold and finery and poised on the edge of the pool with the high priest lifting the sacrificial knife.

'If only it weren't so deep!' Sally exclaimed. 'Ben wanted to get divers to go down, but he says they couldn't work so deep.'

In the area between the inner and outer walls of the temple, where the layer of ash lay thick and where the majority of golden beads and richer ornaments had been discovered, we drew in the quarters of the priests and priestesses. This would be a maze of mud walls with thatched roofs. We reconstructed the streets and courts of the priests and nobles.

'What about the king and his court?' Peter demanded. 'Wouldn't they live within the main walls also?'

So we divided the area between the quarters of the priests and the court of the king, drawing on what little we knew of Knossos, Carthage and Tyre and Sidon to give our paintings life. Ral had found the gate through the outer wall, it was the only opening and it looked towards the west.

'From it a road would have led directly down to the harbour.' Sally drew it in.

'Yes, but there would have been a market, a place of trade beside the harbour,' Ral suggested, and pointed to the map. 'This would be it. The area Peter has been puzzling over.'

'Can you imagine the piles of ivory and copper and gold,' Leslie sighed.

'And slaves standing on the blocks to be sold,' Heather agreed.

'Hold it! Hold it! This is supposed to be a scientific investigation.' I tried to restrain them.

'And the ships lying on the beach.' Sally started to paint them in. 'Huge biremes with their prows shaped like rams' heads, covered with gilt and enamel.'

The walls and towers rose again, the lake refilled with bright waters, and the harbours and taverns were peopled with hosts dead for two thousand years. Warriors strutted, and slaves whined, noble ladies rode in their litters, caravans poured in from the land to the east laden with gold and treasure, and a white king strode out through the great stone gates with a rosetted shield on his shoulder and his armour asparkle in the sun.

The project was fun, and it served also to prod our imagination. By the time Sally had put the last touches to our painting, four weeks had passed, and as a direct result of it Peter had discovered the shipyards suggested by Sally's biremes beached below the city.

There was the keel of a ship laid on the slip, with the main frames in place. The unfinished vessel had been burned, and its charred parts scattered. Only imagination and faith could recognize it as a ship. I knew my scientific opponents would challenge it, but carbon-14 on the charred wood gave us an approximate date of A.D. 300, the date which we had defined as that of the 'great fire'.

The project gave me an excuse to spend more of my time with Sally. I began taking my lunch and bathing costume up to the cavern. At first there was an awkwardness between us, but I worked hard at setting Sally at ease and soon we were back in that friendly bantering relationship that made us such a good working team. Only once I referred back to our more intimate association.

'Have you still got the blues, Sal?' I asked, and she gave me a long frank gaze before replying.

'Please give me time, Ben. There is something I have to work out with myself.'

'Okay.' I smiled as cheerfully as I could, and resigned myself to a long, long wait.

Sometimes the others joined our lunch-time sessions at the pool, for even when the heat was a hissing 115° outside, it was cool in the cavern. We splashed and shouted, and the echoes boomed back at us. One of my indelible memories is that of Leslie clad in a frilly little pink bikini romping skittishly around the pool like a lady hippopotamus in the mating season, pursued by the indefatigable Ral.

Five weeks after my return I went up to the cavern with good news.

'I just received a radio message from Larkin, Sal. Louren is arriving tomorrow.'

I was disappointed in her negative reaction, because I

was sure she had overcome her initial dislike of Louren for my sake – and that she had begun to like him.

I went to meet Louren at the airstrip, and I was shocked. He had lost 20lb in weight, and his skin which usually glowed with golden health was now chalky grey. Beneath his eyes were smears of dark plum that looked like bruises.

'Ben!' He put an affectionate arm around my shoulder and squeezed. 'It's good to see you, you old bastard.' But his voice was weary and I noticed the threads of silver at his temples which were newly acquired.

'My God, Lo, you look terrible.'

'Thanks.' He grinned wryly, and slung his bags into the back of the Land-Rover.

'Seriously, Lo. Are you sick or something?' I was distressed to see him looking so ill and haggard.

'I've been on a rough one, Ben,' he confided as he climbed into the Land-Rover beside me. 'Four weeks at the bargaining table, I had to do it all myself – could not trust anyone else to handle it. The other side sent in teams, changing them when they were worn out.'

'You're going to kill yourself,' I scolded him, sounding a little like a nagging wife. And he leaned across, punched my arm lightly, and laughed.

'You're a shot in the arm, partner.'

'Was it worth it? What was it about?'

'It's big, Ben! E – bloody – normous! Copper and iron, South West Africa, near the Cunene River, massive ore bodies lying in association, low-grade copper and high-grade iron – together they are a treasure chest.' The weary tone was gone from his voice. 'I put those little Jap bastards over the table and I roasted their arses. They will put in the finance for a deep-water harbour and a railway line to get the stuff out. That will cost them 150 million.' He was exultant, colour coming back into the pale cheeks. 'One of my companies will do the construction work, of course.'

He touched a finger to his lips in a conspiratory gesture and I giggled delightedly. I enjoyed him in this mood. 'I'll put up for the pelletization plant and . . .' He went on to outline the scheme, laughing and punching my arm when he recounted each bargaining point on which he had scored.

'What will it make for you?' I asked at last, and he looked at me, slightly put down.

'You mean in terms of money?' he asked.

'Sure! What else?'

'Hell, Ben. I've explained it before. That's not the important thing. It's not the money, it's exports and employment, and opening up new resources, and building for the future, realizing the potential of our country and – and—'

'And getting one hell of a kick out of it,' I suggested.

He laughed again. 'You are too shrewd, Ben. I suppose that's a lot of it. The game not the score.'

'Have you seen last week's *Time* magazine?' I asked. I knew it would needle him.

'Oh, for God's sake, Ben,' he protested.

'Your name is on the list of the world's thirty richest men.'

'Those bastards,' he muttered darkly. 'Now everybody doubles their prices. Why don't they mind their own business and let me get on with mine.'

'And in the process you are killing yourself.'

'You're right, Ben. I do feel a little spent, so I'm taking a week. A whole week's holiday.'

'Big deal,' I sneered, 'a holiday with your B.Y.M. arriving every half-hour for conferences, and the rest of the time with you hanging over the radio set.'

'Forget it,' he smiled. 'I'm getting away, and you're coming with me.'

'What do you mean, Lo?' I asked.

'Tell you later.' He avoided the question for we were

approaching the branch in the dirt track, and I automatically slowed to turn down to the huts.

'Straight on, Ben,' Louren instructed. 'I want to go up to the cavern. I've been thinking of that place for weeks.' His voice went soft and reflective. 'When things got really tough there at the table, I'd think about the peace and tranquillity of that place. It seemed to . . .' He stopped, and coughed with embarrassment. Louren doesn't often talk that way.

Sally was working at the rear wall of the cavern. She wore a green silk blouse and tailored khaki slacks, with her hair loose and shiny. As she looked up to greet Louren, I saw with mild surprise that she wore lipstick for the first time in weeks.

She noticed his haggard features immediately, and I saw the concern in her eyes although she said nothing about it. Her greeting was subdued, almost offhand, and she turned back to her easel. Louren went immediately to the portrait of the white king. I drifted across to join him and we sat in a friendly relaxed silence examining the strange figure. Louren spoke first.

'Do you get the feeling he's trying to tell you something, Ben?'

It was a fanciful question for Louren, but I treated it with respect for he was clearly in deadly earnest.

'No, Lo, I can't say that I do.'

'There is something here, Ben,' he said with certainty. 'Something you – we have overlooked. The key to this place, the whole secret of it is in this cavern.'

'Well, Lo, we could . . .' I began but he wasn't listening. Sally left her easel and came to join us, she sat beside Louren and watched his face with complete attention.

'This feeling has never let me down, Ben. Do you remember the Desolation Valley mine? My geologist gave it a thumbs down, but I had this feeling. Do you remember?'

I nodded. Desolation Valley was now yielding twenty thousand carats of gem diamonds a month.

'There is something here. I am sure of it, but where?' He turned to stare at me, as though I had hidden whatever he was searching for. 'Where is it, Ben? The floor, the walls, the roof?'

'And the pool,' I said.

'All right, let's start with the pool,' he agreed.

'It's too deep, Lo. No diver—'

'What do you know about diving?' he demanded.

'Well, I've dived a couple of times.'

'Oh, for God's sake, Ben!' he interrupted brusquely. 'When I need a heart operation I go to Chris Barnard, not the local vet. Who is the best diver in the world?'

'Cousteau, I suppose.'

'Fine. I'll get my people onto him. That takes care of the pool. Now the floor.'

Dealing with Louren is like being caught in a hurricane. At the end of an hour, he had outlined a scheme for a thorough investigation of the cavern, and at last he suggested casually, 'Okay, Ben. Why don't you go on back to camp? I'd like an hour or so alone here.' I was reluctant to miss a minute of his company but I stood up immediately.

'Are you coming, Sal?' I asked. Louren wanted to be alone.

'Oh, Ben. I'm in the middle of—'

'That's okay, Ben,' Louren told me, 'she won't disturb me.' And I left the cavern.

The guest hut was long ago prepared, but I went with one of the servants to supervise the unpacking of Louren's bags. I noticed that someone had cut a spray of wild cave-lilies that grew under the cliffs, and placed them in a beer tankard beside the bed. I meant to compliment the Matabele who acted as our cook, butler and house-keeper for this thoughtful little touch. It relieved the bleakness of the hut.

After checking Louren's accommodation I went down to the big bungalow and made sure there was ice in the refrigerator and plenty of cold water. Then I cracked the seal on a fresh bottle of Glen Grant – Louren and I have a common fondness for this nectar. While I was busy with the whisky bottle, Ral and Leslie came in off the dig and I heard them clump into the office next door. I did not intend eavesdropping, but the partition walls were paper-thin.

Ral growled like an enraged beast, and Leslie squealed.

'Oh, you are naughty!' she cried breathlessly, and it was clear that she had been physically molested. 'Someone will catch you doing that.'

'As long as they don't catch me doing what I'm going to do tonight,' Ral declared.

'Shh!' Leslie enjoined silence, but to no avail.

'Five weeks. I thought he'd never come. I was going mad.'

'Oh, Rally Dally darling,' wheezed Leslie in high passion.

'Toodles, my little Toodles,' Ral replied, and I blushed for them. Silently I set down the bottle and stole from the room. I was slightly puzzled as to how Louren's arrival, for that was obviously what Ral was referring to, could make such a dramatic improvement in their physical relationship, and I envied them for I had no such expectation.

We were all of us sick to the stomach with a diet of canned and preserved food. Louren had brought with him a full load of fresh fruit, vegetables and meat. That night we had a sucking pig, golden brown in its suit of crackling, with roast potatoes, green peas and a gigantic bowl of fresh salad. There was very little conversation at the dinner-table.

Once the dishes were cleared, Louren lit a cigar. I

refilled the glasses and we all settled down in a circle about Louren. First I reported to Louren the discovery of the quarry, and the deductions we had made from it. This led on to an exhibition of Sally's reconstruction of the city.

I had not expected Louren to react the way he did. I had thought he might be mildly amused, as we were, not that he would accept our fantasy as proven fact. He worked himself into a fever of excitement, jumping up from his chair to examine each illustration, firing his abrupt searching questions at us, or simply sitting hunched forward in his seat staring at the painting with glitter-eyed concentration. His face was still pale and ravaged, which gave an almost demented intensity to his expression.

Sally, with a touch of canny showmanship, had kept the painting of the white king for the last. As she lifted it onto the board I saw Louren stiffen in his seat. The white king was in full battle armour, helmet and breastplate in glistening bronze, shield slung, and a short sword girt around his waist. His red-gold beard was curled and clubbed, and his bearing regal. His attendants followed him through the gates of the high outer wall, one carried his battle-axe, another his bow and a quiver of arrows, a third bore the golden chalice of eternal life.

Sally had lavished patient skill upon this particular illustration, and it was the most impressive of the whole series. We all stared at it in silence until suddenly I uncrossed my legs and leaned forward quickly, spilling a little of my whisky in surprise. I had not noticed it before, the gold beard had masked it, but now I realized suddenly whom Sally had used as her model for the white king. I turned to stare at Louren, and there was the same deep forehead, the noble brow above wide-set piercing pale blue eyes, the same straight nose with delicately chiselled nostrils, and the proud curve of mouth with the slightly sensual pout of the lower lip.

'Ben!' His voice was husky, he did not take his eyes off

the portrait. 'This is remarkable – I hadn't realized until this evening what this meant. Up to now it was just intriguing blocks of stone, and a few beads and scraps of gold. I never really thought about the people. That's the important thing, Ben! These men that voyaged to the ends of the world; that built something magnificent in the wilderness—' He broke off, and shook his head slowly, considering the magnitude, the grandeur of it. Then he turned to me.

'Ben. We have got to find out what happened to them, and their city. I don't care how long it takes, how much it costs. I have got to know.'

Now he stubbed out his cigar and jumped up from his chair, began pacing with a barely controlled violence.

'It's about time we announced this, Ben. I will set up a press conference. I'll want you all there to explain it. The world must know about these men.'

My stomach dropped steeply with alarm, and I stuttered a protest.

'But, Lo, we can't do that. Not now, not yet – please!'

'Why not?' He wheeled on me belligerently.

'We haven't got enough proof yet.' I went chill with horror, as I thought how my critics would hang, draw and quarter me if I went out on stage with such a sorry script. 'They'll scalp us, Lo. They'll tear us to pieces.'

'We'll show them these.' He pointed at the paintings.

'God!' I shuddered at the thought. 'Those are just conjecture, fantasy, in that picture the only single detail we could substantiate would be the chalice.'

Louren stared at me, but I saw the madness fading in his eyes. Suddenly he laughed guiltily, and struck his forehead with the heel of his hand.

'Wow!' he laughed. 'I must be tired! For a moment there those paintings were real, from life!' He went to stand before the painting again and examined it wistfully. 'I've got to know, Ben,' he said again, 'I've just got to know.'

The following day, while we ate lunch beside the emerald pool, Louren told me how he and I were to get away together. He used Sally's charcoal stick to draw on the flat surface of a rock.

'Here we are, and here sixty-five miles to the north-east are the ruins at Domboshaba. If your theories are correct then there was an ancient caravan route between the two cities. You and I are going to take the Land-Rover, and go cross-country, trying to pick up the old trail.'

'It's pretty rough country,' I pointed out, without enthusiasm. 'Completely unexplored, no roads, no water.'

'And no B.Y.M.,' Louren smiled.

'That makes it irresistible.' I returned his smile, remembering that this was therapeutic not scientific. 'When do we leave?'

'Tomorrow morning at first light.'

It was still dark when I awoke, and my bedside clock showed four-thirty. It was too late to go back to sleep and too early to get up. I was pondering the problem when the door of the hut opened stealthily and, as I prepared to repel burglars, Ral's hairy head silhouetted by the moonlight appeared around the jamb.

He had given me a fright so I shouted at him, 'What are you doing?'

If I had been frightened, it was nothing to Ral's reaction to my question. Letting out a howl of terror he leapt about three feet in the air with his arms flapping, rather like a crested crane doing its mating dance. It took him a minute or two to recover himself sufficiently to shamble across to his bed and reply in a shaky voice, 'I've been to the toilet.' Which was just as well, I thought, otherwise my challenge could have had disastrous consequences. I got up, dressed and went out to check the Land-Rover. I suppose I guessed that Ral had been with Leslie, but I did not realize the implications of this.

It took Louren and me most of the first day to find a way

over the Hills of Blood that the Land-Rover could negotiate. We followed the line of cliffs northward until they dwindled away and broke up into low kopjes and we could climb one of the gullies between them. It was a rugged ascent that taxed even that sturdy vehicle, but once on top the going was through open savannah and scattered acacia forest and we made good progress, swinging away southward again to pick up the caravan route that Louren had hopefully drawn in on his large-scale map.

That night we camped astride it, or at least where we hoped it might have been. With the amount of gasoline and water aboard, there was scant room for the luxuries of camp life. Besides it was meant to be a rough trip to dispel the smogs and grimes of civilization, a nostalgic return to the expeditions we had made together in our youth.

We grilled a brace of sand-grouse over the coals, and drank Glen Grant and sun-warmed water from enamel mugs. Then with hollows scraped from the hard earth for hip and shoulder we rolled into our sleeping bags beside the Land-Rover and chatted drowsily and contentedly for an hour before falling asleep.

In the dawn Louren massaged his back and gingerly worked the stiffness out of his muscles.

'I've just remembered I'm not twenty any longer,' he groaned, but by the third day he was looking it. The sun coloured him again, the bruises under his eyes were gone and he laughed freely.

Our progress was slow. Often it was necessary to retrace our spoor out of broken ground whose kopjes and ridges denied us passage. Then we would leave the Land-Rover and go in on foot to try and pioneer a way through. There was no hurry, however, so we could fully enjoy each mile as we groped our way north and east through country that changed its character and mood with the bewitching rapidity that is Africa's alone.

Each hour of eastward travel rewarded us with more

evidence of bird and animal life. The dry-land birds gave way for guinea fowl, francolin, and the gigantic korrie bustard. While amongst the mopani and masasa trees there was the occasional silver-grey flash of a running kudu, with his long corkscrew horns laid flat along his back.

'Water not far away,' Louren commented as we stopped the Land-Rover at the edge of one of those open glades of yellow grass and watched a herd of sable antelope move away into the trees on the far side. The most stately antelope in Africa, proud heads holding the curved scimitar horns high and the dazzling contrast of snowy breast against the black body.

'Another endangered species,' I remarked sadly. 'Making way for the greed and excesses of man.'

'Yes,' Louren agreed. 'And you know something, there's not one single specimen of *homo sapiens* that's half as beautiful, and that,' he said, 'includes Raquel Welch.'

That night we camped in a grove of masasa trees, clad in their outlandish spring foliage which has the colours of no other tree on earth – pinks, soft shiny beige, and flaming reds. Louren had shot a young impala ram during the day and he wrapped the fillets in bacon and roasted them in a heavy iron pot while I made a sauce of onions and tomato and plenty of garlic. We ate it with thick slices of brown bread and yellow tinned butter and it tasted like no other food I had ever known.

'If you ever need a job, Lo, you can come cook for me,' I told him around a mouthful. He grinned and went to the Land-Rover to switch on the radio.

'What was the deal?' I asked.

'Just the news.' He had the grace to look guilty. 'Can't lose touch entirely.'

We listened to the strivings and strugglings of a world gone mad. Somehow, in this remote and tranquil place the affairs of man seemed unimportant, petty and transient.

'Switch it off, Lo,' I said. 'Who needs it?'

He reached for the control knob of the set, but checked his hand as the voice of the announcer spoke a familiar name.

'Lusaka Radio reports that the leader of the terrorist gang which yesterday ambushed a detachment of police in the Wankie district of Rhodesia, killing four and wounding two others, is the self-styled "Colonel" Timothy Mageba who two months ago made world headlines in his dramatic hi-jacking bid. A spokesman for the Rhodesian police said that Mageba is probably one of the most dangerous terrorists in Africa. A reward of 10,000 Rhodesian dollars has been offered for information leading to his death or capture.'

With a savage gesture Louren switched off the set and came back to the fire. He sipped his whisky before speaking.

'He's operating only a hundred miles or so north of here. I'd give anything to get a chance at that one.'

News of Timothy disturbed me deeply, and that night I lay long awake with my hands behind my head staring up at the starry splendour of the night sky. Venus had dropped below the horizon before I fell into a sleep troubled with ugly dreams.

The morning sun lit the crests of the kopjes a fresh gold and inflamed the sky with virulent reds and purples, driving away dark thoughts, and we talked and laughed together as we picked our way slowly towards the east.

In the middle of the morning we saw the vultures circling off towards the north, a vast wheel of specks turning slowly beneath the hard blue sky. Following the flight of these grotesque scavengers is one of the most intriguing invitations that Africa has to offer. For every time they will lead you to the scene of some desperate incident in the never-ending drama of the wilderness.

'A couple of miles off,' Louren commented, peering eagerly ahead through the windscreen. I shared his curiosity. The hell with ruined cities and lost civilizations, this was the stark, raw rule of tooth and claw we were going to witness.

A quarter of a mile ahead of us we saw the hunchbacked bird shapes squatting obscenely in the tree-tops, thick as some devil's fruit in the orchards of hell.

'They are off the kill.' Louren was jubilant. 'Something's keeping them up in the trees and sky.'

He stopped the Land-Rover, and switched off the ignition. We climbed out, and Louren checked the load of his big .375 magnum, changing the solid bullets for soft-nosed ones that would deliver a heavier knock-down blow.

'We'll walk up,' he said. 'I'd love a chance at a big black-maned lion.' He snapped the bolt of the rifle closed. 'Take the shotgun, Ben, load with buckshot.'

This is my sort of thinking. If a lion is far enough away to warrant the use of a rifle then he and I have no quarrel; closer than that I like a weapon that I can't miss with.

Louren set off through the waist-high grass, I followed him, keeping out on his flank to open my line of fire, the shotgun loaded for lion and my pockets bulging with spare shells. We moved in slowly, trying to find the focal point of this gathering of vultures for they were scattered in the trees over an area of half a square mile.

Every step heightened our tension with the expectation of walking on top of a pride of lions lying in the grass. Louren signalled each change of direction to me, as we quartered carefully back and forth over the ground. From the trees around us the birds launched into flight, changing miraculously from ungainly repose into something graceful and beautiful as they entered their true element.

My throat was dry with excitement, and a pleasurable fear. I could see Louren was sweating through the back of his shirt, not entirely from the heat. His every movement was charged with restrained energy, ready to explode at the first sign of the quarry. I loved this part of the hunt, for there is the atavistic urge of hunter still hidden in most of us, it was only the killing that repulsed me.

Louren froze, rifle at high port. He was staring ahead, and I braced myself for the heavy detonation of the shot that I knew must follow; but the seconds passed slowly as dripping oil and still Louren stood with only the slightest movements of his head as he searched.

Quietly I moved up beside him. Ahead of us was an area of flattened and trampled grass. In the centre of it lay the body of a dead buffalo, his belly bloated with gas, and big shiny green flies swarming over his dead eyes and into his open mouth. I could see no marks of claws in the thick hide, with its coarse black hair blotched with patches of shiny baldness and rough scab.

I looked down at the ground, not wishing to tread on a twig as I moved again, and I saw the small childlike human footprint in a patch of ant-turned earth.

I felt the hair at the back of my neck prickle, we had walked into something a damned sight more dangerous than a pride of lions. Quickly I looked back to the dead buffalo, and for the first time noticed two inches of a frail reed stalk protruding from the folded skin of the neck. The flesh around it was swollen tight and hard.

'Lo!' I croaked huskily. 'Let's get the hell out of here – this is a bushman kill.'

Louren's head jerked around and he stared at me. I saw the rim of his nostrils fade to china white.

'How do you know?' he demanded hoarsely.

'Footprints at your feet.' He glanced down. 'Arrow in the buffalo's neck.'

He was convinced. 'This is your shauri, Ben. What do we do?' Now he was sweating as heavily as I was.

I said, 'Slowly, slowly! Don't turn your back and don't move suddenly. They are watching us, Lo. Probably right here.'

We began backing off, clutching our weapons with sweat-greasy hands, eyes darting restlessly from side to side.

'Talk to them, for God's sake, Ben!' Louren whispered. I found time to examine the discovery that the threat of poison could turn even a man like Louren into a coward.

'Can't take the chance. Anything could trigger them.'

'They may be behind us.' His voice shook, and I felt my skin between the shoulder-blades cringe as I listened for the flute of the arrow. With each pace backwards I felt my fear shrinking, and fifty yards from the kill I risked hailing them.

'Peace,' I called. 'We mean you no harm.'

The reply came immediately, birdlike and disembodied, seeming to emanate from the heated air itself.

'Tell the big white-head to lay down his weapon, for we do not know him.'

'Xhai,' I cried out my relief and delight. 'My brother!'

> 'His eye was bright as the yellow moon,
> His hoof struck fire from the iron hills.'

We sang the buffalo song together, the men squatting around the leaping fire, clapping out the complicated rhythm with our hands. The women danced in an outer circle around us, swaying and shuffling, miming the buffalo and his gallant hunter. The firelight shone on their golden-yellow skins, their tiny childlike bodies with the startling bulge of buttocks and the fat little yellow breasts joggling to the dance rhythm.

> 'The arrow-bird flew from my hand
> Swift as a bee, or a stooping hawk.'

The branches of the trees around us were heavy with festoons of raw meat, hung out to dry, and beyond the firelight the jackal and hyena howled their frustrations to the star-bright heavens, as they snuffed the tantalizing odours.

> 'The blood when it flowed was bright as a flower
> And sweet as wild honey was the flesh of his body.'

The dance ended at last, and the women giggled and trilled as they flocked to the fire to cram more meat into their little round bellies. Bushmen and women are awed by physical size, and to them Louren was a huge golden giant. They discussed him in a frank and intimate manner, starting at his golden head and working downwards until I laughed out aloud.

'What's so funny?' Louren demanded, and I told him.

'My God, they didn't say that!' Louren was shocked, staring at the women in horror, and they covered their mouths with their hands as they giggled.

I sat between Xhai and Louren, one of them smoking and the other eating a Romeo and Julieta cigar, and I translated for them. They spoke of the animals and the birds for they had a common love of the chase.

'My grandfather told me that when he was a young man the buffalo in this land below the great river were as locusts, black upon the earth – but then the red sickness came.'

'Rinderpest,' I explained to Louren.

'And they died so that they fell one upon the other, so thick that the vultures could not fly with the load of their bellies, and their bones lay in the sun like the fields of white Namaqua daisies in the spring time.'

They talked on after the women and children had curled up and fallen asleep like little yellow puppies in the dust. They spoke of noble animals and great hunts, and they became friends beside the fire so that at last Xhai told me shyly, 'I should like to share the hunt with such a one. I could show him an elephant, like those that my grandfather knew, with teeth as thick as my waist and as long as the shaft of a throwing spear.'

And there goes any further pretence of looking for ruins and caravan routes, I thought, as I watched Louren's face light up at the suggestion.

'But,' I added, 'he says you must leave the Land-Rover here. They heard us coming for half an hour before we arrived today and he says this elephant is old and cunning. Which means we will have to get some sleep now. We've got a hell of a day ahead of us tomorrow.'

By the time the sun came up we had been on the march for three hours, dew had soaked our trousers to the knees but we had walked the night's chill out of our joints and were extending ourselves, stepping out with full stride to keep the two tiny brown figures in view. Xhai and Ghal were into that loose-limbed trot that would eat away the miles all day without flagging, their little brown forms danced ahead of us through the thickening thorns and jessie bush.

'How you doing, Ben?'

I grunted and changed the shotgun to my other shoulder.

'The little bastards can certainly foot it.'

'Brother, you have only just started,' I warned him. They led us into bad, broken country where harsh black ridges of ironstone thrust from the earth and the thorn was grey and spiny and matted, where deep ravines rent the walls of steep tableland outcrops and the heat was a fierce dazzling thing that sucked the moisture from our bodies and dried it in rings of white salt on our shirts. It was the type of country that a canny old elephant bull, pursued by men all his life, might choose as a retreat.

We rested for half an hour at noon, seeking shade in the lee of a boulder whose black surface was scalding to the touch and drinking a few mouthfuls of lukewarm water, then we went on and almost immediately cut the spoor.

'There and there.' With the point of a poison arrow, Xhai traced the outline of a padmark on the iron-hard earth. 'Do you not see it?' he asked with exasperation, and though we circled the area, tilting our heads learnedly, neither of us could make it out.

'If that's an elephant spoor,' muttered Louren, 'I'm a Chinese tinker.' But Xhai set off confidently on a new bearing through the thorns, and we climbed one of the rocky tablelands, following a trail that Louren and I could not even see. Near the crest of the hill lay a pile of elephant dung, still moist despite the furnace-dry heat, and a cloud of yellow and orange butterflies hovered over it attracted by the wetness. The dung looked like the contents of a coir mattress.

'Velly solly,' I whispered to Louren, 'pleese fixee pottee – chop chop.'

'The man's a bloody magician.' Louren shook his head in amazement, as he unslung the heavy rifle from his shoulder and tucked it under his arm.

We went on again, but slowly now, pausing frequently while Xhai and Ghal searched the impenetrable thickets of thorn ahead of us. It was a gut-aching business in this close bush, each step planned and made only at a signal from Xhai's dainty pink-palmed hand, moving forward when the hand beckoned and freezing when it froze.

'Come,' said the hand and we went on again, then abruptly –

'Stop!' A quick cut-out sign, with the hand like a blade, then balling into a fist and pointing ahead, bad luck to point with a finger at the quarry.

We stood still as death, sweat-shiny faces staring ahead into the wall of thorn – and then suddenly the elephant loomed ghostly grey amongst the grey thorn, moving from us in a leisurely sway-backed shamble, grey skin wrinkled and old, hanging in bags and pouches at the belly and in the crotch of his back legs, the tail bare of tuft hair, the knuckles of the spine showing clearly through the ridged skin on his back. Old elephant. Big elephant.

'Stay here!' Xhai's hand pointed at Ghal and me, and I nodded in acknowledgement.

'Come with me!' Xhai's forefinger crooked at Louren, and they went on together, circling out on the elephant's flank through the thorn. The bushman doll-like beside Louren's bulk, leading him around for a clean shot at the head or shoulder.

The elephant paused, and began feeding from one of the thickets, delicately plucking the pale green shoots with the tip of his trunk, stuffing them into his mouth, completely unaware of danger – while out on his flank Louren reached a firing stance and braced himself, legs spread, leaning forward to meet the recoil of the heavy rifle.

The shot was stunningly loud, shocking in the heat-drugged silence. I heard the bullet slap into flesh, and the elephant spun away from the impact, turning to face Louren, with its long yellow ivories lifted high, the huge grey ears cocked back, and it squealed as it saw the man. It squealed in anger, and a long smouldering hatred now burst into flame.

It crabbed sideways as it began the charge, blanketing Louren's line of fire with a thicket of thorns. I saw Louren turn and run out to the side, trying to open his front for a clear shot. His foot hit an ant-bear hole and he fell in full run, going down heavily, the rifle flying from his hand, lying stunned full in the path of the charge.

'Louren!' I screamed, and then I was running also, armed with only a shotgun, racing to head off the charge of a wounded bull elephant.

'Here!' I screamed at it as I ran. 'Here!' Trying to lead it off him, in the corner of my vision I saw Louren on hands and knees crawling painfully towards his rifle.

'Yah! Yay!' I screamed with all the strength of my lungs, and the bull checked his charge, his head swinging towards me, piggy eyes seeking me, trunk questing for my scent.

I threw up the shotgun, and at thirty yards' range I aimed for his little eyes, hoping to blind him.

Blam! Blam! I fired left and right into his face, and he came at me. I felt a vast sense of relief as his charge exploded towards me, I had taken him off Louren – that was all that counted. With clumsy fingers I groped for fresh cartridges, knowing that before I could reload he would be upon me.

'Run, Ben, run!' Louren's voice, high above the ground-thudding charge of the bull. But I found my legs would not function, and I stood in the path of the charge, groping stupidly for cartridges which were useless as thrown pepper-corns against this grey mountain of flesh.

The blast of Louren's rifle beat against my numbed brain, once – twice, it crashed out and like an avalanche the grey mountain fell towards me, dead already, the brain shattered like an overripe fruit at the passage of the heavy bullet.

My feet were rooted to the earth, I could not move, could not dodge, and the outflung trunk hit me with savage force. I felt myself thrown through the air, and then the cruel impact of earth and my brain burst into bright colours and stabbing lights as I went out.

'You silly bastard! Oh, you silly brave little bastard.' I heard Louren's voice speaking to me down a long dark tunnel, and the sound of it echoed strangely in my head. Cool wetness splashed over my face, blessed wetness on my lips and I opened my eyes. Louren was sitting on the ground, my head cradled in his lap and he was splashing water from the bottle into my face.

'Who are you calling a bastard?' I croaked up at him, and the expression of relief that flooded over his worried features was one of the most satisfying things I have ever seen.

I was stiff and sore, bruised of shoulder and across the small of my back, and there was a lump above my temple that was too painful to touch.

'Can you walk?' Louren fussed over me.

'I can try.' It wasn't too painful, and I even found the inclination to photograph the huge dead beast as it knelt in a prayerful attitude with the head supported on the curved yellow tusks. Louren and the bushman sat on its head.

'We will camp tonight at the Water-In-The-Rocks,' Xhai told me, 'and tomorrow we will return and take the teeth.'

'How far is it?' I asked dubiously.

'Close!' Xhai assured me. 'Very close.' And I scowled at him uncertainly. I had heard him use the same words to describe a march of fifty miles.

'It had bloody well better be,' I said in English, and to my surprise it was much closer than I had expected – and a lot of other things I had not expected either.

We crossed one ridge with me hobbling along on Louren's arm and then came out on a wide granite sheet, a great curved dome of rock almost four acres in extent. I took one look at it, at the lines of shallow rounded holes that dimpled the entire surface, and I let out a whoop of joy. Suddenly I no longer needed Louren's support, and both of us ran down onto the stone floor, chortling with glee, as we examined the regular lines of worn depressions.

'It must have been a big one, Ben,' Louren exulted, he made a guess at the number of holes. 'A thousand?'

'More!' I said. 'More like two thousand.'

I paused then, imagining the long regular lines of naked slaves kneeling on the rock floor, each beside one of the smooth depressions, each of them linked to his neighbours by the iron slave chains, each of them with a heavy iron pestle in his hands, pounding away at the gold-bearing ore in the stone mortar between his knees.

I saw in my imagination the slave masters walking along the lines, the leather whips in their hands as they checked that the rock was crushed to a fine powder. I saw the endless columns of slaves with ore baskets balanced on their heads coming up from the workings. All this had happened here nearly 2,000 years before.

'I wonder where the mine is.' Louren was paralleling my thoughts.

'And the water?' I added. 'They'd need water to wash the gold out.'

'The hell with water,' Louren shouted. 'It's the mine I want, those old boys only worked values of three ounces and over and they stopped at water level – there's a bloody treasure house around here somewhere.'

This was how all the ancient mines had been destroyed. It was a credit to the skill of the ancient metallurgists that the site of nearly every modern mine in central Africa had been discovered by them 2,000 years before. The modern miners ripped out all trace of the ancient workings in their haste to expose the abandoned reef. I made a vow that at the least I would be first into this one, before the vandals with their drills and dynamite.

The water was at the bottom of a fifty-foot well, cut cleanly through the living rock, its walls lined with masonry. It was the finest example of an ancient well I had ever seen; clearly it had been kept in good repair by the bushmen, and I gloated over it while Xhai fetched a raw-hide rope and leather bucket from a hiding place among the rocks. He brought the bucket up brimming with clear water in which floated a few dead frogs and a drowned bush rat. I made a resolution to boil every drop before it passed my lips.

Louren spent a full thirty seconds in admiring the well, before he set off into the narrow valley between the two ridges of granite. I watched him disappear amongst the trees searching diligently, and twenty minutes later his faint shouts drifted up to me.

'Ben! Come here! Quickly!' I dragged myself off the coping of the well and limped down into the valley.

'Here it is, Ben.' Louren was wild with excitement and I was struck again by the power that gold has to quicken the most sluggish pulse, and to put the glitter of avarice in even the most world-weary eyes. I am not a materialistic person, but the lure and magic of it quickened my own breathing as I stood beside Louren and we looked upon the mine of the ancients.

It was not an impressive sight in itself, a shallow depression, a trench sunk about three feet below the level of the surrounding earth, its banks gently rounded, it meandered away amongst the trees like a footpath that had been worn into the earth.

'Open stope,' Louren told me. 'They followed the strike of the reef.'

'And back-filled.' I commented on the peculiar habit that the ancients had of filling in all their workings before abandoning them. This shallow trench was caused by the subsidence of the loose soil with which they had filled it.

'Come on,' said Louren. 'Let's follow it.'

For a mile and a half we followed the old stope through the forest before it petered out.

'If only we could find one of their dumps,' Louren muttered as we searched the rank vegetation for a pile of loose rock. 'Or at least a piece of the ore that they overlooked.'

My back was hurting so I sat on a fallen log to rest, and left Louren to continue the search. He moved away through the trees leaving me alone, and I could enjoy the sense of history which enveloped me when I was alone in a place such as this.

The water level in the well was fifty feet, so I guessed that this was the depth to which the ancients had worked their stope. They did not have the pumps or equipment to evacuate the workings, and as soon as water started pouring in they refilled it and left to find another reef.

This mine had been an open trench, one and a half miles long and fifty feet deep by six feet wide, hacked from the earth with adzes of iron and iron wedges pounded into the grain of the rock with stone hammers. When the rock was hard enough to resist this method, then they built fires upon it and poured water mixed with sour wine on the heated surface to shatter it. This was the same method that Hannibal used to break up the boulders that blocked the passage of his elephants across the Alps – a Carthaginian trick, you might call it. From the sheet of reef they prised lumps of gold quartz and packed it into baskets to be haulted to the surface on raw-hide ropes.

Using these methods they removed an estimated 700 tons of fine gold from workings spread over 300,000 square miles of central and southern Africa, together with vast quantities of iron and copper and tin.

'That's 22 million ounces of gold at $40 an ounce, 880 million dollars.' I worked it out aloud, then added, 'And that's a big loaf of bread.'

'Ben, where are you?' Louren was coming back through the trees. 'I found a piece of the reef.' He had a lump of rock in his hand and he handed it to me.

'What do you make of that?'

'Blue sugar quartz,' I said. And I licked at it to wet the surface, then held it to catch the sunlight. 'Wow!' I exclaimed as the native gold sparkled wetly back at me, filling the cracks and tiny fissures in the quartz like butter in a sandwich.

'Wow, indeed!' Louren agreed. 'This is good stuff. I'll send a couple of my boys in to peg the whole area.'

'Lo, don't forget about me,' I said, and he frowned quickly.

'You'll be cut in on it, Ben. Have I ever tried—'

'Don't be a clot, Lo. I didn't mean that. I just don't want your rock hounds tearing up the countryside before I've had a chance to go over it.'

'Okay, Ben. I promise,' he laughed. 'You can be here when we reopen the workings.' He juggled the lump of quartz in his hand. 'Let's get back, I want to pan this and get some idea of its value.'

Using one of the stone mortars in the granite cap and a lump of ironstone as a pestle, Louren pounded a piece of the quartz to a fine white powder. This he collected in our cooking pot, and with well-water washed off the powdered stone. Swirling the contents of the pot with an easy circular motion, letting a little spill over the rim of the pot with each turn. It took him fifteen minutes to separate the 'tail' of gold. It lay curled around the bottom of the pot, greasy shiny yellow.

'Pretty,' I said.

'They don't come prettier!' Louren grinned. 'This stuff will go five ounces to the ton.'

'You are an avaricious bastard, aren't you,' I teased him.

'Put it this way, Ben,' he was still grinning, 'the profits from this will probably keep your Institute running for another twenty years. Don't kick it, partner, money isn't the root of all evil if you use it right.'

'I won't kick it,' I promised him.

We camped that night beside the well, feasting on boiled elephant tongue and potatoes and keeping a bonfire going to compensate for our lack of blankets. We spent the following morning cutting out the tusks. These we buried beneath a huge pile of rocks to keep off the hyenas, and it was after noon before we started back for the Land-Rover.

Night caught us out again, but we reached the Land-Rover in the middle of the following morning. I had blisters on my heels the size of grapes and my lumps and bruises ached abominably. I collapsed thankfully into the passenger seat of the Land-Rover.

'Up to this moment I have never truly appreciated the invention of the internal combustion engine,' I announced gravely. 'You can take me home now, James.'

We left Xhai and his small tribe to their eternal wanderings in the wilderness and we arrived back at the City of the Moon eight days after we left it. We were blackened by the sun and an accumulation of dirt, we had sprouted beards, and our hair was stiff with dust and grime. Louren's beard came out a burnished red-gold that glistened in the sunlight.

He had been AWOL for three days, and the pack was clamorous. A tall pile of messages waited for him in the radio shack, and before he could shave or bath he had to spend an hour on the radio taking care of the most urgent matters that had arisen in his absence.

'I should get on back to the salt mines right away,' he told me as he came out of the shack. 'It's four-thirty. I could make it.' He hesitated a moment, then his resolve hardened. 'No, damn it! I'm going to steal one more night. Get out the Glen Grant while I take a bath.'

'Now you're talking sense.' I laughed.

'All the way, partner.' He punched my shoulder.

'All the way, Lo,' I assured him.

We talked a lot, and sang a little, and drank whisky until after midnight.

'Bed!' said Louren then, and rose to go, but suddenly he paused. 'Ben, you promised to let me have some photographs of the "white king" painting to take back with me.'

'Sure, Lo.' I stood up a little unsteadily and went through into the office. I took a sheaf of nine-by-six-inch glossy prints from my files and went back with them to Louren. Standing under the light he shuffled through them.

'What's wrong with this one, Ben?' he asked suddenly, and handed it to me.

'What? I can't see anything.'

'The face, Ben. There is a mark.'

I saw it then; a faint shadowy cross which marred the death-white face of the king. I studied it a moment. It puzzled me. I hadn't noticed it before – like a dark grey hot cross bun.

'It's probably a flaw in the printing, Lo,' I guessed. 'Is it on the others?' He glanced through the other prints quickly.

'No. Just that one.'

I handed it back to him. 'Just a faulty print,' I said.

'Okay.' Louren accepted my explanation. 'Good night.'

I poured myself a nightcap while Sally and the others trooped off after Louren, and I drank it slowly, sitting alone, running over in my mind the plans that Louren and I had formulated for the thorough investigation of the cavern.

I will admit that I never gave the mark on the white king's face another thought. My excuse is that I was more than a little drunk.

The next two months passed swiftly. Ral and I devoted ourselves to a thorough excavation of the floor of the cavern.

The results were surprising only in their paucity. The cavern had never been used for human habitation, there was no midden or hearth level. We found an accumulation of animal detritus that extended down to bed-rock. On the bed-rock itself we found a single square block of dressed stone, and that was the total bag.

Our excavations had given the cavern a forlorn and gutted appearance, and the bed-rock was uneven limestone, so I had the dig refilled and neatly levelled. Then we used the ancient blocks to lay a pavement around the emerald pool. I saw this as a concession to the convenience of the thousands of future visitors who would come to view this wonderful gallery of bushman art once its existence was known to the world.

As he had promised, Louren radioed me when his company was ready to begin re-opening the ancient mine we had discovered on the hunt for the elephant. A helicopter fetched me and I spent three weeks with the engineers who were doing the work.

The reef was there below the water-table as we had hoped, and although its values varied widely from place to place along its length, yet the average was exceptionally high. Secretly I was glad of my ten per cent interest in the mine, despite my non-materialist values. We recovered many hundreds of artefacts, mostly mining tools. There were badly rusted adzes and wedges, stone hammers, scraps of chain, a few well-preserved fibre baskets and the usual beads and pottery.

Of these I was most pleased with the fibre baskets which enabled us to obtain a carbon-14 date from the laboratories. This was slightly prior to, if not concurrent with, the date of the great fire, and served to link the elephant mine with the City of the Moon.

However, the most interesting find at the elephant mine was that of fifteen human skeletons lying like a string of beads along the stope at its deepest point. The arrangement of the bodies was so regular as to preclude the idea that they might have been killed in a rockfall. Although the skeletons had been flattened by the weight of earth from above, I was able to determine that five of them were female and ten were males. All of them were elderly, and one of them showed traces of arthritis, another had lost an arm between elbow and wrist but the bone had encysted, proving that it had not been a recent injury. Most of them had lost teeth. On all of them I found traces of iron chains, and the picture I had was that of fifteen elderly and infirm slaves laid deliberately along the bottom of the stope before it was filled.

After supervising the cataloguing, packing and despatch to the Institute of all these finds, I returned to the City of the Moon, and I went immediately to the cavern. As I hoped, Sally was hard at work there. I do not think her pleasure was affected as she came to meet me and kissed me.

'Oh, Ben. I've missed you.' Then she launched immediately into a technical discussion, and while I made the right answers my thoughts were far from bushman paintings.

I watched the way she crinkled her nose as she spoke, and the way she kept pushing her hair back from her cheek with the back of her hand, and my whole being throbbed with love of her. Down in my stomach I felt a squirming dread. Our work at the City of the Moon was almost finished, soon we would be returning to Johannesburg and the hushed halls of the Institute. I wondered how this would affect Sally and me.

'We'll be leaving soon, Sal.' I gave expression to my thoughts.

'Yes,' she agreed, immediately sobered. 'The thought saddens me. I've been so happy here, I'm going to miss it.'

We sat in silence for a while, then Sally stood up and went to stand before the portrait of the white king. She stared at it moodily, her arms folded tightly across her breast.

'We've learned so much here,' she paused for a moment, and then went on, 'and yet there was so much that was denied us. It was like chasing clouds, often I felt we were so close to having it in our hands.' She shook her head, angrily. 'There are so many secrets still locked away from us, Ben. Things we will never know.'

She turned and came back to where I sat; she knelt in front of me with her hands on her knees, staring into my face.

'Do you know that we haven't got proof, Ben! Do you

realize there is nothing we have found here that can't be discredited by the old arguments.' She leaned closer towards me. 'We have a symbol on a scrap of pottery. Imported in the course of trade, they will say. We have the golden chalice, the work of native goldsmiths using the Ankh motif by chance, they will say. We have the paintings – hearsay is not evidence, they will say.'

She sat back on her haunches and stared at me.

'Do you know what we've got, Ben, after it's all been sifted and sorted? We've got a big fat *nothing*.'

'I know,' I said miserably.

'We haven't even a single fact to knock them off their smug little perch. Our City of the Moon – our beautiful city – will be simply another culture of obscure Bantu origin, and there isn't a damn thing we can do about it. We will never know what happened to the great walls and towers, and we will never know where our white king lies buried.'

I planned to shut down the dig on the 1st of August, and we spent the last weeks of July tidying it all, leaving the foundations exposed for others who might follow us, packing our treasures with loving care, making the last entries in the piles of notebooks, typing the long lists of catalogues and attending to the hundreds of other finicky details.

The field investigation was over, but ahead of me lay months of work, filing and correlating everything we had discovered, fitting each fact into its niche and comparing it with evidence gathered by others at other sites, and finally there would be the summation and the book. Months before, I had hoped I might be able to entitle my book *The Phoenicians in Southern Africa*. Now I would have to find another title.

The Dakota arrived to take away the first load of crates, and with it went Peter and Heather Willcox. They would still have two or three months of their European holiday, but we were sorry to see them go, for we had been a happy group.

That evening Louren spoke to me over the radio.

'We have got hold of Cousteau at last, Ben. He's been cruising in the Pacific but my office in San Francisco spoke with him. He thinks he may be able to help, but there is no chance that he will be able to come before next year. He has a full schedule for the next eight months.'

That was my last excuse for staying on at the City of the Moon, and I began packing my own private papers. Sally offered to help me. We worked late, sorting through the thousands of photographs. Now and then we would pause to examine a print of particular interest, or laugh over one that had been taken in fun, remembering the good times we had spent together over the months.

Finally we came to the file of prints of the white king.

'My beautiful mysterious king,' Sally sighed. 'Isn't there anything more you can tell us? Where did you come from? Who did you love? Into what battles did you carry your war shield, and who wept over your wounds when they carried you home from the field?'

We went slowly through the thick pile of prints. They were taken from every angle, with every type of variation in lighting, exposure and printing technique.

A detail of one of the prints caught my eye. I suppose that subconsciously I was alerted to pick it up. I stared at it, with eyes that began to see for the first time. I felt something fluttering inside of me like a trapped bird, felt the electric tickle run up my arms.

'Sal,' I said and then stopped.

'What is it, Ben?' She picked up the quaver of suppressed excitement in my voice.

'The light!' I said. 'Do you remember how we found the city in the moonlight? The angle and intensity of the light?'

'Yes,' she nodded eagerly.

'Do you see it, Sal?' I touched the white king's face. 'Do you remember the print I gave to Lo? Do you remember the mark on it?'

She stared at the photograph. It was fainter than on Louren's print, but it was there, the same shadowy cross shape superimposed upon the death-white face.

'What is it?' Sally puzzled, turning the photograph in her hands to catch the light.

'I don't know,' I said as I hurried across the room to the equipment cupboard, and began scratching around in it, 'but I'm damned well going to find out.'

I came out of the cupboard and handed her one of the four-cell torches. 'Take this and follow me, Watson.'

'We always seem to do our best work at night,' Sally began, and then realized what she had said. 'I didn't mean it that way!' She forestalled any ribald comment.

The cavern was as still as an ancient tomb, and our footsteps echoed loudly off the paving as we skirted the pool and went to the portrait of the white king. The beams of our torches danced upon him and he stared down at us, regal and aloof.

'There's no mark on his face,' Sally said, and I could hear the disappointment in her voice.

'Wait.' I took my handkerchief from my pocket. Folding it in half, and in half again, I masked the glass of my torch. The bright beam was reduced to a steady glow through the cloth. I climbed up on to the timber framework that had been left in position.

'Switch yours off,' I ordered Sally, and in the semi-darkness I stepped up to the portrait and began examining the face with the dimmer light.

The cheek was white, flawless. Slowly I moved the light, lifting higher, lowering it, moving it in a wide circle around the king's head.

'There!' we cried together, as suddenly the hazy mark of the cross appeared over the pale features. I steadied the light in its correct position and examined the mark.

'It's a shadow, Sal,' I said. 'I think there must be an irregularity beneath the paint. A sort of groove, or rather two grooves intersecting each other at right angles to form a cross.'

'Cracks in the rock?' Sally asked.

'Perhaps,' I said. 'But they seem to be too straight, the angles too precise to be natural.'

I unmasked my torch, and turned to her.

'Sal, have you an article of silk with you?'

'Silk?' She looked stunned, but recovered quickly. 'My scarf.' Her fingers went to her throat.

'Lend it to me, please.'

'What are you going to do with it?' she demanded, holding her hand protectively over the scrap of pretty cloth that showed in the neck of her blouse. 'It's genuine Cardin. Cost me a ruddy king's ransom.'

'I won't spoil it,' I promised.

'You'll buy me a new one if you do,' she warned me, as she unknotted the scarf and passed it up to me.

'Give a light,' I requested and she directed her torch onto the king. I spread the scarf over the king's head, holding it in position with the fingers of my left hand.

'What on earth are you doing?' she demanded.

'If you are ever buying a second-hand car, and you want to be sure it has never been in a smash, then this is the way you feel for blemishes that the eye can't see.'

With the finger-tips of my right hand I began feeling the surface of the painting through the silk. The cloth allowed my finger-tips to slip easily over the rock, and seemed to magnify the feel of the texture. I found a faint groove, followed it to a crossroads, moved down the south axis to another cross-roads, moved east, north, and back to my starting point. My finger-tips had traced a regular oblong shape, measuring about nine by six inches.

'Do you feel anything?' Sally could not contain her impatience. I did not answer her for my heart was in my mouth, and my fingers were busy, running all over the rock beneath the silk, moving well away from the portrait, down almost to floor level, and up as high as I could reach.

'Oh, Ben. Do tell me! What is it?'

'Wait!' My heart was drumming like the flight of a startled pheasant, and the track of my finger-tips trembled with excitement.

'I will not wait, damn you,' she shouted. 'Tell me!'

I jumped down off the framework and grabbed her hand. 'Come on.'

'Where are we going?' she demanded as I dragged her across the cavern.

'To get the camera.'

'What on earth for?'

'We are going to take some photographs.'

I had two rolls of Kodak Ektachrome Aero-film type 8443 in the small refrigerated cabinet which housed my stock of films. I had ordered this infra-red film to experiment with photographing the unexcavated foundations of the city from the top of the cliffs, but the results had not been encouraging. There were too many rock strata and too much vegetation confusing the prints.

I filled my Rolleiflex with a roll of the infra-red film, and I fitted a Kodak No. 12 Wratten filter over the lens. Sally pestered me while I worked, but I replied to all her queries with, 'Wait and see!'

I took up two arc-lights, and we arrived back at the cavern a little after midnight.

I used a direct frontal lighting, plugging the arc-lights into the switch-board of the electric water-pump beside the pool. I set the Rolleiflex on a tripod and made twenty exposures at varying speeds and aperture-settings. By this time Sally was on the point of expiring with curiosity, and I took mercy on her.

'This is the technique they use for photographing canvases and picking out the signatures and details overlaid by layers of other paints, for aerial photography through cloud, for photographing the currents of the sea, things which are invisible to the human eye.'

'It sounds like magic.'

'It is,' I said, clicking away busily. 'The filter takes out everything but the infra-red rays, and the film is sensitive to it. It will reflect any temperature or texture differences in the subject and show them in differing colours.'

There was an hour's work in the dark room before I could project the images onto our viewing screen. All colours were altered, becoming weird and hellish. The king's face was a virulent green and his beard purple. There were strange dapplings, speckles, and spots which we had never noticed before. There were irregularities in the surface, extraneous materials in the paint pigments, colonies of lichens and other imperfections. They glowed like outlandish jewels.

I hardly noticed these. What held all my attention, and set my pulses pounding, was the grid of regular oblong shapes that underlaid the entire image. An irregular chequer-board effect; they showed in lines of pale blue.

'We've got to get Louren here immediately,' I blurted.

'What is it? I still don't understand. What does it mean?' Sally pleaded, and I turned to her with surprise. It was so clear to me that I had expected her to understand readily.

'It means, Sal, that beyond our white king is an opening in the rock wall which has been closed off by a master mason with perfectly laid blocks of sandstone. The white king has been painted over it.'

Louren Sturvesant stood before the rock wall in the cavern and stared angrily at the white king. His hands were clasped behind his back. He was balanced on the balls of his feet, with his jaw thrust out aggressively. We stood around him in a semi-circle, Ral, Sally, Leslie and I, and we watched his face anxiously.

Suddenly Louren tore the cigar out of his own mouth and hurled it onto the paved floor. Savagely he ground the stub to powder, then he swung away and went to the edge of the emerald pool and stared down into its shadowy depths. We waited in silence.

He came back, drawn to the painting like a moth to the candle.

'That thing,' he said, 'is one of the world's great works of art. It's two thousand years old. It's irreplaceable. Invaluable.'

'Yes,' I said.

'It doesn't belong to us. It's part of our heritage. It belongs to our children, to generations not yet born.'

'I know,' I said, but I knew more than that. I had watched Louren over the months as his feelings towards the portrait grew. It had developed some deep significance for him, which I could only guess at.

'Now you want me to destroy it,' he said.

We were all silent. Louren swung away and began pacing, back and forth, in front of the portrait. All our heads swung to watch him, like spectators at a tennis match. He stopped abruptly, in front of me.

'You and your fancy bloody photographs,' he said, and began pacing again.

'Couldn't we—' Leslie began timidly, but her voice faded out as Louren spun around and glared at her.

'Yes?' he demanded.

'Well, could you sort of go round behind it, I mean, well—' Her voice faded and then grew stronger again. 'Drill a passage in the wall off to one side, and then turn back behind the king?'

For the first time in my life I felt like throwing my arms around her neck and kissing her.

Louren flew up one of his mine captains with a crack team of five Mashona rock-breakers from the Little Sister gold mine near Welcome. They brought with them an air-compressor, pneumatic drills, jumper bars, and all the other paraphernalia of their trade. The mine captain was a big, ginger-haired man, with cheerful cornflower-blue eyes, and a freckled baby face. His name was Tinus van Vuuren, and he threw himself wholeheartedly into the project.

'Reckon we will be able to cut her fairly easy, Doctor. This sandstone is like cheese, after the serpentine and quartz that I am used to.'

'I want the smallest opening you can work in,' Sally told him sternly. 'I want as little damage as possible done to the paintings.'

'Man,' Tinus turned to her earnestly, 'I'll cut you one no bigger than a mouse's—' he cut the word off, and substituted another, 'ear-hole.'

Sally and I taped the outline of the mouth of the shaft on the wall of the cavern. We positioned it carefully to avoid the most beautiful and significant paintings. Though we took Tinus at his word and made the opening a mere two feet wide by four high – yet we would destroy part of a lovely group of giraffe, and a dainty little gazelle with big listening ears.

We kept thirty feet away from the white king, to avoid undue vibrations from the drills which might have loosened flakes of stone or paint pigments. Tinus would go in for thirty feet, then turn his shaft at right angles to the face and cut in behind the king. Tinus was set to begin first thing the following morning, but that night we entertained him in the common room. The atmosphere was similar to that of a fighter squadron mess on the eve of a dangerous sortie. We were all voluble and tense, and all of us were drinking a little too much.

To begin with, Tinus was very reserved, clearly overawed by the company of the legendary Louren Sturvesant, but the brandy loosened him up and he joined in the conversation.

'What do you want the respirators for, Doc?' he asked. 'You expecting gas or a fire?'

'Respirators?' Louren broke off a private conversation with Sally. 'Who ordered respirators?'

'They specially told me six respirators.' Tinus looked dismayed at Louren's direct questioning. 'They told me that, sir.'

'That's right, Lo.' I rescued the poor man. 'I asked for them.'

'Why?'

'Well, Lo. What we are all hoping to find is a passage, a – ' I was about to say tomb, but I did not want to tempt the gods, ' – cave of some sort.'

He nodded. They were all watching me – and with a receptive audience I can seldom resist a touch of the theatrical.

'That cave will have been sealed, airtight, for two thousand years or so, which means there could be a danger of—'

'The Curse of the Pharaohs!' Sally interjected. 'Of course, do you remember what happened to the men who first entered Tutankhamen's tomb?' She drew a finger across her own throat and rolled her eyes horribly. She was onto her second Glen Grant.

'Sally, you ought to know better,' I cut in severely. 'The Curse of the Pharaohs is of course a myth. But there is a danger of a peculiarly unpleasant lung disease.'

'Well, I must say, I don't believe in curses and all that sort of bulldust,' Tinus laughed, a little too loudly. His inhibitions were way down around his ankles.

'That makes two of us,' agreed Ral Davidson.

'It's not a supernatural thing,' Leslie told them primly. 'It's a fungus disease.'

I seemed to have lost control of the situation completely, so I raised my voice.

'If you are all finished, I'll go on,' which got their attention back to me. 'The conditions would have been ideal for the development of *cryptococcus neuromyces*, a fungoid saphrophitic growth whose air-borne spores are the cause of a fatal disease.'

'What does it do?' Tinus asked.

'The spores are breathed into the lungs, and in the warm moist conditions they germinate almost immediately and develop into dense granulitic colonies.'

'Sies!' said Tinus, which is an expression of the deepest disgust. 'You mean it starts growing on your lungs like that green stuff on mouldy bread?'

'What are the consequences?' Louren asked.

I had it word-perfect. 'Primarily they are extensive lesions of the lung tissue, with haemorrhage, high temperature and rapidly painful breathing, but then the fungoid colonies begin generating wastes which are readily absorbed into the blood and carried to the brain and central nervous system.'

'My God!' Tinus was blanched and horrified, his blue eyes stared out of the white freckled face. 'Then what happens?'

'Well, the wastes act as a virulent neurotoxin and induce hallucination. There is inflammation of the meninges, and severe brain malfunction, similar to the effects of lysergic acid or mescalin.'

'Groovy!' said Ral, and Leslie kicked his shin.

'You mean it drives you crazy?' Tinus demanded.

'Clean out of your little skull,' Sally assured him.

'Fatal?' asked Louren.

'Seventy-five per cent, depending on individual immunity and the rate of antibody formation.'

'In the event of survival, is there permanent damage?'

'Scarring of the lungs similar to healed tuberculosis.'

'Brain damage?'

'No.' I shook my head.

'Hell, man,' said Tinus carefully, setting his glass down. 'I don't know that I am so keen on this deal. Rock falls, methane gas, pressure bursts – those don't worry me. But this fungus thing,' he shuddered, 'it is creepy, man. Just plain bloody creepy.'

'What precautions are you going to take, Ben?' Louren asked.

'The first party in will be protected by respirators,' I explained. 'I will take air and dust samples for microscopic examination.'

Louren nodded, and smiled at Tinus.

'Satisfied?'

'What will you do if you don't find it – but it's sort of lurking there? Like, ready to pounce, you know. Like in those science fiction books,' Tinus hedged.

'If it's there, it will be thick. Every dust sample will be full of it. You can't miss it under the microscope. A black, three-ball structure like a pawnbroker's sign.'

'Are you sure, Doc?'

'I'm sure, Tinus.'

He took a deep breath, hesitated a moment longer, then nodded. 'Okay, Doc. I'll trust you,' he said.

The buffeting, fluttering roar of the rock drills chased my agonized brain into a corner of my skull and started kicking it to a jelly. The party had ended in the early hours.

'How are you feeling, Doc?' Tinus van Vuuren came across to where I stood watching the work and shouted above the din. My nerves vibrated like guitar strings. Tinus looked as fresh and baby-faced as though his nightcap had been hot milk and honey and he had slept twelve hours. I knew the type – Louren was one of them.

'I feel bloody awful, thanks,' I shouted back.

'There won't be anything to see here for a couple of days,' Tinus told me. 'Why don't you go lie down for a bit, Doc?'

'I'll stick around,' I said, which seemed to be the general sentiment. Louren piloted the course of the Sturvesant empire from the radio shack, unable to tear himself away from the City of the Moon. Sally made a few desultory attempts at cataloguing and filing, but these never lasted more than an hour or two and then she was back at the cavern. Ral and Leslie made no pretence, and spent all day in the cavern, except for brief simultaneous absences which Louren and I guessed were exercise periods.

Tinus was a top man in his trade, and his team cut the tunnel swiftly and skilfully. The walls were shaped smoothly and precisely. They were shored with heavy timber baulks, and electric lights were strung along the roof. Thirty feet in, Tinus constructed a large chamber from which a new drive was made, aimed at the area behind the painting of the white king.

Tinus and I had made careful measurements and calculations, and we had decided exactly where we could expect to strike whatever the wall of masonry concealed.

The Bantu drill-men were warned of the need for respirators, and Tinus and I crouched behind them in the cramped rock tunnel as they began the assault on the last few feet of rock. Their backs were naked glistening bunches of black muscles as they worked the heavy drills. The noise in the confined space was thunderous, and despite the ventilation fans circulating air, the heat was appalling. The sweat poured down inside the face-mask of my respirator, and the eye goggles were fogged and blurry.

diameter, it looked like a Catherine wheel with the rays radiating from its circumference. The image evoked in me a strange sense of reverential awe, a hushed feeling of the spirit such as I experience sometimes in a synagogue or the cloisters of a Christian cathedral. Louren and I stood and stared at the image for a long time, then suddenly he turned and looked back to the bricked-in wall 155 feet away.

'Is that all?' he asked, and there was an irritable tone to his voice. 'Just this passage and pots and old bones? There must be something more!'

It came as a shock to me to realize that he was actually disappointed. For me the universe could hold no richer prize, this was the culminating moment of my life – and Louren was disappointed. I felt anger start to hiss and bubble within me.

'What the hell do you want?' I demanded. 'Gold and diamonds and ivory sarcophagi and—'

'Something like that.'

'You don't even know what we've got here yet, and already it's not enough.'

'Ben, I didn't say that.'

'You know what's wrong with you, Louren Sturvesant? You're bloody well spoiled. You've got everything, so nothing is good enough for you.'

'Now, listen here!' I saw my own anger reflected in his eyes, but I rushed on regardlessly.

'I've planned and saved and worked for this all my life. And now I achieve it, and what do you do?'

'Hey, Ben!' I saw comprehension in his eyes suddenly. 'I didn't mean it that way. I'm not knocking your achievement. I really think it's the most incredible discovery ever made in Africa, I was just—'

It took him a few minutes of hard talking to mollify me, but at last I grinned reluctantly.

'Okay,' I relented, 'just don't go saying things like that, Lo. All my life the bastards have been putting down my discoveries and theories, so don't you start!'

'One thing they'll never be able to say about you is that you're frightened to speak your mind!' He punched my shoulder lightly. 'Come on, Ben, let's see what we've got in these pots.'

'We shouldn't disturb them, Lo.' I was ashamed of my outburst now, and eager to make it up to him. 'Not until we have mapped and charted—'

'A couple of them are lying on the floor, knocked off the shelves,' Louren pointed. 'There are thousands of the bloody things. We will just snaffle one of them. Hell, Ben, it won't do that much harm!'

He was not asking permission, not Louren Sturvesant, he was merely giving an order in the pleasantest possible fashion. Already he was making his way back to where the jars were lying beside the dusty bowed corpse, and I hurried after him.

'Okay,' I agreed unnecessarily, in an attempt to keep nominal control of my find. 'We will remove one of them only.' I felt a sneaking sense of relief that the wrong decision had been made for me. I was also in a fever of impatience to find out what was in the jars.

The jar stood in the centre of the work-shop bench in our prefabricated warehouse. Night had fallen outside, but the overhead lights were all on. We stood around the bench, Sally, Ral, Leslie and I. Tinus van Vuuren was still up at the cavern, his status having changed from mine captain to night watchman. Louren had decided to place a twenty-four-hour armed guard over the entrance to the tunnel, and Tinus was it – until we could get others.

Through the thin partition walls of the hut I could hear

Louren's voice as he shouted into the microphone of the radio.

'A vacuum cleaner. *Vacuum cleaner.* VACUUM CLEANER! V for Venereal, A for Alcoholic – that's *right.* Vacuum cleaner. You know the heavy-duty model for cleaning factories. Two of them. Have you got that? Good! Now I want you to get on to Robeson, Head of Security at Sturvesant Diamond Mines. He is to send me his two best men, with half a dozen Bantu guards. Yes, that's right. Yes, I want them armed.'

None of us paid attention to Louren's voice, we were all staring in mesmerized fascination at the earthenware jar.

'Well, it's not filled with gold.' Ral was certain. 'Not heavy enough.'

'Nor is it liquid – not wine or oil,' Leslie agreed. And we relapsed into silence. The pot was about eighteen inches high, and thick around as a pickle jar. It was of unglazed red pottery, without inscription or ornamentation, and the lid was like that of a teapot with a small knob for a handle. It was sealed with a layer of black substance, probably gum or wax.

'Get that lot on the Dakota first thing tomorrow morning, do you hear?' Louren was still busy next door.

'I wish he'd hurry up!' Sally stirred impatiently. 'I'm dying to find out what it is.'

Suddenly I was afraid. I didn't want to know – I didn't want to find the jar filled with African millet or some other indigenous grain. I could hear my critics howling like wolves out there in the wilderness. Suddenly I was doubting my own premonition of some momentous discovery and I sat on the edge of my stool, miserably rubbing my grimy hands together and staring at the jar. Perhaps Louren was right, perhaps we would echo his cry, 'Is that all?'

From the radio shack we heard Louren's voice end the transmission, and he came through into the warehouse. He was still filthy from the work in the tunnel, and his golden hair was stiff with dust and dried sweat. Yet the grime and unruly curls gave him an air of romance, the jaunty look of an old-time pirate. He stood in the doorway with his thumbs hooked into his belt, and all our attention was on him. He grinned at me.

'Okay, Ben. What have you got for us?' he asked and sauntered across the room to stand behind my shoulder. Instinctively the others drew closer, crowding into a circle around me and I picked up the surgical scalpel and touched the point of it to the joint of the lid.

The first touch told me that my guess had been correct.

'Beeswax, I think.'

Carefully I scraped it away, then laid the scalpel aside and gently tried the lid. It came away with surprising ease.

All heads craned forward, but the first view of the contents was disappointing. An amorphous mass of substance that was stained dirty yellow-brown by time.

'What is it?' Louren demanded of his experts, but none of us could answer him. I was not sure whether to be disappointed or relieved. It certainly wasn't corn.

'It smells,' said Sally. There was a faintly unpleasant, but familiar odour.

'I know that smell,' I said.

'Yes,' agreed Leslie.

We stared at the pot trying to place it. Then suddenly I remembered.

'It smells like a tannery works.'

'That's it!' agreed Sally.

'Leather?' asked Louren.

'Let's see,' I said, and carefully tipped the jar onto its side with the mouth facing me. Gently I began easing the contents out of the jar. It became immediately clear that it held something cylindrical in shape and of a hard, brittle texture.

It seemed to have stuck to the inside of the jar, but I twisted carefully and with a faint rending sound it was loose. I inched it out of the jar, and as it emerged, there was a running commentary from the watchers.

'It's a long round thing.'

'Looks like a polony sausage.'

'It's wrapped in cloth.'

'Linen, I hope!'

'It's woven anyway. That will take some explaining away as Bantu culture!'

'The cloth is rotten, it's falling away in patches.'

I laid it on the table, and as I stared at it I knew all my dreams had become reality. *I knew what it was.* A treasure beyond all the gold and diamonds Louren had hoped for. I looked up quickly at Sally to see if she had guessed, her expression was eager but puzzled. Then her eyes met mine and my jubilation must have been obvious.

'Ben!' She guessed then. 'It isn't? Oh, Ben, it couldn't be! Open it, man! For God's sake, open it!'

I took up a pair of tweezers, but my hands were too unsteady to work. I clenched my fists, and drew a couple of deep breaths to try and calm the racing of my blood and the pounding of it in my ears.

'Here, let me do it,' said Ral, and reached to take the tweezers from my grip.

'No!' I snatched my hand away. I think I would have struck him if he had persisted. I saw the shock on Ral's face, he had never before seen the violence that lurks in my depths.

They all waited until I had got control of my hands again. Then carefully I began to peel the wrappings of brittle yellow cloth from the cylinder. I saw it appear from under the wrappings, and there were no more doubts. I heard Sally's little gasp from across the bench, but I did not look up until it was done.

'Ben!' she whispered. 'I'm so happy for you.' And I saw that she was crying, big fat tears sliding slowly down her cheeks. This was what triggered me, I am certain that if she hadn't started it I would have been all right, but suddenly my own eyes were burning and my vision blurred with moisture.

'Thanks, Sal,' I said, and my voice was soggy and nasal. When I felt the droplets start to spill onto my cheeks I struck them away with an angry hand, and groped for my handkerchief. I blew my nose like a bugler sounding the charge, and my heart sang as loudly.

It was a tightly rolled cylindrical scroll of leather. The outer edges of the scroll were tattered and eaten by decomposure. The rest of it, however, was miraculously preserved. There were lines of writing running like columns of little black insects along the length of the scroll. I recognized the symbols immediately, identifying the individual letters of the Punic alphabet. It was written in a flowing Punic script, of which the first thirty lines were exposed on the roll of ancient leather. The language was not one I understood, but I looked up at Sally again. This was her speciality, she had worked with Hamilton at Oxford.

'Sal, can you read it? What is it?'

'It's Carthaginian,' she spoke with complete certainty. 'Punic!'

'Are you sure?' I demanded.

In reply she read aloud in a voice that was still choked up and muffled with tears, '*Into Opet this day a caravan from the* . . .' she hesitated, 'that piece is obscure but it goes on, *In fingers of fine gold one hundred and twenty-seven pieces*, *of which a tenth part unto*—'

'What the hell is going on?' Louren demanded. 'What does all this mean?'

I turned to him. 'It means we have found the archives of our city – completely intact and decipherable. We have the whole written history of our city, of our dead civilization, written by the people themselves in their own language. Their own words.'

Louren was staring at me. It was clear that the significance of our discovery had not yet occurred to him.

'This, Lo, is what every archaeologist prays for. This is proof in its most absolute form, in its most detailed and elaborate form.'

He still didn't seem to understand.

'In one line of writing we have proved conclusively the existence of a people who spoke and wrote the ancient Punic of Carthage, who traded gold, who called their city Opet, who—'

'And that's only in one line of writing,' Sally interrupted. 'There are thousands of jars, each with its scroll of writings. We will know the names and deeds of their kings, their religion, their ceremonial—'

'Their battles and strivings, where they came from and when.' I took the verbal ball from Sally, but just as adroitly she snatched it back.

'And where they went to and why!'

'My God!' Louren understood at last. 'This is everything we've been looking for, Ben. It's the whole bloody shebang and shooting-match rolled into one!'

'The works!' I agreed. 'The whole ruddy lot!'

Within an hour of my triumph, right at the zenith of my career when nothing but the prospect of fame and brilliant success lay ahead of me, Dr Sally Benator managed to bring it all crashing down around me.

We were sitting in the same tight circle around the scroll, still talking eagerly, one of those talk sessions which could only end in the early morning, for already the Glen Grant bottle was out and all our throats were oiled, the words pouring out smoothly.

Sally had translated all the writing visible on the scroll. It was an accounting of trade into the city, a cataloguing of goods and values that in itself held intriguing references to places and peoples.

'Twenty large amphora of the red wines of Zeng, taken by Habbakuk Lal of which a tenth part to the Gry-Lion.'

'What's a gry-lion?' Louren's hunter's instincts were roused.

'Gry is a superlative,' Sally explained. 'So a gry-lion is a great lion. Probably a title of the king or governor of the city.'

'From the grass seas of the south one hundred and ninety-two large tusks of ivory in all two-hundred and twenty-one talents in weight of which a tenth part to the Gry-Lion and the balance outwards on the bireme of Al-Muab Adbm.'

'How much is a talent?' Louren asked.

'About 56 pounds avoirdupois.'

'My God, that's over 10,000 lb. of ivory, in one load,' Louren whistled. 'They must have been great little hunters.'

We had discussed in detail every line of exposed writing, and again Louren's impatience came to the surface.

'Let's unroll a little more,' he suggested.

'That's a job for an expert, Lo.' I shook my head regretfully. 'That leather has been rolled up for nearly 2,000 years. It's so dry and brittle it will fall to pieces if it isn't done correctly.'

'Yes,' Sally agreed with me. 'It will take me weeks to do each one.'

Her presumption left me flabbergasted. Her practical knowledge of palaeography and ancient writings was limited to three years as a third assistant to Hamilton, I doubted if she had actually done much work on preservation and preparation of leather or papyrus scrolls. She could read Punic with about the same aplomb as the average ten-year-old can read Shakespeare, and she was taking it for granted that she would be placed in sole control of one of the greatest hoards of ancient writings ever discovered.

She must have read my expression, for her own alarm showed clearly.

'I *am* to do the work, aren't I, Ben?'

I tried to make it easier for her, I do not like hurting anyone, let alone the girl I love.

'It's an enormous and difficult job, Sal. I really think we should try and get someone like Hamilton himself, or Levy from Tel Aviv, even Rogers from Chicago.' I saw her face starting to fall to pieces, the lips drooping and trembling, the eyes clouding, and I went on hurriedly. 'But I'm sure we can arrange for you to become first assistant to whoever does the work.'

There was a deadly silence for five seconds, and during that time Sally's despair changed swiftly to a blind all-consuming rage. I saw it coming like a build-up of storm clouds but I was powerless to divert it.

'Benjamin Kazin,' she began with deceptive softness of voice, 'I think you are the most unmitigated bastard it has ever been my misfortune to meet. For three long difficult years I have given you my complete and unswerving loyalty—'

Then she lost control and it was a splendid spectacle. Even while her words lashed my soul raw and bleeding I could still admire the flashing eyes, the flushing cheeks and the masterly choice of invective.

'You are a *little* man, in mind as well as body.' She used the adjective deliberately, and I gasped. No one should ever call me that, it is a word that eats away the fabric of my soul and she knew it. 'I hate you. I hate you, you *little* man.'

I felt the blood rush to my face, and I stuttered, trying to find the words to defend myself, but before I could do so Sally had turned on Louren. Her rage still blazed, her tone was not moderated in the least as she shouted at him.

'Make him give it to me. Tell him to do it!'

Even in my own distress I felt alarm for poor Sally. This wasn't a crippled, soft-hearted little doctor of archaeology she was talking to now. This was like prodding a black mamba with a short stick, or throwing stones at a man-eating lion. I could not believe that Sally would be so stupid, would presume so upon the mildly friendly attitude which Louren had shown to her. I could not believe that she would dare that tone with Louren, as though she had some special right to his consideration, as though there was some involvement of emotions or of loyalties which she could call upon in such imperious terms. Even I who had such rights would never misuse them in such a fashion. I knew no one else who would.

Louren's eyes flashed cold blue light, like the glinting of spearheads. His lips drew into grim lines, and the rims of his nostrils flared and turned pale as bone china.

'Woman!' His voice crackled like breaking ice. 'Hold your tongue.'

If it were possible then my despair plunged even deeper as Louren responded precisely as I had expected. Now the two persons I loved were on collision course, and I knew each of them so well, knew their pride and pig-headedness, that neither would deviate. Disaster was certain, inevitable.

I wanted to cry out to Sally, 'Don't, please don't. I'll do what you ask. Anything to prevent this happening.'

And Sally's bravado collapsed. All the fight and anger went out of her. She seemed to cringe beneath the lash of Louren's voice.

'Go to your room and stay there until you learn how to behave.' Louren gave the order in the same coldly furious tone.

Sally stood up and with eyes downcast she left the room.

I could not believe it had happened. I gaped at the door through which she had gone – my saucy, rebellious Sally – as meekly as a chastened child. Ral and Leslie were writhing in a sea of agonized embarrassment.

'Bedtime, I think,' Ral muttered. 'Please excuse us. Come, Les. Good night, all.' And they were gone, leaving Louren and me alone.

Louren broke the long silence. He stood up as he spoke in an easy natural voice. His hand dropped on my shoulder in a casually affectionate gesture.

'Sorry about that, Ben. Don't let it worry you. See you in the morning.' And he strolled out into the night.

I sat alone with my suddenly worthless roll of old leather, and my breaking heart.

'I hate you, you *little* man!' Her voice echoed through the lonely wastes of my soul, and I reached for the Glen Grant bottle.

It took me a long time to get completely drunk, to the stage where the words had lost some of their sting, and when I staggered down the steps into the bright silver moonlight, I knew what I was going to do. I was going to apologize to Sally, and let her do the work. Nothing was important enough to warrant her displeasure.

I went to the hut where Sally now slept alone. Leslie had moved into Peter and Heather's old room. I scratched softly on the door, and there was no reply from within. I knocked louder, and called her name.

'Sally! Please, I must talk to you.'

At last I tried the door, and it opened into the darkened room. I almost went on in, but then my courage deserted me. I closed the door softly, and staggered to my own hut. I fell face down across the bed, and still dirty and fully dressed I found oblivion.

'Ben! Ben! Wake up.' Sally's voice and her hand shaking me gently but insistently. I turned my head and opened my burning eyes. It was bright morning. Sally sat on the edge of my bed, leaning over me. She was fully dressed, although her skin glowed from the bath and her hair was freshly brushed and gay with a scarlet ribbon, yet her eyes were puffy and swollen as though she had slept badly, or had been crying.

'I've come to apologize for last night, Ben. For the stupid, hateful things I said, and my disgusting behaviour—'

As she talked the shattered pieces of my life fell back into place, and the pain in my head and heart abated.

'Even though you've probably changed your mind, and I don't deserve it anyway, I'd be honoured to act as first assistant to Hamilton or whoever does the work.'

'You've got the job.' I grinned at her. 'That's a promise.'

Our first task at the archives was to clean away the thick accumulation of grey dust that blanketed everything. I was puzzled as to the source of this dust in a sealed and airless space like the passage, but I soon found that the joints of the roof lintels were not as tight as those of the walls, and during the centuries a fine sprinkling of dust had filtered down through these cracks.

When the equipment which Louren had ordered arrived on the Dakota, along with a detachment of Louren's security police, we could begin the work.

The security police set up a hut at the entrance to the tunnel, where there was a permanent guard posted. Only the five of us were allowed to enter.

The vacuum equipment simplified the removal of dust from the archives. Ral and I worked from the outer end of the passage like a pair of busy housewives, and the suffocating clouds of grey dust made it necessary to wear respirators until the job was finished.

We were then able to assess our discovery more accurately. There were 1,142 sealed jars of pottery in the stone recesses. Of these 148 had been knocked from their niches and 127 were broken or cracked, with their scrolls exposed to the air and obviously much the worse for it. These we sprayed with paraffin wax to prevent them crumbling, before lifting, labelling and packing them.

We then turned our full attention to the evidence of

the deadly battle that had raged through the archives, and wrought the damage to the shelves of jars.

There were thirty-eight corpses strewn down the passage between the shelves in all the abandoned attitudes of sudden and violent death, and their state of preservation was quite remarkable. A few of them had crawled away into the recesses to die, groaning out their last breaths, and clutching the terrible wounds that still gaped in their mummified bodies. Their dying agonies were clearly stamped into their contorted features. Others had died swiftly, and most of these had received hideous wounds that had severed limbs, or split their skulls down to the shoulders, or, in a few cases, had struck the head clean from the trunk and sent it rolling yards away.

There was evidence here of a diabolical fury, the unleashing of an almost superhuman destructive strength.

All the victims were clearly negroid in type, and wore loin-cloths or aprons of tanned leather, with beadwork or bone decorations. On their feet were light leather sandals, and on their heads caps or head-dresses of leather, feathers or plaited fibre also decorated with beads, shells or bones.

Around them were strewn their weapons; crudely forged iron spearheads bound on shafts of polished hardwood. Many of these shafts were broken, or severed by the blows of some razor-sharp weapon. With them lay hundreds of reed arrows, fledged with the feathers of wild duck and tipped with wickedly barbed heads of hand-forged iron. The arrows had nicked and chipped the soft sandstone walls, and it was easy to determine that they had been fired from outside the mouth of the passage before it had been sealed off. Not one of them had found a mark in a human body, and so we reasoned that a barrage of arrows had preceded the attack by these men who lay scattered in death down the length of the passage.

Fifteen feet from the sealed mouth of the passage there

was evidence of a large bonfire which had blackened the walls, roof and floor around it. A pile of charred logs still lay where the lack of air had stifled the fire when the mouth of the tunnel was sealed. This fire puzzled us until Louren reconstructed the battle for us. He paced restlessly back and forth along the passage, his footsteps ringing on the stone slabs, his shadow falling grotesque and monstrous on the stone walls.

'They drove them into this place, the last of our men of Opet, a small party of the strongest and the bravest.' His voice rang with the truth of it, like a troubadour singing the legends of the old heroes. 'They sent in their champions to finish the slaughter but the men of Opet cut them down and the others fled. Then they drew up their archers at the mouth of the passage, and fired volleys of arrows into it. Again they went in, but the men of Opet were there waiting for them and again they died in their dozens.'

He turned and came down the passage to stand beside me under the swaying electric bulb, and we were silent for a moment imagining it.

'My God, Ben. Think of it. What a fight to end with. What glory these men won on that last day.'

Even I, a man of peace, was stirred by it. I felt my heartbeat quicken and I turned to him like a child at story-time. 'What happened then?' I asked.

'They were dying already, weak with a dozen wounds each. There was no strength left in them to continue and they stood shoulder to shoulder, companions in life, and now in death also, leaning wearily on their weapons, but the enemy would not come again. Instead, they built a fire in the mouth of the passage to smoke them out, and when that did not do it, they abandoned the attack and bricked up the entrance, turning it into a tomb for the dead and the living alike.'

We were all silent then, thinking about Louren's story. It made sense, it fitted the evidence in all but one respect.

I did not want to say it, did not want to spoil such a stirring tale, but Sally had no such compunction.

'If that's true, then what happened to your band of heroes – did they change into moonbeams and flit away?' Her tone was slightly derisive, but of course she was right. I wished she was not.

Louren laughed, a little embarrassed chuckle. 'So *you* think of something better,' he challenged her.

Of the heroes of this ancient drama there was no trace, except that which lay at the foot of the passage below the graven sun image of Baal. It was blanketed by the thick grey dust and it was the final discovery on the archives floor. It was a battle-axe. A weapon of striking beauty and utility. When first I took it up from the paving where it had lain for almost 2,000 years, my hand closed snugly around the haft, the grooves in the handle fitted my fingers as though they had been moulded from them. A broken wrist-strap of leather dangled from the end of the handle.

The haft was forty-seven inches long, and fashioned from lengths of rhinoceros horn that had been laminated into a solid rod of steely resilience and strength. The handle was of ivory and the whole had been bound with electrum wire to reinforce its already surpassing strength and to protect the shaft from the cuts of enemy blades. The blade was shaped like a double crescent moon, each side exposing seven and a half inches of razor edge. From its extreme end protruded an unbarbed spike twelve inches long, thus the weapon could be used on the cut as well as the thrust.

The head was exquisitely worked and engraved, with the shapes of four vultures with wings spread, one on each side of the double blade. The birds were rendered in such detail that every feather was shown, and beyond the figures a sun rose in a burst of rays like a flower. The engravings were inlaid with electrum, an alloy of gold and silver, and from the silvery sheen of the blades it was clear that they had been tempered. The weapon was caked and dulled with what must have been dried blood, it was obviously the author of those horrible wounds that bloomed upon so many of the corpses scattered along the passage.

Holding that beautiful weapon in my hand I was infected by a sudden madness. I was not truly aware of my own intention until the axe was flying in a wide glittering circle around my head. The balance and weight of the great axe was so pure and sweet that no effort was involved as I swung it high, and then into a long overhand killing stroke. The blade whickered eagerly at the kiss of moving air across its bright edge. The flexing of the handle seemed to bring it alive in my hand, alive again after nearly 2,000 long years of sleep.

From some deep atavistic depths of my soul I felt a cry rising, an exultant yell which seemed the natural accompaniment to the deadly song of the axe. With an effort I checked the flight of the axe and the cry before it reached my lips, and looked around at the faces of the others.

They were staring at me as though I had begun raving and frothing at the mouth. Quickly I lowered the axe. I stood there feeling utterly foolish, appalled at my treatment of such a rare treasure. The horn handle could easily have become brittle, and snapped at such harsh usage.

'I was just testing it,' I said lamely. 'I'm sorry.'

That night we pondered and puzzled the riddle of the archives until well after midnight. We found no answer and afterwards Louren walked with me to my hut.

'The Lear is coming to pick me up tomorrow morning, Ben. I've been here two weeks already, and I just cannot stay another day. God, when I think of how I've neglected my responsibilities since we started on this dig!'

We stopped at the door of my hut and Louren lit a cigar.

'What is it about this place that makes us all act so strangely, Ben? Do you feel it also? This strange sense of,' he hesitated, 'of destiny.'

I nodded, and Louren was encouraged.

'That axe. It did something to you, Ben. You weren't yourself for a few minutes there today.'

'I know.'

'I am desperate to discover the contents of the scrolls, Ben. We must start on that as soon as possible.'

'There is ten years' work there, Lo. You will have to be patient.'

'Patience is not one of my virtues, Ben. I was reading of the discovery of Tutankhamen's tomb last night. Lord Carnarvon made the discovery possible, and yet he died before he could look on the sarcophagus of the dead Pharaoh.'

'Don't be morbid, Lo.'

'All right,' Louren agreed. 'But don't waste time, Ben.'

'You get Hamilton for me,' I said. 'We can't do a thing without him.'

'I'll be in London on Friday,' Louren told me. 'I'll see him myself.'

'He is a difficult old codger,' I warned him.

Louren grinned. 'Leave him to me. Now, listen to me, Benjamin my boy, if you find anything else here, you let me know immediately, you understand? I want to be here when it happens.'

'When what happens?'

'I don't know – something. There is something else here, Ben. I know it.'

'I hope you are right, Lo.' And he clapped my shoulder and walked away into the night towards his own hut.

While we worked on in the archives, lifting the human remains and the piles of weapons, a construction crew arrived on the site by Dakota to erect a repository for the scrolls. This was another large prefabricated warehouse, fitted with airtight doors and a powerful air-conditioning unit to maintain the scrolls in an atmosphere of optimum temperature and humidity. A high barbed-wire fence was erected around the building for security reasons, and every precaution for the safety of the scrolls was taken.

At the same time the construction crew erected another half-dozen living quarters for the expanded team, and the first inhabitants of these were four high officials of the Botswana Government. It was the Government who had forbidden the removal of the scrolls from the territory and made the erection of the new buildings necessary. The Government deputation stayed for two days, and left satisfied that their interests in the discovery would be adequately protected, but not before I had exacted a solemn promise of secrecy. The announcement of the site would be at my signal only.

We began labelling and removing the pottery jars from their shelves. Taking the greatest pains to record, both photographically and by written notes, the exact position of each. It seemed likely that they had been stacked in chronological order, and this would assist the work of interpretation.

On the Monday I received a crippling blow to my plans in the form of a laconic message from Louren.

'Hamilton unavailable. Please suggest alternative.'

I was disappointed, hurt and angry. Disappointed because Hamilton was the best in the world, and his presence would have immediately given weight and authenticity to my site. I was hurt because Hamilton obviously believed my claims were spurious, my reputation had been damaged by the vicious attacks of my critics and scientific opponents, Hamilton had clearly been influenced by this.

He did not want to be party to some mistaken or blatantly fraudulent discovery of mine. Finally, I was angry because Hamilton's refusal to undertake the work was a direct insult. He had put the mark of the pariah on me and it would discourage others from giving the assistance I desperately needed. I might find myself discredited before I had even started.

'He didn't even give me a chance,' I protested to Sally. 'He didn't even want to listen to me. Christ, I didn't realize I was such a professional leper. Even talking to me can ruin a reputation!'

'He's a skinny, bald-headed old goat!' Sally agreed. 'He's a lecherous old feeler of bottoms, and—'

'And the greatest living authority on ancient writings in the world,' I told her bitterly. There was no reply to that, and we sat in forlorn silence for a while.

Then Sally perked up. 'Let's go and fetch him!' she suggested.

'He might refuse to see us,' I gloomed.

'He won't refuse to see me,' Sally assured me, and behind the words was an untold story that set my jealousy coursing corrosively through my veins. Sally had worked for him three years, and I could only console myself that her standards were high enough to exclude Eldridge Hamilton.

Seventy-two hours later I sat in the front lounge of the Bell at Hurley with a pint of good English bitter in front of me, and watched the car park anxiously. It was only a fifteen-minute drive from Oxford and Sally should have been here long ago.

I felt tired, irritable and depressed from that soul-destroying overnight flight from Johannesburg to Heathrow. Sally had phoned Hamilton from the airport.

'Professor Hamilton, I do hope you don't mind me phoning you,' she had cooed. 'Sally Benator, do you remember I worked under you in 1966. That's right, Sally Green-Eyes.' And she giggled coyly.

'Well, I am on my way through England. Just here for a day or two. I felt so lonely and nostalgic – those were wonderful times.' Her tones had a hundred intimate shades of invitation and promise.

'Lunch? That's wonderful, Professor. Why don't I pick you up. I have a hire car.' She gave me a triumphant thumbs-up sign.

'The Bell at Hurley? Yes, of course, I remember. How could I forget.' She made a sick face at me. 'I so look forward to it.'

The silver Jaguar slid into the car park, and I saw Sally at the wheel. With a scarf in her hair and laughter on her lips, she didn't look like a girl who had sat fourteen hours in the cramped seat of an intercontinental jet.

She slid out of the car, giving me a flash of those wonderful sun-browned thighs, and then she was coming towards me. Hanging on the arm of Eldridge Hamilton, and laughing gaily.

Hamilton was a tall stoop-shouldered man in his fifties, a baggy Harris tweed suit with leather patches on the elbows hung like a sack on his gaunt frame. His nose was beaky, and his bald pate shone in the pale sunlight as though it had been buffed up with a good wax polish. All in all he was not formidable competition, but his little eyes sparkled behind the heavy horn-rimmed glasses and his lips were slack with desire, exposing a mouthful of bad teeth, as he looked at Sally. I found it a hard price to pay for his services.

Sally led him to my table, and he was six feet from me before he recognized me. He stopped dead, and I saw him blink once. He knew instantly that he had been taken, and for a moment the whole project hung in the balance. He could so easily have turned on his heel and walked out.

'Eldridge!' I leapt to my feet, crooning seductively. 'How wonderful to see you.' And while he still hesitated, I had him by the elbow in a grip like a velvet-lined vice. 'I've ordered you a large Gilbey's gin and tonic – that's your poison, isn't it?'

It was five years since last we had met, and my memory of his personal tastes mollified him slightly. He allowed Sally and I to ease him into a seat and place the gin convenient to his right hand. While Sally and I bombarded him with all our considerable combined charm he maintained a suspicious silence, until the first gin had gone down. I ordered another and he began to thaw; half-way through the third he became skittish and voluble.

'Did you read Wilfred Snell's reply to your book *Ophir* in the *Journal?*' he asked. Wilfred Snell was the most vociferous and merciless of all my scientific adversaries. 'Jolly amusing, what?' And Eldridge neighed like a randy stallion, and clutched at one of Sally's beautiful thighs.

I am a man of peace, but at that moment I was having difficulty remembering it. My expression must have been a sickly grin, my fingernails were driven like claws into the flesh of my palms as I fought down the temptation to drag Eldridge around the room by his heels.

Sally wriggled out from his exploring hand, and I suggested in a strangled voice, 'Let's go through to lunch, shall we?'

There was a quick game of musical chairs at the dining-room table, as Eldridge tried to get a seat within clutching distance of Sally and I tried to prevent it.

We out-foxed him on a cunning double play, allowing him to settle down triumphantly beaming over the top of his menu at Sally who was backed into a corner beside him, before I cried, 'Sally, you are in a draught there.' And smoothly as a pair of ballet dancers we changed seats.

Then I could relax and give the pheasant the attention it deserved, although the burgundy that Eldridge suggested was nothing if not gauche.

With characteristic tact Eldridge brought up the subject we had all been flirting with.

'Met a friend of yours the other day, big flashy chap like a cross between a male model and a professional wrestler. Accent like an Australian with the 'flu. Had some cock-and-bull story about scrolls you'd found in a cave outside Cape Town.' And Eldridge neighed again at a volume that momentarily stopped all other conversation in the room. 'Damned man had the cheek to offer me money. I know the type, not a bean to bless himself with, and talks like he's made of the stuff. He had "shyster" written all over him in letters two feet high.'

Sally and I gaped at him, struck dumb by his astute grasp of the facts and his masterly summation of Louren Sturvesant's character.

'Sent him packing of course,' said Eldridge with relish, and stuffed his mouth with breast of pheasant.

'You probably did the right thing,' I murmured. 'Incidentally the site is in northern Botswana – 1,500 miles from Cape Town.'

'Oh, yes?' Eldridge asked, expressing disinterest as politely as one can with a mouthful of pheasant and rotten teeth.

'And Louren Sturvesant was on *Time* Magazine's list of the thirty richest men in the world,' murmured Sally. Eldridge stopped chewing with his mouth ajar, and afforded us a fine view of a semi-masticated pheasant-breast.

'Yes,' I affirmed. 'He is bank-rolling my dig. He has put in 200,000 dollars already, and he has set no limit.'

Eldridge turned a stricken face towards me. That sort of patron of scientific research was almost as rare as the unicorn, and Eldridge realized suddenly that he had been within range of one and let him escape. All the bumptiousness was gone out of Professor Hamilton.

I signalled the waitress to clear my plate, and I swear that I felt true compassion in my heart for Eldridge as I unlocked my briefcase and took from it a cylindrical bundle wrapped in its protective canvas jacket.

'I have an appointment with Ruben Levy in Tel Aviv tomorrow, Eldridge.' I opened the canvas wrapping.

'We have 1,142 of these leather scrolls. So Ruby will be pretty busy for the next few years. Of course, Louren Sturvesant will make a donation of 100,000 dollars to the Tel Aviv University Faculty of Archaeology for their cooperation, and I shouldn't be surprised if the faculty doesn't have some of the scrolls given to them as well.'

Eldridge swallowed his mouthful of pheasant as though it were broken glass. He wiped his fingers and mouth with his napkin, before leaning forward to examine the scroll.

'*From out of the southern plains of grass*,' he whispered as he read, and I noticed the difference from Sally's translation, '*received 192 large ivory tusks, weighing 221 talents*—' His voice died but his lips moved as he read on. Then he began speaking again, and his voice quavered with excitement.

'Punic in the style of the second century B.C., do you see the use of ligatures to join the median "m", still using the hang of the characters from the line, that's definitely pre-first century B.C. Here, Sally, do you see the archaic crossing of the "A"?'

'We have over a thousand of these scrolls, preserved in chronological order – Levy is very excited,' I interrupted this flow of technicalities with a gentle untruth. Levy didn't know they existed.

'Levy,' Eldridge snorted, and his spectacles flashed with outrage. 'Levy! Take him outside Hebrew and Egyptian and he's a babe in the bloody woods!' He had hold of my wrist now.

'Ben. I insist, I absolutely insist on doing this work!'

'What about Wilfred Snell's criticism of my theories? You seemed to find it amusing.' I had him by the ackers now, and I could afford to be a little cocky. 'How do you feel about working with somebody whose views are so suspect?'

'Wilfred Snell,' said Eldridge earnestly, 'is a monumental jackass. Where did he ever find a thousand Punic scrolls?'

'Waiter,' I called, 'please bring us two large Cordon Argent brandies.'

'Make that three,' said Sally.

As the brandy diffused a gentle warmth through my body, I listened to Eldridge Hamilton effusing about the scrolls and demanding of Sally information as to exactly where, when and how we had discovered them. I found myself beginning to like the man. It was true that he had teeth like the stumps of a pine forest devastated by fire, but then I am not a perfect physical specimen myself. It was also true that he had a weakness for Gilbey's gin and pretty girls – but then he differed from me only in his choice of liquor, and who am I to hold that Glen Grant is in any way superior?

No, I decided, despite my prejudices, I would be able to work with him, just as long as he kept his bony little claws off Sally.

Eldridge followed us out a week after our return to the City of the Moon, and we met him at the airstrip. I was concerned that he might find that the transition from a northern winter to our 110°F summer impaired his abilities. I need not have worried. He was one of those Englishmen who, solar topee cocked, go out in the midday sun without raising a sweat. His luggage consisted of a single small valise which contained his personal effects and a dozen large packing-cases filled with chemicals and equipment.

I gave him the Grade 'A' tour of the site, trying without

success to fan his interest in the city and the cavern. Eldridge was a single-minded specialist.

'Yes,' he said. 'Jolly interesting – now where are the scrolls?' I think even then he had doubts, but I took him into the archives and he purred like an angular old tom cat as he moved down the burdened stone shelves.

'Ben,' he said, 'there's just one thing still to settle. I write the paper on the actual scrolls, agreed?' We are a strange breed, we work not for the gold but for the glory. Eldridge was making certain of his share.

'Agreed.' We shook hands.

'Well then, there is nothing to stop me beginning right away,' he said.

'No,' I said, 'there isn't, is there.'

The treatment of the scrolls was an art form more than an exact science. For each of them the treatment varied, depending on their state of preservation, the quality of the leather, the composition of the ink and other interrelated factors. Sally admitted to me in a weak moment that she would not have been able to handle the task, it required a fund of acquired experience which she did not have at her command.

Eldridge worked like a medieval alchemist, steaming and soaking and spraying and painting. His domain stank of chemicals and other weird smells, and his and Sally's fingers were stained. Sally reported that his absorption with the task had reduced his animal instincts to the level where he made only spasmodic and half-hearted clutches at the protruding parts of her anatomy.

As each scroll was unrolled, its contents were evaluated and the detailed translation begun. One after the other they proved to be either books of account on the city's trade, or proclamations made by the Gry-Lion and the council of the nine families. The authors were nameless clerks, and their style was brisk and economical with little time for poetic flights or unnecessary descriptive passages. This starkly utilitarian outlook echoed the lifestyle which we had so far reconstructed from our finds on the site. We discussed it at the nightly talk sessions.

'It's typically Punic,' Eldridge agreed. 'They had little taste in the visual arts, their pottery was coarse and mass-produced. In my opinion their sculpture, what little there was, was downright hideous.'

'It requires wealth and leisure and security to produce art,' I suggested.

'That's true – Rome and Greece are examples of that. Carthage and, earlier, Phoenicia were often threatened, on occasion struggling for survival – they were the bustlers and hustlers. Traders and warriors, more concerned with wealth and the acquisition of power than the niceties of living.'

'You don't have to go back that far, modern art comes from the great wealthy and secure nations.'

'And we white Africans are like the old Carthaginians,' Sally said, 'when there's gold in them thar hills who gives a hoot about painting pictures.'

The scrolls reinforced the theory. Gold from Zimbao and Punt, ivory from the southern plains of grass or from the forests along the great river, hides and dried meat, salted fish from the lakes, wine and oil from the terraced gardens of Zeng, copper from the hills of Tuya, and salt from pans along the west shores of the lakes, tin from the juncture of the two rivers, corn from the middle kingdom in baskets of woven cane, sun stones from the southern river of the crocodile, iron bars from the mines of Sala – and slaves, thousands upon thousands of human beings treated as domestic animals.

The chronicle was dated from some undisclosed point

in time, we suspected this as the date of the founding of the city, and each entry was prefaced by such dating as, 'In year 169 the month of the elephant.' From these we deduced a ten-month year based on a calendar of 365 days.

Once the nature of the scrolls had been established, I suggested to Eldridge that rather than work systematically through the collection from beginning to end, we sample them and try to establish the overall history of our city.

He fell in with my wishes, and there evolved a picture of a widespread colonization of central and southern Africa by a warlike and energetic people, based on the city of Opet, and ruled by a hereditary king, the 'Gry-Lion', and an oligarchy of nine noble families. The decrees of this Council covered a range as wide as the measures adopted for dredging the channels of the lake and preventing the encroachment of water weed, to the choice of messengers to be sent to the gods Baal and Astarte. Here Astarte seemed to have taken precedence over the more usual Carthaginian form, Tanith. 'Messengers', we suspected, were human sacrifices.

We discovered carefully recorded family trees, based like the Jewish system on a matrilinear system. Each noble man or woman could trace his or her line back to the founding of the city. It was also clear from the chronicle that their religion was part of their scheme of living, and we could reasonably guess that it was a conventional form of polytheism, with leading male and female godheads, Baal and Astarte.

As we moved forward in time so we found new factors intruding, new contingencies occupying the attention of the ruling king. The rapid shrinking of the waters of the lake of Opet began to threaten the city's life line, and in the year 296 the Gry-Lion sent 7,000 slaves to assist with the work of keeping the channels open to the sea. He also despatched a column of 1,000 of his own guards under the war-captain Ramose with orders to 'venture eastwards towards the rising sun stopping not, nor failing in determination' until he had reached the eastern sea and had discovered the route to the lands of the north whose existence was postulated by the sea captain and navigator, Habbakuk Lal.

A year later Ramose returns, with only seventy men, the others having perished in a land of pestilential swamps and putrid fevers. He had, however, reached the eastern sea and there found a city of traders and seafarers 'dark men, and bearded, dressed in fine linens, and binding their brows with the same material'. They come from a land beyond the eastern sea, and Ramose is rewarded with twenty fingers of gold and twenty slaves. Our men of Opet have made their first contact with the Arabs, known to them as 'the Dravs', who are colonizing the Sofala coast.

We learned how the Gry-Lion's search for a new source of slave-labour becomes desperate. Orders are despatched to the mine overseers to take all measures to prolong the working lives of their slaves. Rations of meat and corn are increased, inflating the cost of production but increasing the life expectancy of the slaves. Owners are enjoined to breed all female slaves regularly, and the practice of infibulation is discontinued. The slaving expeditions are sent further and further afield, as the Yuye are hunted down. From the description of these yellow-skinned Yuye we guessed they were the ancestors of Hottentot people.

Then suddenly the Gry-Lion is delighted by the return of a northerly expedition with 500 'savage Nubians, both tall and strong' and the leader of the expedition is rewarded with ten fingers of gold. This delight fades slowly over the following hundred years as a solid mass of black humanity builds up north of the great river. The vast Bantu migrations have begun and now the concern of the Gry-Lion is to dam the flood southwards and his legions march constant patrol upon the northern border.

Our samplings gave us these fleeting glimpses into the

past, but they were recorded as bland impersonal statements of fact. How we longed to find the writings of a Pliny or Livy to give flesh and breath to these meticulous records of acquired wealth.

Each fact seemed to present us with a hundred unanswered questions. Of these the most pressing was: where did they come from these men of Opet, and when? Where did they go to and why? We hoped the answers to the major questions were here somewhere in this maze of writings, and in the meantime we occupied ourselves with finding the lesser answers.

It was easy enough to locate the places mentioned in the chronicles, Zimbao and Punt were the southern and northern territories of modern Rhodesia, the great river was the Zambezi, the lakes had disappeared, the gardens of Zeng were clearly the hundreds of thousands of acres of terraced hillsides in the Inyanga area of eastern Rhodesia, the hills of Tuya must be the copper-rich country above Sinoia; step by step we established the presence of our men of Opet at nearly all of the ancient sites, and at the same time we had a picture of the building-up of an immense treasure. For although the bulk of this wealth was sent 'outwards' yet there re-occurred the words 'a tenth part to the Gry-Lion'.

Where had this treasure been stored, and what had become of it? Had it perished with the city, or was it still here in some secret storehouse carved from the red rock cliffs of the Hills of Blood?

As a mental exercise I made an estimate of the extent of this treasure. Assuming that a 'finger' of gold was one of the finger-like rods of the precious metal we had discovered among the foundations of the city, I listed the total inflow of gold recorded in twenty-odd sample years beginning in the year 345 and ending in the year 501. I found that previous estimates had been hopelessly inadequate. Instead of 750 tons of gold, I found that the total recovery from the ancient mines could not have been less than 4,000 tons – of which a tenth part to the Gry-Lion.

Assuming half of this 400 tons had been spent on the maintenance of his army, the building of the temple and other public works, this still left the staggering figure of 200 tons of gold that might be hidden in or near the city – 200 tons represents a fortune of almost £80,000,000.

When I showed my calculations to Louren on his next visit to the site, I saw the gold-greed glitter in the pale blue eyes. He took away the sheet of paper with my workings on it, and the following morning as he was about to board the Lear for Johannesburg, he remarked casually, 'You know, Ben, I really think that you and Ral should spend more time exploring the area along the cliffs, rather than living in those archives.'

'What should we look for, Lo?' As if I didn't know.

'Well, those old boys were dab hands at hiding things away. They must have been the most secretive people in history, and we still haven't found their burial grounds.'

'So you want me to go grave-hunting.' I grinned at him, and he laughed.

'Of course, Ben, if you happened to stumble on their treasury I wouldn't hate you for it. After all eighty Big M's are a nice piece of petty cash.'

We had transferred 261 jars from the archives to the repository and Eldridge and Sally had sufficient material to keep them busy for the next two or three months, so I decided to follow Louren's suggestion and suspend work in the archives and undertake another detailed search of the area. My timing was impeccable, Ral was within five feet of where the small jars with the sunbird seals on their lids were standing in the darkest corner of the last recess. They were tucked away behind the front rank of jars twice their size and so effectively hidden by them that we had not included them in our original count. Ral was working his way steadily towards them, another three days would have been enough, but I took him away to search the cliffs.

This was November which we call the 'suicide month' in Africa. The sun was a hammer, and the earth an anvil but we worked the cliffs despite it. We rested only for two hours in the middle of the day, when the heat was murderous and the cool green waters of the emerald pool were irresistible.

We were alert now to the tricks and subterfuges of the ancient men of Opet. Having learned from bitter experience how skilfully they could cover their tracks and how cunningly their masons could conceal the joints in their masonry, I went back over ground I had already covered. I used my own tricks to try and out-think them. Ral and I re-photographed every inch of the cavern walls, but this time with infra-red film. We found no more concealed passages.

From there we worked outwards. Each day I marked off a 300-foot section and we combed this minutely. Not content merely to eyeball the rocks, we searched by sense of touch also. Groping our way over them like blind men.

Each day brought its small adventures. I was chased by a black mamba, eight feet of irritability and sudden death, with eyes like glass beads and a flicking black tongue, that resented my prodding around in the crack which was its home and castle. Ral was very impressed with my turn of speed over broken ground, and suggested I took it up professionally.

A week later I could return his sallies in kind by remarking on the improvement that twenty wild bee stings made to his appearance. His face looked like a hairy pumpkin, and his eyes were slits in the swollen flesh. For five days poor Ral was of no use to me at all.

November passed and in mid-December we had a quarter of an inch of rain, which is about par for the course in this part of Africa. It laid the dust for an hour or so, and that was the end of the rainy season. I guessed that the ancient lake of Opet would have ensured a higher and more regular rainfall for the area. Open water encourages rain, both by its evaporation and by cooling the air to aid precipitation.

Ral and I worked on without results, but also without any diminution of our determination or enthusiasm. Despite our days of wearing labour under the killer sun, we spent most of our evenings poring over the map of the foundations of the city. By a process of guess, deduction and elimination, we tried to work out where the ancients would have sited their tombs. I had by now become extremely fond of Ral Davidson, and I saw in this big gangling indefatigable youth the makings of one of the giants of our profession. There would be a permanent post for him at the Institute once this dig was finished, I would see to that.

In contrast to our results, Eldridge Hamilton, assisted by Sally, and Leslie, continued to reap the rich and enchanting harvest of the scrolls. Each evening I would spend an hour in the air-conditioned repository with them, reviewing the day's work. Steadily the sheets of typed translation piled up, the margins thick with notes and references in Eldridge's spidery and untidy hand.

Christmas came and we sat out under a moon as big as a silver gong, exchanging gifts and companionship. I gave them 'White Christmas' in the style of Bing Crosby, even though the night temperature was in the high eighties. Then Eldridge and I did 'Jingle Bells' as a duet. Eldridge had forgotten the words, all except the jingling part. He was a great little jingler was our Eldridge, especially after ten large gins. He was still jingling away merrily when Ral and I carried him off to bed.

Early in the new year we had what amounted to a royal

visit. Hilary Sturvesant had at last prevailed on Louren to bring her to see the site. We had a week to prepare for the family. Hilary was bringing the elder children with her and I was beside myself with excitement at the prospect of having all my favourite women at the City of the Moon. I left the search of the cliffs to Ral, while I rushed about re-arranging the accommodation and checking our stores for such essentials as Coca-Cola and chocolates. Commodities which make life bearable for Bobby Sturvesant.

They arrived in time for the lunch of cold meats and salads which I had personally prepared, and immediately the visit began souring. Sally Benator was not at the meal, she sent a message that she had a headache and was going to lie down. However, I saw her sneaking off with towel and bathing costume towards the emerald pool.

Eldridge Hamilton and Louren Sturvesant took one look at each other, and remembered their last meeting. They were as hostile as a pair of rutting stags. I recalled Eldridge's boast that he had sent Louren packing. They began making elaborately offensive remarks at each other, and I was fully extended in trying to prevent active physical violence breaking out, and when Eldridge spoke about people with 'more money than either breeding or sense', I thought I had lost my expert on ancient writings.

As if this was not sufficient, it was also obvious that Hilary and Louren were engaged in a domestic dispute which made it impossible for them to address each other directly. All communication was conducted through the agency of Bobby Sturvesant and was preceded by remarks of the order, 'Please ask your step-mother if . . .' or 'If your father wants . . .'

Hilary wore dark glasses at the lunch-table, and I could guess her eyes bore the traces of recent weeping. She was silent and reserved, as were both Ral and Leslie. The two youngsters were overcome with shyness in the presence of the Sturvesants, and when Louren and Eldridge also subsided into a smouldering truce, there were only two of us left articulate, Bobby Sturvesant and me.

Bobby took full advantage of the temporary breakdown in parental control to become an utterly impossible little bitch. She spent the entire meal either showing off shamelessly or being insolent to her step-mother. I would dearly have loved to turn her over my knee and paddle her stern.

Immediately after the meal dragged to its tortured conclusion, Eldridge retreated to his repository, Ral and Leslie muttered excuses and fled. Louren asked me for the keys of the Land-Rover and I saw him take his shotgun and drive away towards the north, leaving Hilary and the children to me. I took Hilary through the site museum and she soon forgot her unhappiness in the fascination of our exhibits.

I had carefully cleaned and polished the great battle-axe. It glittered silver, gold and ivory, and we examined the craftsmanship of its manufacture together before going across to the repository of the scrolls. Sally was too busy to talk to us. She hardly lifted her head when we entered, but Hilary turned her gentle charisma on to Eldridge Hamilton and he was not proof against it. When we left an hour later Hilary had another devoted admirer.

We went up to the cavern, and sat together above the emerald pool while the children splashed and shrieked in the cool green water. We talked together like the old and dear friends we were, but even then it was some time before Hilary could bring herself to mention that which was troubling her.

'Ben, have you noticed anything different about him?' The old question of an unhappy woman, and I made the old excuse for him.

'He works so hard, Hil.' And she snatched at it.

'Yes, he's been tied up in this hotel business for months. He's building a chain of luxury vacation hotels across the islands of the Indian Ocean. Comores, Seychelles, Madagascar, ten of them. He is exhausting himself.'

Then as we walked down towards the huts in the dusk, she said suddenly, 'Do you think he has found another woman, Ben?'

I was startled. 'Good Lord, Hil. What on earth makes you think that?'

'I don't know. Nothing I suppose. It's just that—' She stopped and sighed.

'Where would he find more than he has now?' I asked softly, and she took my hand and squeezed it.

'My dear Ben. What would we do without you?'

When I went to tuck Bobby up and kiss her good night, I told her what I thought of her behaviour at lunch and she snuffled a bit and said she was sorry. Then we kissed and hugged and agreed that we still loved each other. She was asleep before I had switched out the light, and with dread in my heart I went across to the common room for a repeat of the midday performance.

At the threshold I blinked with surprise. Louren, Eldridge and Sally were in a friendly and animated huddle over the typed pile of translation sheets, while Ral and Leslie were eagerly discussing their marriage plans with Hilary. The transformation was miraculous. I made my way with relief towards the Glen Grant bottle, and poured a medium-sized one.

'One for me also.' Sally came across to me. I could see no evidence of headache. Her mouth was a hectic slash of bright lipstick, and the silk dress she wore was draped to expose her strong brown back and shoulders. She had piled her hair up on her head, and I thought I had seldom seen her look so lovely.

I poured her a drink, and we went to join the discussion of the scrolls. In contrast to his earlier mood, Louren was at his most charming, and even Eldridge could not resist him.

'Professor Hamilton has done a most remarkable job here, Ben,' he greeted me. 'I can only congratulate you on your choice of a colleague.' Eldridge preened modestly.

'There is something we cannot put off much longer, Ben,' Louren went on. 'We are going to have to make an announcement soon. We can't keep this a secret much longer.'

'I know,' I agreed.

'Have you had any thoughts on it, yet?'

'Well, as a matter of fact—' I hesitated. I hate having to ask Louren to spend money. 'I was thinking of something on a rather grand scale.'

'Yes?' Louren encouraged me.

'Well, I thought if we could have the Royal Geographical Society convene a special symposium on African prehistory. Eldridge is a member of the Council, I'm sure he could arrange it.'

We looked at him, and he nodded.

'Then perhaps Sturvesant International could play host to the delegates, fly them to London and pay their expenses to make sure they all attend, or at least some of them.'

Louren threw his head back and laughed delightedly. 'You are a scheming son-of-a-gun, Ben. I see your plan exactly. You are going to get all your critics and enemies together in one bunch within the hallowed precincts of the R.G.S., and you are going to play the Al Capone of archaeology in a scientific St Valentine's day massacre. In the jargon, you are going to murder da bums. That's right, isn't it?'

I blushed at having my plans so readily exposed.

'Well,' and then I grinned sheepishly and nodded, 'I guess that's about it, Lo.'

'I love it.' Sally clapped her hands with delight. 'We will draw up a guest list.'

'We will do this in style,' Louren promised. 'We'll fly

them in first class and we'll put them up at the Dorchester. We'll give a champagne lunch to lull them and then we'll turn Ben and Eldridge loose amongst them like a pack of ravening wolves.' He had entered fully into the spirit of the thing and he turned to Eldridge.

'How long would it take to arrange?'

'Well, it would have to go before the Council for approval. We would have to give them some idea of the agenda, but of course your offer to pay the expenses would make it a lot easier. I will lobby a couple of the other Council members.' Eldridge was enjoying it also. There is a rather perverse thrill to be had out of planning and executing the professional assassination of one's enemies. 'I think we could arrange it for April.'

'April the first,' I suggested.

'Lovely,' laughed Louren.

'We must have Wilfred Snell,' Sally pleaded.

'He's top of the list,' I assured her.

'And that slimy little Rogers.'

'And De Vallos.'

We were still gloating and scheming when we sat down to eat the fiery curry of wild pheasant that I hoped would make the sultry night air seem cool by comparison. There were pitchers of cold draught beer to go with it, and the meal developed into a festive occasion. We were still gloating on the discomfort of our scientific enemies and planning the confrontation in detail, when Sally turned suddenly to Hilary who had been sitting quietly beside me.

'You must forgive us, Mrs Sturvesant. This must be terribly boring for you. I don't suppose a word of it makes sense to you.' Sally's tone was honeyed and solicitous. I was as surprised as Hilary, for I understand enough of the secret language of women to recognize this as an open declaration of war. I hoped that I was mistaken, but five minutes later Sally attacked again.

'You must find the heat and primitive conditions here most trying, Mrs Sturvesant. Not the sort of weather for your tennis parties, is it?'

The way she said it made tennis seem the pastime of a spoiled and ineffectual social butterfly. But this time Hilary was ready for her, and with a face like an angel and tones every bit as sugary as Sally's, she ripped back in a devastating counter-attack.

'I'm sure it can be most unhealthy, especially after any length of time, Dr Benator. The sun can play havoc with one's skin, can it not? And you are still looking peaky from your headache. We were very worried about you. I do hope you are feeling better now.'

Sally found that despite her gentle nunlike air, Hilary was an opponent worthy of her steel. She changed her attack. She turned all her attention onto Louren, laughing gaily at his every word and not taking her eyes from his face. Hilary was helpless in the face of these tactics. I seemed to be the only one in the party aware of this duel in progress, and I sat silently trying to puzzle out the meaning of it all – until Hilary played her trump.

'Louren, darling, it has been such a busy, exciting day. Won't you take me to bed now, please.'

She swept off the field on Louren's arm, and reluctantly I had to admit that my Sally had received the treatment she deserved.

I woke to the awareness of somebody else in my bedroom with me, and I tensed myself for sudden violent action as I rolled my head stealthily and looked towards the door. It was open. The moonlight outside was bright and clear. Sally stood in the opening.

She wore a flimsy nightdress, which did not conceal the lovely outline of her nude body against the silver moonlight. The long legs, the swelling womanly hips, the nip-in of waist and flare of breast, the long gazelle neck with tilt of dainty head.

'Ben?' she asked softly.

'Yes.' I sat up, and she came quickly to me. 'What is it, Sal?'

In reply she kissed me with open mouth and probing tongue. I was taken completely by surprise, frozen in her arms and she laid her cheek against mine. In a small gusty voice she whispered, 'Make love to me, Ben.'

There was something wrong here, desperately wrong. I felt no awakening of desire, only a warm rise of compassion for her.

'Why, Sal?' I asked. 'Why now?'

'Because I need it, Ben.'

'No, Sally. I don't think you do. I think that is the very last thing in the world you need now.'

And suddenly she was crying, big broken silent sobs. She cried for a long time, and I held her. When she was quiet I laid her on the pillow and covered her with the blankets.

'I am a bitch, aren't I, Ben?' she whispered, and went to sleep. I stayed awake all that night, watching over her. I think I knew then what was happening, but I did not want to admit it to myself.

At breakfast Louren abruptly announced that the family would return immediately to Johannesburg, rather than stay the extra day as had been originally planned. I found it hard to hide my disappointment, and when I asked Louren for a reason as soon as we were alone, he merely looked towards the heavens and shrugged with exasperation.

'You are plain lucky you never married, Ben. My God – women!'

Life at the City of the Moon returned to its normal satisfying routine for a week, during which Ral and I pursued our search for the tombs and the others worked steadily at the scrolls. Then while Ral and I sat in a sizzling midday sun under the meagre shade of a camel thorn, a little puckish figure rose from the grass seemingly at my feet.

'Sunbird,' said Xhai softly, 'I have travelled many days to seek the sunshine of your presence.' He turns the prettiest compliment, and my heart went out to him.

'Ral,' I said, 'let me have your tobacco pouch, please.'

We sat together all that afternoon under the camel thorn and we talked. The conversations of primitive Africa are an art form, with elaborate rituals of question and answer, and it was late before Xhai reached the subject which he had come to discuss.

'Does Sunbird remember the water-in-the-rock at the place where we slew the elephant?'

Sunbird remembered it well.

'Does Sunbird remember the little holes that the white ghosts made in the rock?'

Sunbird would never forget them.

'These holes gave Sunbird and the big golden one much pleasure, did they not?'

They did indeed.

'Since that day I have looked with fresh eyes upon the rocks as I hunted. Would Sunbird wish to visit another place where there are many such holes?'

Would I!

'I will lead you there,' Xhai promised.

'And I will give you as much tobacco as you can carry away,' I promised him in return, and we beamed at each other.

'How far is this place?' I asked, and he began to explain. It was beyond the 'big wire' he told me. This was the 300-mile-long game fence along the Rhodesia border which was erected to control movements of the wild animals as a precaution against foot and mouth disease. We would need clearance from the Rhodesians, and when Xhai went on to describe an area which seemed fairly close to the Zambezi river border with Zambia, I knew I would have to ask Louren to arrange an expedition. It was obviously squarely within the zone of terrorist activity.

Xhai refused to accompany me back to a camp which was filled with his traditional enemies, the Bantu. Instead we arranged to meet under the camel thorn three days later, once Xhai had completed the rounds of his trap line.

I was fortunate enough that evening to find Louren had returned an hour before from Madagascar.

'What's the trouble, Ben?' His voice boomed above the radio static.

'No trouble, Lo. Your little bushman friend has found another ancient gold working site. He's happy to take me to it.'

'That's great, Ben. The elephant mine is in production already, and looking very good indeed.'

'There is only one problem, Lo. It's in Rhodesia, in the closed area.'

'No problem, Ben. I'll fix it.' And the following evening we spoke again.

'It's set up for Monday week. There will be a Rhodesian police escort to meet us at the Panda Matenga border gate.'

'Us?' I asked.

'I'm stealing a couple of days off, Ben. Just couldn't resist it. You take the bushman with you, go by Land-Rover through to Panda Matenga. I will come in from Bulawayo by helicopter. See you there. Monday week, morning, okay?'

The commander of the police escort was one of those beefy, boyish young Rhodesians with impeccable manners, and an air of quiet competence which I found most reassuring. He was an assistant inspector with an askari sergeant and five constables under him. His rank and the composition of the escort gave me some indication of the level to which Louren had applied for co-operation.

We had two Land-Rovers, both with mounted medium machine-guns on the bonnet, and the armament of the rest of the party was impressive, as was to be expected on the borders of a country subjected to unceasing harassment by terrorist infiltrators from the north.

'Dr Kazin.' The inspector saluted and we shook hands. 'My name's MacDonald. Alaistair MacDonald. May I introduce my men?'

They were Matabeles, all of them. The big moon-faced descendants of Chaka's fighting impis, led here 150 years ago by the renegade general, Mzilikazi. They were dressed in camouflage fatigues with soft jungle hats, and they stood to rigid attention as MacDonald led me down the single rank.

'This is Sergeant Ndabuka.' And when I acknowledged the introduction in fluent Sindebele, the stern military expressions dissolved into huge flashing smiles.

Xhai was obviously very ill at ease in this company. He followed on my heels like a puppy.

'Did you know, Doctor, that there is still a field order issued to the British South Africa Police that hasn't been rescinded,' MacDonald told me, as he looked Xhai over with interest. 'It is an instruction to shoot all bushmen on sight. This is the first one I've ever seen. Poor little blighters.'

'Yes.' I had heard of that order which was maintained as a curiosity, but too faithfully reflected the attitude of the last century. The time of the great bushmen hunts, when a hundred mounted men would band together into a commando to hunt and kill these little yellow pixies as though they were dangerous animals.

White and black had hunted them mercilessly. The atrocities committed against them were legion. Shot and speared – and worse. In 1869 King Khama had enticed a whole tribe of them to a feast of reconciliation, and while they sat at his board, with their weapons laid aside, his warriors seized them. The king had supervised the subsequent torture personally. The last bushman died on the fourth day. With this history to remember it was no wonder that Xhai stayed within arm's length of me, and watched these colossal strangers with frightened Chinese eyes.

I explained to MacDonald our approximate destination, pointing out the general area on his map as accurately as I could reckon it from Xhai's description, and the inspector looked grave. He picked a shred of sun-burned skin from the tip of his nose before replying.

'That's not a very good area, Doctor.' And he went off to talk to his men.

It was midday before the helicopter came clattering over the tree-tops from the south-east. Louren jumped from the cabin lugging his own bag.

'Sorry I'm late, Ben. I had to wait for a phone call from New York.'

MacDonald came forward and touched his cap-brim.

'Afternoon, sir.' His attitude was deferential. 'The prime minister asked me to give you his respects, Mr Sturvesant, and I am to place myself at your disposal.'

We left the track before we reached the ranching country near Tete, and we swung away northwards towards the Zambezi. MacDonald was in the leading Land-Rover with a driver and a trooper on the machine-gun. We followed in the central spot, Louren driving and another trooper riding shotgun in the passenger seat, Xhai and I together in the back. The second police Land-Rover took the rearguard with Sergeant Ndabuka in command.

The slow miles ground past, as the column wound through forests of mopane, and climbed the low ranges of granite. At any hesitation in our advance, Xhai's arm would signal the direction and we would move forward, jolting and pitching over the rough places or humming swiftly through open glades of brown grass. I realized that Xhai was guiding us along the elephant trail, the migratory road that the huge beasts had beaten out from the river to the sanctuary of the Wankie game reserve in the south. Skilled trail blazers, they had picked a route that required the minimum effort to negotiate. Always it was the easy gradient, the low pass through the hills, and the river drifts with gentle sloping banks that they chose.

We camped beside one of these drifts. The river-bed was dry, choked with polished black boulders that glittered like reptiles in the sunset. There were banks of sugar-white sand, patches of tall reeds and a pool of slimy green water overhung with the branches of fever trees.

Beyond the river the ground rose steeply in another of those rocky ridges dotted with marula trees and patches of scrub. However, on this side the bush was open, offering a clear field of fire around our camp. MacDonald drew the three vehicles into a defensive triangle, and while he placed his sentries, Louren and I, followed by Xhai, went down the bank to the pool.

We sat on the rocks and watched a colony of yellow weaver birds chattering and fluttering around their nests of woven grass that hung from the fever trees over the green water.

Louren gave Xhai a cigar, and while we talked the little bushman's eyes never left our faces, like those of a faithful dog. The talk was fitful, changing from one subject to another without design. Louren told me about the hotel project on the islands. He was very certain of its success.

'It's one of my really good ones, Ben.' And when I thought about his other good ones – the cattle ranches, the diamond mines, gold, chrome and copper – I knew how big it must be.

I touched lightly on his difficulties with Hilary.

'My God, Ben. If only they understood that they don't buy you with the marriage certificate!' There were three others who had found that out the hard way, I hoped that Hilary would not be the fourth.

It was almost dark when MacDonald came down the bank.

'Excuse me, Mr Sturvesant. Could I ask you to come into the perimeter now. I don't like taking unnecessary chances.' And with good grace Louren flicked the stub of his cigar into the pool, and stood up.

'This used to be a country where a man could range to the full extent of his fancy. Times are changing, Ben.'

When we entered the camp there was coffee brewing on a low screened fire, and while we sipped from the steaming mugs I saw the precautions MacDonald had taken for our safety and I realized that his competent looks were not deceiving. He finished his sentry rounds and came to sit with us.

'I should have asked you sooner, but do you gentlemen know how to use the FN rifle and the 60-calibre machine-gun?' Louren and I both told him we did.

'Good.' MacDonald looked out towards the north. 'The closer we get to the border the more chance there is of a clash. There has been a big step-up in the terrorist activity recently. Something brewing up there.'

He poured a mug of coffee and sipped before he asked:

'Well, gentlemen, what are your plans for tomorrow? How far are we from our destination?'

I looked at Xhai. 'How far is it to the holes in the rock, my brother?'

'We will be there before the sun stands so,' indicating noon with one delicate little hand, 'my people are camped at the waterhole near the holes in the rock. We will go there to find them first, for they have long awaited my coming.'

I stared at him, realizing for the first time the extent of Xhai's friendship. Then I turned to Louren. 'Do you realize, Lo, that this little devil had made a trek of 150 miles on foot merely to tell us something that might give us pleasure.'

'What do you mean?'

'As soon as he discovered the old workings he left his tribe and set off to find me.'

That night Xhai slept between Louren and me. He still didn't trust the big Matabele troopers one little bit.

It was eleven o'clock the following morning when we saw the vultures in the northern sky. MacDonald halted the column, and came back to our vehicle.

'Something up ahead. Probably only a lion kill, but we had better not take any chances.'

Xhai slipped off the seat and clambered up onto the roof of the Land-Rover. For a minute he watched the distant birds, then he came down to me.

'My people have killed a large animal. Perhaps even a buffalo, for the birds are above my camp. There is nothing to fear. Let us go forward.'

I translated for MacDonald, and he nodded.

'Okay, Doctor. But we'll keep our eyes peeled all the same.'

The bushmen had erected five rude shelters beside a hole of mud and filthy water. They had merely bent a number of saplings inwards to form the framework, and then thatched it roughly with leaves and grass. There was no smoke and no sign of the little yellow people as we drove towards the encampment. Xhai was looking puzzled, darting little birdlike glances into the thick bush, and whistling softly through his teeth. The vultures sat in the tree-tops all around the camp, and as we approached there was a sudden commotion from amongst the huts and twenty or thirty of the big ugly birds flapped into the air.

Xhai let out a soft wailing cry. I did not understand what had happened, it merely seemed odd that the vultures were on the ground amongst the huts, but Xhai had guessed it. He began rocking slowly on the seat, hugging his chest and emitting that low-pitched wail.

MacDonald stopped his Land-Rover and climbed out. He stooped over something on the ground, then he straightened up and shouted an order. His troopers jumped from the vehicle and spread out with their weapons held ready. Louren parked our Land-Rover and we went to where MacDonald was standing amongst the huts. Xhai remained in the back seat, still rocking and wailing.

For the Bantu the bushman girls are an object of peculiar lust. I do not know why this should be so, perhaps it is their golden yellow colour, or it may be their tiny doll-like bodies. They had raped Xhai's women, all of them, even the little immature girls. Then they had bayoneted them and left them lying in that pathetically vulnerable attitude of love. Ghal and the other two males they had shot. Bursts of automatic fire had smashed their bodies so that slivers and chips of bone protruded from the mangled flesh. The blood had dried in black splashes and puddles. There were flies everywhere, big green metallic flies that buzzed like hiving bees and came to settle on my lips and eyes. I struck them away angrily. The birds had been at the bodies; that was the truly horrible part of it, the birds.

'God,' said Louren. 'Oh God. Why? Why did they do it?'

'It's their style,' MacDonald answered. 'Frelimo, Mau Mau, all of them hit their own people hardest.'

'But why?' repeated Louren.

'They've got guns. They want to use them. This is easier than going for white ranchers or police posts.' Two of the police troopers carried a tarpaulin from one of the Land-Rovers. They began wrapping the bodies. I walked back to our vehicle and leaned against the door. Suddenly I was sick, an acid bitter flood gushing up my throat, and I retched painfully.

When I was finished I wiped my mouth on my sleeve and looked up to find Xhai watching me. He was a man deprived of everything except the breath of life. There was such agony in those dark eyes, such sorrow twisted that mouth that I felt my own heart breaking for him.

'Let us find who has done this thing, Sunbird,' he whispered, and he led me into the short grass around the camp. He worked quickly, like a gundog.

There were spills of the bright brass cartridge cases scattered on the sandy earth. Shoddily manufactured, and stamped with Chinese characters, hundreds of them. The gunners had fired with childish gusto, pouring a torrent of bullets into the camp. Their boots had left the characteristic chevron-patterned imprints. There seemed to be hundreds of them, for the earth was churned and the grass flattened.

'They came in the night,' Xhai explained softly. 'See! Here is where they waited.' He pointed to the scuffed places amongst the bushes. 'There were many of them.' And he showed both his hands with fingers spread, three times. Thirty of them. A big party. 'They struck in the dawn. Yesterday at dawn.' Thirty-two hours ago. They would be miles away now, I realized. When we returned to the encampment the nine bodies were wrapped in canvas and laid out in a neat line, like parcels ready for posting. Four of the troopers were digging a shallow communal grave.

Xhai went to squat beside the line of dead. He was silent

now, and the silence was more distressing than his despairing wail. Once he leaned forward and timidly touched one of the green canvas-wrapped bundles. How many of these little men had squatted like this in the sun to mourn the massacre of their tribe, I wondered. It is at times such as this that I hate the savage ferocity of this land of ours. I could not watch Xhai's grief and I turned away and went to where Louren and MacDonald stood together talking quietly.

'It's a big party, Ben,' Louren greeted me as I came up.

'Xhai says there are thirty of them,' I told him, and he nodded.

'Very likely. The inspector feels we should turn back, and I reckon I agree with him.'

MacDonald explained, 'Should we run into them, they outnumber us heavily, Doctor. These swine are well trained and armed with the most modern weapons. It's not like a few years ago when they sent in a half-baked rabble. They are really dangerous now, and we aren't an offensive patrol. I think we must get out as quickly as possible, and call in the helicopters. Once they locate them the Hunter jets will give them a whiff of napalm.'

'Yes,' I agreed. The ancient workings were no longer important in the face of this horror. I looked across to where the troopers were lifting the bundles down into the grave. Xhai stood watching them. When the grave was filled with loose earth I went across to Xhai and placed an arm around his shoulder.

'Come, little brother,' I said and led him to the Land-Rover. The column turned and in the same order made its way back into the south.

The journey slowly developed into a nightmare of tension and straining nerves. The revving and gear-changing that was necessary to negotiate the rough and broken ground broadcast our progress far ahead of us. Every mile there was a location ideal for an ambush, with thick cover pressing in closely on either hand. Our trail was laid clearly, and we must follow it on our return. They would know this and wait for us there. It was possible they carried landmines and we watched anxiously for disturbed earth in the trail ahead. The strain was on all of us. Louren drove in grim silence, with an unlit stub of cigar rolling restlessly in the corner of his mouth.

The trooper behind him rode with the butt of the machine-gun pulled into his shoulder, and occasionally he traversed the heavy weapon experimentally. All our heads moved constantly, swinging slowly from side to side, searching, searching.

'Have you noticed there is no sign of game, Ben?' Louren asked suddenly. He was correct. Since leaving the bushman encampment we had seen none of the wildlife which had enlivened our outward journey, not even a herd of the dainty brown impala.

'I don't like it, Lo.'

'Join the club,' Louren grunted.

'In thirty-two hours the bastards could have moved miles. They could be anywhere.' I fiddled restlessly with the rate of fire selector on the rifle in my lap. MacDonald had insisted on us taking the spare weapons from two of the troopers on the heavy machine-guns. I was glad of it now. There was much comfort to be drawn from that hunk of wood and steel.

Suddenly the Land-Rover ahead of us skidded to a halt, and Louren slammed on his own brakes and snatched the automatic rifle from the bracket behind him. We sat with our weapons poised, peering into the wilderness of rock and scrub around us. Waiting for the sudden shuddering roar of machine-guns. The slow seconds passed and my own pulse drummed in my ears deafening me.

'Sorry,' MacDonald called from up front. 'False alarm!'

The engines revved, hideously loud in the vast silence of Africa, and we went on.

'For Christ's sake stop fiddling with that bloody thing!' Louren snapped at me with unnecessary violence. I had not realized that I had been clicking the selector of the rifle.

'Sorry,' I muttered guiltily. The tension was infectious. Louren's outburst was a symptom of it, but almost immediately he glanced over his shoulder and grinned apologetically.

'This is bloody murder.'

It seemed hours later that we crossed a ridge and went twisting down amongst the trees to the pool in the dry water-course where we had camped the previous night. MacDonald signalled the column to a halt on the far bank, and he came back to us.

'We will top up the fuel tanks here, Mr Sturvesant. I'll see to that. Will you take a party down to the pool and refill the water containers.'

Louren went down the bank with two of the troopers lugging the five-gallon jerry cans while I watched MacDonald begin refuelling. The gasoline fumes swirled like a mirage in the heat, and the smell was biting in my throat. One of the troopers splashed the liquid in a spurt down the side of the lead vehicle and MacDonald reprimanded him sharply.

'Stay here,' I told Xhai. 'Do not move.' And he nodded at me from the back seat of the Land-Rover.

I left him and followed Louren down to the edge of the pool. It was a tranquil scene, so typical in Africa. Tall reeds languidly drooping their fluffy heads, black mud, pocked with the hooves of a thousand beasts, water green and thick with slime bubbling sulkily with marsh gas, the weaver birds hanging upside down below their swinging basket nests. The two troopers were talking quietly as they filled the jerry cans, Louren standing over them with the automatic rifle.

'Another hour's travel will see us in the clear,' he

remarked as I joined him. He took a cigar from his top pocket and began unwrapping it without interrupting his search of the surrounding trees and brush.

There was a fleck of white on the rocks at the water's edge. It caught my eye and I glanced at it, and was about to dismiss it as a splash of bird droppings. Then I noticed something else, and I felt the first cool draught of apprehension blow down my spine. Casually I strolled along the edge of the pool averting my eyes from the white object until it was at my feet. Then I glanced down, and my breath jammed in my throat. My first impulse was to scream a warning to Louren and run for the Land-Rover, but I controlled the urge and forced myself to look away casually. Despite the racing of my heart and the difficulty I had in breathing I managed to stoop and pick up a pebble from the water's edge and toss it out into the pool where it fell with a plop in a widening ring of ripples. Quickly I glanced down again.

The white fleck was a piece of domestic soap, with a wet lacework of bubbles still frothing around it. There were damp marks on the rocks, that the sizzling sun had not yet dried, and in the mud at the water's edge, amongst all the thousands of hoof marks was a print. A strange half-human print, like that of a giant bird. The big toes deeply divided from the rest of the foot, split half-way back to the heel, and I knew that Timothy Mageba was watching me over the sights of an automatic weapon.

My skin prickled as from the stings of the myriad insects of fear. They crawled over my body and along the strings of my nerves. Slowly I walked back to Louren. The cigar was in his mouth and he struck a match as I approached. It flared in a puff of blue nitrous smoke in his cupped hands, and he bowed over it.

'Lo,' I said softly. 'Don't do anything suddenly. Behave as naturally as you can. They are here. Right here, watching us.'

He puffed four times then waved the match to extinguish it, and he looked around naturally.

'Where?' he asked.

'I don't know, but they are very close. We must show ourselves here until Mac is ready.'

'Tell the troopers,' Lo said.

The troopers were recapping the jerry cans, and as they moved back past us I stopped them.

'Go very gently. Do not run. Do not look behind you. The evil ones are here. Go to the inspector. Tell him to start the engines, when we hear them we will come running.'

They nodded, expressionlessly, understanding immediately, and I knew then why these were famed as the finest native troops in Africa. They went calmly up the bank, leaning away from the weight of the jerry cans.

'I feel like one of those little mechanical ducks in a shooting gallery,' I said, and tried to smile. It hung all crookedly on my face. 'What are they waiting for?' I asked.

'They probably didn't have time to set it up properly.' Louren laughed, a very good effort. It rang convincingly. 'They'll be moving into position now. Then they wait until we are all together in a bunch, not spread out like this.'

'God, I wish I knew where they are, where to expect it to come from.'

'What tipped you?' Louren asked, anything to keep this conversation flowing naturally.

'Piece of soap, and wet footprints on the rocks. They were bathing when they heard us coming.'

Louren tapped ash from his cigar, and glanced at the rocks, seeing the soap. Then his eyes flicked back to me. Above the bank we heard the starters whirring loudly in the silence, and then the engines running steadily. One, two, and the third one.

Louren ground the fresh cigar into the mud at the edge

of the pool, then turned to me. He let his hand fall onto my shoulder.

'All the way, partner?' he asked.

'All the way, Lo.' And we whirled together and went for the path up the bank, unslinging the rifles as we ran. I felt a lift of relief, the waiting was over. It had begun.

I had the strange sensation of not moving, of marking time, rather than running. The climb up the bank seemed endless, my feet dragged leadenly and a hot hushed silence persisted in which the engines of the Land-Rovers seemed muted, but our footsteps pounded like stampeding hooves.

We came out on top of the bank.

Sergeant Ndabuka was at the wheel of our vehicle swinging in towards us, slowing for the pick up.

The other two Land-Rovers were backing up, ready to cover us, turning for the path with the gunners traversing the heavy machine-guns.

'Jump!' shouted MacDonald. 'Let's hit out!'

I leapt for the side of the Land-Rover and Louren piled in beside me.

'Go!' he snapped urgently at the sergeant. The engine roared and we surged forward. From the moment when we started to run to the moment we boarded the speeding vehicle perhaps six seconds had elapsed. It had all gone very quickly, and I scrambled onto my knees, pushing the automatic rifle forward to cover one flank. In that instant they opened on us. The air around me was torn by the sound of a thousand bull whips, while the gunfire sounded like a stick dragged swiftly across a corrugated-iron fence.

MacDonald's vehicle was leading us out, back along our tracks. It was drawing fire also. I saw the gunner hit. His head snapping backwards as though from a heavy punch and his hat flying from his head. He collapsed over the seat, his untended weapon spiralling idly on its mounting.

They were below the river bank, lining it, hidden in the

reeds and scrub there. I saw the muzzle flashes, glinting like swords. I let off a burst, swinging on them, but with the Land-Rover bucking I was low. Dust flew in a line below the bank as though churned up by a whiplash. I corrected my aim and fired, the weapon shuddering in my hands. Seeing the reeds shake and tremble as my bullets raked them. Someone screamed, a thin passionless sound, and my weapon clicked empty.

I snatched for a fresh magazine, looking ahead, to estimate how much longer we must receive fire. MacDonald was just entering the forest, there were big trees on either side of the path indicating the passage. I saw the loose earth in the path ahead of MacDonald swept neatly, and I knew then why they had held their fire until it served to drive us into the trap.

I opened my mouth to scream a warning, but it was lost in the continuous clamour of gunfire and engine roar.

MacDonald hit the landmines they had laid for us across our old tracks and the detonation was a burst of bright white light that seared the retina of the eye. The concussion slammed painfully into my eardrums, and MacDonald's Land-Rover reared like a wounded lion. Its front end was smashed in, one of the wheels spinning lazily through the air. It toppled backwards, crushing the occupants beneath it. The second Land-Rover drove into it at thirty miles an hour. There was a rending screeching sound of metal as the two came together.

'Look out!' shouted Louren and the sergeant swung the wheel violently to avoid colliding with the mass of wrecked vehicles. Our Land-Rover hung over on two wheels, then flopped over on its side. We were thrown out on to the rocky earth.

There was a silence that lasted for three or four seconds. A stunned silence, even the enemy frozen by the suddenness of the havoc they had created. We were perhaps fifty yards from the river-bed where Timothy's men lay. The intervening ground was sparsely studded with fever trees. These and the bodies of the vehicles gave us a little cover.

I had lost my rifle and as I groped for it I found Xhai huddled next to me. I had one glimpse at his terrified face, as I crawled towards Louren.

'Are you all right?'

For answer he pointed. 'Look!' Twenty feet away Alaistair MacDonald lay on his back with the full weight of the Land-Rover lying across his pelvis. He was pushing the mass of metal with weak fluttering hands. He moaned then softly.

I stood up to go to him, and at that moment the guns opened again. Flailing us, rattling and clanging against the Land-Rovers, lashing billows of dust and storms of stone fragments, ricocheting with the sound of tearing silk – and Louren dragged me down.

I was aware of movement beside me and as I turned towards it little Xhai wailed softly like a restless baby. I put out my hand to calm him, but my touch galvanized him. He jumped to his feet, his dark amber eyes ablaze with terror, and he ran.

'Wait, little brother,' I shouted, and I scrambled up to follow him. Louren grabbed and held me and I watched as Xhai ran out into that hell storm.

He drew all their fire immediately. They hunted him, hosing bullets at him. He ran like a rabbit caught in a car's headlights, making no attempt to hide. I struggled in Louren's grip.

'No!' I shouted. 'Leave him! No! No!' And they hit him, knocking him down so he rolled across the stony earth like a small brown ball. He came up on his feet again, still running but his left arm was shot away above the elbow, holding only by a tatter of wet flesh, and it bounced loosely against his flank. They hit him again, squarely this time, between the shoulder-blades and he went down hard and skidded on his face. He lay very still and small in the harsh white sunlight. I was quiet in Louren's grip, while around me the surviving troopers crawled into position to return the enemy fire. Louren rolled away from me, lying prone and fired a burst around the tailboard of the overturned Land-Rover.

The storm of bullets returned to sweep over us, and MacDonald was still moaning. Nobody could reach him across that bullet-swept space. I knelt on the hard earth staring at Xhai's frail little body, and I felt the hot winds of my rage blow through my soul. They came from deep and far, crescendoèd and overwhelmed my reason.

I jumped up and ran to the mined Land-Rover, I tore the pin from the mounting and hefted the heavy machine-gun out of its seating. Then I threw four loops of the cartridge-belt over my shoulders, draping myself with death as though it were an Hawaiian lei. Then, with my gun on my hip, I went after them, running towards the river-bed, straight at the centre of their line.

I heard myself screaming, and the violent disruption of the air around me as shot passed close, buffeted my ears and fanned my face with a hot dry wind. I ran screaming and the gun shook my body as though it were a giant fist. The spent cartridge cases spewed from the breech in a glittering stream, ringing like silver bells as they bounced off the stony earth. I saw the lip of the bank dissolve in spurting, swirling clouds of dust as I traversed it, saw one of them hit and flung backwards.

Their fire was shrivelling, I saw movement in the reeds as they ran. One of them leapt to his feet and fired a burst. Beside me slabs of white bark exploded from the trunk of a fever tree, and I swivelled the gun onto him. He was in camouflage battledress, a pudding-basin helmet of steel on his head, and he crouched over his weapon, the muzzle winked its hot red eye at me and I wondered that it could miss me at such close range.

One of my bullets caught him in the mouth, spinning his helmet away and the contents of his skull blew out of the back of his head in a pink cloud. He dropped below the bank.

'Follow him! Cover him!' I heard Louren yelling somewhere behind me, but I did not care. I reached the bank of the river and looked down into the dry bed. They were running, panicky, for the far bank and I turned the gun on them. Watching as they fell, with the white sand dancing in sudden soft fountains amongst them. I was still screaming.

The last loop of cartridges flipped off my shoulder and fed into the hungry breech of my weapon. The gun went dead and useless in my hands, and I hurled it after them. Rage and sorrow had driven me far beyond the boundaries of reason and fear. I stood unarmed and unafraid and from the far bank Timothy Mageba turned back towards me. He had a pistol in his right fist, and he aimed at me. I felt the passage of the bullet close beside my head.

'Murderer!' I screamed, and he fired again, twice. It was as though the angels of death had draped their wings around me, shielding me, for I did not even hear the bullets. I saw him glaring at me, those terrible smoky eyes, the great cannon-ball head like that of some wounded beast at bay.

Then suddenly Louren was beside me, he threw up his rifle and snapped a shot at Timothy. I think Louren may have nicked him, for I saw him wince and stagger slightly, but then he was gone into the thick scrub that covered the high ground on the far bank. The police troopers went past us, moving forward in line of skirmishers down the bank and across the river-bed where the dead men lay. They fired a few rounds into the bush, then Louren called them back.

Louren turned to stare at me with a look of disbelief. 'They didn't touch you,' he said with wonder. 'Not a single bullet – my God, Ben, my God!' He shook his head. 'You frightened me, you crazy bastard. You frightened the hell out of me.' He put his arm around my shoulder and led me back to the vehicles.

MacDonald was still moaning softly. We lifted the side of the Land-Rover, Louren and I between us. MacDonald screamed as the troopers drew him out from under the vehicle. His legs were twisted at an odd angle and his face was very pale, his tan a dirty brown over it and little beads of sweat dewed his upper lip.

I left Louren to administer morphine and try to splint the badly shattered bone, and I went across to where Xhai still lay.

The entry hole was a blue-black pucker in the centre of his back, there was no bleeding from it. Yet he lay in a puddle of thick gelatinous blood, and I knew what hideous damage the exit of the bullet from his chest must have caused. I did not turn him over. I could not bring myself to do it, but his head was twisted sideways and I squatted beside him. With my finger-tips I closed the lids over those staring Chinese eyes.

'Go in peace, little brother,' I whispered.

'Come on, Ben. They'll be back. We must hurry,' Louren called.

Two of our troopers were dead, and the sergeant rolled them in their blankets.

'The bushman also,' I told him. He hesitated, but then he saw my expression and went quickly.

We rolled the third vehicle back onto its wheels and while the troopers lifted our dead and wounded aboard, Louren and I checked it out. Two of the tyres were shot through, the petrol tank was riddled, the steering box was severed by a bullet and another had shattered the engine sump cover. Oil poured from it, stinking in the heat.

Quickly Louren placed the sergeant and the three remaining troopers in a defensive perimeter amongst the fever trees and we pushed the crippled Land-Rover into the lee of the wrecked vehicles, giving ourselves some cover to work behind.

There was a tool box in MacDonald's Land-Rover. We changed the wheels as quickly as a pair of Grand Prix mechanics, cannibalizing from the wrecks. As we tightened the last wheel bolts the sniping began. It was long range, from the far ridge a quarter of a mile away. They had learned their lesson well, and kept a respectful distance now. Our troopers answered, blazing away with the two heavy machine-guns to discourage them further.

In the middle of a fire fight Louren and I worked, greasy to the elbows. Smearing skin from knuckles on sharp steel in our haste, burning blisters into our skin on the red-hot manifold and exhaust system.

We pulled the sump cover off the capsized Land-Rover, and lay on our backs with hot oil dripping into our faces as we bolted it back onto our vehicle. The gasket was worn, it would leak, but it would hold oil long enough to get us clear.

Louren changed the steering-box, while I found a cake of soap in my pack and plugged the bullet holes in the fuel tank. As we worked, I blessed the Chinese artisans who had manufactured those shoddy weapons on the far ridge, with their limited range and accuracy.

We refuelled and replaced the engine oil, standing by necessity fully exposed to the marksmen on the hill, forcing ourselves to work methodically and trying to shut from our ears the terrifying sound of passing shot.

Louren jumped into the driver's seat, and pressed the starter; it whirled dismally, on and on, and I closed my eyes tight and prayed. Louren released the starter button and in the silence I heard him swearing with bitter vehemence. He tried again, the battery was weakening now, the whirring of the engine slowed and faltered.

A stray bullet smashed the windscreen, spraying us with

glittering glass fragments. Louren was still swearing. In despair I glanced at the setting sun, only half an hour or so of daylight left. In the darkness the hyenas would come down from the ridge. As though they had read my thoughts the fire from up there intensified. I heard a bullet whine away off the metal of the Land-Rover. Louren jumped out of the driver's seat and opened the bonnet again. As he worked I shouted across to Ndabuka.

'Why aren't you firing, Sergeant? You are letting them have target practice. Keep their heads down, dammit!'

'The ammunition is almost finished, sir,' he called back, and a coldness closed about my guts. No ammunition, and darkness coming on fast.

Louren slammed the bonnet closed, and ducked back into the driver's seat. He looked at me through the shattered windscreen.

'Say another prayer, Ben. The last one was no damned good.' And he pressed the starter. It wheezed wearily but the engine would not turn.

'We've had it, Ben,' Louren told me. 'Both the other batteries are *kaput*.'

'Sergeant – all of you. Shove,' I shouted. 'Come on, help me.'

They ran to me at the rear of the Land-Rover.

'Try her in second,' I shouted at Louren, and a burst of bullets kicked around my legs, stinging them with fragments of stone.

We threw our combined weight on the Land-Rover and it bumped over rough ground, back towards the river.

'Now,' I shouted at Louren. The Land-Rover juddered and slowed and we hurled ourselves against it, keeping it moving against compression.

It fired once. 'Keep going!' I gasped. And abruptly the engine roared into life and we howled with triumph.

'Climb on,' Louren yelled and swung the Land-Rover back towards the trail, but I ran beside him.

'Matches!' I panted.

'What?'

'Give me your matches, damn you.' I snatched them from his hand and ran to the tangled wreckage. Gasoline was dribbling from one of the ruptured tanks and I flicked a match at it. The sucking, roaring torrent of flame licked across my face, singeing my eyelashes away, and I turned and ran after the Land-Rover, scrambling in over the tailboard, falling face forward onto the pile of dead and wounded men in the back.

Louren smashed a new route through a belt of scrub thorn, avoiding the mined trail, and then angled back to pick it up further out.

The firing from the ridge died away as the forest blanketed us. I watched the column of black sooty smoke climbing up into the flushed evening sky, pleased that I had denied them the spoils of victory, and suddenly I found myself shaking like a man in high fever. Icy waves of shock and reaction engulfed me.

'Are you all right, Ben?' Louren called to me.

'Yes, I'm fine,' I answered and looked down at the pathetic blanket-wrapped bundles at my feet.

All that night we crawled southwards, jolting and bumping over the rough ground, often losing the track and having to search for it, shivering in the cold of an African night when the wind blew through the shattered windscreen.

In a dawn that was grape-purple and smoky blue I asked Louren to stop the Land-Rover. The troopers helped me to dig a shallow grave in the sandy bottom land between two kopjes. I lifted Xhai out of the Land-Rover still wrapped in the dark grey police blanket and he was as light as a sleeping child in my arms. I laid him in the earth and we stood around in a circle and looked down at him. Blood had soaked through the blanket and dried in a black stain.

I nodded to the troopers. 'All right. Cover him.' They did it quickly and went back to the Land-Rover. It was still cold, and I shivered in my thin cotton shirt. Up on the kopjes an old bull baboon barked, his cry boomed across the valley.

I followed the troopers back to the Land-Rover and climbed up beside them. As we drove on I looked back, and saw a herd of buffalo moving down out of the bush. They were grazing, heads down and tails swinging towards Xhai's grave. This was where my brother belonged, with the animals in the wilderness he loved.

'I'm very much afraid that they have slipped back across the river,' the assistant commissioner of police told me. 'There is nothing we would have liked more than to get our hands on this fellow Mageba.'

We had flown out with MacDonald in the police helicopter to Bulawayo two days before. Louren had left me to help the Rhodesian police as best I could while he sent for the Lear and went on direct to Johannesburg. Now I was having a final debriefing at police headquarters, while a charter flight stood by to take me back to the City of the Moon.

The assistant commissioner was a tall man with a military set to his shoulders, and a brush of closely cropped grey hair. His face was seamed and furrowed and burned darkly by a thousand suns. There were ribbons on his chest that I recognized, the emblems of courage and honour.

'He is top of our list of the chaps we'd like to meet, actually. A nasty piece of work, but then you'd know that as well as anybody.' And he turned those steely grey eyes onto me, giving me the feeling that I was being interrogated.

'I know him,' I agreed. My part in the hi-jacking incident was common knowledge.

'What do you make of the man?'

'He is an intelligent man, and he has a presence. There is something about him.' I tried to find the words to describe him. 'He's the type of man who sets out to get what he wants, and the type that other men will follow.'

'Yes,' the assistant commissioner nodded. 'That's a fair summation of our own intelligence. Since he joined them there has been an escalation of hostile activity from our friends across the river.' He sighed, and massaged his iron-grey temples. 'I thought we might have got him this time. They left their dead unburied, and made a run for the river. We could only have missed them by minutes.'

He walked down with me to where a police car waited under the jacaranda trees with their clouds of purple blossoms.

'What news have you of MacDonald?' I asked as we stood beside the police car.

'He will be all right. They saved both legs.'

'I am glad.'

'Yes,' agreed the assistant commissioner. 'He is a good type. Wish we had more of them. By the way, Doctor, we would rather you kept mum about this business. We don't like to make too much fuss about these incidents. Rather playing into their hands, you know. Gives them the publicity they want.'

We shook hands and he turned and strode back into the building. As we drove through the busy streets and I saw the smiles on the faces around me I wondered why anybody should want to destroy this society – and if they succeeded, with what would they replace it?

It seemed natural to think then of the City of the Moon.

A great civilization, a nation which held dominion over an area the size of Europe, a people who built great cities of stone and sent their ships in trade to the limits of the known world. All that remained of them were the few poor relics which we had so laboriously gleaned. No other continent was so fickle in the succour it gave to men, to raise them up so swiftly and then to pluck them down and devour them so that they were denied even a place in her memory. A cruel land, a savage and merciless land. It was a wonder that so many of us loved her so deeply.

My return to the City of the Moon was disappointing. After the events of the last few days it was an anticlimax. It seemed that the others had hardly noticed my absence.

'Did you enjoy yourself?' Sally asked over the typewriter and a pile of translation sheets.

'Well, it was interesting.'

'That's good. What happened to your eyelashes?' she asked and without waiting for an answer began pounding the keyboard with two fingers, biting her tongue with concentration, pausing only to push her hair off her cheek with the back of one hand.

'Glad you are back, Ben,' said Eldridge Hamilton. 'I've been wanting to talk to you about this.' And he led me to a table on which a portion of one of the scrolls was spread. I didn't seem to be able to concentrate. Suddenly, for the first time in my life I felt that it was ancient and unimportant compared with the blood that I so recently had seen spurt fresh and red.

Ral and Leslie had obviously used my absence to scheme out an approach. Ral spoke for both of them, with Leslie prompting him when he faltered. 'So you see, Doctor, we don't feel it's right to marry until at least one of us has a steady job. So, well, we thought we'd sort of ask your advice. I mean we love it here, both of us. We'd like to stay on, but we'd also like to get married. It's just that, well, we've got such a high opinion of you, Doctor. We wouldn't like to miss the rest of the investigation, but—'

I spoke to Louren that evening and then called them from the supper table.

'The job is worth three and a half thousand, and Leslie will get two. Of course, there is a free flat at the Institute and I'll help you with the furnishing, as a wedding present.'

Leslie kissed Ral, and then me. A novel way in which to accept the offer of employment, I felt.

Ral threw himself into the search of the cliffs with renewed energy, but I spent little time with him. Instead, I began to prepare my address to the Royal Geographical Society. This should have been a labour of love and excitement, but I found myself floundering. There was so much detail in the scrolls, but all of it seemed irrelevant to those unanswerable questions: where did they come from and when, where did they go to, and why?

Each time, my efforts became so long-winded and convoluted that they bored even me. Then I would rip the sheets from my typewriter, ball them and hurl them at the wall. There is no more lonely place in the world than a blank sheet of paper, and it frightened me that my unruly emotions should intrude and prevent me marshalling my thoughts and facts in orderly ranks. I told myself that it was reaction from the horrors of our journey to the north, that Sally's enigmatic behaviour was worrying me deeply, that it was merely the fear of the imminent confrontation with my enemies.

I tried all the tricks, forcing myself to sit at the typewriter until I had completed 10,000 words or rising at midnight to try and shake loose a flow of words from my stalled brain.

The address remained unwritten, and I found myself mooning about my office polishing the great battle-axe until it gleamed and glittered, painful to the eye, or strumming fitfully on my guitar and composing new songs which all seemed sad and mournful. At other times I would sit for hours before the painting of the white king, dreaming and withdrawn, or I would wander all day along the cliffs, oblivious of the sun and the heat, and it seemed that often a little birdlike presence was near me, moving like a mischievous brown sprite just beyond the fringe of my vision. Or again, I would sit alone in the dim depths of the archives, deep in a trance of despair as I remembered the hatred in Timothy's smoky eyes as he glared at me across the water-course where the dead men lay. Neither Timothy nor I were all of what we seemed to be, there were dark and ugly depths in both of us. I remembered the savagely mauled bodies of the tiny bushmen left lying for the birds, and my own screaming madness as I cut down the running men on the white sand of the river-bed. I do not know how long my despondency might have lasted except for the discovery which uncovered the answer to so many of the mysteries that still shrouded our city.

Eldridge's team had been countering my apathy by an accelerated advance through the scrolls. Practice had sharpened Sally's grasp of the language, until she was as quick and as fluent as Eldridge himself. Even Leslie was now able to make an appreciable contribution to the work, while Eldridge had arrived by a process of trial and error at the most suitable method of unrolling and preserving our scrolls and he was now saving a great deal of time in this procedure.

At breakfast, which seemed to be the only time we spent together these days, Eldridge asked me to resume the work of removing the pottery jars from the archives. To be truthful I welcomed the excuse not to have to face the blank accusing stare of the sheet of paper in my typewriter, and Ral seemed as pleased to have a change from his fruitless search of the cliffs.

In the cool, peaceful gloom of the archives we worked in our established routine, photographing and marking the position of each jar after we had labelled it and entered it in the master notebook. The work was unexacting, and Ral did most of the talking for my mood of lethargy still persisted. Ral lifted down another of the jars from its slab, and then he peered curiously into the space beyond where the wall opened into a squared stone cupboard.

'Hello,' Ral exclaimed. 'What's this?' And I felt my lethargy fall away like a discarded article of clothing. I hurried across to him and I had a feeling of pre-knowledge as I stared at the row of smaller, squatter jars of the same pottery which had been hidden away in this carefully prepared recess. I knew that we had made another major advance, a significant step forward in our search for the ancient secrets. This idea came into my mind fully formed, it was as though I had simply mislaid these small jars and now I had rediscovered them.

Ral moved the arc-light to obtain a better lighting of the recess, and immediately we noticed another unusual feature. Each of the jars that we could see were sealed – a loop of plaited gold wire linked lid and body of the jar, and a clay seal bore the imprinted figure of a bird. I leaned forward and gently blew away the dust that obscured the impression on the seal. It was of the crouching vulture, the classical soapstone bird of Zimbabwe culture with its base of sun discs and rays. It came as a distinct shock to find this emblem of modern Rhodesia upon a seal of indisputably Punic origin 2,000 years old, as it would be to find the lion and unicorn of the British coat of arms in an Egyptian tomb of the twentieth dynasty.

We worked as quickly as was reconcilable with accuracy;

labelling and photographing the large jars which obscured the recess, and when we lifted them down we discovered that there were five of the smaller jars concealed behind them. All this time my excitement had been increasing, my hope of a major discovery becoming more certain. The concealment of the jars, and the seals indicated their importance. It was as though I had been marking time, waiting for these jars, and my spirits surged. When finally we were ready to remove them from the recess, I reserved this honour for myself despite Ral's protests of, 'But I found them!'

Balancing on the top rungs of the step-ladder, I reached in and attempted to lift the first of them.

'It's stuck,' I said, as the jar sat immovably on its slab of stone. 'They must have bolted it down.' And I leaned further into the recess and carefully groped behind the jar for the fixings which held it in place. I was surprised to find that there were none.

'Try one of the others,' Ral suggested, breathing heavily on the back of my neck from his lofty perch atop those lanky legs. 'Can I give you a hand?'

'Look, Ral, if you don't give me a bit of room you're going to suffocate me.'

'Sorry, Doc,' he muttered, moving back a full quarter of an inch.

I tried the next jar and found that it was also solidly anchored to the shelf, as were the next three.

'That's very odd,' Ral understated the position, and I returned to the first jar, and bracing my elbows on the edge of the shelf I began to twist it in an anti-clockwise direction. It required my full strength, and the muscles bulged and knotted in my forearms before the jar moved. It slid towards me an inch, and immediately I realized that the jar was held down on the slab not by bolts but by its own immense weight. It was fifty times heavier than the jars twice its size.

'Ral,' I said. 'You are going to have to give me a hand, after all.'

Between us we moved the jar to the front edge of the shelf, and then I cradled it in my arms like a new-born infant and lifted it down. Later we found that it weighed 122 pounds avoirdupois, and was not much bigger than a magnum of champagne.

Gently Ral helped me to settle it into the fibre-glass cradle we had designed for transporting the jars. We each took a handle and carried it down the archives, out through the access tunnel and past the guard post at the entrance. I was surprised to find it was already dark, and the stars were pricks of light in the high opening above the emerald pool.

Our disparity of heights made it awkward carrying the cradle, but we hurried down the rock passage and down towards the camp. I was relieved to see that lights still burned in the respository. When Ral and I carried in our precious burden the others hardly glanced up from their work.

I winked at Ral, and we carried the jar to the main workbench. Concealing it with our bodies, we lifted it out of the cradle and stood it in the centre of the bench. Then I turned back to the three bent heads across the room.

'Eldridge, would you mind having a look at this one.'

'One moment.' Eldridge went on poring over an unrolled scroll with his magnifying glass, and Ral and I waited patiently until at last he laid the glass aside and looked up. Like I had, he reacted immediately. I saw the glitter of his spectacles, the rosy glow suffuse his bald pate like sunset on the dome of the Taj Mahal. He came quickly to the bench.

'Where did you find it? How many are there? It's sealed!' His hand was actually trembling as he touched the clay tablet. His tone alerted the girls and they almost ran to join us. We stood about the jar in a reverent circle.

'Open it.' Sally broke the short silence.

'It's almost dinner-time.' I glanced at my watch. 'We had better leave it until tomorrow,' I suggested mildly, and both girls turned on me furiously.

'We can't,' Sally began, then she saw my expression, and relief flooded her face. 'You shouldn't joke about things like that,' she told me sternly.

'Well, Professor Hamilton, what are we waiting for?' I asked.

'What indeed?' he demanded, and the two of us went to work on the seal. We used a pair of side-cutters to nip the gold wire, and then carefully worked the seal loose. The lid lifted easily, and there was the usual linen-wrapped cylinder. However, there was not a suggestion of the unpleasant leathery odour. Eldridge, whose arms are like a pair of thin white candles, was unable to lift the jar. I tilted it carefully onto its side, and while he steadied it I withdrew the weighty roll. The wrapping was well preserved and folded off in one piece.

Nobody spoke as we stared at the exposed cylinder. I had guessed what it would contain. There is only one material which is that heavy, but it was still a delicious thrill to have my expectations realized.

It was another writing scroll, but it was not of leather. This scroll was a continuous rolled sheet of pure gold. It was one-sixteenth of an inch thick, eighteen inches wide and a fraction over twenty-eight feet long. It weighed 1,954 fine ounces with an intrinsic value of over $85,000. There were five of them – $425,000, but this was a fraction of the value of the contents.

The beautifully mellow metal unrolled readily as though eager to impart its ancient secrets to us. The characters had been cut with a craftsman's skill into the metal with a sharp engraver's tool, but the reflected light from its surface dazzled the reader.

We all watched with complete fascination as Eldridge spread lamp-black across the blinding surface and then carefully wiped off the excess. Each character stood out now, etched in black against the golden background. He adjusted his spectacles, and pored deliberately over the cramped lines of Punic. He started making non-committal grunts and murmurs, while we crowded closer, like children at story-time.

I think I spoke for all of us when at last I blurted out, 'For God's sake, read the bloody thing!'

Eldridge looked up, and grinned wickedly at me. 'This is very interesting.' He kept us all in aching suspense for a few seconds longer while he lit a cigarette. Then he began to read. It was immediately clear that we had chosen the first scroll in a series, and that Eldridge was reading the author's note.

'Go thou unto my store and take from thence five hundred fingers of the finest gold of Opet. Fashion therefrom a scroll that will not corrupt, that these songs may live for ever. That the glory of our nation may live for ever in the words of our beloved Huy, son of Amon, High Priest of Baal and favourite of Astarte, bearer of the cup of life and Axeman of all the Gods. Let men read his words and rejoice as I have rejoiced, let men hear his songs and weep as I have wept, let his laughter echo down all the years and his wisdom live for ever.

'Thus spoke Lannon Hycanus, forty-seventh Gry-Lion of Opet, King of Punt and the four kingdoms, ruler of the southern seas and keeper of the waterways, lord of the plains of grass and the mountains beyond.'

Eldridge stopped reading, and looked about the circle of our intent faces. We were all silent. This was something far removed from the dry accounts, the list of trade and the Council orders. This scroll was imbued with the very breath, the essence of a people and a land.

'Wow!' Ral whispered. 'They had a pretty good press agent.' And I felt irritation scratch across my nerves at this irreverence.

'Go on,' I said, and Eldridge nodded. He crushed out the stub of his cigarette in the ashtray at his elbow and began to read again. Pausing only to unroll and lamp-black each new turn of the scroll, he read on steadily while we listened, completely entranced. The hours fled on nimble feet, as we heard the poems of Huy Ben-Amon sung again after 2,000 years.

Opet had produced her first philosopher and historian. As I listened to the words of this long-dead poet, I felt a curious kinship of the spirit with him. I understood his pride and petty conceits, I admired his bold vision, forgave his wilder flights of fancy and his more obvious exaggerations, and was held captive by the story-web he wove about me.

His story began with Carthage surrounded by the wolves of Rome, besieged and bleeding, as the legions of Scipio Aemilianus pressed forward on her walls to the chant of 'Carthage must die'.

He told us how Hasdrubal sent a swift ship flying along the shore of the Mediterranean to where Hamilcar, the last scion of the Barcas, a family long since fallen from power and politics, lay with a war fleet of fifty-seven great ships off Hippo on the north African coast.

How the besieged leader called for succour and of the storm and adverse winds that denied it to him. Scipio broke through into the city, and Hasdrubal died with a reeking sword in his hand hacked into pieces by the Roman legionaries below the great altar in the temple of Ashmun upon the hill.

As Eldridge paused, I spoke for the first time in half an hour.

'That gives us our first date. The third Punic war and the final destruction of Carthage, 146 B.C.'

'I think you'll find that is also about the date point of the Opet calendar,' Eldridge agreed.

'Go on,' said Sally. 'Please go on.'

Two biremes escaped the carnage, the sack and rape of Carthage. They fled with the great winds to where Hamilcar lay fretting and storm-bound at Hippo and they told him how Hasdrubal had died and how Scipio had dedicated the city to the infernal gods, had burned it and thrown down the walls, how he had sold the 50,000 survivors into slavery and had sowed the fields with salt and forbidden under pain of death any man to live amongst the ruins.

'So great a hatred, so cruel a deed, could only spring from the heart of a Roman,' cried the poet, and Barca Hamilcar mourned Carthage for twenty days and twenty nights before he sent for his sea captains.

They came to him all nine of them, and Huy the poet named them, Zadal, Hanis, Philo, Habbakuk Lal and the others. Some would fight but most would fly, for how could this pitiful remnant of Carthaginian power stand against the legions of Rome and her terrible fleet of galleys?

There seemed to be no sanctuary for a Carthaginian, Rome ground all the world beneath her armoured heels. Then Habbakuk Lal, the old sea lion and master navigator, reminded them of the voyage that Hanno had made 300 years before beyond the gates of Hercules to a land where the seasons were inverted, gold grew like flowers upon the rocks, and elephants lived in great herds upon the plains. They had all of them read the account that Hanno had written of his voyage inscribed on tablets in the great temple of Baal Hammon at Carthage, now destroyed by Rome. They recalled how he spoke of a river and a mighty lake, where a gentle yellow people had welcomed him and traded gold and ivory for beads and cloth, and how he had lingered there to repair his ships and plant a harvest of corn.

'It is a good land,' he had written. 'And rich.'

Thus in the first year of the exodus Barca Hamilcar had led a fleet of fifty-nine great ships, each with 150 oarsmen and officers aboard, westward beneath the towering gates of Hercules and then southward into an unknown sea. With him went 9,000 men, women and children. The voyage lasted two years, as they made slow progress down the western coast of Africa. There were a thousand hardships and dangers to meet and overcome. Savage tribes of black men, animals and disease when they landed, and shoals and currents, winds and calms upon the sea.

Two years after setting out they sailed into the mouth of a wide, placid river and journeyed up it for sixteen days, dragging their ships bodily through the shallows, until finally they reached the mighty lake of which Hanno had written. They landed upon the furthest shore under a tall red cliff of stone, and Barca Hamilcar died of the shaking fever which he had carried with him from the pestilential lands of the north. His infant son Lannon Hamilcar was chosen as the new king and the nine admirals were his counsellors. They named their new land Opet, after the legendary land of gold, and they began to build their first city at a place where a deep pool of water sprang from the cliffs. The pool and the city were dedicated to the goddess Astarte.

'My God, it's four o'clock.' Ral Davidson broke the spell which had held us all for most of the night, and I realized how tired I was, emotionally and physically exhausted, but well content. I had found my Pliny, now I could go to London in triumph. I had it all.

How swiftly the days passed now. I was at work each morning before sunrise. My typewriter clattered steadily and the filled sheets piled up beside it. I worked until noon each day, and spent the afternoons and evenings in the repository. Listening to the songs from the golden books of the poet Huy. There was no question that the translation could be completed before April the first. Indeed we would be lucky to have the two first scrolls out of the five completed by then. There was equally no possibility that we could postpone the symposium that had been approved by the Council of the Royal Geographical Society for that date. The public relations office of the London branch of Anglo-Sturvesant had completed the arrangements, invitations had been issued and accepted, accommodation, transport and a hundred other details had been arranged and confirmed.

It was a race to marshal and present as much of this incredible plethora of facts and legend as I could in the time left to me. Always I must guard against the temptation to romanticize my subject. The words of Huy were inflammatory to my emotions, I wanted to copy his ebullient style, to laud his heroes and castigate the villains as he did. All of us at the City of the Moon were becoming deeply involved in the story, even Eldridge Hamilton, who was the only one of us not of Africa, was caught up in the grandeur of it. While to the rest of us for whom Africa was, academically and emotionally, the well of our existence, these songs were a compulsive living cavalcade.

How often I found our recent history but an echo of the endeavours and adventures of these men of Opet. How closely they seemed linked to us despite the passage of nearly 2,000 years.

For the first five years the settlement on the shores of the lake prospered. The buildings were of log and mud, the men of Opet came to terms with their new land. They fell into a trading relationship with the Yuye. These were the yellow people that Hanno had described 300 years before, tall graceful men with slanted eyes and delicate features. Clearly they were the ancestors of the Hottentots. They were a pastoral people, with herds of goats and small scrub cattle. They were also hunters and trappers, and gatherers of the flakes of alluvial gold from the gravel beds of the rivers. In the name of the infant king, Habbakuk Lal concluded a treaty with Yuye, King of the Yuye. A treaty that granted all the land between the great river and the hills of Tuya to the men of Opet in return for five bolts of linen and twenty swords of iron.

Well satisfied, Habbakuk Lal, to whom the set and scent of the sea were as the coursing of blood through his own veins, returned with five of his swiftest ships laden with the gold and ivory of Opet to the middle sea. He completed the return journey in nine months, setting up staging posts along the western shores of Africa, and returned with a cargo of beads and linen and the luxuries of civilization. He had pioneered the trade route along which the treasures of southern Africa would pour to the known world, but ever wary of Rome's vengeful eye he covered his tracks like the crafty old sea-fox he was.

He brought with him also new recruits for the colony at Opet. Metallurgists, masons, shipbuilders and gentlemen adventurers. However, the trickle of Yuye gold and ivory shrivelled as the accumulated stores of ages were exhausted. Habbakuk Lal led a company of 100 men to the city of Yuye. He sought the right to prospect and hunt throughout the kingdom of the Yuye, and the king agreed readily, placing his mark at the foot of a leather scroll covered with characters he did not understand. Then he called a feast to entertain his honoured guests. The beer was brought in great gourds, the oxen roasted whole over the pits of glowing coals, and the lithe Yuye maids danced naked, their yellow bodies glistening with oil in the sunlight.

At the height of the revelry Yuye, the king, stood, and pointed his fist at the men whose demands became ever more excessive.

'Kill the white devils,' he cried, and his warriors who had lain in readiness without the mud walls of the city fell upon them.

Habbakuk Lal cut himself a road to safety, his battle-axe swinging in a furious arc about him. Three of his men followed him out, but the rest of them were dragged down and their skulls crushed beneath the war clubs of the Yuye.

Habbakuk Lal and his gallant three outran the warriors that pursued them, and reached the bank of the great river where their ship was moored. Flying on white sails they carried the warning to Opet. When the Yuye regiments, 40,000 strong, swarmed down through the pass of the red cliffs, they found 5,000 men of Opet standing to meet them.

All that day the yellow horde broke like the waves of the sea on the ranks of the Opet archers, and all that day the arrows flew like clouds of locusts. Then at the moment when the Yuye drew back exhausted, their resolve broken, Habbakuk Lal opened his ranks and let his axemen run. Greyhounds on the rabbit, wolves on the sheep herds, they pursued until darkness halted the slaughter. Yuye died in the flames of his burning city, and his people were taken into slavery. This is the law of Africa, a land that favours the strong, where the lion alone walks proud.

Now suddenly the colony which had been quietly establishing itself, putting down its roots and making sure of its base, exploded into growth and bloom.

Her metallurgists sought out the mother lodes of metal, her hunters ranged widely, her ranchers bred the scrub cattle of the Yuye to the blood bulls that Habbakuk Lal's ships brought from the north. Her farmers sowed the corn, and watered it from the lake. To protect her citizens and her gods a start was made on the walls of Opet. The land and its treasures were divided amongst the nine noble families, the sea captains of the exodus, who were now the members of the king's council.

Habbakuk Lal, with his huge frame twisted and tortured by arthritis, and with the flaming red beacon of his hair and beard long ago changed to grey ash, died at last. But his eldest son, already admiral of the fleet of Opet, took his father's name. Another Habbakuk Lal directed the growing fleet of Opet in trade and exploration. His ships still beat the well-worn sea-lanes to the north, but also they voyaged southwards to where the land turned back upon itself and a great flat-topped mountain guarded the southern Cape. Here a sudden gale out of the north-west smashed half the Opet fleet upon the rocks below the mountain. The priests read this as an omen from the gods, and never again would a ship of Opet venture this far southwards.

The centuries pass. Kings take the throne and then pass from it. New customs arise, the ways of the gods and their worship are altered to suit this land, a new breed of man arises from the mixed blood of Opet and Yuye. He is a citizen, but only the noble families may govern. He may enjoy all the privileges and carry all the responsibilities of citizenship, except that of directing the affairs of state. This is reserved for those of the old blood, pure and untainted. As an offshoot of this nobility a clan of warrior priests arises. These are the sons of Amon, and it amused me to learn that the clan has its origin in a man from the old kingdom, that is, the kingdom of Tyre and Sidon, on the borders of Canaan. These priests probably spring from Jewish stock. You cannot keep us out of a good proposition, can you?

New heroes spring up and fight along the borders, or crush a rising of slaves, or slay the wild beasts. The old art of elephant-training is revived, and the king's elephants spearhead his army and lighten the heavy labours of building and mining.

From the golden books we had an occasional exciting flash of physical contact with the past. Huy describes the lay-out of the walls, and the towers of Baal. They tally exactly with the foundations we had exposed. Huy gives the dimensions of walls thirty-five feet high and fifteen thick, and again we wonder how they had disappeared.

At another place he describes a gift of treasure from the Egyptian agents at Cadiz to the Gry-Lion, as the king is now called; amongst the items is a gold cup marvellously worked with the signs of eternal life. It is our chalice found among the ruins of the temple, and that night I went to examine it again. Seeing its battered beauty with new eyes.

Always running through the songs of Huy was the puzzle game of guessing the modern names of the animals and places he mentions. Towns and garrisons had long since gone, or had been reduced to those mysterious piles of old stone which dot the landscape of central Africa. However, we were enthralled to hear how the men of Opet began a search for land where the vine and olive will grow. The oils and wines from the north were more precious than their weight in gold by the time they had completed the journey in the ships of the fifth Habbakuk Lal.

The Gry-Lion's horticulturists and viticulturists discover a range of high mountains far to the east. Mountains of mist and cool pure air. The terracing and developing of the benign slopes begins, with tens of thousands of slaves employed in the project. Living plants in pottery jars are sped southwards in the swiftest ships, then carried on the backs of elephants to the mountains of Zeng, and from them come the sweet red wines of Zeng which the poet Huy so loudly and lovingly extols. Here then is a description of the building of those terraced gardens which cover the Inyanga mountains to this day.

From the descriptions of the animals and wild birds of Punt and the four kingdoms we could recognize most of them. The sacred sunbird, who carried offerings of meat to Baal, flying upwards into a cloudless sky until it disappeared beyond the range of the human eye was obviously the vulture. Then we realized the significance of the carved vulture birds and the seal on the golden scrolls. The vulture had been taken as the emblem of the warrior priests, the sons of Amon, Ben-Amon. Huy had placed his personal seal on the jars which contained the scrolls.

There were other animals described by the poet which could only be extinct species, types which had vanished in the intervening 2,000 years. Chief of these was the Gry-

Lion. For we learned that the king took his title from a real beast. This was a large predatory cat which lived along the southern shores of the lake amongst the reed beds that grew there. As early as the year of Opet 216, laws were passed to protect this animal, already threatened by extinction. This protection was afforded it because of the role it played in the ritual of coronation of a new king; a ceremony which Huy referred to as 'taking the Gry-Lion'. He described it as reddish roan-brown in colour with a face masked in lines of black and white, and standing five feet high at the shoulder. Its eye-teeth protruded from its jaw in a set of great curved fangs ten inches long. Despite the doubts of the others as to Huy's veracity, I thought I recognized a description of the giant sabre-toothed lynx. A skeleton of this animal had been discovered amongst the upper level of bones at Sterkfontein caves.

Huy describes how the trade in live animals begins. Their ancient enemy, Rome, is denuding north Africa of lion and rhinoceros and elephant, for use in her circuses. Hanis, the hunter of the southern plains of grass, develops a method of capturing these animals alive and drugging them with a distillation of the seeds of the wild hemp. In a comatose state they are placed aboard the ships of Habbakuk Lal, and sped swiftly northwards from staging-post to post along the coast. Huy reports an unexpectedly high survival rate of fifty per cent, and these fetch astronomical prices for the entertainment of the sensation-hungry populace of Rome.

In the Opet year of 450, the nation is at the zenith of her wealth and power, but she has outgrown herself. Her boundaries are extended, her slave population hardly sufficient to support her multifarious enterprises. In desperation the Gry-Lion sends a slaving expedition for ten days' march to the north of the great river. Hasmon Ben-Amon returns with 500 superb black Nubian captives, and claims his reward from the Gry-Lion.

We had reached the end of Huy Ben-Amon's second golden book, and the Lear was waiting for us. Reluctantly we had to interrupt our readings and go.

Leaving Ral and Leslie to supervise the site, Eldridge, Sally and I flew out to meet the international flight from Luanda. We had to pay the excess on 200 lb. of overweight luggage, and the fare of the Botswana Police Inspector sent by his Government to guard their interests in the ancient relics we carried with us.

In London we had one free day, one precious day to ourselves and as usual I tried to do it all. The crocuses were out on the lawns of Lincoln's Inn Fields, the bitter at the Barley Mow in Duke Street tasted better than I remembered, and the new crop of girls in the King's Road were prettier than the last. When the National Gallery closed at six o'clock Sally and I took a cab directly to San Lorenzo in Beauchamp Place and ate Lorenzo's wonderful ossobucco washed down with red Chianti. We were only just in time for the curtain at the Queen's Theatre. It was all so different from our life at the City of the Moon.

By the time we returned to the Dorchester it was after midnight, but Sally was still wrought-up with the first impact of that fabulous city.

'I'm too excited to sleep yet, Ben. What shall we do?'

'Well, I've got a bottle of champagne in my suite,' I hinted, and she looked at me with an amused twinkle in her eyes.

'Ben Kazin, my favourite boy scout. Always prepared. Okay, let's go drink it.'

It was Krug, very pale and dry. When the bottle was half finished we made love for the first time in six months. If it were possible this was for me a more cataclysmic experience than our first time. Afterwards I lay exhausted physically and spiritually, and it was Sally who took the empty glasses and carried them through into the lounge. She came back with the brimming pale wine and stood over me naked, and lovely.

'I don't know why I did that,' she said, and gave me a tulip-shaped glass.

'Are you sorry?' I asked.

'No, Ben. I have never regretted anything between us. I only wish – ' But she stopped and instead she sipped at her glass and sat down beside me on the bed.

'You know that I love you,' I said.

'Yes.' She looked at me with an expression I could not fathom.

'I will always love you,' I said.

'No matter what?' she asked.

'No matter what,' I told her.

'I believe you, Ben,' she nodded, her eyes dark brooding green. 'Thank you.'

'Sally—' I began again, but she placed one long tapered finger on my lips, and shook her head so the soft dark wings of her hair swung against her cheeks.

'Be patient, Ben. Please be patient.' But I lifted her finger from my mouth.

'Sally—' She leaned forward and silenced my lips with hers. Still holding the kiss she placed her glass on the floor beside my bed, she took mine from my unresisting fingers and placed it beside hers. Then she made love to me with such devastating skill and subtlety that there were no questions nor protest left in me. At nine o'clock the next morning I got Sally into a taxi headed for Elizabeth Arden in Bond Street, a little apprehensive as to what would happen to that dark silky head of hers. What some of those faggots do to a pretty girl they should be hanged for. Then I climbed into another taxi and headed for the M4 and

Heathrow to become snarled in one of those traffic jams which make British motoring such a leisurely and soothing experience.

Louren's flight had landed by the time I paid off my taxi and ran through into the International Terminal, that seething cauldron of humanity.

I heard someone in the crowd exclaim, 'It must be Dicky and Liz!' and I was immediately alerted to the whereabouts of the Sturvesant party. With the limited horizon that I have from my altitude above ground, I am forced to rely on these gratuitous sighting reports.

I fought my way through to the entourage which had been mistaken for that of the Burtons, and realized that the error was excusable. This was Louren Sturvesant travelling heavy, in the grand manner, with his foreriders running interference and clearing a path for the doors. There was a light screen of the gentlemen of the Press skirmishing along the flanks of the advance, but unable to break through the ranks of B.Y.M. Their methods were too conventional. I got into a head-on position and went in low and dirty, and there were a few yelps and cries of, 'Watch that one,' and, 'Get him,' which changed quickly to, 'Sorry, Doctor.'

And I was through into the soft centre. Bobby Sturvesant let out a shriek and landed around my neck, and the entire advance broke down for the minute it took for us to accomplish the greeting ceremony. Hilary was in a soft wrap of honey mink which was made to look shabby by the lustre of her hair, and over her towered Louren, his mane of hair sun-bleached to white gold and his face burned dark nut-brown.

'Ben, you old bastard.' He grabbed me around the shoulder. 'Thank God you made it. Will you look after Hil and the kids for me. I've got a few things to clear up, then I'll see you back at the Dorchester.'

There were two long shiny black limousines waiting

under the portico and the party split neatly, but not before Louren had doubled back to tell me proudly, 'I got a black marlin in the Seychelles – 900 pounder, Ben. A real beauty.'

'That's the tiger,' I congratulated him.

'Get out the Glen Grant, sport. I won't be long.'

I sat in the jump seat opposite Hilary, having beaten one of the B.Y.M. to it, and I was delighted to see how radiant she looked. It was that bright shiny look of happiness which you cannot fake with cosmetics and eyeliner.

'We had ten days on the islands, Ben. It was wonderful.' She went all misty and soft at the memory. 'Our anniversary. Look!' And she held up her left hand which was overburdened with a ring of red gold and a solitaire diamond. I was accustomed to Louren's style of living, but even I blinked. The diamond was bluey-white in colour and looked good, it was certainly not a shade less than twenty-five carats.

'It's beautiful, Hilary.' And for no good reason I thought, 'The deeper the guilt, the bigger the gift.'

When we reached the Dorchester Hilary gasped and covered her mouth with surprise at the baroque superabundance of the Oliver Messel suite.

'It's not true, Ben,' she laughed. 'It just can't be!'

'Don't laugh,' I warned her. 'We must be costing Louren over £100 per day.'

'Wow!' She flopped into one of the enormous armchairs. 'You can get a drink, Ben, my love. I need it.'

While I poured I asked unnecessarily, 'Your problems were of a temporary nature then, Hil?'

'I have forgotten I ever had any, Ben. He's better than he ever was.'

When Louren arrived I saw what she meant. He was in high humour, laughing and restless with energy, sleek and hard and tanned. He disposed of the last two B.Y.M. while

I poured him a Glen Grant, then he threw his coat and tie over a chair, rolled his sleeves up over brown bulging muscle and settled with the drink.

'Okay, Ben. Show it to me.' And we plunged into an examination and discussion of the scrolls and their translation.

Louren picked on the first line of the first page.

'Go thou unto my store and take from thence five hundred fingers of the finest gold—' He repeated the line, then looked up at me. 'That's right from the old boy's mouth, Ben. My *store*! That's his treasury. That clot Hamilton mistranslated it. It should read "treasury".'

'Suddenly your Punic is pretty hot,' I commended him.

'Well, for cat's sake, Ben, when did you ever send down to a store for your gold?' He tasted the Glen Grant. 'If your theories are correct—'

'Don't give me that *if* bit, Lo. Your name is not Wilfred Snell.'

'All right, let's accept that there was a violent and sudden death to our city. Fire and dead men, the archives which they obviously held so dear are untouched, then there is a better than ever chance the treasury was untouched also. We've just got to find it.'

'Great!' I nodded, and grinned sarcastically. 'This is a major breakthrough. I've been breaking my heart searching for it these last six months.'

'It's there, Ben.' He did not answer my grin.

'Where, Lo? Where?'

'Close. Somewhere within the main walls, probably within the cavern area.'

'Hell, Lo. I've been over every inch of it fifty times.' I spoke with mild but rising irritation.

'And when you've been over it for the hundredth time, you'll realize how blind you've been.'

'Damn it, Lo!' I started. 'I don't think—'

'Get yourself a drink, partner, before you blow up.'

I did as he advised, and Louren went on. 'I'm not knocking what you've done, Ben. But let me just remind you that in 1909 Theodore Davis ended his book by saying, "I fear that the valley of the kings is now exhausted."'

'Yes, I know, Lo, but—'

Ignoring me Louren went on, 'And it was thirteen years later that Howard Carter discovered the tomb of Tutankhamen, the greatest treasure that the valley had ever yielded.'

'Nobody is talking about giving up the search, Lo. I'll go on just as long as you keep paying.'

'And I'll bet that my cheque book is more tenacious than your resolve.'

'That's a bad bet,' I warned him, and we were laughing again.

We parted in the middle of the afternoon, Louren being borne away in a flood of B.Y.M., across the lobby to where a black Rolls waited in front of the hotel, and I slipping out of the side entrance to hail my own taxi in Park Lane.

Eldridge Hamilton was waiting for me on the pavement outside the Royal Geographical Society, having motored up from Oxford in his bright red mini. He was dressed as always in his tweed with the elbow patches, but was feverish with anticipation of the morrow.

'I can hardly wait for it, Ben,' he chortled with malicious glee. 'Have they arrived at the hotel yet?'

'No, but Snell is due in this evening.'

Eldridge did a little hop and skip of excitement and said. 'Like a hippopotamus lumbering into the dead fall.' Cruel but apt, I thought, and we went up through the double oaken doors into the panelled hall which is a high temple of our profession. There is a hushed dignity about the building which I find reassuring and permanent in this insane and transitory modern world.

Side by side we climbed the sweeping staircase, past the portraits of great men and the lists of former medallists honoured by the Society.

'You'll have to give some thought as to who should paint you, Ben.' Eldridge indicated the portraits. 'They do say this foreign Johnny – what's his name, Annigoni? – is not too bad.'

'Don't talk tripe,' I snapped, and he let out one of those startling neighs of laughter that rang like a bugle call through the hallowed precincts. I was irritated by Eldridge's assault on one of my most private and treasured fantasies. I am a modest and almost painfully retiring person, but the very first time I had entered here, and looked up at the portraits, I had imagined my own dark visage peering down from the wall of honour. I had even selected the pose – seated to avoid undue emphasis on my body, with my head turned half away. I have a good right-hand profile. There would be a flecking of dignified grey at the temples, a gay little ribbon of some foreign decoration in my lapel, Legion of Honour, perhaps. The expression pensive, the brow furrowed. . .

'Come on,' said Eldridge, and we went to where the President and a handful of Council Members waited for us with sherry and biscuits, and not a decent whisky in sight. Nevertheless, I was aware that these gentlemen had it in their power to make into reality my imaginings of a few minutes previously. I set out to be as affable and charming as is possible, and it seemed to have the desired effect.

We discussed the opening of the symposium, which was set for two-thirty the following afternoon.

'His Grace will make the opening address,' one of them explained. 'We've asked him to keep it down to forty-five minutes, and if possible to avoid reference to orchid-growing or steeple-chasing.'

I would then read my paper. It would rank as a follow-on to the one I had read six years earlier. 'The Mediterranean Influence on Central and Southern Africa of the Pre-Christian Era', the paper which had afforded Wilfred Snell and his pack so much sport. They had set aside four hours for me.

Eldridge would read his paper the following morning, 'Certain ancient writings and symbols of south-western African origin.' The title Eldridge had chosen was purposely vague, so as not to telegraph my punch.

Eldridge and I reassured ourselves that the exhibits we had brought with us from Africa were safe in the strong-room of the Society, then Eldridge gave me a bad attack of the shakes by driving me back to the Dorchester through London's rush-hour traffic in his satanical red mini. We were carried around Hyde Park Corner four times, with Eldridge cursing fluently and his bald head shining like a warning beacon while I hung terrified to the door handle ready to bale out, before Eldridge managed to break out of the traffic stream into Park Lane.

I led him, both of us still palpitating, into the cocktail bar and shot a pair of double Gilbeys into him, and then left him. I had plans for the evening and it was already past six.

Sally came out of the lifts as I approached them. I mentally apologized to her hairdresser. He had let it lie, still loose and cloudy. They had wrought some sort of magic with her face also. It was all eyes and soft pink mouth. She had on a full-length dress of a floating green material that picked up the green of those eyes.

'Ben,' she came to me quickly. 'I'm so glad I found you. I left a note for you under your door. About this evening, I'm terribly afraid that I won't be able to make it, Ben. I'm sorry.'

'That's all right, Sal. It wasn't definite anyway,' I told her, hiding my disappointment behind a grin as my plans collapsed like soggy pastry.

'I have to see them. They are old friends, Ben. They've come all the way from Brighton.'

I went up to Louren's suite, and hung around waiting for him to return, chatting to Hilary and the children. At seven-thirty he phoned, and Hilary put me on after she had spoken to him.

'I was hoping we could have had dinner, Ben, but I'm screwed up here for heaven knows how long. They have made a complete hash of the tax clause in the contract. We are trying to redraft it. Why don't you take Hilary for dinner, instead?'

But she pleaded exhaustion, and announced her intentions of making it an early night. I ate alone at Isow's, a real kosher meal begun with chopped liver and onions. Afterwards I crossed the alley to Raymond's, and for five pounds watched the loveliest girls in London taking off their clothes. It was a distressing experience. It made me feel even more lonely and despondent, and afterwards, though I am not a lecher, I teetered on the edge of temptation when the girls beckoned from the dark doorways in Wardour Street.

I rang Sally's room when I got in a few minutes before midnight, and again an hour later when I had given up my efforts at sleep. Neither call was answered, and the telephone buzzed dismally like an insect sending out an unanswered mating call. It was almost morning before I found sleep.

Louren woke me, boorishly healthy and hearty at eight, bellowing into the phone, 'It's the big day, Ben. Come and have breakfast up here. I'll order it now, what do you want?'

'Coffee,' I mumbled, and when I arrived in his suite he had a huge platter of steak and bacon, kidneys and eggs, with smoked kippers and porridge to start and toast, marmalade and coffee to end it. An average sort of breakfast for Louren.

'You are going to need your strength, partner. Get in there and eat, boy.'

With my spirits bolstered by this solid bulwark, I was carried through the morning on a cresting wave of expectation and I felt like a lion when we went down to meet our guests at noon. When I say lion, I mean a man-eating lion. I had anointed my smoothly shaven cheeks with a double handful of Dior aftershave, I wore my dark cashmere suit with a white shirt and maroon tie, and Hilary had found a carnation for my button-hole. I smelt like a rose garden, and there was an eager snap to my step and the hunter's warm thrill in my belly.

Louren and I entered the private lounge together, and the buzz of conversation dwindled. I don't pretend that my entrance to a room can command silence, but Louren's certainly can. Only one voice continued raised; in a convincing imitation of the British upper class, it brayed across the lounge. Wilfred Snell stood in a circle of his sycophants, towering above them much bigger than life size, almost like a badly executed monument to himself. His legs were set apart and his body braced in the stance of a heavily pregnant woman to counter-balance his monstrous gut. It was as though he carried a half-filled winesack under his vest. The expanse of pearl-grey suiting material necessary to cover this bulge was as vast as a theatre curtain. His face hung down on his chest in a series of chins like the ripples on a pond. It was white and soft-looking as though a plastic skin had been filled with dirty milk. His mouth was a deep purple gash in the whiteness, loose, perpetually open, even when he was not talking, which was seldom. His hair was a wild curling bush from which a gentle white rain of dandruff sifted down onto his shoulders and lapels, and he was hung with things – a pair of reading glasses around his neck like a tank commander's binoculars, a golden cigar-cutter from his money pocket, from his lapel a monocle on a black ribbon, a watch chain and key ring.

I approached him obliquely, stopping to greet friends, to chat with colleagues, but moving in on him steadily. Someone put a glass in my hand and I looked around.

'Scotch courage,' Sally smiled at me.

'I don't need it, luv.'

'Let's go talk to him,' she suggested.

'I was sort of making the pleasure last.'

We looked at him openly, this self-appointed drummer of archaeology, whose half-dozen books had sold 500,000 copies, books that aimed at and struck squarely in the centre of popular tastes. Books in which he flirted dangerously with the laws of plagiarism and criminal libel; books in which cant masqueraded as erudition, and facts were squeezed, ignored or subtly altered to suit the argument.

I am not a bitter man, not one who bears grudges, but when I looked at this great bloated executioner, this torturer, this – well, when I looked at him I felt the blood bubble and fizz behind my eyes. I started towards him directly.

He saw me coming, but ignored it. The entire room was aware of what was happening, had probably been anticipating this confrontation since the day they received their invitations. The circle about the master opened, giving me space to approach the presence.

'There is no doubt—' Wilfred brayed, his gaze passing several feet over my head. He usually precedes each of his statements with an advertising plug.

'As I have always said—' his voice carried to the furthest corners, and I waited patiently. I have a carefully rehearsed smile which I use at times like this. It is shy, self-effacing.

'It is generally agreed—' Such a recommendation from Wilfred usually means that the theory in question is the subject of a raging controversy.

'To tell the truth—' And he went on to tell a blatant lie.

At last he glanced down, stopped in mid-sentence,

screwed his monocle into his eye, and to his delight and surprise, discovered his old friend and colleague Dr Benjamin Kazin.

'Benjamin, my dear little fellow,' he cried, and the diminutive stung like a dart in the hump of the bull. 'How very good to see you!'

Then Wilfred Snell did a very rash thing. He dangled his great soft white hairy paw languidly in my direction. For an instant I could not believe my good fortune; at the same instant Wilfred remembered the last time we had shaken hands six years before and tried to snatch it back. His reactions are no match for mine, and I had him.

'Wilfred,' I cooed, 'my dear, dear chap.' His hand felt like a glove full of warm jelly, it was only when my fingers had cut in for an inch or two that you could actually feel the bones.

'We were absolutely delighted that you could come,' I told him, and he made a little mooing sound. A few loose drops of spittle spattered from the slack purple lips.

'Did you have a good trip?' I asked, still smiling shyly. Wilfred had begun to do a little jig, skipping from foot to foot. My fingers had almost disappeared in the soft white flesh, I could now feel every knuckle very clearly. It was rather like playing a jelly fish on a trout rod.

'We must make time for a little private chat before the end of the symposium,' I said, and the air started to leak out of Wilfred. He was making a soft hissing sound, and he seemed to shrink like a punctured balloon. Suddenly I was disgusted with my brutality, my weakness in giving in to it. I let him go, and the return of blood to the abused hand must have been more painful than my treatment of it. He held it tenderly to his chest, his big pansy eyes were filled with tears and his lips trembled like those of a petulant child.

'Come,' I told him gently. 'Let me get you another drink.' And I led him away unprotesting like an elephant and its mahout. However, Wilfred Snell is nothing if not resilient, and he came back strongly. Throughout the luncheon snatches of his monologue carried across to our table. He was 'making no bones about it' and 'letting them in on a little secret' in his best form. From what I could hear he was repeating his conviction as to the medieval age and Bantu origin of the central African ruin system, and was lightly and amusingly debunking my own writings. At one stage I glanced across to see that he had *Ophir* open beside his plate and was reading from it to the general merriment of his table companions.

However, I had another crisis threatening which took all my skill to avert. Sally was my lunch partner and we sat opposite the Sturvesants. Within five seconds of seating ourselves, Sally noticed Hilary's new diamond. She could hardly overlook it, it was throwing slivers of light about the room, bright as arrows. Sally was silent for half the meal, but her eyes were drawn to that flaming jewel every few seconds. The rest of us were vying for an opportunity to speak, and there was much laughter and excited banter. Louren seemed to be especially attentive to Hilary, but suddenly there was a momentary silence.

Sally leaned forward, and in her sweetest voice, told Hilary, 'What a pretty ring. You are so lucky to be able to wear costume jewellery, my dear. My bones are too small. It doesn't suit me, I'm afraid.' And she turned back to me and started chattering brightly. She had ruined the mood with one expert thrust. I saw Louren frown, and flush angrily. Hilary pursed her lips, and I saw a hundred retorts pass in review behind her eyes but she withheld them. I plunged gamely into the void, but even my charm and social grace could not restore the mood. I was relieved when at last Louren glanced at his watch, then looked across at the B. Y. M. who was in charge of the arrangements and nodded. Immediately this gentleman was on his feet, shepherding the unwieldy party out to where the cavalcade of cars waited. As we passed through the lobby, Wilfred Snell cleaved a path to my side with a swarm of his admirers following him in grinning anticipation.

'I was glancing through your book again during lunch. I had forgotten how amusing it was, my dear chap.'

'Thank you, Wilfred,' I replied gratefully. 'That's jolly decent of you to say so.'

'You must sign it for me.'

'I will. I will.'

'Looking forward to your paper this afternoon, my dear little chap.' And again I shuddered with the effort of suppressing my feelings and keeping my voice mild.

'I hope you'll find it as amusing.'

'I am sure I will, Benjamin.' He let go a fruity chuckle and moved off like a crowd. I heard him saying to De Vallos as they climbed into their limousine, 'Mediterranean influence! My God, why not Eskimo while he is about it.'

We went through the park like the mourners at a state funeral, a convoy of black limousines, and turned out of the second gate into Kensington Gore.

We were set down at the door of the Society, and moved into the lecture hall. The speakers and Council Members were on the platform, and the body of the hall filled solidly. Wilfred was in his place, front centre, where I could watch every expression on his face. He was surrounded by his hatchet men.

They led in His Grace, smelling of cigars and good port. They pointed him at the audience like a howitzer, and let him go. In forty-five minutes he had covered orchids, and the steeple-chase season. The President began tugging discreetly at his coat-tails, but it was another twenty minutes before I had my chance.

'Six years ago I had the honour of addressing this Society. My subject was "The Mediterranean Influence on Central and Southern Africa of the Pre-Christian Era". I come before you now with the identical subject, but armed with further evidence that has come to light in the intervening period.'

Every few minutes Wilfred would heave himself around in his seat to address a remark to either Rogers or De Vallos in the row behind him. He used a stage whisper, covering his mouth with his programme. I ignored the distraction and ploughed through my introduction. It was a resumé of all the previously known evidence, and the various theories that had been applied to them. I made it purposely dull, pedestrian, letting Wilfred and his party believe that I had nothing further to support my views.

'Then in March of last year a photograph was shown to me by Mr Louren Sturvesant.' Now I changed my delivery, let a little electricity come into my tone. I saw a flare of interest in faces which had taken on glazed expressions. I fanned it steadily. Suddenly, I was telling them a detective story. There were longer intervals between Wilfred's pompous asides. The snickers from his admirers died away. I had the audience by the throat now, they were there with Sally and me in the moonlight looking down on the ghostly outlines of a long-dead city. They shared our thrill as we exposed the first blocks of dressed stone.

At the moment when I needed it, the lights were turned down into darkness and the first image was flashed upon the screen behind me.

It was the white king, proud and aloof, regal in his rampant maleness and golden armour. Out of the darkness the images flashed upon the screen. The audience sat in rapt silence, their fascinated faces lit by the reflected glow of the screen, the only movement was the frantic scribbling of the Pressmen in the front row as my voice went on weaving spells about them.

I carried the story to the point where we had investigated the plain and cavern, but had not yet discovered the walled-up tunnel beyond the portrait of the white king.

At my signal the lights went up, and the audience

stirred back to the present, all except His Grace who had succumbed to the port and was sleeping like a dead man. He was the only one of two hundred who I had not captivated by my tale. Even Wilfred looked groggy and shaken, like a badly beaten prize fighter trying to rouse himself to meet the gong. I had to accord him a grudging admiration, the man was game to the core. He heaved himself around towards De Vallos and in a penetrating whisper told him:

'Typical Bantu stonework of the thirteenth century A.D., of course. But very interesting. Reinforces my theories about the dating of the immigrations.'

I waited silently, clenched fists on the lectern, my head bowed over it. Sometimes I believe I could have been a truly great motion picture actor. I lifted my head slowly and stared at Wilfred, my expression was desolate. He took heart from it.

'The painting means nothing, of course. To tell you the truth it's probably a Bantu initiation candidate, similar to the White Lady of the Brandberg.'

I maintained my silence, letting him take out line as though he were a marlin. I wanted him to swallow it down deep, before I set the hook.

'There is no new evidence here, I'm afraid.'

He looked around him with a satisfied smirk, and his followers' heads started nodding and grinning like puppets.

I addressed him directly then.

'As Professor Wilfred Snell has just remarked, fascinating as all of this was, it presented no new evidence.' They all nodded more vigorously. 'And so, I determined to look deeper.'

And I was away again into a description of the discovery of the blocked tunnel, the decision to preserve the white king and cut through living rock, the hole through into the tunnel, and again I paused, and looked at Wilfred Snell. Suddenly I felt sorry for him; where before he had been my implacable enemy, an open running canker in my professional life, now he was just a fat and rather ridiculous figure.

Like the poet Huy, Axeman of all the Gods, I hacked into him then. Cutting him to pieces with my account of the scrolls, the vulture axe, and the five golden books.

As I spoke, one of the attendants wheeled in a barrow covered with a green velvet cloth. It pulled all their eyes, and at my signal he drew aside the cloth and there lay the great gleaming battle-axe and one of the scrolls.

Wilfred Snell slumped in his seat with his gut in his lap and his purple mouth hanging open slackly while I read the opening words of the first golden book of Huy.

'"Let men read his words and rejoice as I have rejoiced, let men hear his songs and weep as I have wept."'

I ended and looked around at them. They were gripped by the heart strings, every one of them. Even Louren, Hilary and Sally who knew it all were leaning forward in their seats, shiny-eyed and intent.

It was after seven-thirty, I noticed with surprise. I had overrun my time by an hour and there had been no rebuke from the President beside me.

'Our time is finished, but not the story. Tomorrow morning Professor Eldridge Hamilton will read his paper on the scrolls and their contents. I hope you will be able to attend. Your Grace, President, ladies and gentlemen, I thank you.'

The silence was complete, nobody moved nor spoke for a full ten seconds, then suddenly they were on their feet applauding wildly. It was the first time since the formation of the Society in 1830 that a paper had been applauded as though it were a stage performance. They came out of their seats, crowding around me to shake my hand and ask their questions which I could not hope to answer. From my vantage-point on the dais I saw Wilfred Snell rise from his seat and lumber ponderously towards the door. He walked alone, his band of followers had left him to join the crowd around me. I wanted to call out to him, to tell him that I felt sorry for him, that I wished I could have spared him, but there was nothing to say. He had said it all a hundred times before.

Every single national paper had it the following morning, and even *The Times* had allowed itself a touch of the dramatic. 'Discovery of Carthaginian Treasure,' it stated, 'one of archaeology's most significant finds since the tomb of Tutankhamen.'

Louren had sent out for them all, and we sat in a sea of newsprint as we ate another of those gargantuan breakfasts. I was touched by Louren's pride in my achievements. He read each article aloud, interspersing his own comments:

'You rocked them, partner.'

'Ben, you murdered the bums.'

'The way you told it, you even had me wetting my pants, and, hell! I was there!'

He picked one of the left-wing tabloids from the pile and opened it. His expression changed immediately. Suddenly he was scowling furiously, a look of such concentrated venom that I asked quickly, 'What is it, Lo?'

'Here.' He almost flung the sheet at me. 'Read it yourself, while I finish changing.' He went through into the bedroom and slammed the door.

I found it almost immediately. A full page of photographs under a big banner 'The forces of freedom'. Black men with guns, with tanks. Black men marching, rank upon endless rank. Eggshell helmets like evil toadstools of hatred, modern automatic weapons slung on camouflaged shoulders, booted feet swinging. It was not these that held me. In the centre of the page was a picture of a tall man with shoulders wide as the crosstree of a gallows, and a bald cannon-ball head that shone in the bright African sunshine. He walked unsmiling between two grinning Chinamen in those shabby rumpled uniforms that look like pyjamas.

The caption was in bold lettering: 'The Black Crusader. Major-General Timothy Mageba, the newly appointed commander of the People's Liberation Army with two of his military advisors.'

I felt a sinking sensation of dread as I looked at the brooding hatred in that face, the power and terrible purpose in those set shoulders and thrusting gait.

In some inexplicable fashion it seemed to detract from my own personal triumph. What had happened 2,000 years ago seemed of lessened importance when I looked at the picture of this man, and I thought of the dark forces in movement through the length of my land.

Yet it came to me then that this man was not unique, Africa had bred many like him. The dark destroyers who had strewn her plains with the white bones of men, Chaka, Mzilikazi, Mamatee, Mutesa, and hundreds of others that history had forgotten. Timothy Mageba was only the latest in a long line of warriors which stretched back beyond the shadowy, impenetrable veils of time.

Louren came out of the bedroom, and with him was Hilary. She came to kiss me and congratulate me again, and I dropped the sheet of newspaper from my hand, but not my mind.

'I'm sorry I can't be with you to hear your friend Eldridge this morning, Ben. I can't get out of this meeting. Please look after Hil for me. Give her a good lunch, will you?' Louren told me as the three of us went down in the lift.

Eldridge, in his tweeds and elbow patches, massacred his subject. For three and a half hours he mumbled about 'hangs' and 'abridgements', occasionally letting fly with that laugh of his, a sound which woke the sleepers. I was grateful to him as I looked around the slowly emptying hall, and the doodling yawning members of the Press. He certainly wasn't stealing my glory from me.

An hour before lunch Sally slipped me a note from her seat behind me. 'I can't take any more. Going out to do some shopping. See you. S.'

And I smiled as I watched her slide gracefully out of the side exit. Hilary turned and winked at me, and we both smiled.

Eldridge ground to a slow, inconclusive halt and beamed around at his depleted audience.

'Well,' he said. 'I think that covers just about everything.' And there followed a relieved scramble for the doors.

In the lobby of the Society I was once more surrounded by an enthusiastic mob, and we made slow progress towards the door and our lunch.

When at last we reached the taxi, with Eldridge and myself flanking Hilary on the seat, I was just about to give the driver the address of the Trattoria Terrazza when Hilary looked down at her hands in her lap and gave a little stricken cry.

'My ring!' And for the first time we noticed that the great jewel was no longer flamed upon her hand. I stared aghast at the naked finger, a fortune beyond my dreams was missing. That diamond must certainly be worth £30,000.

'When did you last have it?' I demanded of her, and after a second's thought a look of relief replaced her worried frown.

'Oh, I remember now. At the hotel, I was painting my nails. I put it in the alabaster cigarette box beside my chair.'

'Which room? Which chair?'

'The lounge, the tapestry chair beside the television set.'

'Eldridge, will you take Mrs Sturvesant on to the

restaurant, please. I'd better take another cab and dash back to the hotel before one of the cleaning staff discovers it. Have you your key with you, Hil?'

She dug into her handbag and came out with the key.

'Ben, you are an old sweetheart. I'm so sorry about this.' And she handed it to me.

'Damsels in distress are my speciality.' I stepped out onto the pavement. They pulled away and for five minutes I behaved like a berserk semaphorist towards the passing stream of taxis. I can never tell if those little yellow lights on top are burning or not, so I flag them all.

I let myself into the Oliver Messel suite with Hilary's key and hurried down that long passage past the bedrooms. With a little grunt of relief I found the ring amongst the cigarettes in the alabaster box. With it in my hand I moved across the light from the window to admire it for a moment. It was a thing of such brilliant beauty that my stomach turned within me. I felt a fleeting envy, a twinge of unhappiness that I should never own an object of such pure enchantment. Then I pushed the feeling aside and quickly tied the ring into the corner of my handkerchief, and I started back down the passage.

As I came level with the bedroom door I noticed that it was slightly ajar, and I paused with my hand going out towards the handle to draw it closed.

From the room beyond came a woman's voice, a voice husky with emotion, a voice broken by the panting of breath aroused and tremulous.

'Yes, oh God, yes. Do it! Do it!' And a man's voice blended with it, a voice rising in a hoarse cry like a wounded animal.

'Darling! My darling!' The voices washed, and swirled and broke together, the high surf of passion driven by the storm winds of love. With it was another sound, rhythmic, urgent, pounding out the pulse of creation, a sound as old as man, as unchanging as the courses of the stars. As I stood frozen, my hand still out-stretched towards the door handle, the thudding heartbeat of love was arrested and then there was only the sound of ragged breathing and the small sighs and moans of emotions spent and exhausted.

I turned away like a sleep walker. Silently I went to the front door and silently I closed it behind me.

I sat quietly through a lunch I do not remember eating, through conversations I do not remember hearing, for the voices I had heard beyond that door were those of Sally Benator and Louren Sturvesant.

I do not remember the return to the Royal Society, and only vague snatches of the concluding papers and ceremonial remain with me.

I sat in my seat in the front row, hunched down in my chair and stared at a crack in the polished wooden floor. My mind cast back, working over the past like a gun-dog hunting a hidden bird.

I remembered a night at the City of the Moon when I had gone drunk to bed, drunk on whisky poured for me by Sally's own hand. I remembered waking when Louren came into the tent, and seeing the pale flush of dawn in the sky beyond the tent-flap.

I remembered my visit to the cavern in the night, when Louren had dazzled me with the torch beam and sent me away.

I remembered that conversation overheard between Ral and Leslie. I remembered Sally's friends from Brighton, her violent unreasonable attacks on Hilary, her moods and silences, her sudden gaiety and even more sudden depressions, the half-statements, the hovering upon the verge of revelation, the midnight visit to my bedside, and a hundred other clues and hints – and I marvelled at my own blindness. How could I not have seen it, nor sensed it?

My name had been spoken, and I struggled to rouse myself, to try and listen to what was said. It was Graham Hobson, the President of the Society, speaking and looking down at me, smiling. Around me heads were craning, smiling also, friendly kind faces.

'Awarded the Society's Patron's and Founder's Medal,' said Hobson. 'In addition, my Council has instructed me to announce that a sum has been set aside from the fund provided, and that a commission will be awarded to a leading artist to paint a portrait of Dr Kazin. At an appropriate ceremony the portrait will be hung—'

I shook my head to clear it. I felt fuzzy and stupid. Hobson's voice kept fading and I tried to concentrate. Then gentle but insistent hands were pulling me to my feet, pushing me towards the stage.

'Speech!' they called, laughing, applauding.

I stood before them. I felt dizzy, the room turned and steadied again, blurred and refocused.

'Your Grace,' I began and choked, my throat felt flannelly, the words came out thickly. 'I am honoured.' I stopped and groped for words, they were silent, expectant. I looked desperately about the hall, seeking deliverance or inspiration.

Sally Benator was standing beside the side entrance. I did not know how long she had been there. She was smiling, white teeth in her sun-brown and lovely face, dark hair hanging in shining wings to her shoulders, her cheeks aflame and eyes sparkling, a girl freshly arisen from the bed of her lover.

I stared at her. 'I am thankful,' I mumbled, and she nodded and smiled encouragement at me – and my heart broke; it was a physical thing, a sharp pain, tissue tearing in my chest, so intense that I caught my breath. I had lost her, my love, my only love, and all these honours, all this acclaim was meaningless.

I stared across at her, desolate and bereft of purpose. I

felt the tears flood and burn my eyes. I did not want them all to see it, and I stumbled from the stage towards the door. The applause swelled again, and I heard voices in the tumult.

'Poor fellow, he's completely overcome.'

'How touching.'

'He's overwhelmed.'

And I ran out into the street. It was raining a soft drizzle and I ran wildly. Like a wounded animal I wanted to be alone to recover from this hurt. The cold rain soothed my burning eyes.

I craved solitude and surcease from pain, and both I found at the City of the Moon. Eldridge had a month's lecturing commitments to meet in England, and Sally had disappeared. I had not spoken to her since that night, but Louren told me casually that she had taken two weeks of her accumulated vacation time and had joined a tour to Italy and the Greek Islands. At the City of the Moon an airmail letter from Sally reached me, postmarked Padua, confirming this and regretting that her efforts to see me before I left London had failed. This was not surprising, for I had not returned to the Dorchester, but had my luggage sent to Blue Bird House and flown out on the early morning flight for Africa. Sally sent her congratulations, and ended by saying she would return to Johannesburg at the end of the month and take advantage of the first flight to the City of the Moon.

Reading her letter gave me a feeling of unreality, like receiving a message from beyond the grave. For she was dead to me, gone beyond my reach for ever. I burned the letter.

Louren visited the site for one day. I found that I had nothing to say to him. It was as though we were strangers;

his features, once so well remembered and beloved, were unfamiliar to me now.

He sensed the gap that separated us, and tried to reach across it. I could not respond, and he cut short his visit and left. I knew his puzzlement, and vaguely I regretted it. I could not find it in myself to blame or hate him.

Ral and Leslie were shadowy figures on the borders of my solitude. They did not intrude in the private world in which I now lived.

This was the world of Huy Ben-Amon, a place beyond pain and sorrow. During the time that Eldridge worked upon the scrolls, I had followed daily each detail of his translation. Language is my greatest talent, it comes to me without effort. Lawrence of Arabia learned to speak Arabic in four days – in ten I had taught myself Punic, and in so doing had gained the key to the fairyland of the golden books of Huy.

The third book was a continuation of the history of Opet up to the lifetime of the poet. This was as fascinating a document as the two that preceded it, but the true magic for me was in the remaining two golden books.

These were the poems and songs of Huy, poems and songs in the modern sense of the words. This was Huy the warrior, the Axeman of all the Gods, writing an ode to the shiny wing of the bird of the sun, his battle-axe.

He described the ore brought from the mines of the south, and its smelting in the womb-shaped furnace, the smell of the glowing charcoal and the trickle of the molten metal.

How it was purged, and alloyed, forged and shaped, its edging and engraving, and when he described the figures of the four vultures and the four suns I looked up at the great axe that hung above my working desk with wonder.

With Huy I heard the gleaming blade moan in flight, heard the snick of the edge into bone, the sucking withdrawal from living flesh. I read with awe the list of the enemies who had died beneath it, and wondered at their crimes and transgressions.

Then Huy's mood changed and he was a roistering fellow, tipping back the jug of red Zeng wine, roaring with laughter in the firelight with his companions in arms.

Now he was the dandy dressed in white linen, perfumed with sweet oils, his beard twisted and plaited into ropes.

Now the priest, walking with his gods. Sure of them, tending to their mysteries, and rendering unto them their portion of the sacrifice. Huy kneeling alone in silent prayer, Huy in the dawn lifting his arms in greeting to Baal, the sun-god. Huy in a frenzy of religious revelation.

Then again Huy is the friend, the true companion, describing his joy in the company of another man. The interlock of personalities, the spice of shared pleasures, dangers faced together and overcome. There is a strong hint in this poem that Huy is a hero-worshipper, blind to the faults of his friend, describing his physical beauty with an almost womanly insight. He details the breadth of shoulder, the regal curve of flaming red beard down onto a chest where the muscle bulges smooth and hard as the boulders upon the hills of Zimbao, the legs like strong saplings, the smile like the warm blessing of the sun-god Baal, and he ends with the line, 'Lannon Hycanus you are more than King of Opet, you are my friend.' Reading it, I felt that to have the friendship of Huy was to have something of value.

The mood of the poet changes again and he is the observer of nature, the hunter, describing his quarry with loving care, missing no detail, from the curve in the ivory tusk to the creamy softness of a lioness's underbelly.

Then he is a lover, bemused by the beauty of his sweetheart.

Tanith whose wide brow is shining white and full as the

moon, whose hair blows soft and light as the smoke from the great papyrus fires in the swamps, whose eyes shine green as the deep pool in the temple of the goddess Astarte.

Then suddenly Tanith is dead, and the poet cries his grief, seeing her death as the flight of a bird, her ivory arms gleaming like spread wings, her last cry echoing across the vault of heaven to touch the hearts of the gods themselves. Huy's lament was mine, his voice was mine, his terrors and triumphs became my own, and it seemed that Huy was me, and I was Huy.

I rose early and retired late, I ate little and my face grew gaunt and pale, a haunted face that stared back at me from my mirror with wild eyes.

Then suddenly reality caught up with me, shattering the fragile crystal walls of my fairyland. On the same aircraft Louren and Sally arrived together at the City of the Moon. The torment which I had for so long avoided had now begun again.

Again I tried to hide. I chose the archives as my sanctuary, and spent each day there trying to avoid all contact with either Sally or Louren. Still there was that dreaded hour of the evening meal, trying to smile my way through it and join in the banter and discussion, trying not to notice the private intimate exchange of glances and smiles between Louren and Sally until I could reasonably leave.

Twice Louren came to me.

'There is something wrong, Ben.'

'No, Louren. No. I swear to you. You are mistaken.' And I escaped to the stillness of the archives.

There was Ral's quiet company and the physical labour of cataloguing, photographing and packing the jars, and besides these I found another distraction. This cavern sealed for almost 2,000 years had been sterile, devoid of any life form when first we opened it. Now it was establishing its own ecology, first the tiny midge flies, then sand fleas, ants, spiders, moths, and finally the little brown gecko lizards. I had started making a film record of this colonization of the archives.

I spent many hours a day sitting quietly with my camera poised, waiting to obtain some difficult close-up shot of fly or insect and it was thus that I made the last major discovery at the City of the Moon.

I was working alone at the furthest end of the archives, close by the wall on which was graven the image of the sun. One of the gecko lizards ran down the wall, and across the stone floor. At the spot where the great battle-axe had lain when we discovered it, the lizard stopped. It stood poised, the soft skin of its throat pulsing and its little black beady eyes shiny with expectation. I noticed then the insect it was stalking. A white moth that sat quietly with spread wings on the sun image.

Quickly I reached for my camera, and set the flash bulb and exposure. I was anxious to record one of the lizards in the moment of its kill. Slowly I moved into a position from which I could focus on the moth, and I waited while the lizard approached in a series of swift dashes. Twelve inches from the moth it stopped again, and seemed to gather itself for the final assault. I waited breathlessly, my finger on the trigger button. The lizard shot forward and I exploded the bulb.

The lizard froze with the body of the moth crammed in its mouth. Then it turned and darted head-down towards the floor; when it reached the corner formed by wall and floor it disappeared and I laughed at its ludicrous fright.

I wound the film, replaced the flash bulb, returned the camera to its case, and was about to resume my work when a thought occurred to me. I went back to the end wall of the cavern, to the point where the lizard had disappeared and stooped to examine the juncture of floor and wall. It seemed solid, and I could see no hole or crack for the lizard to use as a refuge. Intrigued now by the lizard's disappearance, I went to fetch one of the electric arc-lights on its cable and I set it so that the beam fully illuminated the wall.

Then on hands and knees I crawled along the wall. I felt my heart start to pound like a war drum, and the hum of blood in my ears, the warmth of it in my cheeks. My hand as I reached for my pen-knife was unsteady, and I nearly broke my thumbnail as I tried to open the blade.

Then I was probing the faint crack line, plugged with dust, that separated wall and floor. The blade of my knife slipped into the crack to its full length.

I rocked back on my heels and stared at the wall, seeing the image of the sun throwing weird shadows in the arc-light.

'Perhaps,' I whispered aloud, 'it's just possible . . .' And then I was grovelling again beneath the image of Baal, almost as though I were one of his worshippers. Frantically I probed the crack, following it along the floor, until abruptly it turned ninety degrees, and climbed the wall. Here the crack was secret-jointed, riveted and turned back onto itself, making it all but invisible. The cunning skill with which this joint had been concealed convinced me that it hid something vital. The workmanship of this piece of the wall was a far cry from the rough joints on the roof slabs through which the dust had filtered down.

Now I jumped up and paced restlessly back and forth before the blank wall. I was alive again for the first time since my return to the City of the Moon. My skin tingled, my step was full of spring, my fists clenched and unclenched and my brain was racing with excitement.

'Louren,' I thought suddenly. 'He should be here.' I almost ran back down the archives, and out through the tunnel. In the wooden guard hut which enclosed the entrance to the tunnel one of the security guards was sprawled in a chair with his boots on the desk. The collar of his blue uniform was unbuttoned, his cap pushed back on his head. On the wall behind him his gunbelt hung from a hook, with the black butt of the revolver sticking out of the holster. He looked up from his paperback Western, a thick beaky-nosed face with cold eagle eyes.

'Hi, Doc. You in a hurry?'

'Bols, can you get hold of Mr Sturvesant for me? Ask him to come up here right away.'

I was on my knees below the sun image when Louren arrived.

'Lo, come over here. I want to show you something.'

'Hey, Ben!' Louren laughed, and it seemed to me that his expression was one of relieved pleasure. 'That's the first time I've seen you really smile in two weeks. God, I was worried about you.' He slapped my shoulder, still laughing. 'This is more like the old Ben again.'

'Lo, look at this.' And he knelt beside me.

Ten minutes later he was no longer smiling, his face was cold and intent. He was staring at the wall with those pale blue eyes as though he were seeing through the solid rock.

'Lo,' I began, but he waved me to silence with a peremptory gesture. He never took his eyes from the wall and now it seemed to me that he was listening to a voice I could not hear. I watched that cold god-like face with a sudden feeling of almost superstitious awe. I had a premonition of something unnatural about to happen.

Slowly, step by step, Louren approached the sun image. His hand went out and lay against the centre of the great disc. His fingers were spread, seeming to echo the shape of the image. He began to press against the wall, I saw the tips of his fingers flatten against the rock, changing shape beneath the pressure of his hand.

For a few long seconds nothing happened, then suddenly the wall began to move. There was no sound, no grating or squeal of protesting hinge, but the whole wall began to revolve upon a concealed axis. A ponderous, deliberate movement that revealed the square dark opening to a further passageway concealed beyond the image of Baal.

Staring into that dark prehistoric opening I whispered without glancing at Louren, 'How did you do that, Lo? How did you guess?'

His tone as he replied was puzzled. 'I knew – I just knew, that's all.' We were both silent again, staring into the opening. I was seized by a sudden unaccountable dread of what we would find in there.

'Get the light, Ben,' Louren ordered without taking his eyes from the doorway. I fetched the portable arc-light, and Louren took it from my hand. I followed him as he walked through the doorway.

Before us a passageway slanted down into the earth at an angle of forty-five degrees. The passage was seven foot six inches high, and nine feet wide. There was a flight of stone steps cut into the floor. Each step was worn, with edges smoothed and rounded. The walls and roof of the tunnel were of unadorned stone, and the depths of the tunnel were hidden from us by shadow and darkness.

'What's this?' Louren pointed at two large circular objects which lay at the head of the staircase. I saw the gleam of bronze rosettes upon them.

'Shields,' I told him. 'War shields.'

'Someone dropped them in a hurry.'

We stepped over them carefully and started down the staircase. There were 106 steps, each six inches high.

'No dust in here,' Louren remarked.

'No,' I agreed. 'The seal of the door was tight.'

His words should have acted as a warning, but I was lost in the wonder and excitement of this new discovery. The surface of the stairs was as clean as though freshly swept.

At the bottom of the staircase we reached a T-junction. On our right the passage led to a gate of barred ironwork which was closed and bolted. On the left it descended another twisting staircase that disappeared into the living rock.

'Which way?' Louren asked.

'Let's see what's behind the gate,' I suggested in a voice choking with excitement, and we went to it.

The heavy bolts were not locked but a thread of gold wire was twisted around the jamb of the gate, and a heavy clay seal closed the entrance.

The figure on the seal was of a crudely wrought animal, and the words, 'Lannon Hycanus, Gry-Lion of Opet, King of Punt and the four kingdoms.'

'Give me your knife,' Louren said.

'Lo, we can't,' I began.

'Give it to me, damn you.' His voice was shaking, thick with a peculiar lust and passion. 'You know what this is? It's the treasury, the gold vaults of Opet!'

'Wait, let's do it properly, Lo,' I pleaded, but he took the seal in his bare hands and ripped it from the gate.

'Don't do it, Lo,' I protested, but he pulled the bolts open, and flung his weight against the gate. It was rusted closed, but he attacked it with all his weight. It gave, swinging back far enough for Louren to squeeze through. He ran forward, and I ran after him. The tunnel turned again at right angles and led directly into a large chamber.

'God!' shouted Louren. 'Oh God! Look at it, Ben. Just look at it.'

The treasury of Opet lay before us with all its fabulous wealth untouched. Later we could count and weigh and measure it, but now we stood and stared.

The chamber was 186 feet long and 21 wide. The ivory was stacked along most of one wall. There were 1,016 large elephant tusks. The ivory was rotten and crumbly as chalk, but in itself must have been a vast treasure 2,000 years ago.

There were over 900 large amphorae, sealed with wax.

The contents of precious oils had long since evaporated into a congealed black mass. There were bolts of imported linen and silk, rotted now so that they crumbled to dust at the touch.

The metals were stacked along the opposite wall of the vault – 190 tons of native copper cast into ingots shaped like the cross of St Andrew; 3 tons of tin, cast into the same shape; 16 tons of silver; 96 of lead; 2 of antimony.

We walked down the aisle along the centre of the vault, staring about us at this incredible display of wealth.

'The gold,' Louren muttered. 'Where is the gold?'

There was a stack of wooden chests, carved from ebony, the lids decorated with ivory and mother-of-pearl inlay. These were the only objects of an artistic nature in the vault, and even they were crudely executed battle scenes or hunting scenes.

'No, don't do it, Lo,' I cried another protest as Louren began ripping open the lids.

They were filled with semi-precious stones, amethyst, beryl, tigers' eyes, jade and malachite. Some of these were crudely cut and incorporated in gold jewellery, thick clumsy pieces, collars, brooches, necklaces and rings.

Louren hurried on down the aisle, and then stopped abruptly. In another recess that led off the main chamber, behind another iron gate, the gold was stacked in neat piles. Cast in the usual 'finger' moulds. The piles of previous metal were insignificant in bulk, but when, months later, it was all weighed the total was over sixty tons.

Its value was in excess of £60,000,000 sterling. In the same recess as the gold were two small wooden chests. These yielded 26,000 carats of uncut and rough-cut diamonds of every conceivable colour and shape. Not one of these was smaller than one and a half carats, and the largest was a big sulky yellow monster of thirty-eight carats, and this added a further £2,000,000 to the intrinsic value of the treasure.

Here was the wealth of forty-seven kings of Opet, accumulated painstakingly over the course of 400 years. No other treasure of antiquity could compare with this profusion.

'We'll have to be bloody careful, Ben. No word of this must leak out. You understand what might happen if it did?' He stood with a finger of solid gold in each hand, looking down on the piles of treasure. 'This is enough to kill for, to start a war!'

'What do you want me to do, Lo? I must have help in here. Ral or Sally even.'

'No!' He turned on me ferociously. 'No one else will be allowed in here. I will leave orders with the guards, no one but you and I.'

'I need help, Lo. I can't do it myself, there is too much here.'

'I'll help you,' Louren said.

'It will take weeks.'

'I'll help you,' he repeated. 'No one else. Not a word to anyone else.'

Until six o'clock that evening Louren and I explored the treasure vault.

'Let's find out where the other branch of the tunnel leads to,' I suggested.

'No,' Louren stopped me. 'I want to keep normal hours here. I don't want the others to guess that we are up to something. We will go down to the camp now. Tomorrow we will have a look at the other fork of the tunnel. It can't be anything like this anyway.'

We closed the stone door behind us, sealing off the secret passage, and at the guard post Louren made his orders clear, repeating them and writing them on the guard's instruction sheet. Ral's and Sally's names were removed from the list of those allowed into the tunnel. And later he mentioned it to them at dinner. He explained it away as an experiment that he and I were attempting. It was a difficult evening for me. I was over-wrought by the day's excitement, and now that I had shaken off my mood of apathy I was over-reacting to the normal stimuli of living. I found myself laughing too loudly, drinking too much, and the agony of my jealousy returned more intensely than ever.

When Louren and Sally looked at each other like that, I wanted to shout at them, 'I know. I know about it, and damn you, I hate you for it.'

But then I knew it was not true. I did not hate them. I loved them both and this made it all the harder to bear.

There was no chance of sleep for me, that night. When I get myself into a certain state of nervous tension, then I can go for two or three nights without being able to still the racing of my overheated brain. I did not mean to spy on her. It was a mere coincidence that I was standing at the window of my hut staring out from my darkened room at the moonlit night when Sally left her own hut.

She wore a long pale-coloured dressing-gown and her hair was let down in a dark cloud around her shoulders. She paused in the doorway of her own hut and looked around carefully, making sure that the camp was asleep. Then guiltily, quickly, she hurried across the open moonlit yard to the hut in which Louren was living. She opened the door and went in without hesitating and for me a long harrowing vigil had begun.

I stood by my window for two hours, watching the moon shadows change shape, watching the patterns of the stars swing and turn across the heavens, stars as fat and bright as they are only in the sweet clean air of the wilderness. The beauty of it was wasted on me this night. I was watching Louren's hut, imagining each whispered word, each touch, each movement, and hating myself and them. I thought of Hilary and the children, wondering what madness it is that makes a man gamble his all on a few hours of transient pleasure. In that darkened hut how many confidences were those two betraying, how many people's happiness were they risking.

Then suddenly I realized that I was assuming that this affair was merely play on Louren's part, and I faced the possibility that he was serious. That he would desert Hilary and go to Sally. I found this thought intolerable. I could no longer watch and wait, I must have some distraction and I dressed quickly and hurried across to the repository.

The night-watchman greeted me sleepily, and I unlocked the door and went to the vault in which the golden books were kept. I took out the fourth book of Huy. I carried it across to my own office, and before I settled down to read I went to fetch a bottle of Glen Grant. My two opiates, words and whisky.

I opened the scroll at random and re-read Huy's ode to his battle-axe, the gleaming wing of the bird of the sun. When I had finished I was taken by an impulse and I lifted the great axe down from its place of honour. I caressed the shimmering length of it, studying it with new attention. I was convinced that this was the weapon of the poem. Could there be another answering the description so accurately? I held it in my lap, wishing that I could draw from it the story of the last days of Opet. I was sure it was involved intimately in the final tragedy. Why had it been left abandoned, a thing so well beloved and yet thrown carelessly aside to lie uncared for and discarded for nearly 2,000 years? What had happened to the Axeman Huy, and his king and his city?

I read and dreamed, disturbed less frequently by thoughts of Sally and Louren. However, at every pause in my readings they came to me with a sick little slide of jealousy and despair in my guts. I was torn between the present and the distant past.

I read on, sampling those portions of the scroll which were still unknown territory while the level in the whisky bottle sank slowly and the long night passed.

Then when midnight had flown and the new day was being born, I came upon a small piece of writing which touched a new depth of response in me. Huy makes a sudden heart-felt cry from the depths of his being. It is as though some long-suppressed emotion will no longer be contained and must come out in this appeal to have his physical form discounted when his value is assessed. From base earth flowers the purest gold, Huy cries, in his own poor distorted clay there were treasures concealed.

I re-read the passage half a dozen times, making sure of my translation before I could accept that Huy Ben-Amon was like me. A *cripple*.

Dawn's first promise was tracing the silhouette of the cliff tops with a pale rose colour when I laid the golden book away in its vault and walked slowly back towards my hut.

Sally stepped out of Louren's doorway and came towards me in the darkness. Her gown was ghostly pale and she seemed to float above the ground. I stood still, hoping she would not see me. There was a chance for I stood in the deeper shadow of her hut and I turned my face away, standing quietly.

I heard the rustle of her skirts, the whisper of her feet in the dust very close in the dark, then her startled gasp as she saw me. I looked at her then. She had seen but not recognized me. Her face was a pale moon of fear and her hands were at her mouth.

'All right, Sally,' I said. 'It's only me.'

I could smell her now. On the clean night air of the desert it was a perfumed smell like crushed rose petals, and mingled with it the warm smell of perspiration and love. My heart slid in my chest.

'Ben?' she said, and we were both silent staring at each other.

'How long have you been here?'

'Long enough,' I answered, and again the silence.

'You know, then?' It was said in a small voice, shy and sad.

'I didn't mean to spy,' I said, and another silence.

'I believe you.' She began to move away. Then she turned back. 'Ben, I want to explain.'

'You don't have to do that,' I said.

'Yes, I do. I want to.'

'It doesn't matter, Sal.'

'It does matter.' And we faced each other. 'It does matter,' she repeated. 'I don't want you to think that I, well, that I am so terrible.'

'Forget it, Sally,' I said.

'I tried not to, Ben. I swear to you.'

'It's all right, Sally.'

'I couldn't help it, truly. I tried so hard to fight it. I didn't want it to happen.' She was crying now, silently, her shoulders shaking as she sobbed.

'It doesn't matter,' I said, and went to her. I took her gently to her room and put her on the bed. In the light I saw how her lips were swollen and kiss-inflamed.

'Oh, Ben, I would have given anything for it to be different.'

'I know, Sally.'

'I tried so hard, but it was too much for me. He had me in some kind of spell, from the very first moment I saw him.'

'That evening at the airport?' I could not help but ask the question, remembering how she had watched Louren that first time she met him and how later she had ranted against him.

'That's why – later, with me – that's why we—' I did

not want to hear her answer, and yet I must know if she had first come to me inflamed with thoughts of another man.

'No, Ben.' She tried to deny it, but she saw my eyes, and turned her face away. 'Oh, Ben, I'm sorry. I didn't want to hurt you.'

'Yes,' I nodded.

'I truly didn't want to hurt you. You are so good, so gentle, so different from him.' There were dark shadows of sleeplessness beneath her eyes, and the peach-coloured velvet of her cheek was rubbed pink by Louren's unshaven skin.

'Yes,' I said with my heart breaking.

'Oh, Ben, what shall I do?' she cried in distress. 'I am caught in this thing. I cannot escape.'

'Does Lo – has he said what he is going to do? Has he told you he, well, that he will leave Hilary, and marry you?'

'No.' She shook her head.

'Has he given you reason—'

'No! No!' She caught my hand. 'Oh, Ben. It's just fun for him. It's just a little adventure.'

I said nothing, watching her lovely tortured face, glad at least that she knew about Louren. Realized that he was a hunter and she the quarry. There had been many Sallys in Louren's life, and there would be many more. The lion must kill regularly.

'Is there anything I can do, Sally?' I asked at last.

'No, Ben. I don't think so.'

'If there is, tell me,' I said and moved towards the door.

'Ben,' she stopped me, and sat up. 'Ben, do you still love me?'

I nodded without hesitation. 'Yes, I still love you.'

'Thank you, Ben,' she sighed softly. 'I don't think I could have taken it if you had turned away from me.'

'I'll never do that, Sally,' I said, and walked out into the lemon and rose glow of dawn.

Louren and I descended the staircase beyond the sun image. We went first to the treasure vault. While Louren gloated over the stacks of golden fingers, I watched his face. I was light-headed from lack of sleep, and I could taste the spirits I had drunk in the back of my throat. Watching Louren, I tried to find hatred for him in my heart, I searched diligently without success. When he looked up and smiled at me, I could not but answer him with a smile.

'This will keep, Ben,' he said. 'Let's go and have a look at the rest of it.'

I had guessed what we would find beyond the junction of the tunnels, and once we had descended the last spiralling stairs and come into another short level passage I had my last doubts dispelled.

The passage ended against another solid stone wall. Here, however, there was no attempt at concealment, for carved into the stone was an inscription. We stood before it, and Louren held the arc-lamp full upon it.

'What does it say?' he asked.

I read it through slowly. Even with all my practice I read slowly, for in Punic there are no symbols for the vowels and each must be guessed from the context of the word.

'Come on,' Louren muttered impatiently.

'"You who come here to interrupt the sleep of the kings of Opet, and to despoil their tomb, do so at your peril, and may the curse of Astarte and great Baal hound you to your own graves."'

'Read it again,' Louren commanded, and I did. He nodded.

'Yes,' he said, and stepped to the stone door. He began to seek the pivot point which we knew would trigger the mechanism. Here we were not so fortunate as we had been at the threshold of the sun door. After two hours, our way was still barred by that solid slab of uncompromising stone.

'I'm going to blow the bloody thing open,' Louren warned, but I knew he would not commit such an atrocity in this sacred place. We rested and discussed the problem, before returning to the door. It had to be another simple leverage system, but the trick was to find the pressure point and the angle of movement.

When we found it at last, I cursed my own stupidity. It should have been my first attempt. The symbol for the name of the sun-god Baal was once more the pressure point.

The door swung open, ponderous and slow, and we went through into the tomb of the kings of Opet.

There is only one other place I have known with the same atmosphere. That is Westminster Abbey which contains the tombs of so many of the kings of England. There was the same hushed cathedral sense of time past and history reborn.

Neither of us spoke as we went to the centre of the long narrow vaulted tomb. The silence was an oppressive weight upon my eardrums. Utter silence, so complete as to be sinister and threatening. Here again the air was long disused, but with an even heavier musty quality to it. I thought I detected the faint, stale smell of dust and mushrooms.

Along each wall, parallel to it, stood the sarcophagi of the kings of Opet. They were carved of massive granite. Solid, squat and grey. The lids were held in place by their own immense weight, and the upper surface had been polished and engraved with the name and style of the body that lay within. The mighty names that had echoed through the golden books of Huy. I recognized them, Hamilcar, Hannibal, Hycanus. Forty-seven great coffins, but the last was empty, its lid propped against the wall beside it. Its interior cut out into a man's shape, ready to swallow the last king of Opet.

At the foot of the great stone coffin a man lay stretched

upon his back on the floor of the tomb. His helmet was missing and his red-gold hair and beard formed a soft frame for the wizened, mummified features. His breast-plate had been removed exposing the dried parchment skin stretched over the gaunt skeletal rib-cage. The broken shaft of an arrow protruded from a long-dead chest. He wore a kilt of leather, studded with bronze rosettes and on his shins were greaves of bronze, on his feet light sandals.

His arms lay at his sides, his heels were together. The dead body had been laid out with care and obvious love.

Over him stooped another figure, kneeling like a man in prayer. A figure in full armour, with only the war helmet and breast-plate discarded on the floor beneath the empty sarcophagus. Long black hair hung forward to conceal his bowed face. Both hands clutched at his chest at the level of the diaphragm. From his chest a blade of steel protruded, a reversed sword, with its hilt securely anchored against the stone slabs of the floor, the point driven up under the ribs and lodged in his vitals.

Here was a man in the attitude of final escape from the shame of defeat, a man who in despair had fallen upon his own sword. The weapon had supported his weight these many centuries, propping him up in that kneeling position.

Neither Louren nor I could speak, as we drew closer to this tableau of ancient tragedy. For me there was no doubt as to the identity of these dried-out human husks.

Lannon Hycanus, the last King of Opet, lay stretched on the cold stone floor. Above him knelt his friend and high priest Huy Ben-Amon.

I felt choked with a sense of destiny, with a cold aching dread – for Huy Ben-Amon, the Axeman of the Gods, was a *hunchback*.

I had to see his face. I had to see it! I ran forward, and knelt beside him.

I touched his gaunt bony shoulder, covered by a tunic of brittle yellow linen. It was the lightest touch, a breath almost, but it was enough to shatter that delicately poised mummy.

The corpse of Huy Ben-Amon slid forward and crashed down on the body of the king. Steel and bronze rang on the stone floor, and echoed about the vaulted tomb of Opet.

The two figures burst into dust at the impact, a soft yellow explosion of mustard-yellow dust, swirling like smoke in the arc-light. There was nothing left of them but the metal of armour and sword, and two hanks of gold and sable hair in the puddle of talcum-soft dust.

I stood up, choking with the yellow dust. My eyes were swimming with tears of wonder and burning with the dust. The dust smelled of mushrooms.

Louren Sturvesant and I stared at each other without speaking. We had witnessed a miracle.

I awoke from a screaming nightmare of blood and flame and smoke, a horror of shining black faces and sweat-polished bodies lit by crackling roaring flames and the scream of the dying and the animal roar of blood-crazed voices. I woke panting and choking from the memory, and the terror and horror of it stayed with me long after I had found myself alone in my quiet hut in the silent night.

I switched on the bedside light and looked at my watch. It was still early, a little before eleven. I threw back my sheets and stood up, surprised to find my legs shaky and my breathing ragged. There was a twinge of pain at each breath I drew, and a dull tight sensation behind my eyes. My body felt hot, fever hot. I went to the wash-stand across the hut, and shook three aspirin from the bottle. I swallowed them with a mouthful of water, and then the tickling sensation in my lungs grew stronger. I coughed as though I was on sixty cigarettes a day, and the effort left me sweaty and trembling. My skin seemed to be aflame.

Without really knowing why, I took my dressing-gown off the hook behind the door, pulled it on and went out into the yard. There was half a moon in the sky, horned and yellow. The shadows under the trees and around the buildings were very dark and ugly. I felt the lingering dread and horror of my nightmare still upon me as I hurried across towards my office, and I glanced about me nervously. I could smell the tinge of smoke on the night air, and it troubled me also. I sniffed at it, feeling the faint sting deep in my lungs.

I reached the door of my office, and there was something waiting for me in the deep shadow beside the building. I saw it rush at me from the corner of my vision, a big dark thing, rounded and shapeless and deadly silent. I spun to face it, falling against the wall of the hut, weak with terror. A scream bubbled and died in my throat for there was nothing there. It was gone, I had imagined it, but now the pain in my head beat like hammer blows on the anvil.

I pulled the door open, and fell into my office, slammed the door behind me, locked it, gasping with unnamed and baseless fear. Something scratched against the door from the outside, a terrifying clawing animal sound that ripped my quivering nerves.

I backed away from the door towards my desk, crouching there, trembling, shaking and weak.

The sound came again, but from the wall beside me, I spun to face it, and I heard myself whimper.

I needed a weapon, I looked around desperately and the great battle-axe of Huy hung on the wall above my desk. I snatched it down and backed into a corner, holding it ready, at the present position across my chest. I coughed.

There was a thick sheaf of white paper on my desk. It moved and I felt the gooseflesh crawl all over my hot body.

The white square of paper quivered and wavered, it changed shape, crawled across my desk, and spread white bats' wings. Then suddenly it launched into flight, wings whispering, and it flew at my face. I saw the wide open mouth ringed with needle vampire teeth, heard the shrill squeaks as it attacked. I shouted with horror, and struck with the axe. The white thing fluttered and squeaked against my throat and face, and I fought and shouted, striking it down onto the floor where it crawled and slithered loathsomely. I struck with the edge of the axe, and inky black blood spurted from the thing and puddled the wooden floor of the hut.

I backed away from the thing, and lay back against the wall. I felt weak, and terribly afraid. I began to cough. The cough took hold of my whole body and shook it, rocking me, doubling me against the wall. I coughed until my vision burst into bright lights, and there was a salty sweet taste in my mouth.

I sank to my knees against the wall, my mouth was filled with warm wetness and I spat a thick gob of bright blood onto the floor. I stared at it, not understanding what was happening to me. I lifted my hand to my mouth and wiped my lips. My hand came away smeared with blood.

I knew then what it was. Louren and I had passed beyond two sealed doorways into the depths of a tomb closed for 2,000 years – and we had breathed air loaded with the spores of *cryptococcus neuromyces*, the curse of the Pharaohs.

It was too late now for me to berate myself for overlooking the precautions. I had believed that because the archives were safe, the rest of it was also. In my eagerness and excitement I had not given another thought to the fungus danger, even when Louren and I had discussed the door seals and even when I had smelled the mushroom odour in the tomb of the kings.

Now my lungs were clogged with the horrible colonies

of living fungus, a growing living thing within me, feeding on the soft tissues of my body, and pouring out its poisons into my blood to be carried to my brain.

'Treatment,' I gasped, 'got to find the treatment.' And I staggered across to my bookshelves. I tried to read the letters on the spines of the books, but they changed to little black insects and crawled away. Suddenly a thick mottled snake uncoiled from the top shelf, and dangled down towards my face, a thick bloated puff-adder with a flicking black tongue. I backed away, then turned and fled out into the night.

The smoke was thick, swirling around me, choking me so that I coughed wildly. The flames around me lit all with a lurid satanic glow, a flickering glow. There were dark shapes and strange sounds. I saw Louren's hut, and ran towards it.

'Louren,' I screamed, bursting in through the door. 'Louren!' panting, coughing.

The light went on. Sally was alone in Louren's bed, she sat up, sleepy, soft-eyed, naked, and looked at me with unfocused vision.

'Where is he?' I shouted at her. She looked confused, not understanding.

'Ben, what is it? You're bleeding!'

'Where is Lo?' It was desperately urgent. I had to find him. He had been exposed to the fungus also. I had to find him.

Sally looked down at the bed beside her. There was the indentation on the pillow where Louren's head had lain.

'I don't know,' she said, big-eyed, puzzled. 'He was here. He must have gone out.'

I coughed, great choking sobs, and felt fresh blood in my mouth. Sally was fully awake now. She stared at me.

'Ben, what is it?'

'Neuromyces,' I told her, and she gasped seeing the blood streaming down my chin.

'Louren and I have opened a secret passage beyond the sun image in the archives. It's infected with the spores. We took no precautions. It has got us. I'm sure he's there now. I'm going to him.' I stopped to breathe. Sally was out of bed slipping into her gown, coming to me.

'Get Ral Davidson. Respirators. Take all precautions. Follow us. I will prop the doors open. Down steps. Turn left at bottom. Follow us. Louren will have it also, drives you mad. Crazy. Terrible things. Come quickly – do you understand?'

'Yes, Ben.'

'Get Ral,' I said and turned. I ran out into the smoke and flames and darkness, running for the cliffs and the cavern. The great walls of the temple towered above me, walls long gone. The great phallic towers of Baal pointed to the moon, lit by the flames of a burning city. Towers that stood again after so long. They were screaming, the women, burning alive with their children. Dead men lay strewn in my path, cut down like the harvest of the devil, their dead faces terrible in the moonlight.

'Louren,' I shouted and ran on through the temple. They were in my path, dark and savage, crowding forward to oppose me. Dark, shapeless, terrifying, and I flew at them with a strange battle cry yelled from a blood-glutted throat. The mighty axe spun its silver circles in the firelight, and I was through them, running.

I reached the cavern, saw it lit by the guttering torches, saw the pavement of stone bordering the circular green beauty of the emerald pool. The rows of stone benches, rising in tiers around it as they had 2,000 years before. With a last enormous effort of will, I forced my brain to discount this fantasy and to recognize reality.

The wooden guard hut stood across the cavern from me. I staggered towards it. The guard sat at his desk reading. He looked up, his expression changing to surprise and incredulity.

'Good God, are you all right, Doctor?'

'Mr Sturvesant, is he in the tunnel?'

'Yes.'

'When did he go in?'

'An hour ago.' The guard came towards me. 'Is something wrong? You are bleeding, Doctor!'

'Wait here,' I told him. 'The others are coming. They know what to do.'

I hurried on into the archives, smelling the smoke still and hearing the clamour of a dying city ring in my ears.

Before the image of the sun-god I let the great battle-axe slip from my hand and left it lying on the stone floor. I pushed the stone door open, and propped it with one of the war shields to prevent it swinging closed behind me.

I ran down the staircase. Half-way down I saw the glow of light from the tomb below.

The inscribed doorway with its graven curse of the gods stood open, jammed in the hinge by the cable of the arc-light. The light lay on its side in the centre of the tomb where Louren had dropped it. The bulb still burned, lighting the tomb vividly.

Louren lay on his back at the foot of the huge granite sarcophagus of Lannon Hycanus, the last king of Opet.

He was naked to the waist. His face was deathly pale, his eyes closed, and bright blood stained the corners of his mouth and ran back down his cheeks into his ears and hair.

With the last of my strength I staggered to where he lay and dropped onto my knees beside him. I stooped over him and tried to lift him, my arms around his shoulders.

His skin was moist and burning hot, and his head flopped helplessly backwards. A new bright gush of blood ran out of his mouth, wetting my hands.

'Louren,' I cried, holding him to my chest. 'Oh please, God, help me! Help me!'

There was still life in him, just the last flicker of it. He opened his eyes, those pale blue eyes with the first shadows of death darkening them.

'Ben,' he whispered, choking with his own blood. He coughed, spattering droplets of the bright lung blood.

'Ben,' he whispered so softly I could scarcely hear it. 'All the way?'

'All the way, Lo,' I whispered, holding him like a sleepy child. His head of golden curls cradled against my shoulder. He was quiet for a little while, then suddenly he stirred again, and when he spoke it was in a clear strong voice.

'Fly!' he said. 'Fly for me, Bird of the Sun.' And the life went out of him, he turned to nothing in my arms, the great wild spirit flown – gone.

I knelt over him, feeling my own senses reel. The world turned and swung beneath me. I slipped over the edge of it, down into the swirling darkness of time. Down into a kind of death, a kind of life, for in my dying I dreamed a dream. In my poisoned sleep of death which lasted a moment and a million years I dreamed of long-dead men in a time long passed . . .

PART II

Of the thirty days of the prophecy there were but two remaining when Lannon Hycanus and his train came at last to the Bay of the Little Fish on the furthest southerly shores of the great lake. It was already dark when ten ships of the fleet anchored in the shallow waters of the bay, and their torches and lamps smeared long ruddy paths of light across the black waters.

Lannon stood beside the wooden gunwale of his steering-deck, and looked out across the fields of papyrus and hidden waterways to the south where the open country began and spread away endlessly into the unknown. He knew that here lay his destiny and that of the nation. For twenty-eight days he had hunted and now he felt an unaccustomed chill of fear fan his arms and neck, fear not of the terrible animal he had come to find, but of the consequences of the animal continuing to evade him.

Behind him there were light footsteps on the wooden deck and Lannon turned quickly. His hand on the hilt of the dagger beneath his leather cloak relaxed as he saw the unmistakable shape of the man in the light of the torches.

'Huy,' he greeted him.

'Highness, you must eat now and sleep.'

'Have they come yet?'

'Not yet, but they will before morning,' replied the hunchback, moving closer to his prince. 'Come now. You will have need of a steady hand and clear eye on the morrow.'

'Sometimes it seems I have ten wives, not nine,' laughed Lannon, and regretted the jest when he saw the blood darken the face of the hunchback; quickly he went on.

'You pamper me, old friend, but I think that tonight I will hunt sleep with as little success as I have hunted the gry-lion these twenty-eight days since my father's funeral.' He turned back to the bridge rail and looked across at the other nine ships. The ships of the nine families, come to watch him make good his claim to the throne of Opet and the four kingdoms, come to watch him take his gry-lion.

'Look at them, Huy.' And his friend came to his side. 'How many of them have made sacrifices to the gods for my failure?'

'Three of them, certainly – you know which I mean. There are perhaps more of them.'

'And those who are loyal to house Barca, those we can count upon without question?'

'You know them also, my lord. Habbakuk Lal will stand with you until the seas turn to sand, house Amon, house Hasmon—'

'Yes,' Lannon interrupted. 'I know them, Huy, every one of them, for and against. I was but talking to have the comfort of your voice.' He touched the hunchback's shoulder in a gesture of affection, before turning away to gaze once more into the southern wilderness.

'When the prophecy was made did they ever foresee the day when the great gry-lion would pass from the land? When a prince might search for all thirty of the days allotted to the task without seeing even the marks of the beast's paws in the earth of Opet?' Lannon spoke with sudden anger. He flung his cloak back over his shoulder and folded his arms across his naked chest. His skin was freshly oiled and the muscles glowed in the torch light, he kneaded his own flesh with the long powerful fingers.

'My father killed on the twenty-fifth day, and that was forty-six years ago. They said even then that the gry-lion was finished. Since then how many have the scouts reported?'

'My lord, the gods will decide,' Huy tried to soothe him.

'We have hunted every covert where the gry-lion has been seen in the last 200 years. Five full legions have swept the swamps in the north, three more along the great river.' He broke off and began pacing the deck, pausing to look down into the hull where the tiers of naked slaves slept chained upon their benches, leaning on the mighty oars in the position in which they would die. The stench of the rowing decks came up to him as a solid thing in the humid night. He turned back to Huy.

'This reach of the swamps is the last place in the whole of my kingdoms which might hide a gry-lion. If it does not, then what will happen, Huy? Is there no other way in which I might prove my right? Is there no escape in the scrolls?'

'None, my lord.' Huy shook his head with regret.

'The kingship must fall?'

'Unless there is a gry-lion taken then Opet will have no king.'

'Who will rule without a king?'

'The Council of Nine, alone.'

'And the royal house? What will become of house Barca?'

'Let us not talk of it,' Huy suggested softly. 'Come, my lord. A slave is preparing a jug of hot spiced wine and a stew of fish. The wine will help you to sleep.'

'Will you make an oracle for tomorrow, my priest of Baal?' Lannon asked suddenly.

'If the oracle is unfavourable, will it help you sleep?' asked Huy, and Lannon stared at him a moment before barking with harsh laughter.

'You are right, as always. Come then, I am hungry.'

Lannon ate with vast appetite from the bowl of fish, sitting naked on his fur-covered bed. He had let his hair loose and it hung to his shoulders, curling and gleaming strangely golden in the light of the hanging lamp. He was a god-like figure among his dark-haired people.

The leather awnings were opened, and a light breeze came up from the south-east to cool the cabin and blow out the galley stench. The ship moved to the breeze and the light chop of the surface, her timber popped and creaked softly, a slave cried out in nightmare, and from the deck above came the steps of the night guard – all the familiar comforting sounds of the flagship at sea.

Lannon wiped out the bowl with a piece of millet bread, popped it into his mouth, and washed it down with the last of the wine. He sighed with content, and smiled at Huy.

'Sing for me, my bird of the sun.'

Huy Ben-Amon squatted on the deck at the foot of the prince's bed. He held his lute in his lap, and crouched over it. The curve of his back exaggerated the attitude, the long tar-black tresses of hair hung forward to hide his face, his massively developed arms seemed too powerful for the long delicate fingers that held the lute. He struck a note, and a listening hush fell upon the night. The footsteps overhead ceased, two slave girls ceased their work and came to kneel beside Lannon's bed, the arguing voices from the ship anchored alongside quieted, and Huy sang.

His voice rang sweetly across the dark waters, and the prince and the fleet listened. Dark shapes moved to the rails of the nearest ships and stood quietly there looking across at the flagship. On the cheeks of one of the pretty slave girls stood teardrops that glistened in the lamp light, when Huy sang of a lost love. Then she smiled through her tears when Huy changed the song to one of the bawdy marching tunes of the Sixth Legion.

'Enough.' Huy looked up from his lute at last. 'There will be work tomorrow, my lord.'

Lannon nodded and touched one of the slave girls on the cheek. Immediately she stood up and loosed the shoulder strap of her linen tunic, letting it fall from her body. She was young and lithe, her body almost boyishly slim in the lamp light. She stooped and gathered her robe, dropped it across the bench beside the door and stepped naked into Lannon's bed. The other girl went to snuff the lamp, and Huy rose from the deck with his lute slung on his shoulder.

A voice hailed from the darkness, a great bull bellow from the edge of the papyrus beds that carried across the water to the flagship.

'Open your lines for a friend!'

'Who calls himself friend?' One of the guards shouted a challenge, and the reply was bellowed hoarsely.

'Mursil, huntmaster of house Barca.' And Lannon was out of his bed in one bound.

'He has come!' he exclaimed, flinging his cloak over his shoulders and hurrying to the companion ladder with Huy scampering beside him.

A small canoe bumped alongside and Mursil came up through the entry-port as Lannon and Huy reached the deck, a huge figure, gross and apelike with his big beefy round face ruddy from sun and wine.

The ship was awake now. Her officers swarming up onto the deck, new torches flaring to light the scene as day, the bustle and hum of excitement affecting them all.

Mursil saw Lannon and hurried to him down the aisle which opened for him across the crowded deck. He was followed closely by a pygmy figure, a tiny brown naked manikin that looked about him from slanted eyes in obvious terror at these unfamiliar surroundings.

'My lord.' Mursil opened his cloak and dropped heavily to one knee in front of Lannon. 'I bring good news.'

'Then you are welcome.'

'This one,' Mursil reached behind him and dragged the little bushman forward, 'this one has found what we seek.'

'You have seen it?' Lannon demanded.

'The tracks of his paws only, but this one has seen the beast itself.'

'If it is true, you will be well rewarded, both of you,' promised Lannon Hycanus and turned to grin triumphantly at Huy.

'The gods have decided. House Barca will have its chance once more.'

The sky was only a shade lighter than the black brooding swampland; the dawn-flighting duck ghost-whistled unseen overhead and each minute the light strengthened.

Half a mile out on the open plain a herd of buffalo grazed in a dark bunch. Heads down, tails swinging lazily, they moved back steadily towards the tall dense banks of papyrus reed.

They moved faster as the light strengthened, hurrying to reach the sanctuary of the reedbeds, 200 huge bovine shapes with their armoured heads and bunched black shoulders. Dawn's first light showed the white tick birds which hovered above the dark herd in a cold pink sheen. The swampy earth smoked with mist and the endless banks of papyrus stood frozen in the hush of dawn, for once their fluffy white heads were not nodding and dancing – except where something moved amongst the reeds.

Following its track the papyrus heads stirred, an opening and closing movement that set them nodding briefly before settling into stillness once more. The movement was sedate and yet so weighty that it betrayed the size of the animal which stalked beneath it.

The big bull buffalo that led the herd stopped suddenly fifty yards from the edge of the papyrus bed. He lifted his nose high and spread his ears wide beneath the heavy boss of horn. With little suspicious piggy eyes he examined the bed of reeds ahead of him. Behind him the herd stopped also, alerted by his stillness.

The gry-lion came out of the reeds at full charge, a blur of soft roan-brown, an animal as tall and almost as heavy as the quarry it hunted. It crossed the open ground so swiftly that the bull had only begun to turn away before the gry-lion was on him.

It landed on his back, curved yellow claws hooked through thick black skin and flesh at shoulder and haunch. The long fangs sank into the back of the buffalo's neck, holding it steady while one paw reached forward and grasped the bull's nose. A single powerful wrench twisted the black neck back against the holding fangs, the spine snapped with a sharp report and the bull folded in full run.

Before he went down the gry-lion had left him, dropping lightly to the ground, seeming hardly to touch it before he was in the air again, a long arcing leap, flashing soft brown against the pink dawn sky to land easily across the back of an old black cow that ran beside the bull.

Lightly as a humming bird flashing from flower to flower, the gry-lion had killed again. Bone breaking sharply in the dawn, the victim carrying the great lion forward in the press of galloping buffalo, and as the cow died the gry-lion was gone, flitting to the next, killing again in one fleeting movement and flitting again.

Six times the gry-lion killed before the surging, plunging, panicking herd had run 300 paces. Then he let them run, the thunder of their hooves dwindled, a far bank of papyrus swallowed them and they were gone.

The gry-lion stood in the silky light of dawn. His long, black-tufted tail still slashed from side to side with the thrill of the hunt. Every muscle was tight and swollen and the great beast half crouched, the flat snakelike head lifted as though to counter the weight of those long white fangs that curved down almost to touch the fluffy fur of his chest.

The face mask was elaborately patterned in black and

startling white, an effect that enhanced the golden glowing savagery in the wide-set eyes, but the whiskers and eyelashes were long white bristle, and seemed to soften the animal's expression. However, when it stood up from its crouch, with the short ruff of mulberry-brown mane along its back still fully erect, any illusion of softness vanished.

As tall as a man, and as heavy as a horse, armed with those legendary fangs and claws, this was the most dangerous cat that all nature's twists and evolutions had ever produced.

The cat turned and paced back to where its last victim lay in the short grass of the plain. It stood over the dead buffalo, and it seemed impossible that such a large animal could move as swiftly as this one had at the height of the hunt.

The gry-lion lifted its head, the massive jaws parted, the long pink tongue curled out between those unbelievable fangs, and it roared.

It was a sound that seemed to shake the purple skies of dawn, that made the earth shudder and ruffled the quiet waters of the great lake.

In the dawn, upon the narrow muddy beach beside the reed banks, Huy Ben-Amon greeted his god. Huy wore light hunting armour of leather, a leather breast-plate and arm-guards over a short linen tunic and bronze-studded leather kilt, but his weapons were laid aside, for he was about to offer the sacrifice, to send a messenger to great Baal. A messenger to carry the request of Lannon Hycanus to his god. The prince and his nobles were gathered in a half-circle about the priest, all of them facing the eastern sky. Baal showed the tip of his fiery orb above the horizon, and they lifted their hands to him. Fingers spread in the sun-sign.

'Great Baal,' Huy called the greeting in sweet shimmering tones that seemed must carry to the sky. 'Your children greet you!' Huy's swarthy, beak-nosed features were lit by a mystic glow which gave him a strange beauty.

'We have come to this place to choose a king for your people and we ask your blessing on our endeavours.' Huy knew his gods intimately, and though he loved them yet he knew their all too human weaknesses. They were vain, inconsistent, touchy, greedy, and sometimes bone-lazy. They must be flattered and cajoled, bribed and jollied along, they needed special ceremony and display to capture their jaded interest and attention, sacrifice, which Huy personally found revolting, to assuage their lust for warm blood. It was not enough that sacrifice was made, it must be made in all the correct forms before the gods would accept it, and as one of his lesser priests led the white bull forward Huy wondered if he had done the right thing in persuading Lannon to offer an animal rather than a slave. The gods preferred human blood, but Huy had argued with Lannon that a bull now and the promise of a slave later might be more effective. Huy had no compunction in bargaining with the great immortals, especially if it delayed the moment when he must look into the terrified, pleading eyes of a doomed slave. In the five years that Huy had directed the religious life of Opet, not more than 100 human messengers had been sent to the gods. Whereas there had been times in the city's history when that number had been sent at a single ceremony.

'We send you a fine white bull to carry our message.' Huy turned and approached the animal. It was of the short stocky Opet type, white and grey dappled, with a fat hump on its shoulders and wide straight horns. It stood quietly as Huy took the vulture axe from one of his priests. The circle of nobles drew back a little, giving the axe space to swing and the blood to spurt.

'Great Baal, receive our messenger!' Huy shouted, and

the axe went up, reflecting the low rays of the sun from its flashing blade. It hissed angrily as it fell, and the bull's thick neck severed cleanly, the head seeming to leap from the trunk. Headless, the body fell to its knees and the blood pumped and gushed.

Huy leaned upon his weapon in the typical stance of the resting axeman.

'A sign, great Baal!' Huy shouted, making it more a demand than a request. 'Give your children a sign!' And his voice was tiny in the immensity of swamp and sky and water. The timeless silence of the swamps fell upon them, the silence of the ages in the smoky purple dawn.

A flight of spur-winged geese passed overhead, wings beating heavily, long necks out-stretched, silhouetted darkly against the rosy streamers of sun-touched mist. Huy watched them hopefully, tempted to claim them as god-forms.

'A sign, great Baal!' He thrust aside the temptation, but his irritation was increasing. The sacrifice had been meticulously performed right down to the single clean stroke of the axe – was this to be one of those occasions when the god's attention had wandered, or was he being obstinate, pig-headed? A hippopotamus splashed and snorted out in the bay, and Huy turned towards it expectantly, but the fat grey sea-cow merely fluttered its ears like bees' wings, then submerged with a swirl.

'A sign, great Baal!' The third and final request, and almost immediately it was answered.

A sound rose from beyond the papyrus beds that startled the water birds into flight, that shook the fluffy white heads of the reeds, that seemed to roll across the heavens like thunder. A sound such as none of them had ever heard before. The roaring of the gry-lion.

Huy's dark scowl vanished beneath a beatific smile, and he turned those long-lashed gazelle eyes on his prince.

'The gods have answered you, Lannon Hycanus.' He

was seeing the faces of the priests and nobles and warriors and huntsmen, the superstitious awe with which they gazed at him. He would sacrifice privately to Baal later, nothing ostentatious or expensive, a chicken perhaps, as a gesture of thanks for this magnificent co-operation. It would rank with one of his best performances ever. Huy was so delighted with his success that he could not resist a further histrionic gesture.

'Go out, Prince of Opet, and take your gry-lion,' said Huy.

The little bushman led them along one of the buffalo paths. It was a green tunnel of reeds, the papyrus closing overhead to hide the sky, the damp peaty swamp earth underfoot, the musty animal swamp smell in their nostrils. They came out at last into the open grassland. Short, bright green grass cropped down by the countless herds of buffalo that infested this reach of the shore.

The bushman turned and led them along the edge of the papyrus beds. They were an unwieldy procession, four or five hundred strong, for some of the noble nine would not come ashore to look for the gry-lion without a thick screen of archers and axemen around them. They trailed far behind Lannon's party which consisted of Mursil the huntmaster, smelling richly of fruity Zeng wine, the bushman, Huy, the prince and his two arms-bearers.

The gods were as good as their promise that morning. The bushman led them around the bank of papyrus that thrust out into the plain like an accuser's finger, and as they turned the point of it they came upon another bay of open grassland. It was a natural arena, fenced on three sides by the stands of dark reeds, a huge circular extent of lush grass about half a mile across.

Down the centre of this opening, lying at regular intervals, were six large dark objects, clearly visible on the open plain, but the range was too long for immediate identification.

Mursil, the huntmaster, spoke quickly to the pygmy scout in a formless dialect. Huy made a note to study this language, it was the only spoken word in all the four kingdoms in which he was not fluent.

'My lord, he says they are dead buffalo killed by the gry-lion,' Mursil translated on a warm wave of wine fumes.

'Where is the beast?' Lannon asked, and the bushman pointed.

'It is there, behind the second carcass. It has seen and heard us, and it is lying hidden,' Mursil explained.

'Can he see it?' Lannon demanded.

'Yes, my lord. He can see the tips of its ears and its eyes. It is watching us.'

'At that distance?' Lannon asked with disbelief, looking down at the bushman. 'I do not believe it.'

'It is true, my lord. He has the eyes of an eagle.'

'At your peril, if he is mistaken,' Lannon warned.

'At my peril,' Mursil agreed readily, and Lannon turned to Huy.

'Make ready, my Bird of the Sun.'

While they stripped Lannon of his armour, bound his loins in a cloth of linen, and set light hunting sandals on his feet, the rest of the party straggled up. Some of the older nobles were in litters. Asmun, looking frail and white-haired, stopped his bearers beside Lannon.

'A clean kill,' he wished the prince. 'Like the one your father made.' And they carried him to where he could have a view of the field. The party spread out along the edge of the reed bank, their arms and armour glinting in the sunlight, their robes purple and white and red, spots of gay colour against the dark reed beds. A silence fell upon them as Lannon stepped forward and turned to face them.

His body was naked but for the loin-cloth, and the skin was smooth and startlingly white except where the sun had gilded his face and limbs. It was a beautiful body, tall and gracefully proportioned, heavy in the shoulder and narrow at waist and belly. His curls were bound with a purple headband and his red-gold beard was clubbed and turned up against his throat.

He looked at the waiting ranks before him.

'I make claim to the city of Opet, and all the four kingdoms,' he said with simplicity, and his voice carried clearly to every one of them.

Huy took his weapons to him. The shield. Hide of the buffalo, shaped in a long oval, tall as a man and as wide as his shoulders. In its centre were the 'eyes', a pair of fierce owl eyes painted in white and yellow. When these were exposed to a beast they represented the natural aggressive stare which would usually trigger the charge of a predator.

'May this shield cover you well,' Huy told him softly.

'Thank you, old friend.'

Next Huy offered him the lion-spear. This was such a heavy cumbersome weapon that only a powerful man could handle it. The shaft was of carefully selected hard wood, fire-treated, and bound with green leather which had been allowed to dry and shrink upon it. It was as thick as Lannon's wrist, and twice as tall as he was.

The unbarbed blade was in proportion wide and heavy, bound into the shaft with leather strips, the round point honed to a razor edge. It was designed to allow the maximum penetration into flesh and, once buried, to open a massive wound that would induce heavy bleeding.

'May this blade find the heart,' Huy whispered, and then louder: 'Roar for me, Gry-Lion of Opet.'

Lannon reached out and touched the priest's shoulder. He squeezed it briefly.

'Fly for me, Bird of the Sun,' he said and turned away. With the shield on his back, careful not to show the 'eyes',

Lannon walked out towards the waiting beast. He walked tall and proud in the sunlight, a king in all but name, and Huy's heart went with him. Quietly Huy began to pray, hoping that the gods were still attentive.

Lannon strode through the soft grass that brushed his knees. As he went he remembered the advice of the oldest and best of his huntmasters, rehearsing each move, each word of it.

'Wait until he growls before you show him the eyes.'

'Make him come to you at an angle.'

'He charges with head held low. You must open his chest from the side.'

'The skull is like iron, the bones of the shoulder will turn the finest metal.'

'There is one place only. The base of the neck, between spine and shoulder.'

Then the words of the only man amongst them all who had ever faced the gry-lion, Hamilcar Barca, the forty-sixth Gry-Lion of Opet, 'Once the spear is in, hold it, my son, cling to it with your life. For the gry-lion is still alive and that shaft is all that will keep him from you until he dies.'

Lannon walked on steadily watching the black swollen-bellied carcass of the buffalo, seeing no sign of the beast he was hunting.

'They are mistaken,' he thought. 'There is nothing here.'

He could hear his own heart beating in the silence, his own footfalls, and the hiss and suck of his breath. He watched the dead buffalo and walked on, tucking the butt of the lion spear more firmly under his right armpit.

'There is nothing here. The gry-lion has gone,' he thought, then suddenly he saw movement ahead of him. Just the flick of two ears held erect for a moment then flattened again, but he knew that it was there waiting for him. He felt his steps begin to drag, feet heavy with fear, but he forced himself onwards.

'Fear is the destroyer,' he thought, and tried to force it down, but it was a cold heavy thing like oil in his guts. He walked on, and suddenly the gry-lion stood up beside the carcass of the buffalo. It stood facing him, with ears erect, its tail swinging lazily, head up, watching him, and Lannon gasped aloud. He had not expected it to be so large. He missed a step, hesitating. It was huge, unbelievable, like something from a nightmare.

He was 200 paces from it, and he walked on towards it, concealing the 'eyes', and watching the giant cat's tail swish faster with agitation as he approached.

A hundred paces from it, and now the tail began to slash angrily, like a whip against the gry-lion's flanks. The cat crouched a little, the ears flattening against the skull. Lannon could see the eyes now, hot yellow eyes in the patterned face-mask.

He walked on, and the gry-lion's ruff of mane came erect, swelling out the shape of its head, it sank a little lower into its crouch. Its tail slashed furiously, and Lannon walked on towards it.

Fifty paces separated them now, and the gry-lion growled. It was the muttering menace of distant thunder, the drumming of the earth in quake, a belly-jarring sound like the crash of surf on a storm-swept beach. Lannon stopped, he could not walk on with that sound in his ears. He stood frozen, staring at this terrible animal in its mounting rage.

Long seconds he hesitated, then with an abrupt movement born of fear he swept the shield from his back and showed the 'eyes'. The glaring roundels were all that was needed to precipitate the beast's anger. The black tufted tail froze rigid, lifted slightly above the level of its back, the head dropped low against its chest, and it charged.

At the same moment as the charge began Lannon went up on his toes, and jumped forward. The shackles of fear fell from his limbs, and he bounded towards the charging cat with long light strides. He was angling his run across the gry-lion's front, forcing it to keep turning towards him, bringing it in at an angle, exposing the neck and the side of the chest.

As Lannon ran the spear blade danced above the earth ahead of him, like a firefly of light in the sun.

The gry-lion came fast, and low, head down so that the incredible fangs almost touched its chest, curved and ivory pale. It seemed to snake against the grass as it closed for the kill, and its enormous bulk filled the whole of Lannon's vision.

At the last possible instant Lannon lifted the spear-tip slightly, centring it on the vital spot at the base of the neck, and the gry-lion came onto the spear with its whole weight driving it.

The blade plunged into the brown furry body, sucked into unresisting flesh, and the shock of the impact drove up the shaft and hurled Lannon backwards onto his knees – but he held onto the spear.

A storm raged about him, great waves of sound engulfed him, battering his eardrums, as the gry-lion roared out its death throes. The shaft of the lion-spear whipped and thrashed in his grip, smashing against his ribs, crushing and bruising his flesh, shaking him so his teeth clashed together in his skull, lacerating his tongue. He clung to the spear.

He was lifted from his feet, riding high on the shaft of the spear as the gry-lion reared, then he was smashed down onto the earth again as the great cat plunged. He felt muscle and sinew tear in his arm and shoulders, felt the gry-lion's claws raking the flimsy leather shield, felt weakness in his body and darkness in his head, but still the storm raged and shook him.

Once more the gry-lion roared and reared. Lannon felt himself hurled towards the heavens, the shaft of the lion-spear snapped like a brittle twig, and Lannon was thrown with the butt of it still in his hands. He flew for long seconds, bird free, then earth thumped the breath from his lungs. Painfully he dragged himself into a sitting position, and looked around him stunned, clutching the broken shaft of the spear to his chest.

Ten paces away the gry-lion was crawling towards him through the grass. The broken hilt of the spear protruded from the exact spot in the neck where Lannon had aimed. The gry-lion's throes had worked the blade mercilessly in its own flesh, opening a hideous wound from which the bright heart-blood pumped, but the gry-lion's yellow eyes were still upon him, and those great curved fangs gleamed for his flesh.

Slowly it crawled towards him, its breath drumming in the mighty throat, dragging its paralysed hindquarters, dying but still deadly.

'Die,' thought Lannon, watching it with facination, crushed by the conflict, unable to move. 'Die,' he thought. 'Please die.' And suddenly the final spasm caught the giant cat. Its back arched, the legs stiffened, claws ripping into the earth, the mouth opened wide and pink, and it groaned. One last long pitiful groan, and it died.

The half-circle of watchers shouted, a cheer that was lost in the great silence of the swamps, and they began moving forward slowly towards the tiny figure of the king out on the grassy plain. But Huy was running. On legs too long for his crumpled trunk he seemed to dance over the ground, his long black tresses flowing out behind him and the vulture axe on his shoulder.

He was half-way to where Lannon sat bowed in the grass when the second gry-lion stood up from where it had lain concealed behind the carcass of the nearest buffalo. Huy saw it and shouted as he ran.

'Lannon! Behind you! Beware!'

Lannon looked back and saw it. It was the female,

lighter in colour, daintier in build, but notoriously more savage than the male. It moved towards Lannon with the deadly concentration of a stalking cat.

'Baal speed me!' Huy prayed as he ran towards his prince, and saw him trying to struggle to his feet. The gry-lion was slinking low along the ground, moving forward in short dashes.

Huy ran with all his might, driven by horror and fear for his prince. Lannon was on his feet now, reeling weakly away from the stalking cat. The movement triggered the hunting reflex of the gry-lion; it closed remorselessly.

Huy shouted at it. 'Here!' he yelled. 'Come!' And the cat noticed him for the first time. It lifted its head and looked at him. The fangs glinting long and pale, the eyes yellow and splendid.

'Yes!' shouted Huy. 'Here I am!' He saw Lannon stagger and fall, dropping out of sight into the grass, but he watched the beast. Saw the tail stiffen and the head drop. It began to charge, and Huy checked his advance.

He stood to meet the gry-lion, braced on long powerful legs, with the axe on his shoulder, and he let the cat come straight.

As it closed he fastened his gaze on the black diamond pattern between the gry-lion's eyes, and he adjusted his grip on the axe, settling it carefully.

The axe went up and the gry-lion covered the last few paces in a soft roan-coloured blur of fluid movement, towering over the little hunchback.

'For Baal!' howled Huy and the axe moaned in flight. The blade cracked into skull, buried in the gry-lion's brain and was instantly torn from his grip as the full weight of the dead beast smashed into his chest.

Huy came back from deep down and far away along a tunnel of roaring darkness, and when he opened his eyes Lannon Hycanus, the forty-seventh Gry-Lion of Opet, knelt over him in the sunlight.

'The fool,' said the king, his own face bruised and swollen, caked with drying blood. 'Oh! The brave little fool.'

'Brave, yes,' whispered Huy painfully. 'But fool never, majesty.' And saw the relief dawn in Lannon's eyes.

They spread the wet skins of the two gry-lions on the main mast of the flagship, and Lannon Hycanus received the oaths of allegiance from the heads of the nine houses of Opet while reclining on a couch of soft fur beneath them. Huy Ben-Amon carried the cup of life, despite the protests of his king.

'You must rest, Huy. You are badly wounded, I believe the ribs of your chest are stove—'

'My lord, I am the cup-bearer. Would you deny me that honour?'

Asmun was the first of the nine to make oath. His sons helped him from the litter, but he shrugged away their hands as he approached Lannon.

'In respect of the snow upon your brow, and the scars of your body, you need not kneel, Asmun.'

'I will kneel, my king,' replied Asmun, and went down on the deck in the sunlight. Baal must witness the oath of this frail old man. When Huy held the cup of life to his lips he sipped it, and Huy carried the cup to the king. He drank and then offered it back to Huy.

'Drink also, my priest.'

'It is not the custom,' Huy demurred.

'The King of Opet and the four kingdoms makes the custom. Drink!'

Huy hesitated a moment longer, then lifted the cup and took a long draught. By the time Habbakuk Lal, the last of the nine, came forward the cup had been refilled five times with the heavy sweet wine of Zeng.

'Do your wounds still trouble you?' Lannon asked softly as Huy brought the cup to him for the last time.

'Majesty, I feel no pain,' Huy replied and then giggled suddenly and spilled a drop of wine down the king's chest.

'Fly high, Sunbird,' laughed Lannon.

'Roar loudly, Gry-Lion,' said Huy, and laughed with him. Lannon turned to the nobles who crowded the steering deck.

'There is food and drink.' The ceremony was over, Lannon Hycanus was king. 'Habbakuk Lal!' Lannon picked out the big ginger-bearded seaman with his freckled and sea-brined face.

'My lord.'

'Will you weigh, and set for Opet?'

'A night run?'

'Yes, I wish to reach the city before noon tomorrow, and I trust your seamanship.'

Habbakuk Lal inclined his head at the compliment and the heavy gold ear-rings dangled against his cheek. Then he turned on his heel, and stumped across the deck, bellowing orders at his officers.

The anchors came up over the stern, and the drummer on the forecastle of the flagship struck the hollow tree trunk with the wooden drumstick, beating out the rhythm for the racing start.

Three swift, two slow, three swift. The bank of oars dipped and swung and rose and swung forward and dipped to the beat. In perfect unison, an undulating movement, like the wet silver wing-beats of a great water bird. The long narrow hull slicing boldly through the sunset blush of lake water, the clean run of the wake streaming out behind her, the standard of house Barca hoisted at the crosstree of her masthead and her high castles fore and aft standing tall and proud above the papyrus banks on either hand.

As she swept past the other vessels of the fleet they

dipped their standards, and fell in behind the flagship. Each of them holding their station meticulously in line ahead, the steersmen leaning on the rudder oar and the drum-beats booming out across the lake.

His hobbling gait was all that betrayed Huy's discomfort as he moved from group to group upon the torch-lit deck; with each of them he pointed the bottom of the wine bowl to the starry bright night sky, and bounced the ivory dice across the deck.

'Damn your luck,' laughed Philo, but the laughter did not hide the anger in his brooding gypsy dark features. 'Am I mad to dice with a favourite of the gods?' But he stacked gold upon the board, covering Huy's pile, and Huy scooped the dice and threw the three black fish again. Philo pulled his robes closer about him and moved away with the laughter and the shouted gibes of the watchers following him.

The bright white star of Astarte had set when at last Lannon and Huy stood together beneath the spread skins of the gry-lions and looked about the deck. It was a battlefield when the battle is spent. The bodies lay strewn about in the torch light, lying where they had fallen, loose and senseless. A wine bowl rolled back and forth with the easy motion of the ship that still sped on into the darkness.

'Another victory,' Lannon spoke thickly, peering blearily around at the carnage.

'A notable victory, Majesty.'

'I think,' Lannon began, but did not finish. His legs buckled under him. He swayed and swung forward. Huy caught him neatly as he fell, and settled him across one shoulder. Ignoring the pain in his chest he lifted the king and carried him down to the main cabin below the deck. He dropped Lannon on the bed, and arranged his limbs and head more comfortably. A moment longer he stayed, hanging over the supine figure.

'Sweet sleep, my beautiful king,' he blurted and turned to stagger away to his own cabin. The slave girl rose at his entrance.

'I have set out your writing pallet,' she told him, and Huy peered at the scroll, ink bowl and stylus under the hanging lamp.

'Not tonight.' He started towards the bed, lost direction, crashed into the bulkhead and bounced backwards. The slave girl ran to help him, and steered him into port.

Huy lay on his back and looked up at her. She was one of Lannon's household. Huy wished he could afford one like her, but she would fetch ten fingers of gold at the least.

'Is there anything else, my lord?' she asked. She was a pretty little thing with dark soft hair and pale ivory-yellow skin. Huy closed one eye the better to focus on her.

'Perhaps,' he said shyly. 'If you will help a little.' But his aspirations were too ambitious, and in a few moments his snores shook the ship to its keel. The girl rose, pulled on her robe and for a moment smiled down at him before she slipped out of the cabin.

In the darkness before dawn Huy stood on the forecastle of the galley and worked the axe, keeping it in flight, humming and hissing in the gloom. He felt the sluggish old wine in his veins begin to course faster, the sweat broke out on his body that the cool lake could not quench. He changed hands smoothly on the cut, and the great axe sang. The dullness in his head lightened and the sweat poured now, streaming down his muscled legs and arms, over the bull-humped back, soaking the loin-cloth, running into his eyes, and Huy began to dance, lightly he spun and leapt and waved, and still the axe flew.

Dawn was pinking the sky when at last he stopped and leaned upon the axe. His breath steamed and gasped in the cold stream of air, but his blood raced through his body and he felt like a man again.

In the cabin one of Lannon's slave girls scraped the

sweat from his body with the gold strigil that was a gift from Lannon. Then she rubbed him down with perfumed oil, plaited and set his hair and beard, and held a loose unbelted robe of white linen for him.

He came up on the steering-deck just as the order to heave to was passed to the fleet, and they swung towards the east to await the coming of the sun with the slave oarsmen collapsing thankfully over their oars. As the sun showed over the horizon Huy led the praise chant to Baal. Then there was breakfast on the open deck with the company squatting on mats of plaited reeds. Huy looked at their faces, grey and crumpled, baggy-eyed and bad-tempered. Even Lannon was pale and his hands shook as he breakfasted on a bowl of warm milk and honey.

Huy started on millet cakes dripping with oil and honey, then he ate a large smoked and salted lake bream, and when he called for a broiled duck reeking with rank wild garlic and more millet cakes the company watched him with awe. Huy ripped the duck to pieces and forced an expression of relish as he ate, for he was jealous of his reputation.

Philo spoke for them all when he cried at last, 'Great Baal! You insult not only your own belly but mine as well.' And he jumped up and hurried below.

'He is right.' Lannon laughed for the first time that day. 'You look like a child who has drunk nothing more poisonous than his mother's milk.'

'He was weaned on red Zeng wine, and he cut his teeth on the blade of a battle-axe.'

'If the lake was wine he would lower the level so we could walk across.'

Huy twinkled at them like a mischievous gnome, and tore another leg from the carcass of the duck.

In the middle morning they reached the shallows and Habbakuk Lal went forward to pilot the ship through the narrow channel. Water hyacinth, papyrus and a dozen other varieties of vegetation threatened to clog the life-line of Opet. The channel boats pulled out of the lane as the ten great ships flew past on their silver-wet wings. The officers saluted the standard of Barca at the masthead with a clenched fist, but the slave gangs who were doomed for ever to fight the lake weed stood dumbly and watched with patient animal eyes.

Closer to Opet now they began passing the fishing fleet, the nets coming in over the side with fish shining silver in the mesh like captured stars, and the white clouds of gulls shrieking and fussing overhead.

Then the cliffs came up on the horizon, glowing dusky red in the sunlight, and the rail was crowded with those who were enjoying this moment of homecoming.

Mursil, the huntmaster, came to Lannon on the steering deck and knelt briefly.

'You sent for me, Majesty.'

'Yes – and the pygmy.'

'He is here, King.'

'I promised you a reward. Name it.'

'My lord, I have three wives. All of them avaricious.'

'Gold?'

'If it please you, my lord.'

'Huy, write an order on the treasury for five fingers of gold.'

'May Baal shine upon you always!'

'What of the pygmy?'

Mursil called the little yellow bushman to him, and Lannon examined him with interest.

'What is he named?'

'Xhai, my lord.'

'Does he not understand the language?'

'No, my lord, he speaks only his own primitive tongue.'

'Ask him what he desires – freedom, perhaps?'

'He does not understand the idea of freedom. He is like

a dog, Majesty. Deprive him of a master and you deprive him of the reason for life.'

'Ask him what he wants.'

Mursil and the bushman spoke for a long while in that birdlike chittering tongue, before the huntmaster turned back to the king.

'It is a strange request.'

'Name it.'

'He wishes to hunt with the slayer of the gry-lion.'

Lannon stared at the bushman, who grinned at him with the beguiling candour of a child.

'He thinks, my lord, and you will forgive the impertinence,' Mursil was sweating a little, ill at ease, 'he thinks you are a god, and he wants to belong to you.'

Lannon let out a bull roar of laughter and slapped his thigh.

'So be it then. He is elevated to a master of the royal hunt – with the pay and privileges. Take him, Huy. Teach him to speak the language, or failing that learn to speak his!'

'All the strays and cripples,' thought Huy ruefully. His household was filled with them, whenever he had accumulated sufficient gold for a luscious young slave maid it went on another who was too old or infirm to justify his keep and who was consigned by his master to the pool of Astarte. At least the pygmy would have his pay as a huntmaster to help with the costs.

Lannon dismissed the subject and turned back to the rail. The mother city came up over the horizon at last. The walls of the temple shone a ruddy rose in the sunlight, and the lower city was brilliant white, the walls of the houses painted with the ash of the lake shell-fish.

The war fleet of Opet streamed out from the harbour to meet them. The shields and helmets of the legionaries sparkled in the sun as each ship in turn wheeled across the flagship's bows with the gilt work on her arrow-sharp prow catching the sunlight. They saw the raw skins hanging below the standard of house Barca and a cheer roared out across the water.

The flagship led them into the harbour, still scudding to the drive of her banked oars. Habbakuk Lal aimed at the stone jetty below the city where the crowds thronged the shore. The entire population of the city was out in their best and most brilliant robes, shrieking and cheering their new king from 100,000 throats.

At the last possible moment Habbakuk Lal dropped his hand in a signal to the drummer and steersman. The ship spun on her heel, with every oar clawing at the water to drag her to a halt, her side lightly touching the stone jetty. Lannon Hycanus and his train stepped ashore.

Lannon's wives were the first to greet him. Nine of them, one from each of the noble houses, young matrons of the blood, proud and beautiful. Each one came forward to kneel before Lannon, and call him 'sire' for the first time.

Huy looked at them with a heart that ached. These were not the pliant, brainless slave girls whose company was all he had ever known. These were full women. He needed someone like that to share a life with, and he had tried so hard. He had carried his suit to every one of the great houses of Opet, and had it rejected. They could see no further than his back, and he could not blame them for it.

The dignity of the occasion was abruptly shattered by a loud chorus of 'Hoo! Hoo!' and the twins broke away from their nursemaids and raced each other across the jetty. Ignoring their father and the gathered nobles, they ran to Huy and danced about him, tugging at his robe and demanding his attention. When he picked them up they competed so fiercely for his kisses that it developed into a hair-pulling bout. The nursemaids flew to the rescue and dragged them away.

Imilce's hands still locked in Helanca's golden tresses, and from the scowl on Lannon's face Huy knew that there would be retribution and that those plump little bottoms would soon be glowing red. He wished there was some way he could prevent it.

Huy slipped away into the crowd. On the way to the temple he haggled for a chicken with one of the merchants and struck a good bargain. After he had sacrificed he went to his own house in the precinct of the priests between the outer and inner wall of the temple. His household were all there to meet him, doting and doddering, fussing about him with their grey heads and toothless gums. All agog for the news of his latest exploits, demanding the story of the hunt, while they bathed and fed him.

When at last he escaped to his sleeping quarters to rest, he had not lain for long when the four eldest princesses arrived. Aged from ten to six, they broke through the feeble defences of his slaves and invaded his room as if by right.

With a sigh Huy abandoned rest and sent one of them to fetch his lute, and as he began to sing the slaves, one at a time, crept into the room and sat quietly along the wall. Huy Ben-Amon was home again.

In the year 533 from the founding of Opet, six months after he had taken the gry-lion and claimed the four kingdoms, Lannon Hycanus, the head of house Barca, left the city of Opet and went out to march around his borders, a custom that would bind his claim irrevocably. He was twenty-nine years old in that spring, a year older than his high priest.

He marched with four of his wives, the childless ones, hoping to change their status upon the two-year journey. He took with him two legions each of 6,000 hoplites, light infantry, axemen and archers. The legions were composed mostly of Yuye freedmen with officers from the noble families of Opet. These legions were organized along the Roman lines, in the manner that Hannibal had adopted during his campaign in Italia. There were ten cohorts to a legion and six centuries to a cohort. They were uniformed in leather body armour with conical iron helmets and circular leather shields studded with bronze rosettes. On their legs and feet they wore leather greaves and nailed sandals, and they sang as they marched.

The officers were more magnificently appointed as befitted their noble origins. Their armour was of bronze and their cloaks were of fine linen dyed purple and red, and they marched at the head of their divisions.

There was no cavalry. In 500 years no attempt to bring horses from the north had succeeded. Every one of the animals had succumbed to the sea voyage, or surviving that had died soon after arrival at Opet of a mysterious disease that made their coats stand on end and turned their eyeballs to bloody red jelly.

In place of cavalry were the elephants. Huge, ugly-tempered beasts, who struck terror into the hearts of the enemies of Opet when they charged with the archers in the castles upon their backs loosing a shower of arrows as they came on. In battle frenzy, however, they could wreak as much havoc amongst their own army as that of the enemy, and their handlers were equipped with a mallet and a spike to drive into the brains of the berserk animals. Lannon took twenty-five of these beasts upon his march.

With him went his high priest and a dozen lesser priests, engineers, physicians, armourers, cooks, slaves and a huge flock of camp followers: merchants, prospectors, gamblers, soothsayers, liquor-sellers and prostitutes. The bullock train carrying the tentage and supplies stretched for seven miles, while the whole unwieldy column spread out over fifteen miles. This was no problem in the huge unpeopled grass plains of the south with their plentiful supplies of water and forage, but when Huy Ben-Amon stood on a low hill with his king and saw the slow straggling mass coming down out of the north he thought of the time when they would turn north again in a great circle amongst the forests and broken country along the great river. Such a collection of wealth would be a sore temptation to the pagan war bands from the unknown land beyond the river. He told Lannon his misgivings and Lannon laughed, crinkling his pale blue eyes into the sun.

'You think more like a soldier than a priest.'

'I am both.'

'Of course.' Lannon dropped a hand on his shoulder. 'Not for nothing the command of the sixth legion – well, Huy, I have thought much of this march. In the past, it has always been a great time-waster and a sorry expense on the treasury of Opet. My march will be different. I intend to turn a profit.'

Huy smiled at that magic word, the one understood by all in Opet, noble or commoner, king or priest.

'I intend to make this a different type of march. In the south kingdom we will hunt – hunts such as you have never conceived, and the meat will be smoked and dried and sold to the houses and mines to feed their slaves. We will hunt also for elephant. I would like my army to have 200 of these animals to meet the threats from the north of which you have just reminded me.'

'I had wondered at the multitude of empty wagons that follow us.'

'They will be filled before we turn northwards again,' Lannon promised. 'And when we pass through the gardens of Zeng, I will change the garrisons there, leaving these men in their place. Troops who stay too long in one billet grow lazy and corrupt. At Zeng I will meet the emissaries of the Dravs from the east and renew our treaty with them.'

'But what of the north?' Huy came back to his original question.

'From Zeng we will march north in battle array. The women and the others will be sent home to Opet along the road through the middle kingdom. We will come to the river with two full legions to reinforce the two already there, and we will cross the river on a burning and slave-taking raid that will warn the tribes beyond that a new king reigns in Opet.'

Lannon turned and glared towards the north, and his mane of golden and red hair and beard shone in the sunlight.

'For a hundred years now they have plagued us, and we have been too soft with them. Each year they have grown more numerous, more daring. I will show them the iron of my hand, Sunbird. I will show them that the river is held by a barrier of bright steel, and they will press against it at their cost.'

'Where do they come from, I wonder, and how many of them are there?' Huy asked softly.

'They are the hosts of darkness, black because they are not of the sun-god Baal as we are. They were spawned in darkness in the forests of eternal night to the north, and when you can number the greedy locusts then you will count them also.'

'Are you afraid, Lannon?' Huy asked, and the king turned to him with a fiery anger darkening his face.

'You presume, priest,' he snarled.

'Call me friend, not priest – and I do presume to show you that unreasoning hatred is based on fear.'

Lannon's anger faded, and he fiddled with the hilt of his sword, glancing about to make sure that his aides were out of earshot.

'There is reason for fear,' he said at last.

'I know,' said Huy.

Huy led the praise chant to Baal in the dawn, but they kept the volume of their voices low so as not to alarm the nearest herds, and afterwards Huy asked the gods to look with favour upon the hunt, promising that a part of the spoils would be left for the Sunbirds to carry on high. Then Huy and Lannon drank a bowl of wine and ate a dry millet cake together as they waited for the hunt to develop.

Mursil, the huntmaster of the south, had chosen the ground with cunning and care. From where they sat on the low line of the escarpment they could look down the vast funnel-shaped plain hemmed in by hills on either hand; along the summit of the hills the signal fires smoked in the early morning to show that the warriors were in position to turn any of the game that tried to cross out of the valley.

In the distance, beyond the range of the eye the two legions were spread out across the plain. Already they were moving forward, 10,000 men, sweeping the grassland like a wave across the beach. The dust of their advance rose palely against the eggshell blue of the morning sky, and below the pall an occasional flash of light came from helmet or spear.

'It has begun,' said Lannon with satisfaction.

Huy looked out on the tens of thousands of grazing animals scattered in herds about the plain. This was the tenth great hunt in fifty days, and the slaughter was beginning to sicken him a little.

He glanced down to where the plain narrowed and the river that bisected it ran down into the neck. At the base, squeezed into a wedge shape by the hills, was a gap of 500 paces which promised escape to the limitless expanse of grassland beyond. The whole plain was thinly scattered with tall flat-topped acacia trees.

Even from where they sat above the gap they could barely see the treble line of concealed pits across the gap that joined the spurs of the two ranges of hills. A thousand of Lannon's archers lay in ambush there, each with a bundle of 300 arrows and a spare bow.

Beyond them still was a double line of netting, heavy woven mesh standing on flimsy poles that would collapse when a heavy body charged into it, smothering the animal in its folds until one of the hoplites could jump up from his hiding-place and run forward with a javelin to despatch the animal and reset the net. Here another 1,000 javelin throwers lay in waiting.

'We should go down now.' Lannon finished the last of the wine and brushed a few crumbs from his cloak.

'A little longer,' Huy suggested. 'I should like to watch this.'

A restlessness was running through the herds upon the plain, beginning with the animals nearest the lines of beaters. The long lines of gnu began running in aimless circles with their noses almost raking the ground, black bodies with long flowing manes kicking and frolicking. The herds of zebra grouped themselves in compact masses of some 200 or 300 animals and looked curiously towards the line of approaching beaters. Their close relatives, the quagga, short and sturdier, assembled in lesser herds, a darker bay colour than the grey zebra. Mixed with them were herds of brilliant yellow and red hartebeest, purple sassaby, and the great bovine eland, striped and maned and majestic. This vast multitude began a stirring and moving, a general slow retreat down the valley towards the gap – and the dust rose around them.

'Ah,' said Lannon. 'What a booty.'

'There could never have been a greater in the history of the hunt,' Huy agreed.

'How many, do you think?' Lannon asked.

'I do not know – fifty, a hundred thousand – it would not be possible to count them.'

Now the long-necked giraffe were infected by the

growing alarm, they left the shelter of the acacia trees and their calves followed them as they joined the mass movement down the valley. Amongst the host trotted an occasional rhinoceros, big and cumbersome, horned and snorting, lifting his massive hooves high as he ran.

Like a flux holding the entire mass together moved the smoky brown herds of dainty springbok. They came on down the valley, moving more urgently, like flood waters, and the dust rose thicker, swirling up in choking clouds. The hills squeezed the herds into a denser mass, and when the hartebeest and sassaby tried to cross the ridges on either hand there was a line of screaming, weapon-brandishing men to meet and turn them from the crest. They charged down the slopes again carrying and spreading the panic through the closely packed herds below.

They surged forward, and the sound of their hooves rose like the sound of storm, surf and wind. The ground began to shake. 'Come,' shouted Lannon and he jumped up and went bounding down the slope. For a moment longer Huy watched that unbelievable phalanx of living creatures thundering down on the gap, then he shouldered his axe and went racing down the slope after Lannon. His long black hair streamed out behind him, and he ran goat-footed, rabbit fast, so that he and Lannon came out on the plain together and Huy led the way into the centre of the gap where a pit had been dug for them and a dozen bundles of javelins lay ready.

Lannon jumped down beside him. 'There was no gold on that race,' he laughed.

'There should have been,' said Huy, and they went to the front lip of the pit and looked up the valley. It was a terrifying sight. The entire valley from side to side was clogged with a great tide of living things, and above them rose a high brown wall of dust through which the low sun glared balefully.

The heads and manes of the lead animals tossed and

heaved like the surface of a torrent, and above them rose the stick-like necks of the giraffe and ostrich. The whole bore down upon them, and the earth trembled beneath them and they stared in awe and wonder.

Lannon was judging his moment carefully, waiting for the first wave of game to cross his range-markers. The moment came and he snapped an order to his trumpeter. The single urgent note of the attack rang out, repeated stridently over and over again.

From the earth at the feet of the advancing wall of living things rose the line of archers. They loosed four times before the wall swept over them. Four thousand arrows in twenty seconds and those that followed fell over the wind-rows of dead animals, screaming with the agony of broken bone and arrow-impaled flesh.

Borne by the weight of their own forward momentum the masses of game pressed onwards while flight after flight of arrows decimated their ranks, and the corpses and wounded piled in ridges and huge mounds.

The smaller game were wiped out by the archers, but the larger thick-skinned animals came through with the arrows bristling in their flanks. Great grey rhinoceros, lumbering, wild-eyed towards the line of nets, tossing their long curved nose horns. Giraffe galloping long-legged and terror-driven. A squadron of black buffalo running in a mass, shoulder to shoulder like a team in span.

They came into the nets, and fell struggling and screaming. The javelins whipped into them as they rolled and roared, smothered in the folds of heavy netting. Desperately Lannon and his men worked to clear the dead from the netting and reset the poles, but it was effort wasted. There were too many of them now, and there was death out there in the open beyond the security of the pits. Arrow-maddened, the wounded game charged for any man who showed himself.

Huy saw a soldier tossed by an angry rhinoceros. He

cartwheeled in the air, and fell on the hard earth to be kicked and trampled to a muddy pulp in the dust by the hordes that followed.

From the pit now Lannon hurled his javelins with an uncanny accuracy and power, aiming each bolt for the soft ribs behind the shoulder of the passing game. He piled the bodies about the pit, shouting and laughing in the frenzied excitement of the hunt.

Huy also was infected by it. He danced and shouted and waved his axe, guarding Lannon's back and flank, hurling a javelin when some huge animal seemed about to crash into the pit on top of them.

Both he and Lannon were soaked with their own sweat and caked with the swirling dust; a stone flung by a dashing hoof had cut Huy's forehead open to the bone of the skull and he ripped the hem from his tunic and bound the wound quickly, hardly interrupting his dance of excitement.

In front of them the archers had been overwhelmed by the sheer weight of animal flesh. With their arrows exhausted they cowered in their pits and let the solid ranks pour over them.

Huy saw the fresh ranks driving down on them and he grabbed his blood-crazed king and dragged him struggling to the floor of the pit, and they lay with their heads covered by their arms while the edges of the pit crumbled in on top of them under the impact of hooves. Earth smothered them and they covered their faces with the hems of their tunics and gasped for breath.

A young zebra stallion fell into the pit on top of them, kicking and neighing in terror with its powerful yellow teeth snapping indiscriminately, it was a deadly danger.

Huy rolled away from its flying razor-sharp hooves. He paused a moment to aim and then shot his right arm upwards. The spiked head of the vulture axe lanced up under the terrified animal's jaw, entering the brain cleanly.

It collapsed warm and limp, shivering on top of them, and its corpse was a protection from the storm of hooves that raged about them.

The storm dwindled, passed over, and rumbled away into the distance. In the quiet that followed, Huy rolled towards Lannon.

'Are you safe?' And Lannon crawled with difficulty from under the dead zebra. They dragged themselves from the pit and looked about them with wonder.

Across a front of 500 paces, and to a depth of the same distance the ground was covered by a thick carpet of dead and dying game. From their pits amongst this terrible carnage the archers and javelin-throwers climbed and stood staring with the dazed air of drunken men.

The line of beaters seemed to wade towards them out of a swamp of hanging dust, even the sky was dulled with the dust, and the pitiful cries and the bleating of the dying and wounded animals shamed the silence.

The beaters came forward in lines through the fields of bleeding flesh and their swords rose and fell as they killed the wounded. Huy reached under his tunic and brought out a leather flask of Zeng wine.

'I can always trust you for comfort.' Lannon grinned, and drank greedily. The wine drops shone like blood in his dusty beard.

'Was there ever a hunt like that?' he asked as he handed the flask to Huy.

Huy drank and then looked about him at the field. 'I cannot believe there ever was,' he said softly.

'We will smoke and dry this kill – and then hunt again,' Lannon promised and strode away to order the butchery.

A high dome of orange light hung over the plain, light reflected from 10,000 fires. All afternoon and all that night the army worked to butcher the enormous bag. To cut the flesh into strips and hang it on the racks over the smoking fires. The smell of sweet raw flesh, the musty reek of split entrails, and the sizzle of the cooking meat drifted across the camp where Huy sat beneath the awning of his leather tent and worked by the fluttering light of an oil lamp.

Lannon came out of the darkness, still filthy with dust and dried blood.

'Wine! Sunbird, for the love of a friend.' He pretended to stagger with thirst, and Huy passed both amphora and bowl to him. Scorning the bowl Lannon drank directly from the neck of the jug and wiped his beard on his arm.

'I come with news,' he grinned. 'The bag was 1,700 head.'

'How many of them men?'

'Fifteen men died, and there are some wounded – but was it not worth it?'

Huy did not answer, and Lannon went on.

'There is more news. Another of my javelins has struck the mark. Annel has missed her moon.'

'The southern air must be beneficial. All four of them with child in two months.'

'It is not the air, Sunbird,' Lannon laughed and drank again.

'I am pleased,' said Huy. 'More of the old blood for Opet.'

'When did you ever care for blood, Huy Ben-Amon? You are pleased to have more of my brats to spoil – I know you.' Lannon came to stand behind Huy. 'You are writing,' he said, unnecessarily. 'What is it?'

'A poem,' said Huy modestly.

'What of?'

'The hunt – today's hunt.'

'Sing it to me,' commanded Lannon and dropped onto Huy's fur bed, with the amphora still grasped by the neck.

Huy fetched his lute, and squatted on the reed mat. He sang, and when he had finished Lannon lay quietly on the bed staring out through the opening of the tent into the night.

'I did not see it like that,' he said at last. 'To me it was just a taking, a harvest of flesh.'

He was silent again.

'I have displeased you?' Huy asked, and Lannon shook his head.

'Do you truly believe that what we did today has destroyed something that will never be replaced?' he asked.

'I do not know, perhaps not – but if we hunted like that every day, or even once every ten days, would we not soon turn this land into a desert?'

Lannon brooded quietly over the half-empty amphora for a long while, then he looked up at Huy and smiled.

'We have taken sufficient meat. We will not hunt again this year – only for ivory.'

'My lord, has the wine jug stuck to your hand?' Huy asked softly, and Lannon stared at him for a moment then laughed.

'A trade, Sunbird, another song and I will give you wine.'

'A fair trade,' Huy agreed.

When the amphora was empty, Huy sent one of his ancient slaves for another.

'Bring two,' suggested Lannon. 'It will save time later.'

At midnight Huy was soft from the wine, and desolated by the beauty of his own voice and the sadness of his own song. He wept, and Lannon seeing him weep, wept with him.

'I will not have such beauty recorded on the skin of beasts,' cried Lannon with tears cutting runnels through the dust on his cheeks and pouring into his beard. 'I will have a scroll made of the finest gold, and on it you will inscribe your songs, my Sunbird. Then they will live for ever to delight my children and my children's children.'

Huy stopped weeping. The artist in him aroused, his mind quickly assimilating the offer which he knew Lannon would not remember in the morning.

'I am truly honoured, my lord.' Huy went to kneel at the side of the bed. 'Will you sign the treasury order now?'

'Write it, Huy, write it now, this instant,' Lannon commanded. 'I will sign it.'

And Huy ran for his writing pallet.

The column moved on slowly in a great circle to the south and east through the southern plains of grass. It was a land of such limitless dimensions that the fifteen-mile column was as significant as a file of safari ants. There were rivers and ranges of hills, forests and plains teeming with game. The only men they met were the garrisons of the king's hunting camps. Their task was primarily to provide a steady supply of dried meat for the multitudes of slaves that were the foundation of the nation's prosperity.

They crossed the river of the south* six months after departure from the city of Opet and 100 miles beyond they reached the range of thickly forested blue mountains† which marked the border of the southern kingdom.

They went into camp at the mouth of a dark rocky gorge that tore its way through the heart of the mountains, and Lannon and Huy with a cohort of infantry and archers took the precipitous path through the gorge. It was an eerie place of tall black stone cliffs hanging high above the

* Limpopo River.

† Zoutspansberg.

roaring frothing torrent in the depths below. It was a cold dark place where the warmth of the sun seldom penetrated. Huy shivered, not from the cold, and clutched his axe firmly. He prayed almost continually during the three days that they marched through the mountains for it was most certainly a place frequented by demons.

They camped on the southern slopes of the mountains and built signal fires, sending the smoke aloft in tall columns that could be seen for fifty miles. To the southward stretched a land as vast as that to the north.

Looking out across its golden rolling grasslands and its dark green forests, Huy felt a sense of awe. 'I would like to go down into that land,' he told Lannon.

'You would be the first,' Lannon agreed. 'I wonder what it holds. What treasures, what mysteries?'

'We know there is a Cape to the far south with a flat-topped mountain where the fleet of Hycanus IX was destroyed, but that is all we know.'

'I have a mind to defy the prophecy and lead an expedition southwards beyond these mountains – what say you, Huy?'

'I would not counsel it, my lord,' Huy answered formally. 'No good ever comes of challenging the gods, they have damnably long memories.'

'I expect you are right,' Lannon conceded. 'Yet I am sorely tempted.'

Huy changed a subject which was making him uncomfortable, he should never have broached it.

'I wonder when they will come.' He looked up at the smoke from the signal fires streaming up into the calm blue of the midday sky.

'They will come when they are ready,' Lannon shrugged. 'But I wish they would make it soon. Whilst we wait, we will hunt the leopard.'

For ten days they hunted the big spotted cats which

abounded in the misty cliffs and woody gorges of the mountains. They hunted with specially trained hounds and lion-spears. They would run the quarry with the pack, until it was cornered or bayed and they would then surround it and close in until the charge was provoked.

Then the man selected by the leopard would take the snarling, slashing animal on the point of his spear. Two of the hunters were killed in those ten days – and one of them was a grandson of Asmun, the old nobleman. He was a fine brave lad and they all mourned, although it was a good and honourable death. They cremated his body, for he had died in the field, and Huy sacrificed for a safe passage of his soul to the sun.

On the eleventh day, in the dawn after Huy had greeted Baal, and they had breakfasted and were dressing and arming for the hunt, Huy noticed the agitation and restlessness of the little bushman huntmaster, Xhai.

'What is it that troubles you, Xhai?' he asked him in his own language, which he now spoke with authority.

'My people are here,' the bushman told him.

'How do you know that?' Huy demanded.

'I know it!' Xhai answered simply, and Huy hurried through the camp to Lannon's tent.

'They have come, my lord,' he told him.

'Good.' Lannon laid aside his lion-spear and began stripping his hunting armour. 'Call the stone-finders.' And the royal geologists and metallurgists came hurrying to the summons.

The meeting place was at the foot of the mountains where thick forest ended abruptly at the edge of a wide glade.

Lannon led his party down amongst the rocks and at the edge of the glade they halted, and threw out a protective screen of archers. In the centre of the glade, well out of arrowshot of the forest edge or the rocky slope, a pole had been driven into the soft earth and the tail of a reed buck dangled from it like a standard. It was the sign that the trade could begin.

Lannon nodded to his senior stone-finder, Aziru, and Rib-Addi, master of the royal treasury. The two of them walked out into the glade unarmed and with two slaves following them. The slaves each carried a leather bag.

At the foot of the pole was a dried gourd which contained a handful of bright pebbles and stones of various colours ranging from glassy to fiery red.

The two officials examined each stone, rejecting some by dropping them in a neat pile on the earth, selecting others by returning them to the gourd. Then from the leather bags they doled out glass beads into a pottery jar which they placed beside the gourd. They withdrew to the rocky slope where Lannon and his archers stood.

They waited until a dozen tiny figures left the edge of the forest and approached the pole. The troop of little bushmen squatted beside the gourd and jar and there was a long heated debate before they withdrew to the forest once more. The two officials went out into the glade and found gourd and jar untouched. The offer had been refused. They added a dozen iron arrow heads to the offering.

At the third attempt a bargain was struck when the bushmen accepted the beads and arrow heads and copper bangles, leaving the stones to be collected.

Then another batch of stones was set out beside the pole and haggled over. It was a tedious business which occupied four whole days, and while they waited Huy added considerably to his knowledge of geology.

'From where do these sun-stones come?' he asked Aziru, as he examined a yellow diamond the size of an acorn which had been traded for a pound's weight of glass beads.

'When sun and moon show together in the sky, then it may happen that their rays mingle and become hot and heavy. They fall to earth, and if they strike water then they are quenched and freeze into one of these sun-stones.' Huy found this explanation utterly convincing.

'A love-drop of Baal and Astarte,' he whispered with reverence. 'No wonder then that they are so beautiful.' He looked up at Aziru. 'Where do the pygmies find them?'

'It is said that they search in the gravel beds of the rivers, and also the edge of the lakes,' Aziru explained. 'But they are not adept at recognizing the true sun-stone and their offerings contain many common stones.'

When the bushmen had traded their entire gathering of diamonds, they offered for sale the unwanted children of the tribe. These little yellow mites were left bound and shivering with terror beside the trading pole. The slave masters, experts in appraising human flesh, went out to examine them and offer payment. The pygmies were much in demand as slaves, for they were tractable, loyal and hardy. They made excellent hunters, guides, entertainers, and, strangely, children's companions.

Xhai stood behind his tall yellow-haired king and watched the trade, exactly the bargaining which had been conducted over him as a child.

At the end of the fourth day the treasury of Opet had acquired five large pottery jars of fine diamonds. Trade in these stones was a jealously guarded monopoly of the ruling house of Barca. In addition there were eighty-six bushman children between the ages of five and fifteen years. They were wild slaves, and had to be bound until tamed.

Huy devoted himself almost entirely to their welfare during the return across the mountains. With the help of Xhai and the other tame bushmen he was able to save most of them. Only a dozen of the tiny creatures died of terror and heartbreak before they could be handed over to the slave women of the main camp.

Lannon broke the camp under the southern mountains and they turned north and east, recrossing the river and picking up the mountains of Bar-Zeng* on the horizon. They began passing through the populous kingdom of the east, where the Yuye peasants farmed the corn lands along the Lion River.†

At each settlement the freedmen turned out to welcome them, and make tribute to their new king. They were a cheerful throng, and the mud-walled villages were clean and prosperous-looking. Even the slaves in the fields were sleek and well cared for, only a fool would abuse a valuable possession. The slaves were mostly blacks, taken in the north, but amongst them were those of mixed blood, sired by their own masters, or by selected stud slaves. They were unbound, differing little in dress or ornament from their masters.

Along their way the legionaries who had completed their military service left their regiments and returned to their villages. Their places in the ranks were filled by the young recruits.

They camped each night at one of the walled and fortified garrisons that studded the road to the mountains of Zeng. They were passing now through the fringes of the wide gold belt that ran east and west across the middle kingdom. It was this belt on which the wealth of Opet was based, and the king's stone-finders had developed an almost supernatural ability to find the enriched reefs in which the gold was hidden. The results of their efforts were numerous mines where the ore was prised from the earth by platoons of black slaves working naked in the narrow stifling stopes. At the surface it was crushed and the powdered rock washed from the grains of native gold in specially designed copper basins.

Lannon paused in his march to inspect many of these works, and Huy was impressed by the ingenuity of the

* The Chimanimani Mountains.

† The Sabi River.

engineers who overcame the problems that the extraction of the ore presented at each separate site.

Where the gold-bearing reef was narrow, they kept the headroom in the stopes as low as possible by using only women and children in the workings.

They employed elephants for hauling the ore baskets to the surface, and for carrying water to the mines situated in the drier areas.

They had developed a method of undermining massive ore bodies and collapsing them under their own weight. It was a dangerous procedure, and at one of the mines practising this method Lannon and Huy were kept from sleep the entire night by the mourning wailing from the slave compound. During the day an ore body had collapsed prematurely and over a hundred slaves with a few slave-masters had been crushed beneath it. Huy wondered how much of that hideous sound was on account of the dead slave-masters.

Driven by his insatiable curiosity, Huy had himself lowered in one of the ore baskets to the lower levels of one of the workings. It was a hellish place of foul air, and heat and sweat, lit by the flickering oil lamps. The naked slaves toiled in cramped and dangerous chambers hacked from the living rock. Huy watched an intrusive outcrop of harder rock demolished by the means Hannibal had used hundreds of years before to clear his passage across the alps. A slow fire was lit and kept burning upon the rock until it had heated to a dull glow. It was quenched then with buckets of liquid, a mixture of water and sour wine, that exploded in a swirling cloud of steam, and split the rock into chunks which were hacked out and dragged away by the slaves. Huy went to the face where he saw the native gold shine in the mother lode, rich and yellow, and he mused at the price that must be paid for its extraction.

When Huy was again hoisted to the surface he was soaked with sweat, and filthy with dirt from the stopes.

Lannon shook his head. 'What did you want to do that for? Have the birds got your brain, that you must grovel around in the earth?'

At one of the mines the ore had been exhausted above the level of the subterranean water. It was impossible to go down below this level, for no method had yet been devised to clear the water from the workings. Bucket chains of slaves were seldom able to lower the level by more than a few inches. The mine must be returned to Astarte the mother of moon and earth. She had given of her bounty, and in return she must receive.

Lannon, as was his right, selected the messengers, conferring with his slave-masters to decide which fifteen slaves would be the least loss to the labour force. The gods were not particular about the quality of the sacrifice. To them a life was a life, and therefore acceptable.

Huy's heart went out to them as they were led down into the workings for the last time. They wore the symbolic chains of the sacrifice, and they shuffled along, stooped and maimed and coughing with the lung disease of the miners.

Huy delegated one of his priests to supervise the sending, and when his emissary emerged from the evil dark pit Huy led the praise chant to Astarte, and the work of refilling the mine began. It would continue for many weeks because of the amount of rock that must be carefully repacked into the caverns.

This refilling was necessary to placate the earth mother further and also to allow new gold to grow.

Aziru explained the need for this. 'This is benevolent ground, suitable for the growth of gold. We replace rock in the earth and the action of the sun upon it will, in time, engender a fresh growth of the precious metal.'

'All life is in Baal,' Huy intoned formally.

'Our children's children will one day thank us for this seeding of the earth,' Aziru predicted smugly, and Huy was impressed with this forethought – and he recorded every detail of it all in his neatly flowing script.

Three hundred days after leaving the city of Opet, the column climbed the foothills of the Zeng Mountains.* The air was cool and fresh after the heat of the lowlands, and at night the mist hung heavily along the slopes and woke the fever in men's bones so that they shivered and huddled in their cloaks about the campfires.

Those hills were the gardens of Opet, where tens of thousands of acres of land had been terraced and cultivated, and where tens of thousands of slaves tended the olive groves and vineyards. The centre and citadel of these gardens was a fortified hilltop town named after the twelfth Gry-Lion of Opet, Zeng-Hanno. Here there were temples to both Baal and Astarte, the religious strongholds of the eastern kingdom, and Huy spent twenty days in synod with his priests and priestesses. Huy also exercised and inspected his own personal legion, the sixth Ben-Amon, which was the only one of the eight legions of Opet composed entirely of warriors of the blood. Their standard was a golden vulture set on a shaft of polished ebony.

These religious activities were interrupted when Lannon summoned Huy to accompany him on a short journey to the east, from whence word had come that the Dravs awaited Lannon to renew the five-year treaty.

Three sheikhs of the Drav met them when they descended the mountains of Zeng towards the eastern sea. They were tall, brown-skinned men with fierce eagle features and dark glittering eyes. They wore head-dresses

* Inyanga Mountains.

of white over their long black hair, and they dressed in full-length robes belted with sashes of filigree and semi-precious stones. Each carried a magnificent broad curved dagger at his waist, and wore slippers with long pointed toes.

Their warriors dressed differently, wearing baggy pantaloons, on their heads onion-shaped helmets, body armour of silver breast-plates; and they were armed with round iron shields and long curved scimitars, spears and short oriental bows. Most of them were Negroes, but they had clearly adopted the Drav manner of speech and dress. Two hundred years of relentless warfare had preceded the treaty between the Drav and the kings of Opet.

The two armies bivouacked on each side of a wide valley, with a stream of clear water overhung with shady green trees separating the camps.

Under these trees the council tents were pitched, and here for five days the two delegations feasted and bargained and manoeuvred diplomatically.

Huy spoke the language of the Dravs and he translated for Lannon the negotiations towards a treaty of unrestricted trade and mutual military aid.

'My lord, Prince Hassan is concerned to know how many warriors Opet could put into the field in the event of a threat to the security of the two nations.'

They sat on piles of silken cushions and lovely woven woollen rugs of vivid design and colour, drinking sherbet, for the Drav would not touch even the finest wines, eating a dish of mutton and fish spiced with herbs, smiling at each other and not trusting each other further than the range of the eye.

'Prince Hassan,' replied Lannon, nodding and smiling at him, 'is concerned to know with what force we would oppose an attempt to seize the gardens of Zeng and the gold mines of the middle kingdom.'

'Of course,' Huy agreed. 'What shall I tell him?'

'Tell him I can field fourteen regular legions, as many auxiliaries, and 400 elephants.'

'He will not believe those figures, my lord.'

'Of course not, no more do I believe his. Tell him anyway.' And so the bargaining proceeded in an atmosphere of mutual trust.

They agreed to secure each other's flanks, combine to hold the line of the great river in the north against invasion by the migrant black tribes, and to come to each other's assistance if that border was violated.

'The prince would like to revise the unit of trade, my lord. He suggests that 500 mikthals should equal one Opet finger of gold.'

'Tell him politely to swing on his own testicles,' Lannon replied, smiling at the prince, and the prince nodded and smiled back at him, the gemstones sparkling and glittering on his fingers.

They set the rate of exchange at 590 mikthals per finger, and went on to negotiate the slaving agreement, and the cotton and silk clauses. On the fifth day they ate salt together and exchanged extravagant gifts, while the armies gave displays of archery and swordsmanship and drill. These were intended to impress the other side.

'Their archers are ineffectual,' Lannon appraised them.

'The bow is too short, and they draw to the waist not the chin,' Huy agreed. 'They limit their range and accuracy.'

Then later when the infantry drilled:

'Their infantry are lighter armed and armoured, my lord. They have no axemen, and I doubt those breastplates would turn an arrow.'

'And yet they move fast, and they have a fiery spirit – do not dismiss them lightly, my Sunbird.'

'No, my lord. I will not do that.'

The elephants charged across the open ground with the archers in their castles spraying a shower of arrows ahead of the line. The huge grey beasts tossed and trampled the lines of straw dummies and their squeals and trumpets rang against the crest of the hills.

'See their faces,' Lannon murmured. 'The prince seems to be looking on the eternal seas!' And it was true that the Dravs were silent and subdued for they had no elephants of their own, they had not mastered the art of training them.

They parted and when Lannon and Huy looked back into the valley they saw the Drav army winding away eastwards in column, with the sunlight sparkling on helmets and spearheads.

'Our eastern border is secure for five more years,' Lannon declared with satisfaction.

'Or until the princes change their minds,' Huy qualified.

'No, Sunbird. They must honour the treaty – it is in their own best interest. Trust me, old friend.'

'You, I trust,' said Huy.

On the return to Zeng-Hanno the legions assembled and preparations began for the burning which Lannon planned to lead across the great river.

Huy's legion was one of those chosen, and he spent much time with his priest-officers. They dined with him in the splendid quarters set aside for him within the enclosure of the temple of Baal. Huy invited the reverend priestesses of Astarte, and provided magnificent fare for he had hunted the day before and there was game to add to the beef and chicken and fish seasoned with spices traded from the Drav, while the gardens of Zeng provided the best of their fruits and wines.

Lannon was the guest of honour, and they were all decked with wreaths of flowers and boisterous with wine.

'Reverend Mother,' one of Huy's priests, a handsome young rake named Bakmor, called across the board to the

High Priestess of Astarte. 'Is it true that you have discovered a new oracle among your novices to replace the Lady Imilce who died two years ago of the shivering sickness?'

The reverend mother turned wise old eyes on the young officer. She had pale, brittle-looking skin and her hair was fine and fluffy white. Her arms were thin and pale also and her hands skeletal and corded with blue veins. Up until now she had sat withdrawn from the revelry.

'It is true that one of the temple novices shows wisdom and wit beyond her years or training, it is true also that she has seen beyond the veil and made prophecy, but the sisterhood has not yet decided to send her to the High Priest for examination.'

'Is there doubt then, Reverend Mother?' Bakmor insisted.

'There is always doubt, my son,' the priestess answered, in a tone that clearly rebuked his presumption and the youngster sat back discomfited.

'I have not heard of this,' Huy remarked with interest and a trace of accusation in his tone. For two years the priesthood had been without the services of an oracle, and the search had been diligent. Fees for divination and prophecy formed a significant proportion of the temple income, and there were also political reasons why Huy was anxious to find a successor to Lady Imilce.

'Forgive me, Holy Father. I had determined to discuss this with you privately.' The High Priestess spoke confidentially, but Lannon leaned across Huy to join the discussion.

'Send for the wench,' he said, speaking thickly with wine. The priestess stiffened at his choice of words. 'Send for her, let her entertain us with her prophecies.'

'My lord,' Huy wished to remonstrate but Lannon brushed his protest aside, and raised his voice.

'Send for the oracle – let her speak on the outcome of the campaign to the north.'

Huy turned back to the priestess with an apology in his eyes.

'The king commands,' he said, and the priestess inclined her head then turned to whisper to her body slave. The slave hurried from the hall.

When she came the loud voices and laughter stilled, and they stared at her with curiosity. She was a tall girl with finely boned wrists and ankles. She wore the long green robes of the temple novice which left her arms bare, and her skin had a lustre and smoothness which made it glow in the lamp light. Her hair was dark and soft, so that it floated cloudlike to her shoulders. She wore the gold crescent moon emblem of Astarte on her deep bulging forehead, dangling from a fine chain of gold, and her ear-rings were two small sun-stones that shone like the stars of heaven.

Her eyes were green, a colour that reminded Huy of the pool of Astarte in the cavern of the temple of Opet. Her lips were full and quivered faintly, betraying her agitation at his unexpected summons, while there were spots of colour in her cheeks. However, her manner was calm and controlled, and she moved with dignity to where Huy sat. He saw then that she was very young.

'Pray for me, Holy Father,' she greeted him and bowed her head. Huy studied her avidly, taken with her direct manner and her dignity.

'Greet your king, my child,' he murmured and the girl turned to Lannon. While she made the formal greeting Huy continued to examine her.

'What is your name?' he asked, and the girl turned back to Huy and fixed him with those solemn green eyes.

'Tanith,' she answered. It was the ancient name of the goddess, from the days of the old city of Carthage.

'It is a pretty name,' Huy nodded. 'I have always loved it.' And the girl smiled at him. It was a smile that took him by surprise, for it was as warm and uplifting as the dawn of Baal.

'You are kind, Holy Father,' she said, smiling at him and Huy Ben-Amon fell in love. He felt the bottom fall out of his stomach, and his vitals sucked downwards in a long sliding sensation. He stared at Tanith, unable to speak, feeling his cheeks flush with hot blood, searching desperately for the right word but not finding it.

Lannon broke the spell by shouting at a slave, 'Bring a cushion.' And they seated Tanith before the king and priests.

'Make an oracle,' Lannon commanded, and leaned towards her, breathing heavily and with the wine flushing his face. Tanith looked at him calmly with the faintest trace of a smile on her lips.

'If it were within my power, I would speak an oracle for you, lord, but then there would be a matter of fee and question.'

'What is the fee?' Lannon demanded; he had flushed a little darker with the first stirring of anger. He was not accustomed to this treatment.

'Holy Father, would you set the fee?' Tanith asked of Huy – and the devil took Huy.

'One hundred fingers of fine gold,' he spoke before he realized what he had done. It was an enormous fee, and it constituted a challenge to Lannon, daring him to back down or pay. Tanith smiled again now, a provocative dimple appeared in her cheek and she held Lannon's scowl with a cool amused stare. Huy was suddenly aware that he had placed the girl in a position of peril. Lannon would not forgive this readily, and Huy hastened to give Lannon a graceful escape.

'For this fee the Gry-Lion may put as many questions as he has fingers on his sword hand.'

Lannon hesitated, Huy could see that he was still angry but slightly placated by Huy's amendment.

'I doubt that the wisdom of a child will be worth that much, but it amuses me to test this wench,' Lannon mumbled, looking anything but amused. He took up his wine bowl and drank deeply, then he wiped his beard and looked at Tanith.

'I go northwards on a mission. Speak to me of the outcome,' he ordered, and Tanith settled herself on the leather cushion, spreading her green robe about her. She lowered her head slightly, and her green eyes seemed to look inwards. There was an expectant hush on the guests now, and they watched her eagerly. Huy noticed that her cheeks paled, and her lips also rimmed with white.

'There will be a mighty harvest,' Tanith whispered hoarsely in a strange unnatural monotone, 'more than the Gry-Lion expects or realizes.'

The guests stirred, glancing at each other, whispering, pondering the answer. Lannon frowned over the girl's words.

'Do you speak of a harvest of death?' Lannon asked.

'You will take death with you, but death will return with you unknown and secretly,' Tanith replied. It was an unfavourable oracle, the young officers were restless, sobering rapidly. Huy wanted to intervene – he was regretting the whole business. He knew his king, knew he would not readily forget or forgive.

'What must I fear?' Lannon asked.

'Blackness,' Tanith answered readily.

'How will I find death?' Lannon was shaking with anger now, his voice guttural and his pale blue eyes deadly.

'At the hand of a friend.'

'Who will reign in Opet after me?'

'He who kills the gry-lion,' Tanith replied, and Lannon struck the wine bowl aside and it shattered on the earthen floor, the red wine splattering the feet of a waiting slave.

'The gry-lion is finished,' he shouted. 'I killed the last of them – do you dare prophesy the death of house Barca?'

'That is your sixth question, my lord.' Tanith looked up. 'I cannot see the answer to it.'

'Get her out of here,' Lannon roared. 'Take the witch away.'

And Huy signalled quickly for the High Priestess to take her, for a slave to replace Lannon's wine bowl, and for another to fetch his lute.

After Huy's third song Lannon laughed again.

On the eve of the departure of the legions from Zeng-Hanno, Huy sent for the priestess and the novice Tanith. It was five days since her disastrous prophecies to Lannon Hycanus, and it had taken all Huy's strength of will not to send for her earlier.

When she came she was fresher and lovelier than he remembered. While the priestess sat in the shade, Huy walked with Tanith upon the walls of the city, looking down on the one hand upon the streets and courtyards with the bustle of the army preparing for its march, while on the other hand they looked across the wooded hills and terraces where the slaves tended the neatly laid out vineyards and orchards.

'I have instructed the reverend mother that you will join the convoy to Opet through the middle kingdom. You will travel with the wives of the king, and at Opet you will enter the sisterhood of Astarte – and await my return.'

'Yes, my lord.' Her humble tone was at odds with her saucy expression. Huy stopped and looked into her green eyes, she held his gaze easily, smiling a little.

'Do you truly possess the sight, Tanith?'

'I do not know, my lord.'

'The words you spoke to the king, what did they mean?'

'I do not know. They are words that came into my mind unbidden. I cannot explain them.'

Huy nodded, and paced on in silence. There was an appealing innocence about this girl, coupled with a bright mind and a sunny disposition it was impossible to resist. Huy stopped again, and she waited for him to speak.

'Do you love the gods, Tanith?'

'I do.'

'Do you believe that I am their appointed one?'

'I do, Holy Father,' she answered with such conviction, with such transparent honesty and respect, that Huy's reservations were set at rest. There was no doubt that she was an instrument which could be used, as long as it was used with skill.

'What is your destiny, Tanith?' he asked suddenly.

'I cannot see it,' she answered, but she hesitated then and for the first time Huy knew she was uncertain. 'But this I know, that this – this meeting between you and me is part of that destiny.'

Huy felt his heart swell, but his voice was gruff as he replied, 'Caution, child. You are a priestess, dedicated to the goddess. You know better than to speak like that to a man.'

Tanith dropped her eyes and colour stained her skin a dusky rose. The soft wing of dark hair swung forward against her cheek, and she pushed it away with her hand. Huy felt his soul shrivel with despair. Her presence was a physical agony, for no matter how great his need of her it could never be slaked. She belonged to the gods, forbidden, untouchable.

'You know that,' Huy warned her sternly. 'Do not trifle with the gods.'

She looked up at him demurely, but Huy could have sworn there were glints of laughter and teasing mockery in the green eyes.

'Holiness, you wrong me. I did not mean as man and maid.'

'How then?' demanded Huy, disappointed and with a hollow feeling in his guts at the denial.

'We will find the answer to that when we meet at Opet,

Holiness,' she murmured and Huy knew that the months until then would pass slowly.

Lannon stood over a clay box in which was modelled a relief map of the great river area. In the east rose the Clouds of Baal, a mighty waterfall where the river fell hundreds of feet into a dark gorge and the spray from the torrent rose high into the heavens, a perpetual cloud that stood upon the plains.* From here the river flowed into a deep valley, a hot unhealthy place where rough and rocky ramparts rose on each bank, heavily forested and rich with the ivory-bearing herds. Six hundred miles further east the river entered the territory of the Dravs, and ran through a wide alluvial plain which was inundated in the season of rain. Then at last the river joined the eastern sea through a dozen fan-shaped mouths.

Lannon pointed out the main features of this country on the model to his generals, occasionally turning for verification to his garrison commanders who had held the river during the past year. There were twenty men in the large leather tent, and the sides were lifted to allow a dry breeze to enter – and to show the view across the wide valley below the camp. The great river itself was obscured by the tall dark green growth of trees along its bank. There was an occasional flash of reflected sunlight from the water amongst the trees. Far to the north the opposite escarpment of the valley rose in smoky blue tiers of hills.

'Our spies have marked the main towns at which the tribes are gathered. They are mostly on the high ground, a day's march beyond the river, and it is important that each tribe be attacked on the same day.'

* Victoria Falls.

He went on to assign a target to each of his commanders, a crossing place over the river, and a return route.

'There will be no danger of attack on the return march, as long as you break their spirit on the first day. Each of the tribes is at war with the others, and they will not rally to the assistance of each other. The only way in which we can fail is if warning is carried to the barbarians and they scatter before our thrust.'

He explained the plan in detail, dwelling on the logistics of supply and routes of march, until at last Lannon set a date for the attack.

'Twelve days from now. That will give each of your legions time to march to the crossing places, and reach the towns of the barbarians.'

From the camp on the escarpment of the valley, Huy marched the Sixth Ben-Amon to the garrison fort on the banks of the great river at Sett, and here he put the legion into camp in a forest of mopane trees which would screen them from observers on the opposite bank. Fires were forbidden during the day and were carefully screened at night and the men were kept busy building the rafts for the crossing. Heavy rains in the west had swollen the river and the ford was impassable.

Mago Tellema, the garrison commander, was a tall balding disillusioned man with the yellowish skin and eyes of the shivering sickness which was endemic along the river. He seemed pathetically glad of Huy's company during the waiting days, and Huy found his information valuable, so they dined together every evening – Huy provided the wine out of the ample stocks he had brought from Zeng.

'I have kept my patrols on their usual routine, as you ordered.'

'Good.' Huy nodded over a bowl of baked river fish and wild rice. 'Have they noticed any increase in activity since my arrival?'

'No, Holiness. A war party of a few hundred crossed last night and attacked one of my outposts. We drove them off readily enough, killing fifty of them.'

'What do they gain by these raids?'

'Weapons, and an appraisal of our strength.'

'Is the whole border so active?'

'No, Holy Father. But here at Sett we oppose one of the more warlike tribes, the Vendi – they are exceptional. You recall how four years ago they crossed in strength, 20,000 of them overwhelmed the garrison here and left the valley—'

'Yes,' Huy interrupted. 'I was with the legions when we met them at Bhor.'

'Ah! Of course. I remember now that your legion's number was on the honour list.' The commander chuckled. 'Of that 20,000 not one returned across the river.'

'They fought well, though – for pagans,' Huy conceded.

'Indeed, Holiness, they are exceptional in that respect also and in the years since then they have become more formidable.'

'Have you seen their town?'

'No, Holiness, but I have many spies. It is set on the first slopes of the northern escarpment, where the tributary river Kal comes down from the plateau.'

'What is the population?'

'I believe them to number 50,000.'

'So large!' Huy looked up with a mouthful of fish and stared at the commander.

'They are a numerous tribe – not all of them live in the town. They tend large herds of cattle and are spread over a vast area.'

'Is the town fortified?'

'It is a large and sprawling huddle of huts, Holiness. Some of the huts are ringed with primitive palisades, but these are defence against wild animals only.'

A slave refilled Huy's wine bowl and took away his

empty dish. Huy cupped the bowl in his hands and stared moodily into the dark red liquid. His silence discomfited the commander who at last blurted, 'Is it true that the king will arrive here on the morrow?'

'Yes. Lannon Hycanus will march with my legion in the raid.'

'I have never been presented to him,' the man murmured, and Huy had a penetrating insight into the career of an elderly officer doomed to a minor outpost in the wilderness without patron or prospects.

'I will commend you to him,' Huy promised, and saw the pathetic gratitude in the man's eyes.

One of the biremes that patrolled the river landed a century of axemen and archers on the far bank in the night, and before dawn they had rigged the lines across the river.

The river was 300 paces wide at this point, a dirty green flow of water between steep banks which were thickly wooded and covered with reed and dense vegetation. The rafts were carried down to the river's edge and attached to the looped lines. The legion boarded in groups of fifty, and the elephants walked away with the lines drawing the rafts smoothly across the river.

The crossing went with well-drilled precision – it was not the first time a legion had crossed the great river. There were a few minor incidents – two hoplites fell from their rafts and sank swiftly beneath the weight of their armour, one of the rafts capsized a struggling mass of men and equipment into the shallow water beside the bank but all waded to safety, a legionary entangled his arm in one of the lines and had it neatly severed below the elbow – but the crossing was completed before mid-afternoon and Lannon turned to Huy:

'Bravely done, my Sunbird. Now explain to me your order of march.'

Huy left a cohort to hold the crossing, and to act as a base for his stores, a pile of dried meat and corn in leather bags. His legion would be tired, hungry, and perhaps hard pressed on its return and if all went as was planned, there would also be many thousands of extra mouths to feed.

Then behind a screen of light infantry and archers he began his march on the barbarian town of Kal. Here the weeks of training and hardening during the march from Zeng-Hanno showed. For although the ground was broken and heavily forested, the legion moved swiftly in compact columns, covering the ground at a pace that pushed a steady five miles behind them every hour. Ahead of them the scouts ensured that no one would carry a warning to the town. The few hundred herders and hunters and root gatherers that were met with by the scouts were despatched with a silent shower of arrows or a swift clean axe stroke. Their bodies lay where they had fallen beside the track, and the columns trudged on past them with hardly a sidelong glance. Huy saw that they were well-formed men and women, dressed in kilts of animal skins and with tribal scars on their cheeks and breasts. Like most of the tribes from the north their skins were a very dark blueish black. Some of them had mutilated their teeth by filing them to a sharp point like those of a shark, and the men were armed with throwing spears and light axes with half-moon-shaped blades.

The legion halted after dark, and ate cold cooked meat and corn cakes from their pouches while the wine-carriers moved amongst them filling the bowls.

'Look.' Huy touched Lannon's shoulder and pointed towards the northern hills. The sky glowed, as though the moon was rising from the wrong direction. It was the reflected light from thousands of cooking fires.

'A rich harvest,' Lannon nodded. 'Just as the witch prophesied.'

Huy stirred uncomfortably at the mention of Tanith, but remained silent.

'Her words have troubled me – I've spent many nights pondering them.' Lannon wiped his greasy fingers and lips, before he reached for the wine bowl. 'She preaches death and darkness and betrayal by a friend.' He rinsed his mouth with wine and spat it on the ground before drinking.

Huy murmured, 'She did not preach, Majesty – she replied to a question.'

But Lannon said, 'I believe she is evil.'

'Sire!' Huy protested quickly.

'Do not be misled by a pretty face, Huy.'

'She is young, innocent,' he began but saw Lannon leaning towards him and peering into his face, and he stopped.

'What is this witch to you, my Sunbird?'

'As a maid, she means nothing. How could she, she belongs to the goddess.' Huy denied his love, and Lannon leaned back and grunted sceptically.

'It is as well – you are wise in all things but women, my friend. You must let me guide you.'

'You are always kind,' Huy muttered.

'Keep away from that one, Huy. Be warned by one who loves you, she will bring you nothing but sorrow.'

'We have rested long enough.' Huy stood up and settled the strap of his axe about his wrist. 'It is time to march.'

After midnight they crested the low line of hills that formed the first slope of the escarpment, and before them spread a wide-open basin of land through which the dark river Kal meandered. The basin was moon-washed silver and blue, and the smoke from 10,000 cooking fires spread like a pale sea mist across the river, lying in layers in the still night air.

The fires had died to pin-points of dull red that speckled the town, and the huts were dark and shapeless, scattered thickly without plan or pattern, a vast agglomeration of primitive dwellings.

'He estimated 50,000 – and he's not far wrong.' Huy looked out across the basin, and beside him Lannon asked:

'How will you proceed?' And Huy smiled in the moonlight.

'You taught me how to hunt game, my king.'

His cohort commanders came for their orders, cloaked and helmeted and grim. Huy ordered out a thin screen of light infantry and covering bowmen to the east. During the day the scouts had captured 4,000 of the rangy little scrub cattle belonging to the Vendi.

'Take the cattle with you. You remember Hannibal's ruse in Italia, it will serve us as well upon the great river.'

Lannon laughed delightedly and clapped Huy's shoulder when he had explained it. 'Fly for me, Sunbird.'

'Roar for me, Gry-Lion,' Huy grinned back at him as he settled and buckled his helmet.

Silently Huy led 4,500 of his heavy infantry and axemen around to the west and laid them in a crescent shape at the edge of the forest beyond the town. Huy slept for an hour and when one of his centurions shook him awake he was stiff and cold with the night dew.

'Stand to!' he ordered quietly, and the word was passed from mouth to mouth. There was a stirring and a dark movement along the edge of the forest as the legionaries slung their axes and swords and bows, and took up instead the slavers' wooden clubs.

Huy and Lannon hurried to the command position at the centre of the line, shrugging off their cloaks and flexing cold muscles.

Huy looked out across the sleeping town and the smell of it was wood smoke and cooking food and human excrement, a great sour smell of humanity that wrinkled his nostrils. The town was silent except for the lonely barking of a cur, and the petulant wail of a sleepless baby.

Huy said softly, 'The time is now.' And Lannon nodded. Huy turned and gave the order to one of his centurions and the man stooped over a clay fire pot and blew flame to life on the bunch of pitch-dipped rags that tipped the signal arrow. When the flame had caught and blossomed he notched the arrow and loosed it in a high arching parabola against the dark sky. From along the line the signal was repeated, orange flame soaring briefly in the darkness, but the silence was unbroken and the town slept on.

'They have set no guards, no picket, nothing,' Lannon remarked scornfully.

'They are barbarians,' Huy pointed out mildly.

'They deserve slavery,' Lannon said.

'They will fare better as slaves than free men,' Huy pointed out mildly. 'We will dress them and feed them and show them the true gods.'

Lannon nodded. 'We have come to lead them out of the darkness and into the sun.' And he shifted the heavy slaving club into his right hand.

From the east, appearing suddenly out of the edge of the forest, stampeded a mass of bellowing, maddened cattle. On their horns burned torches of pitch and grass, behind them they dragged flaming dry branches and they were driven by their own terror and by a line of yelling whooping warriors. The whole scene was hellish with dust and smoke and flame. The line of cattle crashed into the town, knocking down the flimsy grass huts, leaving fire to bloom and spread in their wake, trampling the sleep-drugged naked Vendi that stumbled into their path. Behind them ran the warriors, clubbing down the survivors and leaving them lying in the hoof-churned dust.

Huy heard a steady climbing wail from the town, the

sound of thousands of terrified voices. He heard the drumming of running hooves and saw the explosions of yellow flame and sparks mount into the night sky as the tinder-dry huts burned.

'Hold your line,' he called to the men in the darkness around him. 'Leave no gaps in the net for the fish to slip through.'

The night was filled with movement and sound and flame. The flames spread quickly, lighting the scene with a great flickering orange light, and the Vendi darted and milled and screamed as the grim line of marauders moved down upon them. The clubs rose and fell and the sound of the blows against bone was that of woodsmen working in a forest. They fell black and naked, and lay in the glaring firelight, or crawled and wriggled and wailed.

One woman with her infant clutched to her breast saw the relentless line bearing down on her, and she whirled like a doe startled from cover and ran into the tall bellowing flames of burning thatch. She burned like a torch, her hair exploding, and she screamed once and then fell scorched and unrecognizable into the flames. Huy saw it, and his blood madness cooled, congealing into revulsion and disgust.

'Hold!' he shouted. 'Lighten your blows!' And slowly out of this terrible confusion order emerged. The slave-masters were there ordering the captives into squatting lines, the infantry swept the town clear, and the flames burned themselves out, leaving only black mounds of smoking ash.

The dawn came up, a red and angry dawn – across which drifted banks of dark smoke. When Huy led the praise chant to Baal, the cries and wailing of the captives rose with the voice of the legion.

Huy hurried through the devastation ordering and organizing the retreat. Already two cohorts under the young Bakmor had started back towards the great river driving an uncounted herd of captured cattle before them. Huy guessed there might be as many as 20,000 head of the scrubby little beasts. Bakmor had Huy's orders to swim the cattle across the river and return immediately to cover the retreat.

Now his concern was to get the slow unwieldy columns of slaves moving. The approach march that his legion had made in half a day and night would surely take two or three days on the return. The newly captured slaves must be chained, and unaccustomed to their bonds they would move but slowly, retarding the march. Every hour's delay was dangerous, and would make the heavily encumbered legion more vulnerable to attack or reprisal.

One of his centurions accosted him, his tunic blackened with smoke and his beard singed. 'My lord!'

'What is it?'

'The slaves. There are few young men amongst them.'

Huy turned to examine one of the masses of squatting black humanity. They were festooned with the light marching chains, shackled at the neck like hunting dogs in leash.

'Yes.' He saw it now, they were mostly women and immature youths. The slave-masters had weeded out the old and infirm, but there were very few men of warrior age and status. Huy picked a bright-looking youngster from the squatting ranks and spoke to him in the vernacular.

'Where are the warriors?' The youth looked startled at being addressed in his own language, but he dropped his eyes sullenly and would not answer. The centurion half drew his sword, and at the scrape of steel in the scabbard the boy glanced up fearfully.

'A drop more blood will mean nothing,' Huy warned him, and the boy hesitated before replying.

'They have gone to the north to hunt the buffalo.'

'When will they return?' Huy demanded.

'I do not know,' the slave shrugged expressively, and Huy now had a more telling reason for haste. The fighting regiments of the Vendi were intact, and this towering beacon of smoke would draw them as meat draws the vultures.

'Get them up, and moving,' he ordered the centurion and hurried away. Lannon came out of the smoke followed by his armour-bearers and men-at-arms. One glance at his face was enough to warn Huy, for it was flushed and scowling.

'Did you order the slave-masters to spare those they reject?'

'Yes, sire.' Suddenly Huy was impatient with the king's rages and tantrums, there were more important matters to occupy him now.

'By what authority?' Lannon demanded.

'By the authority of a commander of a Royal Legion in the field,' Huy answered him.

'I commanded a burning.'

'But not a massacre of the aged and infirm.'

'I want the tribes to know that Lannon Hycanus passed this way.'

'I leave witnesses to it,' Huy told him shortly. 'If these old ones would burden us, will they not also be a burden upon their tribe?' Lannon drew himself up, Huy saw his rage boil over – and he took Lannon's arm in unexpectedly conspiratorial grip.

'Majesty, there is something of importance I must tell you.' And before Lannon could give vent to his rage Huy had led him aside. 'The regiments of Vendi have escaped us, they are in the field and out in battle array.'

Lannon's rage was forgotten. 'How close are they?'

'I do not know – except that the longer we talk the closer they come.'

It was past noon before the long files of shuffling slaves were all tallied and moving. The slave-masters reported in to Huy's command post, and the final count was almost 22,000 human beings.

Despite Huy's orders to keep the column bunched and under control, the files of chained Vendi stretched over four miles and their pace was that of the slowest. At a laboured crawl like a crippled centipede, they wound through the hills and down into the bad broken ground of the valley bottom.

The first attack hit them a little after midnight on the first night. It came as a shock to Huy, for although he had taken every precaution for a night camp in enemy territory, he had not expected anything like this from the tribes. A few sentries with slit throats, a flight of arrows from ambush, even a swift rush and withdrawal at some weak spot along the line, but not a full-scale night attack which showed every evidence of planning and control, and which was pressed home with murderous intent.

Only training and discipline held his legion together before that howling torrent that hurled itself upon them from the darkness. For two hours they closed up and fought, with the trumpets blowing the standfast and the rallying cries of the centurions ringing out in the darkness.

'On me, the Sixth.'

'Steady, the Sixth.'

'Hold hard, the Sixth.'

When the moon came out and lit the field, the attackers melted away into the forests and Huy could stride among his cohorts and assess his position.

The dead tribesmen were piled chest deep about the square where the cohorts had stood. In the torch light the skirmishers were finishing the enemy wounded with quick sword thrusts, while others were tending their own wounded and laying out their dead for cremation. Huy was relieved to see how small a toll the enemy had exacted from the defence, and how grievous a price they had paid themselves.

In the confusion of the battle many of the files of slaves had responded to the calls of the attackers and, with a concerted rush, had broken out of the square and escaped into the night still linked together. But there were still more than 16,000 of them howling with terror and hunger and thirst.

The legion lit its cremation fires in the dark and sang the praise chant to Baal on the march. Before the sun had been up an hour, it was clear what tactics the Vendi had decided upon for that day. Each feature along the route was contested by groups of archers and spearmen. They had to be laboriously dislodged, always falling back before the charges of Huy's axemen, but at the same time the flanks of the column and the rear were harried and tested by repeated attacks in considerable strength.

'I have never heard of this happening before,' protested Lannon during a lull while he unbuckled his helmet to air his sweat-sodden curls, and wash his mouth out with wine. 'They behave like drilled and trained troops.'

'It is something new,' Huy agreed as he accepted a cloth one of his armour-bearers had wetted for him. Huy's arms and face were speckled with droplets of thrown blood, and blood had dried black and crusty on the blade and shaft of the vulture axe.

'They have direction and purpose – I have never known tribesmen regroup after a charge has broken them. I have never known them come back after a mauling.'

Lannon spat red wine upon the ground. 'We may have better sport than we bargained for before the day is out,' he laughed with anticipation and passed the wine bowl to Huy.

There was a place where the track crossed a narrow stream and then passed between two symmetrical rounded maiden's breast hills. There was a ford at the stream and on the approaches to it sixteen spears had been set in the earth and spiked upon them were the severed heads of legionaries who had been with Bakmor's cohorts that had gone ahead with the cattle.

'Bakmor has not got through unscathed either,' Huy remarked, as he watched the heads taken down and hurriedly wrapped in leather cloaks.

'Sixteen from twelve hundred is hardly a disaster to rank with Lake Trasimene,' Lannon remarked easily. 'And with their grisly display they have warned us of their intention to hold the ford – weak tactics, Sunbird.'

'Perhaps, my lord,' Huy conceded, but he had noticed the faces of his men who had seen the ragged red throats and the dull staring eyes of the trophy heads. Their stomachs had cooled a little.

The ford was held as Lannon had predicted. It was held by a force that Huy guessed was not less than twice his own, and while they attempted to hack their way through the attacks upon the flanks and rear never let up. Twice Huy pulled his axemen and infantry out of the reddened mud of the ford to rest and re-form. By now the day was baking hot and the legionaries were tiring.

Lannon had received a spear-thrust in the face which had opened his cheek to the bone, a wound that looked uglier than it really was, and his beard was thick with blood and dust. A physician was stitching the wet lips of the wound closed when Huy joined the group around the king, and Lannon dismissed his anxious enquiry with a chuckle.

'It will leave an interesting scar.' Then without moving his head he told Huy, 'I have discovered the solution to the mystery, Huy, and there it is!' He pointed across the stream to the closest of the two hills. The crest was just out of random arrow range, perhaps 500 paces away. Although the slopes of the hill were forested the crest was a dome of rounded bare granite, and upon the dome stood a small group of men. They were gathered about a central figure.

Huy would always remember him as he was that fateful noon on the hilltop beside the ford. The distance did not dwarf him as it did the men about him. In some strange fashion it made his physical presence more imposing. He was a huge man, fully a head and shoulder taller than his companions. The sun shone on the oiled black muscles of his chest and arms, and a tall head-dress of blue heron feathers stood wind-tossed and proud upon his head. He wore a short kilt of leopard tails around his waist, but Huy did not need that to know he was a king.

'Ah!' he said softly, and he felt something stir in him, a cold sliding thing like an uncoiling snake. On the hilltop the Vendi king made a sweeping gesture, and then stabbed towards the ford with his heavy war spear. It was clearly the delivery of a command, and from the group around him a messenger broke away and raced down the slope of the hill carrying the order.

'At last the tribes have found a leader,' said Huy. 'I should have guessed it earlier.'

'Take him for me,' Lannon commanded. 'I want him. Nothing else is important. Take that man for me.' And Huy heard a new tone in Lannon's voice. It puzzled him and he glanced at his king. He saw it then. It was not the pain of his crudely stitched cheek that made dark shadows play in the pale blue eyes. For the first time in all the years Huy knew that Lannon was afraid.

Huy timed it carefully for the last hour before dark, for the last of the day when the shadows were long and the light uncertain. During the afternoon he skirmished at the ford in half-cohort strength, but in the thick forest on the banks of the stream he held his main strength in reserve. He let them rest during the heat of the afternoon, let them eat and drink and sharpen their blades while he made his preparations. He chose fifty of his finest, selecting them by name from the ranks, and he took them well back where they would be screened from prying eyes on the heights beyond the stream.

From the bottoms of the cooking-pots they scraped the thick black soot and mixed it into a thick paste with cooking oil. There was not enough to darken the skins of fifty men so for their arms and legs they used the black mud from the river. They were all of them stripped stark naked when the slave chains were shackled about their throats, but instead of the iron pins a thin dry twig was used to close the links on every collar. They could not take shields with them, and they smeared their weapons with a thick coating of black mud to hide the twinkle and flash of naked metal, then they strapped them to their backs so they could run empty-handed.

'You are slaves, not legionaries,' Huy told them. 'Run like a slave, scamper like a beaten dog.'

When they broke from the trees and ran for the river with half a century of legionaries in pursuit, they howled with terror and the carefully aimed arrows patterned around them. They reached the bank 500 paces upstream from the ford. As they blundered across, still linked together by the slave chain, the Vendi king from his vantage point saw their escape and sent two large parties of archers and spearmen to screen their crossing.

A fierce bloody little battle flared up on the river bank, and under cover of the tumult Huy got his group over the river and into the shelter of the forest on the far bank. There was a thin detachment of tribesmen in set positions amongst the trees, but by the time they realized the deception Huy's band had dropped their chains and cut into them in a silent murderous rush.

Then they were through with nothing opposing them to the foot of the command hill. Bunched up, and hidden by the forest, Huy led them at a run around the back of the hill. They had moved fast, and he rested them here for a few minutes. The mud had washed from legs and arms during the crossing of the river and the soot and oil was streaky with sweat giving them a wild and desperate appearance.

The clamour of the fighting at the river had died away and the forest was silent and still as Huy led his band up the back slope of the hill. There were sentries posted here, but they were inattentive and did not see the weird blackened figures amongst the forest shades until it was too late.

Below the bare dome of granite Huy waited again, listening for the diversion which Lannon had promised. The distant yells and tiny scraping sounds of metal from the ford were almost blanketed by the distance and the intervening bulk of the hill.

Huy said softly, 'Now. All together.' And they burst from the forest edge and went racing away up the granite dome. Huy led them easily, bounding ahead with the loping long-armed gait of an old bull baboon.

When he was twenty paces from the crest, the Vendi king sensed his presence and turned to face Huy. He shouted a warning to his staff, and Huy went at him like a terrier at the throat of a lion. Two of the king's bodyguard leapt to intervene, but Huy flicked a casual axe stroke at them, rolling his wrist slightly in midstroke so the blade whimpered as it changed direction, killing the one guard cleanly and taking the spear arm of the other away above the elbow with a single cut. They fell aside and Huy went on to take the king.

He was a big man, perhaps the biggest Huy had ever met, and his skin was a shiny purplish black. The muscles of shoulders and arms were bunched and knotted. The sinews of his neck stood out starkly, corded into the heavy bone of his jaw. His head was round as a river-washed boulder, and without head-dress the scalp was bald and polished black.

He moved to meet Huy, sliding in on thick black legs with his leopard-skin kilts swirling, crouching slightly with the stabbing spear held underhand, the blade glistening hungrily for the softness of Huy's belly. He moved with leopard speed, reacting instantly to Huy's attack, and there was a sense of savage power and energy about him that checked Huy's charge and made him whirl instinctively to the side, just as the blade of the stabbing spear slashed upwards through nothingness where Huy's belly should have been.

The huge black man grunted as his stroke died in air, and his tawny yellow eyes fastened on Huy. He struck again and Huy hopped aside as the point hissed past him, and Huy reached out as he sprang and ran the stabbing point of the axe across the giant's exposed ribs. The purple black skin opened and for an instant white bone showed in the depths of the wound before the rush of dark blood obscured it. The king bellowed at the sting of it, and he struck and slashed and cut at the dancing gadfly before him. Each stroke wilder, each charge more reckless as Huy goaded him, watching for his moment. It came and suddenly Huy was through the circle of the spear. With the point of the axe he probed for the femoral artery in the giant's groin, running the engraved steel into the tight flesh half an inch too far to the right, missing the artery but dropping the king to one knee. Huy twisted out of close contact. The axe flew high and Huy went into the kill stroke aiming at the round black skull of the kneeling king, a stroke which would split him to the chest.

'For Baal!' he shouted, sending the axe down from on high. Then in full stroke he changed. He never knew what impulse it was that made him check, made him twist the weapon, presenting the flat of the blade and not the edge, holding the stroke half back so that the side of the axe cracked against the king's skull with enough force to topple him forward senseless onto his face but not enough to stove in the bone of the great round head.

Huy jumped back and with one quick glance made certain that the Vendi king's train were all lying lifeless on the dome of granite, and his legionaries were grouped around him resting on their bloody swords. The surprise had been complete and overwhelming.

Huy turned and ran to the highest point of the hill. Naked and filthy with soot and mud he brandished his axe above his head, and his band cheered and waved their weapons also. From the ford a trumpet began to blare the advance, and immediately the call was taken up and shrilled from cohort to cohort.

Huy watched Lannon lead the first wave across the ford. The legion crashed into the leaderless tribesmen who opposed them, and drove through them with scarcely a check, splitting them and driving them back against the hills in a disorganized rabble. They had seen their king cut down and there was no spirit left in any of them.

From the hilltop Huy watched Lannon commit his last two reserve cohorts at exactly the right moment. The tribesmen broke and made a rout of it. Throwing aside their weapons they streamed back in a wailing panic-stricken mob into the bottleneck between the hills.

At that moment the handsome young Bakmor, with the two cohorts which had driven the captured cattle to the great river, marched out of the forest. He deployed the cohorts neatly across the only line of retreat open to the tribes. His return was timely indeed, and Huy watched him with grudging professional approval as he made his dispositions. As the sun touched the horizon in a splendour of red and purple the trumpets sounded the advance once again, and the slaughter and the slave-taking lasted until after midnight.

Huy crossed his legion and the host of wild slaves, using the elephant-drawn rafts at Sett. After the battle at the ford the return march had been unopposed. The regiments of the Vendi had been shattered, all their war chiefs killed or captured and Lannon was jubilant.

He told Huy, 'My Sunbird! It was more than I asked of you. Even I did not guess that such a dangerous enemy had grown up upon my borders. If we had left him another year, only the gods know how deadly he might have become.'

'Baal smiled upon me,' Huy disclaimed modestly.

'And so does Lannon Hycanus,' Lannon assured him. 'What was the harvest, Sunbird? Has old Rib-Addi made the accounting yet?'

'I hope so, my lord.'

'Send for him,' Lannon commanded, and Rib-Addi came with his scrolls and his ink-stained fingers and his untrusting little book-keeper's eyes. He read out the lists of cattle and slaves of each grade, every one of them carefully categorized by the slave-masters.

'The prices will be much depressed, sire,' Rib-Addi pointed out pessimistically. 'For the other legions have taken a great tribute from all the tribes across the river. It will be two or three years before the markets of Opet have absorbed this mass of wealth.'

'Nevertheless, the prize money taken by the Sixth Ben-Amon must be considerable, Rib-Addi.'

'As my lord says.'

'How much?' Lannon demanded.

Rib-Addi looked alarmed. 'I could only hazard a guess, Majesty.'

'Guess, then,' Lannon invited him.

'It could be as much as 25,000 fingers – and as low as—'

'You would smell dung in an alabaster jar of perfume,' Lannon chided the old man. 'Do not give me your low figure.'

'As my lord pleases.' Rib-Addi bowed, and Lannon turned to Huy and clasped his shoulder.

'Your share is one part in a hundred, Sunbird. Two hundred and fifty fingers – you are a rich man at last! How does it feel?'

'It does not sicken me,' Huy grinned at him, and Lannon laughed delightedly as he turned back to Rib-Addi.

'Write in your book, old man. Write that Lannon Hycanus sets aside half of his share of the prize. He makes it over as an award to the legion commander, Huy Ben-Amon, for his conduct of the campaign.'

'My lord, that is one part in twenty,' Rib-Addi protested vehemently. 'It is an award of over 1,000 fingers!'

'I have learned my figures also,' Lannon assured him, and the book-keeper might have protested further, but he saw Lannon's expression.

'It shall be written,' he mumbled, and Huy came to kneel before his king in gratitude.

'Up!' Lannon ordered him, smiling. 'Do not grovel for me, old friend.' And Huy went to stand beside Lannon's stool, as the king called each of the officers who had acted with distinction and made the awards.

Huy was lost in a trance of avarice, hardly able to credit his fortune. He was rich – rich! He must sacrifice to the gods this very day. A white bull, at the least. As Rib-Addi had pointed out, the market was flooded and Huy would be able to get one cheaply. Then he remembered that he no longer had to stint.

He could afford any luxury he had ever coveted, and still have enough over for an estate on the terraces of Zeng, a share in one of Habbakuk-Lal's trading galleys. A seat on one of the gold-mining syndicates, a secure income for life. No more patches in his tunics, no more bullying his household to cut down on the consumption of meat, no more of the cheap sour wines from the harbour taverns. And then his mind jumped, no more reliance on Lannon's hospitality and on the goodwill of his young slave girls. He would have one of his own – no damn it, two – three! Young and pretty and pliant. He felt his body stir. He could afford a wife now, even the daughters of the noble houses might turn a blind eye to his back when dazzled by such a pile of the golden metal.

Then suddenly he remembered Tanith, and the phantom slave girls and wives faded back into the mists of his imagining. His spirits plunged sickeningly. The priestesses of Astarte were dedicated to the goddess, they could never marry. Suddenly Huy did not feel as rich as he had a moment before.

'Do you not hear your king when he speaks?' Lannon demanded, and Huy started guiltily.

'My lord, I was dreaming. Forgive me.'

'It is no longer necessary to dream,' Lannon told him.

'What was it the Gry-Lion asked?'

'I said we should send for the barbarian – we can deal with him before the legion assembles.'

Huy looked around at his cohorts drawn up in an open square before the leather awning under which Lannon sat. The legions' standards glittered in the sunlight, and the officers stood at ease before their men. They waited expectantly, and Huy sighed quietly.

'As the Gry-Lion wishes.'

'Order it so,' Lannon commanded.

They had chained him at wrists and ankles, as well as at the throat. The slave-masters could pick a dangerous one at a glance, and two of them held him in leash by the chains from his throat collar.

He was as big as Huy remembered, and his skin even darker, but he was a young man. This came as a shock to Huy, he had thought of him as being in his prime years but this was an illusion. The man's physical bulk and his commanding presence made him older than his years.

Huy saw how he had fought against his bonds, tearing

his own flesh, smearing the skin on the unyielding iron shackles, and the wound in his groin had been crudely dressed with leaves and bark. There were the first watery yellow discharges of putrefaction soiling the dressing, and the flesh around it looked hard and swollen. Although he limped, although the chains jangled mockingly at every pace, and although the slave-masters braced against him as though he were a captured animal, there was no mistaking that he was a king. He stood before Lannon and lowered his head slightly on the thick sinewed neck. His eyes were ferocious, even the whites were smoking yellow and covered with a fine lacework of blood vessels, and he stared at his captors with a hatred that was a palpable thing.

'You captured this – this great black beast, Huy?' Lannon returned the giant's stare. 'Without help, you took him?' Lannon shook his head with wonder and turned to Huy, but Huy was watching the Vendi king.

'What is your name?' Huy asked softly, and the big round head swivelled towards him, the fierce eyes held his.

'How do you have the tongue of Vendi?'

'I have many tongues,' Huy assured him. 'Who are you?'

'Manatassi, King of the Vendi.' And Huy translated for Lannon.

'Tell him he is king no longer,' Lannon snapped, and Manatassi shrugged and smiled. His smile was a frightening thing for although the thick purple lips drew back to expose strong white teeth, yet his eyes still smoked with hatred.

'Fifty thousand warriors of Vendi call me king still,' he answered.

'A slave king of a slave people,' Lannon laughed, and then to Huy, 'What of him, Huy? Is he not a dangerous enemy? Can we afford to let him live?'

Huy tore his gaze from the slave king and considered the question, trying to think logically but finding it difficult. Huy had conceived a sudden but powerful proprietary interest in Manatassi. He was impressed with the man's power and presence, with the military skills he had displayed, with the cunning and cleverness and the strange smouldering depths of him. Huy had taken him, he could claim him, even from Lannon, and he was strongly tempted to do so now, for he sensed that here was some extraordinary opportunity. To take this man and educate him, civilize him – what might be made of him! He felt an excitement as a new idea tried to struggle to the surface of his mind.

'I think not,' Lannon answered himself. 'From the first moment I saw him, on the hill above the ford, I knew he was dangerous. Deadly dangerous. I do not think we can let him live, Huy. He would make a fine messenger to the gods. We will dedicate him to Baal and send him as a messenger to express our gratitude for the outcome of the campaign.'

'My lord,' Huy dropped his voice for Lannon alone, 'I have a feeling about this man. I feel I could enlighten him, teach him the true gods. He is young, my lord, I could work upon him, and when we are ready we could return him to his people.'

'Have the birds picked out your brain?' Lannon looked at Huy in astonishment. 'Why should we return him to his people, when we have spent so much effort on capturing him?'

'We could use him as an ally then.' Huy was trying desperately to get his idea over. 'Through him we could make a treaty with the tribes. We could win him over and use him to secure our northern borders.'

'Treaties with barbarians!' Lannon was angry now. 'What nonsense is this? Secure our northern borders, you say? One thing, and one thing only will secure our northern borders, and that is a sharp sword in a strong hand.'

'My lord, please hear me out.'

'No, Huy. I will have no more of it. He must die – and

quickly.' Lannon stood up. 'Tonight at sunset. Prepare to send him.' And Lannon strode away.

'Dismiss the legion,' Huy ordered his commanders, and nodded to the slave-master to lead the captive away. But Manatassi stepped forward, dragging the slave-masters with him on the chains.

'High born!' Manatassi called Huy, who turned back to him with surprise. He had not expected a title of respect.

'What is it?' Huy looked at him.

'Is it death?' Manatassi asked, and Huy nodded.

'It is death,' he admitted.

'But you argued for me?' Manatassi insisted, and again Huy nodded.

'Why?' demanded the slave king, and Huy could not answer. He spread his hands, a gesture of weariness and incomprehension.

'Twice already,' the slave king said. 'First you turned the blade which should have killed, and now you speak for me. Why?'

'I do not know. I cannot explain.'

'You feel the bond – the bond between us,' Manatassi declared, and his voice sank low, rumbling and soft. 'The bond of the spirits. You felt it.'

'No.' Huy shook his head, and hurried away to his tent. He worked on his scrolls for most of the afternoon, recording the campaign, describing the burning and the battle at the ford, listing the battle honours and the slaves taken, the booty and the glory – but he could not bring himself to describe Manatassi. The man would soon be dead, let his memory die with him, let it not linger on to haunt the living. A phrase that Lannon had used stuck in his mind, 'the black beast', and he used it as the only reference to the doomed slave king.

He ate the noon meal with Bakmor and a few others of his young officers, but his mood infected them all and the meal was awkward, the conversation trivial and stilted. Afterwards Huy spent an hour with his adjutant and quartermaster ordering the legion's affairs, then he worked with the axe until his sweat ran down his body in streams. He scraped and oiled and changed into fresh robes for the sacrifice, and went to Lannon's tent. Lannon was in conference, a group of his advisers and officials sitting in a half-circle around him on the skins and cushions. Lannon looked up and smiled and called Huy to him.

'Sit by me, my Sunbird. There is something here on which I would value your thoughts.' And Huy sat and listened to Lannon directing the affairs of the four kingdoms with a quick and confident logic. He made decisions which would have tormented Huy for days, and he made them easily, without doubts or hesitations. Then he dismissed his court, and turned to Huy.

'A bowl of wine with me, Huy. It will be many days before we have the chance again, for in the morning I leave you.'

'Whither, my lord?'

'I return to Opet, but at speed. I will leave you and your slaves and herds to make the best of it.'

They drank together, exchanging the seemingly easy desultory talk of old friends, but Huy was manoeuvring for an opening to speak of Manatassi, and Lannon was deftly denying it to him. At last Huy in desperation approached the subject directly.

'The Vendi king, my lord.' And he got no further, for Lannon slammed the wine bowl down so that it cracked and a ruby gush of the lees spurted onto the furs on which they sat.

'You presume on friendship. I have ordered his death. Except for the axe-stroke the matter is settled.'

'I believe it is a mistake.'

'To let him live will be a greater mistake.'

'My lord—'

'Enough, Huy! Enough, I say! Go out now and send him.'

In the sunset they brought the Vendi king to a clear place on the river bank below the garrison walls of Sett. He was dressed in a cloak of leather, worked with the symbols of Baal, and he wore the symbolical chains of the sacrifice. Huy stood with the priests and nobles, and when they led the doomed king forward his eyes fastened on Huy's. Those terrible yellow eyes seemed almost to hook into his flesh, seemed to draw Huy's soul out through his eye sockets.

Huy began the ritual, chanting the offertory, making the obeisance to the flaming god image in the western sky and all the while he could feel those eyes eating into the core of his existence.

Huy's assistant offered him the vulture axe, polished and glinting red and gold in the last rays of the sunset. Huy went to where Manatassi stood, and looked up at him.

The slave-masters stepped forward and lifted the cloak from the shoulders of the sacrifice. Except for the golden chains he was naked and magnificent. They had removed the raw-hide sandals from his feet. The slave-masters waited with the chains in their hands, at Huy's signal they would jerk the sacrifice off his feet and stretch him out upon the ground. His neck drawn out for the axe blade.

Huy hesitated, unable to force himself to give the order, held fascinated by those fierce yellow eyes. With an effort he tore his gaze free and looked downwards. He had started to give the signal, but his hand froze. He was staring at Manatassi's bare feet.

Around him the watchers stirred restlessly, glancing towards the horizon where the sun was rapidly sliding below the trees. Soon it would be too late.

Still Huy stared at Manatassi's feet.

'The sun goes, priest. Strike!' Lannon called abruptly, angrily in the silence and the sound of his voice seemed to arouse Huy. He turned to Lannon.

'My lord, there is something you must see.'

'The sun is going,' Lannon called impatiently.

'You must see it,' Huy insisted, and Lannon strode forward to stand beside him.

'Look!' Huy pointed at the Vendi king's feet, and Lannon frowned on a quick intake of breath.

Manatassi's feet were monstrously deformed, deeply divided between the toes so that they resembled the claws of some preternatural bird. Involuntarily Lannon stepped backwards, making the full-handed sun sign to avert evil.

'He is bird-footed,' Huy said, 'he has the feet of the sacred sunbird of Baal.' And there was a rustle and murmur from the watchers. They craned forward with a ghoulish, superstitious curiosity.

Huy raised his voice. 'I declare this man god-marked. He is favoured by the gods – and cannot be sent as a messenger.'

As he spoke the sun dropped below the rim of the world and there was a chill and a dankness in the air.

Lannon was in a towering, shaking rage that paled his lips and face so that the black clotted scab of his wound stood out clearly on his cheek.

'You defied me!' He said it softly, but in a voice that trembled with his rage.

'He is god-marked!' Huy protested.

'Do not try to hide behind your gods, Priest. You and I both know that many of Baal's decisions are made by Huy Ben-Amon, for Huy Ben-Amon.'

'Majesty,' Huy gasped at the accusation, at the dreadful blasphemy of it.

'You defied me,' Lannon repeated. 'You think to place this barbarian beyond my reach, you aspire to play the game of power and politics with me.'

'It is not true, my lord. I would not dare.'

'You *would* dare, Priest. You would dare to steal the teeth from the mouth of the living Gry-Lion, if the fancy came upon you.'

'My lord, I am your true, your most loyal—'

'Tread lightly, Priest. I warn you. You fly high in the four kingdoms, but remember always that you do so by my favour alone.'

'I know this well.'

'I who exalted you, have it in my power to throw you down as readily.'

'I know this also, my lord,' said Huy humbly.

'Then give me this barbarian,' Lannon demanded, and Huy looked up at him with an expression of deep regret.

'He is not mine to give, my lord. He belongs to the gods.'

Lannon let out a bellow of frustrated rage, and snatched up a heavy amphora of wine. He hurled it at Huy's head, and Huy ducked nimbly. The amphora slapped into the leather side of the tent, cushioning the impact and it dropped to the ground without breaking, wine gurgled from the mouth and soaked into the dry earth.

Lannon was on his feet now, towering over Huy, holding out towards him fists bunched into bony clubs, the muscles in his forearms knotted and ridged with exasperation. He held those fists under Huy's nose, and his eyes were pale glittering blue and deadly, the thick red-golden ringlets danced on his shoulders as he shook with the tempests of his rage.

'Go!' he said in a strangled voice. 'Go quickly – before – before I—'

Huy did not wait to hear the rest of it.

Lannon Hycanus marched from Sett with a bodyguard of 200 men, and Huy watched him go from the walls of the garrison. He felt a chill of apprehension, vulnerable now and lonely without the king's favour.

Huy watched the small travelling party march out between the ranks of the legion, and saw that Lannon wore only a light tunic and that he was bare-headed in the early morning sunlight, his hair shining like a beacon fire. His armour-bearers followed him with helmet and breastplate, bow and sword and javelins. At Lannon's heels followed the little pygmy huntmaster, Xhai the bushman; he was attentive as a shadow to the king.

The legion cheered Lannon away, their voices ringing from the escarpment of the valley, and Lannon moved through the gates. He stood taller than those that surrounded him, smiling and proud and beautiful.

He looked up and saw Huy on the wall, and the smile changed to a quick fierce scowl; ignoring Huy's hesitant salute he marched out through the gates and took the road that ran southwards into the pass, and over the hills to the middle kingdom.

Huy watched until the forest hid him from sight, and then he turned away, feeling very alone. He went down to where the slave king lay dying on a bed of dry straw in a corner of Huy's own tent.

In the rising heat of the morning the smell of the wound was the rank, fetid odour of fever swamps and things long dead.

One of the old slave women was bathing his body, trying to lower the fever. She looked up as Huy entered and answered his query with a shake of her head. Huy squatted beside the pallet, and touched the slave king's skin. It was burning hot and dry, and Manatassi moaned in delirium.

'Send for a slave-master,' Huy ordered irritably. 'Have him strike away these chains.'

It was amazing to watch the fever eat away the flesh from that huge black frame, to see the bone appear beneath the skin, to watch the face collapse, and the skin change colour from shiny purple black to dry dusty grey.

The wound in his groin swelled up hot and hard, with a crusty evil-smelling scab from which a watery greenish-yellow fluid wept slowly. Each hour the slave king's hold on life seemed to slacken, his body grew hotter, the wound swelled to the size of a man's bunched fist.

In the noon of the second day Huy left the camp alone and climbed to a high place upon the escarpment where he could be alone with his god. Here in the valley of the great river the sun-god's presence seemed all-pervading and his usually warm benevolent countenance was oppressive. It seemed to fill the entire sky, and to beat down upon the earth like the hammer of a smith upon the anvil.

Huy sang the prayer of approach, but he did so in a perfunctory fashion, gabbling out the last lines, for Huy was very angry with his gods, and he wanted them to be aware of his displeasure.

'Great Baal,' he omitted the more flowery titles, and came swiftly to the main body of his protest, 'following your evident wishes, I have saved this one who bears your marks. Although I do not wish to complain, nor to question your motives, yet you should know that this has been no easy task. I have made serious sacrifices. I have weakened the position of the High Priest of Baal in the king's favour – I think not of myself, naturally, but only of my influence as your agent and servant. What weakens me, weakens the worship of the gods.' Huy said this with relish, that must surely catch their attention, and Huy was delighted with it. He felt it was entirely justified, it was high time that certain things were said and that the reciprocal duties of loyalty were stated.

'You know of old that no command of yours is too difficult of execution, no burden you place upon me but I shoulder it cheerfully, for always I have been secure in the certainty of your wisdom and purpose.'

Huy paused for breath, and thought. He was angry, but he must not let anger run away with his tongue. He had offended the king, best not offend the gods also. Quickly he moderated his closing address.

'However, in the matter of this marked barbarian I have no such certainty. I have saved him at great cost – to what purpose? Is it your intention that he must now die?' Huy paused again, letting his point sink in.

'I ask you now, most humbly,' Huy spread a drop of honey, 'most humbly, to make your intentions plain to your always attentive and obedient servant.'

Huy paused once more, should he dare the use of stronger terms? He decided against it, and instead spread both hands in the sun sign and sang the praise of Baal, with all the skill and beauty at his command. The sound of his voice shimmering and aching sweet in the breathless heat-rush of the wilderness was enough to make the gods weep, and when the last pure note had died upon the heated air Huy went down to the camp and with a bronze razor he lanced the grotesque swelling in the slave king's loin. Manatassi screamed with pain even in his delirium, and the poison gushed out thick and yellow and stinking. Huy poulticed the open wound with boiled corn wrapped in a linen cloth, scalding hot to drain the poisons.

By evening the fever had passed, and Manatassi lay in exhausted, but natural sleep. Huy stood over him smiling and nodding happily. He felt that he had won this wasted giant, wrested him from death's dark jaws with prayer and endeavour. He experienced a proud warmth of ownership and when the old slave crone brought him a brimming bowl of good Zeng wine, Huy lifted it in a salute to the sleeping giant.

'The gods have given you to me. You are mine. You live

under my protection now, and I pledge it to you.' And he drained the bowl.

The weakness of his body smothered him, pressing him down on the hard mattress of straw. It was an effort to lift head or hand, and he hated his body that had failed him now. He rolled his head slowly and opened his eyes.

Across the tent, on a mat of woven reeds sat the strange little man. Manatassi watched him with a quick flaring of interest. He was stooped over a roll of the strange glowing metal that had been beaten out into a thin pliable length, and with a pointed knife he was scratching and cutting marks into the soft surface. He spent many hours of each day at this unusual activity. Manatassi watched him, noticing the quick nervous birdlike movements of head and hands that set the golden ear-rings jangling and the thick black plaits of hair dangling down his back.

The head seemed too large for the oddly hunched body, and the legs and arms were long and thick and brutal-looking, dark hair grew on the forearms and the back of the long tapered hands – and Manatassi remembered the speed and strength of that body in battle. He lifted his head slightly and glanced down at the linen bandages which swathed his lower body.

At the movement Huy was on his feet in one swift movement, and he came to the pallet and stooped over him, smiling.

Huy said, 'You sleep like a breast-fed baby.' And Manatassi looked up at him, wondering that a man could speak such a deadly insult to the paramount king of Vendi – and smile as he said it.

'Aia, bring food,' Huy shouted for the old slave woman,

and settled down on a cushion beside Manatassi's couch. While Manatassi ate with huge appetite he listened with only a small part of his attention to a ridiculous description of the moon as a white-faced woman. He wondered that such a skilled warrior could be so naïve. It was only necessary to look at the moon to see that it was a cake of ground corn, and as the Mitasi-Mitasi the one great god devoured it, so the shape of his bite could clearly be seen cut from the round cake.

'Do you understand this?' Huy asked with deep concern, and Manatassi answered readily:

'I understand, high-born.'

'You believe it?' Huy insisted.

'I believe it.' Manatassi gave the answer which he knew would please, and Huy nodded happily. His efforts to teach the slave king were most rewarding. He had explained the theory of symbolic representation very carefully, showing Manatassi that the moon was not Astarte but her symbol, her coin, her sign and promise. He had explained the waning and waxing as the symbolic subjugation of the female to the male, repeated in the human female by the periodic moon-sickness.

'Now, the great god Baal,' Huy said, and Manatassi sighed inwardly. He knew what was coming. This strange person would now talk about the hole in the sky through which Mitasi-Mitasi made his entrances and exits. He would try to make Manatassi believe that this was a man with a flowing red beard. What a contradictory people they were, these pale ghost-like beings. On the one hand they had weapons and clothes and wonderful possessions and almost magical skills in civil and military matters. He had seen them fight and work, and it had amazed him. Yet these same people could not recognize truths that even the unweaned infants of his tribe understood completely.

Manatassi's first conscious thoughts when he had emerged from the hot mists of fever had been of escape.

But now, forced by his weakness into the role of observer, he had time to reconstruct his plans. He was safe here, this hunchbacked manikin wielded some strange power, and he was under its protection. He knew this now. No one would touch him as long as his new master held his shield over him.

The other thing he knew was that there was much to learn here. If he could acquire the skills and knowledge of this people, he would be armed a thousand times. He would be the greatest war chief the tribes had ever known. They had used these skills to defeat him, he would defeat them with the same skills that he learned from them.

'Do you understand?' Huy asked earnestly. 'Do you understand that Baal is the master of the whole of heaven and earth?'

'I understand,' said Manatassi.

'Do you accept Astarte and great Baal as gods?'

'I accept them,' Manatassi agreed, and Huy looked very pleased.

'They have placed their mark upon you. It is right that you should be dedicated to their service. When we reach the city I will perform the ceremony in the temple of great Baal. I have chosen a god-name for you – you will no longer use the old style.'

'As you wish, high-born.'

'From henceforth you will be called Timon.'

'Timon,' the slave king tested the sound of it.

'He was the priest-warrior in the reign of the fifth Gry-Lion. A great man.'

Timon nodded, not understanding but content to watch and wait and learn.

'High-born,' he asked softly, 'the marks you scratch upon the yellow metal – what are they?'

Huy jumped up and fetched the golden scroll to the couch.

'This is how we store words and stories and ideas.' He

plunged into an explanation of the writing process, and was rewarded by Timon's quick grasp of the principle of the phonetic alphabet.

On a scrap of leather he wrote Timon's name in sooty black ink, and in unison they spelled it out aloud, Timon laughing delightedly at his first achievement.

'Yes,' he thought, 'there is much to learn here – and so little time.'

Across the clay box Caius Terentius Varro, Consul of Rome, fought once more, pressing his legions into Hannibal's soft centre. The centre gave, with the sucky reluctance of dough, the Spaniards and Gauls there withdrew at Hannibal's design.

'Do you see it, Timon? The beauty of it, the sheer genius of it!' Huy called excitedly, speaking in Punic now, manipulating the counters.

'And where was Marhabal now?' Timon demanded as excitedly in the same language. After two years his Punic was fluent, with only the dragging vowels marring its perfection.

'He was here,' Huy touched the cavalry counters, 'holding his horse on a short rein.' Timon understood a horse to be a swift animal like a zebra on whose back armed men rode.

'Varro is entangled now?' Timon asked.

'Yes! Yes! Hannibal has crumpled his front and enveloped him – then what does he do, Timon?'

'The reserves?' Timon guessed.

'Yes! You have it! The Numidians and African reserves.' Huy was hopping up and down in his agitation. 'With the timing of the great master, he unleashes them. Taking Varro in the flanks, squeezing him in a vice, packing his ranks so they cannot manoeuvre nor wield their weapons. Then what, Timon, what then?'

'The cavalry?'

'Ah! The cavalry – Marhabal! The faithful brother. The master of horse, who has waited all that long day. Go! cries Hannibal.' Huy threw his arm in a wide gesture. 'Go! My brother, ride with your wild Iberians! They crash into them, Timon. It is the moment, the exact moment. Five minutes earlier is too soon – five minutes later and it is too late. Timing! Timing! The talent of the great military commander, timing! Of the statesman, the lover, the businessman, the merchant. The right action, at the right time.'

'And the result, high-born, what was the result?' Timon pleaded, in an agony of suspense. 'Was it victory?'

'Victory?' Huy asked. 'Yes, Timon. It was victory. Victory and massacre. Eight legions of vaunting Rome wiped out to the man, two entire consular armies.'

'Eight legions, high-born.' Timon marvelled. 'Forty-eight thousand men in a single battle?'

'More than that, Timon. The auxiliaries were lost also. Sixty thousand men!' Huy swept his hand across the board, exterminating the Roman legions. 'We won the battles, Timon, but they won the wars. Three of them. Three bloody wars, that crushed us—' Huy broke off, his voice choking. He turned away quickly and went to the water jug. Timon hurried across and held the basin for him while Huy washed his hands and combed his beard. 'That brings us to the end of our study of Hannibal's campaigns, Timon. I kept the battle of Cannae for the last.'

'Who will we study next, high-born?'

'The one who Hannibal himself rated the most skilful General of all history.'

'Who was that?'

'Alexander III,' Huy said, 'King of Macedonia, who

smashed the Persian Empire – whom the oracle at Delphi proclaimed invincible, and men called the Great.'

Timon held Huy's cloak for him, and Huy fastened the clasp as he left the precincts of the temple college through the small gate in the inner wall. Timon followed a pace behind him, wearing the short blue tunic of Huy's household with a light gold chain, dagger and purse belting his waist, the mark of high trust as a body slave. He walked a pace behind Huy's left shoulder, so as not to mask his master's sword arm, and he kept his hand on the dagger.

'High-born, the manner in which Hannibal invested Varro?'

'Yes?' Huy encouraged him.

'Could he not have advanced his flanks, and held his centre firm?'

'It is the difference between defence and offence,' Huy explained, and they plunged into discussion of battle tactics and strategy until they left the main gate in the outer wall of the temple area. From here any conversation was impossible, for the crowds spotted this strange couple. Giant black slave and diminutive gnome-like master. They cheered Huy, crowding around him to touch his arm in greeting, to listen to his banter and perhaps receive an alms coin from the purse on Timon's belt.

Huy loved his popularity. He smiled and joked and pushed his way gently through the press. A successful General – there had been two other campaigns since the great slave-taking – a well-beloved priest, a noted wit and song-writer, and a rich philanthropist (Huy's investments had prospered exceedingly in the last two years), he was the object of popular adulation throughout the city.

They crossed the market-place with its fascinating smells and sights and sounds of hides and humanity, of spices and open sewers. On one of the slave blocks was a light-skinned girl of mixed Yuye blood, and the auctioneer spotted Huy in the crowd and called out to him.

'My lord, a work of art for you. A statue in yellow ivory,' opening the girl's cloak to display her body.

Huy laughed and waved a hand in refusal. They moved along the stone jetty at the lakeside where the ships lay with stern almost touching stern, their hatches open and a boiling of stevedores running over them, loading and unloading the merchandise. From the taverns and wine-shops flanking the jetty came the sour stench of cheap wine and gusts of drunken laughter. The street girls beckoned from the narrow lanes between the shops. The uncertain light of dusk softened their raddled features and hectic painted cheeks and lips – Huy wondered what solace a man would find with the likes of them.

Beyond the bustle of the harbour area lay the town houses of the noble families and rich merchants, each protected by the high mud outer wall and a heavy carved wooden gate. Huy's new residence was one of the least pretentious of these, with the entrance off a narrow walled lane, and a view from the flat roof over the lake.

Once through the gate Huy shed his sword and cloak and handed them to Timon with a sigh of pleasure at the moment of homecoming, and he went through into the paved central courtyard.

The princes and princesses were waiting for him, fourteen of them, headed by the twins, Helanca and Imilce. The two of them had grown in the past years, and they were stranded now in that awkward period between girlhood and womanhood. Too young to giggle, yet too old to greet Huy with a kiss.

There were no such inhibitions upon the younger members of house Barca, and they swarmed forward to engulf Huy. The religious instruction of the children of the royal house was a duty Huy had imposed upon himself, and despite the estrangement between king and priest, Lannon had not interfered with this arrangement. He had not sanctioned it, but he had not forbidden it. Huy led his students through into the airy living-room of the house.

In the courtyard one of the royal nursemaids waited until her charges had followed the priest before she turned and her eyes sought those of Timon. She was a tall girl with strong shoulders, long-waisted and with fruitful hips. Her legs also were straight and strong, but her hands were narrow and pink-palmed and delicately shaped. She wore her hair oiled and dressed in the manner of the Vendi, for she was of Timon's tribe. Taken in the great raid, she was not slave born, not of the humble dependent breed that had known nothing but captivity. There was a fierce spirit in her to match Timon's. Her skin was a shade lighter than his, her face was round, moon-shaped, her nose flat and broad, her lips full and pouting, but her teeth were small and even, and very white when she smiled at Timon.

Timon inclined his head sharply in a command, and Sellene the slave girl nodded in acknowledgement. When Timon left the courtyard and went through the kitchens into the slave quarters she followed him.

He was waiting for her in his own tiny room with its single pallet of reed mat and furs. She went to him without hesitation, and lay against the great hard muscles of his chest and belly and thighs. Her round breasts jutting through the purple tunic of house Barca pressed against Timon.

They held their faces together, sniffing softly but eagerly at each other's eyes and mouths and nostrils, clinging to each other in their need and wanting.

'When I hold you, then once again I am King of Vendi, and no slave dog,' Timon whispered, and the girl groaned against him with her love.

With gentle hands that could crush the life from a man Timon loosened her tunic and carried her to the pallet. He laid her upon the bed, and as he came over her he said,

'You shall be the first of my wives. You shall be my queen and the mother of my sons.'

'When shall it be?' she asked him and her voice shook with the emotions locked within her.

'Soon,' he promised. 'Very soon now. I have what I came for, and I will take you back beyond the river. I shall be the greatest king the tribes have ever known, and you shall be my queen.'

'I believe you,' whispered Sellene.

'My royal lords and fair ladies.' The children squealed with glee, it was one of their jokes when Huy addressed them that way. 'Today I have a special treat for you!' Again pandemonium broke out. Huy's treats were usually something special indeed.

'What is it?' Imilce demanded breathlessly.

'This evening you will meet the oracle of Opet,' Huy announced, and thc uproar subsided swiftly. The small ones not understanding but none the less infected by the solemnity of their elders. The bigger children had heard of the oracle, their nurses often frightened them into obedience with the name. Now that they were about to meet this mythical creature the atmosphere was charged with tension. They were all of them suffering from an onset of the creeps and ghostlies.

Anna spoke for all of them when she asked in a very subdued voice, 'She won't eat us, will she?'

When Tanith came she seated herself amongst them, and threw the hood of her cloak back from her face. She smiled at the children, and said softly, 'I am going to tell you a story.' The smile and the promise were enough to ease the tension and they edged in closer to her. 'It's the story of the marriage of the great god Baal to the goddess Astarte.'

Tanith began the tale from religious mythology which was the basis of the Festival of the Fruitful Earth, a festival celebrated every five years. This year of Opet 538 was the 106th ceremony since the founding of the city, and the following day would begin the festivities that would last for ten days.

Tanith held her young audience enthralled, speaking in the compelling voice which Huy had trained so carefully, using the mannerisms and gestures he had taught her. Huy watched her with an unusual mixture of professional appraisal and the adulation of a besotted lover.

In two years she had lost the last traces of gawkiness and uncertainty, and although she was not yet twenty years of age, there was an inner calm, a serenity of mind and expression, that befitted her role of seeress and occult adviser to a nation. No matter that her pronouncements were carefully coached and rehearsed by Huy Ben-Amon, it was she that made the delivery, and made it convincingly. Much of Huy's material success in the last two years stemmed from the questions and requests for guidance addressed to Tanith by the rich merchants and trading syndicates of Opet – and Tanith's replies. The supplicants were usually well satisfied with Tanith's advice, though it was always couched in terms of ambiguity to ensure against recriminations. Did it matter that Huy Ben-Amon was also well satisfied?

In the same way Huy, despite his loss of the king's ear, kept a guiding hand on the rudder of the ship of state. Huy was certain that Lannon Hycanus was fully aware of the ultimate source of the advice and guidance which he received from Tanith. In any event, Lannon visited the oracle regularly in her shrine in the grotto beside the silent green pool of Astarte.

On the morrow Lannon's visit to the oracle would be his first official act that would signal the commencement of the Festival of the Fruitful Earth. This was the true reason why Huy had summoned Tanith to his residence. He must brief her carefully on the replies she would make to the king's queries. Huy knew with a high degree of accuracy what these would be, for his informers were close to the king and again Huy guessed that Lannon intentionally leaked his questions in advance, certain that they would reach Huy and that the replies would come through the oracle.

Thinking of Lannon always brought on a mood of deep melancholy. Two years Huy had been without solace of Lannon's smile and handclasp and companionship, and during that time the sharp edge of his loss had not blunted but grown keener. He would wait for hours for a passing glimpse of his old friend, he would pester others for accounts of the banquets at the palace to which he was not invited. On each anniversary of the king's birth, and also on his throne day Huy had composed a sonnet and sent it with a handsome gift to the palace. The gift had been unacknowledged and the sonnet unsung – as far as he knew.

Huy tore himself out of this sad mood, and looked instead at his love. The children had crowded her now, silent and big-eyed and intent. Four-year-old Hannibal, named after his illustrious ancestor, had crawled into Tanith's lap and was sucking his thumb as he stared up into her face.

Tanith's mask of solemnity had slipped a little, with these children she was childlike, her expression animated and her voice excited. Seeing her thus seemed to add a new dimension to Huy's feelings for her, and his heart swelled in his chest until it seemed his chest must burst. How much longer must he wait, he wondered, and for what? If it had taken two long carefully planned years to win her confidence, how much longer to win her heart, and having won it what could he hope for – for she was dedicated to the goddess and could never belong to mortal man.

Tanith's story ended, and the children exclaimed and clamoured for more, besieging her with demands and entreaties and bribery kisses – but Huy feigned outrage, and scolded them while they laughed and clapped their hands with delight. He shouted for the nursemaids and they came – among them that tall brooding fiery woman who always made Huy feel disquiet when she looked at him from those unfathomably dark eyes.

He said to her. 'Sellene, darkness falls, tell Timon to carry a lamp for you to the palace gate.' And she acknowledged him with an inclination of the head, showing no gratitude at the order nor resentment either.

After the children had gone they ate the evening meal, the three of them, Tanith, Huy and Aina the ancient priestess who was Tanith's chaperone. Huy had selected her for two good reasons. She was half blind and completely deaf. Huy had tested her by making obscene gestures at her from a range of twenty paces. Aina had shown no reaction, nor had she when Huy crept up behind her and shouted a rude name in her ear. She was just the type of chaperone that Huy wanted.

They ate with the lamps trimmed low and the food served by one of the ancient slaves, and when they were finished Huy led Tanith up the outside staircase to the roof and they sat together below the parapet on reed mats and leather cushions. The night wind off the lake was cool and the stars very yellow and bright. Huy crouched over his lute, and strummed softly the rippling tune which he had trained Tanith's unconscious mind to accept as the signal for hypnotic concentration. Before he had finished the last bars of the tune she was breathing slowly and evenly, her body still and her eyes dark green and unseeing.

While his fingers ran over the strings of the instrument,

repeating the tune again and again, Huy began to speak. He kept his voice at a monotonous sing-song tone, speaking softly but insidiously and Tanith sat in the starlight and listened with an inner ear.

On the first day of the 106th Festival of the Fruitful Earth, Lannon Hycanus the forty-seventh Gry-Lion of Opet went in procession to the temple of Astarte to take the oracle.

He passed through the enclosure of the temple of Baal where the sacred towers pointed to the sun, guarded by the carved sunbird monoliths, and where the silent populace of the city waited, but when he reached the cleft in the red cliffs that guarded the entrance to the sacred grotto he unbuckled his sword and handed it to his little pygmy huntmaster, his shield and helmet he gave to his armour-bearers, and bareheaded and unarmed he entered the opening in the cliff.

He passed through the paved tunnel and into the silent beauty of the grotto. The surrounds of the pool were paved with slabs of sandstone and the pool itself was edged with a rounded coping of the same material. Tiers of stone benches rose against the sheer walls of the grotto, and against the far wall the shrine of Astarte was built half into the living rock. Its portals were columned in the Hellenic style, and it contained the cells of the priestesses and the chamber of the oracle.

Beyond the stone throne of the oracle was concealed the entrance to the city archives cut into the rock, and beyond that again, guarded by a massive stone door and the curse of the gods, was the treasury and the tomb of the kings.

Lannon paused beside the pool, and the priestesses came forward to meet him and escort him to the edge of the pool. Here they helped him to shed his armour and undergarments.

He stood tall and naked, golden-headed and beautifully formed, at the head of the steps leading down into the green water. His body was finely muscled as that of a trained athlete, although there was heavy bunched muscle in the shoulders and neck, the mark of the swordsman. His belly and flanks, however, were lean with the shape of muscle beneath the skin but lightly stated. A gilding of red-gold hair ran down from his navel across the flat stomach to explode in a sunny burst of curls in the angle of his legs. The legs were shapely, long and moulded, and balanced his regal bulk easily.

The High Priestess blessed him, and called down the goddess's favour upon him. Then Lannon went down the steps and immersed himself in the sacred, life-giving water.

While two young novices dried his body and dressed the king in robes of fresh linen, Huy Ben-Amon sang the praise chant to the goddess and when it ended all eyes looked up to the opening in the roof of the cavern high above the green pool.

Lannon called out in a loud voice. 'Astarte, mother of moon and earth, receive the messenger we send you – and hear our plea with favour.'

The throng about the pool lifted their hands high in the sign of the sun, and at the signal the body of the sacrifice plunged from the slab that jutted into the opening in the grotto roof. The wail of the doomed soul echoed briefly about the cavern, until he struck the water and was dragged down swiftly into the green depths by the weight of the chains he wore.

Lannon turned from the pool, and passed between the ranks of the priestesses into the entrance of the shrine. The audience chamber of the oracle was only a little larger than the living-room of a rich man's house. The lamps burned with a steady light. The flames were tinted an unnatural greenish hue, and the incense of burning herbs was heavy and oppressive. There were draperies beyond the oracle's throne hanging from roof to flagged floor.

The oracle sat upon the throne, a small figure completely swathed in white robes, the face hidden in the shadows of her hood.

Lannon halted in the centre of the chamber and before he spoke he admired for a moment the arrangements that put the interviewer at such a disadvantage. Bare-footed, damp from the pool, stripped of weapons and finery, dressed in strange robes and forced to look up at the figure on the throne while he inhaled the subtly drugged air – he must be off balance. Lannon felt his anger stir, and his voice was harsh as he made the formal greeting and asked the first question.

Huy watched from his place of concealment behind the draperies. He revelled in the closeness of his friend's physical presence, remembering his mannerisms and voice tones, watching the familiar and well-loved face, smiling at an expected change of expression, the quick smoulder of anger in the pale blue eyes, the quickening of interest at a warning, the glimmer of a smile as he recognized good advice.

Tanith spoke in the same sing-song cadence as Huy had used, picking the answers from the wide selection with which Huy had armed her.

When Lannon was finished and would have left the chamber, Tanith's voice stopped him.

'There is more.'

Lannon turned back with surprise, for he was not accustomed to unsolicited – and unpaid for – counsel from the oracle. But Tanith spoke, 'The lion had a faithful jackal to warn him of the hunter's approach, but drove the jackal away.

'The sun had a bird to carry the sacrifices on high, but turned his countenance away from the bird.

'The hand had an axe to defend it, but cast the axe aside.

'Oh, proud lion! Oh, faithless sun! Oh, careless hand!'

Behind the drapery Huy held his breath. It had sounded very clever when he had composed it, but now spoken out in the bare stone chamber it shocked even him.

Lannon's pale eyes seemed to glaze over as he puzzled the riddle, but it was not that subtle and as the import struck him his eyes cleared to the chill sparkle of sapphire and the blood engorged his face and neck.

'Damn you, witch,' he shouted. 'Must I have it from you also? That cursed priest plagues me at every turn. I cannot walk the streets of my city but I hear the crowds sing his piddling songs. I cannot dine in my own banquet-room but my guests will repeat his empty mouthings. I cannot fight, nor drink a bowl of wine, nor toss a dice but his shadow stands at my shoulder.' Lannon was panting with anger, as he stamped across the audience chamber and shook his fist in the oracle's startled face. 'My children even, he bewitches them also.'

Behind the drapes Huy felt his spirits soar on bright wings, this was not an enemy speaking.

'He struts and lords it in the streets of my city, his name echoes through my kingdoms.'

Lannon's anger was changing to righteous indignation.

'They cheer him when he passes, I have heard it, and, by great Baal, they cheer him louder than they do their own king.'

Lannon swung away from the throne, unable to control his agitation. His eyes swept over the draperies and for an instant seemed to stare into Huy's soul. Huy drew back with a quick intake of breath, but Lannon paced quickly about the chamber before approaching the oracle again.

'He does all this, mark you, *without my favour*. He should be an outcast, a—' He broke off and paced again, and his voice changed, the cutting edge of it dulled, and he said almost inaudibly, 'How I miss that terrible little man.'

Huy doubted for a moment that the words had been spoken, but almost immediately Lannon's voice rose in a bellow.

'But he defied me. He took from me what was mine, and that I cannot overlook!'

Lannon whirled and stormed from the shrine. His gentleman-at-arms and his huntmaster saw the expression on his face and they signalled the warnings ahead of the king's furious progress back to the palace.

On the final day of the festival Lannon Hycanus prayed in the temple of great Baal, alone in the sacred grove among the towers and the sunbird monoliths. Then he emerged to receive the renewed pledges of loyalty from his subjects. Each of the nine noble families would be represented, as well as the order of priesthood, the guilds of craftsmen and the powerful trading syndicates of the kingdom. They would restate their oaths of allegiance to the throne, and present gifts to the Gry-Lion.

Huy Ben-Amon was absent from the ceremony. Bakmor made the oath for the priesthood and presented the gift. Lannon growled softly at the young warrior priest as he made obeisance before him.

'Where is the Holy Father of Ben-Amon?'

'My lord, I speak for him and all the priests of great Baal.' Bakmor avoided the question as Huy had coached him, and Lannon could protest no further in the presence of his assembled nobles.

The ceremony ended the festival and Opet plunged into an orgy of food and wine and frolic and licence. While

Lannon feasted with his nobles in the palace, the commoners thronged the narrow streets singing and dancing. The wine vendors passed freely amongst them, but during the daylight hours the restraints of custom and law checked the behaviour of the crowds. Darkness would bring on the lewd and wanton revels which characterized the festival. In the night the noble matrons and their pretty daughters would slip out, cloaked and hooded, into the streets to join the debauchery – or at the very least to watch it with shining eyes and breathless laughter. For a day and night the rules of society were suspended, and no husband nor wife could demand explanation or accounting from their spouses. It happened but once every five years, and when the festival ended there were wine-sore heads, pale faces and shaking hands, as well as smug and secret smiles.

By the middle of the afternoon Lannon was drunk, expansively and happily drunk, as were most of his guests. The banquet-room of the palace was sweltering. The sun beat down fiercely upon the flat mud roof, while the body heat of 500 excited nobles, and the heat from the steaming dishes of rich food turned it into an oven.

The roar of voices drowned the valiant efforts of the musicians, and the artistry of the naked girl dancers was impaired by a barrage of ripe grapes aimed by a group of young and noble knights. Hits upon various parts of the girls' anatomy scored for the marksmen in a contest upon which large amounts of gold were wagered.

Deep in wine and talk, Lannon was not aware of the change in the feast until almost complete silence had descended upon the hall. He looked up, frowning quickly, and saw that the musicians' hands had frozen upon their instruments, the dancers stood paralysed, and the guests gawked.

Lannon's frown deepened to a scowl as he saw Huy Ben-Amon approaching him down the hall. Huy was dressed in a blue tunic with a border of woven gold wire. He wore a gold belt, and a jewelled dagger. His hair and beard were carefully oiled and curled, and golden ear-rings dangled to his shoulders.

His expression was solemn as he knelt quickly before Lannon, and his voice rang golden and sweet to every corner of the hall.

'My king, I come to renew my allegiance to you. Let all men know that I honour you above all things, and my loyalty is unto death and beyond.'

Lannon was caught off balance, as Huy had intended. His brain was fuddled with surprise and wine. He fumbled for words, but before he found them, Huy had risen swiftly.

'As a mark of my faith, I offer a gift.' He signalled with one hand behind his back, and all heads in the hall swung to the main doors.

The towering figure of Timon stalked into the hall, passed down its length and stopped beside Huy. He stared into Lannon's face with those ferocious smoky eyes.

Huy whispered. 'Down!' And nudged the giant slave, and slowly Timon lowered himself to one knee and bowed his head.

'But he belongs to the gods,' Lannon challenged harshly. 'You declared him god-marked, Priest.'

And Huy gathered his resolve, steeling himself to tell the lie, to commit this sacrilege. Despite the fact that he had already explained it to the gods and to Timon, he was uneasy. It was necessary to regain the king's favour, Huy had explained, there was but one way of doing so. Lannon was bound by his pride. He could not move to break the deadlock. Huy must make the offer. He asked great Baal for permission to deny the bird-footed marking of the slave. He asked aloud, while pacing the roof of his house in the noon day. A distant muttering of summer thunder had been all the answer Huy needed. The gods had answered, but Huy felt nervous, the answer had been in a very minor key, and not without ambiguity. It was also very difficult for Huy to admit that he was wrong – it jarred the very foundations of his soul.

'My lord,' said Huy. 'I was mistaken. The gods have shown me that the markings are not sacred.'

Lannon stared at Huy. He shook his head slightly, as though he doubted the evidence of his own ears.

'You mean – you give him to me without reservation? I can have him despatched immediately, if I wish to?' He leaned forward staring at Huy. 'Do you give him to me without conditions?'

'I have declared my love for the king,' said Huy, and with his foot he nudged Timon.

In a great rumbling bass, Timon spoke his lines in near perfect Punic. 'I come to you as a living proof of that love.'

Lannon rocked back on his cushions. He thought about it, and the scowl reappeared, as he saw it.

'You seek to chain me! There are still conditions – only better concealed,' he growled.

'Nay, my lord. Not chains, but the silken threads of friendship,' Huy told him softly. They held each other's eyes. Lannon beginning to flush with anger, Huy steady and calm.

Then suddenly Huy's face cracked, and the dark eyes sparkled. The ringlets on his cheeks began to dance with suppressed laughter. Lannon opened his mouth to bellow at him, to reject the gift and the offer of friendship. Instead, laughter rattled up his throat and burst from his open lips. He laughed, until the tears poured down his cheeks and between gusts of laughter he moaned with the pain of his aching belly muscles.

'Fly for me, bird of the sun,' he sobbed, and Huy flopped down beside him on the cushions and shook and quivered with laughter.

'Roar for me, Lion of Opet,' he cried and a slave girl filled a wine bowl and brought it to him. Huy quaffed half of it, then passed the bowl to Lannon. He drained it. A little wine ran from the corners of his mouth into his golden beard. He smashed the bowl on the stone floor, then clasped Huy about the shoulders.

'We have wasted much time, my Sunbird. Let us make up for it. What shall we do first?'

'Drink,' said Huy.

'Ah!' cried Lannon. 'And then what?'

'Hunt,' suggested Huy, choosing those activities dearest to the king.

'Hunt!' Lannon echoed. 'Send for my huntmasters – we march tomorrow to hunt the elephant!'

'Astarte, mother of earth, your beauty is multiplied until it floods my soul,' muttered Huy, swaying gracefully, as he looked up at the night sky. He reeled backwards, but fell against a wall. It steadied him, and he went on studying the astronomical phenomena in the heavens. Four silver moons hung above the night-revelling city. Huy closed one eye, and three of the moons vanished – he opened it and they reappeared.

'Astarte, guide your servant's footsteps,' Huy entreated, pushed himself away from the wall and went on down the narrow lane towards the harbour. He stumbled over a body lying in the shadows, and stooped unsteadily to check for signs of life.

The body snored and grunted as he rolled it onto its back, and a warm fruity gust of winey breath came up to Huy. It reminded him of the recumbent figures he had left strewn about the banquet hall at the palace. Lannon chief among them, smiling as he slept.

'Tonight you are in good company, citizen of Opet,' Huy chuckled, and went tottering onwards down the lane. In an angle of the wall a dark shape moved. Huy peered at it curiously, saw one body, two heads, heard broken gusty breathing, soft incoherent cries. The movements were small, but unmistakable. Huy smiled, tripped and nearly fell. He saw a startled girl's face turn towards him from the gloom. 'Let all things be fruitful,' he told her solemnly and went on, and as he went another figure slipped silently from the dark lane and followed Huy. The figure was cloaked and hooded in rough woven brown cloth, and its movements were stealthy and deliberate.

The quayside of the harbour was crowded with revellers, and there were bonfires burning here. The reflections of the flames smeared ruddy and bright upon the still black waters of the lake. Around them, arms linked in a circle, danced the crowds. Some of the women were past all restraint, stripped naked to the waist, spilled wine snaking down their white bodies like blood.

Huy stopped to watch them a while, and the following figure hung back, mingling with the throng of merry-makers.

When Huy started forward, the cloaked figure hurried forward also. The lane that led up to Huy's house was in deep darkness, but a lamp burned dimly in a niche above the gate, left there to welcome the master home.

As Huy groped his way towards the light, the following figure closed with him silently and swiftly. The blundering sounds of his own progress blanketed the rustle of cloth and the light footfalls behind him.

Huy reached the gate, and he stood in the dim lamp-light. His dagger was under his cloak, and his sword hand reached out for the latch of the gate. In that instant while he was unready and off balance, the dark figure flew at him from out of the darkness. A hand closed on his wrist, and he was thrown back against the wall beside the gate. Wine had slowed his reflexes, he twisted his face upwards in surprise and alarm. He saw the dark figure, with its face hidden in the recesses of the hood, come at him – and before he could shout soft lips were pressed against his, and a little muffled chuckle broke through these lips into his startled mouth – and he felt warm breasts and thighs moving against him.

The shock of it paralysed Huy. For long seconds he stood utterly still while lips and cunning hands teased and goaded him. Then with a hoarse cry he reached for the taut warm woman shape, and immediately it was gone, slipping away beyond his reach.

He lunged for it wildly, his hands groping air, and the shape danced away, swirled through the gateway into Huy's house and slammed the gate closed.

Cursing desperately, Huy struggled with the gate, wrenched it open at last and ran into the entrance court.

There was a flash of dark movement across the court, disappearing into the house, and Huy raced after it, tripped over a cushion and fell full length, knocked over a stool on which a house slave had left an amphora and wine bowl. They shattered loudly, splashing wine across the mud floor. A mocking whisper of laughter, from the dim recess of the house, sent Huy scrambling to his feet and charging onwards. He saw the cloaked figure silhouetted against the lamplit doorway of his sleeping quarters.

'Wait!' he shouted. 'Who are you?' And his house slaves roused by the uproar came running, still half asleep, panicky and hastily armed.

'Be gone!' Huy shouted at them furiously. 'All of you – the first one I catch out of his room before morning, I will have flogged.' And they retreated to their quarters, not seriously alarmed by the threat. Huy maintained his dignity until the last of them had disappeared, then he turned and charged towards the doorway of his sleeping quarters.

There was a night lamp burning here also, on a low stool beside his bed. The wick was trimmed low, a soft orange puddle of light which left the furthest reaches of the room in darkness. Beside the lamp stood the cloaked woman. She stood motionless and the face within the hood was completely hidden although Huy thought he caught the sheen of reflected light off watching eyes.

The force of Huy's charge carried him half across the room, but in the wrong direction. He swung towards her, and at that moment she stooped and snuffed the lamp flame. The room was plunged into darkness, and Huy's charge ended against the wall. He gathered himself quickly, he was sobering fast now, and he crouched beside the wall listening.

He heard the rustle of cloth, and he pounced. His fingers closed on a hem of the cloak. There was a muted shriek of surprise, and the fold of material was plucked from his fingers. He swore bitterly, and with arms wide-spread groped like a blind man about the room.

He sensed movements near him, the lightest breathing, the softest stirring in the darkness. He reached out quickly, and his fingers brushed against smooth skin. He recognized the shape of a nude back, and the plump warm bulge of a buttock. A soft chuckle and it was gone again. Huy froze with his heart hammering at his ribs, and his physical arousal making him momentarily dizzy.

Whoever she was, she had discarded the cloak. He was alone with a woman who was elusive as a darting lake pike, and as naked as a new-born babe. Like a stalking leopard he went after her, stripping his own tunic and breech clout as he went, dropping them carelessly on the floor, until, except for the gold rings in his ears, he was bare as his own passion.

She was panicky in the darkness now, unable to control the gasps and nervous giggles. And Huy hunted her by ear, closing in on her, driving her into the corner beside the bed.

She nearly escaped him again, ducking under his searching hands but one of his long arms whipped around her waist and he lifted her easily. She squealed now, kicking like a captive animal, her fists beating against his face and chest.

He carried her to the thick pile of furs that made up his bed.

Huy woke with a sense of peace, a feeling of deep happiness.

His body seemed softened and enervated, but his mind was clear and sharply focused. The soft pinks of dawn suffused his chamber and the cry of the winging lake birds carried clearly to him.

He raised himself on one elbow and looked down at the girl who slept beside him in the storm-tossed bed. She had cast aside her covering in the warm spring night. Her hair was moist at the temples, and a fine sheen of moisture shone on her softly pouting upper lip. Her eyes were closed, and she slept so lightly that her breathing barely stirred the mass of soft dark hair which lay upon her cheeks.

One arm was thrown over her head, pulling the surprisingly large breasts out of shape. Her breasts were big and full and round for the long slim length of her body, and the tips were still flushed dark red from the loving of the night. Her skin was smooth and pale creamy olive, with violent puffs of black silky hair in her armpits and at the base of her belly.

Huy saw all of this in the first startled glance, before his eyes fastened on her calm and sleeping face.

Incredulously Huy stared at her, all sound locked away in his throat. He felt horror, and awe, and superstitious terror.

The girl opened her eyes, and saw him and smiled.

'Baal's blessings on you, Holy Father,' she said softly.

'Tanith!' gasped Huy.

'Yes, my lord.' She was still smiling.

'This is sacrilege,' Huy whispered. 'This is an offence against the goddess.'

'To deny my love for you would have been an offence against all nature.' Tanith sat up on the bed, and kissed him without remorse, without the least sign of guilt.

'Love?' Huy asked, his misgivings temporarily forgotten.

'Yes, my lord,' Tanith nodded, and kissed him again.

'But—' Huy stuttered, and his cheeks turned bright as bush fires. 'You cannot – how can you love me?'

'How can I not, my lord?'

'But my body – my back.'

'Your back I love because it is part of you, part of your goodness and kindness and wisdom.'

He stared at her for many seconds, then clumsily he took her in his arms and buried his face in the fragrant dark cloud of her hair.

'Oh, Tanith,' he whispered. 'What are we going to do?'

Huy stood on the hilltop in the dawn and waited for his god. Below him the camp stirred. The cooking fires paled in the growing light of day. Small sounds carried up to him, the sounds of 6,000 men preparing for the hunt. The 6,000 warriors of Huy's legion, and the king's train. Small wonder that the camp filled the entire valley on both sides of the small river that flowed down the escarpment of the hills. Thirty miles away to the north lay the sluggish green ribbon of the great river, sweltering in its hot and unhospitable valley. One of Lannon's legions was camped there already, and for days now they had been harassing the elephant herds that were feeding along the river. They had attacked them with archers, and javelin-throwers and war elephants.

Under this harassment the herds would leave the valley,

taking to their ancient roads out over the escarpment. Lannon was encamped now astride these well-blazed trails, and scouts from the valley had reported the previous evening that the herds were already on the move. They were massing and moving in towards the escarpment wall, and in the next few days they would come pouring up out of the valley in long majestic files, as the old bulls led them to sanctuary from the persistent hunters who plagued them.

Huy Ben-Amon pondered this as he stood in the dawn. He wore light hunting armour and running sandals, and he leaned comfortably on the shaft of the vulture axe. The splendid blade was covered with a soft leather sheath to protect the finely honed edge and the delicate engravings. It seemed to Huy that the gods had so arranged circumstances as to provide him with this opportunity.

For two weeks, ever since that last night of the Festival of the Fruitful Earth, Huy had spent most of his waking moments pondering his dilemma. He had spent hours poring over the sacred books, examining the roles of priest and priestess, their duties and relationship to the gods, and to each other. He thought that from all this research he had built up a case for his behaviour. He could not bring himself to call it sacrilege. He had come now to plead his case, and to receive judgement.

The sun shot its first golden lance against the crest of the hill, and Huy sang the praise chant with all the beauty at his command. Then he made his plea. It was complicated dialectic, based on the concept of earthly representation, and amounting to a line of reasoning which supposed that what was good behaviour between Baal and his mate Astarte would be equally justifiable between their earthly representatives – although, of course, not between a priestess and any other person than the High Priest of Baal. Huy glossed over the more evidently weak spots in his case.

He ended, 'It may be, however, great Baal and heavenly Astarte, that I am mistaken in my reasoning. It may well be that I have sinned. If this is the case then I deserve your full wrath and despite my life of service and faithful duty, I deserve the most dire punishment!'

Huy paused for effect. 'I go now to hunt the elephant. I swear on my life that wherever the chase is hottest, there I shall be. Wherever the danger is deadliest, there I shall be.

'If I have sinned – then let the tusked beasts strike me down. If I have not sinned then let me live and return to the bosom of your priestess. If you grant me life and love – I swear my duty and service will last to the end of my days, and no man nor woman will ever know of the dispensation you have granted me.' He was quiet a while longer then he spoke again, 'You who have loved, take pity on one who loves also.'

Huy came down the hill well satisfied with his bargain. He would give the gods full measure. He would not hang back in distaste from the slaughter today, the gods would have every opportunity to demonstrate their outrage. In any event, Huy was well aware that only death could keep him out of Tanith's arms. The taste of that fruit had been too sweet for him ever to deny it.

'Huy,' Lannon shouted as Huy entered the camp. 'Where have you been?' He was armed and striding impatiently back and forth outside his tent. He came towards Huy quickly. 'The day wastes away,' he cried. 'Already from the hills our look-outs have seen the approach of the herds.'

The war elephants were ready, drivers sitting on their necks and the tall castles on their backs. Lannon's hunting party was assembled about the tent. Among them Huy noticed some of the king's most renowned huntmasters: Mursil, with his purple boozy face, the lean and saturnine Zadal, Huya the celebrated bowman, and the diminutive yellow Xhai whose fame as a tracker had grown apace in the last few years. Beyond them amongst the horde of body slaves towered the colossal black bulk of Timon. Huy smiled at him, and then he hurried beside Lannon to the elephant lines.

Lannon told him, 'You will ride with me, Sunbird.' And Huy replied, 'I am honoured, my lord.'

Mursil handed Huy one of the elephant bows. Few men could draw these massive weapons. Carved from solid baulks of wild ebony, they were as thick at the centre as a man's wrist and strung with twisted strands of lion gut. It required immense strength in the arms and chest to draw one of the five-foot arrows, that were armed with a heavy steel head and flighted with wild duck feathers. However, once drawn to the limit and loosed, they could fly 100 paces and bury the arrow up to its feathers in the living flesh of an elephant. They could reach the mighty heart in its castle of ribs, they could cut deep into the massive pink lungs, or loosed with skill they could cut through the ear-hole in the great bony skull and find the brain.

'I know you prefer the bow to the spear, Holy Father,' Mursil murmured respectfully. 'As for me, my old arm can no longer draw.'

'Thank you, huntmaster.'

'The quivers are full. I have tested and selected each of the arrows,' Mursil assured him, and Huy followed Lannon to where his war elephant knelt. It was a rangy old cow, more steady than the bull in the heat of battle, more reliable and even-tempered than the bull in the hunt.

Huy followed Lannon up into the castle. There was room for three men in the wooden box. The arrow quivers were fitted to the outside, but with the arrow-heads standing up ready to the hand. The javelins were racked on the front of the castle and Lannon selected one and tested it thoughtfully.

'A nice balance,' he judged it, and then looked down to where his huntmasters waited anxiously. Each of them eager for the honour of riding with the Gry-Lion. Lannon glanced over them, but his eye stopped on Xhai. He nodded, and with pathetic gratitude the pygmy scrambled up the elephant's side.

With a heavy lurch that threw Huy against the edge of the castle, the elephant came up on its feet. They looked down from the majestic height of nearly eighteen feet, and the driver goaded the old cow into a stately swaying walk. They took the trail down towards the escarpment of the valley.

'I have selected a good place for it,' Lannon told Huy. 'Where the steep path comes out suddenly into a small flat bowl. We will wait for them there.'

Huy looked back and saw the other war elephants following them. Twenty of them in single file, ears flapping, trunks swinging, they trundled sedately along. The huntsmen in the castles were checking and testing their weapons, and chattering excitedly.

'For what do we hunt, my lord?' Huy asked. 'Calves or ivory?'

'Calves first. The elephant trainers have asked for two dozen youngsters between five and ten years old. We will capture those this morning, for it will be the breeding herds that come up out of the valley first. Then later we will hunt for ivory. The scouts report many fine bulls scattered along the great river.'

The saucer which Lannon had selected was hemmed in with steep broken ground. It was circular in shape, perhaps 500 paces across. The elephant road came into it through a narrow rocky pass, crossed the saucer and climbed out of it up a steep pitch to the high ground above. The saucer was thickly wooded, and Lannon placed his war elephants in ambush, concealing them about the perimeter of the bowl in the good cover. The war elephants were forced to kneel for better concealment, and while they waited Huy and Lannon breakfasted on cold corn cakes, cheese and roast salt beef washed down with red wine. It was a hunter's meal, taken in cover with the mounting excitement of the chase sharpening their appetites, and as they ate they kept glancing up at the look-outs on the high ground above the saucer whose task it was to watch for and to signal the approach of the herds.

The dew was still on the grass when a figure waved frantically from the skyline above them, and Lannon grunted with satisfaction and wiped the grease from his fingers and lips.

'Come, my Sunbird,' he said, and they mounted the kneeling elephant once more.

It was a long wait that stretched and tightened their nerves, then suddenly little Xhai stirred expectantly beside Huy and his dark amber eyes snapped.

'They are here,' he whispered, and almost immediately a single wild elephant came out through the rocky portals of the pass and paused on the lip of the saucer. It was an old cow, grey and lean and tuskless. Suspiciously she looked about the saucer, lifting her trunk to sample the air and then blowing the sample into her mouth against the olfactory glands in her upper lip. The breeze was behind her, a soft dry movement of air that carried the smell of waiting men away from her, and she lowered her trunk and moved forward.

From the pass behind her poured an avalanche of great grey bodies.

'Breeding herd,' murmured Lannon, and Huy saw the calves at heel. They ranged in size from almost full grown to not much bigger than a large pig. The smaller they were the more noisy and mischievous, squealing and frolicking and chasing between the legs of their mothers. Huy smiled at the attempts of one to suckle from his moving mother, groping for the teats between her front legs with his miniature trunk until in exasperation the mother picked up a fallen branch and swatted him mercilessly across the rump. The calf squealed and fell in at her heels again, demure and chastened.

The saucer was full of wild elephants now, their grey humped backs showing above the thick bush as they streamed along the ancient road to safety.

Lannon leaned forward and touched the driver on the shoulder, and the war elephant rose beneath them, lifting them high so that they could look down from their castle upon the quarry. All around the saucer, the war elephants rose from cover with the armed men upon their backs. They closed in on the herd quietly, the squealing and uproar from the calves blanketing their approach until they were right in amongst the herd.

Lannon selected a young cow with a half-grown calf and leaning out from the castle he hurled his javelin into her neck, aiming for the great arteries there. The cow squealed in pain and alarm, and bright red arterial blood blew in a cloud from the tip of her trunk. She reeled backwards, mortally wounded, and from the other castles a torrent of missiles flew into the herd. Hundreds of huge bodies burst into flight and the forest shook and rang with their trumpeting and their frantic efforts at escape.

Despite his promise to the gods, Huy did not raise his bow, but watched in awful fascination the slaughter of the terrified beasts. He saw an old cow, bristling with arrows and javelins, charge one of the war elephants and knock it down on its knees; the men were hurled from the castle to fall beneath stampeding hoofs, and the old cow tottered away to fall and die, still in her battle rage. He saw a calf, hit in error, trying to tear the arrow from its own flank and squealing pitifully as the barbs clung stubbornly in the flesh. He saw another calf attempting vainly to rouse its dead mother, tugging at her with its little trunk.

Lannon was shouting with excitement, hurling his javelins into the neck and spine with that deadly accuracy that dropped the great grey bodies in profusion about them.

One of the herd mothers charged them from the side; a bad-tempered old queen as big and as strong as their mount, she bore down on them. Lannon swung to face her, braced himself and threw, but the old queen lifted her trunk and the javelin struck it squarely, biting deep into that pulpy sensitive member just below the level of her eyes. She squealed in agony but never faltered in her run, and regretfully Huy lifted his bow. He knew she would charge home, and that only death would stop her.

The old queen lifted her head and trunk high, bracing herself for the impact of her charge. Her mouth was wide open, with the pointed lower lip dangling, and Huy drew, and loosed his shaft into the back of her throat. All five feet of the arrow disappeared into her gaping mouth, and he knew the point had found the brain for she reeled back onto her haunches, shuddering and quivering, a strangled gurgling cry bubbling from her throat. The lids of her eyes twitched violently and she fell forward and was still.

They killed forty-one cows, thirty of them with calf. However, nine of the calves were adjudged by the trainers too young for survival as orphans and they were put down with a single merciful arrow. The others were cut out and rounded up by specially trained nursing cows and led away from the mountainous bleeding carcasses of their mothers. By noon the work was done, and the slaves could busy themselves in butchering the carcasses and carrying the meat away to the smoking racks. The saucer was a reeking charnel-house, and the vultures turned overhead in a dark cloud that almost obscured the sun.

Lannon ate the midday meal with his nobles and huntmasters. Fresh grilled elephant tripe seasoned with hot pepper sauce, broiled elephant heart stuffed with wild rice and olives, platters of golden corn cakes and the inevitable earthen amphorae of Zeng wine made it a meal fit for a hunter's appetite.

Lannon was in a high good humour, striding amongst his men, laughing and jesting with them, picking out one or another for a special commendation. He was still wrought up by the excitement of the chase, and when he paused beside Huy he meant to chaff him when he said:

'My poor Sunbird, you loosed but one arrow during the whole hunt.' And Huy was about to answer lightly that one arrow for one elephant was as good a score as any, when suddenly Zadal the huntmaster from the middle kingdom laughed.

'Was the bow too strong for you, Holiness, or the game too fierce?'

There was sudden and deathly silence on the entire group, and all their faces turned towards the lean dark man with the thin sneering mouth and bright acquisitive eyes.

It took a few seconds of the silence for Zadal to realize what he had said, then he glanced quickly about the circle of watching faces. With a small chill he saw they were looking at him with the same detached curious expression that men looked upon those doomed to sacrifice. Beside him a noble said softly but matter-of-factly, 'You are a dead man.'

Swiftly, with real alarm, Zadal looked back at Huy Ben-Amon. Too late he recalled the reputation of this priest. It was said that no man still lived who had sneered at his back or his height or his courage. With relief he saw that the priest was smiling slightly, and delicately wiping his fingers on the hem of his tunic.

'Thank you, great Baal,' Huy prayed silently, smiling a little. 'It was right that you remind me of my promise. I held back from the hunt. Forgive me, great Baal. I will give you your chance now.'

Zadal's relief was short-lived for when Huy looked directly at him he saw the smile was on the priest's lips only. His eyes were bright and black and cold.

'Zadal,' Huy said softly, and the crowd pressed closer to hear his words. 'Will you fly with me on the wings of the storm?'

They stirred at the challenge, a quick buzz of comment

and they watched Zadal's face. It had paled to a dirty yellow, and his lips compressed into a thin white line.

'I forbid it,' said Lannon loudly. 'I will not let you do this, Huy. You are too valuable to me to waste your life in—'

Huy interrupted him quietly, 'Majesty, it is a matter of honour. This one called me coward.'

'But no man has hunted in that manner for fifty years,' Lannon protested.

'Fifty years is too long,' Huy smiled, 'is it not, Zadal? You and I will revive the custom.'

Zadal stared at him, hating his own unruly tongue.

Huy still smiled at him. 'Or is it that the game is too fierce for you?' he asked softly. For long moments it seemed that Zadal might refuse, then he nodded curtly, his lips still white.

'As you wish, Holiness.' And he knew they were right, he was a dead man.

In two large baskets, slaves had collected from one of the elephant carcasses the contents of the lower intestines. As Huy and Zadal, stripped naked, smeared their bodies with the yellow dung he overheard young Bakmor discussing the hunt with Mursil.

'I do not believe it is possible to kill a full-grown bull elephant with a battle-axe. It sounds to me like an unpleasant form of suicide.'

'That's why they call it flying on the wings of the storm.'

The elephant dung had a rank odour, strong enough to mask the man smell. It was the one protection the hunters would have. Their one chance of getting into close contact with the great beasts without being discovered. The sharp sense of smell of the elephant is its main defence, for its vision is weak and near-sighted.

Timon came over from the king's entourage and assisted Huy, spreading the dung across his back. Quickly Timon had understood the method that they would use.

'High-born, I fear for you,' he said softly.

'I fear for myself,' Huy admitted. 'Spread the dung thickly, Timon. I would prefer to stink, rather than die.'

Huy looked down the steep slope which stretched down into the valley from the saucer. The elephant road zig-zagged up through the sparse forest. They would intercept the next herd here, before it was alarmed by the smell of blood in the saucer.

Huy glanced around him and saw that the huntsmen had spread out along the ridge, selecting vantage points from which to view the sport. His eyes met those of Zadal. The huntmaster was daubed with the yellow filth from his head to his feet, and he gripped the handle of his axe too hard. There was fear in those dark eyes, and fear in the taut manner in which he held himself. Huy smiled at him, enjoying his discomfort, and Zadal looked away. His lips quivered.

'Are you ready, huntmaster?' Huy asked, and Zadal nodded. He could not trust his voice.

'Come,' said Huy, and started down the slope, but Lannon stepped into his path. There was a foreboding in his eyes, and his smile was uncovincing.

'That fool Zadal spoke in haste and without meaning it. No man here doubts your courage, Huy, except you yourself. Do not seek to prove it too convincingly. Life will hold little for me without my Sunbird.'

'My lord,' Huy's voice was hoarse. He was touched to the heart by Lannon's concern.

'The first cut is the dangerous one, Huy. Be careful that when he drops, he does not fall upon you.'

'I will remember.'

'Remember also to bathe before you dine with me this evening.' Lannon smiled and stepped aside.

Twice during the afternoon small herds of elephant passed them, moving swiftly up the slope amongst the trees. Each time Huy shook his head at Zadal and let them pass for they were cows and calves and immature bulls.

The day drew towards its close, and Huy felt an uneasy sense of relief. Perhaps the gods had decided in his favour and would not seek to put him to the test.

There was an hour of light left now. Huy and Zadal sat quietly beside the path, hidden by a screen of monkey apple vines that hung from one of the trees.

The dung had dried upon their bodies, making Huy's skin feel stiff and uncomfortable. He sat with the vulture axe across his lap and watched the path, hoping that nothing would come up it before darkness and he could abandon this mad adventure to which he was committed by honour and hasty choice. It was strange how inactivity dulled even the brightest passion, Huy thought, and grinned wryly as he fondled the handle of the axe.

He saw movement far down the slope, a grey drifting movement like smoke amongst the trees and he felt his skin prickle. Zadal had seen it also, he stopped his restless fidgeting and sat woodenly beside Huy.

They waited, and suddenly two elephants came out of the trees. Two big old bulls, with heavy ivory, stepping lightly up the slope. They were a hundred paces apart, spaced out on the path and there was an alertness and a sense of purpose in their tread that warned Huy they had been freshly disturbed, possibly wounded, by the huntsmen down in the valley.

'We will take these two,' Huy whispered. 'Choose one.'

Zadal was silent a moment, watching the two bulls with an experienced eye. The leading bull was older, and his one tusk was broken off at the lip. He was leaner and rangier-looking than his companion, and his leading position showed he was the more experienced, the more alert, and the broken tusk would make him meaner and his temper more uncertain.

'The second one,' Zadal whispered, and Huy nodded. He had expected it.

'I will move back now. We must try to attack at the same moment.' He left the cover of the hanging vines, and slipped back along the path opening a gap between him and Zadal approximately equal to that between the bulls.

Huy dropped into a patch of coarse grass beside the trail, and looked back. The elephants were striding steadily up towards them. The leading bull passed Zadal's hiding-place, and came on. Huy saw that the gap between the two bulls had closed. Zadal's elephant would reach him before Huy's came level with the clump of grass where he lay.

If one of the hunters launched his attack prematurely the other bull would be alerted, and the danger multiplied many times. Huy knew he could not rely on consideration from Zadal. The man would think only of his own best interests.

As the thought came to him he saw Zadal leave the shelter of the vines, and run silently out into the path behind the second bull. Huy's elephant was still fifty paces from where he lay, and it was facing him.

Zadal was following his elephant, running close upon its heels. Huy felt a moment's admiration for him. Perhaps he had misjudged him. Perhaps Zadal would follow the second bull and wait for Huy to get into position.

Then Huy saw the huntmaster's axe go up and glint at the top of its swing; as it flashed down, Huy transferred all his attention to the leading bull.

There was a squeal of pain and alarm as Zadal's axe struck, and Huy's bull burst into a full run. Sweeping down on him until it seemed to fill the whole field of Huy's vision, an animal as large as the very earth it sprang from.

As Huy rose from his hide he knew he had a few fleeting seconds in which to strike. Then the bull would be gone.

He went bounding along beside the bull, keeping uphill of him for when he fell he would roll down the slope. The pace stretched Huy's long legs to the full, and he was losing ground swiftly, falling back to the bull's hindquarters.

With every pace, as the huge weight of the grey body fell on the hind legs, so the hamstring tendons running down the back of the leg from knee to heel tightened under the coarse eroded skin. The tendon was a thick cord that flexed and bulged, thick as a girl's wrist; it carried the whole weight of the bull at each stride.

Huy swerved in his run, crossing behind the bull and as the tendon in the nearest leg tightened he slashed the blade of the vulture axe across it, severing it cleanly so that the sound of it was a sharp snapping, like the sheet of a sail parting in a gale.

The bull lunged off balance as the leg collapsed under him, he teetered wildly on the edge of the path, his weight held only on the good leg.

'For Baal!' Huy shouted with excitement and the axe went high as he swung. The second tendon parted as sharply, and the huge grey beast dropped heavily. The sound of its fall carried clearly to the watchers on the ridge, and a cloud of dust boiled up from the dry earth. Huy had danced back from under the rolling body and that terrible flailing trunk.

He steeled himself for the final act, as he danced about the rearing floundering animal, knowing he had only seconds to exploit his surprise, seconds before the maimed animal braced itself and saw him, and he searched for his opening desperately.

The bull reared up on its front legs, dragging its crippled hind legs behind it. In its unreasoning rage it was tearing at the trees, and slashing its terrible trunk in wild circles, gouging the earth with its single tusk.

But its back was turned to Huy, it had not recognized its attacker yet. Lightly Huy ran in, ducking under the flailing trunk. He vaulted up on the bull's wide back, landing on his knees with the axe high above his head.

The knotted spine stood out clearly through the wrinkled dry skin, great knuckles of bone braced for the blade. Huy struck, the killing stroke that crashed through the bone, and severed the soft yellow core of the spinal tissue. The bull shrieked, and collapsed, kicking and shaking spasmodically in its death throes.

Huy jumped down from its pulsating body and danced back out of danger from the legs and trunk of the dying beast. He felt a soaring sense of triumph and relief. It was done, he had flown upon the wings of the storm – and lived through it.

He heard the wild shrill trumpeting of the other bull, and he spun around. One glance showed him that the task was not yet completed, the gods were not finished with him.

Zadal had blundered. His second cut had missed the tendon and the bull was on three legs, but moving with agility and speed as it hunted the man. Zadal had thrown his axe aside, and was running, dodging up the slope with the bull close upon him. The bull was shrieking with rage, its trunk out-stretched, gaining swiftly on the fleeing man.

As Huy started forward it caught him. It wrapped its trunk around Zadal's body and flung him high in the air, above the tops of the tallest trees, and his body spun loosely in the air.

He fell face down on the rocky earth, and the bull placed one foot in the small of his back while with its trunk it plucked his head from his body, the way a farmer kills a chicken, and it tossed the head aside. It bounced and rolled down the slope like a child's ball.

Huy ran towards the bull, scrambling up the slope. The bull knelt on the mangled corpse and drove one tusk through Zadal's chest. It was so preoccupied with the mutilation of Zadal's body that Huy came up easily behind it.

He saw the deep gash in the back of the bull's knee

where Zadal's stroke had failed to find the tendon, and the vulture axe moaned softly in flight. This time there was no mistake.

'I give you a new title.' Lannon lifted his wine bowl, and silence fell expectantly on the nobles and knights who sat about his board. 'I give a battle honour for the man who has flown on the wings of the storm.'

Huy dropped his eyes modestly, blushing a little in the torch light under the leather awning of Lannon's campaign tent.

'Huy Ben-Amon – Axeman of the Gods!' Lannon shouted the title, and the nobles echoed it, saluting Huy with clenched fists.

'Drink, Huy! Drink, my Sunbird!' Lannon offered Huy his own wine bowl. Huy sipped the wine, smiling around at the company. Tonight he would not look too deeply in the wine bowl. He did not want to cloud or befuddle this sense of joy. The gods had answered him, and he sat quietly smiling in the midst of noisy revelry, hardly hearing the laughter and the banter, listening instead to the voice deep inside him which sang, 'Tanith! Tanith!'

When he rose to leave, Lannon was outraged, dragging him down into his seat by the hem of his tunic.

'You'll not leave here on your feet, Axeman. You deserve to be carried to your couch this night! Come, I challenge you to a bout with the wine cups.'

Huy shrugged aside the challenge, laughing and shaking his head.

'One challenge a day, my lord, I beg of you.'

Outside the night was still, and the sky was brilliant with the stars. The heat of the day was cooling, and the feel of the night wind in his face was like the caress of Tanith's silky tresses against his cheek.

'Astarte!' The goddess rose out of the valley, the golden disc of her countenance lighting the land with a soft radiance. 'Mother of earth. I thank you,' Huy whispered, and felt the tears of happiness flood his eyes.

He moved on through the camp towards his own tent, hugging the warmth of his love secretly to him.

'Tanith,' he whispered, 'Tanith.'

He moved on through the shadows until movement caught his attention, and he stopped. Beside one of the cooking fires crouched a figure, a slave woman working on the grinding stone, crushing corn for cakes.

The firelight caught her handsome features, and shone on the dark skin of her strong arms. It was the nurse Sellene.

Huy was about to move on, when the slave girl looked up expectantly. A man came towards her out of the darkness, and the girl's face lit with such a look of adoration, such unashamed love, that Huy felt his heart go out to her.

The man stepped into the firelight, and it needed only one glance at the powerful body and rounded bald head for Huy to recognize Timon.

Sellene stood up and went quickly to meet Timon, and they embraced. They sniffed at each other's faces in the strange love greeting of the pagans, holding each other closely. Huy smiled tenderly, feeling the warm sympathy of the lover for all other lovers.

Timon drew back from the girl, holding her at arm's length and he spoke softly. Huy could not catch the words. He heard only the soft rumble of Timon's voice, and the girl nodded quickly.

Timon left her and disappeared amongst the tents. Sellene went to the grinding stone and filled a leather bag with ground corn, then she glanced about furtively and followed Timon into the darkness. Huy watched her go, and smiled.

'I must talk to Lannon,' he thought. 'I could arrange a pairing between those two.'

In his own tent Huy took the golden scroll and spread it upon his writing pallet. He adjusted the lamp wicks, picked up his engraving tool, and began to write the poem to Tanith.

'Her hair is dark and soft as the smoke from the papyrus fires upon the great lake,' he wrote, and the incident between Timon and Sellene was forgotten.

Exhaustion overcame him a little after midnight, and he fell forward across his writing pallet and he slept with one cheek pressed to the love poem to Tanith on the golden scroll. The lamp flames smoked and faded and died.

Rough hands shook him awake in the dawn, and he looked up groggily. It was Mursil, the huntmaster.

'The Gry-Lion sends for you, Holiness. The hounds are in leash, and the slave-masters assembled. Two of the king's slaves have run, and the king bids you join the chase.'

Even in his half-wakening state, Huy knew who the running slaves were, and he felt the sick sliding of his guts.

'The fools,' he whispered. 'Oh, the stupid fools.' Then he looked at Mursil. 'No,' he said. 'I cannot – I will not go with them. I am sick, tell him I am sick.'

Sellene stood in the shadows and listened to the drunken bellowing and laughter from the king's tent. Beneath the short cloak was concealed the leather grain-bag, a bundle of smoked meat dried into hard black sticks, and a small earthen cooking pot. There was food for two of them for four days, and by then they would be across the great river. She was fearful, and elated at the same time. They had planned this moment for two years, and many emotions played behind her round impassive face as she waited.

Timon came at last; quietly he appeared beside her with such suddenness that she gasped with fright. He took her hand, and led her away towards the perimeter of the camp. She saw that he wore a cloak also, and that a bow and quiver stood behind his shoulder and a short iron sword was belted at his waist. These were weapons forbidden to a slave, and death was the penalty for carrying them.

There were two guards at the gate of the stockade, and while Sellene spoke with them, offering favours, Timon came from the darkness behind them. He broke their necks with his bare hands. Taking one in each hand and shaking them the way a dog will shake a rat. There was no outcry, and Timon laid the bodies gently beside the stockade gate and they went through.

They passed through the saucer where the elephant had been butchered, and the night was hideous with the snarling and yammering of the scavengers. Hyena and jackal fought over the bloody scraps and bone chips. With the sword bared in one hand Timon led Sellene through, and though the slinking hump-shouldered hyena followed them, moaning and sniggering, they reached the pass and started down the elephant road into the valley. The moon gave them good light, and they moved fast. They stopped only once at the ford of the stream to rest and drink a little water, then they hurried on towards the north.

Once they came upon a lion in the path. A big male whose body was ghostly grey in the moonlight, with a dark ruff of mane. They stared at each other for long seconds before the lion grunted softly and leapt into the undergrowth beside the path. He had fed recently, and the two human shapes did not interest him.

The moon, four days past full, wheeled across the star-furry sky and sank towards the dark horizon. When it set, there was only the indistinct glow of the stars to light their way, and at a steep and broken place in the path Sellene fell heavily.

Timon heard her cry out and he turned back quickly. She was lying on her side, making a soft moaning sound.

'Are you hurt?' he asked as he dropped to his knees beside her.

'My ankle,' she whispered, agony making her voice husky and Timon groped down her leg. Already the ankle was hot to the touch, and as he held it he could feel it swelling, blowing up into a hard hot ball.

With the sword Timon cut strips from his cloak, and he bound the ankle tightly as Huy had taught him. He worked with frantic haste, and the worms of dread were already gnawing his guts.

When he lifted Sellene to her feet, she cried out as her weight came on the injured foot.

'Can you walk on it?' Timon asked, and she tried a few painful hobbling steps. She was panting with pain and her breathing whistled in her throat. She clung to Timon and shook her head hopelessly.

'I cannot go on. Leave me here.' Timon lowered her to the ground, and then straightened up as he discarded his weapons and her provisions. He kept only the short sword. He folded and knotted the two leather cloaks into a sling seat for Sellene, and placed it about her body. Then he looped the end over his neck and shoulder and lifted her. She was in his arms, with her own clasped about his shoulders. Half of her weight was taken by the sling, hanging about Timon's neck. He started forward, striding out down the steep path towards the valley floor.

By mid-morning the sling had rubbed the skin from his neck, a weeping pink graze through the dark skin. The heat was strong now, that heavy oppressive heat of the valley floor sucking away the last of his energy. The spring had long gone from Timon's step, and he reeled forward with spirit outlasting his physical strength.

On the edge of one of the glades of open grass, Timon stopped and leaned against the trunk of a mhoba-hoba tree. He was afraid to lower the girl's body to the ground lest he could not find the strength to lift it again. His lips were white and rimmed with dried spittle, and his eyes were laced with red veins. His chest heaved and shook with his breathing.

'Leave me, Timon,' Sellene whispered. 'This way both of us will die.'

Timon did not answer, but gestured her to silence with an impatient inclination of his head. He held his breath and listened. She heard it also then, the faint and distant baying of the hound pack.

He said, 'It is too late for that.' And he looked about quickly for a place to stand. They could not hope to outrun the dogs.

'You can still escape,' she urged him. 'The river is not far.'

'Without you there is no escape,' he said, and she clung to him as he carried her across the glade to a place where the mother rock outcropped. A jumble of fragmented granite like the ruins of an ancient castle.

He laid her gently amongst the rocks, with her back against one of the slabs. He folded her cloak and placed it as a pillow for her head, then he squatted beside her and caressed her face and neck with a surprisingly gentle touch for so big a man.

'They will kill us,' Sellene said. 'They always kill those who run.'

Timon did not answer, but his fingers stroked her cheek lightly.

'They kill in the worst way,' Sellene said, turning her head to look at him. 'Would it not be better if we died now, before the dogs come?' But he did not answer, and after a while she went on.

'You have a sword, Timon. Will you not use it?'

'If the little priest is with them, then we have a chance. He has power over the king – and there is a thing between him and me. There is a bond. He will save us.'

The dogs were closer now and it seemed that their baying had become more urgent as the scent ran hotter. Timon stood up and unsheathed the sword. He went out amongst the rocks and looked back towards the escarpment. Half a mile back the pack streamed from the forest into the glade. There were thirty of the tall sinewy hounds, long-legged and with rough ginger-brown coats and the heads and fangs of wolves. They were bred to chase and drag down the quarry.

Timon felt his skin tighten and prickle as he watched them string out across the glade towards him. Behind them, running on the heels of the pack were the handlers, with their distinctive green tunics and the dog-whips over their shoulders.

Beyond them again came the war elephants, five of them with the knights and slave-masters in their castles. The elephants followed the pack easily, in that ambling gait which could cover fifty miles a day.

Timon shaded his eyes and tried to pick out the distinctive figure of the priest amongst the men in the castles. They were too far off still, but the hounds were closing swiftly.

He wrapped his cloak carefully about his left forearm, and settled his grip on the sword. Swinging the weapon in a short arc to stretch his muscles.

The leading hounds saw him amongst the rocks, and immediately the deep regular baying changed to an excited yammering. Their ears flattened as they ran, and long pink tongues flopped over white fangs in the wolf jaws, and they fanned out across his front.

Timon stepped back into the opening where Sellene lay, guarding her from the vicious clamouring rush of brown bodies.

The first hound rushed in at him, with its jaws snapping, and it leapt at his face.

Timon took him on the point, in the base of his throat, killing the dog instantly, but before he could clear his blade another had sprung at him. He thrust his cloaked arm into its jaws, and hacked at a third hound.

They swarmed over him as he stabbed and hacked and thrust. He swung the hound that hung on his arm against the rock beside him, crushing in its ribs, but another had locked its fangs in his calf and was tugging him cruelly off balance. He drove the point into its shaggy back and the hound shrieked and released him.

Another went for his face and he struck at its head with the sword hilt. A great furry body smashed into his chest, a fang ripped his shoulder muscles.

There were too many of them, overwhelming him, ripping and tearing at him, smothering him with their weight and strength. He went down on his knees, holding a frothing slavering animal away from his throat and face with one hand, strangling it – but he felt other teeth slashing at his back and belly and thighs.

Then abruptly the dog-handlers were there, whipping the pack away from him, shouting to the animals by name, dragging them back and leashing them in the strangling collars.

Slowly Timon pulled himself up on to his feet. He had lost his sword, and blood streamed down his shining black body from the deep cuts and lacerations that covered him.

He looked up at the war elephant which towered over him. His last hope faded as he saw that Huy Ben-Amon was not amongst the hunters – and that Lannon Hycanus, the Gry-Lion of Opet was laughing.

'A good run, slave, Lannon laughed. 'I thought that you might reach the river.' He looked beyond Timon to where Sellene lay. 'My huntmasters were correct then. They judged by the sign that the woman had damaged her leg and that you were carrying her. A noble gesture, slave, most unusual for a pagan. All the same it will cost you dear.' Lannon looked away to one of his slave-masters. 'There seems little to be gained by returning with them. Execute them here.'

Timon looked up at the king and spoke in a strong clear voice.

'I am the living symbol of that love,' he said, and Lannon's head jerked around as he remembered the words. With the laughter gone from his lips he stared at the bleeding slave king, meeting those smoky yellow eyes. For long seconds, Timon's life teetered on the verge of extinction, then suddenly Lannon's eyes dropped away from those of Timon.

'Very well,' he nodded. 'You remind me of my duty to a friend. I will honour it, but I swear you will live to curse the moment you spoke those words. You will live – but in life you will long for the sweetness of death.' Lannon's face was a mask of cold anger, as he turned back to his slave-masters. 'This man will not be executed, but he is declared "incorrigible" and he will be chained with a weight of two talents.' Almost a hundred pounds' weight of chains to be carried night and day, waking and sleeping. 'Send him to the mines at Hulya, tell the overseer there that he is to be used at the deep levels.'

Lannon watched Timon's face as he went on. 'The woman cannot claim my protection, but we will take her back with us, none the less. Let her be chained to the castle of one of the war elephants and marched.'

For the first time Timon showed emotion. He stepped forward and in appeal lifted one badly savaged arm from which the dark tattered flesh hung.

'My lord, the woman is hurt. She cannot walk.'

'She will walk,' said Lannon. 'Or she will be dragged. You will ride upon the elephant and encourage her. You will have time to decide if the swift death I offered you would not have been preferable to the life you have chosen.'

They chained Sellene at the wrists with a light marching chain twenty paces long. The other end of the chain was shackled to the rear wall of the elephant castle.

Timon, wearing his massive chains at neck and ankles, was seated in the castle. He was made to face backwards to where Sellene stood swaying slightly on one leg, favouring her grotesquely swollen ankle. Her face was greyish with pain, but she tried to smile up at Timon.

The first jerk of the chain as the elephant started forward pulled her face downwards on the hard earth, with its sharp shales and harsh clumps of razor grass. She was dragged fifty paces before she managed to roll onto her feet again and hop and stumble after the striding elephant. Her knees and elbows were raw, and there were scratches across her belly and breasts.

She fell and regained her feet a dozen times, each time her body was more battered and torn. She went down for the last time a little before sunset.

As Timon sat in the castle, draped in his chains, he swore an oath. In his anger and grief and pain he swore an oath of vengeance, watching Sellene's lifeless body bounce and slide over the rough places, leaving a damp brown smear across the dry red African earth. Then Timon wept, for the last time in his life he succumbed to tears. They ran down his face and dripped from his chin to mingle with the blood and dust that caked his body.

Huy filled a wine bowl from one of his choice amphorae, one that he had set aside for a rare occasion. He was humming softly to himself, and there was a small smile which came and went upon his lips and made his dark eyes sparkle.

He had returned to Opet in the middle of the night, slept five hours and now, bathed and dressed in his best linen, he had sent a slave to summon the oracle of Opet to meet with him. All the blood and passion of these last weeks upon the escarpment of the great river were forgotten now in his anticipation of his reunion with Tanith. Forgotten were the memories of Sellene's mutilated corpse dragged into camp behind the war elephant, the tall figure of Timon bowed beneath his chains and grief, led away by the slave-masters, those terrible accusing eyes turned towards Huy, the manacled wrists lifted in a gesture of menace or of appeal – Huy could not guess which. Then the slave-master's whip hissing and snapping across the purple black shoulders, lifting a welt as thick as a finger without cutting the skin. For the first time since it had happened Huy was free of it, his whole being taken up with the joy of his love.

Pursing his lips thoughtfully he let four drops of the clear liquid drip from the blue glass vial into the wine. He stoppered the bottle and stirred the wine with his forefinger, sucking his finger thoughtfully and wrinkling his nose at the faint musty taste of the opiate. He added a little wild honey to mask it, tasted again and at last satisfied he set the bowl on one of the wooden stools beside the pile of cushions. There was a dish of cakes and sweetmeats there already. Huy covered the wine bowl with a silken cloth, then surveyed his preparations with pleasure. He picked up his lute and climbed the staircase to the parapet of the roof and seated himself. He tuned the instrument and strummed upon it, loosening his voice and fingers, watching the narrow lane that led up to the front gate.

In the bright morning sunlight the lake waters were a cheery blue, only slightly darker than the sky. The breeze had flecked the surface with little floppy waves, and one of Habbakuk Lal's galleys had shipped her oars and was running in towards the harbour under a big lateen sail. The sea birds followed her, planing and soaring across her stern.

High above the lake the midday clouds were building tall, frothy thunder-heads. There would be rain before sunset, Huy thought, feeling the thunder in the air, in the touch of his garments upon his skin and the curl of his beard.

His breath caught, and the music died under his fingers as two figures turned into the lane and came up towards the gate. They wore the coarse brown-hooded robes that the priestesses of Astarte affected while travelling abroad. However, the bulky garment could not disguise the quick step and youthful carriage of the taller figure that hurried ahead, nor the age and aggravation of the bent figure that hobbled after her. The ancient voice, breathless and high, called with exasperation:

'My lady, slower! I pray you.' And Huy grinned. A slave opened the gate, and as they crossed the courtyard Huy struck a single authoritative note on the lute, and Tanith stopped dead. The old chaperone, unhearing, moved on into the house mumbling and muttering while Tanith looked up at Huy upon the parapet of the roof.

He began to sing, and the girl below him lifted the hood from her face and let it fall back on her shoulders. She shook her hair loose, watching his face with large green eyes and her expression was rapt and solemn. He sang the song he had written in the wilderness, the song to Tanith inscribed in the golden book, and as he let the last sweet note fall on the bright morning, Tanith's cheeks were flushed and her lips trembled.

Huy went down the staircase and stood close to her, without touching her.

'You are my soul,' he said gently, and she swayed towards him as if drawn by a force beyond her control.

'My lord, I cannot trust myself to be with you where other eyes may see us. I fear I shall betray my love to the blindest of them. Be strong for me.'

Huy touched her elbow, guiding her towards the house. As they passed through into the main room, Tanith stumbled slightly, for a moment pressed against him.

'Oh! I cannot bear it,' she said, and Huy's voice shook as he answered.

'In a while, my love. In a very short while.'

The old priestess was seated on the cushions already, mouthing a cake with bald gums, dropping crumbs and spittle down her robe and mumbling bitterly about her pains and aches.

Huy moved around behind her, and picked up the prepared wine bowl in both hands. Secure in the old priestess's deafness he asked Tanith, 'Is she strong?'

'As strong as most men,' Tanith smiled. 'Though she'll not admit it.'

'She does not complain of chest pains or shortness of breath?'

'Never.' Tanith was intrigued. 'Why do you ask?'

'I have placed star-drops in her wine,' Huy explained. 'But I do not want her sleep to be eternal.'

Tanith's smile flamed, lighting the green depths of her eyes and sparkling on her teeth. 'Oh, Holy Father, how clever of you.' She clapped her hands, a childlike gesture that never failed to touch Huy to the core of his being.

'How many drops?' Tanith demanded.

'Four,' Huy admitted.

'Perhaps a few more would not hurt her,' Tanith said. 'I have not seen you in many weeks, Holiness. There is much to discuss.'

During this exchange the old priestess had been nodding

and grimacing intelligently, quite as though she had understood every word. Huy studied her a moment, then firmly thrust aside the temptation.

'No,' he said. 'Four is sufficient.' And he came around in front of the priestess. The wrinkled monkey-like face split into a huge toothless grin and she reached for the bowl with a pair of bony claws, on which the old-age blotches and blue veins stood out clearly.

'You have a kind heart, Holiness,' she keened.

They seated themselves in front of her, and while they talked they watched her anxiously. The crone was drawing out her pleasure, sipping the wine and rolling it noisily around her mouth before swallowing and smacking her gums.

'Since we have been apart, I have thought much upon what has happened between us,' Huy admitted, without looking at Tanith.

'I have thought of nothing else.'

'As a man whose life is devoted to the service of the gods, I was greatly troubled that we had sinned against them,' Huy told her.

'There can be no sin in something which gives so much pleasure and happiness.'

'I asked the gods to set a test for me, a trial of my sins.' Huy had still not looked at her, but Tanith glanced at him sharply and her voice snapped.

'You did not indulge in foolish risk, did you?'

'The trial was a fair one – the gods were not cheated.' Huy wanted her to understand, and she understood too well.

'I forbid you to do these stupid male things. I shiver to think of what madness you committed out there in the wilderness.' She was angry now.

'It was necessary. They must have the opportunity to express their wrath.'

'They could as readily express their wrath with a

lightning bolt or a falling tree! I will not have you provoking them to destroy you.'

'Tanith, please let me—'

'I can see, my lord, that you will require stricter supervision in the future. I want a lover not a hero.'

'But, Tanith, the gods' answer was favourable. Don't you see, now we need feel no guilt.'

'I never felt guilt, then or now. But, Holiness, I will feel wrath beside which that of the gods will pale if again you risk your life needlessly.'

Huy turned to her, and shook his head with mock sorrow.

'Oh Tanith, what would I ever do without you?' And her stern expression softened.

'My lord, that question will never arise.' And at that moment the empty wine bowl slipped from the old priestess's fingers and spun on one end across the mud floor. Its circles narrowed, until it settled into silence and the priestess let out a long contented snore and bowed forward. Huy caught her and eased her backwards onto the cushions. He laid her out comfortably, and arranged her robe modestly about her. She was smiling and burbling and whistling in her sleep.

Huy straightened up and Tanith stood close beside him. They turned to each other and embraced, coming together slowly and carefully. Her lips had a glossy feeling, cool and firm. Her soft hair brushed his cheeks, and her body pressed boldly against his.

'Tanith,' he whispered. 'Oh Tanith, there is so much I want to tell you.'

'My lord, your voice is the most beautiful I have ever heard. Your wisdom and wit are celebrated throughout the four kingdoms – but please do not talk now.'

Tanith pulled gently out of his embrace, took his hand and led him softly from the room.

Over the months that followed, Tanith's chaperone developed a peculiar taste for Huy's wine. At the temple feasts she was wont to disparage the quality of the wine served by the Reverend Mother, comparing it most unfavourably against the other, and she would always end with a word of praise for the Holy Father himself.

'A dear, dear man,' she would tell her audience. 'None of the nonsense you find with some of the others. Did I ever tell you about Rastafa Ben-Amon, the Holy Father in the reign of the forty-fourth Gry-Lion when I was a novice. Now there was a one!' Her old eyes went a little misty, and she drooled a thread of saliva.

'Drink!' she said with outraged virtue. 'Fight! And other things.' Then she nodded sagely. 'A terrible, terrible man!' And she grinned fondly at her ancient memories.

From the leather pipe, with its pitch-sealed joints, feeble gusts of air puffed like the dying breaths of a dinosaur. Driven by the great bellows at the surface, the circulation of fresh air had lost most of its force here, seventy feet below.

Timon leaned against the sweating rock surface, pressing his face to the hose outlet, gasping at that scanty trickle of air in the hellish heat and sulphurous atmosphere of the underground workings. He was lean, every rib showed clearly through the black skin, each sinewy muscle was outlined. His head was skull-like, with gaunt cheek-bones and deep eye-sockets in which the smouldering fires of his indomitable spirit still burned.

All fat and spare flesh had been burned off him by the ceaseless toil and the heat. Even now a sheen of moisture squeezed from the pores of his skin, highlighting the scars which criss-crossed his back and curled around his rib-cage – scars that patterned his arms and legs, scars long healed into thick ridges and shiny grooves, scars fresh and pink, scars still thick-scabbed and oozing. The chain shackles hung loosely at his neck and wrists and ankles. They had rubbed coarse calloused circles around his neck and limbs, slave marks that he would carry to his grave.

He sucked in the air, his chest pumping, swelling and subsiding, the ribs beneath the skin fanning open and closing. Around him the smoke swirled, dimming the lamp flames. The heat was a violent shimmering thing, and the rock at the face glowed still, although the fires had burned to thick beds of ash.

For five days now they had been attempting to break up this intrusion of hard green serpentine rock which was obscuring the gold reef. Sixteen men had died in the attempt, suffocated by the steam and smoke, struck down by flying shards of exploding rock or merely overcome by the heat to fall swooning onto the glowing floor and to sizzle while their flesh stuck to the hot rock and came away in stinking slabs from the bone.

From the shaft above him, dangling on a plaited reed rope, one of the water bladders was lowered to him. Made from the whole skin of an ox, carefully stitched and with the joints waterproofed with pitch the bladder contained forty gallons of liquid, a mixture of sour wine and water.

Timon doused his leather cloak in the filthy warm water of the wooden trough beside him, then one at a time he lifted his feet and dipped them into the trough, soaking his leather leggings and the sandals. The soles of the sandals were reinforced with five thicknesses of leather to withstand the heat of the rock floor. Timon threw the cloak across his shoulders, bound the linen cloth over his mouth and nose, took one last breath from the air pipe and held it. Then he ducked under the dangling water bladder and took the weight on his shoulders. Reaching up, he jerked loose the tail of the knot that held it, and, bowed under the weight of the liquid, he staggered up the tunnel.

As he approached the face, the wet soles of his sandals began spluttering and stinking. He could feel the heat through the thick leather. Heat from the rock walls hammered at him, a physical force against which he had to fight his way forward.

There was little time in which to work. Already his abused lungs were pumping painfully, but he dared not draw a breath of this poisonous smoke-laden air. The heat was scalding the exposed skin on his arms and face, his feet were agony as the rock burned away the protective soles.

Against the face of the drive, he eased the bladder from his shoulder. He moaned with the pain as his careless elbow touched the rock, searing away an inch of skin and leaving the pink raw flesh exposed.

He lowered the bladder to the floor, whirled and ran back through swirling fumes and heat down the tunnel with his chains jangling loosely under the cloak. This was the moment when men died, when the hot rock ate through the water bladder too swiftly, before the bearer was out of the danger area.

Behind Timon the bladder popped, forty gallons of liquid drenched the hot rock, the sudden contraction of the strata shattered the surface, the rock burst explosively and a sharp sliver of it hit Timon in the back of the head, a glancing razor touch that sliced down to the bone of his skull. He staggered, knowing that to fall on this burning floor was to die horribly. He kept his feet while with his senses reeling he reached the water trough and plunged his head quickly into the filthy scummy water. Then with dirty water and fresh blood streaming down his back, he clutched the air pipe with both hands and panted into it. He was coughing and retching and his eyes were blinded with the tears of pain.

It took him minutes to recover a little of his strength, and he staggered to the ladder that led to the level above. As he climbed, the next water bladder was being lowered, and he squeezed himself against the side of the narrow shaft to allow it past. He climbed fifty feet in darkness and then crawled over the edge into a dimly lit low-roofed cavern.

The slave-master saw him grovelling on the lip of the shaft.

'Why have you left your station?' And the long lash of the hippo-hide kiboko curled wickedly around Timon's ribs. He writhed at the sting of it.

'My head,' he gasped. 'I'm hurt.' And the slave-master stepped closer to him, stooping to examine the clotted cut in the back of Timon's scalp from which dark blood still welled. He grunted impatiently.

'Rest, then.' And turned to a row of ten squatting slaves. They were all incorrigibles, wearing the same heavy chains as Timon, and their bodies were also scarred and abused. The slave-master selected one of them, prodding him with the sharpened point of the whip.

'You next. Quickly now.' The slave stood, and shuffled to the mouth of the shaft, moving stiffly for the damp of the workings was in all their bones. At the edge of the shaft the slave paused and peered fearfully into that dreadful fuming pit.

'Move!' grunted the slave-master and the kiboko whistled and clapped against his flesh. He went down the ladder.

Timon dragged himself to the low bench against the wall. He sat with his elbows on his knees and his face in his hands. His lungs ached with the smoke and the cut in his scalp burned and stung. None of the other slaves looked at him. Each man was sunk in his own private hell, uncaring and silent. Beside Timon a man began to cough, a monotonous hacking sound, and a little bloody saliva wet his lips and glistened in the lamp light. He was dying of the lung sickness of the miners. The dust of powdered rock had filled his lungs, solidifying like concrete and turning his lungs to stone. None of them moved, none of them spoke.

The younger slave-master paced restlessly back and forth before them. He was a swarthy bearded man, part Yuye, a freed-man as like as not. He wore a linen tunic with light body armour, enough to turn a dagger's point, and an iron helmet to protect his skull from the rough roof of the tunnel. At his waist were belted a short iron sword and a slave club studded with iron nails. He was tall and hard-looking, with flat sinewy muscle in his arms and legs. A cruel man, selected to work with the incorrigibles because of his brutality. There were always two of them. The other slave-master was an older man with a frosting of grey in his beard and a pale sickly-looking face. But he was big in the shoulder, and dangerous, as cruel as the younger man and more experienced. From above, five bladders of liquid were lowered into the shaft, and five times a thick rush of steam swirled from the dark mouth as they were used to quench the heated rock.

'Enough!' the younger slave-master bellowed down, and the slave crawled up out of the pit and lay on the edge coughing and retching. He was filthy with ash and sweat and mud, and he vomited a little yellow bile into the mud.

'Take him away,' ordered the slave-master and two of them shambled forward and dragged him away to the bench.

The younger slave-master's eyes travelled along the row, and they stiffened into awareness, each trying to will the choice away from himself.

'You.' The sharp point of the whip dug spitefully into Timon's ribs. 'You did not finish your shift.'

There was no right of appeal, protest was folly, Timon had learned long ago. He stood up, and shuffled to the shaft. He steeled himself to the descent, but the delay was too long, and the hippo-hide whip seared its white flash of agony across the tenderness beneath his armpit.

It began as a reflex of pain, Timon lifted his arms to protect himself and the chains swung. In a sudden orgasm of anger and pain, Timon whirled the heavy links just as the slave-master swung the next whip stroke. The chain wrapped about the slave-master's forearm and the bone snapped with a sharp brittle sound.

He backed away with a startled cry, and his broken arm dangled loosely at his side. Behind him the older man drew his sword. It came out of the scabbard with a harsh rasp. He was fifty paces away down the tunnel.

Two of them now, for the younger man was groping left-handed for his sword. Somewhere beneath the slave dullness, the blankness of the slave animal mind, a spark burned. Huy Ben-Amon's training came back to Timon: of two enemies – separate them and attack the weaker first.

Flailing the chain Timon leapt at the younger slave-master, and the man went down in the mud.

Timon leapt over him, and caught the second man's sword stroke on the iron shackle at his wrist. The blow jarred him to the shoulder, and numbed his arm, but he ran in under the next stroke and threw a twist of the chain about the man's throat. He drew tight and held it.

The older man dropped his sword and clutched desperately at Timon's hands, at the links of iron that were strangling him.

Timon found that he was growling like a dog as he jerked and twisted the chain tighter. Suddenly the slave-master's hands dropped away, his tongue fell out between slack and swollen lips and there was the sharp acrid odour of faeces as his sphincter muscle relaxed. Timon let him down onto the floor, and picked up his sword from the mud.

He turned to the younger slave-master who had crawled

to his knees, still stunned. He had lost his helmet, and he was cradling his broken arm against his chest.

Timon stood over him and with the short sword chopped his skull open. The slave-master fell face downwards into the mud.

Timon stood back and looked about the drive quickly. From the first blow to the last only ten seconds had passed, and there had been no outcry.

Timon looked down at the sword in his hand, the blade was dulled with mud and blood, but he felt the despondency of abject slavery fall away. He felt the spark burst into flame, felt himself become a man again.

He looked at the other slaves sitting on the bench. Not one of them had moved. Their eyes were dull, incurious. They were not men. Timon felt a chill as he looked at them. He needed men. He must have men.

There was one of them. His name was Zama. A young man of Timon's age. A wild slave, taken beyond the river. He had not worn his chains for a year yet. Timon stared at him, and saw his eyes come into focus, saw his chin lift and the muscles in his jaw clench.

'Hammer!' Timon commanded. 'Bring a hammer!' Zama stirred. It was an effort of will for him to break the pattern of slavery.

'Hurry,' said Timon. 'There is little time.' Zama picked up one of the short-handled iron-headed mining adzes, and stood up from the bench.

Timon felt his heart soar within him. He had found a man. He held out his wrists, with the bloody sword in his hand.

'Strike off these chains,' he said.

Lannon Hycanus was pleased, but trying not to make it obvious. He stood by the window, and looked down towards the harbour where five galleys lay against the stone jetty. Lannon twisted a curl of his beard about one finger, and smiled secretly.

In the room behind him Rib-Addi was reading in his prim and precise voice, combing his fingers through his scraggily grey beard.

'Into Opet this day from the southern plains of grass, fifty-eight large tusks of ivory, in all sixty-nine talents.'

Lannon turned quickly, a scowl masking his pleasure.

'You attended the weighing?' he demanded.

'As always, my lord,' Rib-Addi assured him, and his clerks looked up from their writings, saw the Gry-Lion's expression soften and they grinned and bobbed their heads ingratiatingly.

'Ah!' Lannon grunted, and turned back to the window, while Rib-Addi resumed his reading. The voice was monotonous, and Lannon found his attention wandering although his subconscious was alert for a false note in the bookkeeper's voice. Rib-Addi had the habit of raising his voice slightly whenever he reached a portion of the accounting which might cause the Gry-Lion's displeasure – a lower return, an estimate unfulfilled – and immediately Lannon pounced on him. This convinced Rib-Addi that the Gry-Lion was a financial genius, and that he could hide nothing from him.

Lannon's mind drifted away, picking idly at stray thoughts, turning over mental stones to see what scurried out from under. He thought of Huy, and felt a cold breeze ruffle the surface of his contentment. There was a flaw in their friendship. Huy had changed towards Lannon, and he searched for the reason. He discarded the thought that it might be the aftermath of their long estrangement. It was something else. Huy was withdrawn, secretive. Seldom would he spend his nights in the palace, sharing the dice and wine and laughter with Lannon. Often when Lannon sent for him in the night, instead of Huy arriving with his lute slung on his shoulder and a new ballad to sing, the slave would return with a message that Huy was sick or sleeping or writing.

Lannon frowned now, and at that moment he heard the tell-tale rise in Rib-Addi's voice and he swung around and glared at them.

'What?' he bellowed, and their faces were yellow-white with fright. The clerks ducked their heads over their scrolls.

'My lord, there was a heavy fall of rock in the southern end of the mine,' Rib-Addi stuttered. It never ceased to amaze him that from a mass of figures Lannon would instantly pounce on a ten per cent decrease of output from one of the dozens of tiny mines of the middle kingdom.

'Who is the overseer?' Lannon demanded, and ordered the man replaced.

'It is carelessness, and I will not have it so,' Lannon told him. 'The yield is affected, valuable slaves wasted. I would rather spend more on shoring timber, it is cheaper so in the end.'

Rib-Addi dictated the order to one of the clerks, and Lannon turned back to the window and his thoughts of Huy. He remembered how it had been before, how Huy's presence had provided the zest that made each triumph more valuable, and each disappointment or disaster easier to surmount. All the good things happened when Huy was there.

In a rare moment of self-honesty Lannon realized that Huy Ben-Amon was the only human being that he could look upon as a friend.

His position had isolated him from all others. He could not approach them for the warmth and comfort that even a king needs. His wives, his children feared him. They were uneasy in his presence, and left it with obvious relief.

In all his kingdom there was only one person with the blend of courage, honesty, and disregard of consequence which allowed him to live in the king's presence without shrivelling.

'I need him,' Lannon thought. 'I need him much more than he needs me. Everybody loves him, but he is the only one who truly loves me.' And he grimaced as he remembered how Huy had defied him, and it was he, Lannon Hycanus the forty-seventh Gry-Lion of Opet, who had suffered most during the estrangement.

'I will not let him go again,' he vowed. 'I will not let him draw away from me like this.' And his self-honesty persisted. He saw that he was jealous of his priest. 'I will destroy anything which comes between us. I need him.'

He thought of this latest journey of Huy Ben-Amon's. Was it truly a matter of such urgency that the High Priest must travel 400 miles, taking with him two cohorts of his legion and the priestess and oracle of Opet, to consecrate some minor shrine to the goddess at a desolate garrison outpost in the northern kingdom? Lannon thought it more likely that Huy was leaving Opet for some devious reason of his own, and the result was that Lannon was bored, lonely and irritable. Huy knew that Lannon had planned a feast for his name-day.

The clash of urgent armoured feet interrupted Lannon's thoughts. He turned from the window as three of his high officers burst into the room. With them was a centurion in dusty cloak and unburnished armour. There was dust in his beard and dust coated his sandals and greaves. He had travelled fast.

'My lord. News of the worst possible kind.'

'What is it?'

'A slave rising.'

'Where?'

'At Hulya.'

'How many?'

'A great many. We are not sure. This man,' indicating the centurion, 'has seen it.'

Lannon turned to the weary officer. 'Speak!' he ordered.

'I was on patrol, Majesty. Fifty men on a sweep to the north. We saw the smoke, but by the time we returned to the mine it was finished. They had opened the compounds, slaughtered the garrison.' He paused, remembering the dead men with their bowels ripped open and the bloody mush of castration between their legs. 'They had gone, all except the sick and the lame. Those they left.'

'How many?'

'About 200.'

'What did you do with them?'

'We put them to the sword.'

'Good!' Lannon nodded. 'Continue.'

'We followed after the main party of slaves. There were more than 5,000 when they left Hulya, and they moved northwards.'

'Northwards,' Lannon growled. 'The river, of course.'

'They are moving slowly, very slowly. And they plunder and burn as they go. We could follow them by the smoke and the vultures. The population ahead of them flees, leaving all to them. They devour the land like locusts.'

'How many? How many?' Lannon demanded. 'We must know!'

'They have opened the compounds at Hulya, and Tuye and a dozen other mines – all the field slaves have flocked to join them,' the centurion answered.

One of the officers hazarded, 'There must be 30,000 of them, then?'

'At least, Majesty,' the centurion agreed.

'Thirty thousand, in Baal's holy name,' whispered Lannon. 'Such a multitude!' Then his anger came and he spoke harshly. 'What force have we to oppose their march? How many legions are mobilized?'

'There are two legions at Zeng,' an officer volunteered.

'We could not move them in time,' Lannon answered.

'One legion here at Opet.'

'Too far, too far,' Lannon growled.

'And two more along the south bank of the great river.'

'And they are scattered in garrisons spread over a distance of 500 miles. All the others are disbanded?' Lannon asked. 'How long to call them up?'

'Ten days.'

'Too long,' Lannon snapped. 'We must put down this rising with the uttermost ruthlessness. Rebellion is a plague, it spreads like fire in dry papyrus beds. We must isolate it, and quench it. Every spark of it. What other force have we?'

'There is His Holiness,' one of the officers murmured diffidently, and Lannon stared at him. He had forgotten Huy. 'He is at Sinal, directly in the slaves' lines of march to the north.'

'Huy!' said Lannon softly, and then was silent while his officers plunged into an animated discussion.

'He has only two cohorts with him – 1,200 men – he would not engage an army of 30,000.'

'No army, but a slave rabble.'

'Thirty thousand, none the less.'

'We cannot reinforce him in time.'

'It would be folly to try odds like that – and, my lord, Ben-Amon is no fool.'

'The nearest reserves are at Sett on the river.'

'Ben-Amon will not fight,' one of them declared, and they looked to Lannon for his opinion.

Lannon smiled. 'Content yourselves. Ben-Amen will fight. At a time and a place of his own choosing His Holiness will fight.' Then the smile was gone. 'I will march in four hours with all available troops to support Ben-Amon. Issue mobilization orders to all the disbanded legions, send runners to Zeng.'

'Will there be a battle?' Tanith asked. Her eyes sparkled green with anticipation, and her lips were parted expectantly. 'I mean, a real battle like the ones you sing about?'

Huy grunted without looking up from his writing pallet where he was formulating his orders to the garrison commander at Sett.

'Gather to you all troops within your sector and hold them within your walls. Account to me for your store of javelins, arrows and other weapons. What force of elephant do you command? Command the galleys of the river patrol to anchor beneath your walls and await my orders. Inform me of the level of the river. What fords are passable?

'I will join you within six days to assume command. It is my intention to dispute the enemies' passage of the river at—'

Tanith slipped off the couch and crossed the tent. She came up behind Huy and put a finger in his ear.

'My lord.'

'Please, Tanith. I am busy on affairs of moment. This is urgent.'

'No more urgent than a reply to my question – will there be a battle?'

'Yes,' Huy replied testily. 'Yes, there will.'

'Oh, good!' Tanith clapped her hands. 'I have never watched a real battle.'

'Nor will you now!' replied Huy grimly as he resumed his writing. 'You will leave tomorrow morning on a war elephant with an escort of fifty men. You are going home to Opet until this trouble is over.'

Tanith returned to the couch and plumped herself down upon it with the skirts of her tunic drawn up wantonly about her smooth thighs. She glared at the back of Huy's head, and her lips compressed into a stubborn line.

'That, Holy Father,' she whispered inaudibly, 'may be *your* plan!'

Tanith lay unsleeping and listened to the voices of Huy and his officers as they planned the campaign. Her tent was placed conveniently close to that of the High Priest, and the unlit space between them could be crossed without observation by the sentries. This journey to Sinal had been planned by Huy as a love tryst, an escape for them from the restraints of Opet.

Across the tent from her, Aina, the ancient priestess, burbled and muttered in her sleep. Tanith picked up one of her sandals from beside the couch and threw it at her. Aina hiccupped and subsided into silence.

Tanith was too excited by the momentous events in which she had been caught up for her to even contemplate sleep. A savage slave army was trundling down upon them, tens of thousands of wild men, leaving behind them a wide swathe of rape and slaughter and fire-blackened earth.

All that day the refugees had poured into the camp, each of them bringing fresh tales of horror and death. To oppose these savages was Huy Ben-Amon and his small band of heroes, outnumbered twenty to one. It was the stuff of legend, and Tanith would not miss a moment of it. In her mind the outcome was assured, in the ballads the hero always triumphed. He was the favourite of the gods, and therefore invincible. It was a pity merely that the favourite of the gods in the usual masculine fashion was being tiresome, but Tanith had laid her plans.

It was long after midnight before Tanith heard the officers taking loud leave of Huy, and clumping away to their own tents. She sat up, and started to induce tears to flood her eyes. She could usually achieve this by remembering a puppy she had owned as a child. A leopard had taken it. Tonight the trick would not work and she had to resort to rubbing her eyes with her knuckles.

Huy lay on his couch, with the lamp wick trimmed low so the corners of the tent were in darkness. He came up quickly on one elbow when Tanith slipped in through the tent flap, and before he could speak she had thrown herself on the couch beside him and wrapped her arms about his neck. She was shivering violently.

'What is it, my heart?' Huy was alarmed.

'Oh my lord, a dream. A dream of ill omen.' And Huy felt icy little prickles of dread upon the back of his neck. In two years he had learned that Tanith was truly possessed of the gift of prescience. She was capable of vivid glimpses of the future, from small incidents to matters of the gravest moment. If Huy primed her on the course her prophecies should take, it was only on the more mundane consultations. He had, however, developed a hearty respect for her abilities. Tanith knew this as she whispered, 'I walked upon a night field lit only by the funeral fires.' And Huy held her closer, feeling the chill spreading through his body – night, funeral fires, ill-omens indeed.

'I was weeping, my lord. I do not know why, but there was a great sense of loss. There had been a battle. The field was littered with weapons, and broken shields. I came upon the standard of the sixth legion, the sunbird, broken and discarded in the dirt.' Huy shuddered with awe, the sunbird thrown down! It was not only the symbol of his legion, but his own personal totem.

'Then our Lady Astarte was with me. She also was weeping. Silver tears that ran down across her white face. She was very beautiful and very sad. She spoke to me, chiding me sorrowfully. '"You should have stayed with him, Tanith. This would never have happened if you had stayed with him."'

Huy felt the quick stab of doubt through his superstitious awe. He placed his hands on Tanith's shoulders and held her away to study her face. Her eyes were reddened, and tears had washed her cheeks, but still he was suspicious. It seemed a little too neat, and he had learned that when Tanith set her heart on something she was not easily put off.

'Tanith,' he said severely. 'You know how grave a matter it is to misrepresent the words of the gods.'

Tanith nodded fervently. 'Oh yes, my lord.'

'As a seeress you have a sacred duty,' Huy insisted, and Tanith wiped her cheeks and remembered how Huy had used that sacred duty to steer the political and economic life of the nation, not to mention his personal profit. She could not deny herself a wicked pleasure in paying him in his own coin.

'I know it well, Holy Father.' Huy stared at her but could find no evidence of guile. Unable to withstand the scrutiny of those dark eyes a moment longer, Tanith buried her face in his neck once more and waited silently. The silence lasted a long time, before Huy finally admitted defeat.

'Very well,' he gruffed. 'I will keep you with me, if that is what the goddess wants.' And Tanith hugged him closer and smiled triumphantly into Huy Ben-Amon's curly beard.

For five days Huy probed and tested that moving mass of humanity as it flowed on towards the great river like a vast black jelly-fish. Always he moved back, retreating ahead of it, keeping his tiny force compact and well under his hand, using it with economy and purpose.

On the fifth day he linked up with the garrison at Sett. Mago, the elderly commander, placed himself under Huy with 1,800 archers and light infantry, 12 war elephants, 2 patrol galleys of 100 oars each, and the garrison's considerable arsenal.

Huy greeted him in the heated noonday on a small hill a dozen miles south of the river, and he led Mago aside out of earshot of the staff.

'I am honoured to serve under you, Holy Father. They say there is glory for those that follow the standard of the Sunbird.'

'There will be enough glory for all here, I warrant you,'

Huy told him grimly, and pointed across the open forest land. 'There they are.'

The slave army moved like a thick column of foraging ants, and a pale mist of dust rose above the trees.

'What thought comes first to your mind, Captain?' Huy asked quietly, and Mago studied the distant army.

'From here, my lord, they look like any other army on the march,' he muttered doubtfully.

'And does that not strike you as odd? This is not an army, Mago, it is a rabble of escaped slaves. Yet it moves like an army.'

Mago nodded quickly, understanding. 'Yes! Yes! They are in hand, you can see it. It is true, you would not expect such control.'

'There is more to it than that,' Huy told him. 'You will see it demonstrated in a moment, for I have arranged a little entertainment. I believe in giving these slaves plenty of pepper in their diet. We will raid their baggage in a moment, and then you will see what I mean.'

They were silent for a moment, watching the enemy move slowly down towards them.

Then Huy asked, 'What is the state of the river, Mago?'

'My lord, it is very low.'

'The ford is passable?' Huy insisted. 'How deep is it?'

'It can be crossed on foot. The water at the deepest is neck-deep, but flowing fast. I have had the guide ropes cut.'

Huy nodded. 'They are moving towards the ford at Sett. I have been sure of that from the moment when they chose the Lulule pass of the escarpment.' Huy was silent a moment longer. 'That is where I will destroy them,' he went on firmly, and Mago glanced sideways at him. 'Destroy' seemed a strange word for a General of 3,000 men to use in connection with an army of 30,000.

'My lord!' one of Huy's officers shouted. 'The attack begins!' And Huy hurried across to join the group.

'Ah!' he said with satisfaction. 'Bakmor has chosen his moment well.'

From their carefully prepared ambush, Bakmor's 500 heavy infantry men charged into the flank of the column. Huy's favourite had picked a weak spot in the protective screen of black spearmen. His axemen hacked their way through to the baggage train, and the drivers of the bullock wagons jumped from their seats and ran, the women bearers dropped the baskets of grain from their heads and followed them in a shrieking panic.

Swiftly the attackers slaughtered the oxen in their traces, and piled the grain baskets in heaps. Fire from the earthenware pots was fanned to life and within minutes the plundered food stores of the slave army were ablaze.

'Look!' Huy pointed out to Mago the response of the slaves to this sudden onslaught. From head and tail of the column formations of spearmen were doubling back and forward in the classical manoeuvre of envelopment. The movement was not executed with any of the precision of a trained legion. It was slow and unwieldy, a mere parody of the correct formations, but it was recognizable.

'Remarkable!' Mago exclaimed. 'A soldier commands them, one at least who has read the military statutes. Your officer must be careful now.'

'Bakmor knows what to do,' Huy assured him, and as he spoke the distant axemen formed up quickly into the testudo formation, an armoured tortoise of shields, and they trotted out between the enclosing arms of spearmen, beating the encircling movement with minutes to spare. Behind them the baggage train burned, smearing black smoke across the tree-tops.

'Good! Good!' Huy grinned his pleasure and relief, slapping his thigh with pleasure. 'Sweetly done! Now, let the slave commander show if he is as great a quartermaster as he is a tactician! There will be growling bellies in the enemy camp tonight.' Huy took Mago's arm and led him away. 'A bowl of wine,' he suggested. 'Watching and waiting is almost as thirsty work as swinging the axe.'

Mago smiled. 'Speaking of wine, Holiness. I have a few amphorae of wine that I am sure will give no offence even to a palate as knowledgeable as yours. Will you dine with me this night?'

'I look forward to it with the keenest anticipation,' Huy assured him.

The wine was drinkable, and after the meal Huy and Tanith sang together for the guests. It was a fanciful piece of pornography of Huy's composition, a love duet between Baal and Astarte. Tanith sang the part of the goddess in a sweet and true voice, rendering the more suggestive and ambiguous lines with modestly downcast eyes, that had the guests shouting with laughter and pounding the board with their wine bowls. Huy ignored the pleas for an encore, and setting his lute aside, he became serious. He spoke of the impending battle, warning Mago and his officers not to judge the enemy too lightly.

'I nearly paid dearly for that mistake,' he told them. 'I was tempted to probe their centre in strength, and I found it as soft as freshly kneaded dough. I sensed a quick rout, a chance of victory at a single stroke. With their centre collapsing I would drive through them and split them.' Huy paused, and made the sun sign. 'Praise unto Baal, but a moment before I gave the order to commit and change the probe to a full frontal attack I was warned by an impulse from the gods.' The company assumed expressions of suitable religious solemnity, and a few of them made the sun sign as Huy went on. 'I looked to the enemy's flanks which, naturally, overlapped mine, and I saw how firmly they stood. It seemed to me that the enemy's steadiest and best troops were posted there, and suddenly I remembered Cannae. I remembered how Hannibal had enmeshed the Roman Consul.' Huy broke off suddenly, and an expression of revelation dawned upon his face.

'Cannae! Hannibal!' Clearly he remembered the clay box with the battle counters of Cannae set out upon it. He remembered his own voice lecturing, and a black face intent and listening. 'Timon!' he whispered. 'It's Timon! It must be!'

Around him lay his army, a vast agglomeration of black humanity, hungry and afraid and restless in the night. The fires blossomed like a flower garden upon the southern bank of the great river, and the night sky glowed orange. The fires were for warmth alone, there was no food. There had been no food for two days now, not since they had burned his baggage.

Timon moved silently amongst them, and saw how they huddled about the fires. Hunger had made them cold, and they whispered and moaned, so the sound of his camp was murmurous, a sibilance like the hive sound of wild bees.

He hated them. They were slaves, weaklings. One in fifty of them was a man, one in a hundred was a warrior. When he had longed for a war spear in his hands, they had been a rotten twig. They were slow and clumsy in response to the lightning sallies of the enemy. Fifty of them were no match for one of the splendid warriors that opposed him. He longed for the men of his own tribe, longed to teach them what he had learned, to imbue them with his own sense of purpose, his own dreams of destiny and retribution.

On the bank of the river he stood and looked across the slick black flow of water. The reflection of the stars danced upon the surface, at the shallow place of the ford there were whorls and eddies, a disturbance, as though some monster swam deep.

Three hundred paces out, half-way across the river, was a small islet. The flood waters would cover it, and it was thick with driftwood and mats of stranded papyrus. This was the first stage of the ford. It was here that he would anchor his lines of twisted bark that his men were plaiting now. He would rig the lines at dawn, and attempt to make the crossing in a single day. He knew how heavy his losses must be. They were weak with hunger and wounds and exhaustion, the bark ropes were unreliable, the current was swift and treacherous, and the enemy was as swift and unrelenting.

Timon moved away downstream, passing amongst his sentries, talking quietly with them, stopping to examine the huge coils of bark rope that were laid ready upon the bank, and at last he came to the perimeter of his camp.

Downstream was the garrison of Sett, 1,000 paces away, a Roman mile as Timon now thought of it. There were torches burning upon the walls and Timon could see the sentries moving vigilantly in the light.

Out on the river, anchored in a deep placid pool were the galleys of the river patrol. With oars shipped and sails furled they were saurian in shape, and Timon watched them uneasily. He had never seen warships in action and he did not know what to expect of them. When Huy Ben-Amon had spoken of the great sea battles of the Romans and Greeks and Carthaginians, he had paid scant attention. He regretted it now. He wished he could form some estimate of the threat that these strange craft afforded his crossing.

The sound of voices came faintly to him across the water, and though he could not recognize the words, yet the familiar modulation of the Punic language fanned his hatred. He listened to them and he felt it come up out of the pit of his belly. He wanted to destroy every trace, every memory of this grotesque light-skinned people with their skills and strength and strange gods and monstrous cruelties.

Standing in the darkness and staring at the distant fortress, hearing their voices in the night, he remembered the body of his woman sliding and bouncing over the rough ground, he remembered the slaves wailing in the compounds of Hulya, he remembered the slave smell, the sound and kiss of the lash, the jangling weight of the chains, the searing heat of the rock, the voices of the slave-masters, the thousand other memories burned and branded into his brain. He massaged the thickened chain callouses at his wrist, and stared at his enemies, and from the core of his soul his hatred bubbled and boiled, threatening to flood his reason like the red-hot lava of an active volcano.

He wanted to swing his army about and fall upon them. He wanted to destroy them, destroy every last trace of them.

He found with surprise that he was shaking, his whole body shuddering with the force of his hatred, and with an immense effort of his will, he controlled himself. Sweat poured down his face and chest in the night cool, the rank-smelling sweat of hatred.

'My time is not now,' he thought. 'But it will come.'

There was a presence beside him in the darkness and he turned to it.

'Zama?' he asked, and his lieutenant answered softly.

'The dawn is coming.'

'Yes,' Timon nodded. 'It is time to begin.'

With loving attention Tanith braided his beard, and then twisted it up under his chin and clubbed it out of the way where it would not catch in Huy's breastplate nor afford a grip for a desperate enemy.

She whispered endearments as she worked, the endearments of a childless woman, speaking to him as though he were her infant. Huy sat quietly on his couch, delighting in the deft and gentle touch of her hands, the soft words and the loving tone of her voice; all this contrasted so violently with what the day would bring, and when Tanith rose from the couch and went to fetch his heavy breastplate, he felt a sharp sense of loss.

She helped him to arm, kneeling to buckle the straps of his greaves, fussing with the folds of his cloak, and although she smiled, he could hear the fear in her voice.

He kissed her awkwardly, and the iron crushed her breast as he held her. She made a small movement of protest, half pulling away, then she surrendered to his embrace and, ignoring the pain, pressed herself to him.

'Oh Huy,' she whispered, 'my lord, my love.'

The old priestess pulled aside the hanging reed mat and stepped into the chamber. She saw the two of them clinging to each other, oblivious of all else. Aina stared at them through rheumy old eyes, then her mouth sagged open into a toothless grin and she drew back silently and let the reed mat fall into place.

Tanith drew away at last. She went to the wall against which the vulture axe leaned beside Huy's couch, and she took it up and untied the soft leather sheath from the blade. She came to Huy, standing before him, and she lifted the blade to her lips and kissed it.

'Fail him not!' she whispered to the axe and handed it to Huy.

In the pre-dawn darkness there was an eager group of officers on the ramparts of the fort staring upstream to where the slave army was camped. They were all armed and were eating the morning meal as they stood. They greeted Huy and Tanith with boisterous high spirits, and Tanith watched and listened as they discussed the day. She found it difficult to understand how they could face the possibility of dealing or receiving death with the enthusiasm of small boys for a piece of mischief.

Tanith felt herself excluded from this mysterious male camaraderie, and she was startled by the change which had come over Huy. Her gentle poet, her solemn scholar and shy lover was as inflamed as any of them. She recognized all the signs of his excitement in his fluttering hand gestures, the hectic spots of colour in his cheeks and the high-pitched giggle with which he greeted one of Bakmor's sallies.

'This is the day. Enough waiting,' Huy declared, as he stared upstream into the dawn gloom. There was a heavy mist upon the river, and the smoke from 10,000 campfires obscured the field. He paced restlessly. 'A curse upon this mist! I cannot see if they have strung their lines across the ford yet.'

'Shall I order one of the galleys upstream to investigate?' Mago asked.

'No,' Huy waved the suggestion aside. 'We will know soon enough, and I don't want to draw attention to the galleys yet.' Huy crossed to the parapet on which the food was spread. He poured a bowl of hot wine sweetened with honey and raised it to the company. 'A bright edge to your swords!'

Huy sang the greeting to Baal as the sun came up over a red and smoky horizon, and then standing bare-headed he drew the attention of the gods to the fact that he intended fighting a battle this day. In strong but respectful terms he pointed out that though the men he commanded were the finest, yet the odds were high, and he would need assistance if the day was to be carried. He relied on them for their co-operation. He made the sun sign, and then turned briskly to his staff.

'Very well, you know your stations and duties.' As they dispersed, Huy led Bakmor aside. 'You have a man to attend the priestess?'

Bakmor beckoned to a grizzled old infantry man who stood a short way off, and the man came forward.

'You know your duties?' Huy demanded, and the soldier nodded.

'I will remain with the priestess through the day.'

'Never let her out of your sight,' Huy cautioned him.

'Should the enemy triumph, and it seem that she will fall into their hands, I will—'

'Good,' Huy interrupted him gruffly. 'If it is necessary, make the stroke swift and sure.'

Huy could not look at Tanith; he turned away quickly and went down to where a small boat waited to row him out to the larger of the two galleys.

Huy stood on the castle of the galley and waited. The sun was well up now, and the mist was dispersed. The galley was singled up to a bow anchor, and she faced into the current. The rowers were at their benches, their shields and weapons laid at their feet, the oars feathered and ready.

The slave army was committed to its crossing. Twenty lines had been strung from the south bank to the mid-stream island, and now they were laying the lines from there to the north bank.

The ford was congested with a great struggling mass of humanity. Clinging to the bark ropes, they were wading steadily across towards the island. Only their heads showed, long lines of black dots around which the water swirled and creamed. Already there were fifteen or twenty thousand slaves in the water, and the number increased steadily as the horde on the south side filed down the bank and took to the ropes.

It was happening just the way that Huy had known it

would. The party on the south bank would dwindle to a size which would be a fair match for Bakmor's impatient warriors. Huy smiled as he imagined how Bakmor must be chafing at this delay. He had longer to wait, Huy decided, as he watched the first slaves emerge from the green waters and scramble thankfully out on to the island with their black skins shining wetly in the morning sunlight.

Their thankfulness was premature, Huy thought. There was still the north channel of the river between them and safety. They began filing off the island, while behind them the bark ropes bowed downstream with the weight of human bodies and the island itself swarmed with naked black flesh. It was an awesome spectacle, such a multitude strung across the river, and still a dense mass of black men upon the south bank.

If it is Timon, he will know enough to hold his best men in the rearguard. Huy peered at the men waiting to take their turns upon the ropes, and it seemed that they were steadier and better armed than those in the van. He must let their numbers reduce further before he could risk Bakmor's tiny force against them.

Huy turned his attention back to the ford, from the island the lines of heads were creeping slowly across towards the far bank. He could see now that he would have a difficult choice to make. If he delayed his attack much longer, then many of the fugitives would escape into the dense forests of the north, beyond the reach of his army for ever. However, if he struck before they escaped it would mean committing Bakmor to battle with vastly superior numbers. The choice was a delicate one, and Huy pondered it carefully. His decision was made when he thought suddenly of the day in the future when he would report to his king.

'Not one of them escaped, Majesty.' And he could almost hear the reply. 'I did not doubt it, my bird of the sun.'

Huy turned to the captain of the galley who stood beside him.

'Hoist the standard!' he said quietly, and immediately the order was shouted to the foredeck. The golden battle standard soared to the masthead.

As a hoarse cheer rose from the rowing decks of the galley, Huy saw the battle signal repeated in the other galley anchored on his starboard beam.

In the bows a sailor swung a battle-axe, severing the anchor cable and the galleys spread their wide wings of oars. They dipped and swung and rose, wet and gleaming golden and silver in the sunlight. Under Huy's feet the ship dashed forward against the current, so swiftly that he staggered before he caught his balance. The galleys flew in formation, their great wings beating, arrowing upstream on a diverging course that would carry one through each channel of the river.

'Steer for the centre of their line,' Huy ordered the galley captain, and the order was shouted to the helm.

They raced down on the crowded ropes, strung like black pearls with the heads of struggling men. Above the rush of water, and the creak and dip of oars, Huy heard a mounting hubbub of terror from the men who looked up at the deadly bows that towered above them.

He moved to the bulwark and looked down. He saw their faces turned up towards him, and their eyes showed white in the dark faces. He crushed down the stirrings of his pity, for these were not men. They were the enemy.

The archers in the bows were loosing their arrows into them now. Huy saw an arrow strike one of them squarely in the face and stand there as the man threw his arms high and was swept away by the current.

The galley cut into the heavily laden ropes, slowing slightly and lurching as the weight of them checked the forward dash, then they snapped and burst asunder beneath the iron-shod bows, and the current swept the lines of men away into deep water, washing them close under the walls of the garrison where Huy's archers waited to pick them like windfallen fruit.

The galleys drove through the shallows, scraping their keels against the rock bottom of the ford and then they were into the deep water beyond, and Huy ran to the stern and looked back. The river was filled from bank to bank with screaming, drowning men. Some of them clung to the branches of overhanging trees, others to slippery outcrops of rock, or to floating pieces of driftwood and mats of papyrus. The island was completely hidden by a solid blanket of wet and shivering humanity, and still others were trying to find a foothold upon it, floundering and struggling in the shallows.

There were so many of them that they reminded Huy of a migration of insects, rather than human beings. They were like ants, tens of thousands of ants. He held that thought as he steeled himself to give the next order.

The galley captain was watching him expectantly, he could see the sailors in the bows at the tubes. They were looking up at the castle, waiting for the order.

'Very well, Captain,' Huy said, remembering that they were ants and not men. Instantly the galley captain was shouting his orders, and the ship swung broadside to the current. The other galley conformed to this manoeuvre and from the bows of both of them the deadly jets of Opet's secret weapon, 'Baal's fire', were squirted.

It sprayed upon the surface of the river, spreading smoothly, the sunlight broke into rainbows of colour upon the floating liquid, and the stink of it was oily and rank.

Then magically it burst into flame, the entire surface of the river became a solid sheet of roaring orange flame from which banks of sooty black smoke billowed, and the heat of it was so intense that Huy drew back quickly as he felt his beard singe.

'In Baal's holy name,' Huy whispered, as he watched the

fire, named for the great god Baal, sweep majestically downstream, filling the great river from bank to bank, filling the sky with dark clouds. It flowed over the crowded island, and when it had passed, the blackened bodies lay in high smouldering heaps, while the driftwood and dried papyrus burned like a funeral pyre.

The wall of fire marched downstream, past the fortress walls, searing the vegetation along each bank, sweeping the river clear of life. In ten short minutes 20,000 souls had perished, and their charred bodies floated down towards the sea or washed up as flotsam along the sand banks and back eddies of the river.

After the flames passed, Timon stood appalled and stared at the devastation. He could not believe the dreadful destructive force he had just witnessed, he could not believe that more than half of his army had vanished so swiftly. He was left with a small portion of his original command.

Those left were his best men, but in truth he knew them to be no match for the cohorts that opposed him. Although he realized that he must make his dispositions for the attack which would now surely follow, yet he wasted a few seconds staring longingly across the river to the north where his own land lay. He was cut off from it now, perhaps for ever.

The galleys lay a hundred paces off the bank, with their bows pointed towards him. They were as menacing as two great reptilian monsters, and now he had seen them in action Timon felt fear's chilly breath on his neck when he looked at them.

Behind him rose the roar of challenge and counter-challenge and the clash of shields and weapons. Timon swung about. The second attack had come, as he feared. It had come with the precision and timing he had expected. It had come crashing into his rear at the exact moment when his men's stomachs were cold with the dreadful destruction they had witnessed in the van.

Timon felt his anger swell and buoy him upwards, his hatred rose with it. Anger and hatred, the forces upon which his whole existence depended. Anger that he must fight against men like these with such fragile weapons. Even as he turned to join the conflict he swore an oath that he had sworn a hundred times before. *I will build an army from my own people which will match these pale-skinned devils.*

Timon fought his way towards the rear through the press of his own men. The attack was driving them back steadily, jamming them against the river, packing them so densely that they could neither manoeuvre nor wield their weapons.

It was a nightmare sensation, attempting to find a way through this swaying, surging sea of black bodies. Desperately Timon bellowed his orders, trying to force them forward, trying to make them deploy outwards, but his voice was lost in the battle roar and even his great strength was helpless in this jam of black humanity.

Over the heads of his men he could see the enemy helmets and plumes ringing them. The sword and axe rose and fell to a solemn rhythm, and before them his men dropped their weapons, turned their backs and tried to burrow their way into the massed bodies of their companions. The pressure increased steadily, smothering the ranks behind and driving them steadily back towards the river.

Over the heads of the attackers the archers and javelin men hurled a rain of missiles into Timon's centre, and so densely was it packed that the dead men could not fall but were held upright by their neighbours' striving bodies.

Now the galleys stole in quietly towards the bank and

from the high castles the archers loosed their arrows into the van of Timon's army. The bank began to crumble away beneath the desperate feet, and living and dead slid and fell into the swift waters.

Soon the colour of the water changed from green to brown, and then to the bright scarlet of life blood.

'A river of blood, Holiness,' the galley commander remarked in conversational tones. 'I have heard it sung by the poets before, but this is the first time I have ever seen it.'

Huy nodded without answering. He could see the battle had reached a point of equilibrium. The pressure that Bakmor's cohorts, even strengthened with those of Mago, could exert was insufficient to drive the enemy back another yard. Soon that pressure must relax, for already the axemen were tiring. When that happened the slave army would explode outwards, like a released bowstring. It needed but an ounce more pressure to topple the slaves into the river, but that pressure must come within the next few minutes.

Huy muttered impatiently, 'Come, Bakmor, are you blinded by blood? Has battle-lust drowned your reason? Now is your moment, but it is passing!' And Huy began to pace the wooden deck anxiously. It was so clear to him what should be done, that it amazed him that others could not see it.

'Come, Bakmor, come!' he pleaded, and then he grunted his relief.

'Not a moment too soon!'

Bakmor had charged his war elephants into the massed remnant of Timon's army. Trumpeting and squealing, the huge animals waded through living bodies, crushing them underfoot, lifting men in their trunks and flinging them towards the sky. A terrified screeching of despair went up from 10,000 throats, and Timon's army turned to the water.

'Now!' shouted Huy, and the galleys shot in towards the

bank of the river. They ran aground together, and from them poured 400 heavy axemen, led by Huy Ben-Amon.

His men tried to keep with him. For in the sixth legion the place of honour in battle was at the side of the High Priest. But the vulture axe clave forward so swiftly that it took a good man to pace it.

'For Baal!' And they reaped the bloody harvest so the ground beneath their feet turned to red mud, and the river flowed brightly.

In the midst of it Huy saw Timon. The shock of it slowed his arm for a second, and a spear jabbed at him, scoring his ribs. Huy killed the spearman with a casual back-handed stroke, then cut his way through the press towards Timon. It was slow work, and Timon retreated ahead of him towards the river bank.

'Timon!' Huy shouted in desperation, and those terrible smoky yellow eyes turned to him and held his gaze. They were the eyes of a leopard in the trap, cruel and merciless.

'A challenge!' Huy called. 'Fight me!'

In reply Timon reared to his full height and hurled his spear at Huy. Huy ducked and the point glanced off his helmet and buried itself in the neck of the man beside Huy. The man cried out and fell.

Timon turned and with three strides he had reached the bank of the river. He leapt out into the red waters, and then struck out powerfully in the over-arm stroke that Huy had taught him.

Huy reached the edge of the bank and tore off his helmet and breastplate, he snapped the leather straps of his greaves and kicked off his sandals.

Naked, except for the belt which held his axe, Huy looked out across the river. Timon was out of range of the archers on the bank, he was half-way across to the island in the time which it had taken Huy to strip.

Huy dived cleanly from the bank, and struck the water flat on his belly. Then he was swimming, dragging himself through the bloody water with those long thick arms and churning the surface white with his powerful legs.

On the island Timon had found weapons. The throwing spears of the charred bodies that lay thick upon the ground.

As Huy found his footing and waded ashore, Timon hurled the first of them. Huy deflected the spear with a swing of his axe, catching the spear blade full on the great butterfly-shaped head, swatting the spear out of the air as though it were an insect.

Again Timon threw, and again – but now Huy was charging him across the rocky, corpse-strewn ground, and each thrown spear was caught neatly upon the head of the axe and sent spinning aside to fall harmlessly on the rocky earth.

In desperation Timon stooped and picked up one of the round river boulders as large as a man's head. He lifted it over his head with both hands, and stepped forward as he threw it. The rock caught Huy a glancing blow on his shoulder, and knocked him down on his back with the axe skidding away from his hand.

Timon charged at him, careless in his anger and hatred. Huy bounced off the earth, flipping him forward like a thrown javelin.

The top of Huy's head crashed into Timon's body just below the rib-cage and the air of his lungs rushed out of his throat in a gasp of agony. Timon doubled up and dropped to his knees, clutching at his chest with both hands.

Huy stood over him, and bunched his hand in the manner of the gladiators. He struck Timon with the bony hammer of his fist just below the ear, and Timon toppled forward senseless to the rocks.

'I cannot kill you, Timon,' Huy's voice came to him through the grey mist, and from a great distance. 'Though you deserve death as no one else has done before you. You have betrayed my trust. You have carried the sword against me and my king – you deserve to die.'

Huy's face came into focus, and Timon found himself lying on his back with arms out-stretched. He tried to move and found himself bound. Leather thongs were knotted tightly about his fingers and pegged down to the earth, holding him captive. He rolled his head and found himself on the north side of the island, hidden from watchers on the south bank and alone with Huy.

On the rocks beside him a small fire of driftwood burned. Huy had lit it from a smouldering remnant, and in it was heating a broad spearhead with its shaft snapped off short.

'There is little time. Soon my men will come to find me. And then it will be out of my hands,' Huy explained reasonably. 'I have made an oath to my gods, so I cannot give you the punishment which you have earned. Yet I have a duty to my king and my people. I cannot let you carry the sword against us again.

'The Romans had an answer for this, and though I hate all things of Rome, I must use their methods now.'

Huy stood up, and leaned over Timon.

'I made a mistake with you. No man can ever tame a wild leopard.' Huy held the vulture axe in his right hand. 'You were never Timon, you were always Manatassi. You are as different from me as the colour of my skin is different from yours. There was never a bond between us, it was illusion, for though our mouths speak the same language, our ears hear the sounds differently.

'Your destiny is to seek the destruction of all I hold dear, all that my people have built and tended. My destiny is to protect it, with my very life's blood.' Huy paused, and there was true regret in his heart as he went on. 'I cannot kill you, but I must make sure that you never carry the sword again.'

The vulture axe sang, and Timon screamed once, and then whimpered softly as his severed right hand twitched and trembled like a dying animal on the scorched earth of the island.

Huy fetched the heated spear blade from the fire and sealed off the pumping blood vessels of the stump in a hissing puff of stinking smoke. Then he cut the thongs that still bound Timon.

'Go,' he said. 'You must trust yourself to the river now. My men will come to search the island soon.'

Timon dragged himself down the beach, and at the water's edge he looked back at Huy. His huge black body was scarred and ravaged, and his eyes were terrible.

Slowly he lowered himself into the water, holding the raw stump of his arm across his chest. The current took him, and his head dwindled to a speck upon the wide river, until it was swept beyond the bend below the fort. Huy watched it out of sight, then he stooped and picked up the severed hand from the ground and dropped it onto the fire and piled dry driftwood upon it.

Bakmor had dug his cremation pits along the bank of the river, and he and Huy passed along the ranks of fallen warriors laid upon their last couch of wood. It was the ceremony of farewell, and Huy paused and looked down at old Mago. In death the garrison commander had a dignity which he had lacked in life.

'How sweet is the taste of glory now, Mago?' Huy asked him softly, and it seemed that Mago smiled in his sleep.

Huy sang the praise of Baal, and then he lit the funeral fires with his own hand.

Tanith was not upon the walls to welcome him when they marched back to the fortress of Sett, but Huy found her in her own chamber. She had been weeping and her face was pale, with dark blue smears beneath her eyes.

'I feared for you, my lord. My heart burned within me, but I did not weep. I was very brave through it all. Through all the horror of it. It was only when they told me that you were safe that I cried. Isn't that silly?'

Holding her close, Huy asked, 'Was it like the poets sang it? Was it glorious and heroic?'

'It was horrible,' Tanith whispered. 'Horrible beyond my dreams of horror. It was ugly, my lord, ugly enough to make me despair of beauty.' She was silent then, remembering it all again. 'You poets never tell of the blood, and the wounded screaming and – all the other things.'

'No,' Huy agreed. 'We never do.'

In the night Huy woke and found that Tanith was sitting beside him on the couch. The night lamp was trimmed low and her eyes were dark pools in her face.

'What troubles you?' Huy asked, and she was quiet a few seconds before she spoke.

'Holy Father, you are so gentle, so kind. How could you do what was done today?'

Huy pondered the reply a moment.

'It was my duty,' he explained at last.

'Your duty to slaughter those wretches?' Tanith asked incredulously.

'The law is death to rebel slaves.'

'The law is wrong then,' Tanith declared hotly.

'No.' Huy shook his head. 'The law is never wrong.'

'It is!' Tanith was close to tears again. 'It is!'

'The law is all we have that saves us from the void, Tanith. Obey the laws and the gods and you need never fear.'

'The laws should be changed.'

'Ah!' Huy smiled. 'Change them, by all means, but until they are changed, obey them.'

In the dawn of the next morning Lannon Hycanus arrived at Sett. He arrived at the head of two full legions in battle array, and fifty elephants of war.

'I fear I have been greedy, sire,' Huy told him at the

gates. 'I left you not a single one.' And Lannon shouted with laughter and embraced Huy, turning to his staff with an arm still about Huy's shoulders.

'Which of you was it said that Ben-Amon would not fight?'

That night while he was still sober Huy sang the ballad he had composed to commemorate the Battle of the River of Blood, and Lannon wept at the telling of it, and when it was done he cried out to his own staff.

'Three against 30,000 – it will always be our shame that we did not fight with Huy Ben-Amon that day at Sett.'

Lannon stood. 'I give you the new Commander-in-Chief of all the legions of Opet. I give you Huy Ben-Amon, Axeman of the Gods.'

Then king and priest got very drunk together.

Gondweni was one of the 200 tributary chiefs of the Vendi, and his territory bounded on the broken land of the Kal Gorge, the land of the outcasts. He was fat and prosperous, and because he was a prudent man he regularly left small gifts of salt and meat at a place in the hills where the outcasts came for it. Also because he was a prudent man he gave food and shelter to solitary travellers journeying to the hills or returning from them, and when they left his town the memory of their passing went with them.

Thus a tall gaunt stranger sat one night at his hearth and ate his food and drank his beer. Gondweni sensed power and purpose behind the impassive scarred visage with the fierce yellow eyes. He felt an unusual affinity for this man and he talked more freely than was his wont. Although he spoke the language of Vendi, the traveller seemed to know nothing of the politics and affairs of the tribe, not even the name of the paramount king who had succeeded Manatassi when he was carried off by the white devils from across the river.

'Of Manatassi's six brothers, five died swiftly and mysteriously after drinking of a special brewing of beer, prepared by the middle brother, Khani. Khani alone survived the feast.' And Gondweni chuckled and nodded and winked knowingly at the stranger.

'He is now our king, the Great Black Bull, the collector of the tribute, the Thunder of Heaven, the fat lecher of Vendi with his 500 wives and his 50 young boys.' Gondweni spat forcefully into the fire, and then drank from the beer pot before passing it to the stranger. When he took it Gondweni saw that the stranger's right hand was missing and he steadied the pot with the stump.

'What of Manatassi's counsellors, his war captains, his blood brothers?' the stranger asked. 'Where are they now?'

'Most of them are in the bellies of the birds.' And Gondweni drew a forefinger across his throat expressively.

'Most of them?'

'Some went over to Khani and ate his salt – others spread their wings and flew.' Gondweni pointed out into the hills which showed like the black teeth of an ancient shark against the moon sky. 'Some are my neighbours, chiefs of the outcasts, paying tribute to none, and waiting in the hills for they know not what.'

'Who are they?'

'Zingala.'

'Zingala, the ironsmith?' the stranger demanded eagerly, and Gondweni's expression changed. He turned on the stranger a hard stare.

'It seems to me you know more than is safe,' he said softly. 'Perhaps we should sleep now.' He stood up and pointed out a hut. 'There is a sleeping mat laid out for you, and I will send a young girl for your comfort.'

The stranger's need was like a raging storm on the girl's unresisting body, battering and driving, and Gondweni heard her crying out in pain and fear. He lay awake, troubled and restless, but in the dawn when he went to the stranger's hut the girl lay crumpled in exhausted sleep and the man was gone.

A deep gorge split the mountains, so deep that the path was dark and moss-covered and slippery underfoot. At the head of the gorge a fall of silver plunged down from the cliffs above, and the wind drove it in a fine cold mist into Manatassi's face as he climbed upwards.

At a level place he paused to rest, and the stump of his right arm ached cruelly in the cold. He ignored the pain, pushing it below the surface of his conscious mind, and he looked up the deep dark gut of the gorge.

High above him on the cliff top, outlined against the pale blue of the noon sky was the foreshortened figure of a man. The figure stood very still, and the stillness itself was menacing.

Manatassi ate a little cold millet cake, and drank from the stream of icy clear water, before beginning the climb again. Now there were other figures. They appeared silently and unexpectedly at steep or easily defended places on the trail and they watched him.

One of them stood atop a giant boulder, fully forty feet high, which all but blocked the gorge. He was a tall man, well muscled and heavily armed. Manatassi recognized him, the man had been a captain of one of his old regiments.

Manatassi stopped below the boulder, and let the cloak fall back from his head, exposing his face, but the man did not recognize him, could not see his king in this ravaged face from which pain and hatred had stripped the flesh and which the whip and the club had remoulded.

'Am I so altered?' Manatassi thought grimly. 'Will no man recognize me again?'

He and the man stared at each other for many seconds until Manatassi spoke.

'I seek Zingala, the ironsmith.'

He knew that even though Zingala had joined the outcasts, such a famous craftsman must still have many clients seek him out. He knew that alone and unarmed he would be allowed to pass on such business.

The sentry upon the boulder turned his head slightly and pointed with his chin up the gorge, and Manatassi went on.

There were narrow steps that climbed the black rock cliff beside the waterfall, and when Manatassi came out upon the summit there were armed and silent men waiting. They fell in behind and on each side of him as he strode out along the only path, through the thick forest which covered the crest of the mountain.

The smoke of the furnaces guided Manatassi, and he came at last to a natural amphitheatre of rock, a bowl one hundred paces across, where Zingala worked his art with iron.

The old master was at one of his furnaces, packing the ore into the belly of it, each lump carefully hand selected. His apprentices were gathered around respectfully, ready to add the layers of limestone and charcoal upon the ore.

Zingala straightened up from his task and held aching back muscles as he watched the tall stranger and his escort come down into the bowl. There was something familiar in the man's walk, in the way he carried his shoulders, the tilt of his head, and Zingala frowned. He dropped his hands to his sides, and shuffled uncertainly as the man's features touched a deep memory. The stranger stopped before him and stared into Zingala's face – those eyes, yellow and fierce and compelling. Quickly he looked down at the stranger's feet and he saw the deep cleft between the toes. Zingala wailed and dropped to his face upon the earth. He took one of Manatassi's deformed feet and placed it upon his own grey-frosted pate.

'Command me,' he cried. 'Command me, Manatassi, the great black beast, the Thunder of the Heavens.'

The others heard the name and they fell as though lightning had struck them down.

'Command us,' they cried. 'Command us, black bull of a thousand cows.'

Manatassi looked upon his band of outlaws as they grovelled about him, and he spoke softly but in a voice that cut to the heart of each of them.

'There is but one command I give you, and that is – OBEY!'

The furnace was shaped like the belly of a pregnant woman, and the entrance was slitted like her pudenda between spread thighs of moulded clay.

To fertilize the smelting ore, Zingala introduced the buck-horn nozzle of the bellows into the opening. The nozzle was shaped like a priapus, and the work was done in a strict ritualistic sequence while the apprentices sang the birth chant, and Zingala sweated and laboured like a midwife in his leather apron, pumping away at the leather bellows.

When at last the plug of clay was drawn and the molten metal ran in a fiery stream into the sand moulds there was a murmur of relief and congratulation from the watchers.

Using an anvil of ironstone and a set of special hammers Zingala forged the lion's paw with its five massive iron claws and its pad of solid metal. He filed and dressed and polished it, then he reheated it and tempered it in the blood of a leopard and the fat of a hippopotamus.

One of the skilled leather-workers built a socket of green elephant hide and shaped it to fit the stump of Manatassi's right arm. The iron claw was fixed securely into the leather socket and when it was strapped to Manatassi's stump it made a fearsome artificial limb.

Khani, the paramount ruler of Vendi and foppish half-brother of Manatassi, was with his women when the iron claw tore the top off his skull. The girl beneath him screamed and fainted with the shock of it.

Sondala, the king of Buthelezi, had many subjects, a multitude of cattle, a little grazing land and even less water to carry his people and his kine through a season of drought.

He was a small wiry man, with quick nervous eyes and a ready smile. Of all the tribes along the great river his was the latest to come out of the north, and he was crushed between the powerful Vendi tribe on the one hand and those white-robed, long-bearded, brown-skinned Dravs on the other. He was a desperate man, ready to listen with both ears to any proposition.

He sat in the firelight and grinned and darted quick eyes at the gaunt godlike figure across the hut from him – this king with the ruined face, and bird's feet and clawed hand of iron.

'You have 12 regiments, each of 2,000 men,' Manatassi told him. 'You have five flowerings of maidens each of 5,000. You have, at latest count, 127,000 cattle, bulls, cows, calves and oxen.'

Sondala grinned and wriggled uneasily, amazed at the accuracy of the Vendi king's intelligence.

'Where will you find food and grass and drink for such a multitude?' Manatassi asked, and Sondala smiled and listened.

'I will give you grazing, and land. I will give you a land rich with fruit and lush with grass, a land over which your people will march for ten generations without finding the limits of it.'

'What do you want of me?' Sondala whispered at last, still grinning and blinking his eyes quickly.

'I want your regiments to command. I want your spear in my hand, I want your shield to march beside me.'

'If I refuse?' Sondala asked.

'Then I will kill you,' said Manatassi. 'And take your regiments and all five flowerings of your maidens, and all your 127,000 cattle, except for ten which I will sacrifice upon your grave as a mark of respect to your ghost.' Manatassi grinned then also, and it was such a terrible baring of teeth in that battered face that Sondala's own smile froze.

'I am your dog,' he said hoarsely, and he knelt before Manatassi. 'Command me.'

'There is but one command,' said Manatassi softly. 'And that command is, OBEY!'

In the first year Manatassi made treaties with the Vingo, the Satassa and the Bey. He fought the Xhota in a single devastating battle, employing tactics so revolutionary and relentless that the Xhota king and his wives and courtiers and princes were taken twenty minutes after battle was joined. Instead of massacring the menfolk, and taking the women and cattle as was the custom, Manatassi had only the king and royal family strangled, then he assembled the defeated regiments, still intact and under their own commanders, and he made them swear their allegiance to him. They thundered it in massed voice that seemed to shake the leaves in the trees and rock the hills upon their foundations.

In the second year, after the rains had passed, Manatassi marched westwards as far as that desert coast on which a cold green surf raged eternally. He fought four great battles, strangled four kings – treated with two others, and added almost a hundred thousand warriors to his regiments.

Those close to the great black beast knew that he seldom slept. It seemed there was some driving force within him that denied him rest or pleasure. He ate food without tasting it, in the perfunctory manner in which a man might throw a log upon the fire merely to keep it burning. He never laughed, and smiled only when a task was performed to his satisfaction. He used women with a swift brutality that left them trembling and weeping, and he shared companionship with no man.

Only once did his lieutenants see him show the emotions of a man. They stood upon the tall yellow dunes at the western limit of the land. Manatassi was apart from them, draped in the leopard-skin of royalty and with the blue heron feathers of his head-dress fluttering in the cold breeze that came off the sea.

Suddenly one of the war captains exclaimed aloud and pointed out across the green waters. From out of the banks of silver sea fret, looming like a ghost ship through the mist, sped one of the galleys of Opet. With her single square sail bellied by the trade winds, and her banks of oars beating rhythmically, she sped in silence towards the north on her long voyage of trade to Cadiz.

Again a captain exclaimed, and they all looked towards the king. His face shone and dripped with sweat, and his jaws clenched and ground his teeth together with a sound like rock on rock. His eyes were burning mad as he watched the passage of the galley, and his body shook and shuddered with the strength of his hatred.

The captain ran to aid him, thinking him stricken with sudden fever. He touched the king's arm.

'High-born,' he started, and Manatassi turned upon him

in raging madness and struck him down with the iron claw, ripping half his face away.

'There,' he screamed, pointing with the claw at the disappearing galley. 'There is your enemy. Mark him well.'

Each day brought its own excitements, its secret delights and ventures – and its happiness. It did not seem five years since she and Huy had become lovers, so swiftly had the years sped. Yet it was so, for the Festival of the Fruitful Earth was almost come around once more.

Tanith laughed aloud at the memory of her seduction of Huy, and she made her plans to repeat the performance during the coming Festival. Beside her Aina mumbled a question, peering at her quizzically from the depths of her hood.

'Why do you laugh, child?'

'I laugh because I am happy, old mother.'

'Oh, to be young once again. You do not know what it is like to grow old.' Aina began one of her monologues, and Tanith led her through the bustle of the harbour area, past the low taverns and the taunting street girls to where steps were cut into the stone jetty. She danced down the steps and leapt lightly to the deck of the small sailing craft moored to one of the iron rings in the jetty.

Coming out of the tiny cabin, dressed in rough fisherman's clothes and with a scarf tied about his head, Huy was too late to help her aboard.

'You are late.'

'For your impertinence I shall punish you, just as soon as it is safe,' Tanith warned him.

'I look forward to it,' Huy grinned, and helped old Aina over the gunwale, while Tanith ran forward to cast off the head lines.

Huy was perched in the stern with the steering oar tucked under his arm, and Tanith sitting as close beside him as she could without touching. She had thrown off her cloak, and wore now a light cotton tunic edged with cloth thread and belted with a solid gold chain, a name-day gift from Huy.

Her hair billowed out behind her like black smoke, and her cheeks were flushed. Huy kept glancing at her, and each time she looked at him and laughed for no reason.

The wind was fine on their beam, and as they ran close-hauled for the islands the wind whipped droplets from the bow wave into their faces, and the water was cold in the warmth of the sun. Huy ran the vessel neatly through an almost invisible channel in the reeds, and they emerged into a quiet and sheltered lagoon whose surface was covered with the dark green pads of the water lilies and starred with the blue and gold of their blossoms. Water fowl paddled and dabbled and flighted over and upon the quiet waters.

They were out of the wind here and Huy took up a long pole from the deck and standing in the stern, he poled them across the lagoon to the beach of dazzling white sand. Jumping out into knee-deep water he hauled the vessel up onto the beach.

Amongst the polished black boulders above the beach Huy rigged a sun shelter with a strip of sail, and he helped Aina across the sand and installed her beneath the shelter.

'A bowl of wine, old mother,' he suggested solicitously.

'You are too kind, Holiness.'

They left her there, snoring quietly in the shade, and they walked hand in hand along the ribbon of beach, beyond the curve of the bay. Under the ivory palms Huy spread a cloak on the firm clean sand, and they rid themselves of their clothing and lay together talking and laughing and making love.

Then they bathed together in the clear warm lake water, and, as they lay in the shallows with the wavelets flopping lazily over them, shoals of silvery finger-long fish came to nibble at their naked skin. Tanith laughed and kicked at the tickle of their toothless mouths.

They went to lie in the sun and dry themselves, and Huy looked up at Tanith standing over him. Her hair was sodden and dangled in heavy black ropes down her back and breast. The sun had brought a glow to her shoulders, and there were water drops clinging in her eyelashes. She stood proudly under his scrutiny, and she cupped her breasts, one in each hand.

'Do you see aught different about me, Holy Father?' She asked in her teasing voice, so that Huy smiled and shook his head.

'Look closer,' she invited him, and it seemed then that her breasts were fatter and more pointed, he noticed also that they were marbled with bluish veins beneath the white skin.

'Yes?' Tanith asked, and ran her hands down her body to cradle her belly.

'And here?' she asked. 'Anything different here?' And she puffed out her stomach, laughing at him.

'You are getting fat,' Huy reprimanded her, giving her back her laughter. 'You eat too much.'

Tanith shook her head. 'What I have in here, Holy Father, certainly never went in through my mouth.'

Slowly the laughter dried up in the back of Huy's throat, and he gawked at her.

Huy lay in the darkness and he was still stunned and bemused. It still seemed impossible that some of the seed which he had sown so carelessly should have taken root; were not the priestesses of Astarte instructed in the secret ways of preventing just such an occurrence? This was really an event to rank with earthquake and storm and defeat in battle. Something would have to be done about it, something radical.

Lightly Huy's mind touched upon the thought of the grisly old hags who lived along the harbour front, whose job it was to rectify such blunders. Instantly he rejected the idea.

'No.' He spoke aloud, and then listened to the sound of Tanith's breathing, hoping he had not woken her. He began to moderate his plans; perhaps it was not necessary for such radical action, perhaps he could arrange for another shrine to be consecrated in a remote area of the kingdom, and there, away from prying eyes and busy tongues, she could bear his son. It would be simple enough to find a foster mother, someone he could trust. There were many of the veterans of his legion, men maimed in battle, now living the simple life on one of Huy's estates. Men with fruitful wives, whose breasts were fat and full enough to feed another little lodger.

There they could go as often as the opportunity arose to be with their son. He could imagine it already, the happiness and the laughter, and his son kicking and gurgling, fat-bellied in the sunlight.

Stealthily Huy reached beneath the bed covers, lightly his hand settled on Tanith's naked belly and he began to explore it.

'You cannot feel anything yet,' Tanith whispered, and turned to embrace him. Into his beard she whispered, 'I didn't do the things the priestess taught me. That was very wicked of me, wasn't it? Are you angry with me, my lord?'

'No,' said Huy. 'I am very pleased with you.'

'I thought you would be,' chuckled Tanith contentedly, and snuggled against him, and then she added drowsily, 'I mean, once you got used to the idea.'

The knocking and shouting woke them both and Huy bounded from the couch and snatched up the vulture axe before he was properly awake. Once the initial confusion had quieted, and the house slaves had satisfied themselves by shouted challenge and loud reply that the midnight callers were a contingent of the royal guard, Huy put aside the axe and lit another lamp.

'Holy Father.' One of the body slaves pounded on the door of the bed-chamber.

'What is it?'

'The king's guard. The Gry-Lion cannot sleep. He bids you take your lute and attend him.'

Huy sat on the edge of the couch and cursed softly but meaningfully, running his fingers through his beard and curls, trying to knuckle the sleep from his eyes.

'Did you hear me, Holiness?'

'I heard you,' growled Huy.

'The Gry-Lion said that they were to accept no excuse, and to wait while you dressed, and to escort you to the palace.'

Huy stood up and reached for his tunic, but held his hand as he saw Tanith watching him. Her eyes were enormous in the lamp light, and with her hair in cloudy disorder she looked like a child. Huy lifted the bed clothes and slipped in beside her.

'Tell the king that my picking finger is sore, my throat is raw, my lute strings are broken – and I am drunk,' he shouted, and took Tanith in his arms.

Sheikh Hassan rinsed his fingers in the silver bowl and dried them on a square of silk.

'He seeks to impress us with this show of strength,' Omar, his younger brother, murmured. Hassan glanced at him. His brother was a famous dandy. His beard was washed and perfumed and combed until it glistened, his robes were of the finest silk and his slippers and vest were heavy with embroidery of silk and gold thread. On his finger he wore a pigeon's blood ruby the size of the top joint of a man's thumb. He was misty-eyed from the bhang pipe beside him on the cushions. A dandy perhaps, and a pederast certainly, but nevertheless the possessor of a fine mind and an intuitive perception upon which Hassan relied heavily.

They sat together beneath the ancient fig tree with its widespread branches and its deep dark shade. The dhow that had brought them to this meeting was beached on the white sand of the island below them, and from their vantage point they could look across the channels and sandbanks and slow pools of the great river to the north bank.

There were troops of sea-cow lying on the sandbanks or half submerged in the shallows. Huge grey shapes, like river boulders upon which the white egrets perched unconcernedly.

On the north bank a thin ribbon of dark green vegetation grew along the river, but gave way immediately to the bare brown hills beyond. The country here had a blasted and desolate look to it. The hills were bleak and barren with rounded crests. The earth showed through the sparse dry grass, and the dead trees writhed and held their naked branches to the sky, trees drought-stricken and long dead.

However, as the sheikhs watched so the scene changed. Over the hills spread a dark shadow as though a storm cloud had blotted out the sun.

'Yes,' said Omar. 'This show is to open our ears to his words.'

Hassan spat a stream of bright red juice into the dust, and wiped his beard with silk as he watched the bare hills come to life, watched the dark shadow spread. He had never before seen such a vast concourse of humanity. The regiments and squadrons moved into orderly ranks until they covered the hills. Hassan was nervous, but his face was calm, his eyes grave and only the long brown fingers that fidgeted on the jewelled hilt of his dagger betrayed his disquiet. He had not expected anything like this. He had come to this place expecting to discuss trade and mutual boundaries with the new black emperor who had emerged out of that mysterious and little-known land beyond the river. Instead he had found himself confronted with one of the largest armies the world had ever seen assembled. He wondered if Alexander himself had ever commanded such a multitude.

Omar drew on his bhang pipe, held the smoke and then let it trickle thinly from his nostrils.

'He seeks to impress us,' he repeated, and Hassan's reply was brusque.

'If that is his intention, then he succeeds. I am impressed.'

Still the regiments came pouring over the sky-line in thick but orderly columns. They wheeled and fell into the pattern of the whole as though a single mind directed them, the way shoals of fish or flights of migrating birds react to unspoken commands. Indeed, this seemed to be not a gathering of individuals but a single organism, sprawling but well co-ordinated. Hassan watched it and shivered in the noon heat of the valley.

Upon the north bank all movement ceased, and a massive stillness settled over the serried ranks of black warriors. The stillness seemed more menacing than the preceding movement, and an expectant hush filled the valley, a sense of mounting tension which became unbearable, until Hassan swore and made a gesture as though to rise.

'I will not pander to the whims of a savage. This is an insult. We will go. He must come to us if he wishes to talk.' But the gesture never matured, and he sank back upon the cushions and fretted in silence until his brother spoke.

'It seems,' said Omar, 'that the world we know has changed, brother. What was true yesterday, is true no longer.'

'What is your advice?'

'Let us find the new truths, and examine them. It is possible that we shall still find something to our advantage in all of this.'

On the hills opposite them there was a disturbance, a stirring of the ranks, the way the tops of tall reeds move when a lion passes through. The sheikhs strained their eyes, calling out to their guards for advice of what was happening, but any reply was lost in an ocean of sound. The earth shook beneath the stamp of hundreds of thousands of feet, the air quivered with the drumming of spears on shields, and from the densely packed hills a single voice from the throats of that black multitude roared the royal salute to a king.

The storm of sound rolled across the valley, and died in echoes against the sky and the southern hills. Again the stillness and silence, then a large war canoe with fifty rowers a side was launched from the sandbank and shot across the green waters towards the island.

A man stepped out onto the white beach, and walked alone up the bank to where the sheikhs waited beneath the fig-tree. The very fact that he came without an escort was a mark of contempt, a sign of his strength and invulnerability.

He wore a cloak of leopard-skin and sandals upon his feet but he carried no ornament nor weapon. He stood tall and gaunt over the sheikhs, and they seemed to shrink in significance beside his bulk.

He looked at them with the fierce yellow eyes of a bird of prey, eyes that seemed to rake their souls.

'I am Manatassi,' he said in a soft deep rumble. 'I am the Black Beast.' They had known enough not to be surprised that he spoke their language fluently.

'I am Hassan, Sheikh of Sofala, Prince of Monomatapa and Viceroy of the Chan Emperor.'

'You love the yellow metal.' Manatassi said it like an accusation, and Hassan was taken off balance. He blinked and glanced at Omar.

'Yes,' said Omar. 'We love it.'

'I will give you enough to glut you,' said Manatassi.

Omar licked his lips, an unconscious expression of greed, and he smiled.

'You must have much of the precious stuff?' Hassan asked, this direct approach to trade was distasteful. This man was a savage, he did not understand the niceties of diplomacy. Yet gold was worth a little gaucherie, especially in the quantities this self-styled black beast hinted at. 'Where does it come from?'

'From the treasure house of Lannon Hycanus, Gry-Lion of Opet and king of the four kingdoms,' said Manatassi, and Hassan frowned quickly.

'I do not understand you?'

'Then you are stupid,' said Manatassi, and Hassan flushed dusky rose beneath his brown skin and a retort rose swiftly to his lips, but he felt his brother's cautionary fingers press his wrist.

'Explain it to me,' said Omar. 'Do you intend to war with Opet?'

'I will destroy them – destroy their people, their cities and their gods. I will leave not a trace of them, not a single living one.' The giant Negro began to tremble, a little white spittle wet his full purple lips and a light sheen of sweat greased his battered features.

Omar smiled delicately. 'We heard of a battle at a place named Sett.'

Manatassi roared, a sound of pain. He leaped towards the sheikh and from under his cloak he drew the clawed iron hand and held it in Omar's face. Omar scrambled backwards, and clung to his brother.

'Do not mock me, little brown man, do not mock me, or I will tear out your liver.'

Omar moaned with terror and sweat ran down into his beard.

'Peace,' Hassan intervened hurriedly. 'My brother meant only to remark that the legions of Opet will be difficult to destroy.'

Manatassi gulped for air, still shaking with his rage. He turned away and walked to the edge of the island and stared down into the water. His shoulders heaved, and his chest panted for air, but slowly he calmed himself and came back to them.

'Do you see them?' He pointed to his army that still darkened the hills.

'Numbers alone – will they be sufficient?' Hassan asked. 'You challenge a mighty foe.'

'I will show you,' said Manatassi, and he lifted the iron claw. Instantly one of his war captains ran from the canoe and knelt before him.

Manatassi spoke a few words in the Vendi language and pointed out at the river. The captain sprang to his feet with an expression of joy lighting his dark face. He saluted, went bounding away down the bank, leapt into the bows of the canoe and was sped swiftly across to the north bank.

The sheikhs watched with puzzled interest as a new movement began amongst the massed warriors on the far bank. They moved forward in two thick columns, swarming into the water, and Hassan exclaimed mildly. 'They carry no weapons.'

'They are naked,' added Omar, and his terror ebbed and was replaced by an erotic interest as he watched the black columns move out into the shallows. Like the horns of a buffalo they circled one of the sandbanks, and though the chest-deep water hampered them, yet the manoeuvre was completed before the old bull hippopotamus woke from his gargantuan slumber to find himself surrounded.

He lumbered to his feet and glared about him with his piggy pink eyes. Five tons of solid flesh, clad in a thick grey hide, splotched with pink upon the belly. His legs were short and thick and powerful, and when he opened his jaws to bellow he exposed great yellow fangs of ivory which could bite a war canoe in half.

He broke into a cumbersome gallop, leaving deep hoof-prints in the soft white sandbank, and he charged at the wall of black bodies that cut him off from the deep pool of the river. He entered the shallows, churning up a wake of foaming white water, while ahead of him the wall of black men solidified and thickened as the line bunched up to receive and absorb his charge.

The bull went into them at full gallop, and human bodies were flung about like chaff in the whirlwind. His jaws clashed as he chopped at them, and when he drove forward it seemed that nothing could stay such devastating power. He must burst through them and find safety in the deeps of the river. Yet they swarmed about him, from the sides and rear, and his charge slowed perceptibly, although his bellows seemed louder and the champing of ivory tusks cutting through living flesh carried clearly to the watchers on the island.

Manatassi stood quietly, leaning forward slightly, with a small frown upon his scar-riven brow, and his eyes were yellow and watchful.

In the river the water creamed and flashed and sparkled. The bull's bellows took on a new note, a hint of panic, and he was no longer visible beneath the swarming naked bodies. It was like a scorpion attacked by army ants, creatures only a small fraction of his size smothering him with their numbers. The sunlight glittered on the wet bodies, and the bull's forward progress was arrested. He was transformed into a struggling ball of human bodies, while around him the water turned dark brown with blood, and the mauled bodies fell away like poisoned black ticks from the body of an ox. They floated down on the sluggish current, while others swarmed forward eagerly to replace them.

Now, miraculously, the striving knot of men and beast began to move towards the island; leaving the debris of death behind them, they moved slowly through the shallows.

They reached the island, and came from the water – 1,000, perhaps 2,000 men, carrying the exhausted but still struggling hippopotamus bodily from the river and up the bank. The bull slashed viciously from side to side, and all within reach of his jaws died, while the bull's head and the inside of his mouth was clotted with the bright blood of his victims.

Leaving a thick trail of dead and terribly maimed men behind them, they carried the bull to where Manatassi stood waiting. The war captain came forward unsteadily. He was weak from loss of blood for he had lost one arm above the elbow, taken away by a single bite of those terrible jaws.

He handed a stabbing spear to his king. Manatassi walked forward, and while his men held down the terrified monster, he stabbed it in the throat, finding the jugular vein with the first thrust. The bull died in a burst of dark blood and a cry that rang against the hills.

Manatassi stepped back and watched impassively as his men despatched their wounded with swift mercy, and when the war captain came and knelt before him clutching the severed stump of an arm to his chest and begged for the honour at the hand of his king, a bright pride burned briefly in Manatassi's eyes. He made the mercy stroke, crushing the man's skull with a single blow of the iron claw, then he walked back, and smiled bleakly as he saw the sheikhs' amazement.

'That is my answer,' he said, and after a while Hassan asked, 'What do you want of us?'

'Two things,' Manatassi replied. 'An undefended passage of the river through your territory for my armies. You must forsake your pact of mutual defence with Opet – and I want iron weapons. My smiths will take another ten years to arm so many men. I want weapons from you.'

'In return you will deliver to us the gold of Opet, and the mines of the middle kingdom?'

'No!' Manatassi snarled angrily. 'You may take the gold. I have no use for it. It is a cursed metal, soft and useless. You may take all that Opet has; but,' and he paused, 'the mines of the middle kingdom will never be worked again. No more will men go down to die unnaturally in the earth.'

Hassan wanted to protest. Without the gold of the middle kingdom his own reason for existing would vanish. He could imagine the rage of the Chan Emperor denied his trade routes with the land of gold. Omar's fingers warned him gently, their soft insinuating touch speaking clearly.

'There will be another time to argue.' And Hassan heeded the warning, he choked back the protest and instead he smiled at Manatassi.

'You will have your weapons. I will see to it.'

'When?' demanded Manatassi.

'Soon,' promised Hassan, 'as soon as my ships can return from the land across the eastern seas.'

Lannon had aged these last few years, Huy thought. Yet the change was flattering, the new lines that care had chiselled dispelled the prettiness from his features and had given him dignity. Around the mouth there was the same petulance, the pout of the spoiled child, but one had to look closely to find it.

His body was as young and hard as it ever had been, however, and as he stood now, stark naked in the bows, in the attitude of the harpooner, every muscle in his back and shoulders stood out clearly beneath the oiled skin. The sun had gilded his body to a dark honey gold and only his buttocks were a creamed ivory where his breech clout had protected them. He was a beautiful creature, favoured beyond all others by the gods, and Huy compared this body to his own and felt a despair within him.

Words began to form in his mind, a song to Lannon, an ode to his beauty. As he poled the skiff silently and smoothly over the still waters of the lake the words tumbled about in his mind, like wind-blown leaves, then they began to fall into patterns and the song was born.

In the bows Lannon signalled with his free hand without looking around, still poised, staring down into the waters and Huy turned the skiff with an expert thrust of the pole. Suddenly Lannon's body unleashed its pent-up energy in a fluid explosive thrust, an uncoiling of tensed muscles as he hurled the long harpoon down through the surface. The water bulged and swirled, and the line coiled in the bottom of the skiff began tearing out over the side, hissing away into the water.

'Ha!' shouted Lannon. 'A fair thrust! Help me, Huy!' And together they jumped to the line, laughing with excitement and then swearing at the pain of scorched fingers as the line ran through them. Together they slowed the heavy run of the fish. The skiff was moving out into the lake as the fish sought the deep water, dragging them with it.

'In Baal's holy name, stop him, Huy,' Lannon panted. 'Don't let him get out there and sound on us, we'll lose him for a certainty.' And they threw their combined weight on the line. The muscles in Huy's arms and shoulders bunched and corded like a sack of pythons, and the fish turned.

They brought him up swirling and kicking in circles under the skiff and when his huge whiskered head broke the surface Lannon shouted, 'Hold him!' And Huy took a turn of the line about his wrist and braced his body against the weight, the skiff heeling dangerously as Lannon snatched up the killing club and aimed a blow at the glistening black head.

The surface exploded as the fish went into its death-throes, and water cascaded over them, drenching them both.

'Hit him!' yelled Huy. 'Kill him!' And half blinded with spray, Lannon hammered at the enormous snout. Some of the blows were wild, crunching against the side of the skiff and splintering the planking.

'Not the boat, you fool. Hit the fish!' shouted Huy, and at last the fish was dead, hanging in the water beside the boat.

Laughing and panting and cursing, they got a heavy line through its gills and dragged it aboard, slithering in over the gunwale, slimy and black with a belly of bright silver, and bulging eyes. The whiskers above its gaping mouth still twitched and quivered as it filled the bottom of the boat, twice as long as Huy and with a body too thick to encompass within the circle of his arms.

'It's a monster,' panted Huy. 'The biggest I have ever seen.'

'You called me a fool,' said Lannon.

'Nay, Majesty, I was talking to myself,' grinned Huy, and he unstoppered the amphora and poured wine for them.

Lannon lifted his bowl to Huy, and grinned at him over the rim.

'Fly for me, Bird of the Sun'.

'Roar for me, Gry-Lion.' And they drained the bowls at the same time, then laughed together like children.

'It has been too long, Huy,' Lannon told him. 'We must do this more often. We grow old too swiftly, you and I, our cares and duties envelop us and we are caught in a web of our own making.' A shadow passed across Lannon's eyes, and he sighed. 'I have been happy these last few days, truly happy for the first time in many years.' He looked up at Huy almost shyly. 'You are good for me, old friend.'

He reached out and clasped Huy's shoulder awkwardly. 'I do not know what I would do without you. Don't ever desert me, Huy.'

Huy flushed, clumsy in his embarrassment, this was a mood of Lannon's to which he was unaccustomed. 'Nay, Majesty,' he answered huskily, 'I will be with you always.' And Lannon dropped his hand and laughed, echoing Huy's embarrassment.

'Sweet Baal, but we grow sentimental as girls – is it old age do you think, Huy?' He rinsed his wine bowl over the side, making a great show of it, and avoiding Huy's eyes. 'There are still fish in the lake, and an hour or two of the day left, let us use it.'

In the dusk they returned to where their old shack stood, neglected and forlorn beneath the graceful ivory palms above the beach. As Huy poled the skiff around the point of the island, and they cleared the reed banks, they saw the galley lying at anchor in the bay. The royal standard of house Barca stood at her masthead, and there were lamps burning at stem and stern. The reflections of the lamps danced on the dark waters, and the sound of voices carried clearly to them.

Huy stopped the skiff and leaned on the pole, and in silence they stared at the long ship. Then Lannon spoke.

'The world has found us out, Huy.' And his voice was tired and resigned. 'Hail them for me.'

The lamp hanging in its chain from the roof of the stern cabin lit their faces unnaturally, highlighting cheeks and noses but leaving the eyes in shadow. Their faces were grim as they gathered about the table, and listened to the messenger from the north. Although he was young, an ensign in his first year of military service, yet he had the poise of high birth and he gave his report lucidly.

He described the ripples of unrest that had lapped along the northern borders in the last few weeks, small incidents, movements of large bodies of men seen at a distance, the smoke and fires of vast encampments. Spies reported rumours of strange occurrences, of a new god with the talons of an eagle and the claws of a lion, who would lead the tribes to a land of grass and water. Scouts had watched the sailing of many Drav vessels along the eastern reaches of the great river, an unusual coming and going, talk of secret meetings between nobody knew whom.

There was a restlessness, a vast stirring and muttering, a sense of pressures and tensions building, of secret affairs afoot. The itching of storm clouds gathering and lightning brewing. Things felt but not understood, signs pointing into the unknown.

Lannon listened quietly, frowning a little, his chin propped on his fist and his eyes in shadow.

'My commander bids me tell you of his fears that you might find all this fancy and starting at the hooting of owls.'

'No.' Lannon brushed aside the boy's plea for his report to be taken seriously. 'I know old Marmon better than that. He does not call out snake for an earthworm.'

'There is more,' said the boy, and he laid a leather bag upon the table. He loosed the draw-string and shook out a number of metal objects.

'One of the river patrols surprised a party of pagans attempting to cross in the night. They carried these, all of them.'

Lannon picked up one of the heavy spearheads, and examined it curiously. The shape and workmanship were distinctive and he glanced up at Huy.

'Well?' he asked and had his own opinions confirmed when Huy answered,

'Drav. No doubt of it.'

'Carried by the pagans?'

'Perhaps they were taken from dead Dravs, or stolen.'

'Perhaps,' Lannon nodded. He was silent a while longer then he looked up at the young officer. 'You have done well,' he said and the lad flushed with pleasure. Lannon turned next to Habbakuk Lal. 'Can you take us on another night run to Opet?' And the admiral smiled and nodded.

Lannon and Huy stood together at the stern rail and watched their island merge into the darkness as the galley drew swiftly away, leaving its wake shimmering in the light of the moon.

'I wonder when we will next return here, Huy,' Lannon asked softly, and Huy moved restlessly beside him but did not answer. 'I feel as though I am leaving something behind here. Something valuable which I will never find again,' Lannon went on. 'Do you feel it also, Huy?'

'Perhaps it is our youth, Lannon. Perhaps these last few days were the end of it.' They were silent then, swaying to the easy motion of the galley under oars. When the island was gone Lannon spoke again.

'I am sending you to the border, Huy. Be my eyes and ears, old friend.'

'It is not for long, my heart,' Huy apologized, although Tanith had said nothing, and was fully engaged in daintily devouring a bunch of purple grapes. 'I will be back before you know I have gone.'

Tanith pulled a face as though one of the grapes were sour, and Huy studied her face with exasperation. It was serene and lovely and as unyielding as that of the goddess herself.

Huy had come to know all of Tanith's moods, every expression or tilt of the head that heralded them. He had watched with fascination as she changed from child to full woman, from bud to ripe bloom, and he had studied her with the patience and dedication of love, but this was one mood he had not learned how to distract.

Tanith licked her long tapered thumb and forefinger with the tip of a pink tongue, then examined her hand with interest, twisting it from side to side to catch the light.

'There is nobody else that the king can trust to send on this mission. It is a matter of grave importance.'

'I am sure,' Tanith murmured, still examining her hand. 'Just as there was no other who could go with him to stick fish.'

'Now, Tanith,' Huy explained reasonably. 'Lannon and I have been companions since our childhood. We used to go out to the islands often in the old days. It was like a pilgrimage to revisit our youths.'

'While I sit here with a bellyful of your child, alone.'

'It was but five days,' Huy pointed out.

'But five days!' Tanith mimicked him with her cheeks flushing, signalling the change of her mood from ice to fire. 'I swear on my love of the goddess, that I do not understand you! You profess your love for me, yet when Lannon Hycanus crooks a finger you run to him, panting like a puppy dog and roll on your back that he may tickle your belly!'

'Tanith!' Huy began to grin. 'I swear you are jealous!'

'Jealous, is it!' Tanith cried, and snatched up the fruit bowl. 'I'll give you jealous!' She hurled the bowl, and while it was still in flight she was reaching for fresh missiles.

Old Aina, nodding in the sunlight at the end of the terrace, awoke in the midst of the storm and joined Huy in flight. They found shelter behind an angle of the wall, and from there Huy cautiously reconnoitred the field and found it deserted, but he could hear Tanith weeping somewhere in the house.

'Where is she?' quavered Aina.

'In the house,' answered Huy, combing fruit from his beard and mopping at wine stains on his tunic.

'What is she doing?'

'Weeping,' Huy said.

'Go to her,' commanded Aina.

'And if she attacks me again?' Huy answered nervously.

'Spank her,' instructed Aina. 'Then kiss her.' And she gave him a toothless but utterly knowing grin.

'Forgive me, Holy Father,' whispered Tanith and her tears were warm and wet upon Huy's neck. 'It was childish of me, I know, but every moment I spend away from you is a piece of my life wasted.'

Huy held her, stroking her hair, gentling her, and his chest felt congested and swollen with the strength of his love for her. He was close to tears himself as he listened to her voice.

'Is it not possible for me to go with you this time?' She made one last appeal. 'Please, Holy Father. Please, my love.'

Huy's response was regretful but firm. 'No. I go fast and hard, and you are already in your third month.'

She accepted it at last. She sat up on the couch and dried her eyes. Her smile was only a little lopsided as she asked, 'Won't you tell me again of the arrangements you have made for the baby?'

She sat beside him, soft and warm with her pale skin glowing over the faint bulge of her belly and the new heaviness of her breasts in the lamplight. Her eyes were intent as she listened, and she nodded and smiled and exclaimed as Huy told her how it would be – of the foster mother he had selected in the cool and healthy air of the hills, on the estate at Zeng. He told her how the child would grow healthy and strong, and how they would visit it there.

'It?' Tanith demanded playfully. 'Never *it*, my lord – her!'

'*Him!*' Huy corrected and they laughed. But beneath Tanith's laughter the sadness persisted. This was not the way it would be. She could not see this, she could not catch the happiness of it, could not hear the laughter of a child nor feel the warmth of its little body against her.

For a moment the dark curtains of time opened, and, as sometimes happened, she glimpsed the future, saw dark shapes and men and things that terrified her.

She clung to Huy and listened to his voice. It gave her comfort and strength, and at last she asked softly, 'If I fetch your lute, will you sing for me?'

And he sang the poem to Tanith, but there were new verses now. Every time he sang it, there were new verses.

Marmon was the captain of the north, governor of the northern kingdom and commander of the legions and forts that guarded the northern border.

He was an old friend of Huy's, thirty years his senior but with the bond of scholarship between them. Marmon was a keen military historian, and Huy was helping him with a manuscript history of the third war with Rome. He was a tall bony man with a fine mane of silver hair of which he was inordinately proud. He kept it shampooed and neatly clubbed. His skin was smooth as a girl's and firmly drawn over the prominent bones of his skull, but the shivering sickness had yellowed the tone of his complexion and yellowed the whites of his eyes also.

He was one of the empire's most trusted generals, and for two days he and Huy discussed the situation along the border, poring over a clay-box map of the territory so that Marmon could show Huy exactly where each piece of the puzzle fitted in. Marmon's fine-boned hands touched each of the counters, or drew out the lines and areas of disturbance and dispute, while Huy listened and asked his questions.

At the end of the second day they ate the evening meal together, sitting up on the ramparts of the fortress for the sake of the cool evening breeze. A slave girl anointed their limbs with perfumed oil to discourage the mosquitoes and Marmon filled Huy's wine bowl with his own hands, but did not drink himself. The shivering sickness damages a man's liver, and for him wine turns to poison.

Huy thanked Baal for the immunity that the gods had given him against the ravages of this disease which flourished in the hot lowlands of swamp and river. Huy's mind chased after the thought: Why did the disease kill some, cripple others and leave others untouched? Why did it strike only in the lowlands, and leave the cool uplands untainted? He must think about it more, try and find answers to these questions.

However, Marmon was talking again now and Huy stopped his mind from wandering, brought it back to the problem in hand.

'I am at last building up a system of spies upon which I can rely,' Marmon was saying. 'I have men with the tribes who report to me regularly.'

'I should like to meet some of them,' Huy intervened.

'I would rather that you did not, Holiness,' Marmon

began, then noticed Huy's expression and went on smoothly. 'I expect one of them to report within the next few days. He is my most reliable informant. A man named Storch, a Vendi, an ex-slave. Through him I am recruiting a body of spies across the river.'

'I will speak with him,' said Huy, and the conversation changed, Marmon asking advice of Huy about his manuscript. As old friends they talked on, until darkness had fallen and the servants lit torches for them. At last Marmon asked deferentially:

'My lord, I have been petitioned by my officers. Some of them have never heard you sing, and those who have wish to hear it again. They are importunate, Holiness, but I trust you will bear with them.'

'Send to my quarters for my lute.' Huy shrugged with resignation, and one of the young officers stepped forward with the lute.

'We have already presumed, Holy Father.'

Huy sang the songs of the legions, the drinking and marching songs, the bawdy songs and the songs of glory. They loved it. The officers crowded silently about Huy on the ramparts, and in the courtyard below the common soliders gathered with their faces upturned, ready to come crashing in with the chorus.

It was late when an aide pressed through the throng and spoke quietly to Marmon. He nodded and dismissed the aide before whispering to Huy, 'Holiness, the man I spoke of has come.'

Huy set aside the lute. 'Where is he?'

'In my quarters.'

'Let us go to him,' suggested Huy.

Storch was a tall man, with the distinctive willowy grace displayed by so many of the Vendi, but the smooth velvety black skin of his shoulders was marred by the thickened scars of the slave lash.

He noticed Huy's glance and adjusted his cloak to cover

the ugly cicatrice, and it seemed to Huy there was a flash of defiance in his eyes although his face was handsome and impassive.

'He speaks no Punic,' Marmon explained. 'But I know you speak the dialect.'

Huy nodded, and the spy looked at him a moment longer before he addressed Marmon. His voice was quiet, without either anger or accusation.

'It was in our agreement that no other should see my face,' he said.

'This is different,' Marmon explained quickly. 'This is no ordinary man, but the High Priest of Opet and the General of all the armies of the king.' Marmon paused. 'This is Huy Ben-Amon.'

The spy nodded, his face still showed no expression, not even when Huy spoke in Vendi.

They talked for an hour, and at the end of it Huy turned to Marmon, speaking in Punic.

'This disagrees with much else you have told me.' Huy frowned and knocked his knuckles irritably against the table top. 'This man has heard nothing of a god with lion claws, nor of regiments of trained warriors armed with the weapons of the Drav.'

'No,' Marmon agreed. 'This section of the river is quiet. Our reports come from further east.'

'You have spies there?' Huy asked.

'Some,' Marmon nodded, and Huy thought a moment.

'I will move eastward then,' Huy made up his mind. 'I will march at dawn.'

'The patrol galley will arrive in five days.'

'I will see nothing from the deck of a galley. I will go on foot.'

'I will have an escort waiting for you before the rise of the sun,' Marmon offered.

'No,' Huy rejected the offer. 'I will move faster, and draw less attention to myself if I travel alone.' He glanced again at Storch. 'This man can serve as a guide, if he is as reliable as you say.'

Marmon relayed Huy's order to the spy and ended, 'You may go now. Eat and rest, and be ready before the sun.'

When he was gone Huy looked after Storch for a long moment then asked, 'How much do you pay such a one?'

'Very little,' Marmon admitted. 'Salt, beads, a few copper ornaments.'

'I wonder why he does it,' said Huy softly. 'Why he works for us when the scars of the lash are fresh upon his body.'

'I am no longer amazed by the acts of men,' said Marmon. 'I have seen too much strange behaviour ever to question a man's motives.'

'I never cease to do so,' murmured Huy, still looking after the spy, troubled by the man's treachery which jarred so harshly on Huy's own sense of honour.

Huy's efforts to find out more about the spy over the next four days met with but small sucess. Storch was a silent man, speaking only when he was questioned directly, and then answering with words barely sufficient for the occasion. He never looked directly at Huy; his eyes focused to one side of Huy's face and he looked beyond.

Huy found him a disconcerting companion, though he clearly knew every bend of the river and every fold of the ground over which they travelled.

They called at two of the forts upon the south bank, and from the men who garrisoned them Huy gleaned much first-hand intelligence. Twice they found the sign where large parties of men had crossed the river on mysterious business, and there were other small indications of secret activity which heightened Huy's feelings of unrest.

It disturbed him that these signs were in contradiction of Storch's assurances of quiet and stable conditions beyond the river.

They travelled swiftly and silently, slipping like a pair of forest spirits through the dense valley bush. They travelled much in the cool of evening and night and rested in the hissing heat of noon. They ate little, husbanding the contents of the corn bag and not wasting time upon the hunt.

On the fourth day they reached the summit of a small granite hillock from which they could survey a huge area of the valley floor, a panorama that stretched from escarpment to escarpment and only shaded away into the blue haze of distance. Before them the river made a mighty bight towards the south, a wide glittering loop of many miles that twisted back upon itself.

Although the loop was some twenty or twenty-five miles around, yet across the neck was less than five and beyond it stood the squat solid block of another garrison. The smoke from the cooking fires rose in a pale blue feather into the still, hot air.

Huy looked at the twist of the river for a long time, seeing the choice as between a full day's hard slogging or a quick cut across the neck of the loop with its attendant risk.

'Storch,' he said, 'can we cross the river? Are there men of the tribes here?'

The spy looked away from Huy's scrutiny, hiding any expression. He sat very still, squatting upon the granite dome beside Huy – and Huy thought he had not understood the question.

'It would be shorter to cut across the bend. Is it safe?' he asked again, and Storch replied:

'I will find out. Wait here for me.'

He returned an hour before dark and led Huy down to the river bank. Hidden in the reeds was a narrow dugout canoe. The woodwork was rotten with worm, and it stank of old fish. Huy's suspicion flared.

'Where did you find this?'

'There is a family of fishermen camped downstream.'

'How many?'

'Four of them,' Storch replied.

'Vendi?'

'No, men of Sofala.'

'Warriors?'

'Fishermen. Old men with grey heads.'

'You told them about me?'

'No.'

Huy hesitated, peering into the blank stare of Storch's eyes, trying to find a hint of treachery there.

'No,' said Huy, 'we will not cross. We will go around the long way.' It was a test. He waited for Storch's reaction, waited for him to argue, to attempt to persuade Huy to make the crossing.

'It is for you to say,' Storch nodded, and began to cover the canoe with reeds.

'Very well,' Huy agreed, 'take me across.'

Storch used the current to angle the frail little craft across the river. Ahead of them the cormorants beat the water with their wings in their frenzied efforts to launch into flight, while the chocolate and white jacanas scurried across the lily pads and the sinister log-like shapes of the crocodiles slid down the bank into deep water.

They landed on a muddy beach heavily trodden by the hooves of the game that drank here, and Storch hid the canoe. He led Huy up the bank, and into a glade of bright poisonous green swamp grass. They waded waist-deep through the thick clutching stems, and the ground was soggy and yielding underfoot.

In the centre of the glade Storch stopped abruptly and motioned Huy to stand still. He cocked his head in a listening attitude. They stood frozen for a long time, then

Storch cautioned Huy to remain where he was and he moved forward.

A hundred paces from Huy, Storch stopped again, but now he turned and looked back at Huy.

For the first time his face showed expression, a wild exultation, a bright burst of triumph.

He lifted his right arm and pointed at Huy, a gesture of denunciation, and he shouted out in Vendi, 'There he is! Take him!'

The grass of the glade rustled and shook as though a high wind blew across it, and from their places of concealment rose rank upon rank of Vendi warriors. Their shields overlapped, their lines formed concentric circles about Huy, ringing him in completely, and the plumes of their head-dresses were the foaming crest of a menacing wave about him.

Like the tightening of a strangler's fist upon the throat, the ring of warriors closed in on Huy. Wildly he glared about him, seeking an avenue of escape. There was none, and he stripped the leather guard from the blade of the vulture axe and flew like a terrier at the throat of a black bull.

'For Baal!' he shouted his defiance as he charged into the solid mass of warriors.

'The air in here is foul,' Lannon complained, sniffing at it. 'Is there no way in which we can drive ventilation shafts to the surface?'

'Majesty!' Rib-Addi could not hide his horror. 'Think what that would mean. Workmen in here.' He made a wide gesture that took in the entire length of the treasury. 'Can you imagine what tales they would take with them to inflame the greed of every brigand in the four kingdoms?'

It was for this reason that the location and contents of the royal storehouse was such a closely guarded secret. The best-kept secret in the empire, known only to the king, the High Priest and Priestess, Rib-Addi and four other officials of the treasury.

'I would have them sent to the gods immediately they had completed the task,' Lannon explained reasonably.

Rib-Addi blinked with surprise. He had not envisaged such a sweeping solution to the problem. It took him a moment's beard-scratching and deep thought to unearth his next objection.

'A ventilation shaft would provide entry for thieves and rodents and damp. All these would damage and destroy.'

'Oh, very well.' Lannon dismissed the subject, knowing well that Rib-Addi resisted change merely because it was change. What had been good for the past two hundred years, must be good for the next two hundred.

Lannon watched as the latest shipment of finger ingots from the mines of the middle kingdom was reverently added to the piles of gold already laid down in the recess of the treasury. Rib-Addi noted the quantities meticulously in his scroll, and Lannon affirmed the entry by scrawling his personal sign beside the entry.

The four trusted officials filed out of the long chamber with its piles of treasure. While they climbed the flagged stairs, Rib-Addi sealed the iron gate. He pressed the Gry-Lion's mark into the clay tablet, then he and Lannon climbed the stairs and passed through the sun-door into the state archives. Lannon closed the door, and the massive slab swung into its seating with a solid clunk.

Lannon made the sun sign at the god's image upon the door, then with Rib-Addi beside him discoursing as ever on wealth in its many manifestations, he passed down the length of the archives. The shelves were loaded with the records of the kingdom, and there was little space left. Soon he must turn his mind to an extension of these catacombs, how to enlarge them without destroying or damaging the existing structure.

They went out through the main portals, with their heavy leather curtains, into the guards' ante-chamber where officers of the Sixth Legion guarded the entrance. At all times of the day and night two officers were here, and at their call a century of picked troopers of Legion Ben-Amon waited. The Sixth Legion had originally been formed as a guard to the temples and treasuries of the kingdom and these still formed an important part of its duties.

Within the maze of the temple of Astarte, Rib-Addi took obsequious leave of Lannon and with his four underlings backed away, bowing until he disappeared around the bend of the corridor.

Assisted by four priestesses, Lannon, naked and magnificent, took the ritual bath in the pool of Astarte and while they dressed him in the tunic of the supplicant, Lannon managed to insert a playful hand into the skirts of one of the novices without the others noticing. The novice's expression did not change, but she pressed eagerly onto Lannon's fingers for a moment before drawing away, and while Lannon strode down the passage to the audience chamber of the oracle he made the gesture of stroking his moustache to inhale the girl odour that lingered on his fingers.

They were all as hot as corn cakes sizzling on the griddle, these brides of the gods, having to rely as they did on the embraces of their own kind, or the furtive attentions of a priest or temple guard. Lannon grinned as he wondered how many of them took advantage of the licence of the Festival of the Fruitful Earth. How often had he committed the mortal sin of sacrilege with some heavy-cloaked and disguised priestess. The Festival was imminent, in two weeks it would begin, and as always he looked forward to it. Then with regret he remembered that Huy was unlikely to return from the north in time to join in the celebrations. It would detract from his own enjoyment. Lannon's moods were always mercurial and now within a dozen paces his good spirits evaporated. As he entered the audience chamber he was scowling heavily.

He looked up at the oracle on her throne, sitting like an ivory statue with her hands folded on her lap and her face painted with cosmetics to resemble a mask, forehead white with antimony powder, eyelids metallic shiny blue and the mouth a vivid slash of scarlet in the pale face. He found a focus for his bad temper.

As he made a perfunctory obeisance, he remembered how often this witch had thwarted and unsettled him. He detested these sessions of divination, and yet found that they exerted a weird fascination. He realized that much of her oracle was dross, probably inspired by the politically active priesthood. Yet there was also much shrewd comment and excellent counsel amongst it, and occasionally there were nuggets of purest gold to be gleaned from the witch's lips. During his regular visits he had tuned his ear to catch the nuances of the oracle's voice. As with Rib-Addi, the witch had shades of conviction or hesitation in the manner in which she delivered the oracle. Lannon was sensitive to these, but more particularly so to a rarer tone, a monotonous low-pitched voice which the witch used when she spoke the miraculous god-given truths of real prophecy.

Now he took up his stance before her, legs planted firmly astride and clenched fists on his hips. With the arrogance of royalty heightened by his temper he asked the question.

Tanith hated these sessions with the Gry-Lion. He awed and frightened her. It was like being caged with some beautiful but savage predator, with its restless energy and unpredictable moods. The pale steely blue of his eyes had a predator's cold killing lust, his features were chiselled perfect but cold also with the same relentless passion.

Usually she had the comfort of Huy's presence behind

the curtains to carry her through, but this morning she was alone – and sick.

The night had been hot and airless, and the child in her womb as heavy as a stone. She had risen listless and pale from her couch, her skin damp with night sweat and she had forced down the light morning meal Aina had prepared for her, only to vomit it up again in a dizzy attack of nausea.

The taste of acid-bitter bile was in the back of her throat now, and sweat poured down beneath her cloak, tickling as it slid over her flanks and fruitful belly. She felt herself stifling, her breathing hunting raggedly for air, her body limp and weak, while the king growled his questions.

She was unprepared, her answers were empty words given without conviction, and she struggled to concentrate, to remember what Huy had told her.

The king was becoming restless, he strode back and forth before her, wearying her with his energy. She felt sweat break out beneath her mask of cosmetics. Her skin felt itchy and swollen, the pores blocked with paints and she longed to wipe it away. She had a sudden wondrous image of cool water falling over moss-covered rocks, of plunging her naked body into the green water, of sinking into it with her hair spreading on the surface, like the tendrils of a water plant.

'Come, witch! Come, oh seer of the future. It is a simple question. Answer it!'

The king was stopped before her, one foot on the throne steps, shoulders drawn back and hips thrust forward in masculine hauteur, a sneer on his handsome face and mockery in his voice.

Tanith had not heard the question, she floundered for words, and another wave of nausea washed over her. She felt sweat break through the film of paint on her upper lip, and the nausea changed to dizziness.

Lannon's face receded, and blackness closed about her.

Her vision narrowed, and she looked down a long shaft of darkness at the end of which Lannon's face burned like a golden star. There was a roaring in her ears, the sound of the storm wind through the trees of the forest. Then the sound of the wind died away into silence, and a voice spoke. The voice was husky and low-pitched, even and monotonous, the voice of a deaf woman or one drugged by the smoke of the bhang pipe. With mild surprise Tanith realized that the voice issued from her own throat, and the words shocked her.

'Lannon Hycanus, last Gry-Lion of Opet, question not the future. The future for you is darkness and death.'

She saw her own shock repeated upon Lannon's face, saw the colour fly from his cheeks, and his lips turn to lines of pale marble.

'Lannon Hycanus, prisoner of time, pacing behind the bars of your cage. Blackness waits for you.'

Lannon was shaking his head, trying to deny the words. The golden locks of his hair, still damp from the ritual bath, danced upon his shoulders, and he held up both hands in the sun sign, trying to avert the words which struck his soul like war arrows flighted from the bow.

'Lannon Hycanus, your gods are passing, they fly upwards, and leave you to blackness.'

Lannon retreated from the throne, hands raised to shield his face, but the words sought him out relentlessly.

'Lannon Hycanus, you who seek to know the future, know then that it lies in wait for you as the lion awaits the unwary traveller.'

Lannon cried out, and his terror exploded into violence.

'Evil!' he screamed, and rushed at the oracle, bounding up the steps of the throne. 'Witchcraft!' He struck Tanith in the face with his open hands, knocking her head across and back with heavy blows. The hood of her cloak fell back and her dark hair tumbled loose. The blows rang loudly against her flesh, but Tanith made no sound. Her silence drove Lannon on to further violence.

He caught the front of her cloak and dragged her from the throne.

'Sorceress!' he screamed, and flung her down the steps. She fell heavily and rolled, trying to come to her feet, but Lannon's first kick caught her in the belly and she doubled up, clutching at her middle and groaning as his sandalled feet smashed into her.

Lannon was bellowing as he pursued her about the chamber; between kicks he was looking wildly about for a weapon, something to destroy the woman and the words she had spoken.

Then suddenly the chamber was filled with priestesses, and Lannon drew back panting heavily, the pale eyes bright with madness.

'Majesty!' The Reverend Mother came forward, and Lannon's madness faded, but he was still shaking and his lips were white and quivering.

He turned and strode from the chamber, leaving Tanith whimpering upon the flagged floor.

The Divine Council of Astarte met in the Reverend Mother's chamber, and when she read the Gry-Lion's demand to them they listened quietly, thinking their own thoughts. The Council consisted of the High Priestess and two advisers, both of them senior priestesses who stood in the direct line of succession to the Reverend Mother.

'How can we deliver one of the sisterhood to the temporal body of the Gry-Lion? What precedent would we set by doing so?' Sister Alma asked. She was small and wrinkled with a face like an inquisitive monkey. 'What crime is the child accused of? If she has erred then it is for us to judge and punish. We must protect our own, even if it means defying the king.'

'Can the sisterhood afford such a grand gesture?' asked Sister Haka; dark-skinned and pock-marked, with long raven hair streaked with iron grey, her face was strong-jawed and her voice deep as a man's. She was not yet forty years of age, and certain to outlive the Reverend Mother. Until recently it seemed she must succeed to the head of the sisterhood, a position for which she longed. However, since an oracle had emerged in Opet, her position was less secure. History had proved that every oracle, in time, became Reverend Mother over the claims of all others. In addition, this one had the unquestioned favour of the High Priest, an important consideration when it came to the filling of a vacant position at the head of the Divine Council. In Tanith she had a strong rival, but apart from the political considerations, Sister Haka had a more intimate score to reckon.

Even now as she remembered how her advances had been rejected, she felt hot anger flood her cheeks. She still longed for the girl, dreams of her still troubled her sleep, and often when she was with a young novice in the dark she would pretend that it was Tanith.

'Are we strong enough to resist the demands of the king?' She let the question hang, and looked at their faces. All of them knew what an impetuous, irresistible force ruled in Opet. All of them knew that no one, noble or priest, friend or enemy, had ever denied him his way.

The silence persisted, until Sister Alma coughed gusts of tortured sound, that crescendoed until she spluttered up a lump of bloody phlegm and wiped her lips with a damp cloth, her face strained and her eyes tired and dull.

'Not long for you, old woman,' thought Sister Haka with her grim satisfaction hidden behind a mask of concern.

Again they were silent, until the Reverend Mother

spoke hesitantly. 'Perhaps, if it could be shown that the girl has sinned, committed some crime.'

It was all that Sister Haka needed. Ruthlessly she took charge. 'Send for the girl,' she instructed. 'Let us question her.'

Aina helped Tanith into the chamber, both of them hobbling and doubled over, one with age and the other with pain. They clung to each other, and the ancient priestess was mumbling encouragement to the injured girl, but her face screwed up with anger when she saw the Council, and she screeched at them.

'The child is hurt. Have you no care? Why do you summon her thus?'

'Silence, old hag,' Sister Haka spoke without passion. She was looking at Tanith. Tanith's face was swollen and the bruises were purplish and livid. One eye was closed, the lid puffed and blue, and her lip was cut through and scabbed.

'Let her sit,' Aina demanded. 'She is weak, and sick.'

'Nobody sits before the Council,' said Sister Haka.

'In the name of the goddess.'

'Do not blaspheme here, old crow.'

'I speak not of blasphemy, but of ordinary mercy.'

'You talk too much,' Sister Haka warned her. 'Go! Leave the girl here.'

It seemed Aina might argue still, but Sister Haka rose to her feet and her face was furious and her voice harsh with anger.

'Go!' she repeated, and Aina shuffled out grumbling and whining, leaving Tanith swaying weakly on her feet before the Council. Sister Haka sank down onto her stool and looked at Tanith. She would take her time now, there was all day if she needed it, and besides she was enjoying herself.

Tanith stayed upright by an effort of her will alone, for her senses swam and floated on waves and washes of pain.

The leaden feeling in her legs and lower belly anchored her, but she could make little of the questions with which they pelted her. Sister Haka was leading her onto what it was that she had told the king to infuriate him, she was showing how Tanith had endangered the sisterhood by antagonizing him. She kept coming back to the question, 'What was it you told him?'

'I cannot remember, Sister. I cannot remember,' Tanith whispered.

'You want us to believe that words of such dire consequence can be so easily forgotten. Come, child, what were they?'

'They were not my words.'

'Whose then?' Sister Haka leaned forward attentively, her face blotched with brown speckles of the pox and the wings of grey glowing in her dark hair. 'Whose words were they if not your own? The goddess's?'

'I do not know,' breathed Tanith, and then she gasped as a fist of agony squeezed something within her lower belly.

'Do you speak with the voice of the goddess?' Sister Haka demanded in her hoarse voice, dark and cruel as a bird of prey. The hawk stooping on the sparrow.

'Oh please!' whispered Tanith, bowing slowly forward with both hands pressed to her stomach. 'Oh please, it hurts. Oh how it hurts!'

The three priestesses watching her saw the quick flood of liquid which drenched the front of Tanith's tunic skirts, and splattered in dark red drops upon the flagstones between her feet. With slow grace, Tanith folded and fell forward. She lay on her side with her knees drawn up and she moaned softly.

Sister Haka went quickly to her and stooped over her, drawing up Tanith's skirts and peering with tense lesbian interest as she pulled Tanith's knees roughly apart.

She was smiling as she straightened, and looked at the

other two. 'There is your sin, Holy Mother. There is your proof of crime.' She looked down at the huddled body at her feet. 'Sacrilege!' she accused harshly. 'Sacrilege! A crime against the goddess.'

'I will not answer,' said Tanith gently. The bruises had faded and the swelling abated a little, but there was still a plum-coloured smear under one eye and her lip was distorted and scarred. She had been bed-ridden for ten days and she was still weak. 'I will not tarnish something so dear to me with words. I will not tell you his name.'

'Child, you know this is a matter of mortal sin. Your life is at stake here,' said the Reverend Mother.

'You have taken life from me already. Have done then. Take it all.' Tanith looked directly at Sister Haka, and from her to Lannon Hycanus who stood by the casement of the chamber. 'It is your intention to kill me. Nothing I say will alter that. Very well then, I will cherish the name of my child's father. I shall not let you use this against him also.'

'You are being stupid and stubborn,' said Sister Haka. 'We will find out in the end.'

'Why is it important?' Tanith asked. 'All that matters is that I stand between you and your ambitions.' Tanith looked directly at Sister Haka, and saw her words had struck by the swarthy rose flushing of the priestess's scarred cheeks. Tanith smiled and turned to Lannon. 'All that matters is that I am the source of the prophecy. You seek to destroy that. You seek to have the gods revoke their sentence upon you. It is vain, Lannon Hycanus. The winds of destiny are blowing, the hounds of fate are already hunting.'

'Enough,' snapped Lannon, striding to the centre of the chamber. 'I have no more time to waste. No longer can I listen to your idiot chatter.' He looked at Sister Haka. 'Bring the old priestess, the witch's chaperone.'

When Aina stood blinking and bewildered before the king he looked at her without passion or anger. 'You had duties. You did not discharge them. Name the bull who mounted the goddess's heifer.'

Aina wailed protest, disclaimer, pleading her ignorance. She went down on creaking knees before Lannon, crawling to him, kissing the hem of his tunic, drooling with terror. Lannon pushed her away irritably with one foot and looked at Sister Haka.

'Unless I misjudge your worth, you will not shirk man's work. Have you the belly for it?' he asked, and Sister Haka nodded, licking her lips, her eyes lighting with cruel anticipation.

'Break her arms first,' commanded Lannon. 'And let the witch stand close by to watch it.'

Sister Haka pulled Aina to her feet, holding her easily with her strong brown hands on the back of which grew long silky black hairs. Aina flapped and squawked with terror, and Sister Haka turned and pinned her, twisting one arm backwards against the elbow joint. The arm was thin and white with thick blue cords of vein showing through the skin.

'Wait!' cried Tanith. 'Let her go!'

'Release her,' ordered Lannon.

Tanith went to the old priestess and kissed her gently on the forehead and cheek. Aina was sobbing.

'Forgive me, child. I am sorry. I would have told them. Forgive me.'

'Gently, old mother. Gently now.' Tanith led her to the doorway and pushed her tenderly out of the chamber. She went back to them and spoke to the king.

'I will tell you his name – but you alone.'

'Leave us,' commanded Lannon, and the Divine Council rose and filed from the chamber.

When they were alone Tanith said the name, proudly and defiantly, and she saw Lannon reel as though it had been a physical blow.

'How long has he been your lover?' he asked at last.

'Five years,' she answered.

'So,' he said, seeing the answer to many questions. 'It seems we shared his love then.'

'Nay, Majesty.' Tanith shook her head. 'I had all of it.'

'You are wise to speak of it as past,' Lannon told her. He turned away to stand by the casement, and looked out across the lake. Nothing must come between us, he thought, I need him. I need him.

'What will it be, Majesty? Poison or the secret dagger? How will you kill a priestess of Astarte? Have you forgotten that I belong to the goddess?'

'No,' said Lannon. 'I have not forgotten, and I will send you to her, on the tenth day of the Festival of the Fruitful Earth. You will go as the messenger of Opet to the Gods.'

'Huy will not allow it,' whispered Tanith in horror.

'Huy is in the north – a long way from the pool of Astarte.'

'He will hate you for it, always. You will lose him for ever,' Tanith warned him, but he shook his head.

'He will never know that I ordered it so. He will never know that you betrayed him, and told me his name.' He smiled then, a cold and golden smile. 'No, it is you that will lose him, and I that will have him. You see, I need him, and my need is more important than yours.'

He had been borne in a litter at first, while he was unconscious and then later when he was still too weak to march, so he did not know for how long and in what direction they had travelled.

Even later when he was forced to walk, they bound and blindfolded him, so that he was aware only of the press of their bodies about him and the stench of sweat and the rancid fat with which they smeared their skin. There was no answer when he spoke, and rough hands urged him forward, and a spear blade pricked him when he baulked.

He had been badly beaten and bruised, there were still lumps and gashes in his scalp, and his body was grazed and painfully wrenched, but he had taken no serious wounds, no deep spearthrust nor broken bones. It was as though they had carefully avoided dealing him a killing or crippling injury despite the fact that he had piled the corpses of their comrades in wind-rows about him, the vulture axe taking cruel toll before they overwhelmed him.

On the first night when they camped he began a tentative investigation of his position with escape in mind, but then when he tried to shift his blindfold enough to see out, a heavy blow in the face dissuaded him. They fed him a handful of boiled corn and a strip of badly cured meat, gamey and rank with bacon beetle. Huy ate it hungrily.

In the morning they were marching before the dawn, and when Huy felt the sun's warmth on his cheek and saw the light through his blindfold, he repeated the praise of Baal silently and asked the god for his help.

Later that day he was aware of the ground levelling beneath his feet as though they journeyed across an open plain, and there was the smell of cow dung and smoke and humanity. Over the thudding rhythm of his escorts' bare feet and the swish of their war-kilts he heard a vast susurration of voices and movement. Blending with this was the lowing of many cattle, the air quivered with sound and movement, a hive murmur which warned him of the presence of a great multitude.

At last they stopped him. He stood weary and thirsty in the hot sun with the raw-hide rope cutting into his wrists and his bruises and grazes aching. Time passed slowly in the silence of the waiting men.

At last a voice called out loudly, and Huy's nerves jumped. The voice was in Vendi demanding, 'Who seeks the lion-clawed, who seeks the bird-footed?'

Huy remained silent, waiting for some indication of how to behave, and to his surprise he felt the cool touch of iron at his wrists and a blade sawed through his bonds. He rubbed his fingers, wincing at the flow of blood. Then he lifted his hands to the blindfold, expecting another blow, but none came and he loosed the cloth and blinked uncertainly in the bright sunlight.

His eyes adjusted quickly, and he felt his heart lurch with shock at what he saw. Huy stood at the centre of a wide plain, a slightly concave bowl of land rimmed in with low hills.

Except for a circular open area a hundred paces across, at the centre of which Huy now stood, the land was black with warriors. Huy gazed in awe at this multitude, and he could not begin to reckon their numbers. He would never have believed that the land could support such numbers, it was unreal, completely nightmarish – and the quality of unreality was heightened by the menacing stillness of the black hordes. Only the feathers of their head-dresses stirred in the sluggish wash of heated noonday air.

The heat and the press of humanity threatened to suffocate him, and he looked about him desperately as though seeking an avenue of escape. Storch stood near him, and he carried the vulture axe on his shoulder. Huy felt a weak flutter of anger for the man's treachery, but somehow it seemed unimportant in the enormity of this fresh experience.

Storch was not looking at him, instead he was watching a group of Vendi war captains who stood about a low mound of earth at the end of the clearing. The mound was bare, but compelled the attention of them all, like an empty stage before the principals appear.

Again the voice demanded. 'Who seeks the Great Black Beast, who hunts the lion?'

The heated silence and stillness persisted, then suddenly the multitude stirred and sighed as a man stepped up onto the mound.

The tall crown of heron feathers on his head and the height of the mound upon which he stood made him god-like. His robes of leopard skin hung to the ground about him, and he stood as still as a tall tree in a rustling plain of grass as the royal salute shook the foundations of earth and sky.

Storch carried the vulture axe to the mound and laid it at the king's feet, then he backed away, and the king looked across the open ground at Huy.

Huy drew himself up, trying to ignore the aches of his body, trying not to limp as he approached the mound and looked up at Manatassi.

'I should have guessed,' he said in Punic.

'You should have killed me,' said Manatassi, and from the folds of his robes he lifted the iron claw. 'Instead of arming me with this.'

'You do not understand,' Huy said. 'Your life was not mine to take. I made an oath.'

'Still a man who lives on his word,' Manatassi said, yet Huy looked in vain for the traces of mockery in his voice.

'There is no other way to live.' Huy felt tired now; he faced his certain death with resignation. He did not really have the energy to debate it.

Manatassi made a gesture with the claw, indicating the massed ranks of his army.

'You see what a spear I have forged?'

'Yes,' Huy nodded.

'Who can stand against me?' Manatassi asked.

'Many will try,' said Huy.

'You amongst them?'

And Huy smiled. 'I do not think I will have the chance to do so.'

Manatassi looked down at the little hunchback in his tattered tunic, his beard matted and the bruises on his face and arms, soiled and beaten, but not humble as he discussed his own fate.

'Not one of my men understands us,' Manatassi told Huy. 'We can speak freely.'

Huy nodded, puzzled, but interested in this change of mood.

'I offer you life, Huy Ben-Amon. Come to me, give me the love and duty you have given to the Gry-Lion of Opet and you will live to be an old man.'

'Why do you choose me?' Huy asked.

'I have waited for you. I knew you would come. My spies have watched for you, but it was fate that delivered you so neatly into my hands.'

'Why me?' Huy repeated.

'I need you,' Manatassi said simply. 'I need your learning, I need your understanding, and your humanity.'

'You forgive me the taking of your hand?' Huy asked.

'You could have taken my life,' Manatassi answered.

'You forgive the slave ash and the mines of Hulya?'

'Those I will never forgive,' Manatassi snarled, his face twitching and the eyes glaring smoky yellow. 'But they were not your doing.'

'You forgive the massacre at Sett?' Huy persisted.

'You are a soldier, you could do nothing else.'

Manatassi was still trembling, and Huy sensed how narrowly he skirted the abyss, but he felt compelled to explore this man's strength – and weakness.

'What would you have of me, then?' Huy asked.

'March beside me,' said Manatassi.

'Against?'

'Against Opet and its monstrous cruelties and terrible gods,' Manatassi urged him. 'With you beside me and this army at my back I will rule the world.'

'I cannot do that.' Huy shook his head.

'Why not? Tell me why. It is evil, it must be destroyed.'

'It is mine,' said Huy. 'My land, my people, my gods – therefore they cannot be evil.'

'I thought you were a man of reason,' Manatassi snarled.

'Reason can carry a man just so far, and then he must trust to his heart,' said Huy.

'You refuse me, then?'

'Yes.'

'You know that you choose death?'

'Yes.'

Manatassi raised his hand, the iron claw glowing in the sunlight, and Huy knew that when the hand fell he would die. He steeled himself to meet it as calmly as he had dealt it.

Manatassi turned away. Then after a moment he sighed, and his shoulders beneath the thick scars heaved.

'You spared me,' said Manatassi. 'I shall spare you.'

Huy felt weak with relief. He had not wanted to die, and he allowed himself at last to think of Tanith and the child. Now he would still see his son, and his heart soared.

'Go back to Opet. Go back to your king. Tell him that Manatassi, the Great Black Beast, marches out of the north to destroy him.'

'Should you warn an enemy?' Huy asked. 'Did I teach you that?'

Manatassi smiled. 'A warning will not help him,' he said. 'Tell him what you saw here. Tell him of this army – and let it chill his guts. Tell him I come for him, and I will spare none nor leave a memory of him to taint this land. Tell him I come, and I come swiftly.'

Manatassi picked up the vulture axe and handed it to Huy.

'Go!' he said. 'All debts between us have been paid. You have no call on me, and I have no call upon you. When I meet you again I shall kill you.'

They stared at each other, standing close enough to touch, but separated by a distance wider than the span of the oceans or the vastness of the land.

Huy turned and limped away down the corridor of warriors that opened for him, and no man barred his way.

'Old mother, you must not distress yourself so,' Tanith whispered. 'It was not your fault.'

'I would have told them,' Aina mumbled. 'I know I would have told them. That Sister Haka, she terrifies me.'

'You did not tell,' Tanith comforted her. 'You kept our secret well – even we ourselves did not know you had found out.'

Aina set down the food bowl beside Tanith's bed, and she smiled reflectively. 'You were so happy, the two of you. It made me feel good just to see you. He is a good person, despite his poor crooked back, he is gentle and kind.'

Tanith moved across on the couch, making room for Aina to sit. 'Sit by me for a while, old mother. I am so lonely here, it makes the waiting so much harder.'

Aina glanced fearfully across the narrow chamber at the barred doorway.

'They do not like me to stay too long.'

'Please,' Tanith entreated. 'There is so little time left.' And Aina nodded and gathered up her skirts to sit, creaking at her knee-joints, upon the couch. Tanith leaned close to her, and she whispered eagerly, 'Did you send messengers, did you find someone to go?'

'I sent two young ensigns from Legion Ben-Amon. They worship the Holy Father as though he were himself a god. I told them that you were in mortal danger, and that the Holy Father must return with all speed.'

'Do you think they will find him?'

'There are a hundred roads that he might take, and the land is wide. I would not lie to you, my child. The chance is not good.'

'I know,' said Tanith. 'And if they find him, can he return in time, and if he does, is there aught he can do to dissuade the Gry-Lion?'

'If he returns in time, then you are safe. I know the man.'

'Wait for him, Aina. If he returns, go to him secretly and tell him that the king knows about us. You must warn him of that, for he is also in danger.'

'I will warn him,' promised Aina.

'Oh, I pray to all the gods that he returns swiftly to Opet. I do not want to die, old mother. There is so much I would yet have from life, but the days run out now. It is already the sixth day of the Festival. Unless Huy comes there are but four days of my life left.'

'Gently, child,' Aina crooned and put an arm about Tanith to pat and cuddle her. 'Be brave,' she crooned, 'be brave, child.'

'It is not so easy,' Tanith told her, 'but I will try.' And she pulled away from Aina's embrace and sat up straight. 'You must go now, old mother – or Haka will beat you again.'

On the walls of the fortress at Zanat, south of the great river, a sentry held a javelin lightly in his right hand, concealing it below the level of the parapet, and he looked down on the strange wild figure below him. The man's hair was filthy and matted, he wore no armour, his tunic hung in tatters, and his face was bruised and badly swollen. He seemed to be wounded for he was doubled up painfully in an unnatural posture, bowed beneath the weight of the huge battle-axe he carried.

'What is your name, and what your business?' the sentry hailed, and the traveller looked up at him.

'I am Ben-Amon, High Priest of Baal and warrior of Opet. My business is the king's.'

The sentry started, and thrust the javelin back into its rack. He realized how close he had come to making a fool of himself. The crooked back and the axe were famous throughout the four kingdoms, he should have recognized them immediately, and he berated himself as he ran down into the courtyard shouting for the officer of the guard, warning him of their distinguished caller.

Huy came in through the side gate the moment it swung open, and he cut short the military salutes with a curt, 'Enough of that nonsense.'

The officer of the guard was startled at having the legion's beloved ceremonial dismissed in such a cavalier fashion, and he smothered a grin. Coupled with his appearance and his beggar's garb this story would go to swell the body of legend that already existed about this remarkable little man.

Huy was striding past the hastily assembled guard, demanding of the officer as he passed, 'Where is the general? Is he here?'

'Yes, my lord – Holiness. He is in his quarters.'

'Praise to Baal!' Huy grunted with relief.

Huy wolfed a thick cut of cold meat folded between two corn cakes, and he washed it down with a bowl of red wine, speaking through and around each mouthful of food as he issued his orders.

Marmon's scribe dashed off each article, racing to keep up with the flow of Huy's words. Marmon sat on his stool in the corner, his head of silver hair shining like a summer thunder cloud and his handsome face anxious and worried.

He could hardly believe what he was hearing, yet he knew better than to doubt the word of Huy Ben-Amon. He realized that he was culpable, that he should have been the one to discover this deadly threat that had grown up so swiftly on their borders. Perhaps he had spent too much of his time dreaming over his ancient histories, perhaps he had grown old and feeble without realizing it. He wondered what retribution there would be from Huy Ben-Amon and the Gry-Lion of Opet. Neither of them were men who let failure pass unnoticed.

He listened as Huy issued the orders which would place every garrison and every unit on the alert, would mobilize every disbanded legion, would send messengers racing across the land carrying the scrolls that would place the entire empire on a war footing. Marmon wondered at the courage of a man who could make this battle decision alone, a decision for which he would have to answer to the king and the council of nobles. He might be held responsible for all the losses and damages that would arise when the entire industry and commerce of the nation were suspended. It was a decision upon which his own life might hang, as well as that of Opet.

As he watched Huy signing the orders he doubted that he would have had that much certainty of the rightness of his own actions. He knew he would have sent to Opet for orders, and probably have jeopardized whatever chance there was of survival. For, from what Huy had told him, it was a matter of survival. They were confronted by an enemy so vastly superior in numbers that success lay with the gods.

Huy was finished. He signed the last scroll and the fire went out in him. It was only then that Marmon realized that the man was exhausted. He staggered slightly, his whole body slumping and he seemed to shrivel in size under the burden of his weariness.

Marmon jumped up from his stool and went to him. Huy brushed off the helping arm and tried to gather his strength in hand again.

'I must leave for Opet,' he said, slurring like a drunkard and steadying himself against a corner of the table. 'What day is it, Marmon? I seem to have lost count of the days.'

'It is the seventh day of the Festival, Holiness.'

'The Festival?' Huy looked at him stupidly.

'The Fruitful Earth,' Marmon reminded him.

'Ah!' Huy nodded. 'I did not think it was that late. Have you a war-elephant to carry me to Opet?'

'Nay, Holiness,' Marmon told him regretfully. 'There are no elephant here.'

'Then I must march.' Huy resigned himself.

'You must rest first.'

'Yes,' Huy agreed. 'I must rest.' And he let Marmon lead him to the bed-chamber. As he fell across the couch he asked, 'How long will it take to reach Opet from here, Marmon?'

'If you move fast, six days. Five, if you fly.'

'I shall fly,' said Huy. 'Wake me at dusk.' And he fell asleep.

Looking down on the sleeping figure, Marmon felt the familiar stirring of his affections. He felt his admiration for the great heart of this little fighting man, felt envy for the thrust and drive which always carried him ahead of the pack, and he was glad that Huy Ben-Amon led them at a time of such crisis.

It was then he remembered the messenger from Opet, the young ensign of Legion Ben-Amon who had passed through the garrison the previous day carrying an urgent message for the High Priest. He debated with himself for a moment, then decided not to disturb Huy's rest. He would tell him when he woke at dusk.

At dusk Huy woke, ate a light meal and oiled his body. Twenty minutes later he ran out into the cool of evening through the garrison gate with fifteen legionaries as escort, and it was only after they had disappeared into the dark and silent forests of the south that Marmon again remembered the message that the young ensign had given him.

He thought to send a messenger after Huy, but he knew that no runner of his could hope to catch the priest after he had such a head start. The speed of Huy's long legs was part of the legend.

Marmon thought comfortably, 'He will be in Opet soon enough.' And he paced along the parapet until he reached the far side of the fortress. He stayed there until after darkness had fallen, staring into the turbulent north and wondering how soon they would come.

The Divine Council came to Tanith's cell on the morning of the ninth day of the Festival of the Fruitful Earth. They were led by the Reverend Mother, frail and uncertain, shifty-eyed with guilt.

'We have joyous news for you, my child,' she told Tanith, and Tanith sat up quickly on her couch – her heart leaping within her. The Gry-Lion had changed his mind perhaps.

'Oh, Reverend Mother!' she whispered, feeling the tears of relief at the back of her eyelids. She was still shaky and weak from the loss of the child, and it took little to make her weep now.

The Reverend Mother was gabbling on, not looking at Tanith, unable to meet her eyes, and for a while Tanith was puzzled. She could not understand this talk of precedent and ecclesiastical law, until she glanced at Sister Haka's face and saw how gloating and lustful were the dark features and how brightly the cruel eyes shone.

Then suddenly she realized that this was no reprieve.

'And so in his wisdom the king has chosen you, has given to you the great honour of carrying the message of Opet to the goddess.'

They had not come to release her, but to seal her fate. Sister Haka was smiling.

'You must give thanks, my child. The king has given you life eternal. You will live in glory at the side of the goddess, hers for ever,' said the Reverend Mother, and the priestesses chorused, 'Praise to Astarte. Praise to Baal.'

The Reverend Mother went on, 'You must prepare yourself. I will send Aina to help you. She knows the path of the messenger well, for she has attended many of the chosen ones. Remember to pray, my child. Pray that the goddess will find you acceptable.'

Tanith stared at them, white-faced and afraid. She did not want to die. She wanted to cry out, 'Spare me. I am too young. I want just a little more happiness, just a little more love before I die.'

The Divine Council filed from the chamber, leaving her alone. Now at last the tears flooded her eyes, and she cried out aloud.

'Huy, come to me! Please, come to me.'

Huy struggled up through the glutinous dark swamp of exhausted sleep with the nightmare cry still echoing in his ears. It took him a while to remember where he was and to realize that he had dreamed the horror that had woken him.

He lay in the sparse shade of the wild fig, and through the branches he saw the altitude of the sun and knew that they had slept for only an hour. His legs still felt leaden, his body torpid and completely enervated by two days of hard travel.

He should sleep again for another three or four hours at the least, but the nightmare stayed with him, denying him rest.

He pulled himself up on an elbow, surprised at the effort it required, but then remembering that he had run over two hundred Roman miles in two days. He looked at the remains of his escort, three of them, haggard-faced and finely drawn from their exertions, sleeping like dead men in the attitudes in which they had fallen. The other twelve had dropped along the way, unable to match the blistering pace which Huy had set.

Huy heaved himself to his feet. He could not sleep, could not rest, while dread haunted him and the safety of his king and his land was in jeopardy.

He limped stiffly down to the bed of the small stream, and knelt in the sugary white sand. He splashed his face and body with the clear water, soaking his tunic and beard, then he climbed the bank and looked at his sleeping men. He felt pity for them, pity that did not prevent him calling out, 'Up! On your feet! We march for Opet.'

One of them could not wake, though Huy kicked his ribs and slapped his cheeks with an open hand. They left him lying, whimpering in his sleep.

The other two dragged themselves up, groaning, moving with stiff sore legs, and the glazed expressions of fatigue.

Huy walked the first half-mile to loosen aching muscles, with the escort staggering after him.

Then he went up onto his toes, changed the vulture axe from one shoulder to the other, and went away at a run, bouncing long-legged on a springy stride that covered the ground like the trot of an eland bull.

One of the legionaries cried out as his leg collapsed under him and he went down sprawling in the dust. He was finished, and he lay there groaning with mortification and the pain of cramped and torn muscles.

The other followed Huy, his steps firming as his legs loosened and charged with new blood.

They ran the sun to its zenith, spurning the pitiless heat of the noonday, and they ran on into the afternoon.

Ahead of them, low on the horizon, stood the perpetual bank of cloud which marked the Lake of Opet, a beacon of hope, and Huy ran with his face lifted to it, instinct guiding his feet and his will feeding his exhausted body, allowing him to run on when all physical strength was burned up.

In the last low rays of the sun the walls and towers of Opet glowed with a warm rose colour and the surface of the lake was flaming gold that pained the eye.

Huy plunged on down the caravan road, racing past other dusty travellers who pulled to the side of the track, calling after him as they recognized him.

'Pray for us, Holy Father.'

'Baal's blessing on you, Holiness.'

Half-way down the pass of the cliffs that led to the lake shore and the city, the legionary who followed Huy shouted in a clear strong voice, 'Forgive me, Holy Father, I can go no further.' And his knees buckled under him, he lost direction, blundering to the side of the track; his face contorted at the agony of his bursting heart, he went down face first and lay without movement, dead before he struck the ground.

Huy Ben-Amon ran on alone, and the guard upon the palace gate of Opet saw him afar off, and they swung the gates open to welcome him.

Tanith woke with gentle hands shaking her. There was a lamp burning beside her couch, and Aina leaned over her. Tanith saw that the old face was screwed up into a toothless grin, the monkey eyes twinkling in their web of ancient wrinkles.

'Child, are you awake?'

'What is it, Aina?' Tanith sat up quickly, her spirits leaping upwards like sparks from the bonfire of hope when she saw Aina's smile.

'He has come!' Aina told her jubilantly.

'Huy?'

'Yes, the Holy Father has come.'

'Are you sure?' Tanith demanded.

'I have heard it shouted in the streets. The whole city is agog. They say he ran from Zanat to Opet in three days, they say he killed fifteen men who tried to run with him. He broke their hearts and left them lying on the road.'

'Oh, Aina.' Tanith embraced the old priestess, hugging her to her breast. 'If he came so fast, it must be because he knows.'

'Yes, child. Of course he knows. Why else would he come with such speed? One of the ensigns would have reached him with my message. He knows all right.' Aina drooled and nodded her conviction. 'He knows!'

'Where is he now?' Tanith was laughing with her excitement. 'Do you know where he is?'

'With the king. He went straight to the palace.'

'Oh, praise the goddess and all the gods,' breathed Tanith. 'He has gone to use his influence with the Gry-Lion. Do you think he will succeed, Aina? Will the king change his mind?'

'Of course, child. Do you doubt it? If Huy Ben-Amon set his mind to it, he would make Baal himself change his mind.'

'Oh, I am so happy, old mother.' Tanith clung to Aina,

and they comforted each other in the night. Until at last Tanith drew away.

'Go to him, Aina. Wait for him outside the palace. Tell him everything, and come back to me with his message.'

As Aina was about to leave the chamber Tanith called after her, 'Tell him I love him. Tell him I love him better than life – and all the gods.'

'Hush,' said Aina, 'hush, child. Someone may hear you.'

Alone, Tanith lay back on her couch and smiled.

'I don't care,' she whispered. 'Huy is here, and nothing else matters.'

Lannon listened to Huy in rising consternation. His first thought when Huy had arrived unheralded and unexpected in the night was that he had somehow learned of the sacrifice at tomorrow's ceremony. He had considered refusing Huy an audience, considered all manner of evasion, but while he was considering it Huy had barged his way into Lannon's bed-chamber past the startled and protesting guards.

Lannon had risen naked from the side of his youngest wife, angry words shrivelled on his lips when he saw the state to which Huy was reduced.

'Forgive me, Majesty. I carry dreadful tidings.'

Lannon stared at him, saw the filthy and dusty tunic, the unkempt hair and beard, the skull-like face from which the flesh had wasted, and the wild eyes in their bruised and sunken sockets.

'What is it, Huy?' He went quickly to the priest, and steadied him with a brotherly arm.

The Council of Nine, all the noble families of Opet, met in night session and they heard the report of Huy Ben-Amon in horrified silence. Only when he had croaked out the last of it and slumped wearily on his stool did the babble of fault-finding, and blame-laying, and self-pity and doubt begin.

'We were told he was destroyed at Sett!'

Huy said, 'You were told only that I slew 30,000 at Sett. I did not name them.'

'How could such an army be recruited without our knowledge? Who is to blame?'

Huy answered, 'It was recruited beyond our borders. No one is to blame.'

'What of the mines – we must protect them.'

Huy smiled wearily. 'That is what we intend.'

'Why is there only one legion on the border?'

Huy answered them grimly, 'Because you refused to vote the money for more.'

They turned on him then, their words hammering through the fog of weariness.

'How did you pass unscathed through enemy lines?'

'Was not this Timon once your protégé?'

'You know him well, you taught him, did you not?' And Huy looked at Lannon.

'Enough!' Lannon's voice cut through the tirade. 'His Holiness has called the nation to war. He has shown me copies of the scrolls, and I am about to sign them in ratification.'

'Should we not wait a while?' That was Philo, naturally, 'Are we not being too hasty?'

'What will you wait for?' Huy demanded. 'Until they open your bowels with a spear blade and cut off your testicles?'

Lannon signed the war orders a little before dawn, and he dismissed the Council of Nine with the words:

'We will meet again at noon, after the final ceremony of the Fruitful Earth. See to your arms and take leave of your families.'

To Huy he spoke kindly when they were alone. 'Sleep here. There is nothing more you can do now.'

He was too late. Huy was already asleep, slumped forward on the table with his head on his arms. Lannon picked him up from his stool, and carried him like a sleeping child to a guest chamber.

He placed a sentry at the door.

'No one must wake the Holy Father,' he instructed. 'No one! Do you understand.'

It was almost dawn. The sacrifice would take place in a very few hours, and he knew that Huy was in a kind of death sleep that might last for many days. He left him, and went to bathe and dress for the procession.

Aina lifted the hood of her cloak over her head, covering her face. She thrust her bony old hands into the wide sleeves, and leaned forward to blow out the lamp.

She stood in the darkness, considering what she must do. She would not wait for the High Priest to leave the palace. Aina had access to the palace kitchens. The major domo there was the grandson of her youngest sister, and she often went to eat there as a change from the temple fare. All the palace slaves knew her. It would be a simple matter to find out from one of them whereabouts in the rambling mud-walled building the High Priest was, an even simpler matter to get word to him.

Quietly she drew the curtains of her cell aside, and peered out. There was a single torch guttering in its bracket at the end of the passage, but it threw only a feeble light and Aina did not see the dark figure waiting for her in a shadowy angle of the corridor until it came gliding towards her.

'Not yet asleep, old woman?' a deep, almost masculine voice asked softly, and a strong hand closed on Aina's wrist.

'Are you going visiting so late at night? Is it that you have heard of Huy Ben-Amon's return to Opet?'

'No,' whimpered Aina. 'I swear it.' And she struggled feebly. With her free hand Sister Haka pushed the old priestess's hood back from her face and peered into her eyes.

'You were going to Ben-Amon, were you not?'

'No. I swear it.' Aina saw death in Sister Haka's expression, and she began to scream. It was a thin passionless sound like the sound of the wind, and it was cut off abruptly as Sister Haka's powerful hand whipped over her mouth.

From a doorway opposite a frightened face peered out, and Sister Haka snapped, 'Go back to your couch.' And the young novice obeyed quickly.

Sister Haka forced Aina's frail body back through the curtains and onto her couch. She held her hand over mouth and nostrils, holding Aina down with an arm across her chest.

Aina's struggles exploded feverishly, her heels drummed and kicked against the wall and her arms flapped and clawed at Sister Haka's face. Then swiftly it was over and she subsided and lay still. Sister Haka held her mouth and nostrils closed for a long time after she was quiet, then with one hand she felt the scrawny old chest with its empty pendulant dugs for a heartbeat.

Finding none she nodded with satisfaction, arranged the careless limbs tidily, and left the cell. Through the single window slit the first light of dawn lit Aina's face. Her mouth hung open, her eyes were startled and a wisp of silky silver hair floated on her forehead.

Lannon was conscious of the need to carry through the final ritual of the Festival meticulously. It was apparent that he faced a national emergency of vast proportions, that Opet was opposed by an enemy more powerful and relentless than any in her long history. The oracle had spoken against him, perhaps he or his kingdom had incurred the wrath of the gods.

Lannon knew that the fate of nations hangs not entirely on the actions of men, battles are not won by swords alone. He knew there were influences beyond, sometimes malignant and sometimes benign, which dictated the outcome of earthly affairs. He knew it was possible to placate an angry god, and to enlist the goodwill of one that was kindly disposed.

As the Reverend Mother led him through the catechism beside the pool of Astarte, he paid special concern to the correctness of his responses, and there was no mistaking the sincerity of his voice as he made his pledge to the goddess.

The priestesses closed in about him and light hands helped him shed his robes of purple silk. Currents of cool air stroked his naked body as he strode forward to the edge of the pool, went down the stone steps and lowered himself into the clear green waters.

His body shone white below the surface, and his long golden tresses and beard glistened with water as the priestesses beside him scooped up water in the conch shells and poured it over his head.

They emerged from the pool, and Lannon felt a sense of spiritual cleansing, as though the sacred waters had washed away his cares and armed him against the dangers that lay ahead. He was not a man of deep religious faith, and yet in this moment he felt uplifted. He was happy then that he had chosen such an important messenger for the goddess.

His own petty and personal motives no longer counted. He was sending a priestess of the blood, a god-touched oracle, a person of value and weight. Surely the goddess must find her acceptable, surely Astarte would now turn her countenance upon the children of Opet, spread her wings across the nation in this time of trial and danger.

They dried off his skin, and the muscle was firm and beautifully shaped in leg and arm and wide shoulders. Two priestesses came forward and lifted a white silk robe over his head, the colour of joy and rejoicing. The Reverend Mother placed a garland of flowers about his neck, crimson cave lilies whose scent was sweet and heavy in the hushed cavern.

It was the moment when the praise of the goddess must be sung, and then the offertory. The silence persisted a moment longer and then a voice rang through the cavern.

The voice startled Lannon, and he turned his head searching for the singer. There was no mistaking that voice, the sweet shimmering power of it, the depth and timbre that made the hair on Lannon's forearms come erect and set the echoes flying about the temple, seeming almost to ruffle the quiet surface of the green pool.

Lannon gaped at Huy. He had stepped out of the ranks of nobles and officers and as he sang he paced slowly towards Lannon. His arms spread in the sun sign, his mouth wide open showing the strong white teeth and that achingly beautiful voice pouring from his throat. The praise song ended, and Huy stood close beside the king, looking up at him. His face was still raddled with fatigue, the dark eyes still underscored by bluish purple smears, the skin pale and drawn, but he was smiling at Lannon with an expression of loyal affection.

'Huy!' Lannon whispered in horror. 'Why are you here? I left you resting with orders not to disturb you.'

'At this time my place was with you.'

'You should not have come,' Lannon protested. This was beyond his planning. It was not part of it that Huy should witness the death of the witch. He had not intended torturing him with the deed. Wildly Lannon considered halting the ritual, withdrawing the sacrifice, ordering Huy to leave the temple.

Yet Lannon realized that the safety of the empire might be resolved in these next few moments. Could he halt the sacrifice, dare he risk antagonizing the goddess, was his duty to Huy greater than his duty to Opet, was it not already too late, had he not committed himself long ago to this path? Were the gods and demons mocking him now, could he not hear their hellish laughter echoing in the deserts of his soul?

Bewildered and appalled he stared at Huy. He took a step towards him, reaching out one hand in entreaty as though asking for understanding and forgiveness.

'I need you,' he said hoarsely, and Huy, not understanding, took the hand, thinking it the hand of friendship; proudly he smiled at his king and friend as he began to sing the offertory to the goddess.

His voice rose on eagle's wings, flying up to the sacrificial platform in the roof of the cavern high above them. All the eyes in the temple turned upwards also and a tense expectant hush gripped the throng of worshippers.

Tanith could not believe it was happening to her. When they had come to her cell in the dawn she thought it must be Huy come to fetch her away. She had leapt from her couch and run to meet him.

It was not Huy but Sister Haka. They had taken her from the temple up the secret steps to the top of the cliffs above Opet. There in a stone building with a roof of thatch beside the sacrificial platform over the gaping hole above the pool of Astarte, they had dressed her in the rich embroidered robes of the sacrifice and put flowers in her hair.

Then they had draped her with the heavy gold chains, and bracelets, and leg bangles until Tanith felt she must collapse beneath the weight of them. She knew that this treasure formed part of the sacrifice, and that it was also intended to weight her down swiftly into the green depths of the pool. The pool which had no bottom to it, the pool which would carry her to the bosom of the goddess.

Solemnly and in silence she was seated at the small banquet table, and her sister priestesses waited upon her, pressing her with choice foods and wines. It was the feast of farewell, the feast to someone who goes upon a journey. Tanith sipped a little of the wine, hoping that it might warm her icy spirit.

'Huy,' she thought. 'Where are you, my love?'

At last a priestess came to the door and nodded to the others. There were fifteen of them, all strong young women, more than enough of them to overwhelm any resistance.

They closed in about where Tanith sat, not yet menacing but utterly determined. They looked down on her expressionlessly, their faces closed against pity or regret.

'Come,' said one of them, and Tanith stood up. They led her through the doorway into the sunlight, and ahead of her she saw the carved stone platform jutting out over the dark and gaping hole in the earth.

The path to the sacrificial platform was strewn with blossoms of the yellow mimosa tree, a flower sacred to the goddess. The scent was light and nostalgic on the warm still air, and the blossoms crushed beneath Tanith's bare feet as she passed over them weighted down by her chains of gold, and the heaviness of her dread.

Suddenly she stopped, frozen at the sound of the voice issuing from the pit before her, a voice faint with distance and echoing strangely from the cavern walls; but the voice of such purity and beauty that she could not help but recognize it.

'Huy!' she whispered. 'My lord!' But the upward flight

of her spirits was short-lived, for the voice of Huy Ben-Amon was uplifted in the offertory of the sacrifice.

It was Huy who was sending her to the goddess, and in that moment a vision of hell and desolation opened before her. She found herself caught in the web of some monstrous conspiracy, not understanding it clearly, knowing only that Huy had deserted her. He was against her also. He was the one offering her to the goddess.

There was nothing to live for now. It was easy to take those last few steps up onto the platform.

As she paused on the brink she spread her arms in the sun sign and looked down into the gloom of the cavern. The waters of the pool were still and dark, and beside them stood the king and the priest.

They were looking up at her, but it was too far for her to judge their expressions. All she knew was that Huy's voice was still raised in prayer, offering her to the goddess.

She felt hatred and anger replacing desolation, and she did not want to die with those emotions in her heart. To forestall them she swayed forward over the drop, over the deep green pool, and as she felt her balance go Huy's voice stopped abruptly, cut off in the middle of a word.

Slowly she leaned out over the drop, and then suddenly she was in the air, plunging downwards, hurtling towards the pool by the weight of gold she carried. As her stomach swooped within her she heard Huy's voice again, raised in a shriek of despair as he called her name.

'Tanith!'

She struck the surface of the pool with such force that all life was crushed from her, and the heavy ornaments plucked her beneath the limpid waters so swiftly that Huy saw only the brief gleam of gold deep down as though a great fish had turned upon its side to feed.

Manatassi crossed the great river in the winter of the Opet year 543. He used the cooler weather to carry his armies through the valley where the water was at its lowest levels. He crossed with three armies of varying sizes. The smallest, a mere 70,000 warriors, crossed in the west and overwhelmed the garrisons there. They drove swiftly for the western shores of the lake of Opet where the narrow waterway drained the lake and gave access to the ocean for the galleys of Opet. It was called the River of Life, the artery that fed the heart of Opet.

Manatassi's impis severed the artery, freed the slaves employed at dredging the channel and slaughtered the garrison and slave-masters. Most of Habbakuk Lal's fleet was drawn up on the beach, careened for cleansing of the hulls. The galleys were burned where they lay and the sailors thrown alive on the fires.

Then Manatassi's war captain blocked the channel. His warriors, and the tens of thousands of freed slaves tore down a small granite hill which stood beside the River of Life, and dumped it into the narrowest stretch of the river, rendering it impassable to any vessel larger than a canoe. This was a labour comparable with the construction of the great pyramid of Cheops, and it effectively sealed off the city and population of Opet from the outside world.

At the same time a second larger army crossed in the east, swept unhindered through the territory of the Dravs and burst like a black storm on the hills of Zeng.

The third and largest army, nearly three-quarters of a million strong, surged across the river at Sett. Manatassi commanded them in person and he chose the crossing place as a gesture.

Marmon hurried to oppose him with his single legion of 6,000 men and was crushed in a swift and bloody battle. Marmon fled the field and died on his own sword amidst the burning ruins of Zanat.

Manatassi placed his centre across the road to Opet and rolled along it. His front was three miles wide and twenty deep, a multitude whose own bulk reduced the march to a stately progress.

Manatassi swept the land. He took no prisoner, neither man nor woman nor child. He took no loot, burning cloth and book and leather, smashing pot and cup, throwing it all upon the funeral pyre of a nation. The buildings he burned, and then threw down and scattered the hot stone slabs.

As his hatred fed upon this destruction so it seemed to grow, like the very flames he lit, it burned higher the more was heaped upon it.

The total fighting strength of Opet was nine legions. Of these one had died with Marmon in the north, and two others were hacked to pieces upon the terraces of Zeng, the survivors holding out in a dozen besieged fortresses upon the crest of the hills.

With the remaining six legions Lannon Hycanus marched from Opet to meet Manatassi. They came together 150 miles north-east of Opet, and Lannon won a victory which gained him two miles of territory and one day's respite – but which cost him 4,000 dead and wounded.

Bakmor, who commanded Legion Ben-Amon in the absence of the High Priest, came to Lannon's tent upon the battlefield when the sky still glowed like a furnace from the cremation fires, and the stench of scorching flesh spoiled what little appetite for food that battle fatigue had left.

'The enemy left 48,000 dead upon the field,' Bakmor reported exultantly, and Lannon saw he was a young man no longer. How the years had sped away. 'We took twelve for each of ours,' Bakmor went on.

Lannon looked up at him, sitting on his couch while a physician dressed a minor wound in his arm, and he saw that dried sweat and blood had stiffened Bakmor's hair and beard and that there were new lines and shadows in the handsome face.

'How soon can you fight again?' Lannon asked, and the shadows around Bakmor's eyes deepened.

'It was a hard day,' he said. Legion Ben-Amon had held the centre firm during those desperate hours when it seemed the line must sunder at the pressure of black bodies and darting steel.

'How soon?' Lannon repeated.

'In four or five days,' Bakmor told him. 'My men are weary.'

'It will be sooner than that,' Lannon warned him.

They fought again the following day, a battle as desperate and as costly as the other. Again Lannon won a heavy victory, but he could not hold the field and he must leave over a thousand of his wounded to the hyena and jackal while he fell back to a new defensive line of hills.

They fought again five days later, and five times more in the next seventy days. At the end of that time they were encamped twenty Roman miles from Opet, and Lannon's six fine legions had shrunk to three.

It mattered not that they had won eight great battles, and that they had slain almost 200,000 of the enemy. For Zeng had fallen, only a handful of warriors winning through to describe its fate. The towns were burned and razed to the ground, the gardens cut down and burned also. The mines of the middle kingdom were destroyed, the slaves freed to join Manatassi's horde and the shafts blocked with earth and rock.

The channel of the River of Life was choked with rock, there was no escape upon Habbakuk Lal's galleys now, and from east and west new armies marched to reinforce Manatassi's drive on Opet.

Despite the toll that Lannon had taken from the armies of Manatassi, they seemed unaffected in number or determination. Each time Lannon planted his standards and stood to dispute Manatassi's advance, fresh hordes poured forward to attack him. Though he cut them down by the tens of thousands, they bled his own legions and left them each time more exhausted and with despair more deeply corroding their fighting spirit.

On the seventy-first day one full legion, 6,000 men, stabbed their officers in the night and scattered away into the darkness in small groups. Stopping only to pick up their women from the villages around Opet, they disappeared into the south.

Bakmor pursued them a short distance and dragged a hundred of them back in chains to face Lannon's wrath. They were all men of mixed Yuye blood, one class above that of freed slave, the lowest type of citizen allowed the privilege of bearing arms for the king. It seemed they did not count the privilege dear. Made bold by the certainty of execution, their spokesman told the king:

'If you had given us something to fight for, some station above that of dog, we might have stayed with you.'

Lannon had the man scalded to death with boiling water for his insolence, and retired his two remaining legions on the city.

They camped upon the lake shore without the city wall and Lannon looked to the north in the night and saw the bivouac fires of Manatassi's army spread like a field of yellow Namaqua daisies upon the hills. Manatassi was pressing him hard.

Bakmor found the king on the outskirts of the camp, watching the enemy positions. He approached Lannon eagerly, bearing the first good news they had received in many long days.

'There is word of Huy Ben-Amon, Majesty.' And Lannon felt a lift of his spirits.

'Where is he? Is he alive? Has he returned?' Lannon demanded. It was only now he admitted to himself how he had missed the little priest. He had not seen him since Huy had run out of the cavern of Astarte in the midst of the ceremony of the Fruitful Earth.

Although Lannon had conducted a diligent search, even offering a reward of 100 gold fingers for information about him, Huy had disappeared.

'Has he returned?' How many times in the long nights since then had Lannon longed for his companionship, his counsel and his comfort.

How often in the din of the battle had he listened for Huy's cry, 'For Baal!' and the song of the great axe.

How often had he wished that he could stiffen a crumbling centre or check a pivoting flank with the priest's presence.

'Where is he?' demanded Lannon.

'A fisherman saw him. He is out on the island,' said Bakmor.

The days had drifted past in a haze of grief. Huy had lost count of them, one slid so easily into the next. Most of the time he spent working on the scrolls. He had brought all five of the golden books with him and when he was not in the hut he kept them buried beneath his sleeping mat.

He wrote exclusively of Tanith, of his love for her and her death. In the beginning he worked through the nights as well as the days, but then he used up the last of the oil for the lamp and he spent his nights wandering along the beach and listening to the low surf hiss and growl upon the sands, and the wind across the lake rattle the palm fronds.

He lived on the fresh-water clams and a few fish that he took in the shallows, and he grew lean and unkempt; his beard and hair tangled and uncared for.

His grief showed in his eyes, making them wild and haunted, half mad and uncaring for anything but his own loss. Many of these hopeless days passed before anger and resentment began to work within him. From deep within him rose thoughts dark and dangerous as the shapes of killer sharks rising to the smell of blood.

Brooding over a smoky cooking fire he thought about his land and his gods. It seemed to him that both of them were cruel and greedy. A land devoted to the accumulation of wealth, counting not the toll in human suffering. Frivolous gods demanding the sacrifice, both of them greedy and devouring.

Huy left the fire and went down to the lake shore. He sat in the sand and the water ran up and tugged at his ankles before sliding back. The dark thoughts persisted, and mingled with them were the memories of Tanith.

He pondered the gods who would choose for the sacrifice the beloved of their faithful servant. What more did they demand of him, he wondered. He had given them everything he held dear, and still they wanted more.

How cruel that they should choose Lannon as the instrument to strip him of his love. He wished now that he could have told Lannon about Tanith. If Lannon had known of their love he would have protected her, Huy was sure of this. In the beginning he had hated Lannon, for it was he who had named Tanith as the sacrifice. Then reason had prevailed with Huy. He realized now that Lannon had acted in good faith. He had known nothing of Huy's and Tanith's relationship. He had known only that the nation was in dire danger and a valuable messenger was needed. Tanith was a natural choice then, reluctantly Huy saw that this was so, and knew that he would have done the same.

He no longer hated Lannon, but suddenly he found himself hating those who had forced him to it. The gods – the merciless gods.

Out of the lake great Baal rose in all his splendour of glittering gold and red, and across the waters he could see the rosy cliffs and towers of Opet glowing on the horizon.

From life-long habit Huy rose to his feet and spread his arms in the sun sign, and he opened his mouth to sing the praise of Baal.

Suddenly he was shaking with anger. He felt fiery gusts of it rising through his soul, setting his hatred alight, the funeral fire on which his faith perished.

'Damn you!' he shouted. 'What more do you want of me, you eater of flesh? How much longer must I be your plaything?'

Now his fists were clenched as he shook them in defiance at the rising sun, his face contorted and his tears streaming down into the wild bush of his beard. He walked forward into the lake.

'How much longer must I feed your cruel appetite, man-killer? How many more innocents before you quench your monstrous lust for blood?'

He dropped to his knees in the wet sand, and the running water surged about his waist.

'I reject you!' he shouted. 'You and your bloodless mate. I want no more of you – I hate you. Do you hear me, I hate you!'

Then he fell silent, and bowed his head. The water surged softly about him and after a while he scooped handfuls of it and washed his face. Then he rose and walked back to the hut above the beach. He felt a sense of fateful release, the peace which follows an irrevocable decision. He was priest no longer.

He ate a piece of smoked fish and drank a bowl of lake water, before he began work on the scrolls.

Again he wrote of Tanith, trying to recall every tone of her voice, every smile and frown, the way she laughed, and the way she held her head – as though he could give her immortality in words, as though he could give her life for the next 1,000 years in words cut into a sheet of imperishable gold.

Once he looked up from the scroll with peering shortsighted eyes and saw that the day was passing, and the long shadows of the palms cast tiger-stripes upon the yellow sands of the beach. He stooped again to the scroll and worked on.

There was the crunch of a footstep in the sand outside the hut, and a dark shape blocked out the light.

Again Huy looked up, and Lannon Hycanus stood in the doorway.

'I need you,' he said.

Huy did not reply. He sat hunched over the scroll blinking up at Lannon.

'It was on this island that you promised me you would never desert me,' Lannon went on softly. 'Do you remember?'

Huy stared at him. He saw the deep lines of care and suffering cut into Lannon's flesh, the dark shadowed eye-sockets in the gaunt face. He saw the greyish tone of the skin and the silver glint of old man's hair in the beard and at the temples.

He saw the wounds half healed, and freshly weeping through the linen bindings. He saw a man who was extended to the limits of his strength and determination, and in whose throat was the bitter taste of defeat.

'Yes,' said Huy. 'I remember.' He stood up and went to Lannon.

They came back to Opet in the early morning. All night they had sat together beside the fire in Huy's hut and they had talked.

Lannon told him of the course of the campaign, and the state of the nation. He told him of each battle, every strategy the enemy had deployed.

'I had placed much reliance upon the war-elephants. That trust was ill-founded. We lost most of them in the very first encounter. They used spears dipped in the poison taken from countless bees. I learned from a prisoner how they had smoked out hundreds of hives and laboriously squeezed out the poison sac from each sting. The burning pain of the wounds drove my elephants insane. They raged through our lines, and we had to use spikes on them.

'Also they had trained athletes who could vault onto the elephants' backs. They half leapt and were half thrown by their companions, flipped through the air like professional tumblers to kill the drivers and then stab the beasts in the back of the neck.'

'I was to blame for that,' said Huy. 'I told him of those tactics that the Romans used against Hannibal's elephants. He has not forgotten a single word of my teaching.'

Lannon went on to tell Huy of each battle which, though victorious, left Opet weakened, of the slow retreat before the black hordes, of the mounting despair amongst the legions, of the desertions and mutinies, of the destruction of the greater part of the fleet upon the beaches and the blocking of the channel.

'How many ships remain?'

'Nine galleys,' Lannon replied, 'and an assortment of fishing craft.'

'Enough to carry all of us across the lake, to the southern shores?'

'No,' Lannon shook his head. 'Not nearly enough.'

They talked on through the night, and in the dark hour before the first glimmer of dawn Lannon asked the question that had hovered on his lips all evening. He knew Huy would expect it.

'Why did you desert me, Huy?' Lannon asked softly. If Huy were to believe that Lannon knew nothing of his relationship with the witch, if he were to believe that Lannon's choice of sacrifice was accidental, then Lannon must pretend ignorance.

Huy looked up at the question and the firelight lit his face from below, leaving his eyes as dark pits.

'You do not know?' he asked, watching Lannon intently.

'I know only that you called out the witch's name, and then you were gone.'

Huy went on studying Lannon's face in the firelight, searching for some sign of guilt, some flicker of deceit. There was none. Lannon's face was tired and strained, but the pale blue eyes were direct and steadfast.

'What was it, Huy?' he insisted. 'I have puzzled over it so often now. What drove you from the temple?'

'Tanith. I loved her,' said Huy, and Lannon's expression changed. He stared at Huy for long seconds, appalled and stricken.

'Oh, my friend, what have I done to you? I did not know, Huy, I did not know.'

Huy dropped his gaze to the fire, and he sighed.

'I believe you,' he said.

'Pray Baal's forgiveness for me, Huy,' whispered Lannon and leaned across to grip Huy's shoulder, 'that I should ever have given you grief.'

'No, Lannon,' Huy answered. 'I shall never pray again. I have lost my love, and denied my gods. Now I have nothing.'

'You still have me, old friend,' said Lannon, and Huy smiled shyly at him.

'Yes,' he agreed, 'I still have you.'

They carried the golden scrolls and the vulture axe down to the beach where Bakmor and the crew of the fishing-boat waited patiently, and they came to Opet in the early morning.

The legions cheered them, king and priest, as they moved through the encampment and Huy felt tears scalding his eyelids.

'I do not deserve this,' he whispered. 'I deserted them. I should have been with them.'

Although the two legions were reconstituted from the shattered remnants of the original nine, yet it seemed to Huy they were built around the foundations of Legion Ben-Amon. Everywhere he saw familiar faces, grinning affectionately at him out of the ranks. He stopped to talk with them, trying to keep his tone cheerful as he noted the dented armour and the roughly bound wounds, half healing or suppurating.

He saw how exhausted they were, an exhaustion of the soul as well as the body. The smiles were short-blooming and the cheers were forced from reluctant throats – yet they were in hand, and there was fight left in them. They were lucky that none of the fevers that so often attended an encamped army had not yet weakened them further. It was strange how when they moved regularly, not staying at any one place long enough to foul the water supply or to allow their dung heaps to fester, then the fevers often did not appear.

There were 26,000 men encamped upon the lake shore, and they made a brave show. Huy felt small flames of confidence and hope warming his belly as he passed amongst them. Perhaps there was still something that could be done with this force.

Lannon and Huy ate the noon meal with their officers. There was no shortage of corn or meat or wine so close to the granaries of Opet, and they feasted and toasted each other while their men enjoyed the double wine ration that Lannon had ordered. In the afternoon Lannon allowed the wives into the camp. This was a privilege usually granted only after a great victory, not before a battle. They came streaming out of the city in their thousands, many of them wives for a day – to more than one husband.

'Let them enjoy it,' Lannon remarked with a little regret in his voice, as they strode through the camp with an escort of officers and picked legionaries. 'The gods know well that it may be the last time any of them do so.' Then his voice hardened. 'But see to it that none of the women remain after sundown.'

There was a desperate quality to the mass matings, as though life was trying to ensure its survival on the eve of extinction. As though in the motions of love the morrow's slaughter might be discounted.

Lannon left them to their frenzy and led his party out of the camp at a trot, the easy ground-devouring gait of a legion in forced march. Lannon led them to a spur of high ground which jutted out from the cliffs to overlook the lake shore for twenty miles in each direction. They stayed for many hours, watching Manatassi's hordes debouch from the passes of the cliffs onto the gently sloping lake shore. They watched mainly in silence, for it was a sight to strike ice into the souls of the bravest men.

It was as though a nest of black pythons were uncoiling, flowing outwards in long thick columns. It seemed endless, this massing of men; this stretching and bunching of primeval forces. It seemed as inevitable and undeviating as the tides of the sea, or the march of black storm clouds across a summer sky, and in the face of it they were silent and subdued.

Manatassi went into camp upon the lake shore with his vanguard only five miles from Lannon's own camp. However, the rear of his army had not yet emerged from the hills, and the plain between was thick with his regiments. There was no end to his numbers, no chance of counting them, for they knew not where his columns ended.

Lannon and Huy went down from the high ground in

the dusk. The star of Astarte was a bright prick of light in the indigo sky above Opet. Huy averted his eyes from it.

They went to the harbour and watched the embarkation of the women and children upon the remaining galleys of Habbakuk Lal. They would lie off-shore during the night, and the following day until the battle was decided. If the day went against Opet, as Huy knew it must, then they would be taken across the lake and would strike southwards in an attempt to stay ahead of Manatassi. The men who survived would follow as best they might.

There was not room for all of them aboard the galleys, so the royal and noble women went first, followed by the priestesses and the merchant families. At one stage there was an ugly and fierce moment when a mob of the Yuye women and classless ones tried to rush the harbour and find seats aboard the ferries. They were clubbed down and driven back by Habbakuk Lal's sailors. Huy felt a deep pity for them as they screamed and covered their heads with their hands against the spear butts. One of them, a young Yuye girl, sat dazed upon the flags of the wharf with her head bowed over the baby in her lap and the blood flowing down the ropes of her long black hair to form a dark shadow on the stone.

Lannon took leave of his wives and the children on the deck of Habbakuk Lal's flagship. He was remote and dignified as each woman came to kneel briefly before him. The children followed their mothers, and Lannon barely glanced down at them.

The twins had grown into marriageable young women now. Pretty and vital with long blonde hair plaited and roped. They came to kiss Huy for the last time, and his voice was husky as he said his farewells. The younger children were unaware of the gravity of the moment, and they were tired and petulant, squabbling amongst themselves or squalling in their nurses' arms.

Lannon and Huy were rowed back across the black

waters on which the reflected fire-flies of torchlight danced. The crowds upon the wharf were massed and silent, opening reluctantly to give them passage through, and Huy detected a sullenness close to open hostility. The escort closed in about them and they hurried through the streets of the city towards the encampment.

There were bonfires burning in the streets and about them drunkenness and revelry as the lowly citizens of Opet snatched a few last hours of pleasure before the dreaded morrow. The revels were more wild and grotesque than even those of the religious festivals. Men and women danced naked in the leaping firelight, or lay in puddles of their own vomit besotted with drink, while others rutted unashamedly in open view.

Huy saw a woman reeling drunkenly past them with her tunic torn and stained with red wine hanging in tatters from pale shoulders, and one breast protruding, round and fat with a big copper-coloured nipple. She tripped and fell into one of the fires, her hair exploding in a flare of orange flame.

In the shadows and dark lanes scurried other shapes, bowed under heavy burdens, and Huy knew that the looters were already at work, plundering the empty homes of the rich. Huy knew that his own slaves would still be protecting his house, but none the less he felt a pang of alarm as he remembered the golden books.

'Majesty, grant me an hour,' he said as they came abreast of the turning that led down to his house beside the lake.

'What is it, Huy?' Lannon demanded irritably. 'There is still much to do, and we must rest. What is it that demands your time?'

'I must take leave of my household. My slaves must be released from their duties and my valuables hidden, especially the scrolls – the golden scrolls.'

'As you will,' Lannon conceded bad-temperedly. 'But do not waste time. Return as soon as you can.'

The old slaves could not understand Huy's dismissal.

'This is our home,' they pleaded. 'Do not drive us out.' And Huy could not explain. He left them there sitting huddled together in the kitchens, bewildered and afraid.

With one of the younger slaves to help him, both of them bowed under the immense weight of the scrolls, Huy crossed the temple of Baal and went through the cleft into the cavern of Astarte. It was silent and deserted. The priestesses were all aboard the galleys in the harbour. Huy paused beside the pool and looked down into its depths.

'Wait for me, my love,' he said. 'I will follow close behind you. Keep a place for me at your side.'

He crossed the audience hall of the oracle and found the officers of the temple guards in the chamber beyond. They greeted him joyfully.

'We had heard you were dead, Holiness.'

'Is our duty still at this post, Holy Father?'

'Release us from the temple, Holiness. Let us fight at your side.'

They helped him place the scrolls in the pottery jars and seal them with the golden tablets. Then they carried them through into the archives and placed them upon the stone shelves, hidden by a row of the larger jars.

Huy led the four officers and one hundred men of Legion Ben-Amon back through the city to the camp of the army, leaving the temple unguarded, and Lannon greeted him with relief.

'I doubted you would return, Huy. I thought the fates might keep us apart once more.'

'I gave you a promise, Majesty,' Huy reassured him. 'See what I have for you.' And he led him from the tent to show him the temple guard. One hundred of the finest warriors of Opet, worth as much as a cohort of Yuye troops. Lannon laughed.

'Huy, my worker of miracles.' Then he turned to the

men and looked at them. They were fresh, their armour burnished and bright, and there was a fierce wolfish quality about them which contrasted with the battle weariness of the rest of Lannon's army.

Lannon spoke to their officers. 'You are mine own guard. When the battle begins, stay with me, close with me and Huy Ben-Amon.' Then he dismissed them to eat and rest.

In the big leather tent Lannon and Huy planned the battle, deciding what formations to employ, working out the evolutions for every eventuality, while scribes wrote out the orders.

They were interrupted continually by officers and aides asking for orders, or reporting the movements of the enemy.

Rib-Addi came into the tent begging audience, dry-washing his hands, tugging nervously at his beard and whispering in his secretive book-keeper's voice.

'The treasury, Majesty. Should we not move it to a place of safety?'

'Tell me what place is safe,' Lannon snarled at him, looking up from the clay box in which he and Huy were studying the dispositions. 'Nobody out there knows about the sun door. Leave the treasure where it is, it will remain there until we come for it.'

'The guards have been withdrawn,' Rib-Addi persisted. 'It is not right—'

'Listen to me, old man. It would require 1,000 men and ten days to remove that treasure. I have neither the men nor the time to spare. Go, leave us alone. We have more important matters to employ us now.'

Rib-Addi went, looking very distressed. What more important matters were there than gold and treasure?

Before midnight Lannon straightened up and ran his hands through his thick golden curls, now laced with silver. He sighed, and he looked ill and tired.

'That is all we can do now, Huy. The rest is in the

hands of the gods.' He placed an arm about Huy's shoulders and led him to the flap of the tent. 'A bowl of wine, a breath of lake air – then sleep.'

They stood outside the tent, drinking together and a cool breeze came off the lake, fluttering the tassels upon the golden battle standards.

Something which Huy thought for a moment was a big brown dog sleeping curled against the side of the tent stirred at their voices. Then Huy saw it was the little bushman huntmaster Xhai, faithful as ever, sleeping at the opening of his master's tent. He shook himself awake, grinned when he saw Lannon and Huy, and came to squat beside Lannon.

'I have tried to send him away,' said Lannon. 'He does not understand. He will not leave.' Lannon sighed. 'It seems unnecessary that he should die also, but how can I force him to go.'

'Send him on an errand,' suggested Huy and Lannon glanced at him thoughtfully.

'What errand?'

'Send him to search for sign of the gry-lion upon the southern shores. He will believe that.'

'Yes, he will believe that,' Lannon agreed. 'Tell him, Huy.'

In his own language Huy explained to the little yellow man that the king wanted to hunt the gry-lion once more. Xhai's slanted yellow eyes crinkled and he grinned and nodded with delight, pleased to be of service to the man he considered a god.

'You must go at once,' Huy told him. 'It is an urgent matter.'

Xhai clasped Lannon's knees, bobbing his head, and then he rolled up his sleeping mat and vanished amongst the shadows of the camp. Once he had gone they were silent for a while until Lannon said, 'Do you recall the prophecy, Huy?'

And Huy nodded, remembering it upon Tanith's lips.

'Who shall reign in Opet after me?'

'He who slays the gry-lion.'

He remembered also the prophecy that followed.

'What must I fear?'

'Blackness.'

Huy turned and looked to the north where the great black beast crouched, ready to spring. Lannon's thoughts paralleled his own.

'Yes, Huy,' he murmured. 'Blackness!' And then he drained his wine bowl and hurled it upon the watch fire. A spout of sparks flew upwards.

'At the hand of a friend,' he said, remembering the final prophecy. 'We shall see,' he said. 'We shall see.' Then he glanced at Huy and saw his face.

'Oh, forgive me, old friend. I did not mean to add fuel to the fires of your sorrow. I should not have reminded you of the girl.'

Huy drank the last of his wine and threw the bowl upon the fire. He did not need to be reminded of Tanith, she was ever in his thoughts.

'Let us rest now,' Huy said, but his face was ravished with grief.

The shouting and the trumpets woke Huy, and his first thought was of a night attack upon the camp. He threw on his armour and snatched up the vulture axe, stumbling out of the tent still fumbling with the straps of his breastplate.

The night sky was aglow with a light like that of the dawn, but it was rising from the wrong direction, coming up out of the lake, lighting the towers and walls of Opet.

Lannon joined him, still half-asleep, cursing as he struggled with his armour and helmet.

'What is it, Huy?' he demanded.

'I do not know,' Huy admitted, and they stood staring at the strange light which grew brighter, until they could clearly see each other's features.

'The harbour,' said Huy, understanding at last. 'The fleet. The women.'

'Merciful Baal,' gasped Lannon. 'Come!' And they ran together.

Manatassi had taken the tubes from the beached galleys before he burned them. A little experimentation had shown him how they worked. It was a simple procedure, dependent mostly upon current and wind direction. He had carried the tubes overland, and installed them in the bows of a pair of captured fishing-boats, whose slave crew were skilled seamen and eager to join Manatassi.

The on-shore wind had suited his purpose ideally and carried the boats silently into the mouth of the harbour of Opet. He had personally gone aboard one of the boats and he stood now in the stern wrapped in a leopard-skin robe, watching with fierce and hungry eyes as the jets squirted upon the surface of the wind-chopped water and burst into flame.

Carried on the wind the flame swept into the harbour in a solid wall, roaring like a waterfall and lighting the sky with a false dawn.

Huy stood beside Lannon upon the wharf. The entire basin of the harbour was filled with tall yellow flame, roaring hungrily, the black smoke clouds blocking out the starry sky and rolling in thick evil-smelling billows across the city.

The galleys of Habbakuk Lal stood like islands in a sea of fire. The decks were crowded with the women and children of all the noble families of Opet, and their screams carried over the dull furnace roar of flame.

The watchers upon the shore were unable to offer any escape to them, they looked on helplessly while from the alleyways the lowly ones who had been denied passage hooted and screeched with laughter.

The flames caught upon the wooden hulls and the mooring lines, racing upwards to the crowded decks.

Like ants upon a piece of rotten firewood, they scrambled and milled aimlessly, until the circle of flame tightened about them and shrivelled them.

One of the galleys began drifting in towards the shore. Its anchor lines were burned through, and the wind pushed it so it turned and swung gently, its mast and rigging traced in outlines of yellow fire. Upon the high castle at the stern, clinging together with their blonde hair shining in the firelight, stood Helanca and Imilce, the twin daughters of Lannon Hycanus.

Before the galley touched the stone wall of the quayside, the flames had smothered it, and the girls were gone.

Manatassi watched intently, the firelight glinting on those fierce yellow eyes. When the last flames had died and only the burnt-out hulks of the galleys still smouldered, he lifted his iron hand in command. The two fishing-boats hoisted sail and bore out, close on the wind, northwards to where Manatassi's army was stirring like an awakening monster in the dawn.

This was the mood in which to fight the last battle, this fine blend of sadness and anger, Huy thought as he strode with Lannon along the ranks.

The sun was up, throwing long shadows on the pale brown grass of the plain. On their left stretched the cheerful azure of the lake, flecked with crests of white by the morning breeze. The water fowl flew low in loose V-formations, white against the cloudless blue of the high heavens. On their left rose the rugged rampart of the cliffs, touched with subtle shades of rose and pink and capped with dark green vegetation.

Huy, looking at lake and cliff, saw them only as points on which to anchor his flanks.

Ahead, in front of the walls, the land was open, with

low scrub and a very few big shady trees; it sloped gently from cliff to lake shore, a Roman mile wide. It was a clear front from which no surprise could spring, although it undulated in a series of low rises like the swell of a sleepy ocean.

In their rear were the buildings and streets of the lower city, a maze of low clay walls and flat roofs, while further back rose the massive stone walls of the temple, and above them showed the tops of the sun towers.

This then was a good place in which to fight the last battle, this attenuated front with firm flanks and an open line of retreat.

Lannon strode along the ranks. There was a spring and purpose in his step that belied his tired eyes and grief-sick face; the face of a man who had seen his family burn to death while he stood by. Huy followed a pace behind him, walking with the long-legged crabbing gait which was so familiar to them all. The axe was on his shoulder, and the armour shaped to his bowed back was highly polished and sparkled in the sunlight. Bakmor and a group of officers followed him.

The legions were drawn up into their battle formations, and Huy could find no fault with the placing. The light infantry thrown out in a screen, each man armed with a bundle of javelins as well as his side arms. Behind them were placed the heavy infantry, big men armed with axe and war-spear, carrying a great weight of armour, these men were the backbones of the legions. When hard-pressed, the light infantry could retire through their ranks, and let the enemy spend themselves upon this solid reef of armour.

In the rear were the archers. Drawn up in neat blocks from which they could deliver massed flights of arrows over the heads of the infantry.

Behind them again were the baggage boys, ready with the bundles of fresh javelins and arrows, bags of cold meat and corn cakes, amphorae of water and wine, spare helmets, swords and axes, and those other items which the battle would expend or destroy.

At first Lannon's procession along the ranks was in silence. The men at ease, resting on their weapons, many with their helmets removed, some of them munching a last mouthful of food, all of them with that surface calm of the veteran who has walked many times with old Dame Death, who knows well her whore's face and the smell of her breath. Many of them still showed the recent marks of her claws upon their bodies, but there was no sign of fear on their faces, no shadows in their eyes.

Huy felt a humbleness when he met their steady gaze, a pride when one of them grinned and called out, 'We've missed you, Holiness.'

'It's good to be back,' Huy told him, and there was a growl of assent from those who heard him. Huy passed on, a ripple of animation followed him now.

Quick banter, in which Lannon and the officers joined.

'Leave a few for us, Sunbird,' a grizzled old centurion shouted.

'I think there will be enough for all of us,' Huy grinned at him.

'Too many?' another voice called out.

'Not enough,' Lannon answered. 'For none of those who oppose us is named Ben-Amon.'

They cheered then lustily, and it was taken up all along the line from cliff to lake. New waves of sound and shouting followed them as they went to take their place at the centre of the line upon a rise of higher ground where they could see over the whole field.

Above their heads the standards stood, gaudy with gleaming gold and silken multi-coloured tassels, and at their backs the hundred men of the temple guard. Huy looked over the precisely laid-out cohorts with the sun sparkling on their helmets and weapons, and thought that these were good men with which to fight the last battle, good men in whose company to die.

He loosened his helmet and lifted it from his head, holding it in the crook of his arm.

'Wine here!' he called, and baggage boys came scampering to them with bowls and amphorae. It was the best of Huy's own stocks, rich and red as the blood which would soon soak this field.

Huy saluted his officers with a raised bowl, then turned to Lannon. They looked at each other for a long moment.

'Fly for me, Bird of the Sun,' said Lannon softly.

'Roar for me today, Lion of Opet,' Huy answered him and they drank and broke the bowls and laughed together for the last time. The men about them heard them laugh, and taking courage from it they looked to the north.

Manatassi came in the middle of the bright hot morning. He came on a front that filled the plain from lake shore to cliff foot. He came singing with 500,000 throats, and the rhythmic slapping of bare feet and war rattles which rolled across the sky like the thunder of the heavens. He came in orderly ranks, spaced to give each man fighting space, but the rank behind pressed hard upon that ahead, ready to close any gap in the line, to show a solid unbroken front.

He came in rank upon countless rank, so there was no end to his advance, and the singing was deep and murmurous.

He came like the shadow of storm clouds moving stately and slow across the land, he came dark as night and numerous as the grass of the fields, and the singing took on a harsher more menacing sound.

Huy settled his helmet and tightened the strap. He untied the leather sheath from the vulture axe and watched Manatassi advance on a million moving legs like a single vast black animal topped with a froth of feather headdresses, and the spear blades sparkled like multiple insect eyes in the blackness.

He had never in all his life seen a sight to compare with Manatassi in his full power. This is a worthy foe with whom to fight the last battle, he thought, for there will be no dishonour in defeat by such a one.

Manatassi rolled on deliberately past the markers which Huy had placed on his front to measure the range; 200 paces, 150 – and the dust from a million stamping feet rose as a bank of fire-golden smoke over the horde, blanketing them so that they seemed to appear endlessly out of the moving shifting loom of it.

Huy felt his mouth drying out, and the tingle of his blood as it sped through his tensed body. He lifted the vulture axe high, and glanced left and right to make certain that each commander of the archery had seen the signal.

One hundred and fifty paces, the black tide washed towards him and the singing changed again, rising, shrilling into the blood trill, the high ululation as chilling as any sound Huy had ever heard. He felt the hair on his forearms and at the back of his neck come erect, and his bowels seemed to drop out of his body.

They came on still, trilling, stamping, drumming with spear on shield, head-dresses dipping and tossing, and Huy stood with his axe held aloft.

One hundred paces, and Huy brought down the axe and instantly the air was filled with the soft fluting, the whistle of the wings of wild duck at dusk.

The arrows rose and arched over and fell into them in thick dark flights like that of the locust, and a growl came out of the blackness, the growl of the beast, but it came on steadily into the javelins, seeming to pass through them unscathed for the gaps in the front were instantly filled and the fallen were hidden by the dense mass of bodies passing over them.

Huy's light infantry melted away before this massive advance, falling back through the heavies behind them, and Manatassi rolled weightily into Huy's front.

It seemed as though nothing could check it, it was too heavy, too wide and deep and strong. It must burst through this line of bright helmets.

Then unbelievably the blackness was no longer moving forward, but piling up on itself like a log jam in a river. The ranks pressing forward violated the fighting space of those in the van, catching them in a struggling mass, throwing them onto the prickly metal hedge that was Huy's front line.

Suddenly it was drawing back, sucked away like the wave of the sea from a steep beach.

Immediately the javelin men advanced through the heavies to harass the retreat, while the cry of the centurions carried clearly to Huy as they repaired their line.

'Close up here!'

'Javelins here!'

'Fill that gap!'

'Men here! Men here!'

Manatassi drew back, and bunched, gathered himself like a humping wave and surged forward again, struck and pressed hard, gained a yard of ground and drew back again, gathered himself, started forward gaining momentum and crashing into Huy's front once more.

At noon Lannon and Huy were forced from their vantage point, as the fighting surged about their feet. The standards moved back.

An hour after noon, Huy ordered the last of his reserves into the line, holding only the temple guard under his own hand in a bunch around the battle standards. Still the black waves burst upon the line with a terrible unvarying rhythm, like the ground swell of the ocean.

Huy gave them ground slowly, drawing back each time just enough to reaffirm his line. It was stretched so finely now, that it seemed each new rush of blackness must rip through it, but still it held.

Then they were into the lower city, fighting back along

the streets, and Huy was cut off from visual contact with the battle as a whole. It was merely a narrow street plugged with a knot of legionaries, holding back a steady rush of black warriors.

For the first time that day Huy was drawn into the fighting. A small group of wild-eyed black men burst through the rank ahead of him; they were shiny with sweat and grease, their faces painted with stripes of white ochre, making them appear monstrous and unreal.

Huy cut them down quickly, and ordered a squad of the temple guard into the gap they had opened.

He knew then that the battle was out of his control. He and Lannon were isolated in a cell of fighting men, able only to direct those of their men within sound of their voices.

From some distant part of the field came an animal roar of triumph, and Lannon caught Huy's shoulder and shouted into his ear, 'I think they have broken through.' And Huy nodded.

The set battle was over now. Huy knew that through many gaps in his shattered line the enemy was pouring. It would become a rout now. The miracle had not taken place – the last battle was lost.

'Fall back on the temple?' Lannon shouted the question and again Huy nodded. The army of Opet was no more, it was reduced to hundreds of isolated groups of desperate men locked shoulder to shoulder and back to back in their last fight, a fight from which there would be no surrender, from which death was the only surcease.

They gathered the temple guard about them, and moved back along the street, keeping a steady pace, close up and in hand, offering a solid carapace of shields to the enemy.

Manatassi's hordes were in their rear now, between them and the temple. They had put fire into the lower city, and the flames were taking a swift grip. The streets through which Huy marched were choked with terrified citizens and groups of wild blood-spattered warriors. Huy drove through all of them, his shields locked in the testudo formation, immune to the press of black men at the rear and the greasy billows of black smoke which spread over him.

The main temple gate was open and undefended. The guards had fled, the temple enclosure was empty and silent. Huy and ten men held the steps, while Lannon had the gates swung closed, and at the last instant Huy raced back with his men through the closing gap.

They were resting on the bloody weapons, loosening helmets, wiping the sweat out of their eyes.

'The east gate?' Huy demanded of Lannon. 'It is held? Did you send men to close it?'

Lannon stared at him with dismay, his silence answering Huy's question eloquently.

'You men!' Huy picked a group with a quick wave of his arm. 'Follow me.' But it was too late. Across the temple enclosure black warriors were streaming through the smaller gate.

'Testudo!' shouted Huy. 'Back to the cavern.' They formed the tortoise again, and moved like an armadillo with metal scales across the enclosure while the warriors swarmed about them, unable to pierce the shell. Smoke from the burning city eddied about them, choking them, blinding them.

Suddenly the man beside Huy cried out and grabbed at his groin. Blood spurted out between his fingers and he dropped to his knees. The ground over which they were advancing was strewn with dead warriors cut down by the head of the tortoise. They had to step over them. Dozens of these bodies who had been feigning death came suddenly to life, rolling quickly onto their backs and stabbing up under the skirts of the men above them.

Huy shouted a warning, but it was in vain. The enemy were inside the body of the tortoise, leaping to their feet, thrusting and hacking about them, forcing Huy's men to turn and defend themselves, exposing their backs to the warriors on the outside.

The tortoise disintegrated into a mob of individuals, and the black swarm poured over them as hiving bees.

'With me!' Huy gathered Lannon, Bakmor and a few others about him and they broke out of the mob in a tight bunch and raced for the cleft of the cavern. The smoke was thick and oily, choking them so they coughed as they ran. Huy swung the axe, cutting a path for them and five of them reached the entrance to the cavern but Bakmor had taken a thrust through the ribs. He pressed one fist to it, trying to staunch the flow of life blood. Huy changed the axe to his other hand, and helped Bakmor up the steps into the mouth of the cleft. His blood ran down Huy's side, it felt hot and gelatinous. On the top step Bakmor stumbled to his knees.

'It is finished, Huy,' he choked, but Huy picked him up bodily and carried him into the entrance. He propped him against the wall of the cavern.

'Bakmor,' he panted, and pushed his head back to look into his face. Bakmor's eyes looked back at him without seeing, dead and glazed. Huy let the handsome head drop forward, and stood up.

'Here they come,' shouted Lannon, and Huy hefted the axe and leapt to Lannon's side to meet the first dark rush of bodies into the passage. The four of them – Lannon, Huy and two legionaries – held the entrance long enough to clog it with piles of dead warriors.

Then the archers came up and the first volley of arrows swept the passage. One of them struck a legionary in the throat, and he fell with a dark gush of blood from the mouth.

'No cover in here,' Huy shouted. 'Back to the temple.' They raced back along the passage, and the next volley whistled amongst them. One struck Huy's helmet and glanced away to light sparks off the wall beside him, another found the seam in the last legionary's breastplate and lodged in the bone of his spinal column. His legs collapsed under him. Desperately he clawed his way after Huy, dragging his crippled body by the sheer strength of his arms alone.

'Your favour, my lord,' he screamed, in terror of the castrating blade, the ripping of his bowels while he still lived. 'Don't leave me for them, Holiness.'

Huy checked his run, and shouted, 'Go on, Lannon. I'll follow you.' He went back, and the legionary saw him coming.

'Baal's blessing on you, Holiness,' he cried, and tore his helmet loose, bowing his head forward to expose the neck.

'Find peace!' Huy told him, and cut his head from the trunk with a single stroke of the axe, turning to run again as he did so. An arrow hit Huy in the face below the eye, glancing off the bone and sliced him open to the ear, dangling there by the barb in the fleshy skin.

Huy tore it loose as he ran after Lannon.

Together they crossed the cavern of Astarte, their footsteps echoing from the domed walls; skirting the still green pool, they reached the door of the temple as the next flight of arrows hummed around them. Lannon stumbled slightly, and then they were into the temple.

'Can we hold them here?' Lannon gasped.

'No.' Huy stopped to catch his breath. 'The archives!' Then he looked at Lannon. 'What is it, Majesty?'

'I also am hit, Huy.' The arrow stood out of the joint of his armour near the left armpit. The angle of penetration was such that Huy felt a cold gust of despair. The arrow-head must lie close to the heart. It was mortal, no man could recover from a wound of that nature.

'How is it?' Lannon demanded. 'There is no pain, Huy. It cannot be too bad.'

'You're lucky,' said Huy, and snapped off the shaft, leaving a short stub protruding from the wound.

'Come,' he said, and with a gentle hand on Lannon's arm led him back through the temple into the archives.

'The sun door?' Lannon asked.

'Only at the very end,' said Huy. 'Only when all else fails.' And he steered Lannon into one of the stone recesses.

'Your face.' Lannon stared at Huy in the uncertain light of the torches, as though he had noticed the gaping slash across his cheek for the first time.

'No doubt it's an improvement,' Huy grunted as he tore a strip from his tunic and knotted it into a crude sling for Lannon's left arm.

'Can you use it?' he asked and Lannon worked his fingers, opening and closing them.

'Good,' Huy nodded, and placed the tang of Lannon's shield in his left hand. The sling would help support the weight of it.

Huy cocked his head, listening to the stealthy footsteps, the whispered voices and the clink of weapons within the temple of Astarte.

'They are coming,' he said. 'It will not take them long to find the passage.'

As he spoke the first of them stepped through the entrance from the guard room, and peered into the archives. The wavering light of the smoky torches in their wall brackets emphasized the man's size. He was huge and black, shiny with grease and paint, and Huy smelled him, a warm musky smell like that of a predatory cat.

Huy stepped out of the recess into the light, and in Vendi shouted a challenge at him. The warrior came bounding down the passage at Huy, and their shields came together with a clash that echoed through the temple.

Huy felt the spear blade sting his side, but the lance on the tip of the vulture axe bit in deep, touching bone, and the warrior slid down off the steel.

Lannon limped out of the recess and took his place on Huy's left hand, they stepped over the shivering twitching corpse and went down the passage side by side to meet the rush of dark bodies that came at them.

Manatassi stood in the temple of Astarte. It was after midnight but there were many torches burning and the halls were crowded with warriors, so many that Manatassi had ordered the interior walls torn out of the building to give them access to the mouth of the tunnel.

The dark, evil-looking stone mouth which had already swallowed up so many of his men, was where the two fighting devils of Opet still held out, defying all his efforts to dislodge them. Even now they were dragging dead and badly wounded from the entrance. One of them had his right arm lopped off above the elbow. He made no sound as he clutched at the stump, but his eyes were huge and white in the torchlight.

Manatassi knew what weapon had inflicted that wound, and his anger and his hatred smouldered hotly, warring with the superstitious dread that gripped him.

He had learned enough about the gods of Opet while he was a slave to know their vast powers, their strengths and cruelties. He feared them, and he knew that he stood now in the stronghold of these terrible gods, in their holy place.

He remembered now hearing of this underground place beyond the temple of Astarte, he knew that a death curse guarded it.

Clearly this was the reason why they had taken sanctuary here, in this dark hole.

His anger cooled, chilled by religious awe. He knew the white gods were watching him. He wanted to end it now, destroy this place and go – however, two doomed but stubborn men defied him.

'Fire!' he said. 'Smoke them from their den like wild dogs.'

They built the fire in the entrance of the tunnel, and fed it with green branches, and dense acrid smoke filled the temple and the tunnel. They ringed the tunnel entrance, coughing and choking in the smoke, and they held their weapons ready, knowing that no man could live in there. This must bring them out, surely – but an hour passed with no movement through the smoke.

The fire burned down into a smouldering pile of logs, and the smoke cleared gradually. Manatassi ordered it quenched with water from the pool, and once again they stared into the dark passage from which wisps and streamers of smoke still drifted.

The floor of the passage was still carpeted with the dead, but there was no sign of life.

Manatassi subdued his religious awe, and abruptly snatched a torch from the hand of one of his warriors. Holding it high above his head, he stepped over the hot and sizzling logs and into the passage.

He picked his way amongst the dead, and the floor was puddled and sticky with blood that clung to his bare feet. The torch threw yellow light into each of the stone recesses with their burdened shelves. Manatassi knew what the earthenware pots contained. He had assisted Huy often enough with the scrolls.

He looked for sign of him now, but there was none. Only the black bodies, and the empty recesses.

He reached the end of the passage and the torch lit the engraved image. Manatassi recognized it as the symbol of the sun god, and his courage melted at this tangible evidence of divine influence.

On the floor below the image something caught his eye, sparkling in the torch light.

He suppressed a gasp. It was the vulture axe, laid like an offering before the god image – and the place was empty.

They had gone to their gods. They had cheated him of his revenge, and led him into deadly peril, into a direct confrontation with supernatural forces.

Manatassi backed away, until the god image merged into the darkness and he turned and ran from the place into the hall of the temple of Astarte. There he looked back at the mouth of the tunnel.

'Bring me masons from amongst the freed slaves. Seal off that entrance. It is evil. Seal it.'

They ran to obey, and Manatassi's courage – his anger and his hatred – returned to him.

'I will destroy this evil. I place a curse upon this place, upon these cliffs. A curse that will last for ever.' His voice rose into a scream. 'Burn it. Burn it all. Destroy it. It is an evil to be cleaned from the earth and from the minds of men, for ever.'

So the masons sealed off the entrance to the tomb of the kings. They worked with all the skill that the men of Opet had taught them, and when they were finished the entrance had vanished.

Then Manatassi destroyed the city. He slew every single living thing and threw them on the fires which raged through the lower city for many days. Then he looked at the walls and the towers, and he pointed with his iron claw. They tore it down block by massive block. The walls and the sun towers and the beautiful temple of Astarte. They went down to the very foundations. They lifted the flagged pavings. They tore out the stone wharves of the harbour. Working like a million ants they razed the city until no trace of it remained. They carried each block of masonry up to the cavern and dropped it into the bottomless green pool. They took the entire city and gave it to the goddess, and the pool was so deep – or the goddess so eternally greedy – that it was swallowed without a trace and the level of the green clear waters rose not a finger's width.

When Manatassi marched from Opet, eastwards to complete the destruction of the empire, he left nothing behind him but piles of loose ash which the wind was already scattering in pale runs of dust.

Manatassi spread his regiments like a net across the four kingdoms, with the command to destroy all trace of the cities and the mines and the gardens built by the men of Opet. But his hatred had burned low now, like a forest fire when the trees are gone. The hatred had left him hollow and blackened and dying, his huge battered frame a husk, even the smoky yellow eyes dull and uncaring.

He came to Zimbao, the great walled city of the middle kingdom, and the men of Opet were dead. The city like his own body was untenanted, empty and deserted.

Manatassi wrapped himself in a fur kaross and lay down beside the watch fire, and in the morning his body was stiff and cold.

They buried him outside the walls, and then they quarrelled and fought, for Manatassi had named no successor. Each war captain named himself, and the army of Manatassi split into a hundred tribes.

In time Manatassi and the city of Opet faded from the memory of men.

When Xhai the bushman was an old man and he knew he was dying, he came back to Opet.

The lake had vanished, its shores were twenty miles from the red cliffs and the waters were brackish and shallow and sunwarmed.

Xhai walked over the spot on which the temple of Baal had stood without recognizing it, until he saw the cleft in the red rock leading to the cavern of Astarte.

He camped beside the pool, building a small fire and sitting over it mumbling to himself in the manner of old men. When his memories paraded before him they were magnified and magnificent, and he sought to capture and fix them.

He picked up his belt on which were strung the little horn pots of pigment, each plugged with a piece of wood, and he went to the wall at the rear of the cavern.

He made the outline of the figure in charcoal upon the smoothest place of the wall. He worked slowly and carefully, with great love.

Then he mixed his pigment and began to paint the proud god-like figure with its white face, red-gold beard and majestic vaunting manhood, and as he worked it seemed as though ghost voices whispered deep in the rock, down in the vault of the kings.

'Huy, I am cold. Favour me, old friend. Give me the hand of friendship that the oracle foresaw.'

'I cannot, Lannon. I cannot do it.'

'I am cold and in pain, Huy. If you love me, you will do it.'

'I love you.'

'Fly for me, Bird of the Sun.'

As the old man worked, the wind whispered and sighed along the cliffs, and the sigh was that which a man might make when he has lost his love and his land, has denied his gods and has given mercy to his friend. He might sigh like that as he takes the sword still dulled with his friend's blood and sets the hilt firmly in a niche of the stone floor and places the point up under his ribs, and falls forward on it.

* * *

THE RAND DAILY MAIL
27th May

Death of Multi-Millionaire Financier
Louren Sturvesant Dies of Mystery Disease

BOTSWANA, SATURDAY. The well-known millionaire financier and sportsman, Mr Louren Sturvesant of Kleine Schuur, Sandown, Johannesburg, died here yesterday after a brief illness.

Mr Sturvesant was visiting the site of the recently discovered ancient Carthaginian city in Botswana. The leader of the expedition, Dr Benjamin Kazin, has also contracted the disease which is believed to be infectious.

Dr Kazin has been flown to Johannesburg where a hospital spokesman stated that his condition was critical.

THE FINANCIAL GAZETTE
28th May

Stop Press

Anglo-Sturvesant Crashes 97 Points
Panic on Exchange

HOLLARD STR. MONDAY. Following reports of the death of Mr Louren Sturvesant, Chairman of Anglo-Sturvesant, quoted prices of the Sturvesant Group of Companies fell sharply on the Johannesburg Stock Exchange today.

THE STAR
3rd June

Famous Archaeologist Regains Consciousness

JOHANNESBURG, FRIDAY. After ten days in coma, Dr Benjamin Kazin today regained consciousness, according to a hospital spokesman.

Dr Kazin is the Director of the Institute of Anthropology and African Prehistory, and the discoverer of the ancient Carthaginian city of Opet. He was suffering from a rare fungus infection contracted while working on the site of his recent find.

Today Dr Kazin was visited by his assistant, Dr Sally Benator, who said afterwards that Dr Kazin was 'very much better but still terribly upset by the death of Mr Sturvesant'.

THE STAR
6th September

Well-known Archaeologists Marry

CAPE TOWN, FRIDAY. The discoverer of the city of Opet, Dr Benjamin Kazin, was married to his long-time assistant, Dr Sally Benator, in a brief civil ceremony here today. The bride said that she planned a working honeymoon at the site of the ancient city of Opet.

THE TIMES
20th April

Archaeologist Honoured

LONDON, SATURDAY. At the Royal Geographical Society, an Extraordinary General Meeting of the Society was held today during which Dr Benjamin Kazin was awarded the Society's much-prized Founder's and Patron's Medal.

After the meeting there was a short ceremony at which a portrait of Dr Kazin by the well-known artist Pietro Annigoni was hung in the Society.

Dr Kazin was accompanied by his wife, Dr Sally Kazin, formerly Benator, who is also a well-known figure in archaeological circles. The couple will spend two weeks holidaying in Britain and on the continent before returning to Africa.

WILD JUSTICE

There were only fifteen joining passengers for the British Airways flight at Victoria Airport on the island of Mahé in the oceanic republic of the Seychelles.

Two couples formed a tight group as they waited their turn for departure formalities. They were all young, all deeply tanned and they seemed still carefree and relaxed by their holiday in that island paradise. However, one of them made her three companions seem insignificant by the sheer splendour of her physical presence.

She was a tall girl, with long limbs and her head set on a proud, shapely neck. Her thick, sun-gilded blonde hair was twisted into a braid and coiled high on top of her head, and the sun had touched her with gold and brought out the bloom of youth and health upon her skin.

As she moved with the undulating grace of one of the big predatory cats, bare feet thrust into open sandals, so the big pointed breasts joggled tautly under the thin cotton of her tee-shirt and the tight round buttocks strained the faded denim of her hacked-off shorts.

Across the front of her tee-shirt was blazoned the legend 'I AM A LOVE NUT' and below it was drawn the suggestive outline of a coco-de-mer.

She smiled brilliantly at the dark-skinned Seychellois immigration officer as she slid the green United States passport with its golden eagle across the desk to him, but when she turned to her male companion she spoke in quick fluent German. She retrieved her passport and led the others through into the security area.

Again she smiled at the two members of the Seychelles

Police Force who were in charge of the weapons search, and she swung the net carry bag off her shoulder.

'You want to check these?' she asked, and they all laughed. The bag contained two huge coco-de-mer; the grotesque fruit, each twice the size of a human head, were the most popular souvenirs of the Islands. Each of her three companions carried similar trophies in net bags, and the police officer ignored such familiar objects and instead ran his metal detector in a perfunctory manner over the canvas flight bags which made up the rest of their hand luggage. It buzzed harshly on one bag and the boy who carried it shamefacedly produced a small Nikkormat camera. More laughter and then the police officer waved the group through into the final Departure Lounge.

It was already crowded with transit passengers who had boarded at Mauritius, and beyond the lounge windows the huge Boeing 747 Jumbo squatted on the tarmac, lit harshly by floodlights as the refuelling tenders fussed about her.

There were no free seats in the lounge and the group of four formed a standing circle under one of the big revolving punkah fans, for the night was close and humid – and the mass of humanity in the closed room sullied the air with tobacco smoke and the smell of hot bodies.

The blonde girl led the gay chatter and sudden bursts of laughter, standing inches above her two male companions and a full head above the other girl, so that they were a focus of attention for the hundreds of other passengers. Their manner had changed subtly since they entered the lounge; there was a sense of relief as though a serious obstacle had been negotiated, and an almost feverish excitement in the timbre of their laughter. They were never still, shifting restlessly from foot to foot, hands fiddling with hair or clothing.

Although they were clearly a closed group, quarantined by an almost conspiratorial air of camaraderie, one of the transit passengers left his wife sitting and stood up from his seat across the lounge.

'Say, do you speak English?' he asked, as he approached the group.

He was a heavy man in his middle fifties with a thick thatch of steel-grey hair, dark horn-rimmed spectacles, and the easy confident manner of success and wealth.

Reluctantly the group opened for him, and it was the tall blonde girl who answered, as if by right.

'Sure, I'm American also.'

'No kidding?' The man chuckled. 'Well, what do you know.' And he was studying her with open admiration. 'I just wanted to know what those things are.' He pointed to the net bag of nuts that lay at her feet.

'They are coco-de-mer,' the blonde answered.

'Oh yeah, I've heard of them.'

'They call them "love nuts",' the girl went on, stooping to open the heavy bag at her feet. 'And you can see why.' She displayed one of the fruit for him.

The double globes were joined in an exact replica of a pair of human buttocks.

'Back end.' She smiled, and her teeth were so white they appeared as translucent as fine bone china.

'Front end.' She turned the nut, and offered for his inspection the perfect *mons veneris* complete with a feminine gash and a tuft of coarse curls, and now it was clear she was flirting and teasing; she altered her stance, thrusting her hips forward slightly, and the man glanced down involuntarily at her own plump *mons* beneath the tight blue denim, its deep triangle bisected by the fold of material which had rucked up into the cleft.

He flushed slightly and his lips parted with a small involuntary intake of breath.

'The male tree has a stamen as thick and as long as your arm.' She widened her eyes to the size and colour of blue pansies, and across the lounge the man's wife stood up and came towards them, warned by some feminine instinct. She was much younger than her husband and very heavy and awkward with child.

'The Seychellois will tell you that in the full moon the male pulls up its roots and walks around to mate with the females—'

'As long and as thick as your arm—' smiled the pretty little dark-haired girl beside her, ' – wow!' She was also teasing now, and both girls dropped their gaze deliberately down the front of the man's body. He squirmed slightly, and the two young men who flanked him grinned at his discomfort.

His wife reached him and tugged at his arm. There was a red angry rash of prickly heat on her throat and little beads of perspiration across her upper lip, like transparent blisters.

'Harry, I'm not feeling well,' she whined softly.

'I've got to go now,' he mumbled with relief, his poise and confidence shaken, and he took his wife's arm and led her away.

'Did you recognize him?' asked the dark-haired girl in German, still smiling, her voice pitched very low.

'Harold McKevitt,' the blonde replied softly in the same language. 'Neurosurgeon from Forth Worth. He read the closing paper to the convention on Saturday morning.' She explained. 'Big fish – very big fish,' and like a cat she ran the pink tip of her tongue across her lips.

Of the four hundred and one passengers in the final Departure Lounge that Monday evening three hundred and sixty were surgeons, or their wives. The surgeons, including some of the most eminent in the world of medicine, had come from Europe and England and the United States, from Japan and South America and Asia, for the convention that had ended twenty-four hours previously on the island of Mauritius, five hundred miles to the south of Mahé island. This was one of the first flights out since then and it had been fully booked ever since the convention had been convoked.

'British Airways announces the departure of Flight BA 070 for Nairobi and London; will transit passengers please board now through the main gate.' The announcement was in the soft singsong of the Creole accent, and there was a massed movement towards the exit.

'Victoria Control this is Speedbird Zero Seven Zero request push back and start clearance.'

'Zero Seven Zero you are cleared to start and taxi to holding point for runway Zero One.'

'Please copy amendment to our flight plan for Nairobi. Number of Pax aboard should be 401. We have a full house.'

'Roger, Speedbird, your flight plan is amended.'

The gigantic aircraft was still in its nose-high climb configuration and the seat belt and no-smoking lights burned brightly down the length of the first-class cabin. The blonde girl and her companion sat side by side in the roomy seats 1a and 1b directly behind the forward bulkhead that partitioned off the command area and the first-class galley. The seats that the young couple occupied had been reserved many months previously.

The blonde nodded to her companion and he leaned forward to screen her from the passengers across the aisle while she slipped one of the coco-de-mer from its net bag and held it in her lap.

Through its natural division the nut had been carefully sawn into two sections to allow removal of the milk and the white flesh, then the two sections had been glued together again just as neatly. The joint was only apparent after close inspection.

The girl inserted a small metal instrument into the joint and twisted it sharply, and with a soft click the two sections fell apart like an Easter egg.

In the nests formed by the double husk of the shells, padded with strips of plastic foam, were two smooth, grey, egg-like objects – each the size of a baseball.

They were grenades of East German manufacture, with the Warsaw Pact command designation MK IV(C). The outer layer of each grenade was of armoured plastic, of the type used in landmines to prevent discovery by electronic metal detectors. The yellow stripe around each grenade indicated that it was not a fragmentation type, but was designed for high impact concussion.

The blonde girl took a grenade in her left hand, unlatched her lap belt and slipped quietly from her seat. The other passengers paid her only passing interest as she ducked through the curtains into the galley area. However, the purser and the two stewardesses, still strapped into their fold-down seats, looked up sharply as she entered the service area.

'I'm sorry, madam, but I must ask you to return to your seat until the captain extinguishes the seat-belt lights.'

The blonde girl held up her left hand and showed him the shiny grey egg.

'This is a special grenade, designed for killing the occupants of a battle tank,' she said quietly. 'It could blow the fuselage of this aircraft open like a paper bag or kill by concussion any human being within fifty yards.'

She watched their faces, saw the fear bloom like an evil flower.

'It is fused to explode three seconds after it leaves my hand.' She paused again, and her eyes glittered with excitement and her breath was quick and shallow.

'You—' she selected the purser, ' – take me to the flight deck; you others stay where you are. Do nothing, say nothing.'

When she ducked into the tiny cockpit, hardly large enough to contain the members of the flight crew and its massed banks of instruments and electronic equipment, all three men turned to look back at her in mild surprise – and she lifted her hand and showed them what she carried.

They understood instantly.

'I am taking command of this aircraft,' she said, and then, to the flight engineer, 'Switch off all communications equipment.'

The engineer glanced quickly at his captain, and when he nodded curtly, began obediently to shut down his radios – the very high frequency sets, then the high frequency, the ultra high frequency—

'And the satellite relay,' the girl commanded. He glanced up at her, surprised by her knowledge.

'And don't touch the bug.' He blinked at that. Nobody, but nobody outside the company should have known about the special relay which, when activated by the button beside his right knee, would instantly alert Heathrow Control to an emergency and allow them to monitor any conversation on the flight deck. He lifted his hand away.

'Remove the fuse to the bug circuit.' She indicated the correct box above his head, and he glanced at the captain again, but her voice stung like the tail of a scorpion:

'Do what I tell you.'

Carefully he removed the fuse and she relaxed slightly.

'Read your departure clearance,' she instructed.

'We are cleared to radar departure on track for Nairobi and an unrestricted climb to cruise altitude of thirty-nine thousand feet.'

'When is your next "operations normal" due?'

Operations normal was the routine report to Nairobi

Control to assure them that the flight was proceeding as planned.

'In eleven minutes and thirty-five seconds.' The engineer was a young, dark-haired, rather handsome man with a deep forehead, pale skin and the quick, efficient manner instilled by his training.

The girl turned to the captain of the Boeing and their gazes locked as they measured each other. The captain's hair was more grey than black and cropped close to his big rounded skull. He was bull-necked, and had the beefy, ruddy face of a farmer or of a butcher – but his eyes were steady and his manner calm and unshakeable. He was a man to watch, the girl recognized instantly.

'I want you to believe that I am committed entirely to this operation,' she said, 'and that I would welcome the opportunity to sacrifice my life to my cause.' Her dark blue eyes held his without fear, and she read the first growth of respect in him. That was good, all part of her careful calculations.

'I believe that,' said the pilot, and nodded once.

'Your duty is to the four hundred and seventeen lives aboard this aircraft,' she went on. He did not have to reply. 'They will be safe, just as long as you follow my commands implicitly. That I promise you.'

'Very well.'

'Here is our new destination.' She handed him a small white typewritten card. 'I want a new course with forecast winds, and a time of arrival. Your turn onto the new heading to commence immediately after your next "operations normal" report in—' She glanced back at the engineer for the time.

'Nine minutes fifty-eight seconds,' he said promptly.

' – and I wan' your turn to the new heading to be very gentle, very balanced. We don't want any of the passengers to spill their champagne – do we?'

In the few minutes that she had been on the flight deck

she had already established a bizarre rapport with the captain; it was a blend of reluctant respect and overt hostility and of sexual awareness. She had dressed deliberately to reveal her body, and in her excitement her nipples had hardened and darkened, pushing out through the thin cotton shirt with its suggestive legend, and the musky woman's smell of her body again intensified by her excitement filled the confined cockpit.

Nobody spoke again for many minutes, then the flight engineer broke the silence.

'Thirty seconds to "operations normal".'

'All right, switch on the HF and make the report.'

'Nairobi Approach this is Speedbird Zero Seven Zero.'

'Go ahead Speedbird Zero Seven Zero.'

'Operations normal,' said the engineer into his headset.

'Roger, Zero Seven Zero. Report again in forty minutes.'

'Zero Seven Zero.'

The blonde girl sighed with relief. 'All right, shut down the set.' Then to the captain, 'Disengage the flight director and make the turn to the new heading by hand; let's see how gentle you can be.'

The turn was a beautiful exhibition of flying, two minutes to make a change of 76° of heading, the needles of the turn-and-balance indicator never deviating a hair's breadth, and when it was completed, the girl smiled for the first time.

It was a gorgeous sunny flash of very white teeth.

'Good,' she said, smiling directly into the captain's face. 'What is your name?'

'Cyril,' he replied after a moment's hesitation.

'You can call me Ingrid,' she invited.

There was no set routine to the days in this new command of Peter Stride's, except the obligatory hour on the range with pistol and automatic weapons. No member of Thor Command – not even the technicians – were spared daily range practice.

The rest of Peter's day had been filled with unrelenting activity, beginning with a briefing on the new electronic communications equipment that had just been installed in his command aircraft. This had taken half the morning, and he had been only just in time to join his striker force in the main cabin of the Hercules transport for the day's exercise.

Peter jumped with the first stick of ten men. They jumped from five hundred feet, the parachutes seeming to snap open only seconds before they hit the ground. However, the crosswind had been strong enough to spread them out a little even from that height. The first landing had not been tight enough for Peter. They had taken two minutes fifty-eight seconds from jump to penetration of the deserted administration block standing forlornly in one of the military zones of Salisbury Plain.

'If they had been holding hostages in here, we'd have arrived just in time to start mopping up the blood,' Peter told his men grimly. 'We'll do it again!'

This time they had cut one minute fifty seconds off their time, falling in a tightly steered pattern about the building – beating the time of Colin Noble's No 2 striker team by ten seconds.

To celebrate Peter had scorned the military transports and they had run the five miles to the airstrip, each man in full combat kit and carrying the enormous bundle of his used parachute silk.

The Hercules was waiting to fly them back to base, but it was after dark before they landed and taxied into Thor Command's security compound at the end of the main runway.

For Peter the temptation to leave the debriefing to Colin

Noble had been strong indeed. His driver would have picked up Melissa-Jane at East Croydon Station and she would already be waiting alone in the new cottage, only half a mile from the base gates.

He had not seen her for six weeks, not since he had taken command of Thor, for in all that time he had not allowed himself a single day's respite. He felt a tickle of guilt now, that he should be allowing himself this indulgence, and so he lingered a few minutes after the briefing to transfer command to Colin Noble.

'Where are you going for the weekend?' Colin demanded.

'She's taking me to a pop concert tomorrow night – The Living Dead, no less,' Peter chuckled. 'Seems I haven't lived until I hear the Dead.'

'Give M.J. my love, and a kiss,' Colin told him.

Peter placed high value on his new-found privacy. He had lived most of his adult life in officers' quarters and messes, constantly surrounded by other human beings. However, this command had given him the opportunity to escape.

The cottage was only four and a half minutes' drive from the compound but it might have been an island. It had come furnished and at a rental that surprised him pleasantly. Behind a high hedge of dog rose, off a quiet lane, and set in a sprawling rather unkempt garden, it had become home in a few weeks. He had even been able to unpack his books at last. Books accumulated over twenty years, and stored against such an opportunity. It was a comfort to have them piled around his desk in the small front room or stacked on the tables beside his bed, even though there had been little opportunity to read much of them yet. The new job was a tough one.

Melissa-Jane must have heard the crunch of gravel under the Rover's tyres, and she would certainly have been waiting for it. She came running out of the front door into the driveway, directly into the beam of the headlights, and

Peter had forgotten how lovely she was. He felt his heart squeezed.

When he stepped out of the car she launched herself at him and clung with both arms around his chest. He held her for a long moment, neither of them able to speak. She was so slim and warm, her body seeming to throb with life and vitality.

At last he lifted her chin and studied her face. The huge violet eyes swam with happy tears, and she sniffed loudly. Already she had that old-fashioned English porcelain beauty; there would never be the acne and the agony of puberty for Melissa-Jane.

Peter kissed her solemnly on the forehead. 'You'll catch your death,' he scolded fondly.

'Oh, Daddy, you are a real fusspot.' She smiled through the tears and on tip-toe she reached up to kiss him full on the mouth.

They ate lasagne and cassata at an Italian restaurant in Croydon, and Melissa-Jane did most of the talking. Peter watched and listened, revelling in her freshness and youth. It was hard to believe she was not yet fourteen, for physically she was almost fully developed, the breasts under the white turtle-neck sweater no longer merely buds; and she conducted herself like a woman ten years older, only the occasional gleeful giggle betraying her or the lapse as she used some ghastly piece of Roedean slang – 'grotty' was one of these.

Back at the cottage she made them Ovaltine and they drank it beside the fire, planning every minute of the weekend ahead of them and skirting carefully around the pitfalls, the unwritten taboos of their relationship which centred mostly on 'Mother'.

When it was time for bed she came and sat in his lap and traced the lines of his face with her fingertip.

'Do you know who you remind me of?'

'Tell me,' he invited.

'Gary Cooper – only much younger, of course,' she added hurriedly.

'Of course,' Peter chuckled. 'But where did you ever hear of Gary Cooper?'

'They had *High Noon* as the Sunday movie on telly last week.'

She kissed him again and her lips tasted of sugar and Ovaltine, and her hair smelled sweet and clean.

'How old are you, anyway, Daddy?'

'I'm thirty-nine.'

'That isn't really so terribly old.' She comforted him uncertainly.

'Sometimes it's as old as the dinosaurs—' and at that moment the bleeper beside his empty cup began its strident, irritating electronic tone, and Peter felt the slide of dread in his stomach.

Not now, he thought. Not on this day when I have been so long without her.

The bleeper was the size of a cigarette pack, the globe of its single eye glared redly, insistent as the audio-signal. Reluctantly Peter picked it up and, with his daughter still in his lap, he switched in the miniature two-way radio and depressed the send button.

'Thor One,' he said.

The reply was tinny and distorted, the set near the limit of its range.

'General Stride, Atlas has ordered condition Alpha.'

Another false alarm, Peter thought bitterly. There had been a dozen Alphas in the last month, but why on this night. Alpha was the first stage of alert with the teams embarked and ready for condition Bravo which was the GO.

'Inform Atlas we are seven minutes from Bravo.'

Four and a half of those would be needed for him to

reach the compound, and suddenly the decision to rent the cottage was shown up as dangerous self-indulgence. In four and a half minutes innocent lives can be lost.

'Darling,' he hugged Melissa-Jane swiftly, 'I'm sorry.'

'That's all right.' She was stiff and resentful.

'There will be another time soon, I promise.'

'You always promise,' she whispered, but she saw he was no longer listening. He dislodged her and stood up, the heavy jawline clenched and thick dark brows almost meeting above the narrow, straight, aristocratic nose.

'Lock the door when I'm gone, darling. I'll send the driver for you if it's Bravo. He will drive you back to Cambridge and I will let your mother know to expect you.'

He stepped out into the night, still shrugging into his duffle coat, and she listened to the whirl of the starter, the rush of tyres over gravel and the dwindling note of the engine.

The controller in Nairobi tower allowed the British Airways flight from Seychelles to run fifteen seconds past its reporting time. Then he called once, twice and a third time without reply. He switched frequencies to the channels reserved for information, approach, tower and, finally, emergency, on one at least of which 070 should have been maintaining listening watch. There was still no reply.

Speedbird 070 was forty-five seconds past 'operations normal' before he removed the yellow slip from his approach rack and placed it in the emergency 'lost contact' slot, and immediately search and rescue procedures were in force.

Speedbird 070 was two minutes and thirteen seconds past 'operations normal' when the telex pull sheet landed on the British Airways desk at Heathrow Control, and sixteen seconds later Atlas had been informed and had placed Thor Command on condition Alpha.

The moon was three days short of full, its upper rim only slightly indented by the earth's shadow. However, at this altitude it seemed almost as big as the sun itself and its golden light was certainly more beautiful.

In the tropical summer night great silver cloud ranges towered into the sky, and mushroomed into majestic thunder heads, and the moonlight dressed them in splendour.

The aircraft fled swiftly between the peaks of cloud, like a monstrous black bat on back-swept wings it bored into the west.

Under the port-side wing a sudden dark chasm opened in the clouds like the mouth of hell itself, and deep in its maw there was the faint twinkle of far light, like a dying star.

'That will be Madagascar,' said the captain, his voice over-loud in the quiet cockpit. 'We are on track.' And behind his shoulder the girl stirred and carefully transferred the grenade into her other hand before she spoke for the first time in half an hour.

'Some of our passengers might still be awake and notice that.' She glanced at her wristwatch. 'It's time to wake up the others and let them know the good news.' She turned back to the flight engineer. 'Please switch on all the cabin lights and the seat-belt lights and let me have the microphone.'

Cyril Watkins, the captain, was reminded once again that this was a carefully planned operation. The girl was timing her announcement to the passengers when their resistance would be at its lowest possible ebb; at two o'clock in the morning after having been awoken from the disturbed rest of intercontinental flight their immediate reaction was likely to be glum resignation.

'Cabin and seat-belt lights are on,' the engineer told her, and handed her the microphone.

'Good morning, ladies and gentlemen.' Her voice was warm, clear and bright. 'I regret having to waken you at such an inconvenient hour. However, I have a very important announcement to make and I want all of you to pay the most careful attention.' She paused, and in the cavernous and crowded cabins there was a general stir and heads began to lift, hair tousled and eyes unfocused and blinking away the cobwebs of sleep. 'You will notice that the seat-belt lights are on. Will you all check that the persons beside you are fully awake and that their seat belts are fastened. Cabin staff please make certain that this is done.'

She paused again; the belts would inhibit any sudden movement, any spontaneous action at the first shock. Ingrid noted the passage of sixty seconds on the sweep hand of her wristwatch before going on.

'First let me introduce myself. My name is Ingrid. I am a senior officer of the Action Commando for Human Rights—' Captain Watkins curled his lip cynically at the pompous self-righteous title, but kept silent, staring ahead into the starry, moonlit depths of space ' – and this aircraft is under my command. Under no circumstances whatsoever will any of you leave your seats without the express permission of one of my officers – if this order is disobeyed, it will lead directly to the destruction of this aircraft and all aboard by high explosive.'

She repeated the announcement immediately in fluent German, and then in less proficient but clearly intelligible French before reverting to English once again.

'Officers of the Action Commando will wear red shirts for immediate identification and they will be armed.'

As she spoke her three companions in the front of the first-class cabin were stripping out the false bottoms from their canvas flight bags. The space was only two inches deep by fourteen by eight, but it was sufficient for the broken-down twelve bore pistols, and ten rounds of buckshot cartridges. The barrels of the pistols were fourteen inches long, the bores were smooth and made of armoured plastic. This material would not have withstood the passage of a solid bullet through rifling or any of the newer explosive propellants but it had been designed for use with the lower velocity and pressures of multiple shot and cordite. The breech piece was of plastic as were the double pistol grips, and these clipped swiftly into position. The only metal in the entire weapon was the case-steel firing pin and spring, no bigger than one of the metal studs in the canvas flight bag, so they would not have activated the metal detectors of the security check at Mahé airport. The ten cartridges contained in each bag had plastic cases and bases; again only the percussion caps were of aluminium foil, which would not disturb an electrical field. The cartridges were packed in looped cartridge belts which buckled around the waist.

The weapons were short, black and ugly; they required reloading like a conventional shotgun, the spent shells were not self-ejecting and the recoil was so vicious that it would break the wrists of the user who did not bear down heavily on the pistol grips. However, at ranges up to thirty feet the destructive power was awesome, at twelve feet it would disembowel a man and at six feet it would blow his head off cleanly – yet it did not have the penetrating power to hole the pressure hull of an intercontinental airliner.

It was the perfect weapon for the job in hand, and within a few seconds three of them had been assembled and loaded and the two men had slipped on the bright scarlet shirts that identified them over their tee-shirts and moved to their positions – one in the back of the first-class cabin and one in the back of the tourist cabin, they stood with their grotesque weapons ostentatiously displayed.

The slim, pretty, dark-haired German girl stayed in her seat a little longer, working swiftly and neatly as she opened the remaining coco-de-mer and transferred their contents into two of the netting bags. These grenades differed only from the one carried by Ingrid in that they had double red lines painted around the middle. This signified that they were electronically fused.

Now Ingrid's clear young voice resumed over the cabin address system, and the long rows of passengers – all fully awake now – sat rigid and attentive, their faces reflecting an almost uniform expression of shock and trepidation.

' – The officer of the action commando who is moving down the cabin at this time is placing high explosive grenades—' The dark-haired girl started down the aisle, and every fifteen rows she opened one of the overhead lockers and placed a grenade in it, closed the locker and moved on. The passengers' heads revolved slowly in unison as they watched her with the fascination of total horror. 'A single one of those grenades has the explosive power to destroy this aircraft – they were designed to kill by concussion the crew of a battle tank protected by six inches of armour – the officer is placing fourteen of these devices along the length of this aircraft. They can be detonated simultaneously by an electronic transmitter under my control—' the voice contained a hint of mischief now, a little undercurrent of laughter ' – and if that happened they'd hear the bang at the North Pole!'

The passengers stirred like the leaves of a tree in a vagrant breeze; somewhere a woman began to weep. It was a strangled passionless sound and nobody even looked in her direction.

'But don't worry yourselves. That isn't going to happen. Because everybody is going to do exactly as they are told, and when it's all over you are going to be proud of your part in this operation. We are all partners in a noble and glorious mission, we are all warriors for freedom and for the dignity of man. Today we take a mighty step forward into the new world – a world purged and cleansed of injustice and tyranny and dedicated to the welfare of all its peoples.'

The woman was still weeping, and now a child joined her on a higher, more strident note.

The dark-haired girl returned to her seat and now she retrieved the camera that had activated the metal detector at Mahé airport. She slung it around her neck and crouched again to assemble the two remaining shot pistols; carrying them and the cartridge belts she hurried forward to the flight deck where the big blonde kissed her delightedly and unashamedly on the lips.

'Karen, *Liebling*, you were wonderful.' And then she took the camera from her and slung it around her own neck.

'This—' she explained to the captain ' – is not what it appears to be. It is the remote radio detonator for the grenades in the fuselage.'

He nodded without replying, and with obvious relief Ingrid disarmed the grenade that she had carried for so long by replacing the safety pin. She handed it to the other girl.

'How much longer to the coast?' she asked as she strapped and buckled the cartridge belt around her waist.

'Thirty-two minutes,' said the flight engineer promptly, and Ingrid opened the breech of the pistol, checked the load and then snapped it closed again.

'You and Henri can stand down now,' she told Karen. 'Try and sleep.'

The operation might last many days still, and exhaustion would be the most dangerous enemy they would have to contend with. It was for this reason alone that they had employed such a large force. From now on, except in an emergency, two of them would be on duty and two would be resting.

'You have done a very professional job,' said the pilot, Cyril Watkins, ' – so far.'

'Thank you.' Ingrid laughed, and over the back of his

seat placed a comradely hand on his shoulder. 'We have practised very hard for this day.'

Peter Stride dipped his lights three times as he raced down the long narrow alley that led to the gates of the compound without slowing the Rover, and the sentry swung the gate open just in time for him to roar through.

There were no floodlights, no bustling activity – just the two aircraft standing together in the echoing cavern of the hangar.

The Lockheed Hercules seemed to fill the entire building, that had been built to accommodate the smaller bombers of World War II. The tall vertical fin of its epinage reached to within a few feet of the roof girders.

Beside it the Hawker Siddeley HS 125 executive jet seemed dainty and ineffectual. The differing origins of the machines emphasized that this unit was a co-operative venture between two nations.

This was underscored once more when Colin Noble hurried forward to meet Peter as he cut the Rover's engine and lights.

'A grand night for it, Peter.' There was no mistaking the drawl of mid-Western America, although Colin looked more like a successful used-car salesman than a colonel in the U.S. Marines. In the beginning Peter had believed that this strict apportioning of material and manpower on equal national lines might weaken the effectiveness of Atlas. He no longer had those doubts.

Colin wore the nondescript blue overalls and cloth cap, both embroidered with the legend 'THOR COMMUNICATIONS' which deliberately made him look more of a technician than a soldier.

Colin was Peter's second in command. They had known each other only the six weeks since Peter had assumed command of Thor – but after a short period of mutual wariness the two men had formed one of those fast bonds of liking and mutual respect.

Colin was of medium height, but none the less a big man. First glance might have given the impression that he was fat, for his body had a certain toad-like spread to it. There was no fat upon his frame, however, it was all muscle and bone. He had boxed heavyweight for Princeton and the marines, and his nose above the wide laughing mouth had been broken just below the bridge, it was lumped and twisted slightly.

Colin cultivated the boisterous bluff manner of a career athlete, but his eyes were the colour of burned toffee and were brightly intelligent and all-seeing. He was tough and leery as an old alley cat. It was not easy to earn the respect of Peter Stride. Colin had done so in under six weeks.

He stood now between the two aircraft, while his men went about their Alpha preparation with quick understated efficiency.

Both aircraft were painted in commercial airline style, blue and white and gold, with a stylized portrait of the Thunder God on the tail fin and the 'THOR COMMUNICATIONS' title down the fuselage. They could land at any airport in the world without causing undue comment.

'What is the buzz, Colin?' Peter Stride demanded as he slammed the Rover's door and hurried to meet the American. It had taken him some time and conscious effort to adapt his language and mode of address to fit in with his new second-in-command. He had learned very early not to expect that, merely because he was the youngest major-general in the British army, Colonel Colin Noble was going to call him 'Sir' every time he spoke.

'Missing aircraft.' It could have been a train, an embassy,

even an ocean liner, Peter realized. 'British Airways. For Chrissake let's get out of the cold.' The wind was flapping the legs of Colin's overalls and tugging at his sleeves.

'Where?'

'Indian Ocean.'

'Are we set for Bravo?' Peter asked as they climbed into his command plane.

'All set.'

The interior of the Hawker had been restyled to make it a compact headquarters and communications centre.

There was comfortable seating for four officers directly behind the flight deck. Then the two electronic engineers and their equipment occupied a separate rear compartment, beyond which were the small toilet and galley in the extreme rear.

One of the technicians looked through the communicating door as Peter stooped into the cabin. 'Good evening, General Stride – we have a direct link with Atlas established.'

'Put him on the screen,' he ordered as he sank into the padded leather of his chair behind the small working desk.

There was a single fourteen-inch main television screen in the panel directly facing Peter, and above it four smaller six-inch screens for conference communication. The main screen came alive, and the image of the big noble leonine head firmed.

'Good afternoon, Peter.' The smile was warm, charismatic, compelling.

'Good evening, sir.'

And Dr Kingston Parker tilted his head slightly to acknowledge the reference to the time difference between Washington and England.

'Right at this moment we are in the dark completely. All we have is that BA 070 with four hundred and one passengers and sixteen crew on a flight from Mahé to Nairobi has not reported for thirty-two minutes.'

Parker was Chairman of the Intelligence Oversight Board, among other duties, and he reported directly to the President of the United States in that capacity. He was the President's personal and trusted friend. They had been in the same class at Annapolis, both of them had graduated in the top twenty but, unlike the President, Parker had gone directly into government.

Parker was an artist, a talented musician, the author of four scholarly works of philosophy and politics, and a grand master of chess. A man of overwhelming presence, of vast humanity and towering intelligence. Yet also he was a secret man, avoiding the glaring scrutiny of the media, hiding his ambitions, if ambitions he had – although the presidency of the United States would not be an impossible dream to such a man – only taking up with rare skill and strength any burden that was thrust upon him.

Peter Stride had met him personally on half a dozen occasions since being seconded to Thor. He had spent a weekend with Parker at his New York home, and his respect for the man had become boundless. Peter realized that he was the perfect head for such a complex concept as Atlas: it needed the philosopher's tempering influence over trained soldiers, it needed the tact and charisma of the diplomat to deal directly with the heads of two governments, and it needed that steely intellect to make the ultimate decision that could involve hundreds of innocent lives and incur fearsome political consequences.

Now swiftly and incisively he told Peter what little they knew of Flight 070 and what search and rescue routine was already in force, before going on, 'Without being alarmist, this does seem to be the perfect target. The flight carries most of the world's leading surgeons, and the convention was public knowledge eighteen months ago. Doctors have the necessary image to appeal to public sentiment and their nationalities are nicely mixed – American, British, French, Scandinavian, German, Italian – three of those countries have notoriously *soft* records with militant activity. It's a British aircraft, and the final destination would probably have been chosen to further complicate the issue and inhibit any counter-action.'

Parker paused, and a small crease of worry appeared for a moment in the broad smooth forehead.

'I have put Mercury on condition Alpha as well – if this is a strike the final destination could just as easily be eastwards of the aircraft's last reported position.'

Atlas's offensive arm comprised three identical units. Thor would be used only in Europe or Africa. Mercury was based on the American Naval base in Indonesia and covered Asia and Australasia, while Diana was in Washington itself and ready for counteraction in either of the American continents.

'I have Tanner of Mercury on the other relay now. I will be back to you in a few seconds, Peter.'

'Very well, sir.'

The screen went blank, and in the chair beside him Colin Noble lit one of his expensive Dutch cheroots and crossed his ankles on the desk in front of him.

'Seems the great god Thor came down to earth for a little poontang. When he'd finished pleasuring one of the vestal virgins he thought he'd let her know the honour she'd been given. "I'm Thor," he told her. "Tho am I," she agreed, "but it wath loth of fun."'

Peter shook his head sorrowfully. 'That's funny?' he asked.

'Helps to while away the time.' Colin glanced at his wristwatch. 'If this is another false alarm, it's going to make it thirteen straight.' He yawned. There was nothing to do. It had all been done before. Everything was in the ultimate state of readiness. In the huge Hercules transport, every item of a comprehensive arsenal of equipment was ready for instant use. The thirty highly trained soldiers were embarked. The flight crews of both aircraft were at their stations, the communications technicians had set up their links with satellites and through them to the available intelligence computers in Washington and London. It remained only to wait – the greater part of a soldier's life was spent waiting, but Peter had never become hardened to it. It helped now to have the companionship of Colin Noble.

In a life spent in the company of many men it was difficult to form close relationships. Here in the smaller closed ranks of Thor in shared endeavour they had achieved that and become friends, and their conversation was relaxed and desultory, moving casually from subject to subject, but without relaxing the undercurrent of alertness that gripped both men.

At one stage Kingston Parker came on the screen again to tell them that search and rescue aircraft had found no indications at the last reported position of 070, and that a photographic run by the 'Big Bird' reconnaissance satellite had been made over the same area, but that film would not be ready for appraisal for another fourteen hours. Speedbird 070 was now one hour six minutes past 'operations normal' and suddenly Peter remembered Melissa-Jane. He asked communications for a telephone line and dialled the cottage. There was no reply, so the driver would have collected her already. He hung up and rang Cynthia in Cambridge.

'Damn it, Peter. This really is most inconsiderate of you.' Freshly aroused from sleep, her voice was petulant, immediately awakening only antipathies. 'Melissa has been looking forward to this—'

'Yes, I know, and so have I.'

' – and George and I had arranged—' George, her new husband, was a Political History don; despite himself Peter quite liked the man. He had been very good to Melissa-Jane.

'The exigencies of the service.' Peter cut in lightly – and her voice took on a bitter edge.

'How often I had to listen to that – I hoped never to hear it again.' They were on the same futile old treadmill, and he had to stop it.

'Look, Cynthia. Melissa is on her way—'

In front of him the big television screen lit and Kingston Parker's eyes were dark with regret, as though he mourned for all mankind.

'I have to go,' Peter told the woman whom once he had loved, and broke the connection, leaning forward attentively towards the image on the screen.

'The South African radar defences have painted an unidentified target approaching their airspace,' Kingston Parker told him. 'Its speed and position correspond with those of 070. They have scrambled a Mirage flight to intercept – but in the meantime I'm assuming that it's a militant strike and we'll go immediately to condition Bravo, if you please, Peter.'

'We are on our way, sir.'

And beside him Colin Noble took his feet off the desk and thumped them together onto the floor. The cheroot was still clamped between his teeth.

The target was live and the pilot of the leading Mirage F.1 interceptor had his flight computer in 'attack' mode and all his weaponry – missiles and cannon – were armed. The computer gave him a time to intercept of thirty-three seconds, and the target's heading was constant at 210° magnetic and its ground speed at 483 knots.

Ahead of him the dawn was rising in wildly theatrical display. Avalanches of silver and pink cloud tumbled down the sky, and the sun, still below the horizon, flung long lances of golden light across the heavens. The pilot leaned forward against his shoulder straps and lifted the Polaroid visor of his helmet with one gloved hand, straining ahead for the first glimpse of the target.

His trained gunfighter's eye picked out the dark speck against the distracting background of cloud and sunlight and he made an almost imperceptible movement of the controls to avoid the direct head-on approach to the target.

The speck swelled in size with disturbing rapidity as they converged at combined speeds of nearly fifteen hundred miles per hour, and at the instant he was certain of his identification the leader took his flight, still in a tight 'finger five', up into a vertical climb from which they rolled out neatly five thousand feet above the target and on the same heading, immediately reducing power to conform in speed to the big aircraft far below.

'Cheetah, this is Diamond leader – we are visual, and target is a Boeing 747 bearing British Airways markings.'

'Diamond Leader, this is Cheetah, conform to target, maintain five thousand feet separation and avoid any threatening attitudes. Report again in sixty seconds.'

Major-General Peter Stride's executive jet was arrowing southwards and leaving its enormous protégé lumbering ponderously along in its wake. Every minute increased the distance between the two aircraft, and by the time they reached their ultimate destination – wherever that might be – there would probably be a thousand miles or more separating them.

However, the big Hercules's slow speed became a virtue when the need arose to take its heavy load of men and equipment into short unsurfaced strips in unlikely corners of the earth – perhaps in the 'hot and high' conditions that a pilot most dreads.

It was the Hawker's job to get Peter Stride to the scene of terrorist activity as swiftly as possible, and the general's job once there to stall and procrastinate and bargain until Colin Noble's assault team caught up with him.

The two men were still in contact, however, and the small central television screen in front of Peter was permanently lit with a view of the interior of the Hercules's main hold. When he lifted his head from his work, Peter Stride could see a picture of his troops, all in the casual Thor overalls, lounging or sprawled in abandoned attitudes of relaxation down the central aisle of the Hercules. They also were veterans at the hard game of waiting, while in the foreground Colin Noble sat at his small work desk, going through the voluminous check list for 'condition Charlie' which was the next state of alert when terrorist activity was confirmed.

Watching Colin Noble at work, Peter Stride found a moment to ponder once again the enormous cost of maintaining Atlas, most of it paid by the United States intelligence budget, and the obstacles and resistance that had been overcome to launch the project in the first place. Only the success of the Israelis at Entebbe and of the Germans at Mogadishu had made it possible, but there was still violent opposition in both countries to maintaining a dual national counteraction force.

With a preliminary click and hum the central screen of Peter's communications console came alive and Dr Parker spoke before his image had properly hardened.

'I'm afraid it's condition Charlie, Peter,' he said softly, and Peter was aware of the rush of his blood through his veins. It was natural for a soldier whose entire life had been spent in training for a special moment in time to welcome the arrival of that moment – yet he found contempt for himself in that emotion; no sane man should anticipate violence and death, and all the misery and suffering which attended them.

' – the South Africans have intercepted and identified 070. It entered their airspace forty-five seconds ago.'

'Radio contact?' Peter asked.

'No.' Parker shook his great head. 'It is declining contact, and we must assume that it is under the control of militants – so now I'm going to be at this desk until this thing is settled.' Kingston Parker never used the emotive word 'terrorist' and he did not like to hear it from his subordinates either.

'Never hate your adversary blindly,' he had told Peter once. 'Understand his motives, recognize and respect his strengths – and you will be better prepared to meet him.'

'What co-operation can we expect?' Peter asked.

'All African States that we have so far been able to contact have offered full co-operation, including overflight, landing and refuelling facilities – and the South Africans are being helpful. I have spoken to their defence minister and he has offered the fullest possible co-operation. They will refuse 070 landing clearance, of course, and I anticipate that it will have to go on to one of the black states farther north, which is probably the militants' intention anyway. I think you know my views about South Africa – but in this instance I must say they are being very good.'

Parker brought into the television shot a black briar pipe with a big round bowl, and began to stuff it with tobacco. His hands were large, like the rest of his body, but the fingers were long and supple as those of a pianist – which of course he was. And Peter remembered the scented smell of the tobacco he smoked. Even though he was a non-smoker, Peter had not found the odour offensive. Both men were silent, deep in thought, Parker frowning slightly as he seemed to concentrate on his pipe. Then he sighed and looked up again.

'All right, Peter. Let's hear what you have.'

Peter shuffled through the notes he had been making. 'I have prepared four tentative scenarios and our responses to each, sir. The most important consideration is whether this is a strike "à l'allemande" or "à l'italienne"—'

Parker nodded, listening; although this was well-travelled ground they must go over it again. A strike in the Italian fashion was the easier to resolve, a straight demand for cash. The German tradition involved release of prisoners, social and political demands that crossed national boundaries. They worked on for another hour before they were interrupted again.

'Good God.' It was a measure of Kingston Parker's astonishment that he used such strong language. 'We have a new development here—'

It was only when 070 joined the eastern airway and began to initiate a standard approach and let down, without however obtaining air traffic control clearance, that South African Airforce Command suddenly realized what was about to happen.

Immediately emergency silence was imposed on all the aviation frequencies while the approaching flight was bombarded by urgent commands to immediately vacate national airspace. There was no response whatsoever, and one hundred and fifty nautical miles out from Jan Smuts International Airport the Boeing reduced power and commenced a sedate descent to enter controlled airspace.

'British Airways 070 this is Jan Smuts Control, you are expressly refused clearance to join the circuit. Do you read me, 070?'

'British Airways 070 this is Airforce Command. You are warned that you are in violation of national airspace. You are ordered to climb immediately to thirty thousand feet and turn on course for Nairobi.'

The Boeing was a hundred nautical miles out and descending through fifteen thousand feet.

'Diamond Leader, this is Cheetah. Take the target under command and enforce departure clearance.'

The long sleek aircraft in its mottled green and brown battle camouflage dropped like a dart, rapidly overhauling the huge multi-engined giant, diving down just behind the tailplane and then pulling up steeply in front of the gaily painted red, white and blue nose.

Skilfully the Mirage pilot stationed his nimble little machine one hundred feet ahead of the Boeing and rocked his wings in the 'Follow me' command.

The Boeing sailed on serenely as though it had not seen or understood. The Mirage pilot nudged his throttles and the gap between the two aircraft narrowed down to fifty feet. Again he rocked his wings and began a steady rate-one turn onto the northerly heading ordered by Cheetah.

The Boeing held rock steady on its standard approach towards Johannesburg, forcing the Mirage leader to abandon his attempts to lead her away.

He edged back alongside, keeping just above the jet-blast of the Boeing's port engines until he was level with the cockpit and could stare across a gap of merely fifty feet.

'Cheetah, this is Diamond One. I have a good view into target's flight deck. There is a fourth person in the cockpit. It's a woman. She appears to be armed with a machine pistol.'

The faces of the two pilots were white as bone as they turned to watch the interceptor. The woman leaned over the back of the left-hand seat, and lifted the clumsy black weapon in an ironic salute. She smiled and the Mirage pilot was close enough to see how white her teeth were.

' – a young woman, blonde hair, *mooi*, *baie mooi*—' the Mirage pilot reported. 'Pretty – very pretty.'

'Diamond One, this is Cheetah. Position for head-on attack.'

The Mirage thundered instantly ahead and climbed away swiftly, the other four aircraft of the flight sweeping in to resume their tight 'finger five' formation as they went out in a wide turn ahead of the Boeing.

'Cheetah. We are in position for a head-on attack.'

'Diamond Flight. Simulate. Attack in line astern. Five-second intervals. Minimum separation. Do not, I say again, do not open fire. This is a simulated attack. I say again, this is a simulated attack.'

'Diamond One – understands simulated attack.'

And the Mirage F.1 winged over and dived, its speed rocketing around the mach scale, booming through the sonic barrier in a fearsomely aggressive display.

Cyril Watkins saw him coming from seven miles ahead.

'Jesus,' he shouted. 'This is real,' and he lunged forward to take manual control of the Boeing, to pull her off the automatic approach that the electronic flight director was performing.

'Hold her steady.' Ingrid raised her voice for the first time. 'Hold it.' She swung the gaping double muzzles of the shot pistol onto the flight engineer. 'We don't need a navigator now.'

The captain froze, and the Mirage howled down on them, seemed to grow until it filled the whole view through the windshield ahead. At the last possible instant of time the nose lifted slightly and it flashed only feet overhead, but the supersonic turbulence of its passage struck and tossed even that huge machine like a piece of thistledown.

'Here comes another,' Cyril Watkins shouted.

'I mean it.' Ingrid pressed the muzzles so fiercely into the back of the flight engineer's neck that his forehead struck the edge of his computer console, and there was the quick bright rose of blood on the pale skin.

The jet blasts struck the Boeing one after the other as the Mirages attacked. Ingrid clutched wildly for support with her free hand, but kept the pistol jammed into the navigator's neck. 'I mean it,' she kept shouting. 'I'll kill him,' and they could hear the screams of the passengers even through the bulkhead of the flight deck.

Then the last Mirage was passed and gone and the Boeing's flight director recovered from the battering of close separation and quickly realigned the aircraft on the radio navigational beacons of Jan Smuts Airport.

'They won't buzz us again.' Ingrid stepped back from the flight engineer, allowing him to lift his head and wipe away the trickle of blood on the sleeve of his shirt. 'They can't come again. We are into controlled airspace.' She pointed ahead. 'Look!'

The Boeing was down to five thousand feet, but the horizon was obscured by the haze of smog and summer heat. To the right rose the smooth silhouette of the Kempton Park Power Station cooling towers and, closer at hand, the poisonous yellow tablelands of the mine dumps squatted on the flat and featureless plain of the African highveld. Around them human habitation was so dense that hundreds of windowpanes caught the early morning sun and glittered like beacons.

Closer still was the long, straight, blue streak of the main runway of Jan Smuts Airport.

'Take her straight in on runway 21,' Ingrid ordered.

'We can't—'

'Do it,' snapped the girl. 'Air traffic control will have cleared the circuit. They can't stop us.'

'Yes, they can,' Cyril Watkins answered. 'Just take a look at the runway apron.'

They were close enough now to count five fuel tenders, to see the Shell company insignia on the tanks.

'They are going to block the runway.'

With the tankers were five brilliant red vehicles of the fire service and two big white ambulances. They bumped wildly over the grass verge of the runway and then, one after the other, tenders and fire control vehicles and ambulances parked at intervals of a few hundred yards down the white-painted centre line of the runway.

'We can't land,' said the captain.

'Take her off automatic and fly her in by hand.' The girl's voice was different, hard, cruel.

The Boeing was sinking through a thousand feet, lined up for runway 21 and directly ahead the revolving red beacons on top of the fire vehicles seemed to flash a direct challenge.

'I can't pile into them,' Cyril Watkins decided, and there was no longer hesitation nor doubt in his tone. 'I'm going to overshoot and get out of here.'

'Land on the grass,' the girl shrieked. 'There is open grass on the left of the runway – put her down there.'

But Cyril Watkins had leaned forward in his seat and rammed the bank of throttles forward. The engines howled and the Boeing surged into a nose-high climb.

The young flight engineer had swivelled his stool and was staring ahead through the windscreen. His whole body was rigid, his expression intense and the smear of blood across his forehead was in vivid contrast to the pallor of his skin.

With his right hand he gripped the edge of his desk, and the knuckles of his fist were white and shiny as eggshell.

Without seeming to move the blonde girl had pinned the wrist of that rigid right hand, pressing the muzzles of the pistol into it.

There was a crash of sound, so violent in the confines of the cabin that it seemed to beat in their eardrums. The weapon kicked up as high as the girl's golden head and there was the immediate acrid stench of burned cordite.

The flight engineer stared down incredulously at the desk top. There was a hole blown through the metal as big as a teacup, and the edges were jagged with bright bare metal.

The blast of shot had amputated his hand cleanly at the wrist. The severed member had been thrown forward into the space between the pilots' seats, with the shattered bone protruding from the mangled meat. It twitched like a crushed and maimed insect.

'Land,' said the girl. 'Land or the next shot is through his head.'

'You bloody monster,' shouted Cyril Watkins, staring at the severed hand.

'Land or you will be responsible for this man's life.'

The flight engineer clutched the stump of his arm against his belly and doubled over it silently, his face contorted by the shock.

Cyril Watkins tore his stricken gaze from the severed hand and looked ahead once more. There was wide open grass between the runway markers and the narrow taxiway. The grass had been mown knee-high, and he knew the ground beneath it would be fairly smooth.

Cyril's hand on the throttle bank pulled back smoothly, almost of its own volition, the engine thunder died away and the nose dropped again.

He held his approach aligned with the main runway until he was well in over the threshold lights. He did not want to alert the drivers of the blocking vehicles to his intention while they still had time to counter it.

'You murderous bitch,' he said under his breath. 'You filthy murderous bitch.'

He banked the Boeing steeply, realigned it with the long strip of open grass and cut the throttles completely, bringing her in nose-high and just a fraction above the stall, flaring out deliberately low and banging the Boeing down into the grass for positive touch down.

The huge machine settled to the rough strip, jolting and lurching wildly as Cyril Watkins fought the rudders to keep them lined up, holding his nose wheel off with the control yoke, while his co-pilot threw all her giant engines into reverse thrust and trod firmly down on the main landing gear brakes.

The fire engines and fuel tankers flashed past the starboard wing tip. The startled faces of their crews seemed very close and white – then 070 was past, her speed bleeding off sharply so her nose wheel dropped and she rocked and swayed gradually to a dead stop just short of the brick building which housed the approach and landing beacons, and the main radar installations.

It was 7.25 a.m. local time and Speedbird 070 was down.

'Well, they are down,' intoned Kingston Parker. 'And you can well understand the extreme efforts that were made to prevent them. Their choice of final destination settles one of your queries, Peter.'

'"À l'allemande"—' Peter nodded. 'It's got to be political. I agree, sir.'

'And you and I must now face in dreadful reality what we have discussed only in lofty theory—' Parker held a taper to his pipe and puffed twice before going on. ' – Morally justifiable militancy.'

'Again we have to differ, sir.' Peter cut in swiftly. 'There is no such thing.'

'Is there not?' Parker asked, shaking his head. 'What of the German officers killed in the streets of Paris by the French resistance?'

'That was war,' Peter exclaimed.

'Perhaps the group that seized 070 believes that they are at war—'

'With innocent victims?' Peter shot back.

'The *Haganah* took innocent victims – yet what they were fighting for was right and just.'

'I'm an Englishman, Dr Parker – you cannot expect me to condone the murder of British women and children.' Peter had stiffened in his chair.

'No,' Parker agreed. 'So let us not speak of the MauMau

in Kenya, nor of present-day Ireland then – but what of the French Revolution or the spreading of the Catholic faith by the most terrible persecution and tortures yet devised by man – were those not morally justifiable militancy?'

'I would prefer to call it understandable but reprehensible. Terrorism in any form can never be morally justifiable.' Provoked himself, Peter used the word deliberately to provoke and saw the small lift of Parker's thick bushy eyebrows.

'There is terrorism from above – as well as from below.' Parker picked up the word and used it deliberately. 'If you define terrorism as extreme physical or physiological coercion used to induce others to submit to the will of the terrorist – there is the legal terror threat of the gallows, the religious terror threat of hell fire, the paternal terror threat of the cane – are those more morally justifiable than the aspiration of the weak, the poor, the politically oppressed, the powerless victims of an unjust society? Is their scream of protest to be strangled—'

Peter shifted uncomfortably in his chair. 'Protest outside the law—'

'Laws are made by man, almost always by the rich and the powerful – laws are changed by men, usually only after militant action. The women's suffragette movement, the civil rights campaign in this country—' Parker broke off and chuckled. 'I'm sorry, Peter. Sometimes I confuse myself. It's often more difficult to be a liberal than it is to be a tyrant. At least the tyrant seldom has doubts.' Parker lay back in his chair, a dismissive gesture. 'I propose to leave you in peace for an hour or two now. You will want to develop your plans in line with the new developments. But I personally have no doubts now that we are dealing with politically motivated militants, and not merely a gang of old-fashioned kidnappers after a fast buck. Of one other thing I am certain: before we see this one through we will be forced to examine our own consciences very closely.'

'Take the second right,' said Ingrid quietly, and the Boeing swung off the grass onto the taxiway. There seemed to be no damage to her landing gear, but now that she had left her natural element, the aircraft had lost grace and beauty and became lumbering and ungainly.

The girl had never been on the flight deck of a grounded Jumbo before, and the height was impressive. It gave her a feeling of detachment, of being invulnerable.

'Now left again,' she instructed, and the Boeing turned away from the main airport building towards the southern end of the runway. The observation deck of the airport's flat roof was already lined with hundreds of curious spectators, but all activity on the apron was suspended. The waiting machines and tenders were deserted, not a single human figure on the tarmac.

'Park there.' She pointed ahead to an open area four hundred yards from the nearest building, midway between the terminal and the cluster of service hangars and the main fuel depot. 'Stop on the intersection.'

Grimly silent, Cyril Watkins did as he was ordered, and then turned in his seat.

'I must call an ambulance to get him off.'

The co-pilot and a stewardess had the flight engineer stretched out on the galley floor, just beyond the door to the flight deck. They were using linen table napkins to bind up the arm and try and staunch the bleeding. The stench of cordite still lingered and mingled with the taint of fresh blood.

'Nobody leaves this aircraft.' The girl shook her head. 'He knows too much about us already.'

'My God, woman. He needs medical attention.'

'There are three hundred doctors aboard—' she pointed out indifferently. 'The best in the world. Two of them may come forward and attend to him.'

She perched sideways on the flight engineer's blood-splattered desk, and thumbed the internal microphone.

Cyril Watkins noticed even in his outrage that it needed only a single demonstration and Ingrid was able to work the complicated communications equipment. She was bright and very well trained.

'Ladies and gentlemen, we have landed at Johannesburg Airport. We will be here for a long time – perhaps days, even weeks. All our patience will be tried, so I must warn you that any disobedience will be most severely dealt with. Already one attempt at resistance has been made – and in consequence a member of the crew has been shot and gravely wounded. He may die of this wound. We do not want a repetition of this incident. However, I must again warn you that my officers and I will not hesitate to shoot again, or even to detonate the explosives above your heads – if the need arises.'

She paused and watched a moment as two selected doctors came forward and knelt on each side of the flight engineer. He was shaking like a fever victim with shock, his white shirt splashed and daubed with blood. Her expression showed no remorse, no real concern, and her voice was calm and light as she went on.

'Two of my officers will now pass down the aisles and they will collect your passports from you. Please have these documents ready.'

Her eyes flicked sideways, as movement caught her eye. From beyond the service hangars a line of four armoured cars emerged in line ahead. They were the locally manufactured version of the French Panhard with heavily lugged tall tyres, a raked turret and the disproportionately long barrels of the cannons trained forward. The armoured vehicles circled cautiously and parked three hundred yards out, at the four points – wing tips, tail and nose – around the aircraft, with the long cannon trained upon her.

The girl watched them disdainfully until one of the doctors pushed himself in front of her. He was a short, chubby little man, balding – but brave.

'This man must be taken to a hospital immediately.'

'That is out of the question.'

'I insist. His life is in danger.'

'All our lives are in danger, doctor.' She paused and let that make its effect. 'Draw up a list of your requirements. I will see that you get them.'

'They have been down for sixteen hours now and the only contact has been a request for medical supplies and for a power link-up to the electrical mains.' Kingston Parker had removed his jacket and loosened the knot of his tie, but was showing no other ill effects of his vigil.

Peter Stride nodded at the image on the screen. 'What have your medics made of the supplies?' he asked.

'Looks like a gunshot casualty. Whole blood type AB Positive, that's rare but one of the crew is cross-matched AB Positive on his service record. Ten litres of plasmalyte B, a blood-giving set and syringes, morphine and intravenous penicillin, tetanus toxoid – all the equipment needed to treat massive physical trauma.'

'And they are on mains power?' Peter asked.

'Yes, four hundred people would have suffocated by now without the air-conditioning. The airport authority has laid a cable and plugged it into the external socket. All the aircraft's support system – even the galley heating – will be fully functional.'

'So we will be able to throw the switch on them at any time.' Peter made a note on the pad in front of him. 'But no demands yet? No negotiator called for?'

'No, nothing. They seem fully aware of the techniques of bargaining in this type of situation – unlike our friends, the host country. I am afraid we are having a great deal of trouble with the Wyatt Earp mentality—' Parker paused. 'I'm sorry, Wyatt Earp was one of our frontier marshals—'

'I saw the movie, and read the book,' Peter answered tartly.

'Well, the South Africans are itching to storm the aircraft, and both our ambassador and yours are hard pressed to restrain them. They are all set to kick the doors of the saloon open and rush in with six-guns blazing. They must also have seen the movie.'

Peter felt the crawl of horror down his spine. 'That would be a certain disaster,' he said quickly. 'These people are running a tight operation.'

'You don't have to convince me,' Parker agreed. 'What is your flying time to Jan Smuts now?'

'We crossed the Zambesi River seven minutes ago.' Peter glanced sideways through the perspex bubble window, but the ground was obscured by haze and cumulus cloud. 'We have another two hours ten minutes to fly – but my support section is three hours forty behind us.'

'All right, Peter. I will get back onto them. The South African Government has convened a full cabinet meeting, and both our ambassadors are sitting in as observers and advisers. I think I am going to be obliged to tell them about the existence of Atlas.'

He paused a moment. 'Here at last we are seeing Atlas justified, Peter. A single unit, cutting across all national considerations, able to act swiftly and independently. I think you should know that I have already obtained the agreement of the President and of your Prime Minister to condition Delta – at my discretion.'

Condition Delta was the kill decision.

' – but again I emphasize that I will implement Delta only as a last possible resort. I want to hear and consider the demands first, and in that respect we are open to negotiation – fully open—'

Parker went on speaking, and Peter Stride shifted slightly, dropping his chin into the cup of his hand to hide his irritation. They were into an area of dispute now – and once again Peter had to voice disagreement.

'Every time you let a militant walk away from a strike you immediately create the conditions for further strikes, to free the captive.'

'I have the clearance for condition Delta,' Parker reiterated with a trace of acid in his tone now, 'but I am making it clear that it will be used only with the greatest discretion. We are not an assassination unit, General Stride.' Parker nodded to an assistant off-screen. 'I am going through to the South Africans now to explain Atlas.' The image receded into darkness.

Peter Stride leapt up abruptly and tried to pace the narrow aisle between the seats, but there was insufficient headroom for his tall frame and he flung himself angrily into the seat again.

Kingston Parker stood up from his communications desk in the outer office of his suite in the west wing of the Pentagon. The two communications technicians scurried out of his way and his personal secretary opened the door to his inner office.

He moved with peculiar grace for such a large man, and there was no excess weight on his frame, his big heavy bones lean of flesh. His clothes were of fine cloth, well cut – the best that Fifth Avenue could offer – but they were worn almost to the point of shoddiness, the button-down collar slightly frayed, the Italian shoes scuffed at the toes as though material trappings counted not at all with him. Nevertheless he wore them with a certain unconscious panache, and he looked ten years younger than his fifty-three, only a few silver strands in the thick bushy mane of hair.

The inner office was Spartan in its furnishings, all of it U.S. Government issue, utilitarian and impersonal, only the books that filled every shelf and the grand piano were his own. The piano was a Bechstein grand and much too large for the room. Parker ran his right hand lightly across the keyboard as he passed it – but he went on to the desk.

He dropped into the swivel chair and shuffled through the dozen intelligence folders on his desk. Each of them contained the latest computer print-outs that he had requested. There were personal histories, appraisals, and character studies of all the personalities that had so far become involved in the taking of Speedbird 070.

Both the ambassadors – their pink files signified the highest security ratings, and were marked 'Heads of Departments only'. Four other files in lower echelon green were devoted to the South African Government personalities with decision-making capabilities in an emergency. The thickest file was that of the South African Prime Minister – and once again Parker noted wryly that the man had been imprisoned by the pro-British government of General Jan Smuts during World War II as a militant opponent of his country's involvement in that war. He wondered just how much sympathy he would have for other militants now.

There were files for the South African Ministers of Defence and of Justice, and still slimmer green files for the Commissioner of Police and for the Assistant Commissioner who had been given the on-site responsibility of handling the emergency. Of them all only the Prime Minister emerged as a distinct personality – a powerful bulldog figure, not a man easily influenced or dissuaded, and instinctively Kingston Parker recognized that ultimate authority rested here.

There was one other pink file at the bottom of the

considerable stack, so well handled that the cardboard cover was splitting at the hinge. The original print-out in this file had been requisitioned two years previously, with quarterly up-dates since that time.

'STRIDE PETER CHARLES' it was headed – and reclassified 'Head of Atlas only'.

Kingston Parker could probably have recited its contents by heart – but he untied the ribbons now, and opened it in his lap.

Puffing deliberately at his pipe he began to turn slowly through the loose pages.

There were the bare bones of the subject's life. Born 1939, one of twin war-time babies of a military family, his father killed in action three years later when the armoured brigade of guards he commanded was overrun by one of Erwin Rommel's devastating drives across the deserts of North Africa. The elder twin brother had inherited the baronetcy and Peter followed the well-travelled family course, Harrow and Sandhurst, where he must have disconcerted the family by his academic brilliance and his reluctance to participate in team sports – preferring the loner activities of golf and tennis and long-distance running.

Kingston Parker pondered that a moment. They were pointers to the man's character that had disconcerted him as well. Parker had the intellectual's generalized contempt for the military, and he would have preferred a man who conformed more closely to his ideal of the brass-headed soldier.

Yet when the young Stride had entered his father's regiment, it seemed that the exceptional intelligence had been diverted into conventional channels and the preference for independent thought and action held in check, if not put aside completely – until his regiment was sent to Cyprus at the height of the unrest in that country. Within a week of arrival the young Stride had been seconded, with his commanding officer's enthusiastic approval, to central army intelligence. Perhaps the commanding officer had already become aware of the problems involved in harbouring a wonder-boy in the tradition-bound portals of his officers' mess.

For once the military had made a logical, if not an outright brilliant, choice. Stride in the sixteen years since then had not made a single mistake, apart from the marriage which had ended in divorce within two years. Had he remained with his regiment that might have affected his career – but since Cyprus Stride's progress had been as unconventional and meteoric as his brain.

In a dozen different and difficult assignments since then, he had honed his gifts and developed new talents; rising against the trend of reduced British expenditure on defence, he had reached staff rank before thirty years of age.

At NATO Headquarters he had made powerful friends and admirers on both sides of the Atlantic, and at the end of his three-year term in Brussels he had been promoted to major-general and been transferred to head British Intelligence in Ireland, bringing his own particular dedication and flair to the job.

A great deal of the credit for containing the sweep of Irish terrorism through Britain was his, and his in-depth study of the urban guerrilla and the mind of the militant, although classified departmentally, was probably the definitive work on the subject.

The Atlas concept was first proposed in this study, and so it was that Stride had been on the short list to head the project. It seemed certain the appointment would be made – the Americans had been impressed with his study and his friends from NATO had not forgotten him. His appointment was approved in principle. Then at the last moment there had developed sudden and intense opposition to the appointment of a professional soldier to head such a sensitive agency. The opposition had come from both Whitehall and Washington simultaneously, and had prevailed.

Kingston Parker knocked out his pipe, and carried the file across the room and laid it open on the music rack of the piano. He seated himself at the keyboard and, still studying the printout sheets, began to play.

The stream of music, the lovely ethereal strains of Liszt, did not interrupt his thoughts but seemed to buoy them brightly upwards.

Parker had not wanted Stride, had considered from the very first that he was dangerous, sensing in him ambitions and motivations which would be difficult to control. Parker would have preferred his own nominees – Tanner, who now commanded the Mercury arm of Atlas, or Colin Noble – and had expected that Stride would have declined a command so far below his capability.

However, Stride had accepted the lesser appointment and headed Thor. Parker suspected that there was unusual motivation in this, and had made every effort to study the man at first hand. On five separate occasions he had ordered Stride to Washington, and focused upon him the full strength of his charisma and personality. He had even invited him to stay with him in his New York home, spending many hours with him in deep far-ranging discussions – from which he had developed a prudent respect for the man's mind, but had been able to reach no firm conclusions as to his future in Atlas.

Parker turned a page of the character appraisal. When he looked for the weakness in an opponent, Parker had long ago learned to start at the groin. With this man there was no evidence of any unnatural sexual leanings. Certainly he was not homosexual, if anything too much the opposite. There had been at least a dozen significant liaisons with the opposite sex since his divorce. However, all of these had been discreet and dignified. Although three of the ladies had been married, none of them were the wives of his subordinates in the armed services, nor of brother officers or of men who might be able to adversely affect his career.

The women he chose all had certain qualities in common – they all tended to be tall, intelligent and successful. One was a journalist who had her own syndicated column, another was a former fashion model who now designed and marketed her clothes through her own prestigious outlets in London and on the continent. Then there was an actress who was a leading female member of the Royal Shakespeare Company – Parker skimmed the list impatiently, for Parker himself had no sympathy nor patience with a man who succumbed to the dictates of his body.

Parker had trained himself to be totally celibate, channelling all his sexual energies into pursuits of the mind, while this man Stride, on the other hand, was not above conducting two or three of his liaisons concurrently.

Parker moved on to the second area of weakness. Stride's inheritance had been decimated by the punitive British death duties – yet his private income even after savage taxation was still a little over twenty thousand pounds sterling a year, and when this was added to his salary and privileges as a general officer, it enabled him to live in good style. He could even indulge in the mild extravagance of collecting rare books – and, Parker observed acidly, the greater extravagance of collecting rare ladies.

However, there was no trace of any illicit hoard – no Swiss bank accounts, no deposits of gold bullion, no foreign properties, no shares in off-share companies held by nominees – and Parker had searched diligently for them, for they would have indicated payments received, perhaps from foreign governments. A man like Stride had much to sell, at prices he could set himself – but it seemed he had not done so.

Stride did not smoke; Parker removed the old black briar from his own mouth, regarded it affectionately for a moment. It was his one indulgence, a harmless one despite what the surgeon-general of the United States had determined, and he took the stem firmly between his teeth again.

Stride took alcohol in moderation and was considered knowledgeable on the subject of wine. He raced occasionally, more as a social outing than as a serious punter, and the odd fifty pounds he could well afford. There was no evidence of other gambling. However, he did not hunt, nor did he shoot – traditional pursuits of the English gentleman. Perhaps he had moral objections to blood sports, Parker thought, though it seemed unlikely, for Stride was a superlative marksman with rifle, shotgun and pistol. He had represented Britain at the Munich Olympics as a pistol shot, winning a gold in the fifty metre class, and he spent at least an hour every day on the range.

Parker turned to the page of the print-out that gave the man's medical history. He must be superbly fit as well – his body weight at the age of thirty-nine was one pound less than it had been at twenty-one, and he still trained like a front-line soldier. Parker noticed that he had logged sixteen parachute jumps the previous month. Since joining Atlas he had no opportunity or time for golf, though when he was with NATO Stride had played off a handicap of three.

Parker closed the folder and played on softly, but neither the sensual polished feel of cool ivory beneath his fingertips nor the achingly lovely lilt of the music could dispel his sense of disquiet. Exhaustive as the report was, yet it left unanswered questions, like why Stride had downgraded himself to accept the command of Thor – he was not the kind of man who acted ill-advisedly. Yet the most haunting questions that nagged at Parker were just how strong were his qualities of resilience and independent thought, just how strongly was he driven by his ambitions and that penetrating intellect – and just how great a threat such a man would present to the evolution of Atlas into its ultimate role.

'Doctor Parker, sir—' his assistant knocked lightly and entered, ' – there are new developments.'

Parker sighed softly. 'I'm coming,' he said, and let the

last sad and beautiful notes fall from his long, powerful fingers before he stood up.

The Hawker slid almost silently down the sky. The pilot had closed down power at five thousand feet and made his final approach without touching the throttles again. He was ten knots above the stall as he passed over the boundary fence and he touched down twenty feet beyond the chevron markings of the threshold of runway One Fife, instantly applying maximum safe braking. One Fife was the secondary cross-wind runway and the Hawker's roll-out was so short that every part of the approach and landing had been screened by the buildings of the main airport terminal from where Speedbird 070 stood at the southern intersection of the main taxiway.

The pilot swung the Hawker through 360° and back-tracked sedately up runway 15, using just enough power to keep her rolling.

'Well done,' grunted Peter Stride, crouching behind the pilot's seat. He was almost certain that nobody aboard 070 had remarked their arrival.

'They've prepared a slot for us, with hook up to the electrical mains at the north—' Peter broke off as he saw the apron marshal waving them in with the bats, and beyond him a tight group of four men waiting. Three of them wore camouflage battle dress and the other the trim blue uniform, cap and gold insignia of a senior South African police officer.

The uniformed officer was the first to greet Peter as he came down the Hawker's fold-out air-stairs.

'Prinsloo.' He shook hands. 'Lieutenant-General.'

He ranked Peter, but it was a police, not a military appointment. He was a stocky man, with steel-rimmed spectacles, a little paunchy, and not less than fifty-five years of age. He had the rather heavy features, the fleshiness of jowl and lips, that Peter had noticed so often in Belgian and Dutch peasants during his NATO tour in the Netherlands. A man of the earth, dour and conservative.

'Let me introduce Commandant Boonzaier.' This was a military rank, equivalent to that of colonel, and he was a younger man, but with the same thick accent and his features cast in the same mould. A tall man, however, only an inch or so shorter than Peter – but both of the South Africans were suspicious and resentful, and the reason was immediately apparent.

'I have been instructed to take my orders from you, General,' and there was a subtle shift of position, the two officers ranging themselves beside Peter, but facing each other, and he was aware instantly that not all the hostility was directed at him. There had been friction between police and military already – and the basic value of Atlas was underlined yet again.

A single clean-cut line of command and of responsibility was absolutely essential – Peter's mind flicked back to the shoot-out at Larnaca Airport between Egyptian commandos and Cypriot national guardsmen, from which the hijackers of the grounded jet emerged unscathed while the airfield was littered with the burning wreckage of the Egyptian transport aircraft and dozens of dead and dying Cypriots and Egyptians.

The first principle of terrorist strategy was to strike at the point where national responsibilities were blurred. Atlas cut through that.

'Thank you.' Peter accepted command without flaunting it. 'My back-up team will land in just over three hours' time. We will, of course, use force only as a last resort – but if it comes to that, I will use exclusively Atlas personnel in any counter-strike. I would like to make that quite clear immediately.' And he saw the line of the soldier's mouth harden with disappointment.

'My men are the élite—'

'It's a British aircraft, most of the hostages are British or American nationals – it's a political decision, Colonel. But I would value your help in other areas.' Peter turned him aside tactfully.

'Firstly, I want you to suggest a position where I can place my surveillance equipment – and then we will go over the ground together.'

Peter had no difficulty selecting his forward observation post. The service manager's roomy, sparsely furnished office on the third floor of the terminal building overlooked the entire service area and the southern portion of the taxiway where the Boeing stood.

The windows had been left open when the offices were evacuated, so there was no need to change the external appearance of the room.

The overhang of the observation balcony on the floor above shaded the interior, and the office was deep enough to ensure that an observer out there in the bright glare of sunshine would not be able to see into the room, even with a powerful lens. The militants would expect surveillance from the glass control tower high above – any deception, however trivial, was worth while.

The surveillance equipment was lightweight and compact, the television cameras were neither of them bigger than a super 8-mm home movie camera and a man could carry in one hand both of the aluminium extension tripods. However, the cameras could zoom to 800-mm focal length, and they repeated on the screens of the command console in the cabin of the Hawker, while the image was simultaneously stored on videotape.

The audio intensifier was more bulky, but no heavier. It had a four-foot dish antenna, with the sound collector in the centre. The telescopic sight could aim the intensifier at a sound source with the accuracy of a sniper's rifle – could focus on the lips of a human being at eight hundred yards' distance and clearly record normal conversation at that range, passing sound directly to the command console and at the same time storing it on the big magnetic tape spools.

Two of Peter's communications team were posted here, with a plentiful supply of coffee and doughnuts, and Peter, accompanied by the South African colonel and his staff, went up in the elevator to the glass house of the control tower.

From the air traffic control tower there was an unobstructed view across the airfield and over the apron and service areas around the terminal. The observation platform below the tower had been cleared of all but military personnel.

' – I have road blocks at all the main entrances to the airfield. Only passengers with confirmed reservations and current tickets are being allowed through – no thrill seekers – and we are using only the northern section of the terminal for traffic.'

Peter nodded and turned to the senior controller. 'What is the state of your traffic pattern?'

'We have refused clearance to all private flights, incoming and departing. All domestic scheduled flights have been re-routed to Lanseria and Germiston airports, and we are landing and despatching only international scheduled flights – but the backlog has delayed departures by three hours.'

'What separation are you observing from 070?' Peter asked.

'Fortunately the international departures terminal is the farthest from the aircraft, and we are not using the taxiways or the apron of the southern section. As you see, we have cleared the entire area – except for those three S.A. Airways aircraft which are undergoing overhaul and servicing, there are no other aircraft within a thousand yards of 070.'

'I may have to freeze all traffic, if—' Peter paused, 'or should I say, when we have an escalation.'

'Very well, sir.'

'In the meantime, you may continue as you are at present.' Peter lifted his binoculars and once again very carefully examined the huge Boeing.

It stood in stately isolation, silent and seemingly abandoned. The bright, almost gaudy marking gave her a carnival air. Red and blue and crisp sparkling white in the brilliant sunlight of the highveld. She was parked fully broadside to the tower, and all her hatches and doors were still armed and locked.

Peter traversed slowly along the line of perspex windows down the length of the fuselage – but over each of them the sunshades had been firmly closed from the interior, turning them into the multiple eyes of a blinded insect.

Peter lifted his scrutiny slightly onto the windshield and side panels of the flight deck. These again had been screened with blankets, hung over them from inside, completely thwarting any glimpse of the crew or their captors – and certainly preventing a shot into the flight deck, although the range from the nearest corner of the terminal was not more than four hundred yards, and with the new laser sights one of Thor's trained snipers could pick through which eye of the human head he would put a bullet.

Snaking across the open tarmac of the taxiway was the thin black electrical cable that connected the aircraft to the mains supply, a long, vulnerable umbilical cord. Peter studied it thoughtfully, before turning his attention to the four Panhard armoured cars. A little frown of irritation crossed his forehead.

'Colonel, please recall those vehicles.' He tried not to let the irritation come through in his tone. 'With the turrets battened down, your crews will be roasting like Christmas geese.'

'General, I feel it my duty—' Boonzaier began, and Peter lowered the glasses and smiled. It was a charming, friendly grin that took the man by surprise, after the previous stern set of features – and yet the eyes were devoid of humour, cracking blue and hard in the craggy granite of the face.

'I want to defuse the atmosphere as much as possible.' The necessity to explain irked Peter, but he maintained the smile. 'Somebody with four great cannons aimed at him is more likely to make a bad decision, and pull the trigger himself. You may keep them in close support, but get them out of sight into the terminal car park, and let your men rest.'

With little grace the colonel passed the order over the walkie-talkie on his belt, and as the vehicles started up and slowly pulled away behind the line of hangars, Peter went on remorselessly.

'How many men have you got deployed?' He pointed to the line of soldiers along the parapet of the observation balcony, and then to the heads visible as specks between the soaring blue of the African sky and the silhouette of the service hangars.

'Two hundred and thirty.'

'Pull them out,' Peter instructed, 'and let the occupants of the aircraft see them go.'

'All of them?' incredulously.

'All of them,' Peter agreed, and now the smile was wolfish, 'and quickly, please, colonel.'

The man was learning swiftly, and he lifted the miniaturized walkie-talkie to his mouth again. There were a few moments of scurrying and confusion among the troops on the observation deck below before they could be formed up and marched away in file. Their steel helmets, like a bobbing line of button mushrooms, and the muzzles of their slung weapons would show above the parapet, and would be clearly visible to an observer in the Boeing.

'If you treat these people, these animals—' the colonel's voice was choked slightly with frustration, ' – if you treat them soft—'

Peter knew exactly what was coming, ' – and if you keep waving guns in their faces, you will keep them alert and on their toes, Colonel. Let them settle down a little and relax, let them get very confident.' He spoke without lowering the binoculars. With a soldier's eye for ground he was picking the site for his four snipers. There was little chance that he would be able to use them – they would have to take out every single one of the enemy at the same instant – but a remote chance might just offer itself, and he decided to place one gun on the service hangar roof, there was a large ventilator which could be pierced and would command the port side of the aircraft, two guns to cover the flight deck from both sides – he could use the drainage ditch down the edge of the main runway to get a man into the small hut that housed the approach radar and ILS beacons. The hut was in the enemy's rear. They might not expect fire from that quarter – point by point from his mental checklist Peter planned his dispositions, scribbling his decisions into the small leather-covered notebook, poring over the large-scale map of the airport, converting gradients and angles into fields of fire, measuring 'ground to cover' and 'time to target' for an assault force launched from the nearest vantage points, twisting each problem and evaluating it, striving for novel solutions to each, trying to think ahead of an enemy that was still faceless and infinitely menacing.

It took him an hour of hard work before he was satisfied. Now he could pass his decisions to Colin Noble on board the incoming Herc, and within four minutes of the big landing wheels hitting tarmac his highly trained team with their complex talents and skills would be in position.

Peter straightened up from the map and tucked the notebook under the flap of his button-down breast pocket. Once again he scrutinized every inch of the silent, battened-down aircraft through his glasses – but this time he allowed himself the luxury of gut emotion.

He felt the anger and the hatred rise from some hidden depth of his soul and flush his blood and tighten the muscles of his belly and thighs.

Once again he was confronted by the many-headed monster. It crouched out there in ambush, waiting for him as it had so often before.

He remembered suddenly the shards of splintered glass littering the cobbles of a Belfast street and glittering like diamond chips in the arc lamps, the smell of explosives and blood thick in the air.

He remembered the body of a young woman lying in the gutted interior of a fashionable London restaurant. Her lovely young body stripped by the blast of all but a flimsy pearl-coloured pair of French lace panties.

He remembered the smell of a family, father, mother and three small children, burning in the interior of their saloon car, the bodies blackening and twisting in a slow macabre ballet as the flames scorched them. Peter had not been able to eat pork since that day.

He remembered the frightened eyes of a child, through a mask of blood, a dismembered arm lying beside her, the pale fingers still clutching a grubby little rag doll.

The images flashed in disjointed sequences across his memory, feeding his hatred until it pricked and stung behind his eyes and he had to lower the binoculars and wipe his eyes with the back of his hand.

It was the same enemy that he had hunted before, but his instincts warned him that it had grown even stronger and more inhuman since last he had met and fought it. He tried to suppress the hatred now, lest it cloud his judgement, lest it handicap him during the difficult hours and days that he knew lay ahead – but it was too powerful, had been too long nurtured.

He recognized that hatred was the enemy's vice, that from it sprang their twisted philosophy and their monstrous actions, and that to descend to hatred was to descend to their sub-human levels – yet still the hatred persisted.

Peter Stride understood clearly that his hatred was not only for the ghastly death and mutilation that he had witnessed so often. More it was fostered by the threat that he recognized to an entire society and its civilized rule of law. If this evil should be allowed to triumph, then in the future laws would be made by the wild-eyed revolutionary, with a gun in his fist – the world would be run by the destroyers instead of the builders, and Peter Stride hated that possibility more even than the violence and the blood, and those he hated as a soldier hates. For only a soldier truly knows the horror of war.

His soldier's instinct now was to immediately engage the enemy and destroy him – but the scholar and philosopher in him warned that this was not the moment, and with an enormous effort of will he held that fighting man's instinct in check.

Yet still he was deeply aware that it was for this moment, for this confrontation of the forces of evil, that he had jeopardized his whole career.

When command of Atlas had been plucked away and a political appointee named in his place, Peter should have declined the offer of a lesser position in Atlas. There were other avenues open to him, but instead he had elected to stay with the project – and he hoped that nobody had guessed at the resentment he felt. God knows, Kingston Parker had no cause for complaint since then. There was no harder working officer on Atlas, and his loyalty had been tested more than once.

Now all that seemed worth while, and the moment for which he had worked had arrived. The enemy waited for him out there on the burning tarmac under an African sun, not on a soft green island in the rain nor in the grimy streets of a crowded city – but still it was the same old enemy, and Peter knew his time would come.

His communications technicians had Colin Noble on the main screen as Peter ducked into the Hawker's cabin that was now his command headquarters, and settled into his padded seat. On the top right screen was a panoramic view of the southern terminal area, with the Boeing squatting like a brooding eagle upon its nest in the centre of the shot. On the next screen beside it was a blow-up through the 800-mm zoom lens of the Boeing's flight deck. So crisp was the detail that Peter could read the maker's name on the tab of the blanket that screened the windshield. The third small screen held a full shot of the interior of the air traffic control tower. In the foreground the controllers in shirt sleeves sitting over the radar repeaters, and beyond them through the floor to ceiling windows still another view of the Boeing. All these were being shot through the cameras installed an hour earlier in the terminal building. The remaining small screen was blank, and Colin Noble's homely, humorous face filled the main screen.

'Now if only it had been the cavalry instead of the U.S. Marines,' Peter said, 'you'd have been here yesterday—'

'What's your hurry, pal. Doesn't look like the party has started yet.' Colin grinned at him from the screen and pushed his baseball cap to the back of his head.

'Damned right,' Peter agreed. 'We don't even know who is throwing the party. What's your latest estimate on arrival time?'

'We've picked up a good wind – one hour twenty-two minutes to fly now,' Colin told him.

'Right, let's get down to it,' Peter said, and he began his briefing, going carefully over the field notes he had taken. When he wanted to emphasize a point, Peter called for a change of shot from his cameramen, and they zoomed in or panned to his instruction, picking up the radar shed or the service hangar ventilator where Peter was siting his snipers. The image was repeated not only on the command console but in the cavernous body of the approaching Hercules so that the men who would be called to occupy those positions could study them now and prepare themselves thoroughly for the moment. The same images were hurled across the stratosphere to the circling satellite and from there bounced down to appear, only slightly distorted, on the screens of Atlas Command in the west wing of the Pentagon. Sagging like an old lion in his armchair, Kingston Parker followed every word of the briefing, rousing himself only when a long telex message was passed to him by his assistant, then he nodded a command to have his own televised image superimposed on Peter's command console.

'I'm sorry to interrupt you, Peter, but we've got a useful scrap here. Assuming that the militant group boarded 070 at Mahé, we asked the Seychelles Police to run a check on all joining passengers. There were fifteen of them, ten of whom were Seychelles residents. A local merchant and his wife, and eight unaccompanied children between nine and fourteen years of age. They are the children of expatriate civil servants employed on contract by the Seychelles Government, returning to schools in England for the new term.'

Peter felt the weight of dread bring down upon him like a physical burden. Children, the young lives seemed somehow more important, somehow more vulnerable. But Parker was reading from the telex flimsy in his left hand, the right scratching the back of his neck with the stem of his pipe.

'There is one British businessman, Shell Oil Company, and well-known on the island, and there are four tourists, an American, a Frenchman and two Germans. These last four appeared to be travelling in a group, the immigration and security officers remember them well. Two women and two men, all young. Names Sally-Anne Taylor, twenty-five years, American, Heidi Hottschauser, twenty-four and Gunther Retz, twenty-five, the two Germans and Henri Larousse, twenty-six, the Frenchman. The police have run a back check on the four. They stayed two weeks at the Reef Hotel outside Victoria, the women in one double room and the two men in another. They spent most of the time swimming and sunbathing – until five days ago when a small ocean-going yacht called at Victoria. Thirty-five foot, single-hander around the world, skippered by another American. The four spent time on board her every day of her stay, and the yacht sailed twenty-four hours before the departure of the 070.'

'If the yacht delivered their arms and munitions, then this operation has been planned for a long time,' Peter pondered, 'and damn well planned.'

Peter felt the tingling flush of his blood again, the form of the enemy was taking shape now, the outline of the beast becoming clearer, and always it was uglier and more menacing.

'You have run the names through the computer?' he asked.

'Nothing,' Parker nodded. 'Either there is no intelligence record of them, or the names and passports are false—'

He broke off as there was sudden activity on the screen that monitored the air traffic control tower, and another voice boomed out of the secondary speaker; the volume was set too high, and the technician at the control board adjusted it swiftly. It was a female voice, a fresh, clear young voice speaking English with the lilt and inflexion of the west coast of America in it.

'Jan Smuts tower, this is the officer commanding the task

force of the Action Commando for Human Rights that has control of Speedbird 070. Stand by to copy a message.'

'Contact!' Peter breathed. 'Contact at last.'

On the small screen Colin Noble grinned and rolled his cheroot expertly from one side of his mouth to the other. 'The party has begun,' he announced, but there was the razor edge in his voice not entirely concealed by his jocular tone.

The three-man crew had been moved back from the flight deck, and were held in the first class seats vacated by the group of four.

Ingrid had made the cockpit of the Boeing her headquarters, and she worked swiftly through the pile of passports, filling in the name and nationality of each passenger on the seating plan spread before her.

The door to the galley was open and except for the hum of the air-conditioning, the huge aircraft was peculiarly silent. Conversation in the cabins was prohibited, and the aisles were patrolled by the red-shirted commandos to enforce this edict.

They also ordered the use of the toilets: a passenger must return to his seat before another was allowed to rise. The toilet doors had to remain open during use, so that the commandos could check at a glance.

Despite the silence, there was a crackling atmosphere of tension down the full length of the cabin. Very few of the passengers, mostly the children, were asleep, but the others sat in rigid rows, their faces taut and strained – watching their captors with a mixture of hatred and of fear.

Henri, the Frenchman, slipped into the cockpit.

'They are pulling back the armoured cars,' he said. He was slim, with a very youthful face and dreaming poet's eyes. He had grown a drooping blond gunfighter's moustache, but the effect was incongruous.

Ingrid looked up at him. 'You are so nervous, *chéri.*' She shook her head. 'It will all be all right.'

'I am not nervous,' he answered her stiffly.

She chuckled fondly, and reached up to touch his face. 'I did not mean it as an insult.' She pulled his face down and kissed him, thrusting her tongue deeply into his mouth. 'You have proved your courage – often,' she murmured.

He dropped his pistol onto the desk with a clatter and reached for her. The top three buttons of her red cotton shirt were unfastened, and she let him grope and find her breasts.

They were heavy and pointed and his breathing went ragged as he teased out her nipples. They hardened erect like jelly beans – but when he reached down with his free hand for the zipper of her shorts, she pushed him away roughly.

'Later,' she told him brusquely, 'when this is over. Now get back into the cabin.' And she leaned forward and lifted a corner of the blanket that screened the side window of the cockpit. The sunlight was very bright but her eyes adjusted swiftly and she saw the row of helmeted heads above the parapet of the observation deck. So they were pulling back the troops as well. It was nearly time to begin talking – but she would let them stew in their own juice just a little longer.

She stood up, buttoned her shirt and adjusted the camera on its strap around her neck, paused in the galley to rearrange the shiny mass of golden hair – and then walked slowly back down the full length of the central aisle, pausing to adjust the blanket over a sleeping child, to listen attentively to the complaints of the pregnant wife of the Texan neurosurgeon.

'You and the children will be the first off this plane – I promise you.'

When she reached the prone body of the flight engineer, she knelt beside him.

'How is he?'

'He is sleeping now. I shot him full of morphine,' the fat little doctor muttered, not looking at her, so she could not read the hatred in his expression. The injured arm was elevated to control the bleeding, sticking up stiffly in its cocoon of pressure bandages, oddly foreshortened with the bright ooze of blood through the dressing.

'You are doing good—' She touched his arm. 'Thank you.' And now he glanced at her startled, and she smiled – such a radiant lovely smile, that he began to melt.

'Is that your wife?' Ingrid dropped her voice, so that he alone could hear – and he nodded, glancing at the plump little Jewish woman in the nearest seat. 'I will see she is amongst the first to leave,' she murmured, and his gratitude was pathetic. She stood and went on down the aircraft.

The red-shirted German stood at the head of the tourist cabin, beside the curtained entrance to the second galley. He had the intense drawn face of a religious zealot, dark burning eyes, long black hair falling almost to his shoulders – a white scar twisted the corner of his upper lip into a perpetual smirk.

'Kurt, everything is all right?' she asked in German.

'They are complaining of hunger.'

'We will feed them in another two hours – but not as much as they expect—' and she ran a contemptuous glance down the cabin. 'Fat,' she said quietly, ' – big fat bourgeoisie pigs,' and she stepped through the curtains into the galley and looked at him in invitation. He followed her immediately, drawing the curtains behind them.

'Where is Karen?' Ingrid asked, as he unbuckled his belt. She needed it very badly, the excitement and the blood had inflamed her.

'She is resting – at the back of the cabin.'

Ingrid slipped the button that held the front of her shorts

together and drew down the zipper. 'All right Kurt,' she whispered huskily, 'but quickly, very quickly.'

Ingrid sat in the flight engineer's seat; at her shoulder stood the dark-haired girl. She wore the cartridge belt across the shoulder of her bright red shirt, like a bandolier – and she carried the big ugly pistol on her hip.

Ingrid held the microphone to her lips, and combed the fingers of her other hand through the thick golden tangle of her tresses as she spoke.

' – One hundred and ninety-eight British subjects. One hundred and forty-six American nationals—' She was reading the list of her captives. 'There are one hundred and twenty-two women on board, and twenty-six children under the age of sixteen years.' She had been speaking for nearly five minutes and now she broke off and shifted in her seat, turning to smile at Karen over her shoulder. The dark-haired girl smiled in return and reached across to caress the fine mass of golden hair with a narrow bony hand, before letting it drop back to her side.

'We have copied your last transmission.'

'Call me Ingrid.' She spoke into the mike with the smile turning into a wicked grin. There was a moment's silence as the controller in the tower recovered from his shock.

'Roger, Ingrid. Do you have any further messages for us?'

'Affirmative, Tower. As this is a British aircraft and as three hundred and forty-four of my passengers are either British or American, I want a spokesman, representing the embassies of those countries. I want him here in two hours' time to hear my terms for the release of passengers.'

'Stand by, Ingrid. We will be back to you immediately we have been able to contact the ambassadors.'

'Don't horse around, Tower.' Ingrid's voice snapped. 'We both know damned well they are breathing down your neck.

Tell them I want a man here in two hours – otherwise I am going to be forced to put down the first hostage.'

Peter Stride was stripped down to a pair of bathing trunks, and he wore only canvas sneakers on his feet. Ingrid had insisted on a face-to-face meeting, and Peter had welcomed the opportunity to assess at close range.

'We'll be covering you every inch of the way there and back,' Colin Noble told Peter, fussing over him like a coach over his fighter before the gong. 'I'm handling the gunners, personally.'

The snipers were armed with specially hand-built .222 magnums with accurized barrels that threw small light bullets with tremendous velocity and striking power. The ammunition was match-grade, each round lovingly hand finished and polished. The infra-red telescopic sights were readily interchangeable with the laser sights, making the weapon deadly accurate either in daylight or at night. The bullet had a clean, flat trajectory up to seven hundred yards. They were perfectly designed mankillers, precision weapons that reduced the danger to bystanders or hostages. The light bullet would slam a man down with savage force, as though he had been hit by a charging rhinoceros, but it would break up in his body, and not over-penetrate to kill beyond the target.

'You're getting into a lather,' Peter grunted. 'They want to talk, not shoot – not yet, anyway.'

'The female of the species—' Colin warned, ' – that one is real poison.'

'More important than the guns are the cameras, and sound equipment.'

'I went up there and kicked a few arses. You'll get pictures that will win you an Oscar – my personal guarantee.' Colin checked his wristwatch. 'Time to go. Don't keep the lady waiting.' He punched Peter's shoulder lightly. 'Hang loose,' he said, and Peter walked out into the sunshine, lifting both hands above his shoulders, palms open, fingers extended.

The silence was as oppressive as the dry fierce heat, but it was intentional. Peter had frozen all air traffic, and had ordered the shut down of all machinery in the entire terminal area. He did not want any interference with his sound equipment.

There was only the sound of his own footfalls, and he stepped out briskly – but still it was the longest walk of his life, and the closer he got to the aircraft, the higher it towered above him. He knew that he had been required to strip almost naked, not only to ensure that he carried no weapons, but to place him at a disadvantage – to make him feel ill at ease, vulnerable. It was an old trick – the Gestapo always stripped the victim for an interrogation – so he held himself proud and tall, pleased that his body was so lean and hard and muscled like an athlete's. He would have hated to drag a big, pendulous gut and sagging old-man's tits across those four hundred yards.

He was half-way there when the forward door, just behind the cockpit, slid back and a group of figures appeared in the square opening. He narrowed his eyes: there were two uniformed figures, no three – British Airways uniforms, the two pilots and between them the shorter slimmer feminine figure of a stewardess.

They stood shoulder to shoulder, but beyond them he could make out another head, a blonde head – but the angle and the light were against him.

Closer, he saw that the older pilot was on the right, short-cropped grey curls, ruddy round face – that would be Watkins, the commander. He was a good man, Peter had studied his service record. He ignored the co-pilot and stewardess and strained for a glimpse of the figure beyond them, but it was only when he stopped directly below the open hatch that she moved to let him get a clear view of her face.

Peter was startled by the loveliness of that golden head, by the smooth gloss of young sun-polished skin and the thundering innocence of wide-set, steady, green eyes – for a moment he could not believe she was one of them, then she spoke.

'I am Ingrid,' she said. Some of the most poisonous flowers are the loveliest, he thought.

'I am the accredited negotiator for the British and American Governments,' he said, and switched his gaze to the beefy red face of Watkins. 'How many members of your commando are aboard?' he asked.

'No questions!' Ingrid snapped fiercely, and Cyril Watkins extended four fingers of his right hand down his thigh without a change of expression.

It was vital confirmation of what they already suspected, and Peter felt a rush of gratitude towards the pilot.

'Before we discuss your terms,' Peter said, 'and out of common humanity, I would like to arrange for the well-being and comfort of your hostages.'

'They are well cared for.'

'Do you need food or drinking water?'

The girl threw back her head and laughed delightedly. 'So you can dope it with laxative – and have us knee-deep in shit? Stink us out, hey?'

Peter did not pursue it. The doped trays had already been prepared by his doctor.

'You have a gunshot casualty on board?'

'There are no wounded aboard,' the girl denied flatly, cutting her laughter short – but Watkins made the circular affirmative sign of thumb and forefinger, effectively contradicting her, and Peter noticed the spots of dried blood on the sleeves of his white shirt. 'That's enough,' Ingrid warned Peter. 'Ask one more question and we'll break off—'

'All right,' Peter agreed quickly. 'No more questions.'

'The objective of this commando is the ultimate downfall of the brutally fascist, inhuman, neo-imperialistic regime that holds this land in abject slavery and misery – denying the great majority of the workers and the proletariat their basic rights as human beings.'

And that, thought Peter bitterly, even though it's couched in the garbled jargon of the lunatic left, is every bit as bad as it can be. Around the world hundreds of millions would have immediate sympathy, making Peter's task just that little bit more difficult. The hijackers had picked a soft target.

The girl was still speaking, with an intense, almost religious fervour, and as he listened Peter faced the growing certainty that the girl was a fanatic, treading the thin line which divided sanity from madness. Her voice became a harsh screech as she mouthed her hatred and condemnation, and when she had finished he knew that she was capable of anything – no cruelty, no baseness was beyond her. He knew that she would not stop even at suicide, the final act of destroying the Boeing, its passengers and herself – he suspected she might even welcome the opportunity of martyrdom, and he felt the chill of it tickle up along his spine.

They were silent now, staring at each other, while the hectic flush of fanaticism receded from the girl's face and she regained her breath, and Peter waited, controlling his own misgivings, waiting for her to calm herself and continue.

'Our first demand—' the girl had steadied and was watching Peter shrewdly now, ' – our first demand is that the statement I have just made be read on every television network in Britain and the United States, and also here upon the South African network.' Peter felt his loathing of that terrible little box rise to the surface of his emotions. That mind-bending electronic substitute for thought, that deadly device for freezing, packaging and distributing opinion. He hated it, almost as much as the violence and sensation it purveyed so effectively. 'It must be read at the next occurrence of 7 p.m. local time in Los Angeles, New York, London and Johannesburg—' Prime time, of course, and the media would gobble it up hungrily, for this was their meat and their drink – the pornographers of violence!

High above him in the open hatch the girl brandished a thick buff envelope. 'This contains a copy of that statement for transmission – it contains also a list of names. One hundred and twenty-nine names, all of them either imprisoned or placed under banning orders by this monstrous police regime. The names on this list are the true leaders of South Africa.' She flung the envelope, and it landed at Peter's feet.

'Our second demand is that every person on that list be placed aboard an aircraft provided by the South African Government. Aboard the same aircraft there will be one million gold Kruger Rand coins also provided by the same government. The aircraft will fly to a country chosen by the freed political leaders. The gold will be used by them to establish a government in exile, until such time as they return to this country as the true leaders of the people.'

Peter stooped and picked up the envelope. He was calculating swiftly. A single Kruger Rand coin was worth $170 at the very least. The ransom demand was, therefore, worth one hundred and seventy million dollars.

There was another calculation. 'One million Krugers will weigh well over forty tons,' he told the girl. 'How are they going to get all that on one aircraft?'

The girl faltered. It was a little comfort to Peter to realize that they hadn't thought out everything perfectly. If they made one small mistake, then they were capable of making others.

'The government will provide sufficient transport for all the gold and all the prisoners,' the girl said sharply. The hesitation had been momentary only.

'Is that all?' Peter asked; the sun was stinging his naked shoulders and a cold drop of sweat tickled down his flank. He had never guessed it could be this bad.

'The aircraft will depart before noon tomorrow, or the execution of hostages will begin then.' Peter felt the crawl of horror. 'Execution.' She was using the jargon of legality, and he realized at that moment that what she promised she would deliver.

'When those aircraft arrive at the destination chosen by the occupants, a pre-arranged code will be flashed to us, and all women and children aboard this aircraft will immediately be released.'

'And the men?' Peter asked.

'On Monday the sixth – three days from now, a resolution is to be tabled before the General Assembly of the United Nations in New York. It will call for immediate total mandatory economic sanctions on South Africa – including withdrawal of all foreign capital, total oil and trade embargoes, severance of all transport and communications links, blockade of all ports and air borders by a U.N. peace-keeping force – pending free elections under universal suffrage supervised by U.N. inspectors—'

Peter's mind was racing to keep ahead of the girl's demands. He knew of the U.N. motion, of course, it had been tabled by Sri Lanka and Tanzania. It would be vetoed in the Security Council. That was a certainty – but the girl's timing brought forward new and frightening considerations. The beast had changed shape again, and what he had heard sickened him. It surely could not be merely coincidence that the resolution was to be tabled within three days of this strike – the implications were too horrible to contemplate. The connivance, if not the direct involvement, of world leaders and governments in the strategy of terror.

The girl spoke again deliberately. 'If any member of the Security Council of the U.N. – America, Britain or France

– uses the veto to block the resolution of this General Assembly, this aircraft and all aboard her will be destroyed by high explosive.'

Peter had lost the power of speech. He stood gaping up at the lovely blonde child, for child she seemed, so young and fresh.

When he found voice again, it croaked hoarsely. 'I don't believe you could have got high explosive aboard this aircraft to carry out that threat,' he challenged her.

The blonde girl said something to somebody who was out of sight, and then a few moments later she tossed a dark round object down to Peter.

'Catch!' she shouted, and he was surprised by the weight of it in his hands. It took only a moment to recognize it.

'Electronically fused!' The girl laughed. 'And we have so many I can afford to give you a sample.'

The pilot, Cyril Watkins, was trying to tell him something, touching his own chest – but Peter was occupied with the explosive in his hands. He knew that a single one of these would be fully capable of destroying the Boeing and all aboard her.

What was Watkins trying to tell him? Touching his neck again. Peter transferred his attention to the girl's neck. She wore a small camera slung around her neck. Something connecting camera and grenade – perhaps? Is that what the pilot was trying to tell him?

But now the girl was speaking again. 'Take that to your masters, and let them tremble The wrath of the masses is upon them. The revolution is here and now,' she said, and the door of the hatchway was swung closed. He heard the lock fall into place.

Peter turned and began the long walk back, carrying an envelope in one hand, a grenade in the other, and sick loathing in his guts.

Colin Noble's rugged frame almost filled the hatchway of the Hawker, and for once his expression was deadly serious, no trace of laughter in his eyes or at the corners of the wide friendly mouth.

'Doctor Parker is on the screen.' He greeted Peter who was still buttoning his overalls as he hurried to the command plane. 'We copied every word, and he was hooked into the system.'

'Christ, it's bad, Colin,' Peter grunted.

'That was the good news,' Colin told him. 'When you have finished with Parker, I've got the bad news for you.'

'Thanks, pal.' Peter shouldered his way past him into the cabin, and dropped into his leather command chair.

On the screen Kingston Parker was hunched over his desk, poring over the teleprinter sheet on which the entire conversation between Ingrid and Peter had been recorded, the cold empty pipe gripped between his teeth, the broad brow creased with the weight of his responsibility as he studied the demands of the terrorist commando.

The communications director's voice from off-screen alerted Parker.

'General Stride, sir.' And Parker looked up at the camera.

'Peter. This is you and me alone. I have closed the circuit and we will restrict to single tape recording. I want your first reaction, before we relay to Sir William and Constable—' Sir William Davies was the British Ambassador and Kelly Constable was the United States Ambassador to Pretoria.

'I want your first reaction.'

'We are in serious trouble, sir,' Peter said, and the big head nodded.

'What is the militant capability?'

'I am having my explosives team take down the grenade – but I have no doubt that they have the physical capability to destroy 070, and all aboard. I reckon they have an overkill potential of at least ten.'

'And the psychological capability.'

'In my view, she is the child of Bakunin and Jean Paul Sartre—' Again Parker nodded heavily and Peter went on. 'The anarchist conception that destruction is the only truly creative act, that violence is man recreating himself. You know Sartre said that when the revolutionary kills, a tyrant dies and a free man emerges.'

'Will she go all the way?' Parker insisted.

'Yes, sir.' Peter answered without hesitation. 'If she is pressed she'll go all the way – you know the reasoning. If destruction is beautiful, then self-destruction is immortality. In my view, she'll go all the way.'

Parker sighed and knocked the stem of his pipe against his big white teeth.

'Yes, it squares with what we have on her.'

'You have read her?' Peter asked eagerly.

'We got a first-class voice print, and the computer cross-matched with her facial structure print.'

'Who is she?' Peter cut in impatiently; he did not have to be told that the sound intensifier and the zoom video cameras had been feeding her voice and image into the intelligence computer even as she issued her demands.

'Her born name is Hilda Becker. She is a third-generation American of German extraction. Her father is a successful dentist widowed in 1959. The girl is thirty-one years old—' Peter had thought her younger, that fresh young skin had misled him. ' – I.Q. 138. University of Columbia 1965–68, Master's degree in Modern Political History. Member of SDS – that's Students for a Democratic Society—'

'Yes.' Peter was impatient. 'I know.'

' – Activist in Vietnam war protests. Worker for the draft evasion pipeline to Canada. One arrest for possession of marijuana 1967, not convicted. Implicated with Weathermen – and one of the leaders of on-campus rioting in the spring of 1968. Arrested for bombing of Butler University and released. Left America in 1970 for further study at

Dusseldorf. Doctorate in Political Economics 1972. Known association with Gudrun Ensslin and Horst Mahler of the Baader-Meinhof. Went underground in 1976 after suspicion of implication in the abduction and murder of Heinrich Kohler, the West German industrialist—' Her personal history was an almost classical development of the modern revolutionary, Peter reflected bitterly, a perfect picture of the beast. 'Believed to have received advanced training from the PFLP in Syria during 1976 and 1977. No recorded contact since then. She is a habitual user of cannabis-based drugs, reported voracious sexual activity with members of both sexes—' Parker looked up. 'That's all we have,' he said.

'Yes,' Peter repeated softly 'She'll go all the way.'

'What is your further assessment?'

'I believe that this is an operation organized at high level – possibly governmental—'

'Substantiate!' Parker snapped.

'The co-ordination with U.N.O proposals sponsored by the unaligned nations points that way.'

'All right, go on.'

'For the first time we have a highly organized and heavily supported strike that is not seeking some obscure, partisan object. We've got demands here about which a hundred million Americans and fifty million Englishmen are going to say in unison, "Hell, these aren't unreasonable "'

'Go on,' said Parker.

'The militants have picked a soft target which is the outcast pariah of Western civilization That U.N. resolution is going to be passed a hundred to nil, and those millions of Americans and Englishmen are going to have to ask themselves if they are going to sacrifice the lives of four hundred of their most prominent citizens to support a government whose racial policies they abhor.'

'Yes?' Parker was leaning forward to stare into the screen. 'Do you think they'll do a deal?'

prospect of delivering our discovery to my learned brothers in science, and the idea was as appealing as climbing into a pit full of black mambas. I stood up. 'Let's have a swim, Sal.'

We swam side by side, an easy breaststroke, back and forth across the pool. When we climbed out to sit in the spot of bright sunlight that fell from the roof above, I tried to alleviate my unhappiness by changing the subject. I touched Sally's arm and with all the finesse of a wounded rhinoceros, I blurted out, 'Will you marry me, Sally?'

She turned a startled face to me, her cheeks and eyelashes still bejewelled with water droplets, and she stared at me for fully ten seconds before she began to laugh.

'Oh, Ben, you funny old-fashioned thing! This is the twentieth century. Just because you done me wrong – doesn't mean you have to marry me!' And before I could protest or explain she had stood up and dived once again into the emerald pool.

For the rest of that day she was completely occupied with her paints and brushes, and she had no time to even look in my direction, let alone talk to me. The message was received my end loud and clear – there were some areas of discussion that Sally had put the death curse on. Matrimony was one of them.

It was a very bad day, but I learned the lesson well, and decided to clutch at what happiness I now had without pressing for more.

That evening Larkin had another message from Louren:

'Your samples 1–16 give C.14 average result of 1620 years ± 100. Congratulations. Looks good. When do I get in on the secret? Louren.'

I perked up at this news. Assuming our old bushman artist had been an eye-witness of the subjects he had drawn, then somewhere between A.D. 200 and A.D. 400 an armed Phoenician warrior had led his armies and war-elephants across this beloved land of mine. I felt guilty about all his hatred was suppressed. He felt cold, and functional as the surgeon's blade. Ready to do the job for which he had trained so assiduously, and yet able to assess and evaluate the enemy and the odds against success.

He pressed the call button. Colin had been waiting beyond the soundproof doors of the command cabin, and he came through immediately.

'The explosives boys have taken down the grenade. It's a dandy. The explosive is the new Soviet CJ composition, and the fusing is factory manufacture. Professional stuff – and it will work. Oh, baby, will it ever work.'

Peter hardly needed this confirmation, and Colin went on as he flung himself untidily in the chair opposite Peter.

'We put the list of names and the text of the militant statement on the teleprinter for Washington—' He leaned forward and spoke into the cabin intercom. 'Run that loop – without sound first.' Then he told Peter grimly. 'Here's the bad news I promised.'

The loop of video tape began to run on the central screen. It had clearly been shot from the observation post in the office overlooking the service area.

It was a full shot of the Boeing, the background flattened by the magnification of the lens and swimming and wavering with heat mirage rising from the tarmac of the main runway beyond the aircraft.

In the foreground were Peter's own naked back and shoulders as he strode out towards the aircraft. The lens had again flattened the action so that Peter appeared to be marking time on the same spot without advancing at all.

Suddenly the forward hatch of the Boeing changed shape as the door was slid aside, and the cameraman instantly zoomed in for the closer shot.

The two pilots and the air hostess in the doorway, the camera checked for a few frames and then zoomed closer. The aperture of the lens adjusted swiftly, compensating for the gloom of the interior, and the shot was close and tight on the blonde girl's head for a heartbeat, then the head turned slightly and the lovely line of her lips moved as she spoke – it seemed like three words – before she turned back full face to the camera.

'Okay,' Colin said. 'Run it again – with neutral balance on the sound.'

The entire loop reran, the cabin door opened, there were the three hostages, the fine golden head turned, and then the words 'Let's slide,' from Ingrid, but there was background hiss and clutter.

'"Let's slide"?' Peter asked.

'Run it again with the bass density filter on the sound,' Colin ordered.

The same images on the screen, the golden head turning on the long neck.

'"It's slide."' Peter could not quite catch it.

'Okay,' Colin told the technician. 'Now with full filter and resonance modulation.'

The repetitive images, the girl's head, the full lips parting, speaking to somebody out of sight in the body of the aircraft.

Very clearly, unmistakably, she said, 'It's Stride.' And Peter felt it jolt in his belly like a fist.

'She recognized you,' said Colin. 'No, hell, she was expecting you!'

The two men stared at each other, Peter's handsome craggy features heavy with foreboding. Atlas had one of the highest security classifications. Only twenty men outside the close ranks of Atlas itself were privy to its secrets. One of those was the President of the United States – another was the Prime Minister of Great Britain.

Certainly only four or five men knew who commanded the Thor arm of Atlas – and yet there was no mistaking those words the girl had spoken.

'Run it again,' Peter ordered brusquely.

And they waited tensely for those two words, and when

they came they were in the clear lilt of that fresh young voice.

'It's Stride,' said Ingrid, and the screen went blank.

Peter massaged his closed eyelids with thumb and forefinger. He realized with mild surprise that he had not slept for nearly forty-eight hours, but it was not physical weariness that assailed him now but the suddenly overwhelming knowledge of treason and betrayal and of undreamed-of evil.

'Somebody has blown Atlas,' said Colin softly. 'This is going to be a living and breathing bastard. They'll be waiting for us at every turn of the track.'

Peter dropped his hand and opened his eyes. 'I must speak to Kingston Parker again,' he said. And when Parker's image reappeared on the main screen he was clearly agitated and angry.

'You have interrupted the President.'

'Doctor Parker—' Peter spoke quickly. ' – Circumstances have altered. In my opinion the chances of a successful Delta strike have dropped. We have no better than an even chance.'

'I see.' Parker checked the anger. 'That's important. I will inform the President.'

The lavatories were all blocked by this time, the bowls almost filled, and the stench permeated all the cabins despite the air-conditioning.

Under the strict rationing of food and water most of the passengers were suffering from the lethargy of hunger, and the children were petulant and weepy.

The terrible strain was beginning to show on the hijackers themselves. They were standing a virtual non-stop watch, four hours of broken rest followed by four of ceaseless vigil and activity. The red cotton shirts were rumpled and sweat-stained at the armpits, the sweat of nervous and physical strain, eyes bloodshot and tempers uncertain.

Just before nightfall, the dark-haired girl, Karen, had lost her temper with an elderly passenger who had been slow to respond to her command to return to his seat after using the toilet. She had worked herself up into an hysterical shrieking rage, and repeatedly struck the old man in the face with the short barrel of her shot pistol, laying his cheek open to the bone. Only Ingrid had been able to calm her, leading her away to the curtained tourist galley where she pampered and hugged her.

'It will be all right, *Liebchen* ' She stroked her hair. 'Only a little longer now. You have been so strong. In a few more hours we will all take the pills. Not long now.' And within minutes Karen had controlled the violent trembling of her hands, and although she was pale, she was able to take her position at the rear of the tourist cabin again.

Only Ingrid's strength seemed without limits. During the night she passed slowly down the aisles, pausing to talk quietly with a sleepless passenger, comforting them with the promise of imminent release.

'Tomorrow morning we will have an answer to our demands, and all the women and children will be free – it's going to be all right, you just wait and see.'

A little after midnight the little roly-poly doctor sought her out in the cockpit.

'The navigator is very ill,' he told her. 'Unless we get him to a hospital immediately we will lose him.'

Ingrid went back and knelt beside the flight engineer. His skin was dry and burning hot and his breathing rasped and sawed.

'It's renal failure,' said the doctor, hovering over them. 'Breakdown of the kidneys from delayed shock. We cannot treat him here. He must be taken to hospital.'

Ingrid took the semi-conscious flight engineer's uninjured hand. 'I'm sorry, but that's impossible.'

She went on holding his hand for another minute.

'Don't you feel anything?' the doctor demanded of her bitterly.

'I feel pity for him – as I do for all mankind,' she answered quietly. 'But he is only one. Out there are millions.'

The towering flat-topped mountain was lit by floodlights. It was high holiday season and the fairest cape in all the world was showing her beauty to the tens of thousands of tourists and holidaymakers.

On the penthouse deck of the tall building, named for a political mediocrity as are so many buildings and public works in South Africa, the cabinet and its special advisers had been in session for most of the night.

At the head of the long table brooded the heavily built figure of the Prime Minister, bulldog-headed, powerful and unmovable as one of the granite kopjes of the African veld. He dominated the large panelled room, although he had hardly spoken, except to encourage the others with a nod or a few gruff words.

At the far end of the long table sat the two ambassadors, shoulder to shoulder, to emphasize their solidarity. At short intervals the telephones in front of them would ring, and they would listen to the latest reports from their embassies or instructions from the heads of their governments.

On the Prime Minister's right hand sat the handsome moustached Minister of Foreign Affairs, a man with enormous charisma and a reputation for moderation and common sense – but now he was grim and hard faced.

'Your own governments have both pioneered the policy of non-negotiation, of total resistance to the demands of terrorists – why now do you insist that we take the soft line?'

'We do not insist, minister, we have merely pointed out the enormous public interest that this affair is generating in both the United Kingdom and in my own country.' Kelly Constable was a slim, handsome man, intelligent and persuasive, a democratic appointee of the new American administration. 'It is in your government's interest even more than ours to see this through to a satisfactory conclusion. We merely suggest that some accommodation to the demands might bring that about.'

'The Atlas Commander on the spot has assessed the chances of a successful counter-strike as low as fifty-fifty. My government considers that risk unacceptable.' Sir William Davies was a career diplomat approaching retirement age, a grey, severe man with gold-rimmed spectacles, his voice high pitched and querulous.

'My men think we can do better than that ourselves,' said the Minister of Defence, also bespectacled, but he spoke in the thick blunt accent of the Afrikaaner.

'Atlas is probably the best equipped and most highly trained anti-terrorist group in the world,' Kelly Constable said, and the Prime Minister interrupted harshly.

'At this stage, gentlemen, let us confine ourselves to finding a peaceful solution.'

'I agree, Prime Minister.' Sir William nodded briskly.

'However, I think I should point out that most of the demands made by the terrorists are directly in line with the representations made by the government of the United States—'

'Sir, are you expressing sympathy with these demands?' the Prime Minister asked heavily, but without visible emotion.

'I am merely pointing out that the demands will find sympathy in my country, and that my government will find it easier to exercise its veto on the extreme motion of the General Assembly on Monday if some concessions are made in other directions.'

knew the bushman was considering my claim from every possible angle. At last he spoke again.

'Xhai and I hunt together this season. Even now he comes, before darkness he will be here. We will wait for him.'

'We will wait for him,' I agreed.

'But if you move I will kill you,' warned the bushman, and I took him at his word.

Xhai the old bushman came to my shoulder, and heaven knows I am no giant. He had the characteristically flattened features, with high cheekbones and oriental eyes, but his skin was dry and wrinkled, like an old yellow raisin. The wrinkling extended over his entire body as though he were covered with brittle parchment. The little peppercorns of hair on his scalp were smoky-grey with age, but his teeth were startling white and perfect, and his eyes were black and sparkling. I had often thought that they were pixie eyes, alive with mischief and intelligent curiosity.

When I told him how his friend had tried to kill us, he thought it an excellent joke and went off into little grunting explosions of laughter, at the same time shyly covering his mouth with one hand. The younger bushman's name was Ghal, and he was married to one of Xhai's daughters, so Xhai felt free to josh him mercilessly.

'Sunbird is a white ghost!' he wheezed. 'Shoot him, Ghal, quickly! Before he flies away.' Overwhelmed by his own humour, Xhai staggered in mirth-racked circles, giving an imitation of how he thought a ghost would look as it flew away. Ghal was very embarrassed and looked down at his feet as he shuffled them in the dust. I chuckled weakly, the sound of flighted arrows very fresh in my memory.

Xhai stopped laughing abruptly, and demanded anxiously, 'Sunbird, have you got tobacco?'

'Oh, my God!' I said in English.

'What is it?' Sally was alarmed by my tone, expecting that something else horrifying had happened.

'Tobacco,' I said. 'We haven't any.' Neither Sally nor I used the stuff, but it is very precious to a bushman.

'Louren left a box of cigars in the Land-Rover,' Sally reminded me. 'Is that any use?'

Both Ghal and Xhai were intrigued with the aluminium cylinders in which the Romeo and Julieta cigars were packed. After I showed them how to open them and remove the tobacco, they cooed and chattered with delight. Then Xhai sniffed the cigar like the true connoisseur he was, nodded approvingly and took a big bite. He chewed a while and then tucked the wad of sodden cigar up under his top lip. He passed the stub to Ghal who bit into it and followed Xhai's example. The two of them squatted on their haunches, positively glowing with contentment, and my heart went out to them. It took so little to make them happy.

They stayed with us that night, cooking on our fire a meal of bush-rats threaded on a stick like kebabs, and grilled over the open coals without gutting or removal of the skin. The hair frizzled off in the fire and stank like burning rags.

'I think I'm going to throw up,' murmured Sally palely as she watched the relish with which our two friends ate, but she didn't.

'Why do they call you Sunbird?' she asked later, and I repeated her question to Xhai.

He jumped up and did his celebrated imitation of a sunbird, darting his head and fluttering his hands. It was convincingly done, for bushmen are wonderful observers of nature.

However, when she woke him with a hand down the front of his thin linen slacks, he was bleary-eyed and foul-breathed, not even her skilful kneading could arouse him, and in a minute she turned away with an exclamation of disgust.

As a displacement activity, she picked up the microphone, switched on the loudspeakers of the passenger cabins. She knew she was acting irrationally, but she began to speak.

'Now listen to me, everybody, I have something very important to tell you.' Suddenly she was angry with them. They were of the class that had devised and instituted the manifestly unjust and sick society against which she was in total rebellion. They were the fat, complacent bourgeoisie. They were like her father and she hated them as she hated her father. As she began to speak she realized that they would not even understand the language she was using, the language of the new political order, and her anger and frustration against them and their society mounted. She did not realize she was raving, until suddenly she heard as from afar the shriek of outrage in her own voice, like the death wail of a mortally wounded animal – and she stopped abruptly.

She felt giddy and light-headed, so she had to clutch at the desk top for support and her heart banged wildly against her ribs. She was panting as though she had run a long way, and it took nearly a full minute for her to bring herself under control.

When she spoke again, her tone was still ragged and breathless.

'It is now nine o'clock,' she said. 'If we do not hear from the tyrant within three hours I shall be forced to begin executing hostages. Three hours—' She repeated ominously, ' – only three hours.'

Now she prowled the aircraft like a big cat paces along the bars of its cage as feeding time approaches.

'Two hours,' she told them, and the passengers shrank away from her as she passed.

'One hour.' There was a bright sadistic splinter of anticipation in her voice. 'We will choose the first hostages now.'

'But you promised,' pleaded the fat little doctor as Ingrid pulled his wife out of her seat and the Frenchman hustled her forward towards the flight deck.

Ingrid ignored him, and turned to Karen. 'Get children, a boy and a girl—' she instructed, ' – oh yes, and the pregnant one. Let them see her big belly. They won't be able to resist that.'

Karen herded the hostages into the forward galley and forced them at pistol point to sit in a row upon the fold-down air-crew seats.

The door to the flight deck was open and Ingrid's voice carried clearly to the galley, as she explained to the Frenchman Henri, speaking in English.

'It is of the utmost importance that we do not allow a deadline to pass without retaliating strongly. If we miss one deadline, then our credibility is destroyed. It will only be necessary once, we must show the steel at least once. They must learn that every one of our deadlines are irrevocable, not negotiable—'

The girl began to cry. She was thirteen years old, able to understand the danger. The plump doctor's wife put her arm around her shoulders and hugged her gently.

'Speedbird 070—' the radio squawked suddenly, ' – we have a message for Ingrid.'

'Go ahead, Tower, this is Ingrid ' She had jumped up to take the microphone, pushing the door to the flight deck closed.

'The negotiator for the British and American governments has proposals for your consideration. Are you ready to copy?'

'Negative.' Ingrid's voice was flat and emphatic. 'I say

again negative. Tell the negotiator I will talk only face to face – and tell him we are only forty minutes to the noon deadline. He had better get out here fast,' she warned. She hooked the microphone and turned to Henri.

'All right. We will take the pills now – it has truly begun at last.'

It was another cloudless day, brilliant sunlight that was flung back in piercing darts of light from the bare metal parts of the aircraft. The heat came up through the soles of his shoes and burned down upon Peter's bare neck.

The forward hatch opened, as it had before, when Peter Stride was half-way across the tarmac

This time there were no hostages on display, the hatchway was a dark empty square. Suppressing the urge to hurry, Peter carried himself with dignity, head up, jaw clenched firmly.

He was fifty yards from the aircraft when the girl stepped into the opening. She stood with indolent grace, her weight all on one leg, the other cocked slightly, long, bare, brown legs. She carried the big shot pistol on one hip, and the cartridge belt emphasized the narrow waist.

She watched Peter come on, with a half-smile on her lips. Suddenly a medallion of light appeared on her chest, a dazzling speck like a brilliant insect and she glanced down at it contemptuously.

'This is provocation,' she called. Clearly she knew that the bright speck was the beam thrown by the laser sight of one of the marksmen covering her from the airport building. A few ounces more of pressure on the trigger would send a .222 bullet crashing precisely into that spot, tearing her heart and lungs to bloody shreds.

Peter felt a flare of anger at the sniper who had activated his laser sight without the order, but his anger was tempered by reluctant admiration for the girl's courage. She could sneer at that mark of certain death upon her breast.

Peter made a cut out sign with his right hand, and almost immediately the speck of light disappeared as the gunner switched off his laser sight.

'That's better,' the girl said, and she smiled, running her gaze appraisingly down Peter's body.

'You've a good shape, baby,' she said, and Peter's anger flared again under her scrutiny.

'Nice flat belly—' she said, ' – good legs, and you didn't get those muscles sitting at a desk and pushing a pen.' She pursed her lips thoughtfully. 'You know I think you're a cop or a soldier. That's what I think, baby. I think you're a goddamned pig.' Her voice had a new harsh quality, and the skin seemed drier and drawn – older than it had been before.

He was close enough now to see the peculiar diamantine glitter in her eyes, and he recognized the tension that seemed to rack her body, the abrupt restless gestures. She was onto drugs now. He was certain of it. He was dealing with a political fanatic, with a long history of violence and death, whose remaining humane traits would be now entirely suppressed by the high of stimulant drugs. He knew she was more dangerous now than a wounded wild animal, a cornered leopard, a man-eating shark with the taste of blood exciting it to the killing frenzy.

He did not reply, but held her gaze steadily, keeping his hands in view, coming to a halt below the open hatchway.

He waited quietly for her to begin, and the itch of the drug in her blood would not allow her to stand still; she fidgeted with the weapon in her hands, touched the camera still hanging from around her neck. Cyril Watkins had tried to tell him something about that camera – and suddenly Peter realized what it was. The trigger for the fuses? he pondered, as he waited. Almost certainly, he decided, that was why it was with her every moment. She saw the direction of his eyes, and dropped her hand guiltily, confirming his conclusion.

'Are the prisoners ready to leave?' she demanded. 'Is the gold packed? Is the statement ready for transmission?'

'The South African Government has acceded to urgent representations by the governments of Great Britain and the United States of America.'

'Good.' She nodded.

'As an act of common humanity the South Africans have agreed to release all the persons on your list of detainees and banned persons—'

'Yes.'

'They will be flown to any country of their choice.'

'And the gold?'

'The South African Government refuses categorically to finance or to arm an unconstitutional foreign-based opposition. They refuse to provide funds for the persons freed under this agreement.'

'The television transmission?'

'The South African Government considers the statement to be untrue in substance and in fact and to be extremely prejudicial to the maintenance of law and order in this country. It refuses to allow transmission of the statement.'

'They have accepted only one of our demands—' The girl's voice took on an even more strident tone, and her shoulders jerked in an uncontrolled spasm.

'The release of political detainees and banned persons is subject to one further condition—' Peter cut in swiftly.

'And what is that—' The girl demanded, two livid burning spots of colour had appeared in her cheeks.

'In return for the release of political prisoners, they demand the release of all hostages, not only the women and children, all persons aboard the aircraft – and they will guarantee safe passage for you and all members of your party to leave the country with the released detainees.'

The girl flung back her head, the thick golden mane

flying wildly about her head as she screeched with laughter. The laughter was a wild, almost maniacal sound, and though it went on and on, there was no echo of mirth in her eyes. They were fierce as eagles' eyes, as she laughed. The laughter was cut off abruptly, and her voice was suddenly flat and level.

'So they think they can make demands, do they? They think they can draw the teeth from the U.N. proposals, do they? They think that without hostages to account for, the fascist governments of Britain and America can again cast their veto with impunity?'

Peter made no reply.

'Answer me!' she screamed suddenly. 'They do not believe we are serious, do they?'

'I am a messenger only,' he said.

'You're not,' she screamed in accusation. 'You're a trained killer. You're a pig!' She lifted the pistol and aimed with both hands at Peter's face.

'What answer must I take back?' Peter asked, without in any way acknowledging the aim of the weapon.

'An answer—' Her voice dropped again to an almost conversational level. 'Of course, an answer.' She lowered the pistol and consulted the stainless steel Japanese watch on her wrist. 'It's three minutes past noon – three minutes past the deadline, and they are entitled to an answer, of course.'

She looked around her with an almost bewildered expression. The drug was having side effects, Peter guessed. Perhaps she had overdosed herself, perhaps whoever had prescribed it had not taken into account the forty-eight sleepless hours of strain that preceded its use.

'The answer,' he prodded her gently, not wanting to provoke another outburst

'Yes. Wait,' she said, and disappeared abruptly into the gloom of the interior.

lip of stone, then I dragged her back, and pulled her to safety.

Suddenly she was shaking and weeping hysterically, and I clung to her, for I also was badly scared. Something had happened that was beyond my understanding, something mystical and deeply disturbing.

When Sally's sobs had abated, I asked her gently, 'What happened, Sal? Why did you do it?'

'I don't know. I just felt dizzy, and there was a black roaring in my head, and – oh, I don't know, Ben. I just don't know.'

It was another twenty minutes before Sally seemed sufficiently recovered to begin the journey back to camp, and by then the sun was setting. Before we reached the path down the cliff face it was completely dark.

'The moon will be up in a few minutes, Sal. I don't fancy going down the cliff in the dark. Let's wait for it.'

We sat on the edge of the cliff huddled together, not for warmth, for the air was still hot and the rocks were sunbaked, but because both of us were still a little shaken from the experience we had just come through. The moon was a big silver glow beneath the horizon, then it pushed up fat and yellow and round above the trees, and washed the land with a soft pale light.

I looked at Sally. Her face was silver-grey in the moonlight with dark bruised eyes, and her expression was remote and infinitely sad.

'Shall we go, Sal?' I hugged her lightly.

'In a minute. It's so beautiful.' I turned to stare out over the moon-silver plain. Africa has many moods, many faces, and I love them all. Here, before us, she put on one of her more enchanting displays. We were silent and engrossed for a long time.

Suddenly I felt Sally stir against me, half rising.

'Ready?' I asked her, rising with her.

'Ben!' Her hand closed on my wrist with surprising strength, she was shaking my arm.

'Ben! Ben!'

'What is it, Sal?' I was seized with dread that her earlier mood had returned.

'Look, Ben. Look!' Her voice was choked with emotion.

'What is it, Sal? Are you all right?'

With one hand she was shaking my arm, with the other she was pointing down at the plain below us.

'Look, Ben, there it is!'

'Sally!' I put both arms around her to restrain her. 'Easy, my dear. Just sit down quietly.'

'Don't be a fool, Ben. I'm perfectly all right. Just look down there.'

Still holding her securely, I did as she asked. I stared and saw nothing.

'Do you see it, Ben?'

'No.' And then, like the face in the picture-puzzle, it was there. It was there, as it should have been from the beginning.

'Can you see it?' Sally was trembling. 'Tell me you can see it too, Ben. Tell me I'm not imagining it.'

'Yes,' I mumbled, still not certain, 'yes, I think—'

'It's the City of the Moon, Ben. The ghost city of the bushmen – it's our lost city, Ben. It is – it must be!'

It was vague, hazy. I shut my eyes tightly and opened them again. It was still there.

The double enclosure around the silent grove, vast symmetrical tracings on the silver plain, dark shadowy lines. There were the dark circles that marked the spots on which the phallic towers had stood, some of them obscured by the trees of the grove. Beyond the walls were the honeycomb cells of the lower city, crescent-shaped and spread around the shores of the ancient, vanished lake.

'The moon,' I whispered. 'Low angle. Picking up the

that Peter could hardly catch the words. 'Please, sir. Please help us.'

But Ingrid was there, her voice rising stridently.

'You must believe that what we promise, we mean. You and your evil capitalist masters must understand completely that we will not let a single deadline pass without executions. We have to prove that for the revolution we are without mercy. You must be made to understand that our demands must be met in full, that they are not negotiable. We must demonstrate the price for missing a deadline.' She paused. 'The next deadline is midnight tonight. If our demands are not met in full by then – you must know the price you will be made to pay ' She halted again, and then her voice rose into that hysterical shriek. 'This is the price!' and she stepped back out of sight.

Helpless with dread, Peter Stride tried to think of some way to prevent the inevitable.

'Jump!' he shouted, lifting both hands towards the girl. 'Jump, quickly. I will catch you!'

But the child hesitated, the drop was almost thirty feet, and she teetered uncertainly.

Behind her, ten paces back, the dark-haired Karen and the blonde lion-maned girl stood side by side, and in unison they lifted the short, big bored pistols, holding them in the low double-handed grip, positioning themselves at the angle and range which would allow the mass of soft heavy lead beads with which the cartridges were packed to spread sufficiently to sweep the backs of the four hostages.

'Jump!' Peter's voice carried clearly into the cabin, and Ingrid's mouth convulsed in a nervous rictus, an awful parody of a smile.

'Now!' she said, and the two women fired together. The two shots blended in a thunderous burst of sound, a mind-stopping roar, and blue powder smoke burst from the gaping muzzles, flying specks of burning wadding hurled across the cabin, and the impact of lead shot into living flesh sounded like a handful of watermelon pips thrown against a wall.

Ingrid fired the second barrel a moment before Karen, so this time the two shots were distinct stunning blurts of sound, and in the dreadful silence that followed the two men in the passenger cabins were screaming wildly.

'Nobody move! Everybody freeze!'

For Peter Stride those fractional seconds seemed to last for long hours. They seemed to play on endlessly through his brain, like a series of frozen frames in a grotesque movie. Image after image seemed separated from the whole, so that forever afterwards he would be able to recreate each of them entire and undistorted and to experience again undiluted the paralysing nausea of those moments.

The pregnant woman took the full blast of one of the first shots She burst open like an overripe fruit, her swollen body pulled out of shape by the passage of shot from spine to navel, and she was flung forward so she somersaulted out into space. She hit the tarmac in a loose tangle of pale thin limbs, and was completely still, no flicker of life remaining.

The plump woman clung to the boy beside her, and they teetered in the open doorway – around them swirled pale blue wisps of gunsmoke. Though she kept her balance, the tightly stretched beige silk of her dress was speckled with dozens of tiny wounds, as though she had been stabbed repeatedly with a sharpened knitting needle. The same wounds were torn through the boy's white school shirt, and little scarlet flowers bloomed swiftly around each wound, spreading to stain the cloth. Neither of them made any sound, and their expressions were startled and uncomprehending. The next blasts of sound and shot struck them solidly, and they seemed boneless and without substance as they tumbled forward, still locked together. Their fall seemed to continue for a very long time, and then they sprawled together over the pregnant woman's body.

Peter ran forward to catch the girl-child as she fell, and her weight bore him to his knees on the tarmac. He came to his feet running, carrying her like a sleepy baby, one arm under her knees and the other around her shoulders. Her lovely head bumped against his shoulder, and the fine silken hair blew into his face, half blinding him.

'Don't die,' he found himself grunting the words in time to his pounding feet. 'Please don't die.' But he could feel the warm wet leak of blood down his belly, soaking into his shorts, and dribbling down the front of his thighs.

At the entrance to the terminal buildings Colin Noble ran out a dozen paces and tried to take the child from his arms, but Peter resisted him fiercely.

Peter relinquished the frail, completely relaxed body to the Thor doctor, and he stood by without word or expression of regret as the doctor worked swiftly over her. Peter's face was stony and his wide mouth clamped in a hard line when the doctor looked up at last.

'I'm afraid she's dead, sir.'

Peter nodded curtly and turned away. His heels cracked on the echoing marble of the deserted terminal hall and Colin Noble fell in silently beside him. His face was as bleak and expressionless as Peter's, as they climbed into the cabin of the Hawker command aircraft.

'Sir William, you point at us for holding enemies of the State without trial.' The Foreign Minister leaned forward to point the accuser's finger. 'But you British discarded the citizen's right of Habeas Corpus when you passed the Prevention of Terrorism Act, and in Cyprus and Palestine you were holding prisoners without trial long before that. Now your H block in Ulster – is that any better than what we are forced to do here?'

Sir William, the British Ambassador, gobbled indignantly, while he collected his thoughts.

Kelly Constable intervened smoothly. 'Gentlemen, we are trying to find common ground here – not areas of dispute. There are hundreds of lives at stake—'

A telephone shrilled in the air-conditioned hush of the room and Sir William lifted the receiver to his ear with patent relief, but as he listened, all blood drained from his face, leaving it a jaundiced, putty colour.

'I see,' he said once, and then, 'very well, thank you,' and replaced the receiver. He looked down the length of the long polished imbuia wood table to the imposing figure at the end.

'Prime Minister—' his voice quavered a little ' – I regret to inform you that the terrorists have rejected the compromise proposals offered by your government, and that ten minutes ago they murdered four hostages—'

There was a gasp of disbelief from the attentive circle of listening men.

' – The hostages were two women and two children – a boy and a girl – they were shot in the back and their bodies thrown from the aircraft. The terrorists have set a new deadline – midnight tonight – for the acceptance of their terms. Failing which there will be further shootings.'

The silence lasted for almost a minute as head after head turned slowly, until they were all staring at the big hunched figure at the head of the table.

'I appeal to you in the name of humanity, sir.' It was

Kelly Constable who broke the silence. 'We must save the women and children at least. The world will not allow us to sit by as they are murdered.'

'We will have to attack the aircraft and free the prisoners,' said the Prime Minister heavily.

But the American Ambassador shook his head. 'My government is adamant, sir – as is that of my British colleague—' he glanced at Sir William, who nodded support ' – we cannot and will not risk a massacre. Attack the aircraft and our governments will make no attempt to moderate the terms of the U.N. proposals, nor will we intervene in the Security Council to exercise the veto.'

'Yet, if we agree to the demands of these – these animals—' the last words were said fiercely ' – we place our nation in terrible danger.'

'Prime Minister, we have only hours to find a solution – then the killing will begin again.'

'You yourself have placed the success chances of a Delta strike as low as even,' Kingston Parker pointed out, staring grimly at Peter Stride out of the little square screen. 'Neither the President nor I find those odds acceptable.'

'Doctor Parker, they are murdering women and children out there on the tarmac.' Peter tried to keep his tone neutral, his reasoning balanced.

'Very strong pressure is being brought to bear on the South African Government to accede to the terms for release of the women and children.'

'That will solve nothing.' Peter could not restrain himself. 'It will leave us with exactly the same situation tomorrow night.'

'If we can secure the release of the women and children, the number of lives at risk will be reduced, and in forty hours the situation might have changed – we are buying time, Peter, even if we have to pay for it with a heavy coin.'

'And if the South Africans do not agree? If we come to the midnight deadline without an agreement with the hijackers, what happens then, Doctor Parker?'

'This is a difficult thing to say, Peter, but if that happens—' Parker spread those long graceful hands in a gesture of resignation, ' – we may lose another four lives, but that is better than precipitating the massacre of four hundred. And after that the South Africans will not be able to hold out. They will have to agree to free the women and children – at any cost.'

Peter could not truly believe what he had heard. He knew he was on the very brink of losing his temper completely, and he had to give himself a few seconds to steady himself. He dropped his eyes to his own hands that were interlocked on the desk top in front of him. Under the fingernails of his right hand were black half moons, the dried blood of the child he had carried back from the aircraft. Abruptly he unlocked his fingers and thrust both hands deeply into the pockets of his blue Thor overalls. He took a long deep breath, held it a moment, then let it out slowly.

'If that was difficult to say, Doctor Parker – console yourself that it was a bloody sight harder to listen to.'

'I understand how you feel, Peter '

'I don't think you do, sir.' Peter shook his head slowly.

'You are a soldier—'

' – and only a soldier knows how to really hate violence,' Peter finished for him.

'Our personal feelings must not be allowed to intrude in this.' Kingston Parker's voice had a sharp edge to it now. 'I must once again forcibly remind you that the decision for condition Delta has been delegated to me by the President and your Prime Minister. No strike will be made without my express orders. Do you understand that, General Stride?'

'On the evidence of one bead, and a piece of bone – that has to be the greatest flyer of all time!'

That evening, in reply to Larkin's bellowed queries, I replied, 'Thanks, Peter. We are fine. No, we don't need anything. Yes. Good. Please tell Mr Sturvesant there is no change here, nothing to report.'

I switched off the set, and avoided Sally's eyes.

'Yes,' she told me sternly. 'After a stinking one like that, you should look guilty!'

'Well, you said yourself it's only one bead and a piece of bone.'

But by the evening two days later, I had no such excuse, for I had sunk my trench seven feet five inches and there I uncovered the first of four courses of dry packed masonry. The stones were skilfully dressed, and squared. The joints between each block were so tight that a knife-blade would not go between them. The stones were bigger than those of Zimbabwe, clearly intended to support the weight of a substantial edifice; the average size was approximately four feet, by two, by two. They were cut from red sandstone similar to that of the cliffs and as I examined the workmanship I knew beyond any doubt that they were the work of artisans from a powerful and wealthy civilization.

That night I spoke to Larkin again.

'How soon can you get a message through to Mr Sturvesant, Peter?'

'He should have got back from New York today. I can put a phone call through this evening.'

'Please ask him to come right away.'

'You mean you want him to drop everything and come running – that's a laugh.'

'Just do it, please.'

The helicopter arrived at three o'clock the following afternoon, and I ran to meet it, pulling on my shirt.

'What have you got for me, Ben?' Louren demanded as he climbed, big and blond, out of the cabin.

'I think you are going to like it,' I told him, as we shook hands.

Five hours later we sat around the fire and Louren smiled over the rim of his glass at me.

'You were right, lad. I do like it!' This was the first opinion he had expressed since his arrival. He had followed Sal and me from excavation to cavern to cliff-top, listening attentively to our explanations, shaking his head with a rueful grin when I explained our theory of low-angle light on the ruins, firing a question occasionally in the same tone I had heard him use in a directors' meeting. Each time the question was relevant, incisive and searching, as though he were evaluating a business deal.

When Sally spoke he stood close to her, looking frankly into her face, those marvellous classical features of his rapt and still. Once she touched his arm to enforce a point and they smiled at each other. I was happy to see them so friendly at last, for they were the two people in the world I loved.

He knelt with me in the bottom of the trench and caressed the worked stone with his hands, he held the charred bone and melted glass bead in his palm and frowned at them as though trying to draw their secrets from them by sheer force of concentration.

Just before sunset, at Louren's insistence, we returned to the cavern and went to the rear wall. I lit one of the glass lanterns and placed it so that its light fell full on the painting of the white king. Then the three of us sat around it in a semi-circle and studied it in every detail. The king's head was in profile and Sally pointed out the features, the long straight nose and high forehead.

the long stainless steel probes were attached by flexible armoured couplings – these were the 'sticks' that gave them their name.

The leader carried compressed air in the tank upon his back at a pressure of 250 atmospheres, and on the tip of his twenty-foot probe was the diamond cutting bit of the air-drill. He dropped on one knee under the belly of the aircraft ten feet behind the landing gear and reached up to press the point of the air-drill against the exact spot, carefully plotted from the manufacturer's drawing, where the pressure hull was thinnest and where direct access to the passenger cabins lay just beyond the skin of alloy metal.

The whine of the cutting drill would be covered by the revving of the jet engines of aircraft parked in the southern terminal. Three seconds to pierce the hull, and the second 'stick' man was ready to insert the tip of his probe into the drill hole.

'Power off,' Colin grunted; at that moment electrical power from the mains to the aircraft would be cut to kill the air-conditioning.

The second man simulated the act of releasing the gas from the bottle on his back through the probe and saturating the air in the aircraft's cabins. The gas was known simply as FACTOR V. It smelled faintly of newly dug truffles, and when breathed as a five per cent concentration in air would partially paralyse a man in under ten seconds – loss of motor control of the muscles, unco-ordinated movement, slurred speech and distorted vision, were initial symptoms.

Breathed for twenty seconds the symptoms were total paralysis, for thirty seconds loss of consciousness; breathed for two minutes, pulmonary failure and death. The antidote was fresh air or, better still, pure oxygen, and recovery was rapid with no long-term after-effects.

The rest of the assault group had followed the 'stick' men and split into four teams. They waited poised, squatting under the wings, gas masks in place, equipment and weapons ready for instant use.

Colin was watching his stopwatch. He could not chance exposing the passengers to more than ten seconds of Factor V. There would be elderly people, infants, asthma sufferers aboard; as the needle reached the ten-second mark, he snapped.

'Power on.' Air-conditioning would immediately begin washing the gas out of the cabins again, and now it was 'Go!'

Two assault teams poured up the aluminium scaling ladders onto the wing roots, and knocked out the emergency window panels. The other two teams went for the main doors, but they could only simulate the use of slap-hammers to tear through the metal and reach the locking device on the interior – nor could they detonate the stun grenades.

'Penetration.' The assault leader standing in for Peter Stride on this exercise signalled entry of the cabins, and Colin clicked his stopwatch.

'Time?' asked a quiet voice at his shoulder, and he turned quickly. So intent on his task, Colin had not heard Peter Stride come up behind him.

'Eleven seconds, sir.' The courteous form of address was proof of Colonel Colin Noble's surprise. 'Not bad – but sure as hell not good either. We'll run it again.'

'Rest them,' Peter ordered. 'I want to talk it out a bit.'

They stood together at the full windows in the south wall of the air traffic control tower, and studied the big red, white and blue aircraft for the hundredth time that day.

The heat of the afternoon had raised thunderheads, great purple and silver mushroom bursts of cloud that reached to the heavens. Trailing grey skirts of torrential rain they marched across the horizon, forming a majestic backdrop that was almost too theatrical to be real, while the lowering sun found the gaps in the cloud and shot long groping fingers of golden light through them, heightening the illusion of theatre.

'Six hours to deadline,' Colin Noble grunted, and groped for one of his scented black cheroots. 'Any news of concessions by the locals?'

'Nothing. I don't think they will buy it.'

'Not until the next batch of executions.' Colin bit the end from the cheroot and spat it angrily into a corner. 'For two years I break my balls training for this, and now they tie our hands behind our backs.'

'If they gave you Delta, when would you make your run?' Peter asked.

'As soon as it was dark,' Colin answered promptly.

'No. They are still revved up high on drugs,' Peter demurred. 'We should give them time to go over the top, and start downing. My guess is they will dope again just before the next deadline. I would hit them just before that—' He paused to calculate. ' – I'd hit them at fifteen minutes before eleven – seventy-five minutes before the deadline.'

'If we had Delta,' Colin grunted.

'If we had Delta,' Peter agreed, and they were silent for a moment. 'Listen, Colin, this has been wearing me down. If they know my name, what else does that gang of freaks know about Thor? Do they know our contingency planning for taking an aircraft?'

'God, I hadn't worked it out that far.'

'I have been looking for a twist, a change from the model, something that will give us the jump even if they know what to expect.'

'We've taken two years to set it up tightly—' Colin looked dubious. 'There is nothing we can change.'

'The flares,' said Peter. 'If we went, we would not signal the Delta with the flares, we would go in cold.'

'The uglies would be scattered all through the cabins, mixed up with passengers and crew—'

'The red shirt Ingrid was wearing. My guess is, all four of them will be uniformed to impress their hostages. We would hose anything and everybody in red. If my guess is wrong, then we would have to do it Israeli style.'

Israeli style was the shouted command to lie down, and to kill anyone who disobeyed or who made an aggressive move.

'The truly important one is the girl. The girl with the camera. Have your boys studied the videotapes of her?'

'They know her face better than they do Fawcett Majors',' Colin grunted, and then, 'the bitch is so god-damned lovely – I had to run the video of the executions three times for them, twice in slow motion, to wipe out a little of the old chivalry bit.' It is difficult to get a man to kill a pretty girl, and a moment of hesitation would be critical with a trained fanatic like Ingrid. 'I also made them take a look at the little girl before they put her in a basket and took her down to the morgue. They're in the right mood.' Colin shrugged. 'But what the hell, Atlas isn't going to call Delta. We're wasting our time.'

'Do you want to play make-believe?' Peter asked, and then without waiting for an answer, 'Let's make believe we have a Delta approval from Atlas. I want you to set up a strike timed to "go" at exactly 10.45 local time tonight. Do it as though it was the real thing – get it right in every detail.'

Colin turned slowly and studied his commander's face, but the eyes were level and without guile and the strong lines of jaw and mouth were unwavering.

'Make-believe?' Colin Noble asked quietly.

'Of course,' Peter Stride's tone was curt and impatient, and Colin shrugged.

'Hell, I only work here,' and he turned away.

Peter lifted the binoculars and slowly traversed the length of the big machine from tail to nose, but there was no sign of life, every port and window still carefully covered

– and reluctantly he let his binoculars sink slightly until he was staring at the pitiful pile of bodies that still lay on the tarmac below the forward hatch.

Except for the electrical mains hook-up, the delivery of medicines and the two occasions when Peter himself had made the long trip out there, nobody else had been allowed to approach the machine. No refuelling, no refuse nor sanitary removals, no catering – not even the removal of the corpses of the murdered hostages. The hijackers had learned the lesson of previous hijacking attempts when vital information had been smuggled off the aircraft in refuse and sewerage at Mogadishu, and at Lod where the storming party had come disguised as caterers.

Peter was still gazing at the bodies, and though he was accustomed to death in its most obscene forms, these bodies offended him more deeply than any in his life before. This was a contemptuous flaunting of all the deepest rooted taboos of society. Peter was grimly content now with the decision of the South African police not to allow any television teams or press photographers through the main gates of the airport.

Peter knew that the world media were howling outrage and threats, protesting in the most extreme terms against the infringement of their God-given rights to bring into the homes of all civilized people images of dreadful death and mutilation, lovingly photographed in gorgeous colour with meticulous professional attention to all the macabre details.

Without this enthusiastic chronicling of their deeds, international terrorism would lose most of its impetus and his job would be a lot easier. For sneaking moments he envied the local police the powers they had to force irresponsibles to act in the best interests of society, then as he carried the thought a step further, he came up hard once again against the question of who was qualified to make such decisions on behalf of society. If the police made that decision and exerted it, was it not just another form of the terrorism it was seeking to suppress? 'Christ,' thought Peter angrily, 'I'm going to drive myself mad.'

He stepped up beside the senior air traffic controller.

'I want to try again,' Peter said, and the man handed him the microphone.

'Speedbird 070 this is the tower. Ingrid, do you read me? Come in, Ingrid.'

He had tried a dozen times to make contact in the last few hours, but the hijackers had maintained an ominous silence.

'Ingrid, come in please.' Peter kept trying, and suddenly there was the clear fresh voice.

'This is Ingrid. What do you want?'

'Ingrid, we request your clearance to have an ambulance remove the bodies,' Peter asked.

'Negative, Tower. I say again, negative. No one is to approach this aircraft.' There was a pause. 'We will wait until we have a round dozen bodies for you to remove—' The girl giggled, still on the drug high, ' – wait until midnight, and we'll make it really worth your while ' And the radio clicked into silence.

'We are going to give you dinner now,' Ingrid shouted cheerfully, and there was a stir of interest down the length of the cabin. 'And it's my birthday today. So you're going to have champagne – isn't that great!'

But the plump little Jewish doctor rose suddenly to his feet. His grey sparse hair stood up in comical wisps, and his face seemed to have collapsed, like melting candle wax, ravaged and destroyed by grief. He no longer seemed to be aware of what had been said or what was happening. 'You had no right to kill her.' His voice sounded like a very old with aircraft landing regularly, Land-Rovers kicking up the dust and even the clatter of an electric water-pump shattering the dreaming silence of the cavern and disturbing the still green waters of the emerald pool.

Quickly my group settled into their allotted tasks. Sally worked on at the cavern, with a single young African assistant. Each of the other four was placed in charge of a team of ten labourers and assigned an area in which to work.

Peter and Heather shrewdly elected to work outside the main walls, in the ruins of the lower city. It was here that the ancients would have disposed of their rubbish, broken pottery, old weapons, discarded beads and the fascinating debris of a vanished civilization.

Ral and Leslie with dreams of gold and treasure jumped at the chance of excavating within the enclosure, an area which the ancients would have kept swept and scrupulously clean, and therefore much less likely to yield finds of interest. That is the difference between experience and inexperience, between the impetuosity of youth and the cool calculations of an older head.

I kept myself free, in a supervisory and advisory capacity. Spending my time at those places where it could do the most good. Anxiously I watched Ral and Leslie to assure myself that their approach and technique were satisfactory, then I relaxed as Peter Willcox's recommendation proved correct. They were clever, enthusiastic youngsters and, more important, they knew their way around an archaeological dig.

The four teams shook themselves out as the dullards amongst the African labourers were sorted from the bright ones. In a shorter time than I had hoped for, the firm of Kazin and Company was breaking ground and doing good business.

It was slow, painstaking and thoroughly satisfying work. Each evening, before the nightly singsong in the common ambassador's eyes as he swept the table with a compelling gaze.

'And we all know that no compromise is possible, we must meet the demands in full or not at all.'

'Mr Ambassador—' the Prime Minister broke the silence at last, ' – if we agree to the terms, it will be only as an act of humanity. We will be paying a very high price indeed for the lives of your people – but if we agree to that price, can we be absolutely assured of your support – the support of both Britain and the United States – in the Security Council the day after tomorrow at noon?'

'The President of the United States has empowered me to pledge his support in return for your co-operation,' said Kelly Constable.

'Her Britannic Majesty's Government has asked me to assure you of the same support,' intoned Sir William. 'And our governments will make good the 170 million dollars demanded by the hijackers.'

'Still I cannot make the decision on my own. It is too onerous for one man,' the Prime Minister sighed. 'I am going to ask my ministers, the full cabinet—' he indicated the tense, grim faces around him, ' – to vote. I am going to ask you gentlemen to leave us alone now for a few minutes while we decide.'

And the two ambassadors rose together and bowed slightly to the brooding, troubled figure before leaving the room.

'Where is Colonel Noble?' Kingston Parker asked.

'He is waiting—' Peter indicated with a jerk of his head the sound-proof door of the Hawker's command cabin.

'I want him in on this, please,' Parker said from the screen, and Peter pressed the call button.

Colin Noble came in immediately, stooping slightly under the low roof, a chunky powerful figure with the blue Thor cap pulled low over his eyes.

'Good evening, sir.' He greeted the image on the screen and squeezed into the seat beside Peter.

'I'm glad Colonel Noble is here.' Peter's voice was crisp and businesslike. 'I think he will support my contention that the chances of a successful Delta counterstrike will be greatly enhanced if we can launch our attack not later than ten minutes before eleven o'clock.' He tugged back the cuff of his sleeve, and glanced at his watch. 'That is forty minutes from now. We reckon to catch the militants at the moment when the drug cycle is at its lowest, before they take more pills and begin to arouse themselves to meet their deadline. I believe that if we strike then, we will have an acceptable risk—'

'Thank you, General Stride—' Parker interrupted him smoothly, ' – but I wanted Colonel Noble present so there could be no misunderstanding of my orders. Colonel Noble—' Parker's eyes shifted slightly as he changed the object of his attention. 'Commander of Thor has requested an immediate Delta strike against Speedbird 070. I am now, in your presence, disapproving that request. Negotiations with the South African Government are at a critical state, and under no circumstances must there be either overt or covert hostile moves towards the militants. Do I make myself entirely clear?'

'Yes, sir.' Colin Noble's expression was stony.

'General Stride?'

'I understand, sir.'

'Very well. I want you to stand by, please. I am going to confer with the ambassadors. I will re-establish contact as soon as I have further concrete indications.'

The image receded rapidly, and the screen went dark. Colonel Colin Noble turned slowly and looked at Peter Stride, his expression changed slightly at what he saw, and quickly he pressed the censor button on the command console, stopping all recording tapes, killing the video cameras so there would be no record of his words now.

'Listen, Peter, you're in line for that NATO command, everybody knows that. From there the sky is the limit, pal. Right up there to the joint chiefs – just as far as you want to go.'

Peter said nothing, but glanced once more at the gold Rolex wristwatch. It was seventeen minutes past ten o'clock.

'Think, Peter. For God's sake, man. It's taken you twenty heart-breaking years of hard work to get where you are. They would never forgive you, buddy. You'd better believe it. They'll break you and your career. Don't do it, Peter. Don't do it. You're too good to waste yourself. Just stop and think for one minute.'

'I'm thinking,' said Peter quietly. 'I haven't stopped thinking since—' he checked, ' – always it comes back to this. If I let them die – then I am as guilty as that woman who pulls the trigger.'

'Peter, you don't have to beat your head in. The decision is made by someone else—'

'It would be easier to believe that, wouldn't it,' Peter snapped, 'but it won't save those people out there.'

Colin leaned across and placed a large hairy paw on Peter's upper arm. He squeezed slightly. 'I know, but it eats me to see you have to throw it all away. In my book, you're one of the tops, buddy.' It was the first time he had made any such declaration, and Peter was fleetingly moved by it.

'You can duck this one, Colin. It doesn't have to touch you or your career.'

'I never was very hot at ducking.' Colin dropped his hand away. 'I think I'll go along for the ride—'

'I want you to record a protest – no sense us all getting ourselves fired,' said Peter, as he switched on the recording equipment, both audio and video; now every word would be recorded

'Colonel Noble,' he said distinctly, 'I am about to lead an immediate Delta assault on Flight 070. Please make the arrangements.'

Colin turned to face the camera. 'General Stride, I must formally protest at any order to initiate condition Delta without express approval from Atlas Command.'

'Colonel Noble, your protest is noted,' Peter told the camera gravely, and Colin Noble hit the censor button once again, cutting tapes and camera.

'Okay, that's enough crap for one day.' He came nimbly to his feet. 'Let's get out there and take the bastards.'

Ingrid sat at the flight engineer's desk, and held the microphone of the on-board loudspeaker system to her lips. There was a greyish tone beneath the sun-gilded skin; she frowned a little at the throbbing pulse of pain behind her eyes and the hand that held the microphone trembled slightly. She knew these were all symptoms of the drug hangover. She regretted now having increased the initial dosage beyond that recommended on the typed label of the tablet phial – but she had needed that extra lift to be able to carry out the first executions. Now she and her officers were paying the price, but in another twenty minutes she would be able to issue another round of tablets. This time she would stay exactly within the recommended dosage, and she anticipated the rush of it through her blood, the heightened vision and energy, the tingling exhilaration of the drug. She even anticipated the thought of what lay ahead; to be able to wield absolute power, the power of death itself, was one of life's most worthwhile experiences. Sartre and Bakunin and Most had discovered one of the great truths of life – that the act of destruction, of total destruction, was a catharsis, a creation, a reawakening of the soul. She looked forward, even through the staleness and ache of the drug let-down, she looked forward to the next executions.

'My friends—' she spoke into the microphone, ' – we have not heard from the tyrant. His lack of concern for your lives is typical of the fascist imperialist. He does not concern himself with the safety of the people, though he sucks and bloats himself on the blood and sweat—'

Outside the aircraft the night was black and close. Thunderheads blotted out half the sky, and every few minutes lightning lit the clouds internally. Twice since sundown abrupt fierce downpours of torrential rain had hammered briefly against the Boeing hull, and now the airport lights glinted on the puddled tarmac.

' – We have to show the face of unrelenting courage and iron purpose to the tyrant. We cannot afford to show even a moment's hesitation. We must now choose four more hostages. It will be done with the utmost impartiality – and I want you all to realize that we are now all part of the revolution together, you can be proud of that—'

Lightning exploded suddenly, much closer, a crackling greenish, iridescent flaming of the heavens that lit the field in merciless light, and then the flail of the thunder beat down upon the aircraft. The girl Karen exclaimed involuntarily and sprang nervously to her feet and crossed quickly to stand beside Ingrid. Her dark eyes were now heavily underscored by the dark kohl of fatigue and drug withdrawal; she trembled violently, and Ingrid caressed her absently the way she might calm a frightened kitten as she went on speaking into the microphone.

' – We must all of us learn to welcome death, to welcome the opportunity to take our place and add our contribution, no matter how humble it might be, to man's great reawakening.'

Lightning burst in fierce splendour once again, but Ingrid went on talking into the microphone, the senseless words somehow hypnotic and lulling so that her captives sat in quietly lethargic rows, not speaking, unmoving, seeming no longer capable of independent thought.

'I have drawn lots to choose the next martyrs of the revolution. I will call out the seat numbers and my officers will come to fetch you. Please co-operate by moving quickly forward to the first-class galley.' There was a pause, and then Ingrid's voice again. 'Seat number 63B Please stand up.'

The scarred German in the red shirt and with the lank black hair hanging over his eyes had to force the thin, middle-aged man to his feet, twisting his wrist up between his shoulder blades. The man's white shirt was crumpled and he wore elastic braces over his shoulders and old-fashioned narrow trousers.

'You can't let them,' the man pleaded with his fellow passengers, as Henri pushed him up the aisle. 'You can't let them kill me, please.' And they looked down at their laps. Nobody moved, nobody spoke.

'Seat number 43F.' It was a handsome dark-haired woman in her middle thirties, and her face seemed to dissolve slowly as she read the number above her seat, and she covered her mouth with one hand to prevent herself crying out – but from the seat exactly across the aisle from her a sprightly old gentleman with a magnificent mane of silver-grey hair rose swiftly to his feet and adjusted his tie.

'Would you care to change seats with me, madam?' he said softly in a clipped English accent, and strode down the aisle, on long, thin, stork-like legs, contemptuously brushing past the blond moustached Frenchman who came hurrying forward to escort him. Without a glance to either side, and with thin shoulders thrown back, he disappeared through the curtains into the forward galley

The Boeing had a blind spot that extended back from the side windows of the flight deck at an angle of 20° to the tail, but the hijackers were so well equipped and seemed to have considered every eventuality in such detail that there was no reason to fear that they had worked out some arrangement to keep the blind spot under surveillance.

Peter and Colin discussed the possibility quietly as they stood in the angle of the main service hangar, and both of them carefully studied the soaring shape of the Boeing tailplane and the sagging underbelly of the fuselage for the glint of a mirror or some other device. They were directly behind the aircraft and there was a little over four hundred yards to cover, half of that through knee-high grass and the rest over tarmac.

The field was lit only by the blue periphery lights of the taxiway, and the glow of the airport buildings.

Peter had considered dousing all the airport lights, but discarded the idea as self-defeating. It would certainly alert the hijackers, and would slow the crossing of the assault team.

'I can't see anything,' Colin murmured.

'No,' agreed Peter and they both handed their night glasses to a hovering NCO – they wouldn't need them again. The assault team had stripped all equipment down to absolute essentials.

All that Peter carried was a lightweight eleven-ounce VHF transceiver for communicating with his men in the terminal building – and in a quick-release holster on his right hip a Walther PK 38 automatic pistol.

Each member of the assault team carried the weapon of his own choice Colin Noble favoured the Browning Hi-power 45 for its massive killing power and large fourteen-round magazine, while Peter liked the pinpoint accuracy and light recoil of the 9-mm parabellum Walther with which he could be certain of a snap head-shot at fifty metres.

One item was standard equipment for all members of the assault team. Every one of their weapons was loaded with Super Velex explosive bullets which trebled the knock-down power at impact, breaking up in the human body and thereby reducing the risk of over-penetration and with it the danger to innocents. Peter never let them forget they would nearly always be working with terrorist and victim closely involved.

Beside Peter, Colin Noble unclipped the thin gold chain from around his neck which held the tiny Star of David, twinkling gold on the black bush of his chest hair. He slipped the ornament into his pocket and buttoned down the flap.

'I say, old chap—' Colin Noble gave an atrocious imitation of a Sandhurst accent ' – shall we toddle along then?'

Peter glanced at the luminous dial of his Rolex. It was sixteen minutes to eleven o'clock. The exact moment at which my career ends, he thought grimly, and raised his right arm with clenched fist, then pumped it up and down twice, the old cavalry signal to advance.

Swiftly the two men raced out ahead, absolutely silent on soft rubber soles, carrying their probes at high port to prevent them clattering against tarmac or against the metal parts of the aircraft, dark hunchbacked figures under the burden of the gas cylinders they carried.

Peter gave them a slow count of five, and while he waited he felt the adrenalin charge his blood, every nerve and muscle of his body coming under tension, and he heard his own words to Kingston Parker echo in his ears like the prophecy of doom.

'There is no middle ground. The alternative is one hundred per cent casualties. We lose the aircraft, the passengers and all the Thor personnel aboard her.'

He thrust the thought aside, and repeated the signal to

advance. In two neat files, bunched up close and well in hand, the assault teams went out, at the run. Three men carrying each of the aluminium alloy scaling ladders, four with the sling-bags of stun grenades, others with the slap hammers to tear out the door locks, and each with his chosen weapon – always a big calibre handgun – for Peter Stride would trust nobody with an automatic weapon in the crowded interior of a hijacked aircraft, and the minimum requirement for every member of the assault teams was marksmanship with a pistol that would enable him to pick a small moving target and hit it repeatedly and quickly without endangering innocents.

They ran in almost total silence; the loudest sound was Peter's breathing in his own ears, and he had time now for a moment's regret. It was a gamble which he could never win, the best that could happen was the utter ruin of his life's work, but he steeled himself brutally and thrust aside the thought. He ran on into the night.

Just ahead of him now, silhouetted by the lights of the terminal building, the dark figures of the 'stick' men were in position under the bulging silver belly; and lightning flared suddenly, so that the tall silver thunderheads rippled with intense white fire, and the field was starkly lit, the double column of black-clad figures standing out clearly against the paler grass. If they were observed, it would come now, and the crash of thunder made Peter's nerves jump, expecting detonation and flame of a dozen percussion grenades.

Then it was dark again, and the sponginess of wet grass beneath his feet gave way to flat hard tarmac. Then suddenly they were under the Boeing fuselage, like chickens under the protective belly of the hen, and the two columns split neatly into four separate groups and still in tight order every man dropped onto his left knee, and at the same moment, with the precision of repeated rehearsals, every member of the team lifted his gas mask to cover his nose and mouth.

Peter swept one quick glance back at them, and then depressed the transmit button on his transceiver. He would not speak a word from now until it was over; there was always a remote possibility that the hijackers were monitoring this frequency.

The click of the button was the signal to the members of his team in the terminal – and almost immediately, there was a rising whistling howl of jet engines running up.

Even though the aircraft were parked up in the northern international departures area, they had been turned so the jet exhausts were pointed at the service area, and there were five intercontinental jet liners co-operating. The combined sound output of twenty big jet engines was deafening even at that range – and Peter gave the open hand signal.

The 'stick' man was waiting poised, and at the signal he reached up and placed the drill bit against the belly of the fuselage. Any sound of the compressed air spinning the drill was effectively drowned, and there was only the slight jerk of the long probe as it went through the pressure hull. Instantly the second 'stick' man placed the tip of his probe into the tiny hole, and glanced at Peter. Again the open hand signal, and the gas was spurting into the hull. Peter was watching the sweep hand of his watch.

Two clicks on the transmit button, and the lights behind the row of shaded portholes blinked out simultaneously as the mains power was cut – and the air-conditioning in the Boeing's cabins with it.

The howl of combined jet engines continued a few seconds longer and Peter signalled the ladder men forward.

Gently the rubber-padded tops of the ladders were hooked onto the leading edges of the wings and into the door sills high above them by black-costumed, grotesquely masked figures working with deceptively casual speed.

Ten seconds from discharge of the Factor V gas into the hull, and Peter clicked thrice. Instantly mains power to the Boeing was resumed and the lights flicked on. Now the air-conditioning was running again, washing the gas swiftly from the cabins and flight deck.

Peter drew one long, slow deep breath and tapped Colin's shoulder. They went up the ladders in a concerted silent rush, Peter and Colin leading the teams to each wing surface.

'Nine minutes to eleven,' said Ingrid to Karen. She lifted her voice slightly above the din of jet engines howling somewhere out there in the night. Her throat was dry and sore from the drug withdrawal and a nerve jumped involuntarily in the corner of her eye. Her headache felt as though a knotted rope was being twisted slowly tighter around her forehead. 'It looks as though Caliph miscalculated. The South Africans aren't going to give in—' She glanced with a small anticipatory twist of her lips back through the open door of the flight deck at the four hostages sitting in a row on the fold-down seats. The silver-haired Englishman was smoking a Virginia cigarette in a long amber and ivory holder, and he returned her gaze with disdain, so that Ingrid felt a prickle of annoyance and raised her voice so he could hear her next words. 'It's going to be necessary to shoot this batch also.'

'Caliph has never been wrong before.' Karen shook her head vehemently. 'There is still an hour to deadline—' and at that instant the lights flickered once and then went out. With all the portholes shaded the darkness was complete, and the hiss of the air-conditioning faded into silence before there was a murmur of surprised comment.

Ingrid groped across the control panel for the switch

which transferred the flight deck onto the power from the aircraft's own batteries, and as the soft ruddy glow of the panel lights came on her expression was tense and worried.

'They've switched off the mains,' she exclaimed. 'The air-conditioning – this could be Delta.'

'No.' Karen's voice was shrill. 'There are no flares.'

'We could be—' Ingrid started but she could hear the drunken slur in her own voice. Her tongue felt too large for her mouth, and Karen's face started to distort before her eyes, the edges blurring out of focus.

'Karen—' she said, and now in her nostrils the unmistakable aroma of truffles and on her tongue the taste of raw mushrooms.

'Christ!' she screamed wildly and lunged for the manual oxygen release. Above each seat the panels dropped open and the emergency oxygen masks dangled down into the cabins on their corrugated hoses.

'Kurt! Henri!' Ingrid shrieked into the cabin intercom. 'Oxygen! Take oxygen! It's Delta. They are going to Delta.'

She grabbed one of the dangling oxygen masks and sucked in deep pumping breaths, cleansing the numbing paralysing gas from her system. In the first-class galley one of the hostages collapsed slowly forward and tumbled onto the deck, another slumped sideways.

Still breathing oxygen, Ingrid unslung the camera from around her neck, and Karen watched her with huge terrified dark eyes. She lifted the oxygen mask from her face to ask:

'You're not going to blow, Ingrid?'

Ingrid ignored her and used the oxygen in her lungs to shout into the microphone.

'Kurt! Henri! They will come as soon as the mains are switched on again. Cover your eyes and ears for the stun grenades and watch the doors and wing windows.' Ingrid slapped the oxygen mask back over her mouth and panted wildly.

'Don't blow us up, Ingrid,' Karen pleaded around her mask. 'Please, if we surrender Caliph will have us free in a month. We don't have to die.'

At that moment the lights of the cabin came on brightly, and there was the hiss of the air-conditioning. Ingrid took one last breath of oxygen and ran back into the first-class cabin, jumping over the unconscious figures of the hostages and of two air hostesses. She grabbed another of the dangling oxygen masks above a passenger seat and looked down the long fuselage.

Kurt and Henri had obeyed her orders. They were breathing oxygen from the roof panels. The German was ready at the port wing panel, and Henri waited at the rear doorway hatch – both of them had the short big-mouthed shot pistols ready, but their faces were covered with the yellow oxygen masks, so Ingrid could not see nor judge their expressions.

Only a small number of the passengers had been quick enough and sensible enough to grab the dangling oxygen masks and remain conscious – but hundreds of others slumped in their seats or had fallen sideways into the aisles.

A thicket of dangling, twisting, swinging oxygen hoses filled the cabin like a forest of lianas, obscuring and confusing the scene, and after the darkness the cabin lights were painfully bright.

Ingrid held the camera in her free hand, for she knew that they must continue breathing oxygen. It would take the air-conditioning many minutes longer to cleanse the air of all trace of Factor V, and she held a mask over her mouth and waited.

Karen was beside her, with her shot pistol dangling from one hand and the other pressing a mask to her mouth.

'Go back and cover the front hatch,' Ingrid snapped at her. 'There will be—'

'Ingrid, we don't have to die,' Karen pleaded, and with a

crash the emergency exit panel over the port wing burst inward, and at the same instant two small dark objects flew threw the dark opening into the cabin.

'Stun grenades!' Ingrid howled. 'Get down!'

Peter Stride was light and jubilant as an eagle in flight. His feet and hands hardly seemed to touch the rungs of the ladder, now in the swift all-engulfing rush of action there were no longer doubts, no more hesitations – he was committed, and it was a tremendous soaring relief.

He went up over the smooth curved leading edge of the wing with a roll of his shoulders and hips, and in the same movement was on his feet, padding silently down the broad glistening metal pathway. The raindrops glittered like diamonds under his feet, and a fresh wind tugged at his hair as he ran.

He reached the main hull, and dropped into position at the side of the panel, his fingertips finding the razor-tight joint while his number-two man knelt swiftly opposite him. The grenade men were ready facing the panel, balanced like acrobats on the curved slippery upper surface of the great wing.

'Under six seconds.' Peter guessed at the time it had taken them to reach this stage from the 'go'. It was as swift and neat as it had never been in training, all of them armed by the knowledge of waiting death and horror.

In unison Peter and his number two hurled their combined strength and weight onto the releases of the emergency escape hatch, and it flew inwards readily, for there was no pressurization to resist, and at exactly the same instant the stun grenades went in cleanly, thrown by the waiting grenade men, and all four members of Peter's team bowed like Mohammedans in prayer to Mecca, covering eyes and ears.

Even outside the cabin, and even with ears and eyes

covered, the thunder of the explosions was appalling, seeming to beat in upon the brain with oppressive physical force, and the glare of burning phosphorus powder painted an X-ray picture of Peter's own fingers on the fleshy red of his closed eyelids. Then the grenade men were shouting into the interior, 'Lie down! Everybody down!' They would keep repeating that order Israeli style as long as it lasted.

Peter was a hundredth of a second slow, numbed by the blast, fumbling slightly at the butt of the Walther, thumbing the hammer as it snapped out of the quick-release holster, and then he went in – feet first through the hatch, like a runner sliding for home base. He was still in the air when he saw the girl in the red shirt running forward brandishing the camera, and screaming something that made no sense, though his brain registered it even in that unholy moment. He fired as his feet touched the deck and his first shot hit the girl in the mouth, punching a dark red hole through the rows of white teeth and snapping her head back so viciously that he heard the small delicate bones of her neck crackle as they broke.

Ingrid used both arms to cover eyes and ears, crouching forward into the appalling blast of sound and light that swept through the crowded cabins like a hurricane wind, and even when it had passed she was reeling wildly clutching for support at a seat back, trying to steady herself and judge the moment when the attackers were into the hull.

Those outside the hull would escape the direct force of the explosives she was about to detonate; there was a high survival chance for them. She wanted to judge the moment when the entire assault team penetrated the hull, she wanted maximum casualties, she wanted to take as many with her as possible, and she lifted the camera above her head with both hands.

'Come on!' she shrieked, but the cabin was thick with swirling clouds of white acrid smoke, and the dangling hoses twisted and writhed like the head of the Medusa. She heard the thunder of a shot pistol and somebody screamed, voices were chanting, 'Lie down! Everybody down!'

It was all smoke and sound and confusion, but she watched the dark opening of the emergency hatchway, waiting for it, finger on the detonator button of the camera. A supple black-clad figure in a grotesque mask torpedoed feet first into the cabin, and at that same instant Karen shrieked beside her.

'No, don't kill us,' and snatched the camera from Ingrid's raised hands, jerking it away by the strap, leaving Ingrid weaponless. Karen ran down the aisle through the smoke, still screaming, 'Don't kill us!' holding the camera like a peace offering. 'Caliph said we would not die.' She ran forward screaming frantically. 'Caliph—' and the black-clad and masked figure twisted lithely in the air, arching his back to land feet first in the centre of the aisle; as his feet touched the deck so the pistol in his right hand jerked up sharply but the shot seemed muted and unwarlike after the concussion of the stun grenades.

Karen was running down the aisle towards him, screaming and brandishing the camera, when the bullet took her in the mouth and wrenched her head backwards at an impossible angle. The next two shots blended into a single blurt of sound, fired so swiftly as to cheat the hearing, and from such close range that even the Velex explosive bullets ripped the back out of Karen's shirt and flooded it with a brighter wetter scarlet as they erupted from between her shoulder blades. The camera went spinning high across the cabin, landing in the lap of an unconscious passenger slumped in one of the central seats between the aisles.

Ingrid reacted with the instinctive speed of a jungle cat, diving forward, flat on the carpet aisle below the line of fire;

shrouded by the sinking white smoke of the grenades she wriggled forward on her belly to reach the camera.

It was twenty feet to where the camera had landed, but Ingrid moved with the speed of a serpent; she knew that the smoke was hiding her, but she knew also that to reach the camera she would have to come to her feet again and reach across two seats and two unconscious bodies.

Peter landed in balance on the carpeted aisle, and he killed the girl swiftly, and danced aside, clearing space for his number two to land.

The next man landed lightly in the space Peter had made for him, and the German in the red shirt jumped out from the angle of the rear galley and hit him in the small of the back with a full charge of buckshot. It almost blew his body into two separate parts, and he seemed to break in the middle like a folding penknife as he collapsed against Peter's legs.

Peter whirled at the shot, turning his back on Ingrid as she crawled forward through the phosphorous smoke.

Kurt was desperately trying to pull down the short, thick barrel of the pistol, for the recoil had thrown it high above his head. His scarlet shirt was open to the navel, shiny hard brown muscle and thick whorls of black body hair, mad glaring eyes through a greasy fringe of black hair, the scarred lip curled in a fixed snarl.

Peter hit him in the chest, taking no chance, and as he reeled backwards still fighting to aim the pistol, Peter hit again, in the head through the temple just in front of the left ear; the eyelids closed tightly over those wild eyes, his features twisted out of shape like a rubber mask and he went down face first into the aisle.

'Two.' Peter found that, as always in these desperate moments, he was functioning very coldly, very efficiently.

His shooting had been as reflexively perfect as if he were walking a combat shoot with jump-up cardboard targets.

He had even counted his shots, there were four left in the Walther.

'And two more of them,' he thought, but the smoke was still so thick that his visibility was down to under fifteen feet, and the swirling forest of dangling oxygen hose still agitated by the grenade blasts cut down his visibility further.

He jumped over the broken body of his number two, the blood squelching under his rubber soles, and suddenly the chunky black figure of Colin Noble loomed across the cabin. He was in the far aisle, having come in over the starboard wing. In the writhing smoke he looked like some demon from the pit, hideous and menacing in his gas mask. He dropped into the marksman's crouch, holding the big Browning in a double-handed grip, and the clangour of the gun beat upon the air like one of the great bronze bells of Notre Dame.

He was shooting at another scarlet-shirted figure, half seen through the smoke and the dangling hoses, a man with a round boyish face and drooping sandy moustache. The big Velex bullets tore the hijacker to pieces with the savagery of a predator's claws. They seemed to pin him like an insect to the central bulkhead, and they smashed chunks of living flesh from his chest and splinters of white bone from his skull.

'Three,' thought Peter. 'One left now – and I must get the camera.'

He had seen the black camera in the hands of the girl he had killed, had seen it fall, and he knew how deadly important it was to secure the detonator before it fell into the hands of the other girl, the blonde one, the dangerous one.

It had been only four seconds since he had penetrated the hull, yet it seemed like a dragging eternity. He could hear the crash of the slap-hammers tearing out the door locks, both fore and aft. Within seconds there would be Thor assault teams pouring into the Boeing through every opening, and he had not yet located the fourth hijacker, the truly dangerous one.

'Get down! Everybody down!' chanted the grenade men, and Peter spun lightly, and ran for the flight deck. He was certain the blonde girl would be there at the control centre.

Then, in front of him lay the girl he had shot down, the long, dark hair spread out around her pale, still terrified face. Her hair was already sodden with dark blood, and the black gap in her white teeth made her look like an old woman. She blocked the aisle with a tangle of slim boneless limbs.

The forward hatch crashed open as the lock gave way, but there were still solid curtains of white smoke ahead of him. Peter gathered himself to jump over the girl's body, and at that instant the other girl, the blonde girl, bounded up from the deck, seeming to appear miraculously from the smoke, like some beautiful but evil apparition.

She dived half across the block of central seating, groping for the camera, and Peter was slightly off balance, blocking himself in the turn to bring his gun hand on to her. He changed hands smoothly, for he was equally accurate with either, but it cost him the tenth part of a second, and the girl had the strap of the camera now and was tugging desperately at it. The camera seemed to be snagged, and Peter swung on her, taking the head shot for she was less than ten paces away, and even in the smoke and confusion he could not miss.

One of the few passengers who had been breathing oxygen from his hanging mask, and was still conscious, ignored the chanted orders 'Get down! Stay down!' and suddenly stumbled to his feet, screaming, 'Don't shoot! Get me out of here! Don't shoot!' in a rising hysterical scream. He was directly between Peter and the red-shirted girl, blocking Peter's field of fire, and Peter wrenched the gun off him at the moment that he fired. The bullet slammed into the roof, and the passenger barged into Peter, still screaming.

'Get me out! I want to get out!'

Peter tried desperately to clear his gun hand, for the girl had broken the strap of the camera and was fumbling with the black box. The passenger had an arm around Peter's gun arm, was shaking him wildly, weeping and screaming.

From across the central block of seats, Colin Noble fired once. He was still in the starboard aisle and the angle was almost impossible, for he had to shoot nine inches past Peter's shoulder, and through the forest of dangling hose.

His first shot missed, but it was close enough to flinch the girl's head violently, the golden hair flickered with the passage of shot, and she stumbled backwards, groping with clumsy fingers for the detonator.

Peter chopped the hysterical passenger in the throat with the stiffened fingers of his right hand and hurled him back into his seat, trying desperately to line up for a shot at the girl – knowing he must get the brain and still her fingers instantly.

Colin fired his second shot, one hundredth of a second before Peter, and the big bullet flung the girl aside, jerking her head out of the track of Peter's shot.

Peter saw the strike of Colin's bullet, it hit her high in the right shoulder, almost in the joint of the scapula and the humerus, shattering the bone with such force that her arm was flung upwards in a parody of a communist salute, twisting unnaturally and whipping above her head; once again the camera was flung aside and the girl's body was thrown violently backwards down the aisle as though she had been hit by a speeding automobile.

Peter picked his shot, waiting for a clean killing hit in the head as the girl tried to drag herself upright – but before he could fire, a mass of black-costumed figures swarmed out of the smoke, and covered the girl, pinning her kicking and screaming on the carpet of the aisle. The Thor team had come in through the forward hatch, just in time to save her life, and Peter clipped the Walther into his holster and stooped to pick up the camera gingerly. Then he pulled off his mask with his other hand.

'That's it. That's all of them,' he shouted. 'We got them all. Cease fire. It's all over.' Then into the microphone of the transceiver, 'Touch down! Touch down!' The code for total success. Three of his men were holding the girl down, and despite the massive spurting wound in her shoulder, she fought like a leopard in a trap.

'Get the emergency chutes down,' Peter ordered, and from each exit the long plastic slides inflated and drooped to the tarmac – already his men were leading the conscious passengers to the exits and helping them into the slide.

From the terminal building a dozen ambulances with sirens howling, gunned out across the tarmac. The back-up members of Thor were running out under the glare of floodlights, cheering thinly. 'Touch down! Touch down!'

Like prehistoric monsters the mechanical stairways lumbered down from the northern apron, to give access to the body of the Boeing.

Peter stepped up to the girl, still holding the camera in his hands, and he stood looking down at her. The icy coldness of battle still gripped him, his mind felt needle sharp and his vision clear, every sense enhanced.

The girl stopped struggling, and looked back at him. The image of a trapped leopard was perfect. Peter had never seen eyes so fierce and merciless, as she glared at him. Then she drew her head back like a cobra about to strike, and spat at him. White frothy spittle splattered down the front of Peter's legs.

Colin Noble was beside Peter now, pulling off his gas mask.

'I'm sorry, Peter. I was going for the heart.'

'You'll never hold me,' shrieked the girl suddenly. 'I'll be free before Thanksgiving!'

And Peter knew she was right. The punishment that a befuddled world society meted out to these people was usually only a few months' imprisonment, and that often suspended. He remembered the feel of the dying child in his arms, the warm trickle of her blood running over his belly and legs.

'My people will come for me,' the girl spat again, this time into the face of one of the men who held her down. 'You will never hold me. My people will force you to free me.'

Again she was right, her capture was a direct invitation for further atrocity, the wheel of vengeance and retribution was set in motion. For the life of this trapped and vicious predator, hundreds more would suffer, and dozens more would die.

The reaction was setting in now, the battle rage abating, and Peter felt the nausea cloying his bowels. It had been in vain, he thought; he had thrown away a lifetime's strivings and endeavour to win only a temporary victory. He had checked the forces of evil, not beaten them – and they would regroup and attack again, stronger and more cunning than ever, and this woman would lead them again.

'We are the revolution.' The girl lifted her uninjured arm in the clenched fist salute. 'We are the power. Nothing, nobody can stop us.'

When this woman had fired a load of buckshot through the swollen body of the pregnant woman it had distorted her shape completely. The image was recaptured entire and whole in Peter's memory, the way she had burst open like the pod of a ripe fruit.

The blonde woman shook the clenched fist into Peter's face.

'This is only the beginning – the new era has begun.'

There was a taunt and a sneering threat in her voice, uttered in complete confidence – and Peter knew it was not misplaced. There was a new force unleashed in the world, something more deadly than he had believed possible, and Peter had no illusions as to the role that blind fortune had played in his small triumph. He had no illusion either that the beast was more than barely wounded; next time it would be more powerful, more cunning, having learned from this inconsequential failure – and with the reaction from battle came a powerful wave of dread and despair that seemed to overwhelm his soul. It had all been in vain.

'You can never win,' taunted the woman, splattered with her own blood, but undaunted and unrepentant, seeming to read his very thoughts.

'And we can never lose,' she shrieked.

'Gentlemen.' The South African Prime Minister spoke with painful deliberation. 'My cabinet and I are firmly of the opinion that to accede to the terrorists' demands is to take a seat on the back of the tiger, from which we will never be able to dismount.' He stopped, hung his great granite-hewn head for a moment and then looked up at the two ambassadors. 'However, such is the duty we owe to humanity and the dignity of human life, and such is the pressure which two great nations can bring to bear upon one much smaller, that we have decided unanimously to agree in full to all the conditions necessary for the release of the women and children—'

A telephone on the table top in front of the American Ambassador began to shrill irritatingly, and the Prime Minister paused, frowned slightly.

'However, we place complete faith in the undertaking

given by your governments—' He stopped again for the telephone insisted. ' – You had better answer that, sir—' he told Kelly Constable.

'Excuse me, Prime Minister.' The American lifted the receiver, and as he listened an expression of utter disbelief slowly changed his features. 'Hold the line,' he said into the receiver, and then, covering the mouthpiece with his hand, he looked up. 'Prime Minister – it is a very great pleasure to inform you that three minutes ago the Thor assault team broke into Flight 070 and killed three of the terrorists – they wounded and captured a fourth terrorist, but there were no casualties among the passengers. They got them all out, every last one of them. Safe and sound.'

The big man at the head of the table sagged with relief in his seat, and as the storm of jubilation and self-congratulation broke about him, he started to smile. It was a smile that transformed his forbidding features, the smile of an essentially fatherly and kindly man. 'Thank you, sir,' he said, still smiling. 'Thank you very much '

'You are guilty of blatant dereliction of your duty, General Stride,' Kingston Parker accused grimly

'My concern was entirely with the lives of hostages and the force of moral law.' Peter answered him quietly; it was less than fifteen minutes since he had penetrated the hull of the Boeing in a blaze of fire and fury. His hands were still shaking slightly and the nausea still lay heavily on his guts.

'You deliberately disobeyed my specific orders.' Parker was an enraged lion, the mane of thick shot-silver hair seemed to bristle, and he glowered from the screen; the vast power of his personality seemed to fill the command cabin of the Hawker. 'I have always had grave reservations as to your suitability for the high command with which you have been entrusted. I have already expressed those reservations in writing to your superiors, and they have been fully justified.'

'I understand by all this that I have been removed from command of Thor,' Peter cut in brusquely, his anger seething to the surface, and Parker checked slightly.

Peter knew that even Kingston Parker could not immediately fire the hero of such a successful counter-strike. It would take time, a matter of days, perhaps, but Peter's fate was sealed. There could be no doubt of that, and Parker went on to confirm this.

'You will continue to exercise command under my direct surveillance. You will make no decision without referring directly back to me, no decision whatsoever. Do you understand that, General Stride?'

Peter did not bother to reply; he felt a wildly reckless mood starting to buoy his sagging spirits, a sense of freedom and choice of action such as he had never known before. For the first time in his career he had deliberately disobeyed a superior officer, and luck or not, the outcome had been a brilliant success.

'Your first duty now will be to withdraw all Thor units, and swiftly and in as good an order as possible. The militant you have taken will be returned to London for questioning and trial—'

'Her crimes were committed here. She should be tried here for murder – I have already had demands from the local—'

'Arrangements are being made with the South African authorities.' Parker's anger had not abated but he had it better under control. 'She will return to Britain aboard your command aircraft, with the Thor doctor in attendance.'

Peter remembered what had happened to the terrorist Leila Khaled, dragged from the El Al airliner where she was being held by Israeli security agents. As a guest of the British police, she had spent six short days in captivity, and then been released in a blaze of publicity and glory, heroine of the communications media, Joan of Arc of terror – released to plan and execute the death and destruction of hundreds more innocents, to lead the attack on the foundations of civilization, to shake the columns that held aloft the rule of law and society.

'I want this woman in London within twenty-four hours. She is to be strictly guarded at all times against retaliation. We cannot afford another bloodbath – like the one you led on 070.'

Peter Stride walked very erect, very tall into the echoing, marble-columned domestic departures hall of the airport, and his men called to him as he came.

'Well done, sir.'

'Great stuff, General.'

'Way to go—'

They were tending the released passengers, re-assembling their scattered gear, dismantling the security and communications equipment and packing it away – within the hour they would be ready to pull out – but now they left their tasks to crowd about him, competing to shake his hand.

The passengers realized that this must be the architect of their salvation and they cheered him as he passed slowly through the hall, and now he was smiling, acknowledging their pitiful gratitude, stopping to talk with an old lady, and submitting to her tearful embrace.

'God bless you, my boy. God bless you.' And her body trembled against him. Gently Peter set her aside and went on, and though he smiled it was with his lips only, for there was steel in his heart.

There were Thor guards on the main administrative offices on the mezzanine floor armed with submachine guns, but they stood aside for him and Peter went through.

Colin Noble was still in his black skin-tight assault suit with the big .45 on his hip, and a cheroot clamped between his teeth.

'Take a look at this lot,' he called to Peter. The desk was covered with explosives and weapons. 'Most of it's iron-curtain stuff – but God alone knows where they got these.' He indicated the double-barrelled shot pistols. 'If they had these custom built, it would have cost them plenty.'

'They have got plenty,' Peter answered drily. 'The ransom for the OPEC ministers was one hundred and fifty million dollars, for the Braun brothers twenty-five million, for Baron Altmann another twenty million – that's the defence budget for a nation.' He picked up one of the shot pistols and opened the breech. It had been unloaded.

'Is this the one she used to gun down the hostages?'

Colin shrugged 'Probably, it's been fired through both barrels.' Colin was right, there were black specks of burned powder down the short smooth bores.

Peter loaded it with buckshot cartridges from the pile on the desk, and walked on down the long office with the covered typewriters on the deserted desks and the airline travel posters decorating the wall.

Along one wall the three bodies of the hijackers were laid out in a neat row, each encapsulated in its separate translucent plastic envelope.

Two Thor men were assembling the contents of their pockets – personal jewellery, meagre personal effects – and they were packing them into labelled plastic bags.

The body of Peter's Number Two was against the far wall, also in his plastic body-bag, and Peter stooped over him. Through the plastic he could make out the features of the dead man's face. The eyes were wide and the jaw hung open slackly. Death is always so undignified, Peter thought, and straightened up.

Still carrying the shot pistol, Peter went on into the inner office, and Colin Noble followed him.

They had the girl on another stretcher, a plasma drip suspended above her, and the Thor doctor and his two orderlies were working over her quietly, but the young doctor looked up irritably as Peter pushed open the door, then his expression changed as he recognized Peter.

'General, if we are going to save this arm, I have to get her into theatre pretty damned quickly. The joint of the shoulder is shattered—'

The girl rolled the lovely head towards Peter. The thick springing golden hair was matted with drying blood, and there was a smear of it across one cheek.

Now her face was completely drained of all colour, like the head of an angel carved out of white marble. The skin had a waxen, almost translucent, lustre and only the eyes were still fierce, not dulled by the painkilling drugs that they had injected into her.

' – I have asked the South Africans for co-operation—' the doctor went on, ' – they have two top orthopaedic surgeons standing by, and they have offered a helicopter to fly her into the Central Hospital at Edenvale.'

Already she was being treated, even by Thor, as the major celebrity she was. She had taken her first step along the rose-strewn pathway to glory, and Peter could imagine how the media would extol her beauty – they had gone berserk with extravagant praise for the swarthy ferrety-eyed Leila Khaled with her fine dark moustache – they would go over the top for this one.

Peter had never known any emotion so powerful as the emotion that gripped him now.

'Get out,' he said to the doctor.

'Sir?' The man looked startled.

'Get out,' Peter repeated, 'all of you.' And he waited until the opaque glass door closed behind them, before he spoke to the girl in conversational tones.

'You have made me abandon my own principles, and descend to your level.'

The girl watched him uncertainly, her eyes flickered to the shot pistol that Peter held dangling from his right hand.

'You have forced me, a career soldier, to disobey the orders of a superior officer in the face of the enemy.' He paused. 'I used to be a proud man, but when I have done what I must do now I will no longer have much of which to be proud.'

'I demand to see the American Ambassador,' said the girl huskily, still watching the pistol. 'I am an American citizen. I demand the protection—'

Peter interrupted her, again speaking quickly. 'This is not revenge. I am old and wise enough to know that revenge has the most bitter taste of all human excesses.'

'You cannot do it—' The girl's voice rose, the same strident tones, but now shriller still with fear. 'They will destroy you.'

But Peter went on as though she had not spoken. 'It is not revenge,' he repeated. 'You, yourself, gave the reason clearly. If you continue to exist, they will come to get you back. As long as you live, others must die – and they will die stripped of all human dignity. They will die in terror, the same way you murdered—'

'I am a woman. I am wounded. I am a prisoner of war,' screamed the girl, trying to struggle upright.

'Those are the old rules,' Peter told her. 'You tore up the book, and wrote a new one – I am playing to your rules now. I have been reduced to your level.'

'You cannot kill me,' the girl's voice range wildly. 'I still have work—'

'Colin,' Peter said quietly, without looking at the American. 'You'd better get out now.'

Colin Noble hesitated, his right hand on the butt of the Browning, and the girl rolled her head towards him imploringly.

'You can't let him do it.'

'Peter—' Colin said.

'You were right, Colin,' Peter spoke quietly. 'That kid did look a lot like Melissa-Jane.'

Colin Noble dropped his hand from the pistol and turned to the door. Now the girl was shrieking obscenity and threat, her voice incoherent with terror and hatred.

Colin closed the door softly and stood with his back to it. The single crash of shot was shockingly loud, and the stream of filthy abuse was cut off abruptly. The silence was even more appalling than the harrowing sounds which had preceded it. Colin did not move. He waited four, five seconds before the door clicked open and General Peter Stride came out into the main office. He handed the shot pistol to Colin and one barrel was hot in his hand.

Peter's handsome aristocratic features seemed ravaged, as though by a long wasting disease. The face of a man who had leapt into the abyss.

Peter Stride left the glass door open, and walked away without looking back. Despite the terrible expression of despair, he still carried himself like a soldier and his tread was firm.

Colin Noble did not even look through the open door.

'All right,' he called to the doctor. 'She's all yours now.' And he followed Peter Stride down the broad staircase.

There was a long hard gallop over good going and open pasture to the crest of the ridge, with only one gate. Melissa-Jane led on her bay filly, her Christmas gift from Uncle Steven. She was in the midst of the passionate love affair that most pubescent girls have with horses, and she looked truly good astride the glistening thoroughbred. The cold struck high colour into her cheeks and the braid of honey-coloured hair thumped gaily down her back at each stride. She had blossomed even in the few weeks since last Peter had seen her – and he realized with some awe and considerable pride that she was fast becoming a great beauty.

Peter was up on one of Steven's hunters, a big rangy animal with the strength to carry his weight, but the gelding was slogging hard to hold the flying pair that danced ahead of him.

At the hedge, Melissa-Jane scorned the gate, gathered the filly with fine strong hands and took her up and over. Her little round bottom lifted out of the saddle as she leaned into the jump, and clods of black earth flew from the filly's hooves.

As soon as she was over she swivelled in the saddle to watch him, and Peter realized that he was under challenge. The hedge immediately appeared to be head-high and he noticed for the first time how the ground fell away at a steep angle beyond. He had not ridden for almost two years, and it was the first time he had been up on this gelding – but the horse went for the jump gamely, and they brushed the top of the hedge, landed awkwardly, stumbled with Peter up on his neck for an appalling instant of time in which he was convinced he was to take a toss in front of his daughter's critical eye; caught his balance, held the gelding's head up and they came away still together.

'Super-Star!' Melissa-Jane shouted laughing, and by the time he caught her she had dismounted under the yew tree at the crest, and was waiting for him with her breath steaming in the crisp calm air.

'Our land once went right as far as the church—' Peter pointed to the distant grey needle of stone that pricked the belly of the sky, ' – and there almost to the top of the downs.' He turned to point in the opposite direction.

'Yes.' Melissa-Jane slipped her arm through his as they stood close together under the yew. 'The family had to sell it when Grandfather died. You told me And that's right too. One family shouldn't own so much.'

Peter glanced down at her, startled. 'My God, a communist in the family. An asp in the bosom.'

She squeezed his arm. 'Don't worry, Daddy darling. It's Uncle Steven who is the bloated plutocrat. You're not a capitalist – you aren't even employed any more—' And the instant she had said it, her laughter collapsed around her and she looked stricken. ' – Oh, I didn't mean that. I truly didn't.'

It was almost a month now since Peter's resignation had been accepted by the War Office, but the scandal had not yet run out of steam.

The first heady paeans of praise for the success of Thor's Delta strike had lasted only a few days. The glowing editorials, the full front pages, the lead news item on every television channel, the effusive messages of congratulations from the leaders of the Western governments, the impromptu triumph for Peter Stride and his little band of heroes, had quickly struck an odd note, a sudden souring of the ecstasies.

The racist Government of South Africa had actually agreed to the release of political prisoners *before* the assault, one of the hijackers had been taken alive, and died of gunshot wounds received in the terminal buildings. Then one of the released hostages, a freelance journalist who had been covering the medical convention in Mauritius and was returning aboard the hijacked aircraft, published a sensational eye-witness account of the entire episode, and a dozen other passengers supported his claims that there had been screams from the fourth hijacker, screams for mercy, before she was shot to death after her capture.

A storm of condemnation and vilification from the extreme left of the British Labour Government had swept through the Westminster parliament, and had been echoed by the Democrats in the American Congress. The very existence of the Thor Command had come under scrutiny and been condemned in extravagant terms. The Communist parties of France and Italy had marched, and the detonation of an M.26 hand grenade – one of those stolen by the Baader-Meinhof gang from the American base in Metz – amongst the crowd leaving the Parc des Princes football stadium in Paris had killed one and injured twenty-three. A telephone call to the offices of *France Soir* by a man speaking accented French claimed that this fresh atrocity was revenge for the murder of four hijackers by the Imperialist execution squad.

Pressure for Peter's discharge had come initially from the Pentagon, and there was very little doubt that Dr Kingston Parker was the accuser, though, as head of Atlas, he was never identified, total secrecy still surrounding the project. The media had begun to demand an investigation of all the circumstances surrounding Thor. ' – And if it is ascertained that criminal irregularities did indeed exist in the conduct of the operation, that the person or persons responsible be brought to trial either by a military tribunal or the civil courts.' Fortunately the media had not yet unravelled the full scope of Atlas Command. Only Thor was under scrutiny; they did not yet suspect the existence of either Mercury or Diana.

Within the War Office and the governments of both America and Britain, there had been much sympathy and support for Peter Stride – but he had made it easier for his friends and for himself by tendering his resignation. The resignation had been accepted, but still the left was clamouring for more. They wanted blood, Peter Stride's blood.

Now Melissa-Jane's huge pansy violet eyes flooded with the tears of mortification. 'I didn't mean that I truly didn't '

'One thing about being out of a job – I have more time to be with my favourite girl.' He smiled down at her, but she would not be mollified.

'I don't believe the horrible things they are saying. I know you are a man of honour, Daddy '

'Thank you.' And he felt the ache of it, the guilt and the

sorrow. They were silent a little longer, still standing close together, and Peter spoke first.

'You are going to be a palaeontologist—' he said.

'No. That was last month. I've changed my mind. I'm not interested in old bones any more. Now I'm going to be a doctor, a child specialist.'

'That's good.' Peter nodded gravely. 'But let's go back to old bones for a moment. The age of the great reptiles. The dinosaurs – why did they fade into extinction?'

'They could not adapt to a changing environment.' Melissa-Jane had the answer promptly.

Peter murmured, ' – A concept like honour. Is it outdated in today's world, I wonder?' Then he saw the puzzlement, the hurt in her eyes, and he knew they had wandered onto dangerous ground. His daughter had a burning love for all living things, particularly human beings. Despite her age, she had a developed political and social conscience, distinguished by total belief in shining ideals and the essential beauty and goodness of mankind. There would be time in the years ahead for the agony of disillusion. The term 'man or woman of honour' was Melissa-Jane's ultimate accolade. No matter that it could be applied to any of her current heroes or heroines – the Prince of Wales, or the singer of popular songs with an outrageous name that Peter could never remember, to Virginia Wade, the former Wimbledon champion, or to the Fifth Form science teacher at Roedean who had aroused Melissa-Jane's interest in medicine – Peter knew that he should feel proper gratitude for being included in this exalted company.

'I will try to live up to your opinion of me.' He stooped and kissed her, surprised at the strength of his love for this child-woman. 'And now it's too cold to stand here any longer, and Pat will never forgive us if we are late for lunch.'

They clattered over the stone cobbles of the stable yard, riding knee to knee, and before he dismounted, Peter indulged himself in the pleasure of his favourite view of the house that had always been home, even though it belonged now, together with the title, to Steven, the older brother, older by three hours only, but older none the less.

The house was red brick with a roof that ran at fifty different unlikely angles. It missed being hideous by a subtle margin and achieved a fairytale enchantment. Peter could never grudge it to Steven, who loved the sprawling edifice with something close to passion.

Perhaps the desire to own the house and to restore it to its former magnificence was the goad which had pricked Steven to the superhuman effort that a British resident must make against taxation and socialist restrictions in order to amass anything like a fortune.

Steven had made that effort and now Abbots Yew stood immaculate and well-beloved in glorious gardens, and Sir Steven kept baronial style.

His affairs were so complicated, spread over so many continents that even the British taxman must have been daunted Peter had once skirted this subject with his twin brother, and Steven had replied quietly.

'When a law is patently unjust, such as our tax law is, it's the duty of an honest man to subvert it.'

Peter's old-fashioned sense of rightness had baulked at such logic, but he let it pass.

It was strange that it had worked this way for the two brothers, for Peter had always been the brilliant one, and the family had always referred to 'Poor Steven'. Nobody was very surprised when Steven left Sandhurst amid dark whispers halfway through his final year – but two years later Steven was already a millionaire while Peter was a lowly second lieutenant in the British Army Peter grinned without rancour at the memory. He had always been particularly fond of his elder brother – but at that moment his train of thought was interrupted as his eye caught the mirror-like finish of the silver limousine parked at the end of the stable yard. It was one of those long Mercedes-Benz favoured by pop stars, Arab oil men, or heads of state. The chauffeur was uniformed in sober navy blue and was busy burnishing the paintwork to an even higher gloss. Even Steven did not run to that sort of transportation, and Peter felt mildly intrigued. House guests at Abbots Yew were always interesting. Steven Stride did not concern himself with those who did not wield either power, wealth or extraordinary talent. Beyond the Mercedes 600 was parked another smaller model; this one was black and the two men in it had the hard closed faces that marked them as bodyguards.

Melissa-Jane rolled her eyes at the automobile. 'Another bloated plutocrat, I expect,' she muttered. It was the currently favoured term of extreme disapproval, a great advance on 'grotty' which had preceded it, Peter could not help thinking as he helped his daughter unsaddle and then rub down the horses. They went up through the rose garden, arm in arm, and then laughing together into the main drawing-room.

'Peter old boy!' Steven came to meet him, as tall as his brother, and once he had been as lean, but good living had thickened his body while at the same time the strains of being a professional deal maker had greyed his hair at the temples and laced his moustache with silver bristles. His face was not quite a mirror image of Peter's, slightly more fleshy and florid – but the twin resemblance was still strongly marked, and now his face was alive with pleasure

'Thought you'd broken your bloody neck, what!' Steven carefully cultivated the bluff manner of the country squire to shield his quick and shrewd intelligence.

Now he turned to Melissa-Jane and hugged her with barely a touch of incestuous pleasure. 'How did Florence Nightingale go?'

'She's a darling, Uncle Steven. I will never be able to thank you.'

'Peter, I would like you to meet a very charming lady—'

She had been talking to Patricia Stride, Steven's wife, and now as she turned, the winter sunshine through the bay windows behind lit her with a soft romantic aura.

Peter felt as though the earth had tilted under his feet, and a fist closed around his ribs constricting his breathing and inhibiting the action of his heart.

He recognized her immediately from the photographs in the official file during the long-drawn-out kidnapping and subsequent murder of her husband. At one stage it had seemed that the kidnappers had crossed the Channel with their victim, and Thor had gone to condition Alpha for almost a week. Peter had studied the photographs that had been assembled from a dozen sources, but even the glossy coloured portraits from *Vogue* and *Jours de France* had not been able to capture the magnificence of the woman.

Surprisingly, he saw his own immediate recognition reflected. There was no change in her expression, but it flared briefly like dark-green emerald fire in her eyes. There was no question in Peter's mind but that she had recognized him, and as he stepped towards her he realized she was tall, but the fine proportion of her body had not made that immediately apparent. Her skirt was of a fine wool crêpe which moulded the long, stately legs of a dancer.

'Baroness, may I present my brother. General Stride.'

'How do you do, General.' Her English was almost perfect, a low husky voice, the slight accent very attractive, but she pronounced his rank as three distinct syllables.

'Peter, this is Baroness Altmann.'

Her thick glossy black hair was scraped back severely from the forehead with a perfect arrowhead of widow's peak at the centre, emphasizing the high Slavic cheekbones and the unblemished perfection of her skin – but her jawline was too square and strong for beauty, and the mouth had an arrogant determined line to it. Magnificent, but not beautiful – and Peter found himself violently attracted. The breathless wholesale feeling he had not experienced for twenty years.

She seemed to epitomize everything he admired in a woman.

Her body was in the condition of a trained athlete. Beneath the oyster silk of her blouse her arms were delicately sculpted from toned muscle, the waist narrow, the breasts very small and unfettered, their lovely shape pressing clearly through fine material, her clean lightly tanned skin glowed with health and careful grooming. All this contributed to his attraction.

However, the greater part was in Peter's own mind. He knew she was a woman of extraordinary strength and achievement, that was pure aphrodisiac for him, and she exuded also the challenging air of being unattainable. The regal eyes mocked his evident masculinity with the untouchable aloofness of a queen or a goddess. She seemed to be smiling inwardly, a cool patronizing smile at his admiration, which she realized was no more than her due. Quickly Peter reviewed what he knew of her.

She had begun her association with the Baron as his private secretary, and in five years had become indispensable to him. The Baron had recognized her ability by rapidly elevating her to the boards of directors, first of some of the group's lesser subsidiaries, and finally to that of the central holding company. When the Baron's physical strength had begun to decline in his losing battle with an inexorable cancer, he came to rely more upon her, trust well placed as it soon turned out. For she ran the complex empire of heavy industrial companies, of electronics and armaments corporations, of banking and shipping and property developments, like the son he never had. When he married her he was fifty-eight years of age, almost thirty years her senior, and she had been a perfect wife as she had been a perfect business partner.

She had assembled and personally delivered the massive ransom demanded by his abductors, against the advice of the French police, going alone and unguarded to a meeting with merciless killers, and when they had returned the Baron's fearfully mutilated corpse to her, she had mourned him and buried him and continued to run the empire she had inherited, with vision and strength so far beyond her years.

She was twenty-nine years old. No, that had been two years ago, Peter realized, as he bowed over her hand, not quite touching the smooth cool fingers with his lips. She would be thirty-one years old now. She wore a single ring on her wedding finger, a solitaire diamond, not a particularly large diamond, not more than six carats but of such a perfect whiteness and fire that it seemed to be endowed with its own life. It was the choice of a woman of immense wealth and even greater style.

As Peter straightened, he realized that she was appraising him as carefully as he was her. It seemed that he would be unable to conceal anything from those slanted emerald eyes, but he returned her gaze steadily, knowing without conceit that he could withstand any such scrutiny; still intrigued, however, with the certainty that she had known him.

'Your name has been much in the news recently,' she said, as if in explanation.

There were sixteen for lunch, including Steven and Pat's three children and Melissa-Jane. It was a happy, relaxed meal, but the Baroness was seated at a distance that made it impossible for Peter to speak directly to her, and though he strained to follow her conversation, her voice was low and addressed mostly to Steven and the editor of one of the national daily newspapers who flanked her. Peter found himself fully occupied in fending off the breathless attention of the pretty but feather-brained blonde on his left. She was a starlet who had married well and divorced even better. She had been handpicked by Pat Stride. Peter's sister-in-law was indefatigable in her efforts to find him a suitable replacement for Cynthia. Twelve years of straight failures had not daunted her in the least.

There was still time for Peter to notice that though the Baroness sipped once or twice at her wine, the level in the glass never fell, and she picked only lightly at her plate.

Though Peter watched her covertly, the Baroness never glanced once in his direction. It was only as they went through for coffee that she came directly and unaffectedly to his side.

'Steven tells me there are Roman ruins on the estate,' she said.

'I could show them to you. It is a lovely walk up through the woods.'

'Thank you. I do have some business to discuss with Steven before that; shall we meet at three o'clock?'

She had changed into a loose tweed skirt and jacket that would have looked bulky on a shorter or plumper woman, and high boots in the same lavender tinted brown. Under it she wore a cashmere roll-neck jersey, and a scarf of the same fine wool hung down her back. A wide-brimmed hat with a bright feather in the band was pulled down over her eyes.

She walked in silence, hands thrust deeply into the big pockets of her jacket, making no effort to protect the expensive boots from mud, thorns of damp bracken. She moved with a flowing, long-legged grace, swinging from the hips so that her shoulder and head seemed to float beside Peter, at a not much lower level than his own. Had she not been a world leader in finance and industry, she might have made a great model, he decided. She had a talent for making clothes look important and elegant, while treating them with indifference.

Peter respected her silence, pleased to be able to step out to match her pace, as they went up through the dark dripping woods that smelt of leaf mould and cold rain, the oaks bare and moss-pelted, seeming to beseech a purple-grey sky with arthritic limbs held high.

They came out on the higher open ground without having stopped once, although the path had been steep and the ground soft underfoot.

She was breathing deeply but evenly, and she had coloured just sufficiently to flatter the high Slavic cheeks. She must be in peak physical condition, he thought.

'Here they are.' Peter indicated the barely discernible grass-covered ditch that circled the hilltop. 'They are not very impressive, but I didn't want to warn you in advance.'

She smiled now. 'I have been here before,' she said in that intriguing husky accent.

'Well, we are off to a flying start. We have both deceived each other at our first meeting—' Peter chuckled.

'I came all the way from Paris,' she explained. 'It was most inconvenient really – the business I had to discuss with Sir Steven could have been completed by telephone in five minutes. What I had to discuss with you could only be done face by face—' She corrected herself immediately. 'I am sorry, face to face.' It was a rare slip Steven had been strangely insistent that Peter spend this particular weekend at Abbots Yew, and was certainly party to this encounter.

'I am flattered by the interest of such a beautiful lady—'

Instantly she frowned, and with a gesture of irritation cut short the compliment as frivolous.

'Very recently you were approached by the Narmco section of Seddler Steel with an offer to head their Sales Division,' she said, and Peter nodded. Since his resignation had been accepted by the War Office, there had been many offers. 'The terms of employment offered were extraordinarily generous.'

'That is true.'

'You prefer the cloistered academic life, perhaps?' she asked, and though Peter's expression did not change, he was taken off balance. It seemed impossible that she could know of the offer of the Chair of Modern Military History that he had been offered by a leading American university, an offer with which he was still toying idly.

'There are some books I want to read and write,' Peter said.

'Books. You have an important collection, and I have read those you have written. You are an interesting contradiction, General Stride. The man of direct action, and at the same time of deep political and social thought.'

'I confuse myself at times,' Peter smiled. 'So what chance do you have to understand me?'

She did not rise to the smile. 'A great deal of your writing coincides with my own conviction. As for your action, if I had been a man and in your position, I might have acted as you did.'

Peter stiffened, resenting any allusion to the taking of Flight 070, and again she seemed to understand instinctively.

'I refer to your entire career, General. From Cyprus to Johannesburg – and including Ireland.' And he relaxed slightly.

'Why did you refuse the Narmco offer?' she asked.

'Because it was presented with the unstated conviction that I could not refuse. Because the terms were so generous that they left a strange unsatisfying odour in my nostrils. Because I believe that I would have been required to perform duties in line with the reputation I seem to have acquired since the taking of Flight 070.'

'What reputation is that?' She leaned slightly towards him, and he smelled her particular aroma. The way perfume reacted upon that petally-smooth skin, heated by the exertion of the climb up the hill. She smelled faintly of crushed lemon blossom and clean healthy mature woman. He felt himself physically aroused by it, and had an almost undesirable impulse to reach out and touch her, to feel the warmth and glossiness of her skin.

'A man who makes accommodations, perhaps,' he answered her.

'What did you think you might have been asked to do?'

This time he shrugged. 'Perhaps carry bribes to my one-time colleagues in NATO Command, to induce them to consider favourably the products of Narmco.'

'Why would you believe that?'

'I was once a decision-making officer in that Command.'

She turned away from him and looked out across the special greens of an English winter landscape, the orderly fields and pastures, the dark wedges and geometrical shapes of the woods and copses.

'Do you know that through Altmann Industries and other companies I control a majority shareholding in Sedler Steel, and naturally in Narmco?'

'No,' Peter admitted. 'But I cannot say I am surprised.'

'Did you know that the offer from Narmco was in reality from me personally?'

This time he said nothing.

'You are quite right, of course, your contacts with the upper echelon of NATO and with the British and American high commands would have been worth every centime of the extravagant salary you were offered. As for bribes—' She smiled then suddenly, and it altered her face entirely, making her seem many years younger, and there was a warmth and a sense of fun that he would not have suspected, ' – this is a capitalist society, General. We prefer to talk about commissions and introducer's fees.'

He found himself smiling back at her, not because of what she had said, but simply because her smile was irresistible.

'However, I give you my solemn word that you would never have been expected to offer or carry – no, since Lockheed were indiscreet, it has changed. Nothing disreputable could ever be traced back to Narmco, and certainly not to the top men there. Certainly not to you.'

'It's all academic now,' Peter pointed out. 'I've refused the offer.'

'I disagree, General Stride.' The brim of the hat covered her eyes as she looked down. 'I hope that when you hear what I had hoped to achieve you may reconsider. I made the error of trying to keep us at arms' length to begin with. I relied on the generosity of the offer to sway you. I do not usually misjudge people so dismally—' and she looked up and smiled again, and this time reached out and touched his arm. Her fingers were like her limbs, long and slim, but they were delicately tapered and the nails were shaped and lacquered to a glossy fleshy pink. She left them on his arm as she went on speaking.

'My husband was an extraordinary man. A man of vast vision and strength and compassion. Because of that they tortured and killed him—' her voice had sunk to a hoarse catchy whisper ' – they killed him in the most vile manner—' She stopped, but made no attempt to turn her head away, she was unashamed of the tears that filled both eyes but did not break over the lower lids. She did not even blink, and it was Peter who looked away first Only then she moved her hand, slipping it lightly into the crook of Peter's elbow and coming beside him so her hip almost touched his.

'It will rain soon,' she said, her voice level and controlled. 'We should go down.' And as they started, she went on talking.

'The butchers who did that to Aaron went free, while an impotent society looked on. A society which has systematically stripped itself of defence against the next attack. America has virtually disbanded its intelligence system, and so shackled and exposed what is left that it is powerless. Your own country is concerned only with its particular problems, as are we in the rest of Europe – there is no international approach to a problem that is international in scope. Atlas was a fine concept, limited as it was by the fact that it was a force that could only be used in retaliation and then only in special circumstances. However, if they ever suspect that it exists, the denizens of the left will mass to tear it down like a hunting pack of hyena.' She squeezed his arm lightly, and looked sideways at him with a solemn slant of the emerald eyes. 'Yes, General, I do know about Atlas – but do not ask me how.'

Peter said nothing, and they entered the forest, stepping carefully, for the path was slick and steep.

'After the death of my husband, I began to think a great deal about how we could protect the world that we know, while still remaining within the laws which were first designed to do that. With Altmann Industries I had inherited a comprehensive system of international information-gathering; naturally it was attuned almost entirely to commercial and industrial considerations—' She went on talking in that low intense voice that Peter found mesmeric, describing how she had gradually used her massive fortune and influence to reach across borders closed to most to gain the overall view of the new world of violence and intimidation. ' – I was not tied by considerations such as that of Interpol, forbidden by suicidal laws to involve itself in any crime that has political motivation. It was only when I was able to pass on what I had learned that I found myself coming up against the same self-destructive state of mind that masquerades as democracy and individual freedom. Twice I was able to anticipate a terrorist strike and to warn the authorities, but intention is not a crime, I was told, and both the culprits were quietly escorted to the border and turned free to prepare themselves almost openly for the next outrage. The world must wait and cringe for the next stroke, prohibited from making any pre-emptive strike to prevent it, and when it comes they are hampered by confused national responsibilities and by the complicated concept of minimum force—' The Baroness broke off. 'But you know all this! You have written in depth of the same subject.'

'It's interesting to hear it repeated.'

'I will come soon enough to the interesting part – but we are almost back at the house.'

'Come,' Peter told her, and led her past the stables to the swimming pool pavilion. The surface of the heated pool steamed softly, and lush tropical plants were in odd contrast to the wintry scene beyond the glass walls.

They sat side by side on a swing seat, close enough to be able to talk in subdued tones, but the intense mood was broken for the moment. She took off her hat, scarf and jacket, and tossed them onto the cane chair opposite, and she sighed as she settled back against the cushions.

'I understand from Sir Steven that he wants you to go into the bank.' She slanted her eyes at him. 'It must be difficult to be so sought after.'

'I don't think I have Steven's reverence for money.'

'It's a readily acquired taste, General Stride,' she assured him. 'One that can become an addiction.'

At that moment the children of both Stride brothers arrived in a storm of shouted repartee and laughter, which moderated only marginally when they realized that Peter and the Baroness were in the swing seat.

Steven's youngest son, bulging over the top of his costume with puppy-fat and with silver braces on his front teeth, rolled his eyes in their direction and in a stage whisper told Melissa-Jane, '*Je t'aime, ma chérie*, swoon! swoon!' His accent was frighteningly bad and he received a hissed rebuke and a shove in the small of the back that hurled him into the deep end of the pool.

The Baroness smiled. 'Your daughter is very protective—' she turned slightly to examine Peter's face again ' – or is it merely jealousy?' Without waiting for an answer she went straight on to ask another question. Against the background of shouts and splashes, Peter thought he had misheard.

'What did you say?' he asked carefully, certain that his expression had revealed nothing, and she repeated.

'Does the name Caliph mean anything to you?'

He frowned slightly, pretending to consider, while his memory darted back to the terrible micro-seconds of mortal combat, of smoke and flame and gunfire and a dark-haired girl in a scarlet shirt screaming:

'Don't kill us! Caliph said we would not die. Caliph—' And his own bullets stopping the rest of it, smashing into the open mouth. The word had haunted him since then, and he had tried a thousand variations, looking for sense and meaning, considering the possibility that he had misheard. Now he knew he had not.

'Caliph?' he asked, not knowing why he was going to deny it, merely because it seemed vital that he keep something in reserve, that he were not carried headlong on the torrent of this woman's presence and personality. 'It's a Mohammedan title – I think it literally means the heir of Mohammed, the successor to the prophet.'

'Yes.' She nodded impatiently. 'It's the title of a civil and religious leader – but have you heard it used as a code name?'

'No. I am sorry, I have not. What is the significance?'

'I am not sure, even my own sources are obscure and confused.' She sighed, and they watched Melissa-Jane in silence. The child had been waiting for Peter's attention, and when she had it she ran lightly out along the spring-board and launched herself, light as a swallow in flight, into a clean one-and-a-half somersault, entering the water with hardly a ripple and surfacing immediately with fine pale hair slick down across her face, immediately looking again for Peter's approval.

'She's a lovely child,' said the Baroness. 'I have no

children. Aaron wanted a son – but there was not one.' And there was real sorrow in the green eyes that she masked quickly. Across the pool Melissa-Jane climbed from the pool and quickly draped a towel around her shoulders, covering her bosom which was now large enough and yet so novel as to provide her with a constant source of embarrassment and shy pride.

'Caliph,' Peter reminded the Baroness quietly, and she turned back to him.

'I first heard the name two years ago, in circumstances I shall never forget—' She hesitated. 'May I take it that you are fully aware of the circumstances surrounding my husband's kidnapping and murder? I do not wish to repeat the whole harrowing story – unless it is necessary.'

'I know it,' Peter assured her.

'You know that I delivered the ransom, personally.'

'Yes.'

'The rendezvous was a deserted airfield near the East German border. They were waiting with a light twin-engined aircraft, a Russian-built reconnaissance machine with its markings sprayed over—' Peter remembered the meticulous planning and the special equipment used in the hijacking of 070. It all tallied. ' – There were four men, masked. They spoke Russian, or rather two of them spoke Russian. The other two never spoke at all. It was bad Russian—' Peter remembered now that the Baroness spoke Russian and five other languages. She had a Middle European background. Peter wished he had studied her intelligence file more thoroughly. Her father has escaped with her from her native Poland when she was a small child. ' – Almost certainly, the aircraft and the Russian were intended to cover their real identity,' she mused. 'I was with them for some little time. I had forty-five million Swiss francs to deliver and even in notes of large denomination it was a bulky and heavy cargo to load aboard the aircraft After the first few minutes, when they realized that I had no police escort, they relaxed and joked amongst themselves as they worked at loading the money. The word "Caliph" was used in the English version, in a Russian exchange that roughly translates as "He was right again" and the reply "Caliph is always right". Perhaps the use of the English word made me remember it so clearly—' She stopped again, grief naked and bleak in the green eyes.

'You told the police?' Peter asked gently, and she shook her head.

'No. I don't know why not. They had been so ineffectual up to that time. I was very angry and sad and confused. Perhaps even then I had already decided that I would hunt them myself – and this was all I had.'

'That was the only time you heard the name?' he asked, and she did not reply immediately. They watched the children at play – and it seemed fantasy to be discussing the source of evil in such surroundings, against a background of laughter and innocent high spirits.

When the Baroness answered, she seemed to have changed direction completely.

'There had been that hiatus in international terrorism. The Americans seemed to have beaten the hijacking problem with their Cuban agreement and the rigorous airport searches. Your own successful campaign against the Provisional wing of the IRA in this country, the Entebbe raid and the German action at Mogadishu were all hailed as breakthrough victories. Everybody was beginning to congratulate themselves that it was beaten. The Arabs were too busy with the war in the Lebanon and with inter-group rivalries It had been a passing thing ' She shook her head again. 'But terrorism is a growth industry – the risks are less than those of financing a major movie. There is a proven sixty-seven per cent chance of success, the capital outlay is minimal, with outrageous profits in cash and publicity, with instant results – and potential power not even calculable. Even in the event of total failure, there is still a better than fifty per cent survival rate for the participants.' She smiled again, but now there was no joy and no warmth in it. 'Any businessman will tell you it's better than the commodity markets.'

'The only thing against it is that the business is run by amateurs,' Peter said, 'or by professionals blinded by hatred or crippled by parochial interests and limited goals.'

And now she turned to him, wriggling around in the canvas swing seat, curling those long legs up under her in that double-jointed woman's manner, impossible for a man.

'You are ahead of me, Peter.' She caught herself. 'I am sorry, but General Stride is too much to say, and I have the feeling I have known you so long.' The smile now was fleeting but warm. 'My name is Magda,' she went on simply. 'Will you use it?'

'Thank you, Magda.'

'Yes.' She picked up the thread of conversation again. 'The business is in the hands of amateurs – but it is too good to stay that way '

'Enter Caliph,' Peter guessed

'That is the whisper that I have heard; usually there is no name. Just that there was a meeting in Athens, or Amsterdam or East Berlin or Aden – only once have I heard the name Caliph again But if he exists already he must be one of the richest men in the world, and soon he will be the most powerful.'

'One man?' Peter asked.

'I do not know. Perhaps a group of men – perhaps even a government. Russia, Cuba, an Arab country? Who knows yet?'

'And the goals?'

'Money, firstly. Wealth to tackle the political objectives – and finally power, raw power.' Magda Altmann stopped herself, and made a self-deprecating gesture. 'This is guesswork again, my own guessing – based only on past performance. They have the wealth now, provided by OPEC and – myself amongst others. Now he or they have started on the political objectives, a soft target first. An African racist minority government unprotected by powerful allies. It should have succeeded. They should have won an entire nation – a mineral-rich nation – for the price of a dozen lives. Even had they failed to gain the main prize, the consolation prize was forty tons of pure gold. That's good business, Peter. It should have succeeded. It *had* succeeded. The Western nations actually put pressure on the victims, and forced them to accede to the demands – it was a trial run, and it worked perfectly, except for one man.'

'I am afraid,' said Peter softly, 'as afraid as I have ever been in my life.'

'Yes, I am also, Peter. I have been afraid ever since that terrible phone call on the night they took Aaron, and the more I learn the more afraid I become.'

'What happens next?'

'I do not know – but the name he has chosen has the hint of megalomania, perhaps a man with visions of godlike domination—' She spread her fine narrow hands and the diamond flashed white fire. ' – We cannot hope to fathom the mind of a man who could embark on such a course. Probably he believes that what he is doing is for the eventual good of mankind. Perhaps he wants to attack the rich by amassing vast wealth, to destroy the tyrant with universal tyranny, to free mankind by making it a slave to terror. Perhaps he seeks to right the wrongs of the world with evil and injustice.'

She touched his arm again, and this time the strength of those long fingers startled Peter. 'You have to help me find him, Peter I am going to put everything into the hunt, there will be no reservations, all the wealth and influence that I control will be at your disposal.'

'You choose me because you believe that I murdered a wounded woman prisoner?' Peter asked. 'Are those my credentials?' And she recoiled from him slightly, and stared at him with the slightly Mongolian slant of eyes, then her shoulders slumped slightly.

'All right, that is part of it, but only a small part of it. You know I have read what you have written, you must know that I have studied you very carefully. You are the best man available to me, and finally you have proved that your involvement is complete. I know that you have the strength and skill and ruthlessness to find Caliph and destroy him – before he destroys us and the world we know.'

Peter was looking inwards. He had believed that the beast had a thousand heads, and for each that was struck off a thousand more would grow – but now for the first time he imagined the full shape of the beast, it was still in ambush, not clear yet, but there was only a single head. Perhaps, after all, it was mortal.

'Will you help me, Peter?' she asked.

'You know I will,' he answered quietly. 'I do not have any choice.'

She flew in the brilliance of high sunlight reflected from snowfields of blazing white, jetting through her turns with flowing elegance, carving each turn with a crisp rush of flying snow, swaying across the fall line of the mountain in an intricate ballet of interlinked movement.

She wore a slim-fitting skin suit of pearly grey, trimmed in black at the shoulders and cuffs, she was shod with gleaming black Heierling snowbirds, and her skis were long, narrow, black Rossignol professionals.

Peter followed her, pressing hard not to lose too much ground, but his turns were solid Christies without the stylish fallback unweighting of the jet turn which gave her each time a fractional gain.

The dun he ran like a stag of ten
But the mare like a new roused fawn

Kipling might have been describing them, and she was a hundred yards ahead of him as they entered the forest.

The pathway was barred with the shadows of the pines, and sugary ice roared under his skis as he pushed the narrow corners dangerously fast. Always she was farther ahead, flickering like a silver-grey wraith on those long lean legs, her tight round buttocks balancing the narrow waist and swinging rhythmically into the turns, marvellous controlled broadsides where the icy roadway denied purchase, coming out fast and straight, leaning into the rush of the wind, and her faint sweet laughter came back to Peter as he chased. There is an expertise that must be learned in childhood, and he remembered then that she was Polish, would probably have skied before she was weaned, and suppressed the flare of resentment he always felt at being outclassed by another human being, particularly by the woman who was fast becoming his driving obsession.

He came round another steeply banked turn, with the sheer snow wall rising fifteen feet on his right hand and on his left the tops of the nearest pines at his own level, so steep the mountain fell away into the valley.

The ice warning signs flashed past, and there was a wooden bridge, its boards waxen, opalescent with greenish ice. He felt control go as he hit the polished iron-hard surface. The bridge crossed a deep sombre gorge, with a frozen waterfall skewered to the black mountain rock by its own cruel icicles, like crucifixion nails

To attempt to edge in, or to stem the thundering rush across the treacherous going, would have invited disaster, to lean back defensively would have brought him down instantly and piled him into the sturdy wooden guide rails. At the moment he was lined up for the narrow bridge Peter flung himself forward so that his shins socked into the pads of his boots, and in a swoop of terror and exhilaration he went through, and found that he was laughing aloud though his heart leaped against his ribs and his breathing matched the sound of the wind in his own ears.

She was waiting for him where the path debouched onto the lower slopes. She had pushed her goggles to the top of her head, and stripped off her gloves, both sticks planted in the snow beside her.

'You'll never know how much I needed that.' She had flown into Zurich that morning in her personal Lear jet. Peter had come in on the Swissair flight from Brussels, and they had motored up together. 'You know what I wish, Peter?'

'Tell me,' he invited.

'I wish that I could take a whole month, thirty glorious days, to do what I wish. To be ordinary, to be like other people and not feel a moment's guilt.'

He had seen her on only three occasions in the six weeks since their first meeting at Abbots Yew. Three too brief and, for Peter, unsatisfying meetings.

Once in his new office suite at the Narmco headquarters in Brussels, again at La Pierre Bénite, her country home outside Paris, but then there had been twenty other guests for dinner. The third time had been in the panelled and tastefully decorated cabin of her Lear jet on a flight between Brussels and London.

Though they had made little progress as yet in the hunt for Caliph, Peter was still exploring the avenues that had occurred to him and had cast a dozen lines, baited and hooked

During their third meeting Peter had discussed with her the need to restructure her personal safety arrangements. He had changed her former bodyguards, replacing them with operatives from a discreet agency in Switzerland which trained its own men The director of the agency was an old and trusted friend

They had come to this meeting now so that Peter might report back on his progress to Magda. But for a few hours the snow had seduced them both.

'There is still another two hours before the light goes.' Peter glanced across the valley at the village church. The gold hands of the clock showed a little after two o'clock. 'Do you want to run the Rheinhorn?'

She hesitated only a moment. 'The world will keep turning, I'm sure.' Her teeth were very white, but one of them was slightly crooked, a blemish that was oddly appealing as she smiled up at him. 'Certainly it will wait two hours.'

He had learned that she kept unbelievable hours, beginning her day's work when the rest of the world still slept, and still hard at it when the offices of Altmann Industries in Boulevard Capucine were deserted, except her own office suite on the top floor. Even during the drive up from Zurich she had gone through correspondence and dictated quietly to one of her secretaries. He knew that at the chalet across the valley her two secretaries would be waiting already, with a pile of telex flimsies for her consideration and the line held open for her replies

'There are better ways to die than working yourself to death.' He was suddenly out of patience with her single-mindedness, and she laughed easily with high colour in her cheeks and the sparkle of the last run in the green eyes.

'Yes, you are right, Peter I should have you near to keep reminding me of that.'

'That's the first bit of sense I've had from you in six weeks ' He was referring to her opposition to his plans for her security He had tried to persuade her to change established behaviour patterns, and though the smile was still on her lips, her eyes were deadly serious as she studied his face

'My husband left me a trust—' she seemed suddenly sad beneath the laughter ' – a duty that I must fulfil. One day I should like to explain that to you – but now we only have two hours.'

It was snowing lightly, and the sun had disappeared behind the mountains of rock and snow and cloud as they walked back through the village. The lights were burning in the richly laden shop windows and they were part of the gaily clad stream returning from the slopes, clumping along the frozen sidewalks in their clumsy ski boots, carrying skis and sticks over one shoulder and chattering with the lingering thrill of the high piste that even the lowering snow-filled dusk could not suppress.

'It feels good to be free of my wolves for a while.' Magda caught his arm as her snowbirds skidded on dirty ridged ice, and after she had regained her balance she left her gloved hand there.

Her wolves were the bodyguards that Peter had provided, the silent vigilant men who followed her either on foot or in a second car. They waited outside her offices while she worked, and others guarded the house while she slept.

That morning, however, she had told Peter, 'Today I have as a companion a gold medal Olympic pistol champion, I don't need my wolves.'

Narmco marketed its own version of the 9-mm parabellum pistol. It was called 'Cobra', and after a single morning in the underground range Peter had taken a liking to the weapon. It was lighter and flatter than the Walther he was accustomed to, easier to carry and conceal, and the single action mechanism saved a flicker of time with the first shot, for there was no need to cock the action. He had had no trouble obtaining a permit to carry one as a trade sample, although it was necessary to check it before every commercial flight, but it carried neatly in a quick-release shoulder holster.

He had felt theatrical and melodramatic at first, but with a little sober thought had convinced himself that to follow on Caliph's tracks unarmed was shortening the odds against himself.

Now it was becoming habit, and he was barely aware of the comforting shape and weight in his armpit, until Magda spoke.

'I am close to dying from thirst,' she went on, and they racked their skis and went into the jovial warmth and clouds of steam that billowed from one of the coffee shops that lined the main street.

They found a seat at a table already crowded with young people, and they ordered glasses of steaming hot *Glühwein*

Then the four-piece band thumped out a popular dance tune and their table companions swarmed onto the tiny dance floor.

Peter raised a challenging eyebrow at her and she asked with amusement, 'Have you ever danced in ski boots?'

'There has to be a first time for everything.'

She danced like she did everything else, with complete absorption, and her body was strong and hard and slim against his.

It was completely dark as they climbed the narrow track above the village and went in through the electronically controlled gate in the protective wall around the chalet.

It was somehow typical of her that she had avoided the fashionable resorts, and that externally the chalet seemed not much different from fifty others that huddled in the edge of the pine forest.

There was patent relief amongst her entourage at her return, and she seemed almost defiant at their concern as though she had just proved something to herself – but still she did not change from her sports clothes before disappearing into the office suite on the first floor with her two male secretaries. 'I work better with men,' she had explained to Peter once. As Peter dressed in slacks, blazer and silk roll-neck after a scalding shower, he could still hear the clatter of the telex machine from the floor below, and it was an hour later when she called him on the house telephone.

The entire top floor was her private domain and she was standing at the windows looking out over the snow-fuzzed lights of the valley as he entered.

She wore green slacks tucked in après-ski boots, and a blouse of the same colour, a perfect match for her eyes. The moment Peter entered, she pressed a concealed switch and the curtains slid silently closed, then she turned to him.

'A drink, Peter?' she asked.

'Not if we are going to talk.'

'We are going to talk,' she said positively, and indicated the soft squashy leather armchair across from the fireplace. She had resisted the traditional Swiss cuckoo-clock and knotty pine decor, and the carpeting was thick Wilton to match the curtains, the furniture low and comfortable but modern, sporty and good fun, the very best made to appear natural and unaffected, blending easily with the modern art on the walls and abstract sculpture in marble and grained wood.

She smiled suddenly at him. 'I had no idea that I had found myself a gifted Sales Director for Narmco – I really am impressed with what you have done in so short a time.'

'I had to establish a plausible cover—' Peter deprecated the compliment. 'And I used to be a soldier – the job interests me.'

'You English!' she told him with mock exasperation. 'Always so modest.' She did not seat herself but moved about the room; although never at rest, neither did she give the feeling of restlessness 'I am informed that there is to be a definite NATO testing of Kestrel – after almost two years of procrastination.'

Kestrel was Narmco's medium-range ground-to-ground infantry portable missile.

'I am further informed that the decision was made to test after you had met with some of your former colleagues.'

'The whole world runs on the old boy system—' Peter chuckled, ' – you should know that.'

'And you are on old boy terms with the Iranians?' She cocked her head at him.

'That was a small stroke of luck. Five years ago I was on a staff college course with their new military adviser.'

'Luck again.' She smiled. 'Isn't it strange that luck so often favours those who are clever and dedicated and who move faster than the pack?'

'I have had less luck in other directions,' Peter pointed out, and immediately there was no trace of laughter left upon her lips nor in the emerald eyes, but Peter went on. 'So far I have been unsuccessful with the contact we spoke about on our last meeting—'

They had discussed the possibility of access to the Atlas computer link, of requisitioning a printout on 'Caliph' from the Central Intelligence bank, if there was one programmed.

'As I explained, there was the one remote possibility of access, somebody who owed me a favour. He was of no help. He believes that if there is a "Caliph" listing, it's blocked and buzzed.' Which meant that any unauthorized requisition would sound an alarm in intelligence control. 'We'd trigger a Delta condition in Atlas if we put in a printout requisition.'

'You did not give him the name?' Magda asked sharply.

'No. No names, just a general discussion over dinner at Brooks's – but all the implications were there.'

'Do you have any further avenues – ?'

'I think so One more, but it's a last resort,' Peter said. 'Before we come to that, though, perhaps you can tell me if you have anything further from your sources '

'My sources—' Magda had never made more explicit descriptions, and Peter had instinctively known not to pry. There was a certain finality to the way she said it. 'My sources have been mostly negative. The seizure of the Netherlands Embassy in Bonn was unconnected with

Caliph. It was exactly what it purported to be – South Moluccan extremists. The hijackers of Cathay Airlines and Transit Airlines were both enthusiastic amateurs, as evidence the methods and the outcome—' She smiled drily and drifted back across the room to touch the Hundedwasser collage that hung on the side wall, rearranging the hang of the frame in an essentially feminine gesture. ' – There is only one recent act that has the style of Caliph '

'Prince Hassied Abdel Hayek?' Peter asked, and she turned to face him, thrusting out one hip with her hand upon it, the nails very red against the light-green cloth and the marquise cut diamond sparkling.

'What did you make of it?' she asked. The Prince had been shot dead, three bullets of .22 calibre in the back of the head while asleep in his rooms on the Cambridge campus. A nineteen-year-old grandson of King Khalid of Saudi Arabia, not one of the particular favourites of the king, a bespectacled scholarly youth who seemed content to remain outside the mainstream of palace power and politics. There had been no attempt at abduction, no sign of a struggle, no evidence of robbery – the young Prince had no close friends nor apparent enemies.

'It does not seem to have reason or motive,' Peter admitted. 'That's why I thought of Caliph.'

'The deviousness of Caliph—' Magda turned away and her haunches rippled under the elastic of her green slacks. There was no ruck line of panties, and her buttocks were perfect spheres, with the shadow of the deep cleft between them showing through the thin material. Peter watched her legs as she paced, realizing for the first time that her feet were long and narrow as her hands, fine and graceful bones in perfect proportion.

'If I told you that Saudi Arabia last week made clear to the other members of OPEC that, far from supporting a rise in the price of crude, she will press for a *five per cent* reduction in the world price at the organization's next meeting—'

Peter straightened up in his chair slowly and Magda went on softly ' – and that she will be supported by Iran in her proposal. If I told you that, what would you think?'

'The King has other, more favoured grandchildren – grandsons and sons as well, brothers, nephews—'

'Seven hundred of them,' Magda agreed, and then went on musing. 'The Shah of Iran has children that he divorced one wife to obtain—'

'The Shah paid his hundred-million-dollar ransom promptly to save his oil minister during the Carlos abduction – what would he do for his own children?' Peter stood up now, unable to stay still with the itch of new ideas.

'And the King of Saudi-Arabia is an Arab. You know how Mohammedans are about sons and grandsons.' Magda came to stand so close to him that he could feel the warmth of her flesh through the narrow space between them, and her perfume subtly underlined the ripe sweet woman's smell of her body, disturbing him, but strangely heightening his awareness. 'Perhaps King Khalid has also been reminded of his own mortality.'

'All right.' Peter hunched his shoulders and frowned in concentration. 'What are we suggesting? That Caliph has struck another easy formula? Two men who control the economic destiny of the Western world? Two men who make decisions at the personal level, who are not answerable to cabinets or causes or governments?'

'Men who are therefore vulnerable to personal terrorism, who have records of appeasement to terrorist pressure.' Magda paused 'The old truths are still good. "Uneasy lies the head that wears a crown." Both the Shah and the King will be no strangers to the fear of the assassin's blade. They will understand the law of the knife, because they have always lived by it.'

'Hell, you have to admire it.' Peter shook his head. 'There is no need to take and hold hostages. No need for exposure. You kill one obscure member of a large royal family, and you promise that there will be others, each one more important, closer to the head.'

'Both families have a high profile. The Shah loves the bright lights. He's up at Gstaad right this moment. It would need only a sniper up in the treeline to pick one of his children. His sister Shams is in Mauritius now. As for the King's family – any time you want to drop into the Dorchester you'll find one of his sons or grandsons sipping coffee in the public lounge. They are soft targets, and there are plenty of them. You might even have to kill two princelings or three – but secretly the world will feel that they had it coming to them anyway. There will not be oceans wept for men who have themselves held the world to ransom.'

Peter's frown smoothed away, and he grinned wryly. 'Not only do you have to admire it – you've got to have a sneaking sympathy for the object. A dead brake to the crippling inflation of the world, a slowing of disruptive imbalance in trade.'

And Magda's expression was fierce as he had never seen it before. 'That is the trap, Peter. To see the end only, and to harden yourself to the means. That was the trap that Caliph set with the taking of 070. His demands coincided with those of the Western powers, and they placed additional pressure on the victim. Now, if we are correct and Caliph is pressuring the oil dictators for a moderation of their demands, how much more support can he expect from the Western capitalist powers?'

'You are a capitalist,' Peter pointed out. 'If Caliph succeeds you will be one of the first to benefit.'

'I'm a capitalist, yes. But before that I am a human being, and a thinking human being. Do you really believe that if

Caliph succeeds now that this will be the last we hear of him?'

'Of course not.' Peter spread his hands in resignation. 'Always his demands will be harsher – with each success he must become bolder.'

'I think we can have that drink now,' Magda said softly, and turned away from him. The black onyx top of the coffee table slid aside at her touch to reveal the array of bottles and glasses beneath.

'Whisky, isn't it?' she asked, and poured a single malt Glenlivet into one of the cut glass tumblers. As she handed it to him their fingers touched and he was surprised at how cool and dry her skin felt.

She poured half a flute glass of white wine and filled it with Perrier water. As she replaced the wine bottle in the ice bucket, Peter saw the label. It was Le Montrachet 1969. Probably the greatest white wine in the world, and Peter had to protest at the way in which she had desecrated it.

'Alexander Dumas said it should be drunk only on bended knee and with head reverently bared—'

' – He forgot the mineral water,' Magda purred with throaty laughter. 'Anyway you can't trust a man who employed other people to write his books for him.' She lifted the adulterated wine to him 'Long ago I decided to live my life on my own terms. To hell with Messrs Dumas and Caliph.'

'Shall we drink to that?' Peter asked, and they watched each other over the rims. The level of Magda's glass had not lowered and she set the glass aside, moving across to adjust the bowl of hothouse tulips in the chunky free-form crystal bowl.

'If we are right. If this is Caliph at work – then it disturbs the instinctive picture I had formed of him.' Peter broke the silence.

'How?' she asked without looking up from the flowers.

'Caliph – it's an Arabic name. He is attacking the leader of the Arab world.'

'The deviousness of Caliph. Was the name deliberately chosen to confuse the hunters – or perhaps there are other demands apart from the oil price – perhaps pressure is also being put on Khalid for closer support of the Palestinians, or one of the other extremist Arab movements. We do not know what else Caliph wants from Saudi Arabia.'

'But then, the oil price. It is Western orientated. Somehow it has always been accepted that terrorism is a tool of the far left,' Peter pointed out, shaking his head. 'The hijacking of 070 – even the kidnapping of your husband – were both aimed against the capitalist society.'

'He kidnapped Aaron for the money, and killed him to protect his identity. The attack on the South African Government, the attack on the oil cartel, the choice of name, all point to a person with god-like pretensions.' Magda broke the head off one of the tulips with an abrupt, angry gesture, and crushed it in her fist. She let the petals fall into the deep onyx ashtray. 'I feel so helpless, Peter. We seem to be going round in futile circles.' She came back to him as he stood by the curtained windows. 'You said earlier that there was one sure way to flush out Caliph?'

'Yes,' Peter nodded.

'Can you tell me?'

'There was an old trick of the Indian shikari. When he got tired of following the tiger in thick jungle without a sight of the beast, he used to stake out a goat and wait for the tiger to come to it '

'A goat?'

'My Zodiacal sign is Capricorn – the goat.' Peter smiled slightly.

'I don't understand.'

'If I were to put the word out that I was hunting Caliph—' He smiled again. 'Caliph knows me. The hijacker spoke my name, clearly, unmistakenly. She had been warned. So I believe that Caliph would take me seriously enough to consider it necessary to come after me.'

He saw the lingering colour drain dramatically from her high cheeks, and the sudden shadow in the depths of her eyes.

'Peter—'

'That's the only way I'm going to get close to him.'

'Peter—' She placed her hand on his forearm, but then she could not go on. Instead she stared at him silently and her eyes were green and dark and unfathomable. He saw there was a pulse that throbbed softly in her long graceful neck, just below the ear. Her lips parted, as though she were about to speak. They were delicately sculptured lips, and she touched them with the pink tip of her tongue, leaving them moist and soft and somehow defenceless. She closed them, without speaking, but the pressure of her fingers on his arm increased, and the carriage of her whole body altered. Her back arched slightly so her lower body swayed towards him and her chin lifted slightly.

'I have been so lonely,' she whispered. 'So lonely, for so very long. I only realized how lonely today – while I was with you '

Peter felt a choking sensation in his throat, and the prickle of blood behind his eyes.

'I don't want to be lonely again, ever.'

She had let her hair come down. It was very thick and long. It fell in a straight rippling curtain shot through with glowing lights, to her waist.

She had parted it in the centre; a thin straight line of white scalp divided the great black wings and they framed her face, making it appear pale and childlike with eyes too large and vulnerable, and as she came towards where Peter lay the glossy sheets of hair slid silently across the brocade of her gown.

The hem of the gown swept the carpet, and her bare toes peeped out from under it with each step. Narrow finely boned feet, and the nails were trimmed and painted with a colourless lacquer. The sleeves of the gown were wide as batwings and lined internally with satin, the collar buttoned up in a high Chinese style.

Beside the bed she stopped and her courage and poise seemed to desert her, her shoulders slumped a little and she clasped the long narrow fingers before her in a defensive gesture.

'Peter, I don't think I am going to be very good at this.' The throaty whisper was barely audible, and her lips trembled with the strength of her appeal. 'And I want so badly to be good.'

Silently he reached out one hand towards her, palm upwards. The bedclothes covered him to the waist, but his chest and arms were bare, lightly tanned and patterned with dark wiry body hair. As he reached for her the muscle bunched and expanded beneath the skin, and she saw that there was no surplus flesh on his waist, nor on his shoulders and upper arms. He looked lean and hard and tempered, yet supple as the lash of a bullwhip, and she did not respond immediately to the invitation, for his masculinity was overpowering.

He folded back the thick down-filled duvet between them, and the sheet was crisp and smoothly ironed in the low rosy light.

'Come,' he ordered gently, but she turned away and with her back to him she undid the buttons of the embroidered gown, beginning at the throat and working downwards.

She slipped the gown from her shoulders, and held it for a moment in the crook of her elbows. The smooth pale flesh gleamed through the fall of dark hair, and she seemed to steel herself like a diver bracing for the plunge into unknown depths.

She let the gown drop with a rustling slide down the full length of her body, and it lay around her ankles in a shallow puddle of peacock colours.

She heard him gasp aloud, and she threw the hair back from her shoulders with a toss of the long, swan-white neck. The hair hung impenetrably to the small of her back; just above the deep cleft of her lower body it ended in a clean line and her buttocks were round and neat and without blemish, but even as he stared the marble smoothness puckered into a fine rash of gooseflesh as though his eyes had physically caressed her, and she had responded with an appealingly natural awareness that proved how her every sense must be aroused and tingling. At the knowledge Peter felt his heart squeezed. He wanted to rush to her and sweep her into his arms, but instinct warned him that she must close the last gap herself, and he lay quietly propped on one elbow, feeling the deep ache of wanting spread through his entire body.

She stooped to pick up the gown, and for a moment the long legs were at an awkward coltish angle to each other and the spheres of her buttocks altered shape. No longer perfectly symmetrical, but parted slightly, and in the creamy niche they formed with her thighs there was an instant's heart-stopping glimpse of a single dense tight curl of hair and the light from beyond tipped the curl with glowing reddish highlights, then she had straightened again, once more lithe and tall, and she dropped the robe across the low couch and in the same movement turned back to face Peter.

He gasped again and his sense of continuity began to break up into a mosaic of distinct, seemingly unconnected images and sensations.

Her breasts were tiny as those of a pubescent child, but

the nipples were startlingly prominent, the colour and texture of ripening young berries, dark wine-red, already fully erect and hard as pebbles.

The pale plain of her belly, with the deep pit of the navel at its centre, that ended at last on the plump darkly furred mound pressed into the deep wedge between her thighs, like a small frightened living creature crouching from the stoop of the falcon.

The feel of her face pressed to his chest, and the tickle of her quick breath stirring his body hair, the almost painful grip of slim powerful arms locked with desperate strength around his waist.

The taste of her mouth as her lips parted slowly, softly, to his and the uncertain flutter of her tongue becoming bolder, velvety on top and slick and slippery on the underside.

The sound of her breathing changing to a deep sonorous pulse in his ears, seeming to keep perfect time with his own.

The smell of her breath, heavy with the aromatic musk of her arousal, and blending with the orangy fragrance of her perfume and the ripe woman smell of her body.

And always the feel of her – the warmth and the softness, the hardness of toned muscle and the running ripple of long dark hair about his face and down his body, the crisp electric rasp of tight, tense curls parting to unbearable heat and going on for ever to depths that seemed to reach beyond the frontier of reality and reason

And then later the stillness of complete peace that reached out from the centre where she lay against his heart and seemed to spread to the farthest corners of his soul.

'I knew that I was lonely,' she whispered. 'But I did not realize just how terribly deeply.' And she held him as though she would never relinquish her grip.

Magda woke him in the cold utter darkness three hours before dawn, and it was still dark when they left the chalet. The headlights of the following Mercedes that carried her wolves swept the interior of their saloon through each bend in the steep twisting road down from the mountains.

On take-off from Zurich Magda was in the Lear jet's left-hand seat, flying as pilot-in-command, and she handled the powerful machine with the sedate lack of ostentation which marks the truly competent aviator. Her personal pilot, a grizzled and taciturn Frenchman, who was flying now as her co-pilot, evidently held her skill in high regard and watched over her with an almost fatherly pride and approval as she cleared Zurich controlled airspace and levelled out at cruise altitude for Paris Orly before she left him to monitor the auto-pilot and came back to the main cabin. Though she sat beside Peter in the black calfskin armchairs, her manner was unchanged from the way it had been during their last flight together in this machine – reserved and polite – so that he found it difficult to believe the wonders they had explored together the previous night.

She worked with the two dark-suited secretaries opposite her, speaking her fluent rippling French with the same enchanting trace of accent that marked her English. In the short time since he had joined Narmco, Peter had been forced to make a crash revision of his own French. Now once again he could manage, if not with éclat, at least with competence, in technical and financial discussion. Once or twice Magda turned to him for comment or opinion, and her gaze was serious and remote, seeming as impersonal and efficient as an electronic computer – and Peter understood that they were to make no show of their new relationship before employees.

Immediately she proved him wrong, for her co-pilot called her over the cabin speaker.

'We will join the Orly circuit in four minutes, Baroness.'

And she turned easily and naturally and kissed Peter's cheek, still speaking French.

'Pardon me, *chéri*. I will make the landing. I need the flying time in my logbook.'

She greased the sleek swift aircraft onto the runway as though she was spreading butter on hot toast. The co-pilot had radioed ahead so that when she parked in the private hangar there were a uniformed immigration *policier* and a *douanier* already waiting.

As they came aboard, they saluted her respectfully and then barely glanced at her red diplomatic passport. They took a little longer with Peter's blue and gold British passport, and Magda murmured to Peter with a trace of a smile.

'I must get you a little red book. It's so much easier.' Then to the officials. 'It is a cold morning, gentlemen, I hope you will take a glass.' And her white-jacketed steward was hovering already. They left the two Frenchmen removing their kepis and pistol belts, settling down comfortably in the leather armchairs to make a leisurely selection of the cigars and cognac that the steward had produced for their approval.

There were three cars waiting for them, parked in the back of the hangar with drivers and guards Peter's lip curled as he saw the Maserati.

'I told you not to drive that thing,' he said gruffly. 'It's like having your name in neon lights.'

They had argued about this vehicle while Peter was reorganizing her personal security, for the Maserati was an electric silver-grey, one of her favourite colours, a shimmering dart of metal. She swayed against him with that husky little chuckle of hers.

'Oh, that is so very nice to have a man being masterful again. It makes me feel like a woman.'

'I have other ways of making you feel like that.'

'I know,' she agreed, with a wicked flash of green eyes.

'And I like those even better, but not now – please! What in the world would my staff think!' Then seriously, 'You take the Maserati, I ordered it for you, anyway. Somebody may as well enjoy it. And please do not be late this evening. I have especially made it free for us. Try and be at La Pierre Bénite by eight o'clock – will you please?'

By the time Peter had to slow for the traffic along the Pont Neuilly entrance to Paris, he had accustomed himself to the surging power and acceleration of the Maserati, and, as she had suggested, he was enjoying himself. Even in the mad Parisian traffic he used the slick gear box to knife through the merest suspicion of an opening, bulling out of trouble or overtaking with the omnipotent sense of power that control of the magnificent machine bestowed upon its driver.

He knew then why Magda loved it so dearly, and when he parked it at last in the underground garage on the Champs-Elysées side of Concorde he grinned at himself in the mirror.

'Bloody cowboy!' he said, and glanced at his Rolex. He had an hour before his first appointment, and as a sudden thought unclipped the holster of the Cobra and, with the pistol still in it, locked it in the glove compartment of the Maserati. He grinned again as he pondered the inadvisability of marching into French Naval Headquarters armed to the teeth.

The drizzle had cleared, and the chestnut trees in the Elysèe gardens were popping their first green buds as he came out into Concorde. He used one of the call boxes in the Concorde Metro station to make a call to the British Embassy. He spoke to the Military Attaché for two minutes, and when he hung up he knew the ball was probably already in play. If Caliph had penetrated the Atlas Command deeply enough to know him personally as the commander of Thor – then it would not be too long before he knew that the former commander had picked up the spoor. The

Military Attaché at the Paris Embassy had other more clandestine duties than kissing the ladies' hands at diplomatic cocktail parties.

Peter reached the main gates of the Marine Headquarters on the corner of the rue Royale with a few minutes to spare, but already there was a secretary waiting for him below the billowing Tricolour. He smoothed Peter's way past the sentries, and led him to the armaments committee room on the third floor overlooking a misty grey view of the Seine and the gilded arches of the Pont Neuf. Two of Peter's assistants from Narmco were there ahead of him with their briefcases unpacked and the contents spread upon the polished walnut table.

The French Flag captain had been in Brussels, and on one unforgettable evening he had conducted Peter on a magic carpet tour of the brothels of that city. He greeted him now with cries of Gallic pleasure and addressed him as 'tu' and 'toi' – which all boded very well for the meeting ahead.

At noon precisely, the French captain moved that the meeting adjourn across the street to a private room on the first floor of Maxim's, blissful in the certainty that Narmco would pick up the tab, if they were really serious about selling the Kestrel rocket motors to the French Navy.

It required all Peter's tact not to make it obvious that he was taking less than his share of the Clos de Vougeot or of the Rémy Martin, and more than once he found that he had missed part of the discussion which was being conducted at a steadily increasing volume. He found that he was thinking of emerald eyes and small pert bosoms.

From Maxim's back to the Ministry of Marine, and later it required another major act of diplomacy on Peter's part when the captain smoothed his moustache and cocked a knowing eye at Peter. 'There is a charming little club, very close and wonderfully friendly—'

By six o'clock Peter had disentangled himself from the

Frenchman's company, with protestations of friendship and promises to meet again in ten days' time. An hour later Peter left his two sales assistants at the Hôtel Meurice after a quick but thorough summation of the day's achievements. They were, all three, agreed that it was a beginning but a long, long road lay ahead to the ending.

He walked back along Rivoli; despite the frowsiness of a long day of endless talk and the necessity for quick thinking in a language which was still strange on the tongue, despite a slight ache behind the eyes from the wine and cognac and despite the taste of cigar and cigarette smoke he had breathed, he was buoyed by a tingling sense of anticipation, for Magda was waiting, and he stepped out briskly.

As he paused for traffic lights, he caught a glimpse of his own reflection in a shop window. He was smiling without realizing it.

While he waited on the ramp of the parking garage for his turn to pay and enter the traffic stream, with the Maserati engine whispering impatiently, he glanced in the rear view mirror. He had acquired the habit long ago when one of the captured Provo death lists had begun with his name; since then he had learned to look over his shoulder.

He noticed the Citroën two back in the line of vehicles because the windshield was cracked and there was a scrape which had dented the mudguard and exposed a bright strip of bare metal.

He noticed the same black Citroën still two back as he waited for pedestrian lights in the Champs-Elysées, and when he ducked his head slightly to try and get a look at the driver, the headlights switched on as though to frustrate him and at that moment the lights changed and he had to drive on.

Going around the Étoile, the Citroën had fallen back four places in the grey drizzling dusk of early autumn, but he spotted it once again when he was halfway down the Avenue de la Grande Armée, for by now he was actively searching for it. This time it changed lanes and slipped off the main thoroughfare to the left. It was immediately lost in the maze of side streets and Peter should have been able to forget it and concentrate on the pleasure of controlling the Maserati, but there lingered a sense of foreboding and even after he had shot the complicated junction of roads that got him onto the periphery route and eventually out on the road to Versailles and Chartres, he found himself changing lanes and speed while he scanned the road behind in the mirror.

Only when he left Versailles and was on the Rambouillet road did he have a clear view back a mile down the straight avenue of plane trees, and he was certain there was no other vehicle on the road. He relaxed completely and began to prepare himself for the final turn off that would bring him at last to La Pierre Bénite.

The shiny wet black python of road uncoiled ahead of him and then humped abruptly. Peter came over the rise at 150 kilometres an hour and instantly started to dance lightly on brake and clutch, avoiding the temptation of tramping down hard and losing adhesion on the slippery uneven tarmac. Ahead of him there was a gendarme in a shiny white plastic cape, wet with rain, brandishing a torch with a red lens; there were reflective warning triangles bright as rubies, a Peugeot in the ditch beside the road with headlights glaring at the sky, a dark blue police Kombi van half blocking the road, and in the stage lit by the Kombi's headlights two bodies were laid out neatly, and all of it hazed by the soft insistent mantle of falling rain – a typical roadside accident scene.

Peter had the Maserati well in hand, bringing her neatly down through the gears to a crawl, and as he was lowering the side window, the electric motor whining softly and the icy gust of night air into the heated interior, the gendarme gestured with the flashlight for him to pull over into the narrow gap between hedge and the parked Kombi, and at that moment the unexpected movement caught Peter's eye. It was one of the bodies lying in the roadway under the headlights. The movement was the slight arch of the back that a man makes before rising from the prone position.

Peter watched him lift his arm, not more than a few inches, but it was just enough for Peter to realize he had been holding an object concealed down the outside of his thigh, and even in the rain and the night Peter's trained eye recognized the perforated air-cooled sleeve enclosing the short barrel of a fold-down machine pistol.

Instantly his brain was racing so that everything about him seemed to be taking place in dreamy slow motion.

The Maserati! he thought. They're after Magda.

The gendarme was coming round to the driver's side of the Maserati, and he had his right hand under the white plastic cape, at the level of his pistol belt.

Peter went flat on the gas pedal, and the Maserati bellowed like a bull buffalo shot through the heart. The rear wheels broke from the wet surface, and with a light touch Peter encouraged the huge silver machine to swing like a scythe at the gendarme. It should have cut him down, but he was too quick. As he dived for the hedge, Peter saw that he had brought the pistol out from under his cape but was too busy at that moment to use it.

The side of the Maserati touched the hedge with a fluttering rustle of foliage, and Peter lifted his right foot, caught the enraged charge of the machine and swung her the other way. The moment she was lined up he hit the gas again, and the Maserati howled. This time she burned blue rubber smoke off her rear wheels.

There was a driver at the wheel of the blue police Kombi, and he tried to pull across to block the road completely, but he was not fast enough.

The two vehicles touched, with a crackle and scream of metal that jarred Peter's teeth, but what concerned him was that the two bodies in the headlights were no longer flat.

The nearest was on one knee and he was swinging the short stubby machine pistol – it looked like a Stirling or the new Sidewinder, but he was using the fold-down wire butt, wasting vital fractions of a second to get the weapon to his shoulder. He was also blocking the field of fire of the man who crouched behind him with another machine pistol pinned to his hip, pointing with index finger and forearm, ready to trigger with his second finger – 'That's the way it should be done.' Peter recognized professional skill, and his brain was running so swiftly that he had time to applaud it.

The Maserati cannoned off the police Kombi, and Peter lifted his right foot to take traction off the rear wheels, and spun the wheel the hard lock to the right. The Maserati swung her tail with a screech of rubber and went into a left side slide towards the two figures in the road, and Peter ducked down below the level of the door. He had deliberately induced the left-hand slide, so that he had some little protection from the engine compartment and bodywork.

As he ducked he heard the familiar sound, like a giant ripping heavyweight canvas, an automatic weapon throwing bullets at a cyclic rate of almost two thousand rounds a minute, and the bullets tore into the side of the Maserati, beating in the metal with an ear-numbing clangor, while glass exploded in upon Peter like the glittering spray as a storm-driven wave strikes a rock. Glass chips pelted across his back, and stung his cheek and the back of his neck. They sparkled like a diamond tiara in his hair.

Whoever was doing the shooting had certainly emptied the magazine in those few seconds, and now Peter bobbed up in his seat, slitting his eyes against the cloud of glass splinters. He saw a looming nightmare of dark hedges and spun the wheel back to hold the Maserati. She swayed to the limits of her equilibrium and Peter had a glimpse of the two gunmen in the road rolling frantically into the half-filled ditch, but at that moment his offrear wheel hit the lip and he was slammed up short against his safety belt with a force that drove the air from his lungs, and the Maserati reared like a stallion smelling the mare and tail-walked, swinging in short vicious surges back and forth across the road, as he desperately fought for control with gear and brake and wheel. He must have spun full circle, Peter realized, for there was a giddy dazzle of light beams and of running and rolling figures, everything hazy and indistinct in the rain, then the open road ahead again, and he sent the car at it with a great howling lunge, at the same moment glancing up at his mirror.

In the headlights he saw the burned blue clouds of smoke and steam thrown up by his own tyres, and through it the figure of the second gunman obscured from the waist by the ditch. He had the machine pistol at his waist, and the muzzle flash bloomed about him.

Peter heard the first burst hit the Maserati and he could not duck again, for there was a bend ahead in the rain, coming up at dazzling speed and he clenched his jaws waiting for it.

The next burst hit the car, like the sound of hail on a tin roof, and he felt the rude tugging, numbing jerk in his upper body.

'Tagged!' he realized. There was no mistaking it, he had been hit before. The first time when he led a patrol into an EOKA ambush a very long time ago, and at the same moment he was evaluating the hit calmly finding he still had use of both hands and all his senses. Either it was a ricochet, or the bullet had spent most of its force in penetrating the rear windshield and seat back.

The Maserati tracked neatly into the bend, and only then he felt the engine surge and falter. Almost immediately the sharp stink of gasoline filled the cab of the Maserati.

'Fuel line,' he told himself, and there was the warm, uncomfortable spread of his own blood down his back and side, and he placed his wound low in the left shoulder. If it had penetrated it would be a lung hit, and he waited for the coppery salt taste of blood in his throat or the bubbling froth of escaping air in his chest cavity.

The engine beat checked again, surged and checked, as it starved for fuel. That first traversing burst of automatic fire must have ripped through the engine compartment, and Peter thought wryly that in the movies the Maserati would have immediately erupted in spectacular pyrotechnics like a miniature Vesuvius – though in reality it didn't happen like that, still gasoline from the severed lead would be spraying over plugs and points.

One last glance backwards, before the bend hid it and he saw three men running for the police van – three men and the driver, that was lousy odds. They would be after him immediately, and the crippled machine made a final brave leap forward that carried them five hundred yards more, and then it died.

Ahead of him, at the limits of the headlight beam, Peter saw the white gates of La Pierre Bénite. They had set the ambush at the point where they could screen out most extraneous traffic, and gather only the silver Maserati in their net.

He cast his mind back swiftly, recalling the lie of the land beyond the main gates of the estate. He had been here only once before, and it had been dark then also – but he had the soldier's eye for ground, and he remembered thick forest on both sides of the road, down to a low bridge over a narrow fast flowing stream with steep banks, a hard left hander and a climb up to the house. The house was half a mile beyond the gates, a long way to go with a body hit and at least four armed men following, and no guarantee that he would be safe there either.

The Maserati was coasting down the slight incline towards the gates, slowing as it ran out of momentum, and now there was the hot smell of oil and burning rubber. The paintwork of the engine hood began to blister and discolour. Peter switched off the ignition to stop the electric pump spraying more fuel onto the burning engine and he slipped his hand into his jacket. He found the wound where he had expected it – low and left. It was beginning to sting and his hand came away sticky and slick with blood. He wiped it on his thigh.

Behind him was the reflected glow of headlights in the rain, a halo of light growing stronger. At any moment they would come through the bend, and he opened the glove compartment.

The 9-mm Cobra gave some little comfort as he slipped it from its holster and thrust it into the front of his belt. There was no spare magazine and the breech was empty, a safety consideration which he now regretted, for it left him with only nine rounds in the magazine – one more might make a lot of difference.

Pretty little fingers of bright flame were waving at him from under the bonnet of the engine compartment, finding the hinge and joint, probing the ventilation slot on the top surface. Peter released his seat belt, held open the door and steered with his other hand for the verge. Here the road was banked and dropped away steeply.

He flicked the wheel back the opposite way and let the change of direction eject him neatly, throwing him clear, while the Maserati swerved back into the centre of the road and rolled away, slowing gradually.

He landed as though from a parachute drop, feet and knees together cushioning the impact and then rolled into it. Pain flared in his shoulder and he felt something tear. He came up in a crouch and ran doubled over for the edge of the woods, and the burning auto lit the dark trees with flickering orange light.

The fingers of his left hand felt swollen and numb as he pumped a round into the chamber of the Cobra, and at that moment the headlights beyond the bend flared with shocking brilliance and Peter had the illusion of being caught in front stage centre of the Palladium. He went down hard on his belly in the soft rain-sodden earth, but still his wound jarred and he felt the warm trickle of running blood under his shirt as he crawled desperately for the tree line.

The police van roared down the stretch of road. Peter flattened and pressed his face to the earth, and it smelled of leaf mould and fungus. The van roared past where he lay.

Three hundred yards down the road the Maserati had coasted to a halt, two wheels still on the road, the offside wheels over the verge so she stood at an abandoned angle, burning merrily.

The van pulled up at a respectful distance from it, aware of the danger of explosion, and a single figure, the gendarme in his plastic cape, ran forward, took one look into the cab and shouted something. The language sounded like French, but the flames were beginning to drum fiercely and the range too long to hear clearly.

The van locked into a U-turn, bumped over the verge, and then started back slowly. The two erstwhile accident victims, still carrying their machine pistols, running ahead like hounds on leash, one on each side of the road, heads down as they searched for signs in the soft shoulders of the road. The white-caped gendarme rode on the running-board of the van, calling encouragement to the hunters.

Peter was up again, doubled over, heading for the edge of the forest, and he ran into the barbed wire fence at full stretch. It brought him down heavily. He felt the slash of steel through the cloth of his trousers, and as he gathered himself again, he thought bitterly. One hundred and seventy guineas. The suit had been tailored in Savile Row. He crawled between the strands of armed wire, and there was a shout behind him. They had picked up his spoor, and as he dodged across the last few yards of open ground, another sharper, more jubilant shout.

They had spotted him in the towering firelight of the blazing Maserati, and again there was the tearing rip of automatic fire; but it was extreme range for the short barrel and low velocity ammunition. Peter heard passing shot like a whisper of bats' wings in the darkness above him and then he reached the first trees and ducked behind one of them.

He found he was breathing deeply, but with a good easy rhythm. The wound wasn't handicapping him yet, and he was into the cold reasoning rage that combat always instilled in him.

The range to the barbed wire fence was fifty metres, he judged, it was one of his best distances – International pistol standard out-of-hand with a 50-mm X circle – but there were no judges out here and he took a double-handed grip, and let them run into the fence just as he had done.

It brought two of them down, and the cries of angry distress were definitely in French; as they struggled to their feet again they were precisely back-lit by the flames, and the Cobra had a luminous foresight. Peter went for the mid-section of one of the machine gunners.

The 9-mm had a vicious whipcrack report, and punched into flesh and bone with 385 foot-pounds of energy. The strike of the bullet sounded like a watermelon hit with the full swing of a baseball bat. It lifted the man off his feet, and threw him backwards, and Peter swung onto the next target, but they were pros. Even though the fire from the edge of the woods had come as a complete surprise, they reacted instantly, and disappeared flat against the dark earth. They gave him no target, and Peter was too low on ammunition to throw down holding fire.

One of them fired a burst of automatic and it tore bark and wood and leaves along the edge of the trees. Peter fired at the muzzle flash only once as a warning and then ducked away and, keeping his head down to avoid lucky random fire, sprinted back into the woods.

They would be held up for two or three minutes by the fence and by the threat of coming under fire again, and Peter wanted to open some ground between them during that time.

The glow of the burning Maserati kept him well orientated and he moved quickly towards the river; however, before he had covered two yards he was starting to shiver uncontrollably. His two-piece city suit was soaked by the persistent drizzle and by the shower from each bush he brushed against. His shoes were light calf leather with leather soles and he had stepped in puddles of mud, and the knee-high grass was sodden. The cold struck through his clothing; he could feel his wound stiffening agonizingly and the first nauseating grip of shock tightened his belly, but he paused every fifty yards or so and listened for sounds of pursuit. Once he heard the sound of a car engine from the direction of the road, passing traffic probably, and he wondered what they would make of the abandoned police vehicle and the blazing Maserati. Even if it was reported to the real police, it would be all over before a patrol arrived and Peter discounted the chance of assistance from that quarter.

He was beginning now to be puzzled by the total lack of any sign of further pursuit, and he looked for and found a good stance in which to wait for it. There was a fallen oak tree and he wriggled in under the trunk, with a clear avenue of retreat, good cover and a low position from which any pursuer would be silhouetted against the sky glow of the burning Maserati. There were only three pursuers now, and seven cartridges in the Cobra. If it were not for the cold and the demoralizing ache through his upper body, he might have felt more confident, but the nagging terror of the hunted animal was still on him.

He waited five minutes, lying completely still, every sense tuned to its finest, the Cobra held out in extended double grip, ready to roll left or right and take the shot as it came. There was no sound but the drip and plop of the rain-soaked woods.

Another ten minutes passed before it occurred to him suddenly that the pursuers must now realize that the wrong quarry had sprung their trap. They were setting for Magda Altmann, and it must be clear to them that they had a man, and an armed one at that. He pondered their reaction. Almost certainly they would pull out now, or had already done so.

Instead of a lady worth twenty or thirty million dollars in ransom money, they must realize they had one of her employees, probably an armed bodyguard, who was driving the Maserati either as a decoy or merely as delivery driver. Yes, he decided, they would pull out – take their casualty and melt away, and Peter was sure they would leave no clues to their identity. He would have enjoyed the opportunity to question one of them, he thought, and grimaced at a new lance of pain in the shoulder.

He waited another ten minutes, utterly still and alert, controlling the spasms of cold and reaction that shook him, then he rose quietly and moved back towards the river. The Maserati must have burned out completely now for the sky was black again and he had to rely on his own sense of direction to keep orientated. Even though he knew he was alone, he paused every fifty yards to listen and look.

He heard the river at last. It was directly ahead and very close. He moved a little faster and almost walked off the bank in the dark. He squatted to rest for a moment, for the shoulder was very painful now, and the cold was draining his energy.

The prospect of wading the river was particularly uninviting. The rain had fallen without a break for days now, and the water sounded powerful and swift – it would certainly be icy cold, and probably shoulder deep rather than waist deep. The bridge must be only a few hundred yards downstream, and he stood up and moved along the bank.

Cold and pain can sap concentration very swiftly, and Peter had to make a conscious effort to keep himself alert, and he felt for every foothold before transferring his weight forward. He held the Cobra hanging at full stretch of his right arm, but ready for instant use, and he blinked his eyes clear of the fine drizzle of rain and the cold sweat of pain and fear.

Yet it was his sense of smell that alerted him. The rank smell of stale Turkish tobacco smoke on a human body, it was a smell that had always offended him, and now he picked it up instantly, even though it was just one faint whiff.

Peter froze in mid stride while his brain raced to adjust to the unexpected. He had almost convinced himself that he was alone.

Now he remembered the sound of a car engine on the main road, and he realized that men who had set up such an elaborate decoy – the faked motor accident, the police van and uniform – would certainly have taken the trouble to plot and study the ground between the ambush point and the victim's intended destination.

They would know better than Peter himself the layout of woods and river and bridge, and would have realized immediately they had taken their first casualty that futility of blundering pursuit through the dark. It was the smart thing to circle back and wait again, and they would choose the river bank or the bridge itself.

The only thing that troubled Peter was their persistence. They *must* know it was not Magda Altmann, and then even in this tense moment of discovery he remembered the Citroën that had followed him down the Champs-Elysées – nothing was what it appeared to be, and slowly he completed the step in which he had frozen.

He stood utterly still, poised every muscle and every nerve screwed to its finest pitch, but the night was black and the rush of the river covered all sound. Peter waited. The other man will always move if you wait long enough, and he waited with the patience of the stalking leopard, although the cold struck through to his bones and the rain slid down his cheeks and neck.

The man moved at last. The squelch of mud and the unmistakeable brush of undergrowth against cloth, then silence. He was very close, within ten feet, but there was no glimmer of light, and Peter shifted his weight carefully to face the direction of the sound. The old trick was to fire one shot at the sound and use the muzzle flash to light the target for a second shot which followed it in almost the same instant of time – but there were three of them and at ten feet that machine pistol could cut a man in half. Peter waited.

Then from upstream there was the sound of a car engine again, still faint but fast approaching. Immediately somebody whistled faintly, a rising double note in the night up towards the bridge, clearly some prearranged signal. A car door banged shut, much closer than the sound of the approaching engine and a starter whirred, another harsher engine roared into life, headlights flared through the rain, and Peter blinked as the whole scene ahead of him lit up.

A hundred yards ahead the bridge crossed the stream, the surface of the water was shiny and black as new-mined coal as it flowed about the supporting piles.

The blue van had parked on the threshold of the bridge, obviously to wait for Peter, but now it was pulling out, probably alarmed by the approach of the other more powerful engine from the direction of La Pierre Bénite. The driver was heading back towards the main road, the phoney gendarme scrambling alongside with his cape flapping as he tried to scramble through the open offside door – and out of the darkness, close to Peter, a voice cried out with alarm.

'*Attendez!*' The third man had no desire to be left by his companions, and he ran forward, abandoning all attempt at concealment. He had his back to Peter now, waving the machine pistol frantically, clearly outlined by the headlights of the van, and the range was under ten feet. It was a dead shot, and Peter went for it instinctively – and only at the very instant of trigger pressure that would have sent a 95 gram bullet between his shoulder blades was Peter able to check himself.

The man's back was turned and the range would make it murder; Peter's training should have cured him of such nice gentlemanly distinctions. However, what really held his trigger finger was the need to know. Peter had to know who these people were and who had sent them, and what they had been sent to do, who they were after.

Now that the man was being deserted, he had abandoned all stealth and was running as though he were chasing a bus, and Peter saw the chance to take him. Roles had been exchanged completely, and Peter darted forward, transferring the Cobra to his injured left hand.

He caught the man in four paces, keeping low to avoid his peripheral vision, and he whipped his good right arm around the throat, going for the half nelson and the spin that would disorientate the man before he slammed the barrel of the Cobra against the temple.

The man was quick as a cat, something warned him – perhaps the squelch of Peter's sodden shoes, and he ducked his chin onto his chest rolling his shoulders and beginning to turn back into the line of Peter's attack.

Peter missed the throat and caught him high, the crook of his elbow locking about the man's mouth, and the unexpected turn had thrown him slightly off balance. If he had had full use of his left arm, he could still have spun his victim, but in an intuitive flash he realized that he had lost the advantage, already the man was twisting his head out of the armlock, bulking his shoulders, and by the feel of him, Peter knew instantly that he was steel-hard with muscle.

The barrel of the machine pistol was short enough to enable him to press the muzzle into Peter's body just as soon as he completed his turn; it would tear Peter to pieces like a chain saw.

Peter changed his grip slightly, no longer opposing the man's turn, but throwing all his weight and the strength of his right arm into the same direction; they spun together like a pair of waltzing dancers, but Peter knew that the moment they broke apart the man would have the killing advantage again.

The river was his one chance, he realized that instinctively, and before the advantage passed back from him to his adversary, he hurled himself backwards, keeping his grip on the man's head.

They went out into black space, falling together in a short gut-swooping drop with Peter underneath. If there was rock below the steep bank of the river, he realized he would be crushed by the other's weight.

They struck the surface of the fast black water, and freezing cold struck like a club so that Peter almost released the air from his lungs as a reflex.

The shock of cold water seemed to have stunned the man in his grip momentarily, and Peter felt the whoosh of air from his lungs as he let go. Peter changed his grip, wedging his elbow under the chin, but not quite able to get at the throat – immediately the man began the wild panic-stricken struggles of somebody held under icy water with empty lungs.

He had lost the machine pistol, for he was tearing at Peter's arms and face with both hands as the water swirled them both end over end down towards the bridge.

Peter had to keep him from getting air, and as he held his own precious single breath, he tried to get on top and stay there.

Fingers hooked at his closed eyes, and then into his mouth as the man reached back desperately over his own shoulders. Peter opened his mouth slightly and the other man thrust his fingers deeply in, trying to tear at his tongue. Immediately Peter locked his teeth into the fingers with a force that made his jaw ache at the hinges, and his mouth filled with the sickening warm spurt of the other man's blood.

Fighting his own revulsion, he hung on desperately with teeth and arms. He had lost his own weapon, dropping it into the black flood from numbed and crippled fingers, and the man was fighting now with the animal strength of his starved lungs and mutilated fingers; every time he tried to yank his hand out of Peter's mouth the flesh tore audibly in Peter's ears and fresh blood made him gag and choke.

They came out on the surface and through streaming eyes Peter had one glimpse of the bridge looming above him. The blue van had disappeared, but Magda Altmann's Mercedes limousine was parked in the centre of the bridge, and in the wash of its headlights he recognized her two bodyguards. They were leaning far out over the guardrail, and Peter had a moment's dread that one of them might try a shot – then they were flung into the concrete piles of the bridge with such force that they lost the deathlock they had upon each other.

The back eddy beyond the bridge swung them in towards the bank. Gasping and swallowing with cold and exhaustion and pain, Peter fought for footing on gravel and rock. The machine-gunner had found bottom also and was stumbling desperately towards the bank. In the headlights of the limousine Peter saw Magda's two bodyguards racing back across the bridge to head him off.

Peter realized that he would not be able to catch the man before he reached the bank.

'Carl!' he screamed at the bodyguard who was leading. 'Stop him. Don't let him get away.'

The bodyguard vaulted over the guardrail, landing cat-like in complete balance, with the pistol double-handed at the level of his navel.

Below him the machine-gunner dragged himself waist deep towards the bank. It was only then that Peter realized what was going to happen.

'No!' He choked on blood and water. 'Take him alive. Don't kill him, Carl!'

The bodyguard had not heard, or had not understood. The muzzle blast seemed to join him and the wallowing figure in the river below him, a blood-orange rope of flame and thunderous explosion. The bullets smacked into the machine-gunner's chest and belly like an axeman cutting down a tree.

'No!' Peter yelled helplessly. 'Oh Jesus, no! No!'

Peter lunged forward and caught the corpse before it slid below the black water, and he dragged it by one arm to the bank. The bodyguards took it from him and hauled it up, the head lolling like an idiot's, and the blood diluted to pale pink in the reflected headlights.

Peter made three attempts to climb the bank, each time slithering back tiredly into the water, then Carl reached down and gripped his wrist.

Peter knelt on the muddy bank, still choking with the water and blood he had swallowed, and he retched weakly.

'Peter!' Magda's voice rang with concern, and he looked up and wiped his mouth on the back of his forearm. She had slipped out of the back door of the limousine and was running back along the bridge, long-legged in black boots and ski-pants, her face dead white with concern and her eyes frantic with worry.

Peter pushed himself onto his feet and swayed drunkenly. She reached him and caught him, steadying him as he teetered.

'Peter, oh God, darling. What happened—'

'This beauty and some of his friends wanted to take you for a ride – and they got the wrong address.'

They stared down at the corpse. Carl had used a .357 magnum and the damage was massive. Magda turned her head away.

'Nice work,' Peter told the bodyguard bitterly. 'He's not going to answer any questions now, is he?'

'You said to stop him.' Carl growled as he reloaded the pistol.

'I wonder what you would have done if I'd said to really clobber him.' Peter began to turn away with disgust, and pain checked him. He gasped.

'You're hurt.' Magda's concern returned in full strength. 'Take his other arm,' she ordered Carl, and they helped him over the parapet to the limousine.

Peter stripped off the torn and sodden remains of his clothing and Magda wrapped him in the Angora wool travel rug before examining his wound under the interior light of the cab.

The bullet hole was a perfect little blue puncture in the smooth skin, already surrounded by a halo of inflammation, and the bullet was trapped between his ribs and the sheet of flat, hard trapezium muscles. She could see the outline of it quite clearly, the size of a ripe acorn in his flesh, swollen out angry purple.

'Thank God—' she whispered, and unwound the Jean Patou scarf from her long pale throat. She bound the wound carefully. 'We'll take you directly to the hospital at Versailles. Drive fast, Carl.'

She opened the walnut-fronted cocktail cabinet in the bodywork beside her and poured half a tumbler of whisky from the crystal decanter.

It washed the taste of blood from Peter's mouth and then went warmly all the way down his throat to soothe the cramps of cold and shock in his belly.

'What made you come?' he asked, his voice still rough with the fierce spirit, the timely arrival nagged at his sense of rightness.

'The police at Rambouillet had a report of a car smash – they knew the Maserati, and the inspector rang La Pierre Bénite immediately. I guessed something bad—'

At that moment they reached the gates at the main road. The remains of the Maserati lay smouldering on the side of the road; around it like boy scouts around a camp fire were half a dozen gendarmes in their white plastic capes and pillbox kepis. They seemed uncertain of what they should do next.

Carl slowed the limousine and Magda spoke tersely through the window to a sergeant, who treated her with immense respect. '*Oui*, madame la Baronne, *d'accord Tout à fait vrai*—' She dismissed him with a final nod, and he and his men saluted the departing limousine.

'They will find the body at the bridge—'

'There may be another one on the edge of the forest there—'

'You are very good, aren't you?' She slanted her eyes at him.

'The really good ones don't get hit,' he said, and smiled at her. The whisky had taken some of the sting and stiffness out of the wound and unknotted his guts. It was good to still be alive, he started to appreciate that again.

'You were right about the Maserati then – they were waiting for it.'

'That's why I burned it,' he told her, but she did not answer his smile

'Oh, Peter. You'll never know how I felt. The police told me that the driver of the Maserati was still in it and had been burned. I thought – I felt as though part of me had been destroyed. It was the most terrifying feeling—' She shivered. 'I nearly did not come, I didn't want to see it. I nearly sent my wolves, but then I had to know – Carl saw you in the river as we turned onto the bridge. He said it was you, I just couldn't believe it—' She stopped herself and shuddered at the memory. 'Tell me what happened, tell me all of it,' she demanded and poured more whisky into his tumbler.

For some reason that he was not sure of himself, Peter did not mention the Citroën that had followed him out of Paris. He told himself that it could not have been relevant. It must have been a coincidence, for if the driver of the Citroën had been one of them he would have been able to telephone ahead and warn the others that Baroness Magda Altmann was not in the Maserati, so that would have meant that they were not after her – but after him, Peter Stride, and that didn't make sense because he had only set himself up as bait that very morning, and they would not have had time yet. He stopped the giddy carousel of thoughts – shock and whisky, he told himself. There would be time later to think it all out more carefully. Now he would simply believe that they were waiting for Magda, and he had run into their net. He told it that way, beginning from the moment that he had seen the police van parked in the road. Magda listened with complete attention, the huge eyes clinging to his face, and she touched him every few moments as if to reassure herself.

When Carl parked under the portico of the emergency entrance of the hospital, the police had radioed ahead and there were an intern and two nurses waiting for Peter with a theatre trolley.

Before she opened the door to let them take Peter, Magda leaned to him and kissed him full on the lips.

'I'm so very glad to have you still,' she whispered, and then with her lips still very close to his ear she went on. 'It was Caliph again, wasn't it?'

He shrugged slightly, grimaced at the stab of pain, and answered, 'I can't think of anyone else offhand that would do such a professional job.'

Magda walked beside the trolley as far as the theatre doors, and she was beside his bed in the curtained cubicle as he struggled up through the deadening, suffocating false death of the anaesthetic.

The French doctor was with her, and he produced the gruesome blood-clotted souvenir with a magician's flourish.

'I did not have to cut,' he told Peter proudly. 'Probe only.' The bullet had mushroomed impressively, had certainly lost much of its velocity in penetrating the bodywork of the Maserati. 'You are a very lucky man,' the doctor went on. 'You are in fine condition, muscles like a racehorse that stopped the bullet going deep. You will be well again very soon.'

'I have promised to look after you, so he is letting you come home now.' Magda hovered over him also. 'Aren't you, doctor?'

'You will have one of the world's most beautiful nurses.' The doctor bowed gallantly towards Magda with a certain wistfulness in his expression.

The doctor was right, the bullet wound gave him less discomfort than the tears in his thighs from the barbed wire, but Magda Altmann behaved as though he were suffering from an irreversible and terminal disease.

When she did have to go up to her office suite in the Boulevard des Capucines the next day, she telephoned three times for no other reason than to make sure he was still alive and to ask for his size in shoes and clothing. The cavalcade of automobiles carrying her and her entourage were back at La Pierre Bénite while it was still daylight.

'You are keeping civil service hours,' he accused when she came directly to the main guest suite overlooking the terraced lawns and the artificial lake.

'I knew you were missing me,' she explained, and kissed

him before beginning to scold him. 'Roberto tells me you have been wandering around in the rain. The doctor said you were to stay in bed. Tomorrow I will have to stay here to take care of you myself.'

'Is that a threat?' he grinned at her. 'For that sort of punishment I would let Caliph shoot another hole—'

Swiftly she laid her fingers on his lips. 'Peter, *chéri*, don't joke like that.' And the shadow that passed across her eyes was touched with fear, then immediately she was smiling again. 'Look what I have bought you.'

Peter's valise had been in the trunk of the Maserati, and she had replaced it with one in black crocodile from Hermes. To fill it she must have started at the top end of the Faubourg St Honoré and worked her way down to the Place Vendôme.

'I had forgotten how much fun it is to buy presents for one who you—' She did not finish the sentence, but held up a brocade silk dressing-gown. ' – Everybody in St Laurent knew what I was thinking when I chose this.'

She had forgotten nothing. Shaving gear, silk handkerchiefs and underwear, a blue blazer, slacks and shoes from Gucci, even cufflinks in plain gold, each set with a small sapphire.

'You have such blue eyes,' she explained. 'Now I will go and make myself respectable for dinner I told Roberto we would eat here, for there are no other guests tonight.'

She had changed from the gunmetal business suit and turban into floating cloud-light layers of gossamer silk, and her hair was down to her waist, more lustrous than the cloth.

'I will open the champagne,' she said. 'It needs two hands.'

He wore the brocade gown, with his left arm still in a sling, and they stood and admired each other over the top of the champagne glasses.

'I was right.' She nodded comfortably. 'Blue is your

colour. You must wear it more often.' And he had to smile at the quaint compliment, and touched her glass with his. The crystal pinged musically and they saluted each other before they drank. Immediately she set the glass aside, and her expression became serious.

'I spoke with my friends in the Sûreté. They agree that it was a kidnap attempt against me, and because I asked it, they will not trouble you to make a statement until you feel better. I told them to send a man tomorrow to speak to you. There was no sign of the second man you shot at on the edge of the woods, he must have been able to walk or been carried by his friends.'

'And the other man?' Peter asked. 'The dead one.'

'They know him well. He had a very ugly past. Algeria with the paras. The mutiny.' She spread her hands eloquently. 'My friends were very surprised that he had not killed you when he tried to do so. I did not say too much about your own past. It is better, I think?'

'It's better,' Peter agreed

'When I am with you like this, I forget that you also are a very dangerous man.' She stopped and examined his face carefully. 'Or is it part of the reason I find you so—' she searched for the word ' – so compelling? You have such a gentle manner, Peter. Your voice is so soft and—' She shrugged. 'But there is something in the way you smile sometimes, and in certain light your eyes are so blue and hard and cruel. Then I remember that you have killed many men. Do you think that is what attracts me?'

'I hope it is not.'

'Some women are excited by blood and violence – the bullfight, the prize ring, there are always as many women as men at these, and I have watched their faces. I have thought about myself, and still I do not know it all. I know only that I am attracted by strong men, powerful men. Aaron was such a man. I have not found many others since then.'

'Cruelty is not strength,' Peter told her.

'No, a truly strong man has that streak of gentleness and compassion. You are so strong, and yet when you make love to me it is with extreme gentleness, though I can always feel the strength and cruelty there, held in bate, like the falcon under the hood.'

She moved away across the room furnished in cream and chocolate and gold, and she tugged the embroidered bell-pull that dangled from the corniced ceiling with its hand-painted panels, pastoral scenes of the type that Marie Antoinette had so admired. Peter knew that much of the furnishing of La Pierre Bénite had been purchased at the auction sales with which the revolutionary committee dispersed the accumulated treasures of the House of Bourbon. With the other treasures there were flowers, wherever Magda Altmann went there were flowers.

She came back to him as Roberto, the Italian butler, supervised the entry of the dinner trolley, and then Roberto filled the wine glasses himself, handling the bottles with white gloves as though they were part of the sacrament, and stationed himself ready to serve the meal, but Magda dismissed him with a curt gesture and he bowed himself out silently.

There was a presentation-wrapped parcel at Peter's place setting, tissue paper and an elaborately tied red ribbon. He looked up at her inquiringly as she served the soup into fragile Limoges bowls.

'Once I began buying presents, I could not stop myself,' she explained. 'Besides, I kept thinking that bullet might have been in my back.' Then she was impatient. 'Are you not going to open it?'

He did so carefully, and then was silent.

'Africa, it is your speciality, is it not?' she asked anxiously. 'Nineteenth-century Africa?'

He nodded, and reverently opened the cover of the volume in its bed of tissue paper. It was fully bound in maroon leather, and the state of preservation was quite extraordinary, only the dedication on the flyleaf in the author's handwriting was faded yellow.

'Where on earth did you find this?' he demanded. 'It was at Sotheby's in 1971. I bid on it then.' He had dropped out of the bidding at five thousand pounds.

'You do not have a first edition of Cornwallis Harris?' she asked again anxiously, and he shook his head, examining one of the perfectly preserved colour plates of African big game.

'No, I do not. But how did you know that?'

'Oh, I know as much about you as you do yourself,' she laughed. 'Do you like it?'

'It is magnificent. I am speechless.' The gift was too extravagant, even for someone of her fortune. It troubled him, and he was reminded of the comedy situation of the husband who brings home flowers unexpectedly and is immediately accused by his wife. 'Why do you have a guilty conscience?'

'Do you truly like it? I know so little about books.'

'It is the one edition I need to complete my major works,' he said. 'And it is probably the finest specimen left outside the British Museum.'

'I'm so glad.' She was genuinely relieved. 'I was truly worried.' And she put down the silver soup ladle and lifted both arms to welcome his embrace.

During the meal she was gay and talkative, and only when Roberto had wheeled away the trolley and they settled side by side on the down-filled couch before the fire did her mood change again.

'Peter, today I have been unable to think of anything but this business – you and me and Caliph. I have been afraid, and I am still afraid. I keep thinking of Aaron, what they did to him – and then I think of you and what nearly happened.'

They were silent, staring into the flames and sipping

coffee from the demi-tasses, then suddenly she had changed direction again. He was growing accustomed to these mercurial switches in thought.

'I have an island – not one island, but nine little islands – and in the centre of them is a lagoon nine kilometres wide. The water is so clear you can see the fish fifty feet down. There is an airstrip on the main atoll. Just under two hours' flying time to Tahiti. Nobody would ever know we were there. We could swim all day, walk in the sand, make love under the stars. You would be king of the islands, and I would be your queen. No more Altmann Industries – I would find somebody as good or better than myself to run it. No more danger. No more fear. No more Caliph – no more—' She stopped abruptly, as though she had been about to commit herself too far, but she went on quickly. 'Let's go there, Peter. Let's forget all this. Let's just run away and be happy together, for ever.'

'It's a pretty thought.' He turned to her, feeling deep and genuine regret.

'It would work for us. We would make it work.'

And he said nothing, just watching her eyes, until she looked away and sighed.

'No.' She mirrored his regret. 'You are right. Neither of us could ever give up living like that. We have to go on – but, Peter, I am so afraid. I am afraid of what I know about you and of what I do not know I am afraid of what you do not know about me, and what I never can tell you – but we must go on. You are right. We have to find Caliph, and then destroy him. But, oh God, I pray we do not destroy ourselves, what we have found together – I pray we will be able to keep that intact.'

'The best way to conjure up emotional disaster is to talk about it.'

'All right, let's play riddles instead. My turn first. What is the most miserable experience known to the human female?'

'I give up.'

'Sleeping alone on a winter's night.'

'Salvation is at hand,' he promised her.

'But what about your poor shoulder?'

'If we combine our vast talents and wisdom, I am sure we will manage something.'

'I think you are right,' she purred and nestled against him like a sleek and silken cat. 'As always.'

There is always a delightfully decadent feeling about buying underwear for a beautiful woman, and Peter was amused by the knowing air of the middle-aged sales lady. She clearly had her own ideas about the relationship, and slyly produced a tray filled with filmy lace and iniquitously expensive wisps of silk.

'Yes,' Melissa-Jane approved rapturously. 'Those are exactly—' She held one of them to her cheek, and the sales lady preened at her own foresight. Peter hated to disillusion her, and he played the role of sugar-daddy a few moments longer as he glanced up at the mirror behind her head.

The tail was still there, a nondescript figure in a grey overcoat, browsing through a display of brassieres across the hall with the avid interest and knowledgeable air of a closet queen.

'I don't really think your mother will approve, darling,' Peter said, and the sales woman looked startled.

'Oh, please, Daddy. I will be fourteen next month '

They had had a tail on him since he had arrived at Heathrow the previous afternoon, and Peter could not decide who they were. He began to regret he had not yet replaced the Cobra he had lost in the river

'I think we'd better play it safe—' Peter told his daughter, and both Melissa-Jane and the sales lady looked crestfallen.

'Not bloomers!' Melissa-Jane wailed. 'Not elastic legs.'

'Compromise,' Peter suggested. 'No elastic legs – but no lace, not until you're sixteen. I think painted fingernails is enough for right now.'

'Daddy, you can be so medieval, honestly!'

He glanced at the mirror again, and they were changing the guard across the sales hall. The man in the shabby grey overcoat and checked woollen scarf drifted away and disappeared into one of the lifts. It would take some little time for Peter to spot his replacement – and then he grinned to himself; no it would not. Here he came now. He wore a tweed sports jacket in a frantic hounds tooth pattern, above Royal Stewart tartan trews and a grin like an amiable toad.

'Son of a gun. This is a surprise.' He came up behind Peter and hit him an open-handed blow between the shoulder blades that made Peter wince. At least he knew who they were at last.

'Colin.' He turned and took the massive paw with its covering of wiry black hair across the back. 'Yes, it is a surprise. I've been falling over your gorillas since yesterday.'

'Oafs,' Colin Noble agreed amiably. 'All of them, oafs!' And turned to seize Melissa-Jane. 'You're beautiful,' he told her and kissed her with more than avuncular enthusiasm.

'Uncle Colin. You come straight from heaven.' Melissa-Jane broke from the embrace and displayed the transparent panties. 'What do you think of these?'

'It's you, honey. You've just got to have them '

'Tell my father, won't you?'

Colin looked around the Dorchester suite and grunted. 'This is really living. You don't get it this good in this man's army.'

'Daddy is truly becoming a bloated plutocrat – just like Uncle Steven,' Melissa-Jane agreed.

'I notice that you and Vanessa and the other comrades all wear lace panties,' Peter counter-attacked his daughter.

'That's different.' Melissa-Jane back-tracked swiftly, and hugged the green Harrod's package defensively. 'You can have a social conscience without dressing like a peasant, you know.'

'Sounds like a good life.' Peter threw his overcoat across the couch and crossed to the liquor cabinet. 'Bourbon?'

'On the rocks,' said Colin.

'Is there a sweet sherry?' Melissa-Jane asked.

'There is Coke,' Peter answered. 'And you can take it through to your own room, young lady.'

'Oh Daddy, I haven't seen Uncle Colin for ages.'

'Scat,' said Peter, and when she had gone, 'sweet sherry, forsooth.'

'It's a crying bastard when they start growing up – and they look like that.' Colin took the glass from Peter and rattled the ice cubes together as he lay back in the armchair. 'Aren't you going to congratulate me?'

'With pleasure.' Peter took his own glass and stood at the windows, against the backdrop of bare branches and grey misty skies over Hyde Park. 'What did you do?'

'Come on, Pete! Thor – they gave me your job, after you walked out.'

'Before they fired me.'

'After you walked out,' Colin repeated firmly. He took a sip of the Bourbon and gargled it loudly. 'There are a lot of things we don't understand – "Ours not to reason why, ours but to do and die." Shakespeare.'

He was still playing the buffoon, but the small eyes were as honey bright and calculating as those of a brand new teddy bear on Christmas morning. Now he waved his glass around the suite.

'This is great. Really it's great. You were wasted in Thor – everybody knew that. You must be pulling down more than all the joint-chiefs put together now.'

'Seven gets you five that you've already seen a Xeroxed copy of my contract of employment with Narmco.'

'Narmco!' Colin whistled. 'Is that who you're working for? No kidding, Pete baby, that's terrific!'

And Peter had to laugh, it was a form of capitulation. He came across and took the seat opposite Colin.

'Who sent you, Colin?'

'That's a lousy question—'

'That's just an opener.'

'Why should somebody have sent me? Couldn't I just want to chew the fat with an old buddy?'

'He sent you because he worked it out that I might bust the jaw of anybody else.'

'Sure now and everybody knows we love each other like brothers.'

'What's the message, Colin?'

'Congratulations, Peter baby, I am here to tell you that you have just won yourself a return ticket to the Big Apple.' He placed one hand across his heart and sang with a surprisingly mellow baritone. 'New York, New York, it's a wonderful town.'

Peter sat staring impassively at Colin, but he was thinking swiftly. He knew he had to go. Somehow he was certain that something was surfacing through muddied waters, the parts were beginning to click together. This was the sort of thing he had hoped for when he put the word on the wind.

'When?'

'There is an airforce jet at Croydon right now.'

'Melissa-Jane?'

'I've got a driver downstairs to take her home.'

'She's going to hate you.'

'Story of my life,' Colin sighed. 'Only the dogs love me.'

They played gin-rummy and drank teeth-blackening airforce coffee, all the way across the Atlantic. Colin Noble did most of the talking, around the stub of his cheroot. It was shop, Thor shop, training and personnel details, small anecdotes about men and things they both knew well – and he made no effort to question Peter about his job and Narmco, other than to remark that he would have Peter back in London for the series of Narmco meetings he had arranged starting on the following Monday. It was a deliberate and not very subtle intimation of just how much Atlas knew about Peter and his new activities.

They landed at Kennedy a little after midnight, and there was an army driver to take them to a local Howard Johnson for six hours' sleep, that kind of deep black coma induced by jet-lag.

Peter still felt prickly-eyed and woollen-headed as he watched with a feeling of disbelief as Colin devoured one of those amazing American breakfasts of waffles and maple syrup, wieners and bacon and eggs, sugar cakes and sticky buns, washed down with countless draughts of fruit juice and coffee. Then Colin lit his first cheroot and announced, 'Hell, now I know I'm home. Only now I realize I've been slowly fading away with malnutrition for two years'

The same army driver was waiting for them at the front entrance of the motel. The Cadillac was an indication of their status in the military hierarchy. Peter looked out with detachment from the air-conditioned and padded interior onto the brooding ghettoes of Harlem. From the elevated highway along the East River, it reminded Peter of a deserted battle ground – where a few survivors lurked in dark doorways or scuttled along the littered and pitted sidewalks in the cold misty morning. Only the graffiti that adorned the bare brick walls had passion and vitality.

Their drive caught the junction of Fifth and One Hundred and Eleventh Street, and ran south down the park past the Metropolitan Art Museum in the thickening rush-hour traffic, then slipped off and into the cavernous mouth of a parking garage beneath one of the monolithic structures that seemed to reach to the grey cold heavens.

The garage entrance was posted 'Residents Only', but the doorman raised the electronically controlled grid and waved them through. Colin led Peter to the bank of elevators and they rode up with the stomach-dropping swoop while the lights above the elevator door recorded their ascent to the very top of the building.

There they stepped out into a reception area protected by ornamental, but none the less functional screens.

A guard in military police uniform and wearing a side-arm surveyed them through the grille and checked Colin's Atlas pass against his register before allowing them through.

The apartment occupied the entire top level of the building, for there were hanging gardens beyond the sliding glass panels and a view across the sickening canyons of space to the other tall structures farther down Island – the Pan Am building and the twin towers of the World Trade Center.

The decor was Oriental, stark interiors in which were displayed works of art that Peter knew from his previous visit were of incalculable value – antique Japanese brush paintings on silk panels, carvings in jade and ivory, a display of tiny netsuke – and in an atrium through which they passed was a miniature forest of Bonsai trees in their shallow ceramic bowls, the frozen contortions of their trunks and branches a sign of their great age.

Incongruously, the exquisite rooms were filled with the thunder of von Karajan leading the Berlin Philharmonic Orchestra through the glories of the Eroica.

Beyond the atrium was a plain door of white oak, and Colin Noble pressed the buzzer beside the lintel and almost immediately the door slid open.

Colin led into a long carpeted room, the ceiling of which was covered with acoustic tiles. The room contained besides the crowded bookshelves and work table an enormous concert piano, and down the facing wall an array of hi-fi turntables and loudspeakers that would have been more in place in a commercial recording studio.

Kingston Parker stood beside the piano, a heroic figure, tall and heavy in the shoulder, his great shaggy head hanging forward onto his chest, his eyes closed and an expression of almost religious ecstasy glowing upon his face.

The music moved his powerful frame the way the storm wind sways a giant of the forest. Peter and Colin stopped in the doorway, for it seemed an intrusion on such a private, such an intimate moment, but it was only a few seconds before he became aware of them and lifted his head. He seemed to shake off the spell of the music with the shudder that a spaniel uses to shake itself free of water when it reaches dry land, and he lifted the arm of the turntable from the spinning black disc.

The silence seemed to tingle after the great crashing chords of sound.

'General Stride,' Kingston Parker greeted him. 'Or may I still call you Peter?'

'Mr Stride will do very nicely,' said Peter, and Parker made an eloquent little gesture of regret, and without offering to shake hands indicated the comfortable leather couch across the room.

'At least you came,' he said, and as Peter settled into the couch, he nodded.

'I have always had an insatiable curiosity.'

'I was relying on that,' Kingston Parker smiled. 'Have you breakfasted?'

'We've had a snack,' Colin cut in but Peter nodded.

'Coffee then,' said Parker, and spoke quietly into the intercom set, before turning back to them.

'Where to begin?' Parker combed the thick greying hair back with both hands, leaving it even more tousled than it had been.

'Begin at the beginning,' Peter suggested. 'As the King of Hearts said to Alice.'

'At the beginning—' Parker smiled softly. ' – All right, at the beginning I opposed your involvement with Atlas.'

'I know.'

'I did not expect that you would accept the Thor command, it was a step backwards in your career. You surprised me there, and not for the first time.'

A Chinese manservant in a white jacket with brass buttons carried in a tray. They were silent as he offered coffee and cream and coloured crystal sugar and then, when he had gone, Parker went on.

'At that time, my estimate of you, General Stride, was that although you had a record of brilliance and solid achievement, you were an officer of rigidly old-fashioned thought. The Colonel Blimp mentality more suited to trench warfare than to the exigencies of war from the shadows – the kind of wars that we are fighting now, and will be forced to fight in the future.'

He shook the great shaggy head and unconsciously his fingers caressed the smooth cool ivory keyboard, and he settled down on the stool before the piano.

'You see, General Stride, I saw the role of Atlas to be too limited by the original terms of reference placed upon it. I did not believe that Atlas could do what it was designed for if it was only an arm of retaliation. If it had to wait for a hostile act before it could react, if it had to rely entirely on other organizations – with all their internecine rivalries and bickerings – for its vital intelligence. I needed officers who were not only brilliant, but who were capable of unconventional thought and independent action. I did not believe you had those qualities, although I studied you very carefully. I was unable to take you fully into my confidence.'

Parker's slim fingers evoked a fluent passage from the keyboard as though to punctuate his words, and for a moment he seemed completely enraptured by his own music, then he lifted his head again.

'If I had done so, then the conduct of your rescue operation of Flight 070 might have been completely different. I have been forced radically to revise my estimate of you, General Stride – and it was a difficult thing to do. For by demonstrating those qualities which I thought you lacked, you upset my judgement. I admit that personal chagrin swayed my reasoned judgement – and by the time I was thinking straight again you had been provoked into offering your resignation—'

'I know that the resignation was referred to you personally, Doctor Parker – and that you recommended that it be accepted.' Peter's voice was very cold, the tone clipped with controlled anger – and Parker nodded.

'Yes, you are correct. I endorsed your resignation.'

'Then it looks as though we are wasting our time here and now.' Peter's lips were compressed into a thin, unforgiving line, and the skin across his cheeks and over the finely chiselled flare of his nostrils seemed tightly drawn and pale as porcelain.

'Please, General Stride – let me explain first.' Parker reached out one hand to him as though to physically restrain him from rising, and his expression was earnest, compelling. Peter sank back into the couch, his eyes wary and his lips still tight.

'I have to go back a little first, in order to make any sense at all.' Parker stood up from the piano and crossed to the rack of pipes on the work table between the hi-fi equipment. He selected one carefully, a meerschaum mellowed to the colour of precious amber. He blew through the empty pipe and then tramped back across the thick carpet to stand in front of Peter.

'Some months before the hijacking of 070 – six months to be precise, I had begun to receive hints that we were entering a new phase in the application of international terrorism. Only hints at first, but these were confirmed and followed by stronger evidence.' Parker was stuffing the meerschaum from a leather wallet as he spoke, now he zipped this closed and tossed it onto the piano top. 'What we were looking at was a consolidation of the forces of violence under some sort of centralized control – we were not sure what form this control was taking.' He broke off and studied Peter's expression, seemed to misinterpret it for utter disbelief, for he shook his head. 'Yes, I know it sounds far-fetched, but I will show you the files. There was evidence of meetings between known militant leaders and some other shadowy figures, perhaps the representatives of an Eastern government. We were not sure then, nor are we now. And immediately after this a complete change in the conduct and apparent motivation of militant activity. I do not really have to detail this for you. Firstly the systematic accumulation of immense financial reserves by the highly organized and carefully planned abduction of prominent figures, starting with the ministers of OPEC, then leading industrialists and financial figures—' Parker struck a match and puffed on his pipe and perfumed smoke billowed around his head. ' – So that it appeared that the motivation had not really changed and was still entirely self gain or parochial political gain. Then there was the taking of 070. I had not confided in you before and once you were on your way to Johannesburg it was too late. I could do nothing more than try to control your actions by rather heavy-handed commands. I could not explain to you that we suspected that this was the leading wave of the new militancy, and that we must allow it to reveal as much as possible. It was a terrible decision, but I had to gamble a few human lives for vital information – and then you acted as I had believed you were incapable of acting.' Parker removed his pipe from his mouth and he smiled; when he smiled you could believe anything he said and forgive him for it, no matter how outrageous. 'I admit, General Stride, that my first reaction was frustrated rage. I wanted your head, and your guts also. Then suddenly I began using my own head instead. You had just proved you were the man I wanted, my soldier capable of unconventional thought and action. If you were discredited and cast adrift, there was just a chance that this new direction of militancy would recognize the same qualities in you that I had been forced to recognize. If I allowed you to ruin your career, and become an outcast – an embittered man, but one with vital skills and invaluable knowledge, a man who had proved he could be ruthless when it was necessary—' Parker broke off and made that gesture of appeal. ' – I am sorry, General Stride, but I had to recognize the fact that you would be very attractive to—' he made an impatient gesture ' – I do not have a name for them, shall we just call them "the enemy". I had to recognize the fact that you would be of very great interest to the enemy. I endorsed your resignation.' He nodded sombrely. 'Yes, I endorsed your resignation, and without your own knowledge you became an Atlas agent at large. It seemed perfect to me. You did not have to act a role – you believed it yourself. You were the outcast, the wronged and discredited man ripe for subversion.'

'I don't believe it,' Peter said flatly, and Parker went back to the work table, selected an envelope from a Japanese ceramic tray and brought it back to Peter.

It took Peter a few moments to realize that it was a Bank Statement – Crédit Suisse in Geneva – the account was in his name, and there were a string of deposits. No withdrawals or debits. Each deposit was for exactly the same amount, the net salary of a major-general in the British Army.

'You see,' – Parker smiled – 'you are still drawing your Atlas salary. You are still one of us, Peter. And all I can say is that I am very sorry indeed that we had to subject you to the pretence – but it seems it was all worth while.'

Peter looked up at him again, not entirely convinced, but with the hostility less naked in his expression.

'What do you mean by that, Doctor Parker?'

'It seems that you are very much back in play again.'

'I am Sales Director for Northern Armaments Company,' he said flatly.

'Yes, of course, and Narmco is part of the Altmann Industrial Empire – and Baron Altmann and his lovely wife are, or rather were, an extraordinarily interesting couple. For instance, did you know that the Baron was one of the top agents of Mossad in Europe?'

'Impossible,' Peter shook his head irritably. 'He was a Roman Catholic. Israeli intelligence does not make a habit of recruiting Catholics.'

'Yes,' Parker agreed. 'His grandfather converted to Catholicism – and changed the name of the family home to La Pierre Bénite. It was a business decision, that we are certain of, there was not much profit in being Jewish in nineteenth-century France. However, the young Altmann was much influenced by his grandmother and his own mother. He was a Zionist from a very early age, and he unswervingly used his enormous wealth and influence in that cause – right up until the time of his murder. Yet he did it so cunningly, with such subtlety that very few people were aware of his connections with Judaism and Zionism. He never made the mistake of converting back to his ancestral religion, realizing that he could be more effective as a practising Christian.'

Peter was thinking swiftly. If this was true, then it all had changed shape again. It must affect the reasons for the

Baron's death – and it would change the role of Magda Altmann in his life.

'The Baroness?' he asked. 'Was she aware of this?'

'Ah, the Baroness!' Kingston Parker removed his pipe from between his teeth, and smiled with reluctant admiration. 'What a remarkable lady. We are not certain of very much about her – except her beauty and her exceptional talents. We know she was born in Warsaw. Her father was a professor of medicine at the university there, and he escaped to the West when the Baroness was still a child. He was killed a few years later, a traffic accident in Paris. Hit and run driver, while the professor was leaving his faculty in the Sorbonne. A small mystery still hangs around his death. The child seems to have drifted from family to family, friends of her father, distant relatives. She already was showing academic leanings, musical talent, at thirteen a chess player of promise – then for a period there is no record of her. She seems to have disappeared entirely. The only hint is from one of her foster mothers, a very old lady now, with a fading memory. "I think she went home for a while – she told me she was going home."' Parker spread his hands. 'We do not know what that means. Home? Warsaw? Israel? Somewhere in the East?'

'You have researched her very carefully,' Peter said. What he had heard had left him uneasy.

'Of course, we have done so to every contact you have made since leaving Atlas Command. We would have been negligent not to do so – but especially we have been interested in the Baroness. She has been the most fascinating, you understand that, I am sure.'

Peter nodded, and waited. He did not want to ask for more. Somehow it seemed disloyal to Magda, distrustful and petty – but still he waited and Parker went on quietly.

'Then she was back in Paris. Nineteen years of age now – a highly competent private secretary, speaking five languages fluently, beautiful, always dressed in the height of fashion, soon with a string of wealthy, influential and powerful admirers – the last of these was her employer, Baron Aaron Altmann.' Parker was silent then, waiting for the question, forcing Peter to come to meet him.

'Is she Mossad also?'

'We do not know. It is possible – but she has covered herself very carefully. We are rather hoping you will be able to find that out for us.'

'I see.'

'She must have known that her husband was a Zionist. She must have suspected that it had something to do with his abduction and murder. Then there are the missing six years of her life – from thirteen to nineteen, where was she?'

'Is she Jewish?' Peter asked. 'Was her father Jewish?'

'We believe so, although the professor showed no interest in religion and did not fill in the question on his employment application to the Sorbonne. His daughter showed the same lack of religious commitment – we know only that her marriage to the Baron was a Catholic ceremony followed by a civil marriage in Rambouillet.'

'We have drifted a long way from international terrorism,' Peter pointed out.

'I do not think so.' Kingston Parker shook his big shaggy head. 'The Baron was a victim of it, and almost as soon as you – one of the world's leading experts on militancy and urban warfare – as soon as you are associated with her there is an assassination attempt, or an abduction attempt made on the Baroness.'

Peter was not at all surprised that Parker knew of that night on the road to La Pierre Bénite – it was only a few days since Peter's arm had been out of the sling.

'Tell me, Peter. What was your estimate of that affair? I have seen an excerpt of the statement that you made to the French police – but what can you add to that?'

Peter had a vivid cameo memory of the Citroën that had

followed him out of Paris, and then almost simultaneously the tearing sound of automatic fire in the night.

'They were after the Baroness,' Peter said firmly.

'And you were driving her car?'

'That's right.'

'You were at the place at the time that the Baroness usually passed?'

'Right.'

'Who suggested that? You?'

'I told her that the car was too conspicuous.'

'So you suggested taking it down to La Pierre Bénite that night.'

'Yes.' Peter lied without knowing why he did so.

'Did anybody else know that the Baroness would not be driving?'

'Nobody.' Except her bodyguards, the two chauffeurs who had met them on their return from Switzerland, Peter thought.

'You are certain?' Parker persisted.

'Yes,' Peter snapped. 'Nobody else.' Except Magda, only Magda. He pushed the thought aside angrily.

'All right, so we must accept that the Baroness was the target – but was it an assassination or an abduction attempt? That could be significant. If it was assassination, it would indicate that it was the elimination of a rival agent, that the Baroness was probably also a Mossad agent, recruited by her husband. On the other hand, an abduction would suggest that the object was monetary gain. Which was it, Peter?'

'They had blocked the road—' he said, but not completely he remembered. 'And the police impersonator signalled me to stop—' or at least to slow down, he thought, slow down sufficiently to make an easy target before they started shooting ' – and they did not open fire until I made it clear that I was not going to stop.' – But they had been ready to begin shooting at the instant Peter made the decision to send the Maserati through the roadblock. The intention of the two machine-gunners had seemed evident. ' – I would say the object was to seize the Baroness alive.'

'All right,' Parker nodded. 'We will have to accept that for the time being.' He glanced at Colin. 'Colonel Noble? You had a question?'

'Thank you, Doctor. We haven't heard from Peter in what terms he was approached by Narmco or the Baroness. Who made the first contact?'

'I was approached by a London firm who specializes in making top executive placements. They came directly from the Narmco Board—' And I turned them down flat, he thought. It was only later at Abbots Yew—

'I see.' Colin frowned with disappointment. 'There was no question of a meeting with the Baroness?'

'Not at that stage.'

'You were offered the sales appointment – no mention of any other duties, security, industrial intelligence—'

'No, not then.'

'Later?'

'Yes. When I met the Baroness, I realized her personal security arrangements were inadequate. I made changes.'

'You never discussed her husband's murder?'

'Yes, we did.'

'And?'

'And nothing.' Peter was finding it difficult to improvise answers, but he used the old rule of telling as much of the truth as possible.

'There was no mention by the Baroness of a hunt for her husband's murderers? You were not asked to use your special talents to lead a vendetta?'

Peter had to make a swift decision. Parker would know of his leak to the British military attaché in Paris – the bait he had so carefully placed to attract Caliph. Of course Parker would know: he was head of Atlas with access to the

Central Intelligence computer. Peter could not afford to deny it.

'Yes, she asked me to relay any information which might point to her husband's murderers. I asked G.2 in Paris for any information he might have. He couldn't help me.'

Parker grunted. 'Yes. I have a note that G.2 filed a routine report – but I suppose her request was natural enough.' He wandered back to his work table to glance at a pad on which was scribbled some sort of personal shorthand.

'We know of eight sexual liaisons that the Baroness formed prior to her marriage, all with politically powerful or wealthy men. Six of them married men—'

Peter found himself trembling with anger so intense that it surprised him. He hated Parker for talking like this of Magda. With a huge effort he kept his expression neutral, the hand in his lap was relaxed and the fingers spread naturally, though he felt a driving desire to bunch it and drive it into Parker's face.

' – all these affairs were conducted with utmost discretion. Then during her marriage there is no evidence of any extra-marital activity. Since the Baron's murder there have been three others, a minister in the French Government, an American businessman – head of the world's second largest oil company—' He dropped the pad back on the desk and swung back to face Peter. 'And recently there has been one other.' He stared at Peter with a bright penetrating gaze. 'The lady certainly believes in mixing business with pleasure. All her partners have been men who are able to deliver very concrete proof of their affections. I think this rule probably applies to her latest choice of sexual partner.'

Colin Noble coughed awkwardly, and shifted in his chair, but Peter did not even glance at him, he went on staring impassively at Kingston Parker. He and Magda had made very little secret of their relationship – still it was bitterly distasteful to have to discuss it with anybody else.

'I think that you are in a position now to gather vital intelligence. I think that you are very near the centre of this nameless and formless influence – I think that you will be able to make some sort of contact with the enemy, even if it is only another military brush with them. The only question is whether or not you find any reason, emotional or otherwise, that might prevent you fulfilling this duty?' Kingston Parker cocked his head on one side, making the statement into a question.

'I have never let my private life interfere with my duty, Doctor,' Peter said quietly.

'No,' Kingston Parker agreed. 'That is true. And I am sure that now you know a little more about Baroness Altmann you will appreciate just how vital is our interest in that lady.'

'Yes, I do.' Peter had his anger under control completely. 'You want me to use a privileged relationship to spy on her. Is that correct?'

'Just as we can be sure she is using the same relationship to her own ends—' Parker broke off as an odd thought seemed to occur. 'I do hope I have not been too blunt, Peter. I haven't destroyed some cherished illusion.' Now Parker's attitude was dismissive. The interview was over.

'At my age, Doctor – a man has no more illusions.' Peter rose to his feet. 'Do I report to you direct?'

'Colonel Noble will make the arrangements for all communications.' Kingston Parker held out his hand. 'I would not have asked this of you if I had a choice.'

Peter did not hesitate, but took the hand. Parker's hand was cool and dry. Although he made no show of it, Peter could sense the physical power in those hard pianist's fingers.

'I understand, sir,' said Peter – and he thought grimly, and even if that is also a lie, I'm going to understand pretty damned soon.

Peter made the excuse of tiredness to avoid the gin-rummy game, and pretended to sleep during most of the long trans-Atlantic flight. With his eyes closed he tried to marshal his thoughts into some sort of pattern, but always they seemed to come around full circle and leave him chasing his tail. He could not even achieve any certainty about his feelings and loyalties to Magda Altmann. They seemed to keep changing shape every time he examined them, and he found himself brooding on irrelevancies. 'Sexual liaisons' – what a ridiculously stilted expression Parker had used, and why had it angered Peter so much? Eight liaisons before marriage, six with married men, two others since marriage – all wealthy or powerful. He found himself trying to flesh out these bare statistics, and with a shock of bitter resentment imagined those faceless, formless figures with the slim smooth body, the tiny, perfectly shaped breasts, and the long smoky fall of shimmering hair. He felt somehow betrayed, and immediately scorned himself for this adolescent reaction.

There were other more dire questions and chances that Kingston Parker had raised, the Mossad connection, the six missing years in Magda's life – and yet he came back again to what had happened between them. Was she capable of such skilful deception, or was it not deception? Was he merely suffering from hurt pride now, or somehow unbeknown to him had she been able to force him into a more vulnerable position? Had she succeeded in making him fall in love with her?

How did he feel about her? At last he had to face that question directly and try to answer it, but when they landed again he still had no answer, except that the prospect of seeing her again pleased him inordinately and the thought that she had deliberately used him to her own ends and was capable of discarding him as she had done those others left him with an aching sense of dismay. He dreaded the answer for which he had to search, and suddenly he remembered her suggestion of an island to which they could escape together. He realized then that she was a victim of the same dread, and with a clairvoyant shudder he wondered if they were somehow preordained to destroy each other.

There were three separate messages from her at the Dorchester. She had left the Rambouillet number, each time. He telephoned immediately he reached the suite.

'Oh, Peter. I was so worried. Where were you?' And it was hard to believe her concern was faked, and it was even harder to discount the pleasure when, the following noon, she met him at Charles de Gaulle Airport herself instead of sending a chauffeur.

'I needed to get out of the office for an hour,' she explained, and then she tucked her hand into the crook of his elbow and pressed herself against him. 'That's a lie, of course. I came because I couldn't wait the extra hour to see you.' Then she chuckled huskily. 'I am behaving shamelessly, I can't imagine what you must think of me!'

They were with a party of eight that evening, dinner at Le Doyen and then the theatre at the Palais de Chaillot. Peter's French was still not up to Molière, so he took his pleasure in surreptitiously watching Magda, and for a few hours he succeeded in suppressing all those ugly questions; only on the midnight drive back to La Pierre Bénite did he begin the next move in the complicated game.

'I couldn't tell you on the telephone—' he said in the intimate darkness and warmth of her limousine. 'I had an approach from Atlas. The head of Atlas summoned me to New York. That's where I was when you called. They are also onto Caliph.'

She sighed then, and her hand stole into his. 'I was waiting for you to tell me, Peter,' she said simply, and she sighed again. 'I knew you'd gone to America, and I had a terrible premonition that you were going to lie to me. I don't know what I would have done then.' And Peter felt a lance of conscience driven up under his ribs, and with it the throb of concern – she had known of his journey to New York, but how? Then he remembered her 'sources'.

'Tell me,' she said, and he told her – everything, except the nagging question marks which Kingston Parker had placed after her name. The missing years, the Mossad connection with the Baron, and those ten nameless men.

'They don't seem to know that Caliph uses that name,' Peter told her. 'But they seem to be pretty certain that you are hunting him, and you've hired me for that purpose.'

They discussed it quietly as the small cavalcade of cars rushed through the night, and later when she came to his suite, they went on talking, holding each other as they whispered in the night, and Peter was surprised that he could act so naturally, that the doubts seemed to evaporate so easily when he was with her.

'Kingston Parker still has me as a member of Atlas,' Peter explained. 'And I did not deny it, nor protest. We want to find Caliph, and if I still have status with Atlas it will be useful, of that I am certain,'

'I agree. Atlas can help us – especially now that they are also aware that Caliph exists.'

They made love in the dawn, very deeply satisfying love that left bodies and minds replete, and then keeping her discretion she slipped away before it was light, but they met again an hour later for breakfast together in the Garden Room.

She poured coffee for him, and indicated the small parcel beside his plate.

'We aren't quite as discreet as we think we are, *chéri*.' She chuckled. 'Somebody seems to know where you are spending your evenings.'

He weighed the parcel in his right palm; it was the size of a roll of 35-mm film, wrapped in brown paper, sealed with red wax.

'Apparently it came special delivery yesterday evening.' She broke one of the crisp croissants into her plate, and smiled at him with that special slant of her green eyes.

The address was typed on a stick-on label, and the stamps were British, franked in south London the previous morning.

Suddenly Peter was assailed with a terrifying sense of foreboding; the presence of some immense overpowering evil seemed to pervade the gaily furnished room.

'What is it, Peter?' Her voice cracked with alarm.

'Nothing,' he said. 'It's nothing.'

'You suddenly went deadly pale, Peter. Are you sure you are all right?'

'Yes. I'm all right.'

He used his table knife to lift the wax seal and then unrolled the brown paper.

It was a small screw-topped bottle of clear glass, and the liquid it contained was clear also. Some sort of preservative, he realized immediately, spirits or formaldehyde.

Hanging suspended in the liquid was a soft white object.

'What is it?' Magda asked.

Peter felt cold tentacles of nausea closing around his stomach.

The object turned slowly, floating free in its bottle, and there was a flash of vivid scarlet.

'Does your mother allow you to wear nail varnish now, Melissa-Jane?' He heard the question echoed in his memory, and saw his daughter flirt her hands, and the scarlet flash of her nails. The same vivid scarlet.

'Oh yes – though not to school, of course. You keep forgetting I'm almost fourteen, Daddy.'

The floating white object was a human finger. It had been severed at the first joint, and the preservative had bleached the exposed flesh a sickly white. The skin had puckered and wrinkled like that of a drowned man. Only the painted fingernail was unaltered, pretty and festively gay.

The nausea caught Peter's throat, choking him and he heaved and retched drily as he stared at the tiny bottle.

The telephone rang three times before it was answered.

'Cynthia Barrow.' Peter recognized his ex-wife's voice, even though it was ragged with strain and grief.

'Cynthia, it's Peter.'

'Oh, thank God, Peter. I have been trying to find you for two days.'

'What is it?'

'Is Melissa-Jane with you, Peter?'

'No.' He felt as though the earth had lurched under his feet.

'She's gone, Peter. She's been gone for two nights now. I'm going out of my mind.'

'Have you informed the police?'

'Yes, of course.' The edge of hysteria was in her voice.

'Stay where you are,' Peter said. 'I'm coming to England right now, but leave any message for me at the Dorchester.' He hung up quickly, sensing that her grief would overflow at any moment and knowing that he could not handle it now.

Across the ormolu Louis Quatorze desk Magda was pale, tense, and she did not have to ask the question, it was in the eyes that seemed too large for her face.

He did not have to reply to that question. He nodded once, an abrupt jerky motion, and then he dialled again and while he waited he could not take his eyes from the macabre trophy that stood in its bottle in the centre of the desk.

'Colonel Noble.' Peter snapped into the mouthpiece. 'Tell him it's General Stride and it's urgent.'

Colin came on within the minute. 'Peter, is that you?'

'They've taken Melissa-Jane.'

'Who? I don't understand.'

'The enemy. They've taken her.'

'Jesus God! Are you sure?'

'Yes, I'm sure. They sent me her finger in a bottle.'

Colin was silent for a few seconds, and then his voice was subdued. 'That's sick. Christ, that's really sick.'

'Get onto the police. Use all your clout. They must be keeping quiet on it. There has been no publicity. I want to be in on the hunt for these animals. Get Thor involved, find out what you can. I'm on my way now. I'll let you know what flight I am on.'

'I'll keep a listening watch at this number round the clock,' Colin promised. 'And I'll have a driver meet you.' Colin hesitated. 'Peter, I'm sorry. You know that.'

'Yes. I know.'

'We will all be with you, all the way.'

Peter dropped the receiver onto its arm, and across the desk Magda stood up resolutely.

'I'll come with you to London,' she said, and Peter reached out and took her hand.

'No,' he said gently. 'Thank you, but no. There will be nothing for you to do.'

'Peter, I want to be with you through this terrible thing. I feel as though it's all my fault.'

'That's not true.'

'She's such a lovely child.'

'You will be more help to me here,' said Peter firmly. 'Try through all your sources, any little scrap of information.'

'Yes, very well.' She accepted the decision, without further argument. 'Where can I find you if I have anything?'

He gave her Colin Noble's private number at Thor, scribbling it on the pad beside the telephone. 'Either there or at the Dorchester,' he said.

'At least I will come with you as far as Paris,' she said.

The news had broken by the time Peter landed at Heathrow Airport. It was on the front page of the *Evening Standard* and Peter snatched a copy off the news stand and read it avidly during the drive up to London.

The victim was abducted at the front gate of her home in Leaden Street, Cambridge at eleven o'clock on Thursday. A neighbour saw her speak to the occupants of a maroon Triumph saloon car, and then enter the back door of the vehicle, which drove off immediately.

'I thought there were two people in the car,' Mrs Shirley Callon, 32, the neighbour, told our correspondent, 'and Melissa-Jane did not seem alarmed. She appeared to enter the Triumph quite willingly. I know that her father, who is a senior officer in the army, often sends different cars to fetch her or bring her home. So I thought nothing about it.'

The alarm was not raised for nearly twenty-four hours, as the missing girl's mother also believed that she might be with her ex-husband.

Only when she was unable to contact Major-General Stride, the girl's father, did she inform the police. The Cambridge police found a maroon Triumph abandoned in the car park at Cambridge railway station. The vehicle had been stolen in London the previous day, and immediately a nation-wide alert was put in force for the missing girl.

Chief-Inspector Alan Richards is the police officer in charge of the investigation and any person who may be able to provide information should telephone—

There followed a London number and a detailed description of Melissa-Jane and the clothes she was wearing at the time she disappeared.

Peter crumpled the newspaper and dropped it on the front seat. He sat staring ahead, cupping his anger to him like a flame, husbanding it carefully – because the heat was infinitely more bearable than the icy despair which waited to engulf him.

Inspector Alan Richards was a wiry little man, more like a jockey than a policeman. He had a prematurely wizened face, and he had combed long wisps of hair across his balding pate to disguise it. Yet his eyes were quick and intelligent, and his manner direct and decisive.

He shook hands when Colin Noble introduced them. 'I must make it very clear that this is a police matter, General. However, in these very special circumstances I am prepared to work very closely with the military.'

Swiftly Richards went over the ground he had already covered. He had mounted the investigation from the two offices set aside for him on the third floor of Scotland Yard, with a view over chimney pots of the spires of Westminster Abbey and the Houses of Parliament.

Richards had two young policewomen answering the telephone calls coming in through the number they had advertised in the Press and on television. So far they had accepted over four hundred of these. 'They range from long shots to the completely crazy, but we have to investigate all of them.' For the first time his expression softened. 'It's going to be a long, slow process, General Stride, but we have a few more leads to follow – come through.'

The inner office was furnished in the same nondescript Public Works Department furniture, solid and characterless, but there was a kettle boiling on the gas ring, and Richards poured the tea as he went on.

'Three of my men are taking the kidnap car to pieces. We are sure it is the right car. Your ex-wife has identified a purse found on the floor of the vehicle. It is your daughter's. We have lifted over six hundred fingerprints, and these are being processed. It will take some time until we can isolate each and hope for an identification of any alien prints. However, two of these correspond to prints lifted from your daughter's room – Sugar? Milk?'

Richards brought the cup to Peter as he went on.

' – The neighbour, Mrs Callon, who saw the pick-up, is working on an identikit portrait of the driver, but she did not get a very good view of him. That is a very long shot.'

Richards sipped his tea. 'However, we will show the final picture on television and hope for another lead from it. I am afraid that in cases like this, this is all we can do. Wait for a tip, and wait for the contact from the kidnappers. We do not expect the contact will be made through your ex-wife but of course we have a tap on her telephone and men watching over her.' Richards spread his hands. 'That's it, General Stride. Now it's your turn. What can you tell us? Why should anybody want to snatch your daughter?'

Peter exchanged a glance with Colin Noble, and was silent as he collected his thoughts, but Inspector Richards insisted quietly:

'I understand you are not a very wealthy man, General – but your family? Your brother?'

Peter dismissed the idea with a shake of his head. 'My brother has children of his own. They would be the more logical targets.'

'Vengeance? You were very active against the Provos in Ireland. You commanded the recapture of Flight 070.'

'It's possible.'

'You are no longer connected with the army, I understand.'

Peter was not going to be drawn further in that direction. 'I do not think this type of guesswork will profit us much. We will know the motive as soon as the kidnappers make their demands known.'

'That is true.' Richards rattled his teacup, a little nervous gesture. 'They could not have sent you her—' He broke off as he saw Peter's expression change. ' – I'm sorry, General. It is horrible and terribly distressing, but we have to accept the finger as proof that your daughter is still alive and that the contact, when it comes, will be made to you. It was an expression of their earnest intention, and a threat – but—'

The telephone on his desk rang shrilly and Richards snatched it up.

'Richards!' he snapped, and then listened at length, occasionally grunting encouragement to the caller. When he hung up the receiver he did not speak immediately, but offered Peter a rumpled pack of cigarettes. When Peter refused, the policeman lit one himself and his voice was diffident.

'That was the laboratory. You know your daughter was a white cell donor, don't you?'

Peter nodded. It was part of Melissa-Jane's social commitment. If she had not been tactfully dissuaded, she would have donated her blood and marrow by the bucketful.

'We were able to get a tissue typing from the Cambridge hospital. The amputated finger matches your daughter's tissue type. I'm afraid we must accept that it is hers – I cannot imagine that the kidnappers would have gone to the lengths of finding a substitute of the same type.'

Peter had been secretly cherishing the belief that it was a bluff. That he had been sent the fingertip from a corpse, from a medical sample, from the casualty ward of a city hospital – and now as that hope died he was assailed by the cold spirit-sapping waves of despair. They sat in silence for fully a minute, and now it was Colin Noble who broke it.

'Inspector, you are aware of the nature of the Thor Command?'

'Yes, of course. There was a great deal of publicity at the time of the Johannesburg hijacking. It is an anti-terrorist unit.'

'We are probably the most highly trained specialists in

the world at removing hostages safely from the hands of militants—'

'I understand what you are trying to tell me, Colonel,' Richards murmured drily. 'But let us track down our militants first, and then any rescue attempts will be entirely under the control of the Commissioner of Police.'

It was after three o'clock in the morning when Peter Stride checked in with the night receptionist at the Dorchester Hotel in Park Lane.

'We have been holding your suite since midday, General.'

'I'm sorry.' Peter found himself slurring his words, exhaustion and nervous strain, he realized. He had only left Police Headquarters when he could convince himself that everything possible was being done, and that he could place complete trust in Chief-Inspector Richards and his team. He had Richards's solemn undertaking that he would be informed, no matter at what time of day or night, as soon as there was any new development.

Now he signed the register, blinking at the gritty swollen feeling of his eyelids.

'There are these messages for you, General.'

'Thank you again, and goodnight.'

In the elevator he glanced at the mail the clerk had given him.

The first was a telephone slip.

'Baroness Altmann asks you to return her call to either the Paris or Rambouillet number.'

The second was another telephone slip.

'Mrs Cynthia Barrow called. Please call her at Cambridge 699 – 313.'

The third was a sealed envelope, good-quality white paper, undistinguished by crest or monogram.

His name had been printed in capitals, very regular lettering, an old-fashioned copper-plate script. No stamp, so it would have been delivered by hand.

Peter split the flap with his thumb, and withdrew a single sheet of lined writing paper, again good but undistinguished. There would be a stack of these sheets in any stationery department throughout the United Kingdom.

The writing was the same regular, unnatural script, so that Peter realized that the writer had used a stencil to form each letter, one of those clear plastic cut-out stencils obtainable from any toy store or stationery department. A completely effective method of disguising handwriting.

> A finger you have already, next you will have the hand, then another hand, then a foot, then another foot – and at last the head.
>
> The next package will arrive on April 20th, and there will be another delivery every seven days.
>
> To prevent this you must deliver a life for a life. The day Dr Kingston Parker dies, your daughter will return to you immediately, alive and suffering no further harm.
>
> Destroy this letter and tell nobody, or the head will be delivered immediately.

The letter was signed with the name which had come to loom so largely in Peter's life:

'CALIPH'

The shock of it seemed to reach to the extremities of his soul. To see the name written. To have complete confirmation of all the evil that they had suspected, to see the mark of the beast deeply printed and unmistakable.

The shock was made greater, almost unbearable, by the contents of the letter. Peter found that such cruelty, such utter ruthlessness, tested his credibility to its limits.

The letter was fluttering in his hands, and he realized with a start of surprise that he was shaking like a man in high fever. The porter carrying his black crocodile valise was staring at him curiously, and it required a huge physical effort to control his hands and fold the sheet of white paper.

He stood rigidly, as though on the parade ground, until the elevator door opened and then he marched stiffly down the passage to his suite. He gave the porter a banknote, without glancing at it, and the moment the latch clicked closed, he unfolded the sheet again, and standing in the centre of the living-room floor scanned the stilted script again, and then again until the words seemed to melt together and lose coherence and meaning.

He realized that for the first time in his life he was in complete panic, that he had lost all resolution and direction.

He took a deep breath and closed his eyes, counting slowly to one hundred, emptying his mind completely, and then giving himself the command:

'Think!'

All right, Caliph knew his movements intimately. Even to when he was expected at the Dorchester. Who knew that? Cynthia, Colin Noble, Magda Altmann and the secretary at Rambouillet who had made the reservation, Colin's secretary at Thor, the Dorchester staff, and anybody else who had made even an idle study of Peter's movements would know he always stayed at the Dorchester. That was a cul-de-sac.

'Think!'

Today was April fourth. There were sixteen days before Caliph sent him Melissa-Jane's severed hand. He felt the panic mounting again, and he forced it back.

'Think!'

Caliph had been watching him, studying him in detail, assessing his value. Peter's value was that he could move unsuspected in high places. He could reach the head of Atlas by simply requesting an audience. More than that, he could probably get access to any head of state if he wanted it badly enough.

For the first time in his life Peter felt the need for liquor. He crossed quickly to the cabinet and fumbled with the key. A stranger's face stared at him out of the gilt-framed mirror above it. The face was pale, haggard, with deep parentheses framing the mouth. There were plum-coloured bruises of fatigue below the eyes, and the gaunt, bony jaw was gun-metal blue with a new beard – and the sapphire blue of the eyes had a wild deranged glitter. He looked away from his own image. It only increased his sense of unreality.

He poured half a tumbler of Scotch whisky, and drank half of it straight off. He coughed at the sting of the liquor and a drop of it broke from the corner of his mouth and trickled down his chin. He wiped it away with his thumb, and turned back to study the sheet of white paper again. It was crumpled already, where he had gripped it too hard. He smoothed it carefully.

'Think!' he told himself. This was how Caliph worked, then. Never exposing himself. Picking his agents with incredible attention to detail. Fanatics, like the girl, Ingrid who had led the taking of Flight 070. Trained assassins, like the man he had killed in the river at La Pierre Bénite. Experts in high places, like General Peter Stride. Studying them, assessing them and their capabilities, and finally finding their price.

Peter had never believed the old law that every man had his price. He had believed himself above that general rule. Now he knew he was not – and the knowledge sickened him.

Caliph had found his price, found it unerringly. Melissa-Jane. Suddenly Peter had a vivid memory of his daughter on horseback, swivelling in the saddle to laugh and call back to him.

'Super-Star!' And the sound of her laughter on the wind.

Peter shivered, and without realizing it he crumpled the sheet of paper to a ball in his fist.

Ahead of him he saw the road that he was destined to follow. With a new flash of insight, he realized that he had already taken his first steps along the road. He had done so when he had put the gun to the blonde killer in the terminal of Johannesburg Airport, when he had made himself judge and executioner.

Caliph had been responsible for that first step on the road to corruption, and now it was Caliph who was driving him farther along it.

With a sudden prophetic glimpse ahead, Peter knew it would not end with the life of Kingston Parker. Once he was committed to Caliph, it would be for ever – or until one of them, Peter Stride, or Caliph, was completely destroyed.

Peter drank the rest of the whisky in the tumbler.

Yes, Melissa-Jane was his price. Caliph had made the correct bid. Nothing else would have driven him to it.

Peter picked the booklet of matches off the liquor cabinet and like a sleepwalker moved through to the bathroom. He twisted the sheet of paper into a taper and lit the end of it, holding it over the toilet bowl. He held it until the flame scorched his fingers painfully, then dropped it into the bowl and flushed the ash away.

He went back into the lounge, and refilled the glass with whisky. He picked the comfortable armchair below the window and sank into it. Only then did he realize how very weary he was. The nerves in his thighs quivered and twitched uncontrollably.

He thought about Kingston Parker. A man like that had an incalculable amount to offer mankind. It will have to look like an assassination attempt aimed at me, Peter thought. One that finds the wrong victim.

'A bomb,' Peter thought. He hated the bomb. Somehow

it seemed to be the symbol of the senseless violence which he hated. He had seen it used in Ireland and in London town, and he hated it. The undirected destruction, mindless, merciless.

'It will have to be a bomb,' he decided, and with surprise he found that his hatred had found a new target. Again for the first time ever, he hated himself for what he was going to do.

Caliph had won. He knew that against an adversary of that calibre there was no chance they would find where Melissa-Jane was hidden. Caliph had won, and Peter Stride sat the rest of the night planning an act which he had dedicated his life, until then, to prevent.

'I cannot understand why we haven't had the demand contact yet.' Inspector Richards ran his hand distractedly across his pate, disturbing the feathery wisps that covered it and leaving them standing out at a startled angle. 'It's five days now. Still no demands.'

'They know where to contact Peter,' Colin Noble agreed. 'The interview he gave covered that.'

Peter Stride had appeared on BBC TV to broadcast an appeal to the kidnappers not to maim his daughter further, and to the general public to offer any information that might lead to her rescue.

On the same programme they had displayed the police identikit portrait of the driver of the maroon Triumph prepared by the one witness.

The response had been overwhelming, jamming the switchboard at Inspector Richards's special headquarters, and a mixed bag had fallen into the net.

A fourteen-year-old runaway had the police barge into the Bournemouth apartment where she was in bed with her thirty-two-year-old lover. She was returned weeping bitterly to the bosom of her family, and had again disappeared within twenty-four hours.

In North Scotland the police sadly bungled a raid on a remote cottage hired by a man with the same lank dark hair and gunfighter's moustache as the identikit portrait. He turned out to be a cottage-industry manufacturer of LSD tablets, and he and his four assistants, one of them a young girl who vaguely fitted the description of Melissa-Jane in that she was female and blonde, had scattered across the Highlands before being overtaken and borne to earth by sweating pounding members of the Scottish Constabulary.

Peter Stride was furious. 'If it had been Melissa-Jane, they would have had fifteen minutes in which to put her down—' He raged at Richards. 'You've got to let Thor go in to the next raid.'

Through the Thor communications net he spoke directly to Kingston Parker on the video screens.

' – We'll put all our influence into it,' Parker agreed, and then with deep compassion in his eyes, 'Peter, I'm living every minute of this with you. I cannot escape the knowledge that I have placed you into this terrible situation. I did not expect the attack would come through your daughter. I think you know that you can call on me for any support you need.'

'Thank you, sir,' said Peter and for a moment felt his resolve weaken. In ten days he would have to execute this man. He steeled himself by thinking of a puckered dead-white finger floating in its tiny bottle.

Kingston Parker's influence worked immediately. Six hours later the order came down from Downing Street via the Commissioner of Police, that the next raid on a suspect hideout would be conducted by Thor Command.

The Royal Air Force placed two helicopters at Thor's disposal for the duration of the operation, and Thor's assault unit went into intensive training for penetration and removal under urban conditions. Peter trained with them, he and Colin swiftly re-establishing the old rapport of concerted action.

When they were not practising and refining the exit and assembly from the hovering helicopters, Peter spent much of his time in the enclosed pistol range, trying to drown his awareness in the crash of gunfire, but the days passed swiftly in a series of false alarms and misleading clues.

Each night when Peter examined his face in the mirror above the liquor cabinet, it was more haggard, the blue eyes muddied by fatigue and terrible gut-eroding terror of what the next day might bring forth.

There were six days left when Peter left the hotel room before breakfast, caught the tube at Green Park and left it again at Finsbury Park. In a garden supplies shop near the station he purchased a twenty-pound plastic bag of ammonium nitrate garden fertilizer. He carried it back to the Dorchester in a locked Samsonite suitcase and stored it in the closet behind his hanging trenchcoat.

That night, when he spoke to Magda Altmann, she pleaded once again to be allowed to come to London.

'Peter, I know I can be of help to you. Even if it's just to stand beside you and hold your hand.'

'No. We've been over that.' He could hear the brutal tone in his own voice, but could not control it. He knew that he was getting very close to the edge. 'Have you heard anything?'

'I'm sorry, Peter. Nothing, absolutely nothing. My sources are doing all that is possible.'

Peter bought the dieseline from a pump at the Lex Garage in Brewer Street. He took five litres in a plastic screw-topped container that had contained a household detergent. The pump attendant was a pimply teenager in dirty overalls. He was completely uninterested in the transaction.

In his bathroom Peter worked on the dieseline and the nitrate from the garden shop. He produced twenty-one pounds of savagely weight-efficient high explosive that was, none the less, docile until activated by a blasting cap – such as he had devised with a flashlight bulb.

It would completely devastate the entire suite, utterly destroying everybody and everything in it. However, the damage should be confined to those three rooms.

It would be a simple matter to lure Kingston Parker to the suite under the pretence of having urgent information about Caliph to deliver, information so critical that it could only be delivered in person and in private.

That night the face in the mirror above the liquor cabinet was that of a man suffering from a devouring terminal disease, and the whisky bottle was empty. Peter broke the seal on a fresh bottle; it would make it easier to sleep, he told himself.

The wind came off the Irish Sea like the blade of a harvester's scythe, and the low lead-coloured cloud fled up the slopes of the Wicklow hills ahead of it.

There were weak patches in the cloud layer through which a cold and sickly sun beamed swiftly across the green forested slopes. As it passed so the rain followed – icy grey rain slanting in on the wind.

A man came up the deserted street of the village. The tourists had not yet begun the annual invasion, but the 'Bed and Breakfast' signs were already out to welcome them on the fronts of the cottages.

The man passed the pub, in its coat of shocking salmon pink paint – and lifted his head to read the billboard above the empty car park. 'Black is Beautiful – drink Guinness' it proclaimed, and the man did not smile but lowered his head and trudged on over the bridge that divided the village in two.

On the stone balustrades of the bridge a midnight artist

had used an aerosol paint can to spray political slogans in day-glo colours.

'BRITS OUT' on the left-hand balustrade and 'STOP H BLOCK TORTURE' on the other. This time the man grimaced sourly.

Below him the steely grey water boiled about the stone piers before hissing down towards the sea.

The man wore a cyclist's plastic cape and a narrow-brimmed tweed cap pulled down over his eyes. The wind dashed at him, flogging the skirts of the cape against his Wellington boots.

He seemed to cringe to the wind, hunching down against its cold fury, as he trudged on past the few buildings of the village. The street was deserted, though the man knew that he was being watched from curtained windows.

This village on the lower slopes of the Wicklow hills, a mere thirty miles from Dublin, would not have been his choice. Here isolation worked against them, making them conspicuous. He would have preferred the anonymity of the city. However, his preferences had never been asked for.

This was only the third time he had left the house since they had arrived. Each time it had been for some emergency provision, something that a little more forethought might have prevented, which should have been included when the old house was stocked for their stay. That came from having to rely on a drinking man, but here again he had not been consulted.

He was discontented and in a truculent, smouldering mood. It had rained most of the time, and the oil-fired central heating was not working, the only heating was the smoking peat fires in the small fireplaces in each of the two big rooms they were using. The high ceilings and sparse furnishings had made the rooms more difficult to warm – and he had been cold ever since they had arrived. They were using only the two rooms, and had left the rest of the house locked and shuttered. It was a gloomy building, with the smell of damp pervading it. He had only the company of a whining alcoholic, day after cold rainy day. The man was ripe and over-ripe for trouble, for any diversion to break the grinding monotony – but now he was reduced to errand boy and house servant, roles for which he was unsuited by temperament and training, and he scowled darkly as he trudged over the bridge towards the village store, with its row of petrol pumps standing before it like sentries.

The storekeeper saw him coming, and called through into the back of the shop.

'It's himself from down at the Old Manse.'

His wife came through, wiping her hands on her apron, a short plump woman with bright eyes and ready tongue.

'City people have no more sense than they need, out in this weather.'

'Sure and it's not baked beans nor Jameson whiskey he's after buying.'

Speculation about the new occupant of the Old Manse had swiftly become one of the village's main diversions, with regular bulletins broadcast by the girl on the local telephone exchange – two overseas telephone calls, by the postman – no mail deliveries, by the dustman – the disposals into the dustbins were made up mainly of empty Heinz baked beans cans and Jameson whiskey bottles.

'I still think he's from the trouble up north,' said the shopkeeper's wife. 'He's got the look and the sound of an Ulster man.'

'Hush, woman.' Her husband cautioned her. 'You'll bring bad luck upon us. Get yourself back into the kitchen now.'

The man came in out of the rain and swept the tweed cap off his head, beating the water from it against the jamb of the door. He had black straight hair, cut into a ragged fringe above the dark Irish visage and fierce eyes, like those of a falcon when first the leather hood is slipped.

'The top of the morning to you, Mr Barry,' the shopkeeper greeted him heartily. 'Like as not it will stop raining, before it clears.'

The man they knew as Barry grunted, and as he slipped the waterproof cape from his shoulders, swept the cluttered interior of the little general dealer's store with a quick, all-embracing glance.

He wore a rough tweed jacket over a cable-stitched jersey and brown corduroys tucked into the top of the Wellington boots.

'You finished writing on your book, have you?' Barry had told the milkman that he was writing a book about Ireland. The Wicklow hills were a stronghold of the literary profession, there were a dozen prominent or eccentric writers living within twenty miles, taking advantage of Ireland's tax concessions to writers and artists.

'Not yet,' Barry grunted, and went across to the shelves nearest the till. He made a selection of half a dozen items and laid them on the worn counter top.

'When it's good and wrote I'm going to ask the library to keep a copy for me,' the shopkeeper promised, as though that was exactly what a writer would want to hear, and began to ring up the purchases on his register.

Barry's upper lip was still unnaturally smoother and paler than the rest of his face. He had shaved away the dark droopy moustache the day before arriving in the village, and at the same time had cut the fringe of his hair that hung almost to his eyes.

The shopkeeper picked up one of the purchases and looked inquiringly at Barry, but when the dark Irish face remained impassive and he volunteered no explanation, the shopkeeper dropped his eyes self-consciously and rang up the package with the other purchases and dropped it into a paper carrier.

'That will be three pounds twenty pence,' he said, and closed the cash drawer with a clang, waiting while Barry slung the cape over his shoulders and adjusted the tweed cap.

'God be with you then, Mr Barry.'

There was no reply and the shopkeeper watched him set off back across the bridge before he called his wife again.

'He's a surly one, all right, he is.'

'He's got him a girlfriend down there.' The shopkeeper was bursting with the importance of his discovery. 'He's up to a nice little bit of hanky-panky.'

'How do you know that?'

'He was after buying women's things – you know.' He hooded a knowing eye.

'No, I don't know,' his wife insisted.

'For the curse – you know. Women's things,' and his wife glowed with the news, and began to untie her apron.

'You're sure now?' she demanded.

'Would I ever be lying to you?'

'I think I'll go across to Mollie for a cuppa tea,' said his wife eagerly; the news would make her the woman of the hour throughout the village.

The man they knew as Barry trudged into the narrow, high-walled lane that led up to the Old Manse. It was only the heavy boots and voluminous cape that gave him a clumsy gait, for he was a lithe, lean man in prime physical condition, and under the brim of his cap the eyes were never still, hunter's eyes probing and darting from side to side.

The wall was twelve feet high, the stonework blotched with silver-grey lichen, and although it was cracked and sagging at places, yet it was still substantial and afforded complete privacy and security to the property beyond.

At the end of the lane there was a pair of rotten and warping double doors, but the lock was a bright new brass Yale and the cracks in the wood and the gaping seams had been covered with fresh white strips of pine so that it was impossible to see into the interior of the garage.

Barry unlocked the brass Yale lock and slipped through, pulling the latch closed behind him.

There was a dark blue Austin saloon car parked facing the doors for immediate departure. It had been stolen in Ulster two weeks before, resprayed and fitted with a roof rack to alter its appearance, and with new licence plates. The engine had been tuned and checked and Barry had paid nearly twice its market value.

Now he slipped behind the wheel and turned the key in the ignition. The engine fired and caught immediately. He grunted with satisfaction; seconds could mean the difference between success and failure, and in his life failure and death were synonymous. He listened to the engine beat for half a minute, checking the oil pressure and fuel gauges before switching off the engine again and going out through the rear door of the garage into the overgrown kitchen yard.

The old house had the sad unloved air of approaching dereliction. The fruit trees in the tiny orchard were sick with fungus diseases and surrounded by weed banks.

The thatch roof was rotten-green with moss, and the windows were blindman's eyes, unseeing and uncaring.

Barry let himself in through the kitchen door and dropped his cape and cap on the scullery floor and set the carrier on the draining board of the sink. Then he reached into the cutlery drawer and brought out a pistol. It was a British officer's service pistol, had in fact been taken during a raid on a British Army arsenal in Ulster three years previously.

Barry checked the handgun with the expertise of a long familiarity and then thrust it into his belt. He had felt naked and vulnerable for the short time that he was without the weapon – but he had reluctantly decided not to risk carrying it in the village.

Now he tapped water into the kettle, and at the sound a voice called through from the dim interior.

'Is that you?'

'None other,' Barry answered drily, and the other man came through and stood in the doorway to the kitchen.

He was a thin, stooped man in his fifties with the swollen inflamed face of the very heavy drinker.

'Did you get it?' His voice was husky and rough with whiskey, and he had a seedy run-down air, a day's stubble of grey hairs that grew at angles on the blotchy skin.

Barry indicated the package on the sink.

'It's all there, doctor.'

'Don't call me that, I'm not a doctor any more,' the man snapped irritably.

'Oh, but you are a damned fine one. Ask the girls who dropped their bundles—'

'Leave me alone, damn you.'

Yes, he had been a damn fine doctor. Long ago, before the whiskey, now however it was the abortions and the gunshot wounds of fugitives, and jobs like this one. He did not like to think about this one. He crossed to the sink and sorted through the packages.

'I asked you for adhesive tape,' he said.

'They had none. I brought the bandage.'

'I cannot—' the man began, but Barry whirled on him savagely, his face darkening with angry blood.

'I've had a gutsful of your whining. You should have brought what you needed, not sent me to get it for you.'

'I did not expect the wound—'

'You didn't expect anything but another dram of Jamesons, man. There is no adhesive tape. Now get on with it and tie the bitch's hand up with the bandage.'

The older man backed away swiftly, picked up the packages and shuffled through into the other room.

Barry made the tea and poured it into the thick china mug, spooned in four spoons of sugar and stirred noisily, staring out of the smeared panes. It was raining again. He thought that the rain and the waiting would drive him mad.

The doctor came back into the kitchen, carrying a

bundle of linen soiled with blood and the yellow ooze of sepsis.

'She is sick,' he said. 'She needs drugs, antibiotics. The finger—'

'Forget it,' said Barry.

From the other room there was a long-drawn-out whimper, followed by the incoherent gabble of a young girl deep in the delirium induced by fever and hypnotic drugs.

'If she is not taken to proper care, I won't be responsible.'

'You'll be responsible,' Barry told him heavily. 'I'll see to that.'

The doctor dropped the bundle of linen into the sink and let the water run over it.

'Can I have a drink now?' he asked.

Barry made a sadistic display of consulting his watch.

'No. Not yet,' he decided.

The doctor poured soapflakes into the sink.

'I don't think I can do the hand,' he whispered, shaking his head. 'The finger was bad enough – but I can't do the hand.'

'You'll do the hand,' said Barry. 'Do you hear me, you whiskey-guzzling old wreck? You'll do the hand, and anything else I tell you to do.'

Sir Steven Stride offered a reward of fifty thousand pounds to anyone giving information that led to the recovery of his niece, and the offer was widely reported on television and in the press with reprints of the identikit portrait. It led to a revival of the flagging public interest in the case.

Inspector Richards had been able to reduce his telephone answering staff to one the last few days, but with the renewed spate of informers and speculators, he had to ask for the other policewoman to return to the third floor, and he had two sergeants processing the material that flowed in.

'I feel like Littlewoods,' he growled to Peter. 'Everybody taking a ticket on the pools, or getting his three-pence worth of advertising.' He picked up another message slip. 'Here is another claim for responsibility – the Democratic People's Party for the Liberation of Hong Kong – Have we ever heard of them before?'

'No, sir.' The senior sergeant looked up from his lists. 'But that makes one hundred and forty-eight confessions or claims for responsibility so far.'

'And 'Enry the Eighth was on again half an hour ago.' One of the girls at the switchboard turned and smiled around her mouthpiece. 'Hasn't missed a day.'

'Enry the Eighth was a sixty-eight-year-old pensioner who lived in a council estate in South London. His hobby was confessing to the latest spectacular crime from rape to bank robbery, and he had called regularly every morning.

'Come and get me,' he challenged each time. 'But I warn you I won't come peaceful like—' When the local constable had made a courtesy call, while on his regular beat, 'Enry the Eighth had his suitcase packed and ready to go. His disappointment was heart-rending when the bobby tactfully explained that they weren't going to arrest him, but when the bobby assured him that they would be keeping him under close surveillance as the Commissioner considered him a very dangerous man, he brightened up considerably and offered the constable a cup of tea.

'The trouble is we dare not dismiss any of it, even the real loonies, it all has to be checked out,' Richards sighed, and motioned Peter to go through to the inner office.

'Still nothing?' Richards asked. It was an unnecessary question. They had a tap on his telephone, at the hotel and at Thor Headquarters, to record any contact from the kidnappers.

'No, nothing,' Peter lied, but the lie had become easy now – just as he had learned to accept whatever else was necessary for Melissa-Jane's release.

'I don't like it, General. I really don't like the fact that there has been no attempt to contact you. I don't want to be despondent, but every day of silence makes it look more like an act of vengeance—' Richards broke off and covered his embarrassment by lighting a cigarette. 'Yesterday the Deputy-Commissioner telephoned me. He wanted my opinion as to how much longer I thought it necessary to maintain this special unit.'

'What did you tell him?' Peter asked.

'I told him that if we did not have some firm evidence within ten days, at least some sort of demand from the kidnappers – then I would have to believe that your daughter was no longer alive.'

'I see.' Peter felt a fatalistic calm. He knew. He was the only one who knew. There were four days to Caliph's deadline, he had worked out his timetable. Tomorrow morning he would request his urgent meeting with Kingston Parker. He expected it would take less than twelve hours to arrange it, he would make it too attractive for Parker to refuse.

Parker would have to come, but against the remote possibility that he did not, Peter had left himself three clear days before the deadline in which to put into action his alternative plan. This would mean going to Kingston Parker. The first plan was the better, the more certain – but if it failed, Peter would accept any risk.

Now he realized that he had been standing in the centre of Richards's office, staring vacantly at the wall above the little inspector's head. He started as he realized that Richards was staring at him with a mingling of pity and concern.

'I am sorry, General. I understand how you feel – but I cannot keep this unit functioning indefinitely. We just do not have enough people—'

'I understand.' Peter nodded jerkily, and wiped his face with an open hand. It was a weary, defeated gesture.

'General, I think you should see your doctor. I really do.' Richards's voice was surprisingly gentle.

'That won't be necessary – I'm just a little tired.'

'A man can take just so much.'

'I think that's what these bastards are relying on,' Peter agreed. 'But I'll be all right.'

From the next door office there was the almost constant tinkle of telephone bells, and the murmur of female voices as the two policewomen answered the incoming stream of calls. It had become a steady background effect, so that when the call for which they had prayed and pleaded and waited finally came, neither of the two men was aware of it, and there was no excitement on the switchboard.

The two girls sat side by side on swivel stools in front of the temporary switchboard. The blonde girl was in her middle twenties, she was pretty and pert, with big round breasts buttoned primly under her blue uniform jacket. The blonde hair was twisted into a bun at the back of her neck to free her ears, but the headset made her appear older and businesslike.

The bell pinged and a panel lit in front of her; she plugged in the switch and spoke into the headset.

'Good morning. This is the Police Special Information Unit—' She had a pleasant middle-class accent, but was unable to keep the trace of boredom out of it. She had been on this job for twelve days now. There was the warning tone of a public telephone and then the click of small change fed into the slot.

'Can you hear me?' The accent was foreign.

'Yes, sir.'

'Listen carefully. Gilly O'Shaughnessy has her—' No, it was an imitation, the foreign accept slipped a little with the pronunciation of the name.

'Gilly O'Shaughnessy,' the police girl repeated.

'That's right. He's holding her at Laragh.'

'Spell that, please.' Again the accent slipped as the man spelled the name.

'And where is that, sir?'

'County Wicklow, Ireland.'

'Thank you, sir. What is your name, please?'

There was the clack of a broken connection and the hum of the dialling tone. The girl shrugged, and scribbled the message on the pad before her, glancing at her wrist-watch simultaneously.

'Seven minutes to tea time,' she said. 'Roll on death, battle with the angels.' She tore the sheet off the pad and passed it over her shoulder to the burly, curly-headed sergeant who sat behind her.

'I'll buy you a sticky bun,' he promised.

'I'm on a diet,' she sighed.

'That's daft, you look a treat—' The sergeant broke off. ' – Gilly O'Shaughnessy. Why do I know that name?'

The older sergeant looked up sharply.

'Gilly O'Shaughnessy?' he demanded. 'Let me see that.' And he snatched the sheet, scanning it swiftly, his lips moving as he read the message. Then he looked up again.

'You know the name because you've seen it on the wanted posters, and heard it on the telly. Gilly O'Shaughnessy, strewth man, he's the one who bombed the Red Lion at Leicester, and shot the Chief Constable in Belfast.'

The curly-headed policeman whistled softly. 'This looks like a hot one. A real hot one—' But his colleague was already barging into the inner office without the formality of knocking.

Richards had the connection to the Dublin police within seven minutes.

'Impress upon them that there must be no attempt—' Peter fretted, while they waited, and Richards cut him short.

'All right, General. Leave this to me. I understand what has to be done—' At that moment the Dublin connection was made, and Richards was transferred quickly to a Deputy-Commissioner. He spoke quietly and earnestly for nearly ten minutes before he replaced the receiver.

'They will use the local constabulary, not to waste time in sending a man down from Dublin. I have their promise that no approach will be made if a suspect is located.'

Peter nodded his thanks. 'Laragh,' he said. 'I have never heard of it. It cannot have a population of more than a few hundred.'

'I've sent for a map,' Richards told him, and when it came they studied it together.

'It's on the slopes of the Wicklow hills – ten miles from the coast—' And that was about all there was to learn from the large-scale map.

'We'll just have to wait for the Dublin police to call back—'

'No,' Peter shook his head. 'I want you to call them again, and ask them to contact the surveyor-general. He must have trig maps of the village, aerial photographs, street layouts. Ask them to get them down with a driver to Enniskerry Airfield—'

'Should we do that now? What if this turns out to be another false alarm.'

'We'll have wasted a gallon of petrol and the driver's time—' Peter was no longer able to sit still, he jumped out of the chair and began to pace restlessly about the office; it was too small for him suddenly, he felt as though he were on the point of suffocation. 'I don't think it is, however. I have the smell of it. The smell of the beast.'

Richards looked startled and Peter deprecated the exaggerated phrase with a dismissive gesture. 'A manner of speech,' he explained, and then stopped as a thought struck him. 'The helicopters will have to refuel, they haven't got the range to make it in one hop, and they are so bloody slow!' He paused and reached a decision, then leaned across Richards's desk to pick up the telephone and dialled Colin Noble's private number at Thor.

'Colin.' He spoke curtly with the tension that gripped him like a mailed fist. 'We've just had a contact. It's still unconfirmed, but it looks the best yet.'

'Where?' Colin broke in eagerly.

'Ireland.'

'That's to hell and gone.'

'Right, what's the flight time for the whirly birds to reach Enniskerry?'

'Stand by.' Peter heard him talking to somebody else – probably one of the R.A.F. pilots. He came back within the minute.

'They will have to refuel en route—'

'Yes?' Peter demanded impatiently.

'Four and a half hours,' Colin told him.

'It's twenty past ten now – almost three o'clock before they reach Enniskerry. With this weather it will be dark before five.' Peter thought furiously; if they sent the Thor team all the way to Ireland on a false trail – and while they were there the correct contact was made in Scotland, or Holland, or—

'It's got the smell. It's got to be right,' he told himself, and took a deep breath. He could not order Colin Noble to go to Bravo. Peter was no longer commander of Thor.

'Colin,' he said. 'I think this is it. I have the deep-down gut feel for it. Will you trust me and go to Bravo now? If we wait even another half hour we'll not get Melissa-Jane out before nightfall – if she is there.'

There was a long silence, broken only by Colin Noble's light quick breath.

'Hell, it can only cost me my job,' he said easily at last. 'Okay, Pete baby, it's Bravo, we'll be airborne in five minutes. We'll pick you up from the helipad in fifteen minutes; be ready.'

The cloud was breaking up, but the wind was still bitter and spiteful, and up on the exposed helipad it cut cruelly through Peter's trench coat, blazer and roll-neck jersey. They looked out across the churned surface of the River Thames, eyes watering in the wind, for the first glimpse of the helicopters.

'What if we have a confirmation before you reach Enniskerry?'

'You can reach us on the R.A.F. frequencies, through Biggin Hill,' Peter told him.

'I hope I don't have bad news for you.' Richards was holding his bowler hat in place with one hand, the skirts of his jacket slapping around his skinny rump and his face blotchy with the cold.

The two ungainly craft came clattering in, low over the rooftops, hanging on the whirling silver coins of their rotors.

At a hundred feet Peter could plainly recognize the broad shape of Colin Noble in the open doorway of the fuselage, just forward of the brilliant R.A.F. roundels, and the down-draught of the rotors boiled the air about them.

'Good hunting.' Richards raised his voice to a shout. 'I wish I was coming with you.'

Peter ran forward lightly, and jumped before the helicopter gear touched the concrete pad. Colin caught him by the upper arm and helped to swing him aboard without removing the cheroot from his wide mouth.

'Welcome aboard, buddy. Now let's get this circus on the road.' And he hitched the big .45 pistol on his hip.

'She's not eating.' The doctor came through from the inner room and scraped the plate into the rubbish bin below the sink. 'I'm worried about her. Very worried.'

Gilly O'Shaughnessy grunted but did not look up from his own plate. He broke a crust off the slice of bread and very carefully wiped up the last of the tomato ketchup. He popped the bread into his mouth and followed it with a gulp of steaming tea, and while he chewed it all together, he leaned back on the kitchen chair and watched the other man.

The doctor was on the verge of cracking up. He would probably not last out the week before his nerve went completely; Gilly O'Shaughnessy had seen better men go to pieces under less strain.

He realized then that his own nerves were wearing away.

It was more than just the rain and the waiting that was working on him. He had been the fox for all of his life, and he had developed the instincts of the hunted animal. He could sense danger, the presence of the pursuers, even when there was no real evidence. It made him restless to stay longer in one place than was necessary, especially when he was on a job. He had been here twelve days, and it was far too long. The more he thought about it the more uneasy he became. Why had they insisted he bring the brat to this isolated, and therefore conspicuous, little dead-end? There was only one road in and out of the village, a single avenue of escape. Why had they insisted that he sit and wait it out in this one place? He would have liked to keep moving. If he had had the running of it, he would have bought a second-hand caravan, and kept rolling from one park to another – his attention wandered for a few moments as he thought how he would have done it – if he had been given the planning of it.

He lit a cigarette and gazed out of the rain-blurred window panes, hardly aware of the muttered complaints and misgivings of his companion. What they should have done was crop the brat's fingers and bottle all of them to send to her father at intervals, and then they should have held a pillow over her face and buried her in the vegetable garden or weighted her and dumped her out beyond the hundred-fathom line of the Irish Sea – that way they would not have had to bother with a doctor, and the nursing—

Everything else had been done with professional skill, starting with the contact they had made with him in the *favela* of Rio de Janeiro, where he was hiding out in a sleazy one-room shack with the half-caste Indian woman, and down to his last fifty quid.

That had given him a real start, he thought he had covered his tracks completely, but they had him made. They had the passport and travel papers in the name of Barry, and they did not look like forgeries. They were good papers, he was sure of it, and he knew a lot about papers.

Everything else had been as well planned, and swiftly delivered. The money – a thousand pounds in Rio, another five thousand the day after they grabbed the brat, and he was confident that the final ten would be there as it was promised. It was better than an English gaol, the 'Silver City' as the Brits called their concentration camp at the Maze. That was what Caliph had promised, if he didn't take the job.

Caliph, now that was a daft name, Gilly O'Shaughnessy decided for the fiftieth time as he dropped the stub of his cigarette into the dregs of his teacup and it was extinguished with a sharp hiss. A real daft name, but somehow it had the ability to put a chill on the blood, and he shivered not only from the cold.

He stood up and crossed to the kitchen window. It had all been done with such speed and purpose and planning – everything so clearly thought out, that when there was a lapse it was more troubling.

Gilly O'Shaughnessy had the feeling that Caliph did nothing without good reason – then why had they been ordered to back themselves into this dangerously exposed bottleneck, without the security of multiple escape routes, and to sit here and wait?

He picked up the cyclist cape and tweed cap. 'Where are you going?' the doctor demanded anxiously. 'I'm going to take a shufti,' Gilly O'Shaughnessy grunted as he pulled the cap down over his eyes.

'You're always prowling around,' the doctor protested. 'You make me nervous.'

The dark Irishman pulled the pistol from under his jacket and checked the load before thrusting it back into his belt. 'You just go on playing nursemaid,' he said brusquely. 'And leave the man's work to me.'

The small black Austin crawled slowly up the village street, and the rain hammered on the cab and bonnet in tiny white explosions that blurred the outline, giving the machine a softly focused appearance, and the streaming windscreen effectively hid the occupants. It was only when the Austin parked directly in front of Laragh's only grocery store and both front doors opened that the curiosity of watchers from behind the curtained windows all down the street was satisfied.

The two members of the Irish constabulary wore the service blue winter uniform with darker epaulettes. The soft rain speckled the patent leather peaks of their caps as they hurried into the shop.

'Good morning, Maeve, me old love,' the sergeant greeted the plump red-faced lady behind the counter.

'Owen O'Neill, I do declare—' She chuckled as she recognized the sergeant – there had been a time, thirty years before, when the two of them had given the priest some fine pickings at the confessional. 'And what brings you all the way up from the big city?'

That was a generous description of the quaint seaside resort town of Wicklow, fifteen miles down the road.

'The sight of your blooming smile—'

They chatted like old friends for ten minutes, and her husband came through from the little storeroom when he heard the rattle of teacups.

'So what is new in Laragh, then?' the sergeant asked at last. 'Any new faces in the village?'

'No, all the same faces. Nothing changes in Laragh, bless the Lord for that.' The shopkeeper wagged his head. 'No, indeed – only new face is the one down at the Old Manse, he and his lady friend—' he winked knowingly ' – but seeing as how he's a stranger, we aren't after counting him.'

The sergeant ponderously delved for his notebook, opened it and extracted a photograph from it; it was the usual side view and full face of police records. He held the name covered with his thumb as he showed it to them.

'No.' The woman shook her head positively. 'Himself down at the manse is ten years older than that, and he does not have a moustache.'

'This was taken ten years ago,' said the sergeant.

'Oh, well, why didn't you say so.' She nodded. 'Then that's him. That's Mr Barry for certain sure.'

'The Old Manse, you say.' The sergeant seemed to inflate visibly with importance, as he put the photograph back into his notebook. 'I'm going to have to use your telephone now, dear.'

'Where will you be after telephoning?' The shopkeeper asked suspiciously.

'Dublin,' the sergeant told him. 'It's police business.'

'I'll have to charge you for the call,' the shopkeeper warned him quickly.

'There,' said the wife as they watched the sergeant making his request to the girl on the village switchboard. 'I told you he had the look of trouble, didn't I. The first time I laid eyes on him I knew he was from up in the North, and carrying trouble like the black angel.'

Gilly O'Shaughnessy kept close in under the stone wall, keeping out of the slanting rain and out of the line of sight of a casual watcher on the slope beyond the river. He moved carefully and quietly as a tomcat on his midnight business, stopping to examine the earth below the weakened or tumbled places in the wall where a man could have come over, studying the wet drooping weeds for the brush marks where a man might have passed.

At the farthest corner of the garden, he stepped up onto the leaning main stem of an apple tree to see over the wall, wedging himself against the lichen-encrusted stone, so that the silhouette of his head did not show above the wall.

He waited and watched for twenty minutes, with the absolute animal patience of the predator, then he jumped down and went on around the perimeter of the wall, never for a moment relaxing his vigilance, seemingly oblivious to the discomfort of the cold and the insistent rain.

There was nothing, not the least sign of danger, no reason for the nagging disquiet – but still it was there. He reached another vantage point, the iron gate that led into the narrow walled alley, and he leaned against the stone jamb, cupping his hands to protect match and cigarette from the wind, and then shifting slightly so he could see through the crack between wall and gate and cover the walled lane, and the road beyond as far as the bridge.

Once again he assumed the patient watching role, closing his mind against the physical discomfort and letting his eyes and his brain work at their full capacity.

Not for the first time he pondered the unusual system of signals and exchanges of material that Caliph had insisted upon.

The payments had been made by bearer deposit certificates, in Swiss francs, sent through the post to his Rio address and then to his collection address in London.

He had made one delivery to Caliph, the bottle and its contents – and two telephone calls. The delivery had been made within two hours of grabbing the girl, while she was still under the effects of the initial shot of the drug. The doctor – Dr Jameson, as Gilly O'Shaughnessy liked to think of him – had done the job in the back of the second car. It had been waiting in the car park at Cambridge railway station, a little green Ford delivery van with a completely enclosed rear compartment. They had moved the girl from the maroon Triumph to the Ford in the covering dusk of the autumn evening, and they had parked again in the lot of a roadside café on the A10 while Dr Jameson did the job. All the instruments had been ready for him in the van, but he had botched it badly, his hands shaking with nerves and the need for liquor. The brat had bled copiously, and now the hand was infected.

Gilly O'Shaughnessy felt his irritation rising sharply when he thought of the doctor. Everything he touched seemed to turn to disaster.

He had delivered the bottle to a pick-up car that had been exactly where he was told it would be, and it had dipped its headlights in the prearranged signal. Gilly had hardly stopped, but merely drawn up alongside and handed the bottle across, then driven straight into the West, and caught the early morning ferry long before any general alarm was out for the girl.

Then there were the telephone calls. They worried Gilly O'Shaughnessy as much as anything else in this whole bloody business. He had made the first call immediately they reached Laragh. It was an international call, and he had to say one sentence: 'We arrived safely.' And then hang up. A week later a call to the same number, and again only one sentence: 'We are enjoying ourselves.' And then immediately break the connection.

Gilly remembered how each time the girl on the local exchange had called him back to ask if the contact had been satisfactory – and each time she had sounded puzzled and intrigued.

It was not the way Caliph had worked up until then, it was leaving a trail for the hunters to follow and he would have protested – if there had been somebody to protest to, but there was only the international telephone number, no other way of contacting Caliph. He decided as he stood by the gate that he would not make the next telephone call to that number which was due in four days' time.

Then he remembered that was the day the hand was due – and he would probably receive his orders for delivery of the hand when he made the call – but he didn't like it. Not even for the money – and suddenly his mind went back to an incident long ago.

They had wanted to pass false information to the English, details of an intended operation – which would in fact take place at a different place and a different time. They had fed the detailed but duff information to a young unreliable Provo, one who they knew would not hold out under interrogation, and they had put him in a safe house in the Shankhill Road – and that was where the English took him.

Gilly O'Shaughnessy felt a little electric prickle run down his spine like ghost-fire, and that feeling had never let him down before – never. He looked at his cheap Japanese wristwatch; it was almost four o'clock, and evening was lowering on the hills of grey and cold green. When he looked up again, there was movement on the road.

From the top of the hill a vehicle was following the curve of the road, down towards the bridge. It was a small black saloon car, and it went out of sight behind the hedge.

Gilly O'Shaughnessy watched for it to reappear without particular interest, still worrying about those two telephone calls. Trying to find the need for them, why Caliph should want to take that chance.

The small black car turned onto the bridge, and came directly down towards the Manse, but the light was wrong and Gilly could make out only the shape of two heads beyond the rhythmically flogging windscreen wipers.

The car began to slow up, coming down almost to walking speed, and Gilly straightened up instinctively, suddenly completely alert as he peered through the slit. There was the pale blur of faces turned towards him, and the car slowed almost to a halt. The nearest side window was lowered slowly and for the first time he could see clearly into the interior. He saw the peak of the uniform cap, and the silver flash of a cap badge above the straining white face. The ghost-fire flared up Gilly O'Shaughnessy's spine and he felt his breath suddenly scalding his throat.

The small black car disappeared beyond the corner of the stone wall, and he heard it accelerate away swiftly.

Gilly O'Shaughnessy whirled with the cape ballooning around him and he ran back to the house. He felt very cold and sure and calm now that the moment of action had come.

The kitchen was empty and he crossed it in half a dozen strides, and threw open the door to the second room.

The doctor was working over the bed and he looked up angrily.

'I've told you to knock.'

They had argued this out before. The doctor still retained some bizarre vestige of professional ethics in his treatment of his patient. He might surgically mutilate the child for the money he so desperately needed, but he had protested fiercely when Gilly O'Shaughnessy had lingered at the doorway to ogle the maturing body whenever the doctor stripped it for cleansing, treatment or for the performance of its natural functions

The dark Irishman had half-heartedly attempted to force him to back down, but when he had encountered surprisingly courageous opposition he had abandoned his voyeuristic pleasures and had returned to the inner room only when called to assist.

Now the child lay face down on the soiled sheets. Her blonde hair was matted and snarled into greasy tresses; the doctor's attempts at cleanliness were as bumbling and ineffectual as his surgery.

The infection and the use of drugs had wasted the flesh off the tender young body, each knuckle of her spine stood out clearly and her naked buttocks seemed pathetically vulnerable, shrunken and pale.

Now the doctor pulled the grubby sheet up to her shoulders, and turned to stand protectively over her. It was an absurd gesture, when you looked at the untidy, stained dressing that bound up her left hand – and Gilly O'Shaughnessy snarled at him fiercely.

'We are getting out.'

'You can't move her now,' protested the doctor. 'She's really sick.'

'Suit yourself,' Gilly agreed grimly. 'Then we'll leave her.' He reached under the dripping cape, and brought out the pistol. He thumbed back the hammer and stepped up to the bed. The doctor grabbed at his arm, but Gilly pushed him away easily, sending him reeling back against the wall.

'You are right, she'll be a nuisance,' he said, and placed the muzzle of the pistol against the base of the child's skull.

'No,' shrieked the doctor. 'No, don't do that. We'll take her.'

'We are leaving as soon as it's dark.' Gilly stepped back and uncocked the pistol. 'Be ready by then,' he warned.

The two helicopters flew almost side by side, with the number two only slightly behind and higher than the leader; below them the Irish Sea was a sheet of beaten lead flecked with feathers of white water.

They had refuelled at Caernarvon and had made good time since leaving the Welsh coast, for the wind drove them on, but still the night was overtaking them and Peter Stride fretted, glancing at his wristwatch every few seconds.

It was only ninety miles of open water to cross, but to Peter it seemed like the entire Atlantic. Colin slumped beside him on the bench that ran the length of the hold, with the cold stump of a cheroot in the corner of his mouth in deference to the 'No smoking' light that burned on the bulkhead behind the flight deck. The rest of the Thor team had adopted their usual attitudes of complete relaxation, some of them sprawled on the deck using their equipment as pillows, the others stretched out full length on the benches.

Peter Stride was the only one tensed up, as though his blood fizzed with nervous energy. He stood up once again to peer through the perspex window, checking the amount of daylight and trying to judge the height and position of the sun through the thick cloud cover.

'Take it easy,' Colin counselled him as he dropped back into his seat. 'You will give yourself an ulcer.'

'Colin, we've got to decide. What are our priorities on this strike?' He had to shout above the racket of wind and motor.

'There are no priorities. We have only one object – to get Melissa-Jane out, and out safely.'

'We aren't going to try for prisoners to interrogate?'

'Peter baby, we are going to hit anything and everything that moves in the target area, and we are going to hit them hard.'

Peter nodded with satisfaction. 'They will only be goons anyway, you can be certain that their paymaster will not let them connect to him – but what about Kingston Parker, he would want prisoners?'

'Kingston Parker?' Colin removed the stub of cheroot from his mouth. 'Never heard of him – around here it's Uncle Colin makes the decisions.' And he grinned at Peter, that friendly lopsided grin, and at that moment the flight engineer crossed the cabin and yelled at Colin.

'Irish coast ahead – we'll be landing at Enniskerry in seven minutes, sir.'

Air traffic control at Enniskerry had been apprised of the emergency. They stacked the other traffic in holding pattern above circuit altitude and cleared the two R.A.F. helicopters for immediate landing.

They came clattering out of the low grey cloud and rain, and settled on the hangar apron. Immediately a police car with headlights burning in the gloom, sped out from between the hangars and parked beside the leading machine. Before the rotors had stopped turning, two members of the Irish Constabulary and a representative of the surveyor general's office were scrambling up into the camouflaged fuselage.

'Stride.' Peter introduced himself quickly. He was dressed now in Thor assault gear, the one piece fitted black suit and soft boots, the pistol on its webbing belt strapped down to his right thigh.

'General, we've had a confirmation,' the police inspector

told him while they were still shaking hands. 'Local people have identified O'Shaughnessy from a police photograph. He is staying in the area all right.'

'Have they found where?' Peter demanded.

'They have, sir. It's an old rambling building on the edge of the village—' He motioned the bespectacled surveyor to come forward with the file he was clutching to his chest. There was no chart table in the stripped-out hull of the helicopter, and they spread the survey map and photographs on the deck.

Colin Noble ordered across the team from the second helicopter, and twenty men crowded into a huddle about the maps. 'There, that's the building.' The surveyor placed a circle on the map with a blue pencil.

'Right,' grunted Colin. 'We've got good fixes – we pick up either the river or the road and follow it to the bridge and the church. The target is between them.'

'Haven't we got a blow-up of the building, a plan of the interior?' one of the Thor team asked.

'Sorry, there wasn't time to do a proper search,' the surveyor apologized.

'The local police reported again a few minutes ago, and we got a relay on the radio. They say the house is enclosed by a high stone wall and that there are no signs of activity.'

'They haven't been near it?' Peter demanded. 'They were strictly ordered not to approach the suspects.'

'They drove past once on the public road.' The inspector looked slightly abashed. 'They wanted to make certain that—'

'If it's O'Shaughnessy, he needs only one sniff and he'll be gone—' Peter's expression was stony, but his eyes sparkled blue with anger. ' – Why can't these people do what they are told?' He turned quickly to the helicopter pilot in his yellow life jacket and helmet with its built-in microphone and earphones.

'Can you get us in?'

The pilot did not answer immediately but glanced up at the nearest window; a fresh gout of rain splashed against the pane.

'It will be dark in ten minutes, or even earlier, and the ceiling is down to the deck now, we only got down here using the airport V.O.R. beacons—' He looked dubious. ' – There is nobody aboard who will recognize the target, hell – I don't know – I could get you in at first light tomorrow.'

'It has to be tonight, now. Right now.'

'If you could get the local police to mark the target—' the pilot suggested, ' – with torches or a flare.'

'There is no chance of that – we have to go in cold, and the longer we sit here talking the less our chances. Will you give it your best shot?' Peter was almost pleading, the go decision is one that cannot be forced on a pilot, even air traffic control cannot force a pilot-in-command to operate beyond his personal judgement.

'We will have to try and keep ground contact all the way; it's classic conditions for trouble, rising terrain and deteriorating weather—'

'Try it—' Peter said, ' – please.'

The pilot hesitated five seconds longer.

'Let's go!' he said abruptly, and there was a concerted rush for the hatchway as the second Thor team made for the other machine, and the police and surveyor made certain they were not included on the passenger list.

Turbulence slogged the helicopter like the punches of a heavyweight prize fighter, and she dipped and staggered to them with a nauseatingly giddy action.

The ground flickered past under them, very close, and yet darkly insubstantial in the wild night. The headlights of a solitary vehicle on a lonely country road, the cluttered lights of a village, each a distinct yellow rectangle they were so close, these were the only landmarks with any meaning – the rest was dark patches of woods, the threads of hedges and stone walls drawn lightly across sombre fields, and every few minutes even that was gone as a fresh squall of grey clouds and rain washed away all vision, and the pilot concentrated all his attention on the dull glow of the flight instruments arranged in their distinctive T layout in front of him.

Each time they emerged from cloud, the light seemed to have diminished and the dark menace of earth loomed more threateningly as they were forced lower and lower to keep contact.

Peter was squeezed into the jump seat of the helicopter's flight deck, between the two pilots, and Colin crowded in behind him, all of them peering ahead, all silent and tense as the ungainly machines lumbered low and heavy over the earth, groping for the shoreline.

They hit the coast, the ghostly white line of surf flared with phosphorescence only fifty feet below them, and the pilot swung them to run south with it – and seconds later another brighter field of lights appeared below them.

'Wicklow,' said the pilot, and his co-pilot called the new heading; now they had made a fix they could head for Laragh directly.

They swung onto the new heading, following the road inland.

'Four minutes to target,' the co-pilot shouted at Peter, stabbing ahead with his finger, and Peter did not try to answer in the clatter and roar of the rotors, but he reached down and checked the Walther in its quick-release holster; it came out cleanly in his fist.

Gilly O'Shaughnessy threw his few personal possessions into the blue canvas airways grip, a change of underclothing and his shaving gear. Then he pulled the iron bedstead away from the wall, ripped back the skirting board and cleared out the hiding-place he had made there by removing a single brick.

There were the new papers and passports. Caliph had even provided papers for the brat – Helen Barry – his daughter. Caliph had thought of everything. With the papers was six hundred pounds sterling in travellers' cheques, and a package of spare ammunition for the pistol. He thrust these into the pocket of his jacket, and took one last look around the bare bleak room. He knew that he had left nothing to lead the hunters, because he never carried anything that could be used to identify him. Yet he was obsessed by the need to destroy all sign of his passing. He had long ago ceased to think of himself by the name of Gilly O'Shaughnessy. He had no name, and only one purpose – that purpose was destruction. The magnificent passion to reduce all life to decay and mortification.

He could recite by heart most of Bakunin's *The Revolutionary Catechism*, especially the definition of the true revolutionary:

> The lost man, who has no belongings, no outside interest, no personal ties of any sort – not even a name. Possessed of but one thought, interest and passion – the revolution. A man who has broken with Society, broken with its laws and conventions. He must despise the opinions of others, and be prepared for death and torture at any time. Hard towards himself, he must be hard to others, and in his heart there must be no place for love, friendship, gratitude or even honour.

As he stood now in the empty room, he saw himself in a

rare moment of revelation, as the man he had set out to become – the true revolutionary, and his head turned for a moment to indulge in the vanity of regarding his own image in the mirror screwed to the peeling wallpaper above the iron bedstead.

It was the dark cold face of the lost man, and he felt proud to belong to that élite class, the cutting edge of the sword, that was what he was.

He picked up the canvas grip, and strode through into the kitchen.

'Are you ready?' he called.

'Help me.'

He dropped the grip and stepped to the window. The last of the light was fading swiftly, glowing pink and mother-of-pearl within the drooping, pregnant belly of the sky. It seemed so close he could reach out and touch it. Already the trees of the unkempt orchard were melding into the darkness as the night encroached.

'I cannot carry her on my own,' the doctor whined, and he swung away from the window. It was time to go again. In his life there was always the moving onwards, and always the hunters baying hard upon his scent. It was time to run again, run like the fox.

He went through into the second room. The doctor had the child wrapped in a grey woollen blanket, and he had tried to lift her from the bed, but had failed. She was sprawled awkwardly, half onto the floor.

'Help me,' repeated the doctor.

'Get out of the way.' Gilly O'Shaughnessy pushed him roughly aside, and stooped over the girl. For a second their faces were within inches of each other.

Her eyes were opened, half conscious, although the pupils were widely dilated by the drug. The lids were pink-rimmed and there were little butter-yellow lumps of mucus in the corners. Her lips were dried to white scales, and cracked through to the raw flesh at three places.

'Please tell my daddy,' she whispered. 'Please tell him I'm here.'

His nostrils flared at the sick sour smell of her body, but he picked her up easily with an arm under her knees and the other under her shoulders, and carried her out across the kitchen, kicking open the door so the lock burst and it slammed back against its hinges.

Quickly he carried her across the yard to the garage, with the doctor staggering along after them carrying a carton of medical supplies and equipment against his chest, cursing miserably at the cold, and sliding and slipping in the treacherous footing.

Gilly O'Shaughnessy waited while the doctor opened the rear door of the car, and then he bundled her in so roughly that the child cried out weakly. He ignored her and went to the double garage doors and dragged them open. It was so dark now that he could not see as far as the bridge.

'Where are we going?' bleated the doctor.

'I haven't decided yet,' Gilly told him brusquely. 'There is a safe house up North, or we might go back across the sea to England—' He thought of the caravan again, that was a good one—

'But why are we leaving now, so suddenly?'

He did not bother to reply but left the garage and ran back into the kitchen. Always he was obsessed by the need to cover his tracks, to leave no sign for the hunters.

Though he had brought little with him, and was taking that now, yet he knew the old house contained signs, even if it was only his fingerprints. There was also the single remaining appetite for destruction to assuage.

He ripped the wooden doors off the kitchen cupboards and smashed them to splinters under his heel, piled them in the centre of the wood floor. He crumpled the newspapers piled on the table and added them to the pile, threw the table and chairs upon it.

He lit a match and held it to the crumpled newsprint. It flared readily, and he straightened and opened the windows and doors. The flames fed on the cold fresh air and climbed greedily, catching on the splintered doors.

Gilly O'Shaughnessy picked up the canvas grip and stepped out into the night, crouching to the wind and the rain – but halfway to the garage he straightened again abruptly and paused to listen.

There was a sound on the wind, from the direction of the coast. It might have been the engine note of a heavy truck coming up the hills, but there was a peculiar thin whistling sound mingled with the engine beat, and the volume of sound escalated too sharply to be that of a lumbering truck. It was coming on too swiftly, the sound seemed to fill the air, to emanate from the very clouds themselves.

Gilly O'Shaughnessy stood with his face lifted to the fine silver drizzle, searching the belly of the clouds, until a throbbing regular glow began to beat like a pulse in the sky, and it was a moment until he recognized it as the beacon light of a low-flying aircraft, and at the same moment he knew that the shrill whistle was the whirling of rotors bringing the hunters.

He cried aloud in the certainty of betrayal and onrushing death. 'Why? God, why?' He called to the god he had so long ago denied, and he began to run.

'It's no good.' The pilot twisted his neck to shout at Peter without taking his eyes from the flight instruments which kept the great ungainly machine level and on course. They had lost contact with the other machine.

'We are socked in, blind.' The cloud frothed over the

canopy like boiling milk over the lip of the pot. 'I'm going to have to climb out, and head back for Enniskerry before we run into my number two.'

The risk of collision with the other helicopter was now real and imminent.

The beacon light throbbed above them, reflected off the impenetrable press of soft cloud – but the other pilot would not see it until too late.

'Hold on. Just another minute,' Peter shouted back at him, his expression tortured in the glow of the instrument panel. The entire operation was disintegrating about him, would soon end in tragedy or in fiasco, but he must go on.

'It's no good—' the pilot began, and then shouted with fright and hurled the helicopter over onto its side, at the same instant altering pitch and altitude so the machine shuddered and lurched as though she had run into a solid obstruction, and then bounded upwards, gaining a hundred feet in a swoop.

The spire of a church had leapt at them out of the cloud, like a predator from ambush, and now it flickered by only feet from where they crouched in the flight deck, but it had disappeared again instantly as they roared past.

'The church!' Peter yelled. 'That's it! Turn back.'

The pilot checked the machine, hovering blindly in the chaos of rain and cloud churned to a fury by the down-draught of their own rotor.

'I can't see a damned thing,' shouted the pilot.

'We've got one hundred and seventy feet on the radio altimeter,' his co-pilot called; that was actual height from the ground and still they could see nothing below them.

'Get us down. For God's sake, get us down,' Peter pleaded.

'I can't take the chance. We don't have any idea of what is under us.' The pilot's face was sickly orange in the instrument glow, his eyes the dark pits of a skull. 'I'm climbing out and heading back—'

Peter reached down and the butt of the Walther jumped into his hand, like a living thing. He realized coldly that he was capable of killing the pilot, to force the co-pilot to land – but at the moment there was a hole in the cloud, just enough to make out the dark loom of the earth below them.

'Visual,' Peter shouted. 'We've visual, get us down!' And the helicopter sank swiftly, breaking out suddenly into the clear.

'The river.' Peter saw the glint of water. 'And the bridge—'

'There's the churchyard—' Colin roared eagerly, ' – and that's the target.'

The thatched roof was a black oblong, and light spilled from the windows of one side of the building, so they could see the high enclosing wall. The pilot spun the helicopter on its axis like a compass needle, and dived towards the building.

Colin Noble scrambled down into the cabin, shouting to his team. 'Delta! We are going to Delta—' And the flight engineer slid the hatch cover open. Immediately a fine swirling mist filled the cabin as the down-draught of the rotors churned the rain filled air.

The Thor team were on their feet, forming up on each side of the open hatch, while Colin towered over the flight engineer as he took lead position – 'point' as he always called it.

The dark earth rushed up to meet them, and Colin spat out the cheroot stub and braced himself in the doorway.

'Hit anything that moves,' he yelled. 'But for Chrissake watch out for the kid. Let's go, gang. Let's go!'

Peter was jammed into the jump seat by the swooping drop of the machine, unable to follow, wasting precious seconds – but he had a clear view ahead through the canopy.

The light in the windows of the building wavered unnaturally, and Peter realized that it was burning. Those were flames, and his concern was heightened by the knowledge, but he did not have a chance to ponder this new development. In the shadows of the walled yard he saw movement, just the dark blur of it in the glow of the flames, and what was left of the daylight – but it was the shape of a man, running, crouched low, disappearing almost immediately into one of the outbuildings that flanked the narrow stone walled lane.

Peter dragged himself out of the seat against the G force, scrambling awkwardly down into the cabin as the helicopter dropped the last few feet, and then hung, swaying slightly, suspended ten feet above the open yard at the rear of the house – and black-clad figures spilled out of her, dropping lightly onto their feet and racing forward as they touched ground, seeming to disappear again miraculously through the doors and windows of the building. Even in the grinding tension of the moment Peter felt the flare of pride in the way it was done, instant and seemingly effortless penetration, the lead man using the sandbags to break in glass and wooden shutters and the man behind him going in with a clean controlled dive.

Peter was the last man left aboard, and something made him check in the open hatchway before jumping. Perhaps it was that glimpse of movement outside the main building that he had been given; he looked back that way, and suddenly lights leapt in solid white lances down the walled lane – the headlights of a motor vehicle, and at the same moment the vehicle launched itself from the dark derelict outbuilding and rocketed away down the lane.

Peter teetered in the open hatch, for he had been in the very act of jumping, but he caught his balance now, grabbing wildly at the nylon line above the door. The vehicle slowed for the turn into the main road at the bridge – and Peter caught the flight engineer and shook his shoulder violently, pointing after the escaping vehicle. His lips were inches from the man's face.

'Don't let it get away!' he screamed, and the flight engineer was quick and alert; he spoke urgently into his microphone, directly to the pilot in the flight deck above them, and obediently the helicopter swung around and the beat of the engines changed as the rotors altered pitch and roared in forward thrust – the machine lunged forward, skimming the garage roof by mere feet and then hammered out into the night in pursuit of the dwindling glow of headlights.

Peter had to hang out of the hatchway to see ahead, and the wind clamoured around his head and tore at his body, but they were swiftly overhauling the vehicle as it raced down the twisting narrow road towards the coast.

It was two hundred yards ahead, and the dark tree tops seemed to rush by at the same level as the hatch in which Peter stood. A hundred yards ahead now, the headlights blazing through the drivel of rain, etching fleeting cameos of hedges and starkly lit stone walls from the night.

They were close enough now for Peter to make out that it was a smallish vehicle with an estate car body, not quite large enough to be a station wagon – the driver was throwing it through the curves and twists of the road with reckless skill, but the helicopter crept up behind him.

'Tell him to switch off the beacon light.' Peter swung inboard to shout in the flight engineer's ear. He did not want to warn the driver that he was being followed, but as the engineer lifted the microphone to his mouth the headlights snapped out into darkness. The driver had become aware, and after the brilliance of the headlights the night seemed totally dark, and the car disappeared into it.

Peter felt the helicopter lurch, as the pilot was taken by surprise, and his own dismay was a lance.

We have lost them, he thought, and he knew that it was suicide to fly on in darkness only a few feet above the treetops, but the pilot of the helicopter steadied the craft and then suddenly the earth below them was lit by a blaze of stark white light that startled Peter until he realized that the pilot had switched on his landing lights. There were two of them, one on each side of the fuselage; they were aimed down and slightly forward.

The escaping car was caught fairly in their brilliance.

The helicopter dropped lower, edging in between the telegraph poles and trees that lined the narrow road.

Now Peter could see that the car was a dark blue Austin, with a carrying rack bolted to the long roof. It was that carrying rack which decided him. Without it no human being could have hoped for purchase on the smooth rounded roof of the lurching, swaying car.

The doctor in the back seat of the Austin had been the one who spotted the helicopter. The engine noise and the drumming of the wind had covered the whistling whine of the rotors, and Gilly O'Shaughnessy had chuckled with grim triumph and self-congratulation. He had deliberately waited for the helicopter to discharge its load of fighting men before he had switched on his headlights and roared out of the garage into the lane.

He knew it would be many minutes before the assault team realized that the burning house was empty and that it would take as long again to regroup and board the helicopter to continue the hunt – and by that time he would be clear; there was a safe house in Dublin – or there had been, four year previously. Perhaps it was blown now; in that case he would have to get rid of the brat and Dr Jameson, a bullet each in the back of the head, and drive the Austin into the Irish Sea.

The wild exhilaration of danger and death was upon him again, the waiting was over at last and he was living again the way he had chosen – the fox running ahead of the hounds, he was alive again, with his right foot thrust flat to the floor boards and the Austin rocketing through the night.

The girl was screaming weakly from the back seat, in pain and panic; the doctor was trying to quieten her, and Gilly laughed aloud. The tyres screeched wildly as he skidded out in the turn, brushing the hedge with the side before he was through.

'They are following,' screamed the doctor, as he straightened the car into the next stretch, then Gilly glanced back over his shoulder. He could see nothing through the rear windows.

'What?'

'The helicopter—'

Gilly lowered his window and, driving with one hand, thrust his head out. The flashing aircraft beacon was close behind and above, and he ducked back in and looked ahead to make sure that the road ran straight, then he switched off the headlights.

In total darkness he did not diminish speed, and now when he laughed it was a wild and reckless sound.

'You're mad,' the doctor shrieked. 'You'll kill us all!'

'Right you are, doctor!' But his night vision was clearing and he caught the Austin before she wandered into the stone wall on the left-hand side, and at the same moment he jerked the pistol from under his cape and laid it on the seat beside him.

'There is not going to be—' he began and then broke off as the blinding light burst over them. The helicopter had switched on its landing lights – the road ahead was brightly lit, and he skidded into the next turn with rubber squealing.

'Stop!' the doctor pleaded, trying to hold the semiconscious child from being hurled about in the swaying cab. 'Let's give up now, before they kill us.'

'They've got no fighting men on board,' Gilly yelled back at him. 'There's nothing they can do.'

'Give up,' the doctor whined. 'Let's get out of this alive.'

And Gilly O'Shaughnessy threw back his head and roared with laughter.

'I'm keeping three bullets, doctor, one for each of us—'

'They're right on top of us.'

Gilly snatched up the pistol and once again thrust his head and right shoulder out, twisting to look upwards.

The eye-searing lights beamed down upon him, very close above. It was all he could see and he fired at them, the crash of the shots lost in the clattering whistling roar of the rotors and the tearing rush of the wind.

Poised in the hatchway, Peter counted the bright orange spurts of gunfire. There were five of them, but there was no sound of passing shot, no thump of the strike.

'Get lower!' he shouted at the engineer, reinforcing the order with urgent hand signals, and obediently the big machine sank down upon the racing Austin.

Peter gathered himself, judging his moment carefully, and when it came he launched himself clear of the hatchway, and his guts seemed to cram into his throat as he dropped.

He dropped with all four limbs spread and braced to land together, but for a moment he thought he had misjudged it and would fall behind the Austin, into the metalled roadway, to be crushed and shredded by the forward impetus of the low-flying helicopter.

Then the Austin swerved and checked slightly and Peter crashed into its roof with stunning force; he felt the metal buckle and sag under him, and then he was rolling and slipping sideways. His whole left side was numbed by the force of impact, and he clutched wildly with his right hand, his fingernails tearing at the paintwork, but still he slid towards the edge, his legs kicking wildly in dark rushing space.

At the last instant before he was hurled into the roadway, his clawed fingers hooked in the framework of the roof rack, and he hung bat-like from his one arm. It had taken only a small part of a second, and immediately the driver of the Austin realized that there was a man on the roof. He slewed the little car from one side of the road to the other, short wrenching turns that brought her over on two outside wheels before slamming back and twisting the other way. The tyres squealed harsh protest, and Peter was flung brutally back and forth, the muscle and tendons of his right arm popping and creaking with the strain of holding on – but feeling was flooding swiftly back into his numbed left side.

He had to move quickly, he could not survive another of those wrenching swerves, and he gathered himself, judged the Austin's momentum, and used it to roll and grab with his free hand; at the same moment the toes of his soft boots found purchase on one of the struts of the roof carrier, and he pressed himself belly down, clinging with both arms and legs to the wildly swinging machine.

The Austin checked and steadied as a steep turn appeared ahead in the arc lights of the helicopter which still hung over them. The driver shot the car into the corner, and ahead of them was a long extended drop as the road twisted down the hills towards the coast.

Peter half lifted himself and was about to slide forward when the metal six inches in front of his nose exploded outwards, leaving a neatly punched hole through the roof, and tiny fragments of flying metal stung his cheek; at the same moment the concussion of the pistol shot beat in upon his eardrums. The driver of the Austin was firing blindly up through the coachwork, and he had misjudged Peter's position above him by inches. Peter threw himself desperately to one side, for an instant almost losing his grip on the struts of the carrier – and another pistol bullet clanged out through the metal roof, that one would have taken him through the belly, and Peter had a fleeting image of the kind of wound that it would have inflicted, the bullet would have been mushroomed and deformed by the roof and would have broken up inside his body.

Desperately Peter threw himself back the opposite way, trying to outguess the gunman below him, and once again the crash of the shot and the metal roof erupted in a little jagged pockmark, flecking the paintwork away so the rim of the bullet hole shone like polished silver shilling. Again it would have hit him, if he had not moved.

Peter rolled again, tensing his belly muscles in the anticipation of the tearing, paralysing impact, expecting the gun shot – which did not come. Only then he remembered the wasted pistol fire the driver had thrown up at the hovering helicopter. He had emptied his pistol and as the realization dawned on Peter there was another completely compelling sound, very faint in the drumming rush of the wind and the engine roar – but unmistakable. It was the sound of a young girl screaming and it galvanized Peter as nothing else, even the threat of death, could have done.

He came up on toes and fingers, like a cat, and he went forward and to the right, until he was directly above the driver's seat

The girl screamed again, and he recognized Melissa-Jane's voice. There was no question of it, and he slipped the Walther from its quick-release holster and cocked the hammer with the same movement, one glance ahead and they were rushing down on another turn in the narrow road. The driver would be using both hands to control the swaying and bucking little machine.

'Now!' he told himself, and dropped forward, so that he was peering backwards and upside-down through the windscreen directly into the driver's pale face and at a distance of only eighteen inches.

In the thousandth part of a second Peter recognized the dark, wolfish features and the cold, merciless eyes of the killer. He had hunted this man for many years and studied his photograph endlessly when the hunting of the Provo terrorists had been his life's work.

Gilly O'Shaughnessy was driving with both hands, the pistol still gripped in one of them and the chamber open for reloading. He snarled at Peter like an animal through the bars of its cage, and Peter fired with the muzzle of the Walther touching the glass of the windscreen.

The glass starred into a glittering sheet, white and opaque, and then it collapsed inwards with the force of the wind, filling the interior of the Austin with flying diamond chips of sparkling glass.

Gilly O'Shaughnessy had thrown up both hands to his face, but bright blood burst from between them, spattering his chest and soaking swiftly into the lank black hair.

Still hanging upside down across the Austin's cab, Peter thrust the Walther in through the shattered windscreen until it almost touched the man's body and he fired twice more into his chest, where the explosive Velex bullets would break up against bone, and would not overpenetrate to harm anybody else in the interior. Melissa-Jane's screams still rang clearly in his ears, as he killed Gilly O'Shaughnessy. He did it as coldly as a veterinary surgeon would put down a rabid dog, and with as little pleasure, and the bullets punched Gilly O'Shaughnessy back on the bucket seat, head lolling from side to side, and Peter expected the howl of the engine to cut out now as the dead man's foot slipped from the accelerator.

It did not happen. There was no change in the engine beat, the body had slid forward and jammed, the knee under the dashboard bearing down fully on the pedal, and the little car flew down the slope of the hill, the stone walls on each side blurring past as though down a tunnel in the depths of the earth.

Peter wriggled forward and thrust both arms through the shattered windscreen and caught the untended wheel as it began to spin aimlessly. He checked the Austin and swung her back into the road but she had been driven to her limits, rocking and swaying crazily before she righted herself and flew down the hill.

It was almost impossible to judge the control needed to keep her on the road.

Peter was hanging head down, gripping only with knees and toes, and he had to manipulate the wheel from this inverted position with his upper arms sawing across the teeth of jagged glass still remaining in the frame of the windscreen.

The wind whipped and clawed him, and Gilly O'Shaughnessy's body flopped forward bonelessly onto the wheel, jamming it at a critical moment, so that while Peter used one hand to shove him backwards, the side of the Austin touched the stone wall with a screech of rending metal and a shower of orange sparks. Peter wrenched her back into the road, and she began a series of uncontrolled broadsides, swinging wildly from side to side, touching the wall with another jarring shock, then swinging back sideways to bounce over the verge, then back again.

She was going over, Peter knew it, and he would be crushed under the metal roof and smeared along the abrasive surface of the macadam road. He should jump now, and take his chances – but grimly he stayed with the crazed machine, for Melissa-Jane was in her and he could not leave.

She survived one more skid, and ahead Peter had the glimpse of a barred wooden gate in the wall. Deliberately he turned the front wheels into the direction of the next skid, no longer trying to counteract it, but aggravating it –

steering directly for the gate, and the Austin smashed into it.

A wooden beam cartwheeled over Peter's head, and a scalding cloud of steam from the shattered radiator stung his face and hands, and then the Austin was into the open field, bouncing and thudding over the rocks that studded it, the drag of soft muddy earth slowing her, and the steep slope of the hillside against her – within fifty feet the front end dropped heavily into a drainage ditch, and the little car shuddered to a halt, canted at an abandoned angle.

Peter slipped over the side and landed on his feet. He jerked open the rear door and a man half fell from the cab. He dropped onto his knees in the mud, blubbering incoherently and Peter drove his right knee into his face. Bone and cartilage crunched sharply and there was the crackle of breaking teeth. His voice was cut off abruptly and, as he dropped, Peter chopped him with the stiffened blade of his right hand, a controlled blow – judged finely to immobilize but not to kill, and before the unconscious body dropped, Peter had gone in over it.

He lifted his daughter out of the Austin, and the frail wasted body felt unsubstantial in his arms, and the heat of fever and infection burned against his chest.

He was possessed by an almost uncontrollable desire to crush her body to him with all the strength of his arms, but instead he carried her as though she was made of some precious and fragile substance, stepping carefully over the uneven rocky surface of the field to where the helicopter was settling cumbersomely out of the darkness.

The Thor doctor was still aboard her; he jumped clear before the helicopter touched and ran towards Peter in the brilliant glare of the landing lights.

Peter found he was crooning softly.

'It's all right now, darling. It's all over now. It's all finished, my baby – I'm here, little one—'

Then Peter made another discovery. It was not sweat running down his cheeks and dripping from his chin, and he wondered unashamedly when last it was he had wept. He could not remember, and it did not seem important, not now, not with his daughter in his arms.

Cynthia came down to London, and Peter relived some of those horrors from their marriage.

'Everybody around you always has to suffer, Peter. Now it's Melissa-Jane's turn.'

He could not avoid her, nor her martyred expression, for she was always at Melissa-Jane's bedside. While he bore her recriminations and barbed accusations, he wondered that she had ever been gay and young and attractive. She was two years younger than he was but she already had the shapeless body and greying mind that made her seem twenty years older.

Melissa-Jane responded almost miraculously to the antibiotics, and although she was still weak and skinny and pale, the doctor discharged her on the third day, and Peter and Cynthia had their final degrading haggling and bargaining session which Melissa-Jane settled for them.

'Mummy, I'm still so afraid. Can't I go with Daddy – just for a few days?'

Finally Cynthia agreed with sighs and pained airs that left them both feeling a little guilty. On the drive down to Abbots Yew, where Steven had invited them for as long as was necessary for Melissa-Jane's convalescence, she sat very quietly beside Peter, her left hand still in the sling and the finger wearing a small neat white turban. She spoke only after they had passed the Heathrow turn off on the M4.

'All the time I knew you were going to come. I can't remember much else. It was always dark and giddymaking –

things kept changing. I'd look at a face and it would fade away, and then we'd be somewhere else—'

'It was the drug they were giving you,' Peter explained.

'Yes, I know that. I remember the prick of the needle—' Reflexively she rubbed her upper arm, and shivered briefly. 'But even with the drug I always knew you were going to come. I remember lying in the darkness listening for your voice—'

There was the temptation to try to pretend it had never happened, and Melissa-Jane had not spoken about it until now – but Peter knew she must be allowed to talk it out.

'Would you like to tell me about it?' he invited gently, knowing that it was essential to the healing process. He listened quietly as she spilled out drug-haunted memories, disjointed scraps of conversation and impressions. The terror was back in her voice when she spoke of the dark one.

'He looked at me sometimes. I remember him looking at me—' And Peter remembered the cold killer's eyes.

'He is dead now, darling.'

'Yes, I know. They told me.' She was silent for a moment, and then went on. 'He was so different from the one with grey hair. I liked him, the old one. His name was Doctor Jameson.'

'How did you know that?' Peter asked.

'That's what the dark one called him.' She smiled. Doctor Jameson, I remember he always smelled like cough nixture and I liked him—'

The one who had done the amputation, and would have aken her hand as well, Peter thought grimly.

'I never saw the other one. I knew he was there, but I never saw him.'

'The other one?' Peter turned to her sharply. 'Which ther one, darling?'

'There was another one – and even the dark one was fraid of him. I knew that, they were all afraid of him.'

'You never saw him?'

'No, but they were always talking about him, and arguing about what he would do—'

'Do you remember his name?' Peter asked, and Melissa-Jane frowned in concentration.

'Did he have a name?' Peter prompted.

'Usually they just talked about *him*, but, yes, I remember now. The dark one called him "Casper".'

'Casper?'

'No, not that, not Casper. Oh, I can't remember.' Her voice had risen, a shrill note in terror that ripped at Peter's nerves.

'Don't worry about it.' He tried to soothe her, but she shook her head with frustration.

'Not Casper, a name like that. I knew he was the one who really wanted to hurt me – they were just doing what he told them. He was the one I was truly afraid of.' Her voice ended with a sob, and she was sitting bolt upright in the seat.

'It's over now, darling.' Peter swung into the verge of the road and braked to a halt. He reached for her but she was rigid in his arms and at his touch she began to shake uncontrollably. Peter's alarm flared, and he held her to his chest.

'Caliph!' she whispered. 'That's his name. Caliph.' And she relaxed against him softly, and sighed. The shaking stopped slowly. Peter went on holding her, trying to control the terrible consuming waves of anger that engulfed him, and it was some little time before he realized suddenly that Melissa-Jane had fallen asleep.

It was as though uttering the name had been a catharsis for her terror, and now she was ready to begin the healing inside.

Peter laid her gently back in the seat and covered her with the angora rug before he drove on, but every few seconds he glanced across to make sure she was at peace.

Twice Peter called Magda Altmann from Abbots Yew, both times to her private number, but she was unobtainable and there was no message for him. That was five days he had not been able to reach her, not since the Delta Strike which had freed Melissa-Jane. She seemed to have disappeared completely, and Peter pondered the implications during the quiet days when he was almost always alone with his daughter.

Then Dr Kingston Parker arrived at Abbots Yew, and Sir Steven Stride was delighted to have as his guest such a distinguished statesman.

Kingston Parker's giant personality seemed to fill the beautiful old home. When he put himself out, his graciousness was irresistible. Steven was delighted with him, particularly when he discovered that despite Parker's image as a liberal and his well-known concern with human rights, he was also a champion of the capitalist system, and determined that his country should take more seriously its responsibilities as leader of the Western world. They both deplored the loss of the B1 bomber and the delaying of the neutron bomb programme, and the restructuring of America's intelligence agencies. They spent much of the first afternoon in Steven's redwood-panelled study exploring each other's views, and came out of it fast friends.

When they emerged, Parker completed his conquest of the Stride household by showing he shared with Patricia Stride a scholarly knowledge and love of antique porcelain. His concern and warmth for Melissa-Jane and his relief at her safety were too spontaneous not to be entirely genuine. His conquest of that young lady's affections was complete when he went down with her to the stables to meet Florence Nightingale and prove that he was also a fair judge of horseflesh.

'He's a lovely man. I think he is truly an honourable man,' Melissa-Jane told Peter, when he went up to her bedroom to bid her goodnight – 'And he's so kind and funny—' Then, lest there be any question of disloyalty, 'But you are still my most favourite man in all the world.'

Her cure and convalescence seemed almost complete, and as Peter went down to rejoin the company he marvelled again at the resilience of young flesh and young minds.

As usual at Abbots Yew there was glittering and stimulating company at dinner, with Kingston Parker at its centre, but afterwards he and Peter exchanged a single glance down the length of Pat Stride's silver- and candle-decorated table and they left them to the port and cognac and cigars and slipped out unobtrusively into the walled rose garden.

While they paced side by side on the crunching gravel pathway, Kingston Parker stoked his meerschaum and then began to talk quietly. Once his bodyguard coughed in the shadows where he waited just out of range of their subdued voices, but that was the only intrusion and the spring night was still and balmy. Their conversation seemed utterly incongruous in these surroundings, talk of death and violence, the use and abuse of power, and the manipulations of vast fortunes by a single mysterious figure.

'It's been five days since I arrived in England—' Kingston Parker shrugged. 'One does not rush through the echoing passages of Whitehall. There was much to discuss—' Peter knew that he had met with the Prime Minister on two separate occasions ' – and it wasn't just Atlas business, I'm afraid—' Parker was one of the President's confidants. They would have taken full advantage of his visit to exchange views with the British Government. 'However, we did discuss Atlas in depth and detail. You know very well that Atlas has opponents and critics on both sides of the Atlantic. They tried very hard to squash it, and when they could not they saw to it that its power and duties were severely curtailed—' Parker paused and his pipe gurgled. He flicked out the juices from the mouthpiece onto the gravel path. 'The opponents of Atlas are all highly intelligent concerned and informed men. Their motives and their reasoning in opposing Atlas are laudable. I find myself a little in sympathy despite myself. If you create a strike force such as Atlas, where enormous powers are placed in the hands of a single man or a small élite leadership, you could very well be creating a Frankenstein – a monster more frightening than you are setting out to destroy.'

'That depends on the man who controls it, Dr Parker. I believe that they have the right man.'

'Thank you, Peter.' Parker turned his big shaggy head and smiled. 'Won't you please call me Kingston.'

Peter nodded agreement, while Parker went on. 'Atlas has had some spectacular successes – at Johannesburg and now in Ireland – but that makes it more dangerous. There will be a readier acceptance of the whole concept by the public; if Atlas asks for wider powers, it is more likely they would be granted. And, believe me, if it is to do the job it needs wider powers, Peter. I find myself torn down the centre—'

'And yet,' Peter pointed out, 'we cannot take on the most dangerous animal in the world, man the killer, we cannot do it without arming ourselves in every possible way.'

Kingston Parker sighed. 'And if Atlas achieves those powers, who can say when they will be abused, when will the rule of force supersede the rule of law?'

'The rules have changed. The rule of law is so often powerless in the face of those who have no respect for the law.'

'There is another aspect, Peter. One that I have thought about half my life. What about the rule of unjust law? The laws of oppression and greed. A law that enslaves or deprives a man because of the colour of his face or the god he worships? If a duly constituted parliament makes racial laws – or if the General Assembly of the United Nations declares that Zionism is a form of Imperialism and must be outlawed. – What if a handful of men gain control of the world's resources and legally manipulate them in a manner dictated by personal greed to the detriment of all mankind, such as the Committee of the OPEC, the Shah and the King of Saudi Arabia—' Kingston Parker made a helpless gesture, spreading those long sensitive fingers. 'Must we respect those laws? The rule of law, even unjust law, is it sacrosanct?'

'Balance,' said Peter. 'There has to be a balance between law and force.'

'Yes, but what is the balance, Peter?' He abruptly closed his hands into fists. 'I have asked for greater powers for Atlas, wider scope for its use, and I think these will be granted. When they are, we will have need of good men, Peter.' Kingston Parker reached out and took Peter's shoulder in a surprisingly powerful grip. 'Just men, who can recognize when the rule of law has either failed or is unjust, and who have the courage and the vision to act to restore the balance that you spoke of a moment ago.'

His hand was still on Peter's shoulder and he left it there. It was a natural gesture, without affectation.

'I believe you are one of those men.' He let the hand drop, and his manner changed. 'Tomorrow I have arranged that we meet with Colonel Noble. He has been busy breaking down and examining the entire Irish operation, and I hope he will have come up with something for us to get our teeth into. Then there is much else to discuss. Two o'clock at Thor Command, will it suit you, Peter?'

'Of course.'

'Now let's go in and join the company.'

'Wait.' Peter stopped him. 'I have something I must tell you, Kingston. It's been tearing at my guts, and after you have heard it you may alter your opinion of me – my suitability for my role at Atlas.'

'Yes?' Parker turned back and waited quietly.

'You know that the people who kidnapped my daughter

made no demands for her return, made no attempt to contact me or the police to negotiate.'

'Yes,' Parker answered. 'Of course. It was one of the puzzling things about the whole business.'

'It was untrue. There was a contact and a demand.'

'I don't understand.' Parker frowned and thrust his face closer to Peter's, as though trying to study his expression in the poor light from the windows.

'The kidnappers contacted me A letter which I destroyed—'

'Why?' Parker shot at him.

'Wait. I'll explain,' Peter replied. 'There was a single condition for my daughter's release, and a deadline of two weeks. If I did not meet the condition by that time, they would have sent me parts of my daughter's body – her hands, her feet, and finally her head.'

'Diabolical,' Parker whispered. 'Inhuman. What was the condition?'

'A life for a life,' said Peter. 'I was to kill you in exchange for Melissa-Jane.'

'Me!' Parker started, throwing back his head with shock. 'They wanted me?'

Peter did not reply, and they stood staring at each other, until Parker raised his hand and combed at his hair, a distracted gesture.

'That changes it all. I will have to think it out carefully – but it makes a whole new scenario.' He shook his head. 'Me. They were going for the head of Atlas. Why? Because I was the champion of Atlas, and they opposed its formation? No! That's not it. There seems only one logical explanation. I told you last time I saw you that I suspected the existence of a central figure – the puppetmaster who was taking control of all known militant organizations and welding them into a single cohesive and formidable entity. Well, Peter, I have been hunting this figure. I have learned much to confirm my suspicions since last we met. I believe this person, or assembly of persons, does in fact exist – part of the new powers I have asked for Atlas were to be used to hunt and destroy this organization before it does grave damage – before it succeeds in so terrifying the nations of the world that it becomes itself a world power—' Parker stopped as though to gather his thoughts, and then went on in quiet, more measured tones. 'I think now that this is absolute proof that it does exist, and that it is aware of my suspicions and intentions to destroy it. When I set you up as Atlas agent at large, I believed you would make contact with the enemy – but, God knows, I did not expect it to come like this.'

He paused again, considering it. 'Incredible!' he marvelled. 'The one person whom I would never have suspected, you Peter. You could have reached me at any time, one of the few people who could. And the leverage! Your daughter – the protracted mutilations – I may have just misjudged the cunning and ruthlessness of the enemy.'

'Have you ever heard the name Caliph?' Peter asked.

'Where did you hear that?' Parker demanded harshly.

'The demand letter was signed Caliph, and Melissa-Jane heard her captors discussing it.'

'Caliph.' Parker nodded. 'Yes, I have heard the name, Peter. Since I last spoke to you. I have heard the name. Indeed I have.' He was silent again, sucking distractedly on his pipe, then he looked up. 'I will tell you how and when tomorrow when we meet at Thor, but now you have given me much to keep me awake tonight.'

He took Peter's arm and led him back towards the house. Warm yellow light and laughter spilled out from the downstairs windows, welcoming and gay, but both of them were withdrawn and silent as they trudged up the smoothly raked path.

At the garden door Kingston Parker paused, holding Peter back from entering.

'Peter, would you have done it?' he asked gruffly.

Peter answered him levelly without attempting to avoid his eyes. 'Yes, Kingston, I would have done it.'

'How?'

'Explosives.'

'Better than poison,' Parker grunted. 'Not as good as the gun.' And then angrily, 'We have to stop him, Peter. It is a duty that supersedes every other consideration.'

'What I have just told you does not alter our relationship?' Peter asked. 'The fact that I would have been your assassin – does not change it?'

'Strangely enough, it merely confirms what I have come to believe of you, Peter. You are a man with the hard ruthless streak we need, if we are to survive.' He smiled bleakly. 'I might wake up sweating in the night – but it doesn't alter what we have to do – you and I.'

Colin Noble with his cheroot, and opposite him Kingston Parker with the amber meerschaum, seemed to be in competition as to who could soonest render the air in the room incapable of supporting human life. It was already thick and blue, and the temporary headquarters of Thor Command lacked air-conditioning – but within minutes Peter had become so immersed in what he was hearing that the discomfort was forgotten.

Colin Noble was going over the details of the Irish operation, and all that had been gleaned from it.

'The house, the Old Manse, was burned to the ground, of course. The Irish constabulary had twenty men sifting through the ashes—' He spread his hands. 'A big nix. Nothing at all.'

'Next the contents of the Austin and its – provenance – now do you like that word, Peter baby? Provenance, that's a classy word.'

Parker smiled indulgently. 'Please go on, Colin.'

'The Austin was stolen in Dublin, and resprayed and fitted with the roof carrier. It contained nothing, no papers, nothing in the glove compartment or boot, it had been stripped and cleaned out by an expert—'

'The men,' Parker prompted him.

'Yes, sir. The men. The dead one first. Name of Gerald O'Shaughnessy, also known as "Gilly", born Belfast 1946—' As he spoke Colin picked up the file that lay on the table in front of him. It was five inches thick. ' – Do we want to read all of it? It's a hell of a story. The guy had a track record—'

'Only as far as it concerns Atlas,' Parker told him.

'There is no evidence as to when or how he became involved with this business—' Colin sketched the facts swiftly and succinctly. ' – So we end with the contents of his pockets. Six hundred pounds sterling, thirty-eight rounds of .38 ammunition, and papers in the name of Edward and Helen Barry – forged, but beautifully forged.' Colin closed the file with a slap. 'Nothing,' he repeated. 'Nothing we can use. Now the other man Morrison – Claude Bertram Morrison – celebrated abortionist and dedicated alcoholic Struck off the medical rolls in 1969—' Again he recounted the sordid history swiftly and accurately. ' – His price for the digital surgery was three thousand pounds – half in advance Hell, that's cheaper than the Blue Cross.' Colin grinned but his eyes were black and bright with anger. 'I am pleased to report that he can expect a sentence of approximately fifteen years. They are going to throw the book at him. There is only one item of any possible interest which he could give us. Gilly O'Shaughnessy was the leader from whom he took his orders, O'Shaughnessy in turn took his orders from somebody called—' He paused dramatically. 'Yes, that's right. The name we have all heard before. Caliph.'

'Just one point here,' Kingston Parker interrupted.

'Caliph likes to use his name. He signs it on his correspondence. Even his lowliest thugs are given the name to use. Why?'

'I think I can answer that.' Peter stirred and raised his head. 'He wants us to know that he exists. We must have a focal point for our fear and hatred. When he was merely a nameless, faceless entity he was not nearly as menacing as he is now.'

'I think you are right.' Parker nodded his head gravely. 'By using the name he is building up a store of credibility which he will draw upon later. In future when Caliph says he will kill or mutilate we know he is in deadly earnest, there will be no compromise. He will do exactly as he promises. The man, or men, are clever psychologists.'

'There is just one aspect of the Irish operation we have not yet considered,' Peter broke in, frowning with concentration. 'That is – who was it that tipped us off, and what was the reason for that telephone call?'

They were all silent, until Parker turned to Colin.

'What do you think of that one?'

'I have discussed it with the police, of course. It was one of the first things that puzzled us. The police believe that Gilly O'Shaughnessy picked his hideout in Ireland because he was familiar with the terrain, and had friends there. It was his old stamping ground when he was with the Provos. He could move and disappear, get things fixed.' Colin paused and saw the sceptical expression on Peter's face. 'Well, look at it this way, Peter baby. He had a woman negotiate the lease on the Old Manse – Kate Barry, she called herself and signed it on the lease – so that was one ally. There must have been others, because he was able to buy a stolen and reworked automobile – he would have had difficulty doing that in Edinburgh or London without the word getting about.'

Peter nodded reluctantly. 'All right, having the Irish connection helped him—'

' – But there was the other side of the coin. O'Shaughnessy had enemies, even in the Provos. He was a ruthless bastard with a bloody record. We can only believe that one of those enemies saw the chance to make a score – the one who sold him the stolen auto, perhaps. We have had the recording of the tip-off call examined by language experts and had a run against the voice prints on the computer. Nothing definite. The voice was disguised, probably through a handkerchief and nose plugs, but the general feeling is that it was an Irishman who made the call. The boffins from the telephone department were able to test the loading of the line and guess it was a call from a foreign country – very likely Ireland, although they cannot be certain of that.'

Peter Stride raised one eyebrow slightly, and Colin chuckled weakly and waved the cheroot at him in a wide gesture of invitation.

'Okay. That's my best shot,' he said. 'Let's hear you do better. If you don't like my theories, you must have one of your own.'

'You are asking me to believe it was all a coincidence; that O'Shaughnessy just happened to run into an old enemy who just happened to tip us off twenty-four hours before the deadline for Melissa-Jane's hand to be amputated. Then it just so happened that we reached Laragh at exactly the same moment as O'Shaughnessy was pulling out and making a run for it. Is that what you want me to believe?'

'Something like that,' Colin admitted.

'Sorry, Colin. I just don't like coincidence.'

'Shoot!' Colin invited. 'Let's hear how it really happened.'

'I don't know,' Peter grinned placatingly. 'It is just that I have this feeling that Caliph doesn't deal in coincidence either. I have this other feeling that somehow Gilly O'Shaughnessy had the death mark on his forehead from the beginning. I have this feeling it was all part of the plan.'

'It must be great fun to have these feelings.' Colin was prickling a little. 'But they sure as hell aren't much help to me.'

'Take it easy.' Peter held up one hand in surrender. 'Let's accept tentatively that it happened your way, then—'

'But?' Colin asked.

'No buts – not until we get some more hard evidence—'

'Okay, buster.' There was no smile on Colin's face now, the wide mouth clamped in a grim line. 'You want hard evidence, try this one for size—'

'Hold it, Colin,' Parker shot in quickly, authoritatively. 'Wait for a moment before we come to that.' And Colin Noble deflated with a visible effort, the cords in his throat smoothing out and the line of mouth relaxed into the old familiar grin as he deferred to Kingston Parker.

'Let's backtrack here a moment,' Parker suggested. 'Peter came up with the name Caliph. In the meantime we had picked up the same name – but from an entirely different source. I promised Peter I would tell him about our source – because I think it gives us a new insight into this entire business.' He paused and tinkered with his pipe, using one of those small tools with folding blades and hooks and spikes with which pipe smokers arm themselves. He scraped the bowl and knocked a nub of half-burned tobacco into the ashtray, before peering into the pipe the way a rifleman checks the bore of his weapon. Peter realized that Parker used his pipe as a prop for his performances, the way a magician distracts his audience with flourishes and mumbo-jumbo. He was not a man to underestimate, Peter thought again for the hundredth time. Kingston Parker looked up at him and smiled, a conspiratorial smile as if to acknowledge that Peter had seen through his little act.

'Our news of Caliph comes from an unlikely direction – or rather, considering the name, a more likely direction. East. Riyadh to be precise. Capital city of Saudi Arabia, seat of King Khalid's oil empire. Our battered and beleaguered

Central Intelligence Agency has received an appeal from the King following the murder of one of his grandsons. You recall the case, I'm sure—' Peter had a strange feeling of *déjà-vu* as he listened to Kingston Parker confirming exactly the circumstances that he and Magda Altmann had discussed and postulated together, was it only three weeks before? ' – You see the King and his family are in a very vulnerable position really. Did you know that there are at least seven hundred Saudi princes who are multi-millionaires, and who are close to the King's affections and power structure? It would be impossible to guard that many potential victims adequately. It's really damned good thinking – you don't have to seize a hostage with all the attendant risks. There is virtually an unlimited supply of them walking around, ripe for plucking, and an inexhaustible supply of assassins to be either pressured or paid to do the job, just as long as you have the information and leverage, or just enough money. Caliph seems to have all that.'

'What demand has been made upon Khalid?' Peter asked.

'We know for certain that he has received a demand, and that he has appealed to the CIA for assistance to protect and guard his family. The demand came from an agency or person calling himself Caliph. We do not know what the demand is – but it may be significant that Khalid and the Shah of Persia have both agreed that they will not support a crude oil price increase at the next pricing session of OPEC, but on the contrary they will push for a five per cent decrease in the price of crude.'

'Caliph's thinking has paid off again,' Peter murmured.

'It looks like it, doesn't it.' Parker nodded, and then chuckled bitterly. 'And once again you get the feeling, as with his demands to the South African Government, that his final objective is desirable – even if the way he goes about procuring it is slightly unconventional, to say the least.'

'To say the very least,' Peter agreed quietly, remembering

the feel of Melissa-Jane's fever-racked body against his chest.

'So there is no doubt now that what we feared, is fact. Caliph exists—' said Parker.

'Not only exists, but flourishes,' Peter agreed.

'Alive and well with a nice house in the suburbs.' Colin lit the stub of his cheroot before going on. 'Hell! He succeeded at Johannesburg. He is succeeding at Riyadh – where does he go from there – why not the Federation of Employers in West Germany? The Trade Union leaders in Great Britain? – Any group powerful enough to affect the fate of nations, and small enough to be terrorized as individuals.'

'It's a way to sway and direct the destiny of the entire world – you just cannot guard all the world's decision-makers from personal attack,' Peter agreed. 'And it's no argument to point out that because his first two targets have been South Africa and the oil monopoly, then the long term results will be to the benefit of mankind. His ultimate target will almost certainly be the democratic process itself I don't think there can be any doubt that Caliph sees himself as a god. He sees himself as the paternal tyrant. His aim is to cure the ills of the world by radical surgery, and to maintain its health by unrestrained force and fear.'

Peter could remain seated no longer. He pushed back his chair and crossed to the windows, standing there in the soldier's stance, balanced on the balls of his feet with both hands clasped lightly behind his back. There was an uninspiring view of the high barbed-wire fence, part of the airfield and the corrugated sheet wall of the nearest hangar A Thor sentry paced before the gates with a white M.P. helmet on his head and side arm strapped to his waist. Peter watched him without really seeing him, and behind him the two men at the table exchanged a significant glance. Colin Noble asked a silent question and Parker answered with a curt nod of affirmative.

'All right, Peter,' Colin said. 'A little while back you asked for hard facts. I promised to give you a few.'

Peter turned back from the window and waited.

'Item One. During the time that Gilly O'Shaughnessy held Melissa-Jane in Laragh, two telephone calls were made from the Old Manse. They were both international calls. They both went through the local telephone exchange. The first call was made at seven p.m. local time on the first of this month. That would have been the first day that they could have reached the hideout. We have to guess it was an "All Well" report to the top management. The second call was exactly seven days later again at seven o'clock local time precisely. To the same number. We have to guess that it was another report, "All is still well". Both calls were less than one minute in duration. Just time enough to pass a pre-arranged code message—' Colin broke off and looked again at Kingston Parker.

'Go on,' Parker instructed.

'The calls were to a French number. Rambouillet 47–87–47.'

Peter felt it hit him in the stomach, a physical blow, and he flinched his head, for a moment closing both his eyes tightly. He had called that number so often, the numerals were graven on his memory.

'No.' He shook his head, and opened his eyes. 'I'm not going to believe it.'

'It's true, Peter,' Parker said gently

Peter walked back to his seat. His legs felt rubbery and shaky under him. He sat down heavily.

The room was completely silent. Neither of the other two looked directly at Peter Stride.

Kingston Parker made a gesture to Colin and obediently he slid the red box file, tied with red tapes, across the cheap vinyl-topped table.

Parker untied the tapes and opened the file. He shuffled the papers, scanning them swiftly. Clearly he was adept at speed reading and was able to assimilate each typed double-spaced page at a glance – but now he was merely waiting for Peter to recover from the shock. He knew the contents of the red file almost by heart.

Peter Stride slumped in the steel-framed chair with its uncushioned wooden seat, staring sightlessly at the bulletin board on the opposite wall on which were posted the Thor rosters.

He found it hard to ride the waves of dismay that flooded over him. He felt chilled and numbed, the depth of this betrayal devastated him, and when he closed his eyes again he had a vivid image of the slim, tender body with the childlike breasts peeping through a silken curtain of dark hair.

He straightened in his seat, and Kingston Parker recognized the moment and looked up at him, half closing the file and turning it towards him.

The cover bore the highest security gradings available to Atlas Command – and below them was typed:

ALTMANN MAGDA IRENE Born KUTCHINSKY

Peter realized that he had never known her second name was Irene. Magda Irene. Hell, they were really ugly names – made special only by the woman who bore them.

Parker turned the file back to himself and began to speak quietly.

'When last you and I met, I told you of the special interest we had in this lady. That interest has continued, unabated, since then, or rather it has gathered strength with every fresh item of information that has come to us.' He opened the file again and glanced at it as if to refresh his memory. 'Colin has been very successful in enlisting the full co-operation of the intelligence agencies of both our countries, who in turn have been able to secure that of the French and – believe it or not – the Russians. Between the four countries we have been able to at last piece together the woman's history—' He broke off. 'Remarkable woman,' and shook his head in admiration. 'Quite incredible really. I can understand how she is able to weave spells around any man she chooses. I can understand, Peter, your evident distress. I am going to be utterly blunt now – we have no time nor space in which to manoeuvre tactfully around your personal feelings. We know that she has taken you as a lover. You notice that I phrase that carefully. Baroness Altmann takes lovers, not the other way around. She takes lovers deliberately and with careful forethought. I have no doubt that once she has made the decision, she accomplishes the rest of it with superb finesse.'

Peter remembered her coming to him and the exact words she had used. 'I am not very good at this, Peter, and I want so badly to be good for you.'

The words had been chosen with the finesse that Kingston Parker had just spoken of. They were exactly turned to make herself irresistible to Peter – and afterwards she had given the gentle lie to them with the skill and devilish cunning of her hands and mouth and body.

'You see, Peter. She had special and expert training in all the arts of love. There are probably few women in the Western world who know as much about reading a man, and then pleasing him. What she knows she did not learn in Paris or London or New York—' Kingston Parker paused and frowned at Peter. 'This is all theory and hearsay, Peter. You are in a better position to say just how much of it is false?'

The ultimate skill in pleasing a man is to fuel his own belief in himself, Peter thought, as he returned Parker's inquiring gaze with expressionless eyes. He remembered how with Magda Altmann he had felt like a giant, capable of anything. She had made him feel like that with a word, a smile, a gift, a touch – that was the ultimate skill.

He did not answer Parker's question. 'Go on please,

Kingston,' he invited. Externally, he had himself completely under control now. His right hand lay on the table top, with the fingers half open, relaxed.

'I told you that even as a child she showed special talents. In languages, mathematics – her father was an amateur mathematician of some importance – chess and other games of skill. She attracted attention. Especially she attracted attention because her father was a member of the Communist Party—' Parker broke off as Peter lifted his head in sharp inquiry. ' – I'm sorry, Peter. We did not know that when last we met. We have learned it since from the French, they have access to the party records in Paris it seems, and it was confirmed by the Russians themselves. Apparently the child used to accompany her father to meetings of the Party, and soon showed a precocious political awareness and understanding. Her father's friends were mostly party members, and after his death – there still remains a mystery around his death. Neither the French nor the Russians are forthcoming on the subject. – Anyway, after his death, Magda Kutchinsky was cared for by these friends. It seemed she was passed on from family to family—' Kingston Parker slid a postcard-sized photograph from a marbline envelope and passed it across the table to Peter, ' – from this period.'

It showed a rather skinny girl in short skirts and dark stockings, wearing the yoked collar and straw bonnet of the French schoolgirl. Her hair was in two short braids, tied with ribbons, and she held a small fluffy white dog in her arms. The background was a Parisian summer park scene, with a group of men playing *boule* and chestnut trees in full leaf.

The child's face was delicately featured with huge beautiful eyes, somehow wise and compassionate beyond her age, and yet still imbued with the fresh innocence of childhood.

'You can see she already had all the markings of spectacular beauty.' Kingston Parker grunted, and reached across to take back the photograph. For a moment Peter's fingers tightened instinctively; he would have like to have kept it, but he relaxed and let it go. Parker glanced at it again and then slipped it back into the envelope.

'Yes. She attracted much interest, and very soon an uncle from the old country wrote to her. There were photographs of her father and the mother she had never known, anecdotes of her infancy and her father's youth. The child was enchanted. She had never known she had an uncle. Her father had never spoken of his relatives, but now at last the little orphan found she had family. It took only a few more letters, exchanges of delight and affection, and then it was all arranged. The uncle came to fetch her in person – and Magda Kutchinsky went back to Poland.' Parker spread his hands. 'It was easy as that.'

'The missing years,' Peter said, and his voice sounded strange in his own ears. He cleared his throat and shifted uncomfortably under Parker's piercing but understanding gaze.

'No longer missing, Peter. We have been fed a little glimmering of what happened during those years – and we have been able to fill in the rest of it from what we knew already.'

'The Russians?' Peter asked, and when Parker nodded, Peter went on with a bitter tang to his voice. 'They seem to be very forthcoming, don't they? I have never heard of them passing information – at least not valuable information – so readily.'

'They have their reasons in this case,' Parker demurred. 'Very good reasons as it turns out – but one will come to those in due course.'

'Very well.'

'The child returned with her uncle to Poland, Warsaw. And there was an extravagant family reunion. We are not certain if this was her real family, or whether the child was provided with a foster family for the occasion. In any event, the uncle soon announced that if Magda would submit to examination there was an excellent chance that she would be provided with a scholarship to one of the élite colleges of the USSR. We can imagine that she passed her examination with great distinction and her new masters must have congratulated themselves on their discovery.

'The college is on the shores of the Black Sea near Odessa. It does not have a name, nor an old school tie. The students are very specially selected, the screening is rigorous and only the brightest and most talented are enrolled. They are soon taught that they are an élite group, and are streamed in the special direction that their various talents dictate. In Magda's case it was languages and politics, finance and mathematics. She excelled and at the age of seventeen graduated to a higher, more specialized branch of the Odessa college. There she was trained in special memory techniques, the already bright mind was honed down to a razor edge. I understand that one of the less difficult exercises was to be given access to a list of a hundred diverse items for sixty seconds. The list had to be repeated from memory, in the correct order, twenty-four hours later.' Parker shook his head again, expressing his admiration.

'At the same time she was also trained to fit naturally into upper-class international Western society. Dress, food, drink, cosmetics, manners, popular music and literature, cinema, theatre, democratic politics, business procedures, the operation of stocks and commodities markets, the more mundane secretarial skills, modern dancing, the art of love-making and pleasuring men – that and much else, all of it taught by experts – flying, skiing, weapons, the rudiments of electronics and mechanical engineering and every other skill that a top-class agent might have to call upon.

'She was the star of her course and emerged from it much as the woman you know. Poised, skilled, beautiful, motivated – and deadly.

'At the age of nineteen she knew more, was capable of

more, than most other human beings, male or female, twice her age. The perfect agent, except for a small flaw in her make-up that only showed up later. She was too intelligent and too personally ambitious.' Kingston Parker smiled for the first time in twenty minutes. ' – Which of course is a pseudonym for greed. Her masters did not recognize it in her, and perhaps at that age it was only latent greed. She had not yet been fully exposed to the attractions of wealth – nor of unlimited power.'

Kingston Parker broke off, leaned across the table towards Peter. He seemed to change direction then, smiling an inward knowledgeable smile, as though pondering a hidden truth.

'Greed for wealth alone belongs essentially to the lower levels of human intelligence. It is only the developed and advanced mind that can truly appreciate the need for power—' He saw the protest in Peter's expression. ' – No, no, I don't mean merely the power to control one's own limited environment, merely the power of life and death over a few thousand lives – not that, but true power. Power to change the destiny of nations, power such as Caesar or Napoleon wielded, such as the President of the United States wields – that is the ultimate greed, Peter. A magnificent and noble greed.'

He was silent a moment, as though glimpsing some vision of splendour. Then he went on:

'I digress. Forgive me,' and turned to Colin Noble. 'Do we have some coffee, Colin? I think we could all do with a cup now.'

Colin went to the machine that blooped and gurgled and winked its red eye in the corner, and while he filled the cups, the charged atmosphere in the room eased a little, and Peter tried to arrange his thoughts in some logical sequence. He looked for the flaws and weak places in the story but could find none – instead he remembered only the feel of her mouth, the touch of her hands on his body. Oh

God, it was a stab of physical pain, a deep ache in the chest and groin, as he remembered how she had coursed him like a running stag, driving and goading him on to unvisited depths of his being. Could such skills be taught, he wondered, and if so, by whom? He had a horrifying thought of a special room set on the heights above the Black Sea, with that slim, vulnerable tender body practising its skills, learning love as though it were cookery or small arms practice – and then he shut his mind firmly against it, and Kingston Parker was speaking again, balancing his coffee cup primly with his pinky finger raised, like an old maid at a tea party.

'So she arrived back in Paris and it fell at her feet. It was a triumphant progress.' Kingston Parker prodded in the file with his free hand, spilling out photographs of Magda – Magda dancing in the ballroom of the Elysée Palace, Magda leaving a Rolls-Royce limousine outside Maxim's in the rue Royale, Magda skiing, riding, beautiful, smiling, poised – and always there were men. Rich, well-fed, sleek men.

'I told you once there were eight sexual liaisons.' Kingston Parker used that irritating expression again. 'We have had reason to revise that figure. The French take a very close interest in that sort of thing, they have added to the list.' He flicked over the photographs. 'Pierre Hammond, Deputy Minister of Defence—' And another. 'Mark Vincent, head of mission at the American Consulate—'

'Yes,' Peter cut in short, but still there was a sickly fascination in seeing the faces of these men. He had imagined them accurately, he realized, without particular relish.

'Her masters were delighted – as you can imagine. With a male agent it is sometimes necessary to wait a decade or more for results while he moles his way into the system. With a young and beautiful woman she has her greatest value when those assets are freshest. Magda Kutchinsky gave them magnificent value. We do not know the exact extent of her contributions – our Russian friends have not bared everything to us, I'm afraid, but I estimate that it was about this time they began to realize her true potential. She had the magical touch, but her beauty and youth could not last for ever—' Kingston Parker made a deprecating gesture with the slim pianist's hands. ' – We do not know if Aaron Altmann was a deliberate choice by her masters. But it seems likely. Think of it – one of the richest and most powerful men in Western Europe, one who controlled most of the steel and heavy engineering producers, the single biggest armaments complex, electronics – all associated and sensitive secondary industries. He was a widower, childless, so under French law his wife could inherit his entire estate He was known to be fighting a slowly losing battle with cancer, so his life term was limited – and he was also a Zionist and one of the most trusted and influential members of Mossad. It was beautiful. Truly beautiful,' said Kingston Parker. 'Imagine being able to undermine a man of that stature, perhaps being able to double him! Though that seemed an extravagant dream – not even the most beautiful siren of history could expect to turn a man like Aaron Altmann. He is a separate study on his own, another incredible human being with the strength and courage of a lion – until the cancer wore him out. Again I digress, forgive me. Somebody, either the Director of the NKVD in Moscow, or Magda Kutchinsky's control at the Russian Embassy in Paris, who was, incidentally, the Chief NKVD Commissar for Western Europe, such was her value, or Magda Kutchinsky herself, picked Aaron Altmann. Within two years she was indispensable to him. She was cunning enough not to use her sexual talents upon him immediately Altmann could have any woman who took his fancy, and he usually did. His sexual appetites were legendary, and they probably were the cause of his remaining childless. A youthful indiscretion resulted in a venereal disease with complications. It was later completely cured, but the damage was irreversible, he never produced an heir.'

He was a man who would have toyed with her and cast her aside as soon as he tired of her, if she had been callow enough to make herself immediately available to him.

First, she won his respect and admiration. Perhaps she was the first woman he had ever met whose brain and strength and determination matched his own—

Kingston Parker selected another photograph and passed it across the table. Fascinated, Peter stared at the black and white image of a heavily built man with a bull neck, and a solid thrusting jaw. Like so many men of vast sexual appetite, he was bald except for a Friar Tuck frill around the cannon ball dome of his skull. But there were humorous lines chiselled about his mouth, and his eyes, though fierce, looked as though they too could readily crinkle with laughter lines. Portrait of Power, Peter thought.

'When at last she gave him access to her body, it must have been like some great electrical storm.' Kingston Parker seemed to be deliberately dwelling on her past love affairs, and Peter would have protested had not the information he was receiving been so vital. 'This man and woman must have been able to match each other once again. Two very superior persons, two in a hundred million probably – it is interesting to speculate what might have happened if they had been able to produce a child.' Kingston Parker chuckled. 'It would probably have been a mongolian idiot – life is like that.'

Peter moved irritably, hating this turn in the conversation, and Parker went on smoothly.

'So they married, and NKVD had a mole in the centre of Western industry. Narmco, Altmann's armaments complex, was manufacturing top secret American, British and French missile hardware for NATO. The new Baroness was on the Board, was in fact Deputy Chairman of Narmco. We can be sure that armaments blueprints were passed, not by the sheet but by the truckload. Every night, the leaders and decision-makers of the Western world sat at the new

Baroness's board and swilled her champagne. Every conversation, every nuance and indiscretion was recorded by that specially trained memory, and slowly, inevitably, the Baron's strength was whittled away. He began to rely more and more upon her. We do not know exactly when she began to assist him with his Mossad activities – but when it happened the Russians had succeeded in their design. In effect they had succeeded in turning Baron Aaron Altmann, they had his right hand and his heart – for by this time the dying Baron was completely besotted by the enchantress. They could expect to inherit the greater part of Western European heavy industry. It was all very easy – until the latent defect in the Baroness's character began to surface. We can only imagine the alarm of her Russian masters when they detected the first signs that the Baroness was working for herself alone. She was brighter by far than any of the men who had up until that time controlled her, and she had been given a taste of real power. The taste seemed very much to her liking. We can only imagine the gargantuan battle of wills between the puppetmasters and the beautiful puppet that had suddenly developed a mind and ambitions of her very own – quite simply her ambition now was to be the most wealthy and powerful woman since Catherine of Russia, and the makings were almost within her pretty hands – except—'

Kingston Parker stopped; like a born storyteller, he knew instinctively how to build up the tension in his audience. He rattled his coffee cup.

'This talking is thirsty business.' Colin and Peter had to rouse themselves with a physical effort. They had been mesmerized by the story and the personality of the storyteller. When Parker had his cup refilled, he sipped at it, then went on speaking.

'There was one last lever her Russian masters had over her. They threatened to expose her. It was quite a neat stroke, really. A man like Aaron Altmann would have acted like an enraged bull if he had known how he had been deceived. His reaction was predictable. He would have divorced Magda immediately. Divorce is difficult in France – but not for a man like the Baron. Without his protection Magda was nothing, less than nothing, for her value to the Russians would have come to an end. Without the Altmann Empire her dreams of power would disappear like a puff of smoke. It was a good try – it would have worked against an ordinary person, but of course they were not dealing with an ordinary person—'

Parker paused again; it was clear he was as wrapped up by the story as they were, and he was drawing out the pleasure of the telling of it.

'I have been doing a lot of talking,' he smiled at Peter. 'I'm going to let you have a chance now, Peter. You know her a little, you have learned a lot more about her in the last hour. Can you guess what she did?'

Peter began to shake his head – and then it crashed in upon him with sickening force, and he stared at Parker, the pupils of his eyes dilating with the strength of his revulsion.

'I think you have guessed.' Parker nodded. 'Yes, we can imagine that by this stage she was becoming a little impatient herself. The Baron was taking a rather long time to die.'

'Christ, it's horrible.' Peter grunted, as though in pain.

' – From one point of view, I agree.' Parker nodded. 'But if you look at it like a chess player, and remember she is a player of Grand Master standard, it was a brilliant stroke. She arranged that the Baron be kidnapped. There are witnesses to the fact that she insisted on the Baron accompanying her that day. He was feeling very bad, and he did not want to go sailing, but she insisted that the sun and fresh air would be good for him. He never took his bodyguard when he went sailing. There were just the two of them. A very fast cruiser was waiting offshore—' He spread his hands. ' – You know the details?'

'No,' Peter denied it.

'The cruiser rammed the yacht. Picked the Baron out of the water, but left the Baroness. An hour later there was a radio message to the coastguard; they went out and found her still clinging to the wreckage. The kidnappers were very concerned that she survived.'

'They may have wanted a loving wife to bargain with,' Peter suggested swiftly.

'That is possible, of course, and she certainly played the role of the bereaved wife to perfection. When the ransom demand came it was she who forced the Board of Altmann Industries to ante up the twenty-five million dollars. She personally took the cash to the rendezvous – alone.' Parker paused significantly.

'She didn't need the money.'

'Oh, but she did,' Parker contradicted. 'The Baron was not in his dotage, you know. His hands were still very firmly on the reins – and the purse strings. Magda had as much as any ordinary wife could wish for, furs, jewellery, servants, clothes, cars, boats – pocket money, around two hundred thousand dollars a year, paid to her as a salary from Altmann Industries. Any ordinary wife would have been well content – but she was not an ordinary wife We must believe she had already planned how to carry forward her dreams of unlimited power – and it needed money, not thousands but millions. Twenty-five million would be a reasonable stop-gap, until she could get her pretty little fingers on the big apple. – She drove with the cash, in thousand-Swiss-franc bills, I understand; she drove alone to some abandoned airfield and had a plane come pick it up and fly it out to Switzerland. Damned neat.'

'But—' Peter searched for some means of denial. ' – But the Baron was mutilated. She couldn't—'

'Death is death, mutilation may have served some obscure purpose. God knows, we're dealing with an Eastern mind, devious, sanguinary – perhaps the mutilation was merely to make any suspicion of the wife completely far-fetched – just as you immediately used it to protect her.'

He was right, of course. The mind that could plan and execute the rest of such a heinous scheme would not baulk at the smaller niceties of execution. He had no more protest to make.

'So let us review what she had achieved by this stage. She was rid of the Baron, and the restrictions he placed upon her. An example of these restrictions, for we will find it significant later: she was very strongly in favour of Narmco banning the sale of all weapons and armaments to the South African Government. The Baron, ever the businessman, looked upon that country as a lucrative market. There was also the South African sympathy for Zionism. He overruled her, and Narmco continued to supply aircraft, missiles and light armaments to that country right up until the official UN resolution to enforce a total arms embargo, with France ratifying it. Remember the Baroness's anti-South African attitude. We come to it again later.

'She was rid of the Baron. She was rid of her Russian control, well able to maintain a small army to protect herself. Even her former Russian masters would hesitate to take revenge on her. She was a French Grande Dame now. She had gained significant working capital – twenty-five million for which she was not accountable to another living human being. She had gained an invincible power base at Altmann Industries. Although she was still under certain checks and safeguards from the Board of Directors, yet she had access to all its information-gathering services, to its vast resources. As the head of such a colossus she had the respect of and sympathy of the French Government, and as a fringe benefit – limited but significant access to their intelligence systems. Then there was the Mossad connection: was she not the heir to Aaron Altmann's position—'

Peter suddenly remembered Magda speaking of her 'sources' – and never identifying them. Was she really able to use the French and Israeli intelligence as her own private agencies? It seemed impossible. But he was learning swiftly that when dealing with Magda Altmann, anything was possible – as Kingston Parker had pointed out, she was not an ordinary person – but Parker was speaking again.

'There was a period then of consolidation, a time when she gathered up the reins that Aaron had dropped. There were changes amongst the top management throughout Altmann Industries as she replaced those who might oppose her with her own minions. A time of planning and organizing, and then the first attempt to govern and prescribe the destiny of nations. She chose the nation which most offended her personal view of the new world she was going to build. We will never know what made her choose the name of Caliph—'

'You have to be wrong.' Peter squeezed his eyelids closed with thumb and forefinger. 'You just don't know her.'

'I don't think anybody knows her, Peter,' Kingston Parker murmured, and fiddled with his pipe. 'I'm sorry, we are going pretty fast here. Do you want to back up and ask any questions?'

'No, it's all right.' Peter opened his eyes again. 'Go on, will you, Kingston?'

'One of the most important lessons that Baroness Altmann had learned was the ease with which force and violence can be used, and their tremendous effect and profitability. Bearing this lesson in mind, the Baroness chose her first act as the new ruler of mankind, and the choice was dictated by her early political convictions, those convictions formed at her father's knee and at the Communist Party meetings that she had attended as a precocious child in Paris. There is a further suggestion that the choice was reinforced by the Altmann banking corporation's interests in South African gold sales, for by this time the Baroness had tempered her socialist and communist leanings with a good healthy dollop of capitalistic self-interest. We can only guess, but if the scheme to bring out forty tons of gold – and a black-based government-in-exile – had succeeded, it would not have taken very long for Caliph to gain control of both government and gold—' Parker shrugged. ' – We just cannot say how ambitious, even grandiose, those plans were. But we can say that Caliph, or the Baroness, recruited her team for the execution of the plan with the skill she brought to anything she handled.' He broke off, and smiled. 'I think all three of us remember the taking of Flight 070 vividly enough not to have to go once more over the details. Let me just remind you that it would have succeeded, in fact it had actually succeeded, when Peter here made his unscheduled move that brought it all down. But it succeeded. That was the important thing. Caliph could afford to congratulate herself. Her information was impeccable. She had chosen the right people for the job. She even knew the name of the officer who would command the anti-terrorist force which would be sent to intervene, and her psychology had been excellent. The execution of the four hostages had so shocked and numbed the opposition that they were powerless – the cup had been dashed from her lips by one man alone. Inevitably her interest in that man was aroused. Possibly with feminine intuition she was able to recognize in him the qualities which could be turned to her own purpose. She had that indomitable streak in her make-up that is able to recognize even in the dust of disaster that material for future victory—' Parker shifted his bulk, and made a small deprecatory gesture. ' – I hope this will not seem immodest if I bring myself into the story as this stage. I had been given the hint that something like Caliph existed. In fact this may not have been her first act after the killing of Aaron Altmann. Two other successful kidnappings have her style – one of them the OPEC ministers in Vienna – but we cannot be sure. I had been warned and I was waiting for Caliph to surface. Dearly I would have loved a chance to interrogate one of the hijackers—'

'They would have had nothing to tell you,' Peter interjected brusquely. 'They were merely pawns, like the doctor we captured in Ireland.'

Parker sighed. 'Perhaps you are right, Peter. But at the time I believed that our only lead to Caliph had been severed. Later when the thing had been done and I had recovered from the shock of it, it suddenly occurred to me that the lead was still there – stronger than ever. You were that lead, Peter. That was why I recommended that your resignation be accepted. If you had not resigned, I would have forced you out anyway, but you played along superbly by resigning—' He smiled again. ' – I have never thanked you for that.'

'Don't mention it,' said Peter grimly. 'I like to be of service.'

'And you were. Almost immediately you were on the loose, the Baroness began making her approach. First she collected every known fact about you. Somehow she even got a computer run on you. That's a fact. An unauthorized run was made on the Central Intelligence computer four days after your resignation. She must have liked what she got, for there was the Narmco offer – through conventional channels. Your refusal must have truly excited her interest, for she used her connections to have herself invited down to Sir Steven's country house.' Parker chuckled. 'My poor Peter, you found yourself without warning in the clutches of one of history's most accomplished enchantresses. I know enough about the lady to guess that her approach to you was very carefully calculated from the complete information that she had on you. She knew exactly what type of woman attracted you. Fortunately, she fitted the general physical description—'

'What is that?' Peter demanded. He was unaware that he had a specific type of physical preference.

'Tall, slim and brunette,' Parker told him promptly.

'Think about it,' he invited. 'All your women have been that.'

He was right, of course, Peter realized. Hell, even at thirty-nine years of age it was still possible to learn something about yourself.

'You're a cold-blooded bastard, Kingston. Did anybody ever tell you that?'

'Frequently.' Kingston smiled. 'But it's not true, and compared to Baroness Altmann I am Father Christmas.' And he became serious again. 'She wanted to find out what we at Atlas know about her activities. She knew by this stage that we had our suspicions, and through you she had an inside ear. Of course, your value would deteriorate swiftly the longer you were out of Thor – but you could still be useful in a dozen other ways. As a bonus you could be expected to do a good job at Narmco. All her expectations were fulfilled, and exceeded. You even thwarted an assassination attempt on her life—'

Peter lifted an eyebrow in inquiry.

' – On the road to Rambouillet that night. Here we are only guessing, but it's a pretty well-informed guess. The Russians had by this time despaired of returning her to the fold. They had also suspicions as to her role as Caliph. They decided on a radical cure for their one-time star agent. They either financed and organized the assassination attempt themselves, or they tipped off Mossad that she had murdered Aaron Altmann. I would be inclined to believe that they hired the killers themselves – because the Mossad usually do their own dirty work. Anyway, with NKVD or Mossad as paymasters, an ambush was set up on the Rambouillet road and you drove into it. I know you don't like coincidence, Peter, but I believe it was merely coincidence that you were driving the Baroness's Maserati that night.'

'All right,' Peter murmured. 'If I swallow the rest of the hog, that little crumb goes down easily enough.'

'That attempt severely alarmed the Baroness. She was not certain who had been the author. I think she believed it was Atlas Command, or at the very least that we had something to do with it. Almost immediately after that you were able to confirm our interest in her, and our knowledge that Caliph existed. I invited you to America, Colin brought you to meet me, and when you returned you either told her about it, or in some way confirmed her suspicions of Atlas Command and Kingston Parker. I am guessing again – but how close am I, Peter? Be honest.'

Peter stared at him, trying to keep his face expressionless while his mind raced. That was exactly how it had happened.

'We were all hunting Caliph. You saw no disloyalty in discussing it with her.' Parker prompted him gently, and Peter nodded once curtly.

'You believed that we had common goals,' Parker went on with deep understanding and compassion. 'You thought we were all hunting Caliph. That is right.'

'She knew I had been to America to see you before I told her. I don't know how – but she knew,' Peter said stiffly. He felt like a traitor.

'I understand,' Parker said simply. He reached across the table and once again placed his hand on Peter's shoulder. He squeezed it while he looked into Peter's eyes, a gesture of affirmation and trust. Then he laid both hands on top of the table.

'She knew who was the hunter then, and she knew enough about me to know I was dangerous. You were probably the only man in the world who could reach me and do the job – but you had to be motivated. She picked the one and only lever that would move you. She picked it unerringly – just as she had done everything else. It would have worked – in one stroke she would have gotten rid of the hunter, and she would have acquired a top-class assassin. When you had done the job, you would have belonged to

Caliph for all time. She would have used you to kill again and again, and each time you killed you would be more deeply enmeshed in her net. You really were a very valuable prize, Peter. Valuable enough for her to find it worthwhile to use her sexual wiles upon you.'

He saw the lumps of clenched muscle at the corner of Peter's jaw, and the fire in his eyes.

'You are also a very attractive man, and who knows but she felt the need to combine business and pleasure? She is a lady with strongly developed sexual appetites.'

Peter felt a violent urge to punch him in the face. He needed some outlet for his rage. He felt belittled, soiled and used.

'She was clever enough to realize that the sex was not enough of a hold to force you to commit murder. So she took your daughter, and immediately had her mutilated – just as at Johannesburg she had executed hostages without hesitation. The world must learn to fear Caliph.'

There was no smile on Parker's face now.

'I truly believe that if you had not been able to deliver my head by the deadline, she would not have hesitated to carry out the next mutilation, and the one after that.'

Again Peter was assailed by a wave of nausea as he remembered that shrivelled white lump of flesh with the scarlet fingernail floating horribly in its tiny bottle.

'We were saved from that by the most incredible piece of luck. The Provo informer,' said Parker 'And again the understandable eagerness of the Russians to co-operate with us. It is a wonderful opportunity for them to hand us their problem. They have let us have an almost full account of the lady and her history.'

'But what are we going to do about it?' Colin Noble asked. 'Our hands are tied. Do we just have to wait for the next atrocity – do we have to hope we will get another lucky break when Caliph kills the next Arab prince, or machine-guns the Shah's sister?'

'That will happen – unless they push through the OPEC decision,' Parker predicted levelly. 'The lady has converted very easily to the capitalist system now that she owns half of Europe's industry. A reduction in the oil price would benefit her probably more than any other individual on earth – and at the same time it will also benefit the great bulk of humanity. How nicely that squares all her political and personal interests.'

'But if she gets away with it—' Colin insisted, ' – what will be her next act of God?'

'Nobody can predict that,' Parker murmured, and they both turned their heads to look at Peter Stride.

He seemed to have aged twenty years. The lines at the corners of his mouth were cut in deeply like the erosion of weathered granite. Only his eyes were blue and alive and fierce as those of a bird of prey.

'I want you to believe what I am going to say now, Peter. I have not told you all this to put pressure on you,' Parker assured him quietly. 'I have told you only what I believe is necessary for you to know – to protect yourself if you should elect to return to the lion's den. I am not ordering you to do so. The risks involved cannot be overestimated. With a lesser man I would term it suicidal. However, now that you are forewarned, I believe you are the one man who could take Caliph on her own ground. Please do not misunderstand what I mean by that. I am not for a moment suggesting assassination. In fact I expressly forbid you to even think in that direction. I would not allow it, and if you acted independently, I would do my utmost to see that you were brought to justice. No, all I ask is that you keep close to Caliph and try to outguess her. Try to expose her so we can lawfully act to take her out of action. I want you to put out of your mind the emotional issues – those hostages at Johannesburg, your own daughter – try to forget them, Peter. Remember we are neither judge nor executioner—' Parker went on speaking quietly and insistently, and Peter watched his lips with narrowed eyes, hardly listening to the words, trying to think clearly and see his course ahead – but his thoughts were a children's carousel, going around and around with fuss and fury but returning with every revolution to the one central conclusion.

There was only one way to stop Caliph. The thought of attempting to bring someone like Baroness Magda Altmann to justice – in a French court – was laughable. Peter tried to force himself to believe that vengeance had no part in his decisions, but he had lived too long with himself to be able to pull off such a deceit. Yes, vengeance was part of it – and he trembled with the rage of remembrance, but it was not all of it. He had executed the German girl Ingrid, and Gilly O'Shaughnessy – and had not regretted the decision to do so. If it was necessary for them to die – then surely Caliph deserved to die a thousand times more.

And there is only one person who can do it, he realized.

Her voice was quick and light and warm, with just that fascinating trace of accent; he remembered it so well, but had forgotten the effect it could have upon him. His heart pounded as though he had run a long way.

'Oh, Peter. It's so good to hear your voice. I have been so worried. Did you get my cable?'

'No, which cable?'

'When I heard that you had freed Melissa-Jane. I sent you a cable from Rome.'

'I didn't get it – but it doesn't matter.'

'I sent it to you via Narmco – in Brussels.'

'It's probably waiting for me there. I haven't been in touch.'

'How is she, Peter?'

'She is fine now—' He found it strangely difficult to use

her name, or any form of endearment. He hoped that the strain would not sound in his voice. 'But we went through a hell of a time.'

'I know. I understand. I felt so helpless. I tried so hard, that's why I was out of contact, Peter *chéri*, but day after day there was no news.'

'It's all over now,' Peter said gruffly.

'I don't think so,' she said swiftly. 'Where are you calling from?'

'London.'

'When will you come back?'

'I telephoned Brussels an hour ago. Narmco wants me back urgently. I am taking a flight this afternoon.'

'Peter, I have to see you. I've been too long without you – but, oh *mon Dieu*, I have to be in Vienna tonight. – Wait, let me see, if I sent the Lear to fetch you now we could meet, even for an hour. You could take the late flight from Orly to Brussels and I could go on to Vienna with the Lear – please, Peter. I missed you so. We could have an hour together.'

One of the airport sub-managers met Peter as he disembarked from the Lear and led him to one of the VIP lounges above the main concourse.

Magda Altmann came swiftly to meet him as he stepped into the lounge – and he had forgotten how her presence could fill a room with light.

She wore a tailored jacket over a matching skirt, severe gun-metal grey and tremendously effective. She moved like a dancer on long graceful legs which seemed to articulate from the narrow waist – and Peter felt awkward and heavy-footed, for the awareness that he was in the presence of evil sat heavily upon him, weighting him down.

'Oh, Peter. What have they done to you?' she asked with quick concern flaring in those huge compassionate eyes. She reached up to touch his cheek.

The strain and horror of the last days had drawn him out to the edge of physical endurance. His skin had a greyish, sickly tone against which the dark new beard darkening his jaws contrasted strongly. There were more fine silver threads at his temples, gull's wings against the thicker darker waves of his hair, and his eyes were haunted. They had sunk deeply into their sockets.

'Oh, darling, darling,' she whispered, low enough so that the others in the room could not hear her, and she reached up with her mouth for his.

Peter had carefully schooled himself for this meeting. He knew how important it was that he should not in any way betray the knowledge he had. Magda must never guess that he had found her out. That would be deadly dangerous. He must act completely naturally. It was absolutely vital, but there was just that instant's remembrance of his daughter's pale wasted fever-racked features, and then he stooped and took Magda's mouth.

He forced his mouth to soften, as hers was soft and warm and moist, tasting of ripe woman and crushed petals. He made his body welcoming as hers was melting and trusting against his – and he thought he had succeeded completely until she broke from his embrace and leaned back, keeping those slim strong hips still pressed against his. She studied his face again, a swift probing, questioning gaze, and he saw it change deep in her eyes. The flame going out of them leaving only a cold merciless green light, like the beautiful spark in the depths of a great emerald.

She had seen something; no there had been nothing to see. She had sensed something in him, the new awareness. Of course, she would have been searching for it. She needed only the barest confirmation – the quirk of expression on his mouth, the new wariness in his eyes, the slight stiffness and reserve in his body – all of which he thought he had been able to control perfectly.

'Oh, I am glad you are wearing blue now.' She touched the lapel of his casual cashmere jacket. 'It does suit you so well, my dear.'

He had ordered the jacket with her in mind, that was true – but now there was something brittle in her manner. It was as though she had withdrawn her true self, bringing down an invisible barrier between them.

'Come.' She turned away, leading him to the deep leather couch below the picture windows. Some airport official had been able to find flowers, yellow tulips, the first blooms of spring, and there was a bar and coffee machine.

She sat beside him on the couch, but not touching him, and with a nod dismissed her secretary. He moved across the room to join the two bodyguards, her grey wolves, and the three of them remained out of earshot, murmuring quietly amongst themselves.

'Tell me, please, Peter.' She was still watching him, but the cold green light in her eyes had been extinguished – she was friendly and concerned, listening with complete attention as he went step by step over every detail of Melissa-Jane's kidnapping.

It was an old rule of his to tell the complete truth when it would serve – and it served now, for Magda would know every detail. He told her of Caliph's demand for Kingston Parker's life, and his own response.

'I would have done it,' he told her frankly, and she hugged her own arms and shuddered once briefly.

'God, such evil can corrupt even the strongest and the best—' and now there was understanding softening her lips.

Peter went on to tell her of the lucky tip-off and the recovery of Melissa-Jane. He went into details of the manner in which she had been abused, of her terror and the psychological damage she had suffered – and he watched

Magda's eyes carefully. He saw something there, emphasized by the tiny frown that framed them. He knew that he could not expect feelings of guilt. Caliph would be far beyond such mundane emotion – but there was something there, not just stagey compassion.

'I had to stay with her. I think she needed those few days with me,' he explained.

'Yes. I am glad you did that, Peter.' She nodded, and glanced at her wristwatch. 'Oh, we have so little time left,' she lamented. 'Let's have a glass of champagne. We have a little to celebrate. At least Melissa-Jane is alive, and she is young and resilient enough to recover completely.'

Peter eased the cork and when it popped he poured creaming pale yellow Dom Perignon into the flutes, and smiled at her over the glass as they saluted each other.

'It's so good to see you, Peter.' She was truly a superb actress; she said it with such innocent spontaneity that he felt a surge of admiration for her despite himself. He crushed it down and thought that he could kill her now and here. He did not really need a weapon. He could use his hands if he had to, but the Cobra parabellum was in the soft chamois leather holster under his left armpit He could kill her, and the two bodyguards across the room would gun him down instantly He might take one of them, but the other one would get him. They were top men. He had picked them himself. They would get him.

'I'm sorry we will not be together for very long,' he countered, still smiling at her.

'Oh, *chéri*. I know, so am I.' She touched his forearm, the first touch since the greeting embrace. 'I wish it were different. There are so many things that we have to do, you and I, and we must forgive each other for them.'

Perhaps the words were meant to have a special significance; there was a momentary flash of the warm green fire in her eyes, and something else – perhaps a deep and unfathomable regret. Then she sipped the wine, and lowered the long curled lashes across her eyes, shielding them from his scrutiny.

'I hope we will never have anything terrible to forgive—'

For the first time he faced the act of killing her. Before it had been something clinical and academic, and he had avoided considering the deed itself. But now he imagined the impact of an explosive Velex bullet into that smooth sweet flesh. His guts lurched, and for the first time he doubted if he were capable of it.

'Oh, Peter, I hope so. More than anything in life, I hope that.' She lifted her lashes for a moment, and her eyes seemed to cling to his for an instant, pleading for something – forgiveness, perhaps. If he did not use the gun, then how would he do it, he wondered. Could he stand the feeling of cartilage and bone snapping and crackling under his fingers, could he hold the blade of knife into her flat hard belly and feel her fight it like a marlin fights the gleaming curved hook of the gaff?

The telephone on the bar buzzed, and the secretary picked it up on the second ring. He murmured into it.

'*Oui, oui D'accord.*' And hung up. 'Ma Baronne, the aircraft is refuelled and ready to depart.'

'We will leave immediately,' she told him, and then to Peter, 'I am sorry.'

'When will I see you?' he asked.

She shrugged, and a little shadow passed over her eyes. 'It is difficult. I am not sure – I will telephone you. But now I must go, Peter. Adieu, my darling.'

When she had gone, Peter stood at the windows overlooking the airfield. It was a glorious spring afternoon, the early marguerites were blooming wild along the grassy verges of the main runways, like scattered gold sovereigns, and a flock of black birds hopped amongst them, probing and picking for insects, completely undisturbed by the jet shriek of a departing Swissair flight.

Peter ran his mind swiftly over the meeting. Carefully

identifying and isolating the exact moment when she had changed. When she had ceased to be Magda Altmann and become Caliph.

There was no doubt left now. Had there ever been, he wondered, or had it merely been his wish to find doubt?

Now he must harden himself to the act. It would be difficult, much more difficult than he had believed possible. Not once had they been alone, he realized then – always the two grey wolves had hovered around them. It was just another sign of her new wariness. He wondered if they would ever be alone together again – now that she was alerted.

Then abruptly he realized that she had not said 'Au revoir, my darling' but instead she had said 'Adieu, my darling'.

Was there a warning in that? A subtle hint of death – for if Caliph suspected him, he knew what her immediate reaction must be. Was she threatening, or had she merely discarded him, as Kingston Parker had warned that she would?

He could not understand the desolate feeling that swamped him at the thought that he might never see her again – except through the gunsight.

He stood staring out of the window, wondering how his career and his life had begun to disintegrate about him since first he had heard the name Caliph.

A polite voice at his shoulder startled him and he turned to the airport sub-manager. 'They are calling the KLM flight to Brussels now, General Stride.'

Peter roused himself with a sigh and picked up his overcoat and the crocodile skin Hermes briefcase that had been a gift from the woman he must kill.

There was such a volume of correspondence and urgent business piling the long desk in his new office that Peter had an excuse to put aside the detailed planning of the pre-emptive strike against Caliph.

To his mild surprise he found himself enjoying the jostle and haggle, the driving pace and the challenge of the market place. He enjoyed pitting wits and judgement against other sharp and pointed minds, he enjoyed the human interaction – and for the first time understood the fascination which this type of life had exerted over his brother Steven.

Three days after arriving back at his desk, the Iranian Air Force made their first order of the Narmco Kestrel missiles. One hundred and twenty units, over a hundred and fifty million dollars' worth It was a good feeling, and could grow stronger, could finally become addictive, he realized.

He had always looked upon money as rather a nuisance, those degrading and boring sessions with bank managers and clerks of the income tax department, but now he realized that this was a different kind of money. He had glimpsed the world in which Caliph existed, and realized how once a human being became accustomed to manipulating this kind of money, then dreams of godlike power became believable, capable of being transmuted into reality.

He could understand, but could never forgive, and so at last, seven days after his return to Brussels, he forced himself to face up to what he must do.

Magda Altmann had withdrawn. She had made no further contact since that brief and unsatisfactory hour at Orly Airport.

He must go to her, he realized. He had lost his special inside position which would have made the task easier.

He could still get close enough to kill her, of that he was certain. Just as he had the opportunity to do so at Orly. However, if he did it that way it would be suicidal. If he survived the swift retribution of her guards, there would be the slower but inexorable processes of the law. He knew without bothering to consider it too deeply that he would be unable to use the defence of the Caliph story. No court would believe it. It would sound like the rantings of a maniac without the support of Atlas or the Intelligence systems of America and Britain. That support would not be forthcoming – of that he was certain. If he killed Caliph they would be delighted, but they would let him go to the guillotine without raising a voice in his defence. He could imagine the moral indignation of the civilized world if they believed that an unorthodox organization such as Atlas was employing assassins to murder the prominent citizens of a foreign and friendly nation

No. He was on his own, completely. Parker had made that quite clear. And Peter realized that he did not want to die He was not prepared to sacrifice his life to stop Caliph – not unless there was no other way. There had to be another way, of course

As he planned it he thought of the victim only as Caliph – never as Magda Altmann. That way he was able to bring a cold detachment to the problem. The where, the when, and the how of it.

He had complicated the task by replanning her personal security, and his major concern when he did so had been to make her movements as unpredictable as possible. Her social calendar was as closely guarded as a secret of state, there were never any forward press reports of attendance at public or state events.

If she were invited to dine at the Élysée Palace, the fact was reported the day after, not the day before – but there were some annual events that she would never miss. Together they had discussed these weaknesses in her personal security.

'Oh, Peter – you cannot make a convict of me.' She had laughed in protest when he mentioned them. 'I have so few real pleasures – you would not take them from me, would you?'

The first seasonal showing of Yves St Laurent's collections, that she would never miss – or the Grande Semaine of the spring racing season which culminates with the running of the Grand Prix de Paris at Longchamp. This year she had high hopes of victory with her lovely and courageous bay mare, Ice Leopard. She would be there. It was absolutely certain.

Peter began to draw up the list of possible killing grounds, and then crossed off all but the most likely. The estate at La Pierre Bénite, for instance. It had the advantage of being familiar ground for Peter. With a soldier's eye he had noticed fields of fire across the wide terraced lawns that dropped down to the lake; there were stances for a sniper in the forests along the far edge of the lake, and in the little wooded knoll to the north of the house which commanded the yard and stables. However, the estate was well guarded and even there the victim's movements were unpredictable. It would be possible to lie in ambush for the week when she was in Rome or New York. Then again the escape route was highly risky, through a sparsely populated area with only two access roads – both easily blocked by swift police action. No, La Pierre Bénite was crossed from the list.

In the end Peter was left with the two venues that had first sprung to mind – the members' enclosure at Longchamp or Yves St Laurent's premises, at 46 Avenue Victor Hugo.

Both had the advantages of being public and crowded, circumstances favouring pickpockets and assassins, Peter thought wryly. Both had multiple escape routes, and crowds into which the fugitive could blend. There were good stances for a sniper in the grandstands and buildings overlooking the members' enclosure and the saddling paddock at Longchamp or in the multi-storied buildings opposite No 46 in Avenue Victor Hugo.

It would probably be necessary to rent an office suite in one of the buildings – with the attendant risks, even if he used a false name, which put the probability slightly in favour of the racecourse. However, Peter delayed the final decision until he had a chance to inspect each site critically.

There was one last advantage in doing it this way. It would be a stand-off kill. He would be spared the harrowing moments of a kill at close range, with handgun or knife or garrotte.

There would be the detached view of Caliph through the lens of a telescopic sight. The flattened perspectives and the altered colour balances always made for a feeling of unreality. The intervening distance obviated the need for confrontation. He would never have to watch the green light go out in those magnificent eyes, nor hear the last exhalation of breath through the soft and perfectly sculptured lips that had given him so much joy – quickly he thrust those thoughts aside. They weakened his resolve, even though the rage and the lust for vengeance had not abated.

If he could get one of the Thor .222 sniper rifles it would be the perfect tool for this task. With the extra long, accurized barrels designed for use with match grade ammunition and the new laser sights, the weapon could throw a three-inch group at seven hundred yards.

The sniper had only to depress the button on the top of the stock with the forefinger of his left hand. This activated the laser and the beam swept precisely down the projected flight of the bullet. It would show as a bright white coin the size of a silver dime. The sniper looked for the spot of light through the telescopic lens of the sight, and the moment it was exactly on the target he pressed the trigger. Even an unskilled marksman could hardly miss with this sight, in Peter's hands it would be infallible – and Colin Noble would give him one. Not only would Colin give him one, hell, he would probably have it delivered with the compliments of the American Marine Corps by the senior military attaché of the U.S. Embassy in Paris.

Yet Peter found himself drawing out the moment of action, going over his plans so often and with such a critical eye that he knew he was procrastinating.

The sixteenth day after his return to Brussels was a Friday. Peter spent the morning on the NATO range north of the city at a demonstration of the new electronic shield that Narmco had developed to foil the radar guidance on short-range anti-tank missiles. Then he helicoptered back with the three Iranian officers who had attended the demonstration and they lunched at Épaule de Mouton, a magnificent and leisurely meal. Peter still felt guilty spending three hours at the lunch table, so he worked until eight o'clock that evening, on the missile contracts.

It was long after dark when he left through the rear entrance, taking all his usual precautions against the chance that Caliph had an assassin waiting for him in the dark streets. He never left at the same time nor followed the same route, and this evening he bought the evening papers from a *marchand du tabac* in the Grand'Place and stopped to read them at one of the outdoor cafés overlooking the square

He began with the English papers, and the headlines filled the page from one side to the other; black and bold, they declared:

DROP IN PRICE OF CRUDE OIL

Peter sipped the whisky thoughtfully as he read the article through, turning to Page Six for the continuation.

Then he crumpled the newsprint in his lap, and stared at the passing jostle of spring tourists and early evening revellers.

Caliph had achieved her first international triumph.

From now on there would be no bounds to her ruthless rampage of power and violence.

Peter knew he could delay no longer. He made the go decision then, and it was irrevocable. He would arrange to visit London on Monday morning, there was excuse enough for that. He would ask Colin to meet him at the airport, and it would be necessary to tell him of his plan. He knew he could expect full support. Then he could move on to Paris for the final reconnaissance and choice of killing ground. There was still two weeks until the showing of the spring collections – two weeks to plan it so carefully that there would be no chance of failure.

He felt suddenly exhausted, as though the effort of decision had required the last of his reserves. So exhausted that the short walk back to the hotel seemed daunting. He ordered another whisky and drank it slowly before he could make the effort.

Narmco maintained two permanent suites at the Hilton for their senior executives and other important visitors. Peter had not yet made the effort of finding private accommodation in the city, and he was living out of the smaller of the two suites. It was merely a place to wash and sleep and leave his clothes, for he could not shake off the feeling of impermanence, of swiftly changing circumstances by which he found himself surrounded.

My books are in storage again, he thought with a little chill of loneliness. His collection of rare and beautiful books had been in storage for the greater part of his life, as he roamed wherever his duty took him, living out of barracks and hotel rooms. His books were his only possessions, and as he thought about them now he was filled with an unaccustomed longing to have a base, a place that was his own – and immediately he thrust it aside, smiling cynically at himself as he strode through the streets of another foreign city, alone again.

It must be old age catching up with me, he decided.

There had never been time for loneliness before – but now, but now? Unaccountably he remembered Magda Altmann coming into his arms and saying quietly:

'Oh, Peter, I have been alone for so long.'

The memory stopped him dead, and he stood in the light of one of the street lamps, a tall figure in a belted trench coat with a gaunt and haunted face.

A blonde girl with lewdly painted lips sauntered towards him down the sidewalk, pausing to murmur a proposition, and it brought Peter back to the present.

'*Merci.*' He shook his head in curt refusal and walked on.

As he passed the bookstall in the lobby of the Hilton, a rack of magazines caught his attention and he stopped at the shelf of women's magazines. There would be announcements of the Paris haute couture showings soon, and he thumbed the pages of *Vogue* looking for mention of Yves St Laurent's show – instead he was shocked by the image of a woman's face that leapt out of the page at him.

The elegant cheekbone structure framing the huge slanted Slavic eyes. The shimmering fall of dark hair, the feline grace of movement frozen by the camera flash.

In the photograph she was in a group of four people. The other woman was the estranged wife of a pop singer, the sulky expression, slightly skew eyes and bee-stung lips a landmark on the Parisian social scene. Her partner was a freckled, boyish-faced American actor in a laid-back velvet suit with gold chains around his throat, more famous for his sexual exploits than his film roles. They were not the type of persons with whom Magda Altmann habitually associated, but the man beside her, on whose arm she leaned lightly, was much more her style. He was fortyish, dark and handsome in a fleshy heavily built way, with dense wavy hair, and he exuded the special aura of power and confidence that befitted the head of the biggest German automobile manufacturing complex.

The caption below the photograph had them attending

the opening of an exclusive new Parisian discotheque – again this was not Magda Altmann's habitual territory, but she was smiling brilliantly at the tall handsome German, so obviously enjoying herself that Peter felt a stinging shaft of emotion thrust up under his ribs. Hatred or jealousy – he was not certain – and he slapped the magazine closed and returned it to its rack.

In the impersonal antiseptically furnished suite he stripped and showered, and then standing naked in the small lounge of the suite he poured himself a whisky. It was his third that evening.

Since the kidnapping he had been drinking more than ever before in his life, he realized. It could exert an insidious hold when a man was lonely and in grave doubt. He would have to begin watching it. He took a sip of the smoky amber liquid and turned to look at himself in the mirror across the room.

Since he had been back in Brussels, he had worked out each day in the gymnasium at the NATO officers' club where he still had membership, and his body was lean and hard with a belly like a greyhound's – only the face was ravaged by strain and worry – and, it seemed, by some deep unutterable regret.

He turned back towards the bedroom of the suite, and the telephone rang.

'Stride,' he said into the mouthpiece, standing still naked with the glass in his right hand.

'Please hold on, General Stride. We have an international call for you.'

The delay seemed interminable with heavy buzzing and clicking on the line, and the distant voices of other operators speaking bad French or even worse English.

Then suddenly her voice, but faint and so far away that it sounded like a whisper in a vast and empty hall.

'Peter, are you there?'

'Magda?' He felt the shock of it, and his voice echoed

back at him from the receiver; there was the click before she spoke again, that switch of carrier wave that told him they were on a radio telephone link.

'I have to see you, Peter. I cannot go on like this. Will you come to me, please, Peter?'

'Where are you?'

'Les Neuf Poissons.' Her voice was so faint, so distorted, that he asked her to repeat it.

'Les Neuf Poissons – The Nine Fishes,' she repeated 'Will you come, Peter?'

'Are you crying?' he demanded, and the silence echoed and clicked and hummed so he thought they had lost contact, and he felt a flare of alarm so his voice was harsh as he asked again. 'Are you crying?'

'Yes.' It was only a breath, he might have imagined it.

'Why?'

'Because I am sad and frightened, Peter. Because I am alone, Peter. Will you come, please will you come?'

'Yes,' he said. 'How do I get there?'

'Ring Gaston at La Pierre Bénite. He will arrange it. But come quickly, Peter. As quickly as you can.'

'Yes. As soon as I can – but where is it?'

He waited for her reply, but now the distances of the ether echoed with the sound of utter finality.

'Magda? Magda?' He found himself shouting desperately, but the silence taunted him and reluctantly he pressed a finger down on the cradle of the telephone.

'Les Neuf Poissons,' he repeated softly, and lifted the finger 'Operator,' he said, 'please get me a call to France Rambouillet 47–87–47.' And while he waited he was thinking swiftly.

This was what he had been subconsciously waiting for, he realized. There was a feeling of inevitability to it, the wheel could only turn – it could not roll sideways. This was what had to happen.

Caliph had no alternative. This was the summons to

execution. He was only surprised that it had not come sooner. He would see why Caliph would have avoided the attempt in the cities of Europe or England. One such attempt well planned and executed with great force had failed that night on the road to Rambouillet. It would have been a warning to Caliph not to underestimate the victim's ability to retaliate – for the rest, the problems would have been almost the same as those that Peter had faced when planning the strike against Caliph herself.

The when and the where and the how – and Caliph had the edge here. She could summon him to the selected place – but how incredibly skilfully it had been done. As he waited for the call to Rambouillet, Peter marvelled at the woman afresh. There seemed no bottom to her well of talent and accomplishments – despite himself, knowing full well that he was listening to a carefully rehearsed act, despite the fact that he knew her to be a ruthless and merciless killer, yet his heart had twisted at the tones of despair in her voice, the muffled weeping perfectly done, so he had only just been able to identify it.

'This is the residence of Baroness Altmann.'

'Gaston?'

'Speaking, sir.'

'General Stride.'

'Good evening, General. I was expecting your call. I spoke to the Baroness earlier. She asked me to arrange your passage to Les Neuf Poissons. I have done so.'

'Where is it, Gaston?'

'Les Neuf Poissons – it's the Baroness's holiday island in the Îles sous le Vent – it is necessary to take the UTA flight to Papeete-Faaa on Tahiti where the Baroness's pilot will meet you. It's another hundred miles to Les Neuf Poissons and unfortunately the airstrip is too short to accommodate the Lear jet – one has to use a smaller aircraft.'

'When did the Baroness go to Les Neuf Poissons?'

'She left seven days ago, General,' Gaston answered, and

immediately went on in the smooth, efficient secretarial voice to give Peter the details of the UTA flight. ' – The ticket will be held at the UTA check-in counter for you, General, and I have reserved a non-smoking seat at the window.'

'You think of everything. Thank you, Gaston.'

Peter replaced the receiver, and found that his earlier exhaustion had left him – he felt vital and charged with new energy. The elation of a trained soldier facing the prospect of violent action, he wondered, or was it merely the prospect of an end to the indecision and the fear of unknown things? Soon, for good or for evil, it would be settled and he welcomed that.

He went through into the bathroom and pitched the whisky that remained in his glass into the handbasin.

The UTA DC 10 made its final approach to Tahiti-Faaa from the east, slanting down the sky with the jagged peaks of Moorea under the port wing. Peter remembered the spectacularly riven mountains of Tahiti's tiny satellite island as the backdrop of the musical movie *South Pacific* that had been filmed on location here. The volcanic rock was black and unweathered so that its crests were as sharp as sharks' fangs

They arrowed down across the narrow channel between the two islands, and the runway seemed to reach out an arm into the sea to welcome the big silver machine.

The air was heavy and warm and redolent with the perfume of frangipani blossoms, and there were luscious brown girls swinging and swaying gracefully in a dance of welcome. The islands reached out with almost overpowering sweetness and friendliness – but as Peter picked his single light bag out of the hold luggage and started for the exit doors, something unusual happened. One of the Polynesian customs officers at the gate exchanged a quick word with his companion and then politely stepped into Peter's path.

'Good afternoon, sir.' The smile was big and friendly, but it did not stretch as far as the eyes. 'Would you be kind enough to step this way.' The two customs men escorted Peter into the tiny screened office.

'Please open your bags, sir.' Swiftly but thoroughly they went through his valise and crocodile-skin briefcase; one of them even used a measuring stick to check both cases for a hidden compartment.

'I must congratulate you on your efficiency,' said Peter, smiling also, but his voice tight and low.

'A random check, sir.' The senior officer answered his smile. 'You were just unlucky to be the ten thousandth visitor Now, sir, I hope you won't object to a body search?'

'A body search?' Peter snapped, and would have protested further, but instead he shrugged and raised both arms. 'Go ahead.'

He could imagine that Magda Altmann was as much the Grande Dame here as she was in mother France. She owned the entire island group, and it would need only a nod to have an incoming visitor thoroughly searched for weapons of any sort.

He could imagine also that Caliph would be very concerned that the intended victim should be suitably prepared for execution, lest he should inadvertently become the executioner.

The one customs officer checked his arms and flanks from armpit to waist, while the other knelt behind him and checked inside the outside of his legs from crotch to ankle.

Peter had left the Cobra in the safe deposit box in the Hilton in Brussels. He had anticipated something like this, it was the way Caliph would work.

'Satisfied?' he asked.

'Thank you for your co-operation, sir. Have a lovely stay on our island.'

Magda's personal pilot was waiting for Peter in the main concourse, and hurried forward to shake his hand.

'I was worried that you were not on the flight.'

'A small delay in customs,' Peter explained.

'We should leave immediately, if we are to avoid a night landing on Les Neuf Poissons – the strip is a little difficult.'

Magda's Gates Lear was parked on the hardstand near the service area, and beside it the Norman Britten Tri-Islander looked small and ungainly, a stork-like ugly aircraft capable of the most amazing performance in short take-off and landing situations.

The body of the machine was already loaded with crates and cartons of supplies, everything from toilet rolls to Veuve Cliquot champagne, all tied down under a wide-meshed nylon net.

Peter took the right-hand seat, and the pilot started up and cleared with control, then to Peter:

'One hour's flying. We will just make it.'

The setting sun was behind them as they came in from the west and Les Neuf Poissons lay like a precious necklace of emeralds upon the blue velvet cushion of the ocean.

There were nine islands in the characteristic circular pattern of volcanic formation, and they enclosed a lagoon of water so limpid that every whorl and twist of the coral outcrops showed through as clearly as if they were in air.

'The islands had a Polynesian name when the Baron purchased them back in 1945,' the pilot explained in the clearly articulated rather pedantic French of the Midi. 'They were given by one of the old kings as a gift to a missionary he favoured and the Baron purchased them from his widow. The Baron could not pronounce the Polynesian name so he changed it—' The pilot chuckled. ' – The Baron was a man who faced the world on his own terms.'

Seven of the islands were merely strips of sand and fringes of palms, but the two to the east were larger with hills of volcanic basalt glittering like the skin of a great reptile in the rays of the lowering sun.

As they turned onto their downwind leg, Peter had a view through the window at his elbow of a central building with its roof of palm thatch elegantly curved like the prow of a ship in the tradition of the islands, and around it half-hidden in luscious green gardens were other smaller bungalows. Then they were over the lagoon and there were a clutter of small vessels around the long jetty which reached out into the protected waters – Hobie-cats with bare masts, a big powered schooner which was probably used to ship the heavy stores such as dieseline down from Papeete, power boats for skiing and diving and fishing. One of them was out in the middle of the lagoon, tearing a snowy ostrich feather of wake from the surface as it ran at speed; a tiny figure towed on skis behind it lifted an arm and waved a greeting. Peter thought it might be her, but at that moment the Tri-Islander banked steeply onto its base leg and he was left with only a view of cumulus cloud bloodied by the setting sun.

The runway was short and narrow, hacked from the palm plantation on the strip of level land between beach and hills. It was surfaced with crushed coral. They made their final approach over a tall palisade of palm trees. Peter saw that the pilot had not exaggerated by calling it a little difficult. There was a spiteful crosswind rolling in and breaking over the hills and it rocked the Tri-Islander's wings sickeningly. The pilot crabbed her in, heading half into the wind, and as he skimmed in over the palm tops, closed the throttles, kicked her straight with the rudders, lowered a wing into the wind to hold her from drifting and dropped her neatly fifty feet over the threshold, perfectly aligned with the short runway so she kissed and sat down solidly; instantly the pilot whipped the wheel to full lock into the crosswind to prevent a ground loop and brought her up short.

'*Parfait*!' Peter grunted with involuntary admiration, and the man looked slightly startled as though the feat deserved no special mention. Baroness Altmann employed only the very best.

There was an electric golf cart driven by a young Polynesian girl waiting at the end of the strip amongst the palm trees. She wore only a pareo wrapped around her body below the armpits, a single length of crimson and gold patterned cloth that fell to mid thigh. Her feet were bare, but around her pretty head she wore a crown of fresh flowers – the maeva of the islands.

She drove the golf cart at a furious pace along narrow winding tracks through the gardens that were a rare collection of exotic plants, skilfully laid out, so that there was an exquisite surprise around each turn of the path.

His bungalow was above the beach with white sand below the verandah and the ocean stretching to the horizon, secluded as though it were the only building on the island. Like a child the island girl took his hand, a gesture of perfect innocence, and led him through the bungalow, showing him the controls for the air-conditioning, lighting and the video screen, explaining it all in lisping French patois, and giggling at his expression of pleasure.

There was a fully stocked bar and kitchenette, the small library contained all the current best-sellers, and the newspapers and magazines were only a few days old. The offerings on the video screen included half a dozen recent successful features and Oscar winners.

'Hell, Robinson Crusoe should have landed here,' Peter chuckled, and the girl giggled and wriggled like a friendly little puppy in sympathy

She came to fetch him again two hours later, after he had showered and shaved and rested and changed into a light cotton tropical suit with open shirt and sandals.

Again she held his hand and Peter sensed that if a man had taken the gesture as licence the girl would have been hurt and confused. By the hand she led him along a path that was demarcated by cunningly concealed glow lights, and the night was filled with the murmur of the ocean and the gentle rustle and clatter of palm fronds moving in the wind.

Then they came to the long ship-roofed building he had seen from the air. There was soft music and laughter, but when he stepped into the light the laughter stopped and half a dozen figures turned to him expectantly.

Peter was not sure what he had expected, but it was not this gay, social gathering, tanned men and women in expensive and elegant casual wear, holding tall frosted glasses filled with ice and fruit.

'Peter!' Magda Altmann broke from the group, and came to him with that gliding hip-swinging walk.

She wore a soft, shimmering, wheaten-gold dress, held high at the throat with a thin gold chain, but completely nude across the shoulders and down her back to within an inch of the cleft of her buttocks. It was breathtaking for her body was smooth as a rose petal and tanned to the colour of new honey. The dark hair was twisted into a rope as thick as her wrist and piled up onto the top of her head, and she had touched her eyes with shadows so they were slanting and green and mysterious.

'Peter,' she repeated, and kissed him lightly upon the lips, a brush like a moth's wing, and her perfume touched him as softly, the fragrance of Quadrille flowering with the warmth and magic of her body.

He felt his senses tilt. With all he knew of her, yet he was still not hardened to her physical presence.

She was cool and groomed and poised as she had ever been, there was no trace at all of the confusion and.fearsome loneliness that he had heard in those muffled choked-down sobs from halfway across the world – not until she stepped back to tilt her head on one side, surveying him swiftly, smiling lightly.

'Oh, *chéri*, you are looking so much better. I was so worried about you when last I saw you.'

Only then he thought he was able to detect the shadows deep in her eyes, and the tightness at the corners of her mouth.

'And you are more beautiful than I remembered.'

It was true, so he could say it without reserve, and she laughed, a single soft purr of pleasure.

'You never said that before,' she reminded him, but still her manner was brittle. Her show of affection and friendliness might have convinced him at another time, but not now. 'And I am grateful.'

Now she took his arm, her fingers in the crook of his elbow, and she led him to the waiting group of guests as though she did not trust herself to be alone with him another moment lest she reveal some forbidden part of herself.

There were three men and their wives: an American Democrat senator of considerable political influence, a man with a magnificent head of silver hair, eyes like dead oysters, and a beautiful wife at least thirty years his junior who looked at Peter the way a lion looks at a gazelle and held his hand seconds longer than was necessary.

There was an Australian, heavy in the shoulder and big in the gut. His skin was tanned leathery and his eyes were framed in a network of wrinkles. They seemed to be staring through dust and sun glare at distant horizons. He owned a quarter of the world's known uranium reserves, and cattle stations whose area was twice the size of the British Isles. His wife was as tanned and her handshake was as firm as his.

The third man was a Spaniard whose family name was synonymous with sherry, an urbane and courtly Don, but with that fierce Moorish rake to his thin features. Peter had read somewhere that the sherry and cognac ageing in this man's cellars was valued at over five hundred million dollars, and that formed only a small part of his family's investments. His wife was a darkly brooding Spanish beauty with an extraordinary streak of chalk white through the peak of her otherwise black hair.

As soon as the group had assimilated Peter, the talk turned back easily to the day's sport. The Australian had boated a huge black marlin that morning, a fish over one thousand pounds in weight and fifteen feet from the point of its bill to the tip of its deep sickle tail, and the company was elated.

Peter took little part in the conversation, but watched Magda Altmann covertly. Yet she was fully aware of his scrutiny; he could see it in the way she held her hand, and the tension in her whole long slim body, but she laughed easily with the others and glanced at Peter only once or twice, each time with a smile, but the shadows were in the green depths of her eyes.

Finally she clapped her hands. 'Come, everybody, we are going to open the feast.' She linked arms with the senator and the Australian and led them down onto the beach. Peter was left to cope with the senator's wife, and pushed her bosom against his upper arm and ran her tongue lightly over her lips as she clung to him.

Two of the Polynesian servants were waiting beside a long mound of white beach sand, and at Magda's signal they attacked it with shovels, swiftly exposing a thick layer of seaweed and banana leaves from which poured columns of thick and fragrant steam. Below that was a rack of banyan wood and palm fronds which suspended the feast over another layer of seaweed and live coals.

There were exclamations of delight as the aroma of chicken and fish and pork mingled with those of breadfruit and plantains and spices.

'Ah, a success,' Magda declared gaily. 'If any air is allowed to enter the bake we lose it all. It burns, poof! And we are left with only charcoal.'

While they feasted and drank the talk and laughter became louder and less restrained, but Peter made the single drink last the evening and waited quietly – not joining the conversation and ignoring the blandishments of the senator's wife.

He was waiting for some indication of when and from what direction it would come. Not here, he knew, not in this company. When it came it would be swift and efficient as everything else that Caliph did. And suddenly he wondered at his own conceit, that had allowed him to walk, entirely unarmed and unsupported, into the arena selected and prepared by his enemy. He knew his best defence was to strike first, perhaps this very night if the opportunity offered. The sooner the safer, he realized, and Magda smiled at him across the table set under the palm trees and laden with enough food to feed fifty. When he smiled back at her, she beckoned with a slight inclination of her head, and then while the men argued and bantered loudly, she murmured an apology to the women and slipped unobtrusively into the shadows.

Peter gave her a count of fifty before he followed her. She was waiting along the beach. He saw the flash of her bare smooth back in the moonlight and he went forward to where she stood staring out across the wind-ruffled waters of the lagoon.

He came up behind her, and she did not turn her head but her voice was a whisper.

'I am so glad you came, Peter.'

'I am so glad you asked me to.'

He touched the back of her neck, just behind her ear. The ear had an almost elfin point to it that he had not noticed before and the unswept hair at her nape was silken under his fingertips. He could just locate the axis, that delicate bone at the base of the skull which the hangman aims to crush with the drop. He could do it with the pressure of thumb and it would be as quick as the knot.

'I am so sorry about the others,' she said. 'But I am getting rid of them – with almost indecent haste, I'm afraid.' She reached up over her shoulder and took his hand from her neck, and he did not resist. Gently she spread the hand, and then pressed the open palm to her cheek. 'They will leave early tomorrow. Pierre is flying them back to Papeete, and then we will have Les Neuf Poissons to ourselves – just you and I—' And then that husky little chuckle.' – And thirty-odd servants.'

He could understand exactly why it would be that way. The only witnesses would be the faithful retainers of the Grande Dame of the islands.

'Now we must go back. Unfortunately my guests are very important, and I cannot ignore them longer – but tomorrow will come Too slowly for me, Peter – but it will come.'

She turned in the circle of his arms and kissed him with a sudden startling ferocity, so his lips were crushed against his teeth, and then she broke from him and whispered close to his ear.

'Whatever way it goes, Peter, we have had something of value, you and I Perhaps the most precious thing I have had in my life. They can never take that away from me.'

And then she was out of his arms with that uncanny speed and grace of movement and gliding back along the path towards the lights. He followed her slowly, confused and uncertain as to what she had meant by those last words, concluding finally that the purpose had been exactly that – to confuse and unbalance him, and at that moment he sensed rather than heard movement behind him, and instantly whirled and ducked.

The man was ten paces behind him, had come like a leopard, silently from the cover of a fall of lianas and flowering creepers beside the path; only some animal instinct had warned Peter – and his body flowed into the fighting stance, balanced, strung like a nocked arrow, at once ready both to attack and meet attack.

'Good evening, General Stride.' Peter only just managed to arrest himself, and he straightened slowly but with each hand still extended stiffly at his side like the blade of a meat cleaver, and as lethal.

'Carl!' he said. So the grey wolves had been close, within feet of them, guarding their mistress even in that intimate moment.

'I hope I did not alarm you,' said the bodyguard – and though Peter could not see the man's expression, there was a faint mockery in his voice. If there was confirmation needed, complete and final, this was it. Only Caliph would have need of a guard on a romantic assignment. Peter knew then beyond any doubt that either he or Magda Altmann would be dead by sunset the following evening.

Before going into the bungalow he made a stealthy prowling circuit of the bushes and shrubs that surrounded it. He found nothing suspicious but in the interior the bed had been prepared and his shaving gear cleaned and neatly rearranged. His soiled clothing had been taken for cleaning and the other clothing had been pressed and rearranged more neatly than his own unpacking. He could not therefore be certain that his other possessions had not been searched, but it was safe to presume they had. Caliph would not neglect such an elementary precaution.

The locks on doors and windows were inadequate, had probably not been used in years, for there had been no serpents in this paradise, not until recently. So he placed chairs and other obstacles in such a way that an intruder should stumble over them in the dark, and then he rumpled the bed and arranged the pillows to look like a sleeping figure, but took a single blanket to the long couch in the private lounge. He did not really expect an attempt before the other guests left the island, but if it came he would confuse Caliph's scenario as much as possible.

He slept fitfully, jerking awake when a falling palm frond rattled across the roof, or the moon threw picture shadows on the wall across the room. Just before dawn he fell into a deeper sleep and his dreams were distorted and nonsensical, only the sharp clear image of Melissa-Jane's terror-stricken face and her silent screams of horror remained with him when he woke. The memory roused in him the cold lust for vengeance which had abated a little in the weeks since her rescue, and he felt reaffirmed, possessed of a steely purpose once more, determined to resist the softening, fatal allure of Caliph.

He rose in the slippery pearl light of not yet dawn, and went down to the beach. He swam out a mile beyond the reef, and had a long pull back against a rogue current, but he came ashore feeling good and hard and alert as he had not been in weeks.

All right, he thought grimly. Let it come. I'm as ready as I'll ever be.

There was a farewell breakfast for the departing guests, on the sugary sands of the beach that had been swept smooth by the night tide – pink Laurent Perrier champagne and hothouse strawberries flown in from Auckland, New Zealand.

Magda Altmann wore brief green pants that showed off her long shapely legs to perfection, and a matching 'boob tube' across her small neat breasts – but her belly and shoulders and back were bare It was the body of a finely trained athlete, but drawn by a great artist.

She seemed unnaturally elated to Peter, her gaiety was slightly forced and the low purring laughter just a little too ready – and with a saw-edge to it. It was almost as though she had made some hard decision, and was steeling herself to carry it through. Peter thought of them as true opponents who had trained carefully for the coming configuration – like prize fighters at the weigh-in.

After the breakfast they rode up in a cavalcade of electric carts to the airfield. The senator, revved-up with pink champagne and sweating lightly in the rising heat, gave Magda an over-affectionate farewell, but she skilfully avoided his hands and shunted him expertly into the Tri-Islander after the other passengers.

Pierre, Magda's pilot, stood on the brakes at the end of the runway while he ran all three engines up to full power. Then he let her go, and the moment she had speed he rotated her into a nose-high obstacle-clearance attitude. The ungainly machine jumped into the sky and went over the palms at the end of the short strip with five hundred feet to spare – and Magda turned to Peter ecstatically.

'I hardly slept last night,' she admitted, as she kissed him.

'Neither did I,' Peter told her – and then he added silently ' – for the same reasons, I'm sure.'

'I've planned a special day for us,' she went on. 'And I don't want to waste another minute of it.'

The head boatman had Magda's big forty-five-foot Chris-craft Fisherman singled up at the end of the jetty. It was a beautiful boat, with long low attacking lines that made it seem to be flying even when on its mooring lines, and loving care had very obviously been lavished upon it. The paintwork was unmarked and the stainless steel fittings were polished to a mirror finish. The boatman beamed happily when Magda commended him with a smile and a word.

'Tanks are full, Baronne. The scuba bottles are charged and the light rods are rigged. The water-skis are in the main racks, and the chef came down himself to check the ice-box.'

However, his wide white smile faded when he learned that Magda was taking the boat out alone.

'Don't you trust me?' she laughed.

'Oh, of course, Baronne—' But he could not hide his

chagrin at having to give over his charge – even to such a distinguished captain.

He handled the lines himself, casting her off, and calling anxious last-minute advice to Magda as the gap between jetty and vessel opened.

'*Ne t'inquiet pas!*' she laughed at him, but he made a dejected figure standing on the end of the jetty as Magda slowly opened up both diesels and the Chris-craft came up on the plane and seemed almost to break free of the surface. Her wake was scored deep and clean and straight through the gin-clear water of the lagoon, a tribute to the design of her hull, and then it curved out gracefully behind them as Magda made the turn between the channel markers and lined her up for the passage through the reef, and out into the open Pacific.

'Where are we going?'

'There is an old Japanese aircraft carrier lying in a hundred feet of water beyond the reef. Yankee aircraft sank her back in 'forty-four – It is a beautiful site for scuba diving. We will go there first—'

How? Peter wondered. Perhaps one of the scuba bottles had been partially filled with carbon monoxide gas. It was simply done, with a hose from the exhaust of the diesel generator: simply pass the exhaust gases through a charcoal filter to remove the taste and smell of unconsumed hydrocarbons and the remaining carbon monoxide gas would be undetectable. Fill the bottle to 30 atmospheres of pressure then top it up with clean air to its operating pressure of 110 atmospheres. It would be swift, but not too swift to alarm the victim, a gentle long sleep. When the victim lost his mouthpiece, the bottles would purge themselves of any trace of the gas. That would be a good way to do it.

'After that we can go ashore on Île des Oiseaux. Since Aaron stopped the islanders stealing the eggs to eat, we've got one of the biggest nesting colonies of terns and noddies and frigate birds in the Southern Pacific—'

Perhaps a speargun. That would be direct and effective. At short range, say two feet, even below the surface, the spear arrow would go right through a human torso – in between the shoulder blades and out through the breast bone.

'– And afterwards we can water-ski—'

With an unsuspecting skier in the water, awaiting the pick-up, what could be more effective than opening up both those tremendously powerful diesels to the gates and running the victim down? If the hull did not crush him, the twin screws turning at 500 revolutions per minute would cut him up as neatly as a loaf of pre-sliced bread.

Peter found himself intrigued with the guessing-game. He found himself regretting the fact that he would never know what she intended, and he looked back from where they stood side by side on the tall flying bridge of the Chris-craft. The main island was lowering itself into the water; already they were out of sight of anybody who did not have a pair of powerful binoculars.

Beside him Magda pulled the retaining ribbon out of her hair, and shook loose a black rippling banner that streamed in the wind behind her.

'Let's do this for ever,' she shouted above the wind and the boom of the engines.

'Sold to the lady with the sexy backside,' Peter shouted back, and he had to remind himself that she was one of the most carefully trained killers he would ever meet. He must not allow himself to be lulled by the laughter and the beauty – and he must not allow her to make the first stroke. His chances of surviving that were remote.

He glanced back again at the land. Any minute now, he thought, and moved as though to glance over the side, getting slightly into her rear, but still in the periphery of her vision; she shifted slightly towards him still smiling.

'At this state of the tide there are always amberjack in the channel. I promised the chef I would bring him a couple of them kicking fresh,' she explained. 'Won't you go down and get two of the light rods ready, *chéri*? The feather lures are in the forward starboard seat locker.'

'Okay,' he nodded.

'I'll throttle back to trolling speed when I make the turn into the channel – put the lines in then.'

'*D'accord*.' And then on an impulse. 'But kiss me first.'

She held up her face to him, and he wondered why he had said that. It was not to take farewell of her. He was sure of that. It was to lull her just that fraction, and yet as their lips met he felt the deep ache of regret that he had controlled for so long and as her mouth spread slowly and moistly open under his, he felt as though his heart might break then. For a moment he felt that he might die himself before he could do it; dark waves of despair poured over him.

He slid his hand over her shoulder to the nape of her neck and her body flattened against his; he caressed her lightly, feeling for the place, and then settling thumb and forefinger – a second, another second passed, and then she pulled him back softly.

'Hey, now!' she whispered huskily. 'You stop that before I pile up on the reef.'

He had not been able to do it with his bare hands He just could not do it like that – but he had to do it quickly, very quickly. Every minute delayed now led him deeper and deeper into deadly danger

'Go!' she ordered, and struck him a playful blow on the chest 'We've got time for that later – all the time in the world. Let's savour it, every moment of it.'

He had not been able to do it, and he turned away It was only as he went down the steel ladder into the cockpit of the Chris-craft that it suddenly occurred to him that during the lingering seconds of that kiss the fingers of her right hand had cupped lovingly under his chin. She could have crushed his larynx, paralysing him with a thumb driven up into the soft vulnerable arch of his throat at the first offensive pressure of his thumb and forefinger.

As his feet hit the deck of the cockpit another thought came to him. Her other hand had lain against his body, stroking him softly under the ribs. That hand could have struck upwards and inwards to tear through his diaphragm – his instincts must have warned him. She had been poised for the stroke, more so than he was; she had been inside the circle of his arms, inside his defences, waiting for him – and he shivered briefly in the hot morning sun at the realization of how close he had been to death.

The realization turned instantly to something else, that slid down his spine cold as water down a melting icicle. It was fear, not the crippling fear of the craven, but fear that edged him and hardened him. Next time he would not hesitate – he could not hesitate.

He was instinctively carrying out her instructions as his mind raced to catch up with the problem. He lifted the lid of the seat locker. In the custom-fitted interior were arranged trays of fishing gear, swivels of brass and stainless steel in fifty different sizes; sinkers shaped for every type of water and bottom; lures of plastic and feathers, of enamel and bright metal; hooks for gigantic bill fish or for fry – and in a separate compartment in the side tray a bait knife.

The knife was a fifty-dollar Ninja with a lexan composition handle, chequered and moulded for grip. The blade was seven inches of hollow ground steel, three inches broad at the hilt and tapering to a stiletto point. It was a brutal weapon, you could probably chop through an oak log with it, as the makers advertised. Certainly it would enter human flesh and go through bone as though it were Cheddar cheese.

It balanced beautifully in Peter's fist as he made one testing slash and return cut with it. The blade hissed in the air, and when he tested the edge too hurriedly it stung like a razor and left a thin line of bright blood across the ball of his thumb.

He kicked off his canvas sneakers, so the rubber soles did not squeak on the deck. He was dressed now in only a thin cotton singlet and boxer-type swimming trunks, stripped down for action.

He went up the first three rungs of the ladder on bare silent feet, and lifted his eyes above the level of the flying bridge.

Magda Altmann stood at the controls of the Chris-craft, conning the big vessel into the mouth of the channel, staring ahead in complete concentration.

Her hair still flew in the wind, snaking and tangling into thick shimmering tresses. Her naked back was turned to him, the deeply defined depression running down her spine and the crest of smooth hard muscle rising on each side of it.

One leg of her pants had rucked up slightly exposing a half-moon of round white buttock, and her legs were long and supple as a dancer's as she balanced on the balls of her narrow feet, raising herself to see ahead over the bows.

Peter had been gone from the bridge for less than ten seconds, and she was completely unaware, completely unsuspecting.

Peter did not make the same mistake again; he went up the ladder in a single swift bound, and the bellow of the diesels covered any sound he might have made.

With the knife you never take the chance of the point turning against bone, if you have a choice of target.

Peter picked the small of the back, at the level of the kidneys where there was no bone to protect the body cavity.

It is essential to put the blade in with all possible power; this decreases the chance of bone-deflection and it peaks the paralysing effect of impact-shock.

Peter put the full weight of his rush behind the thrust.

The paralysis is total if the blade is twisted a half-turn at the same instant that the blade socks in hilt-deep.

The muscles in Peter's right forearm were bunched in anticipation of the moment in which he would twist the blade viciously in her flesh, quadrupling the size and the trauma of the wound.

The polished stainless steel fascia of the Chris-craft's control panel reflected a distorted image, like those funny mirrors of the fairground Only at the moment that Peter had committed himself completely, at the moment when he had thrown all his weight into the killing stroke, did he realize with a sickening flash that she was watching him in the polished steel control panel; she had been watching him from the moment he reappeared at the head of the ladder.

The curved surface of the steel distorted her face, so that it appeared to consist only of two enormous eyes; it distracted him in that thousandth part of a second before the point of the blade entered flesh. He did not see her move

Blinding, numbing agony shot down his right flank and arm, from a point in the hollow where his collar bone joined the upper arm, while at the same instant something hit him on the inside of his forearm just below the elbow The knife stroke was flung outwards, passing an inch from her hip, and the point of the blade crashed into the control panel in front of her, scoring the metal with a deep bright scratch, but Peter's numbed fingers could not keep hold on the hilt The weapon spun from his grip, ringing like a crystal wine glass as it struck the steel handrail and rebounded over the side of the bridge into the cockpit behind him. He realized that she had struck backwards at him, not turning to face him but using only the reflection in the control panel to judge her blow with precision into the pressure point of his shoulder.

Now pain had crippled him and the natural reaction was

to clutch at the source of it. Instead with some reflexive instinct of survival he flung up his left hand to protect the side of his neck and the next blow, also thrown backwards, felt as though it had come from a full-blooded swing of a baseball bat. He hardly saw it, it came so fast and hard there was just the flicker of movement across his vision, like the blur of a hummingbird's wing, and then the appalling force of it crushing into the muscle of his forearm.

Had it taken him in the neck where it was aimed, it would have killed him instantly; instead it paralysed his other arm, and she was turning into him now effortlessly, matching his bull strength with a combination of speed and control.

He knew he must try and keep her close, smother her with his weight and size and strength and he hooked at her with the clawed crippled fingers of his knife hand; they caught for a moment and then she jerked free. He had ripped away the flimsy strip of elasticized cloth that covered her breasts, and she spun lightly under and out of the sweep of his other arm as he tried desperately to club her down with his forearm.

He saw that her face was bone-white with the adrenalin overdose coursing her blood. Her lips were drawn back into a fixed snarl of concentration and fury and her teeth seemed as sharp as those of a female leopard in a trap.

It was like fighting a leopard; she attacked him with an unrelenting savagery and total lack of fear, no longer human, dedicated only to his total destruction.

The long hair swirled about him, at one moment flicking like a whiplash into his eyes to blind and unbalance him, and she weaved and dodged and struck like a mongoose at the cobra, every movement flowing into the next, her taunting red-tipped breasts dancing and jerking with each blow she hurled at him.

With a jar of disbelief, Peter realized that she was beating him down. So far he had managed barely to survive each blow that he caught on arm and shoulder; each time her bare feet crashed into his thigh or lower belly, each time her knees drove for his groin and jarred against the bone of his pelvis, he felt a little more of his strength dissipate, felt his reactions becoming more rubbery, just that instant slower. He had countered her attack with luck and instinct, but any instant she must land solidly and drop him, for she was never still, cutting him with hands and feet, keeping him off balance – and he had not hurt her yet, had not touched her with any of his counter-strokes. Still there was no feeling in his hands and fingers. He needed respite, he needed a weapon, and he thought desperately of the knife that had fallen into the cockpit behind him.

He gave ground to her next attack, and the bridge rail caught him in the small of the back; at the same moment another of her strokes – aimed at the soft of his throat – deflected off his arm and crunched into his nose. Instantly his eyes flooded with tears, and he felt the warm salt flood of blood over his upper lip and down the back of his throat; he doubled over swiftly, then in the same movement he threw himself backwards, like a diver making a one-and-a-half from the three-metre board. The rail behind him helped his turn in the air, and he had judged it finely. He landed like a cat on both feet on the deck of the cockpit ten feet below the bridge, flexing at the knees to absorb the shock, and flicking the tears from his eyes, wringing his arms to return blood and feeling.

As he spun into a crouch he saw the knife. It had slid down the cockpit into the stern scuppers. He went for it.

The dive had taken her by surprise, just as she was poised for the final killing stroke to the back of his exposed neck, but she swirled to the head of the ladder and gathered herself while below her Peter launched himself across the cockpit for the big ugly Ninja knife.

She went for him feet first, dropping from ten feet, and the bare soles of her feet hit him together, the impetus of her falling body enhanced by the stabbing kick that she released at the moment that she hit him.

She caught him high in the back, hurling him forward so that the top of his head cracked into the bulkhead and darkness rustled through his head. He felt his senses going, and it required all of his resolve to roll over and pull his knees swiftly to his chest, to guard himself against the next killing stroke. He caught it on his shins, and once again launched himself after the knife. His fingers felt swollen and clumsy on the rough chequered surface of the hilt, and at the moment they touched he unwound his doubled-up body like a steel coil spring, lashing out with both feet together. It was a blind stroke, delivered in complete desperation.

It was the first solid blow he had landed; it caught her at the moment when she had already launched herself into her next onslaught; both his feet slammed into her belly just below the ribs, and had the flesh there been soft or yielding it would have ended it; but she was just able to absorb the force of it with flat hard muscle – though it hurled her backwards across the cockpit with the breath hissing from her lungs and the long slim body doubling over in an agonized convulsion.

Peter realized that this was the only chance that he had had, and the only one he would ever have – yet his body was racked with such pain that he could hardly drag himself up onto his elbow, and his vision swam and blurred with tears and blood and sweat.

He did not know how he had managed it, some supreme exertion of will, but he was on his feet with the knife in his hand, instinctively extending the blade down the back of his right thigh to keep it protected until the moment it had to be used, crouching as he went in, left arm raised as a shield – and knowing that now he had to end it swiftly, he could not go on longer. This was his last effort.

Then she had a weapon also. Moving so swiftly that it had happened before she was halfway across the cockpit, she had knocked the retaining clip off the boat hook that stood in the rack beside the cabin entrance.

It was eight feet of heavy varnished ash, with an ornate but vicious brass head, and she cut at him with it, a low swinging warning blow to hold him off while she forced air back into her empty lungs.

She was recovering swiftly, much more swiftly than Peter himself. He could see the cold killing light rekindle in her eyes. He knew he could not go on much longer, he must risk it all in one last total effort.

He threw the knife, aiming at her head. The Ninja, not designed as a throwing weapon, rolled out of line of flight, hilt foremost – but still it forced her to lift the staff of the boat hook and deflect it. It was the distraction he had wanted.

Peter used the momentum of his throw to go in under the swinging staff, and he hit her with his shoulder while her arms were raised.

Both of them reeled backwards into the cabin bulkhead, and Peter groped desperately for a grip. He found it in the thick lustrous tresses of her hair, and he wove his fingers into it

She fought like a dying animal with strength and fury and courage that he could never have believed possible, but now at last he could pit his superior weight and strength directly against hers.

He smothered her against his chest, trapping one arm between their bodies, while he was able to pull her head backwards at an impossible angle, exposing the long smooth curve of her throat

And then he scissored his thighs across her, so that those lethal feet and legs were unable to reach him, and they crashed over onto the deck.

She managed with an incredible effort to swing her weight so that she landed on top of him, her breasts sliding against his chest, lubricated by sweat and blood that dribbled down from his nose, but Peter heaved all his remaining strength into his shoulders and rolled back on top of her.

They were locked breast to chest and groin to groin in some bizarre parody of the act of love, only the stock of the boat hook between them.

Peter twisted down hard on the rope of hair in his left hand, pinning her head to the deck so that her eyes were only six inches from his and blood from his nose and mouth dripped onto her upturned face.

Neither of them had spoken a word, the only sound the hiss and suck of laboured breathing, the explosive grunt of a blow delivered or the involuntary gasp of pain as it landed.

They glared into each other's eyes, and at that moment neither of them was a human being, they were two animals fighting to the death, and Peter shifted quickly so the stock of the boat hook fell across her unprotected throat. She had not been ready for that and she ducked her chin too late.

Peter knew he could not dare to release his grip on her hair, nor the arm around her body, nor the scissors that enfolded her legs. He could feel the steely tension of her whole body, that required all his own strength to hold. If he relaxed his grip in the slightest, she would twist away, and he would not have the strength to go on after that.

With the elbow of the hand that held her hair, he began to bear down on the ash staff of the boat hook, slowly crushing down into her throat.

She knew it was over then, but still she fought on. As she weakened Peter was able to transfer more and more of his weight onto the stock of the boat hook. Slowly blood suffused her face, turning it dark mottled plum, her lips quivered with each painful rasping breath and a little frothy saliva broke from the corners of her mouth and ran back down her cheek.

Watching her die was the most horrible thing Peter had ever had to do. He shifted cautiously, going for the few extra ounces of weight which would force the heavy wooden stock down that last eighth of an inch and crush in her throat, and she recognized the moment in her eyes.

She spoke for the first time. It was a croak slurred through swollen and gaping lips.

'They warned me.' He thought he had misheard her, and he checked the final thrust downwards which would pinch out the last spark of life 'I couldn't believe it.' The faintest whisper, only just intelligible. 'Not you.'

Then the last resistance went out of her, her body relaxed, the complete acceptance of death at last. The fierce green light went out in her eyes, replaced at the very end with a sadness so heavy that it seemed to acknowledge the ultimate betrayal of all goodness and trust

Peter could not force himself to make the final thrust downwards that would end it. He rolled off her and flung the heavy wooden stock across the cockpit. It crashed into the bulkhead and he sobbed as he crawled painfully across the deck, turning his back to her completely, knowing that she was still alive and therefore still as dangerous as she had ever been – yet no longer caring. He had gone as far as he could go. It didn't matter any more if she killed him; something in him even welcomed the prospect of release.

He reached the rail and tried to drag himself onto his feet, expecting at any moment the killing blow into the nape of his neck as she attacked him again.

It did not come, and he managed to get onto his knees, but his whole body was trembling violently so that his teeth chattered in his jaws and every strained and bruised tendon and muscle screamed for surcease. Let her kill me, he thought, it doesn't matter. Nothing matters now.

Half supporting himself on the rail, he turned slowly and his vision swam and flickered with patches of darkness and little shooting stars of crimson and white flame.

Through the swirl of senses at the end of their usefulness,

he saw that she was kneeling in the centre of the cockpit, facing him.

Her naked torso was splattered and smeared with his blood and the smooth tanned skin oiled with slippery sweat of near death. Her face was still and swollen and inflamed, wreathed in a great tangle of matted and disordered hair. There was a flaming livid weal across her throat where the stock had crushed her, and as she fought for breath her small pert breasts lifted and dropped to the painful pumping of her chest.

They stared at each other, far beyond speech, driven to the very frontiers of their existence.

She shook her head, as though trying desperately to deny the horror of it all, and at last she tried to speak; no sound came and she licked her lips and lifted one slim hand to her throat as though to ease the pain of it.

She tried again, and this time she managed one word. 'Why?'

He could not reply for fully half a minute, his own throat seemed to have closed, grown together like an old wound. He knew that he had failed in his duty and yet he could not yet hate himself for it. He formed the words in his own mind, as though he were trying to speak a foreign language, and when he spoke his voice was a stranger's broken and coarsened by the knowledge of failure.

'I couldn't do it,' he said.

She shook her head again, and tried to frame the next question. But she could not articulate it, only one word came out, the same word again.

'Why – ?'

And he had no answer for her.

She stared at him, then slowly her eyes filled with tears; they ran down her cheeks and hung from her chin like early morning dew on the leaf of the vine.

Slowly she pitched forward onto the deck, and for many

seconds he did not have the strength to go to her, and then he lurched across the deck and dropped to his knees beside her; he lifted her upper body in his arms suddenly terrified that he had succeeded after all, that she was dead.

His relief soared above the pain of his battered body as he felt her breathing still sawing through her damaged throat, and as her head lolled against his shoulder he realized that fat oily tears still welled out from between her closed eyelids.

He began to rock her like a child in his arms, a completely useless gesture, and only then did her words begin to make any sense to him.

'They warned me,' she had whispered.

'I couldn't believe it,' she had said.

'Not you.'

He knew then that had she not spoken he would have gone through with it. He would have killed her and weighted her body and dropped it beyond the 1,000-fathom line – but the words, although they did not yet make sense, had reached deep into some recess of his mind.

She stirred against his chest. She said something, it sounded like his name. It roused him to reality. The big Chris-craft was still roaring blindly through the channels and reefs of the outer passage.

He laid her back gently on the deck, and scrambled up the ladder to the flying bridge. The whole of that horrific conflict had taken less than a minute, from his knife-stroke to her collapse under him.

The steering of the Chris-craft was locked into the automatic pilot and the vessel had run straight out through the channel into the open sea. It reinforced his knowledge that she had been ready for his attack. She had been acting that total concentration in steering the vessel, luring him into the attack while the Chris-craft was on automatic pilot and she was ready to throw that backward blow at him.

It did not make sense, not yet. All that he knew was that

he had made some terrible miscalculation. He threw out the switch of the automatic steering, and shut down both throttles to the idle position before disengaging the main drive. The diesels burbled softly, and she rounded up gently into the wind and wallowed beam-on to the short steep blue seas of the open ocean.

Peter took one glance back over the stern. The islands were just a low dark smudge on the horizon, and then he was stumbling back to the ladder.

Magda had dragged herself into a half sitting position, but she recoiled swiftly as he came to her and for the first time he saw fear pass like cloud shadow across her eyes.

'It's all right,' he told her, his own voice still ragged. Her fear offended him deeply. He did not want her ever to be afraid of him again.

He took her up in his arms, and her body was stiff with uncertainty, like that of a cat picked up against its will, but too sick to resist.

'It's all right,' he repeated awkwardly, and carried her down into the saloon of the Chris-craft. His own body felt battered as though his very bones were bruised and cracked, but he handled her so tenderly that slowly the resistance went out of her and she melted against him.

He lowered her onto the leather padded bench, but when he tried to straighten up she slid one arm around his neck and restrained him, clinging to him.

'I left the knife there,' she whispered huskily. 'It was a test.'

'Let me get the medicine chest.' He tried to pull away.

'No.' She shook her head and winced at the pain in her throat. 'Don't go away, Peter. Stay with me. I am so afraid. I was going to kill you if you took the knife. I nearly did. Oh, Peter, what is happening to us, are we both going mad?'

She held him desperately and he sank to his knees on the deck and bowed over her.

'Yes,' he answered her, holding her to his chest. 'Yes, we

must be going mad. I don't understand myself or any of it any more.'

'Why did you have to take the knife, Peter? Please – you must tell me. Don't lie, tell me the truth, I have to know why.'

'Because of Melissa-Jane – because of what you had done to her—'

He felt her jerk in his arms as though he had struck her again She tried to speak but now her voice was only a croak of despair, and Peter went on to explain it to her.

'When I discovered that you were Caliph, I had to kill you.'

She seemed to be gathering herself for some major effort, but then when she spoke it was still in that scratchy broken whisper.

'Why did you stop yourself, Peter?'

'Because—' He knew the reason then. ' – Because suddenly I knew that I loved you. Nothing else counted.'

She gasped and was silent again for nearly a minute.

'Do you still think that I am Caliph?' she asked at last.

'I don't know. I don't know anything any more – except that I love you. That's all that matters.'

'What happened to us, Peter?' She lamented softly 'Oh God, what has happened to us?'

'Are you Caliph, Magda?'

'But Peter, you tried to kill me. That was the test with the knife. You are Caliph.'

Under Magda's direction Peter took the Chris-craft in through a narrow passage in the coral reef that surrounded Île des Oiseaux, while the seabirds wheeled about them in a raucous cloud, filling the air with their wingbeats.

He anchored in five fathoms in the protected lee, and

then called the main island on the VHF radio, speaking to the head boatman.

'The Baronne has decided to sleep on board overnight,' he explained. 'Don't worry about us.'

When he went down to the saloon again Magda had recovered sufficiently to be sitting up. She had pulled on one of the terry towelling track suits from the clothes locker, and she had wound a clean towel around her throat to protect it and to hide the fierce fresh bruise that was already staining her skin like the squeezed juice of an over-ripe plum.

Peter found the medicine box in a locker above the toilet bowl of the heads, and she protested when he brought two Temprapain capsules for the pain, and four tablets of Brufin for the swelling and bruising of her throat and body.

'Take them,' he commanded and held the glass while she did so

Then he carefully unwrapped the towel from her throat and lightly rubbed a creamy salve into the bruise with his fingertips

'That feels better already,' she whispered, but now she had lost her voice almost entirely

'Let's have a look at your stomach.' He pushed her down gently on her back on the long padded bench and unzipped the top of the towelling suit to the waist. The bruise where he had kicked her had spread from just below her small pale breasts to the tiny sculpted navel in the flat hard plane of her belly; again he massaged the soothing cream into her skin and she sighed and murmured with the comfort of it When he finished she was able to hobble, still painfully doubled over, to the heads. She locked herself in for fifteen minutes while Peter tended his own injuries, and when she emerged again she had bathed her face and combed out her hair

He poured two crystal old-fashioned glasses half full of Jack Daniel's Bourbon and he handed one to her as she sank onto the padded bench beside him. 'Drink it. For your throat,' he ordered, and she drank and gasped at the sting of the liquor and set the glass aside.

'And you, Peter?' she husked with sudden concern. 'Are you all right?'

'Just one thing,' he said. 'I'd hate you to get really mad at me.' Then he smiled, and she started to chuckle but choked on the pain and ended up clinging to him.

'When can we talk?' he asked her gently. 'We have to talk this out.'

'Yes, I know, but not yet, Peter. Just hold me for a while.' And he was surprised at the comfort that it afforded him. The warm woman shape pressed to him seemed to ease the pain of body and of mind, and he stroked her hair as she nuzzled softly against his throat.

'You said you loved me,' she murmured at last, making it a question. Seeking reassurance, as lovers always must.

'Yes. I love you. I think I knew it all along, but when I learned that you were Caliph, I had to bury it deep. It was only there at the end I had to admit to myself.'

'I'm glad,' she said simply. 'Because you see I love you also. I thought I would never be able to love. I had despaired of it, Peter. Until you. And then they told me you would kill me. That you were Caliph. I thought then I would die – having found you and then lost you. It was too cruel, Peter. I had to give you the chance to prove it wasn't true!'

'Don't talk,' he commanded. 'Just lie there and listen. There is nothing wrong with my voice, so I will tell it first. The way it was with me, and how I knew you were Caliph.'

And he told it to her, holding her to him and speaking softly, steadily. The only other sounds in the cabin were the slap of the wavelets against the hull and the subdued hum of the air-conditioning unit.

'You know everything up to the day Melissa-Jane was taken, all of it. I told you all of it, without reservation and without lying, not once—' He started, and then he went on to tell her in detail of the hunt for Melissa-Jane.

' – I think something must have snapped in my mind during those days. I was ready to believe anything, to try anything to get her back. I would wake up in the night and go to the toilet and vomit with the thought of her hand in a glass jar.'

He told her how he had planned to kill Kingston Parker to meet Caliph's demands, exactly how he intended doing it, the detailed how and where, and she shuddered against him.

'The power to corrupt even the best,' she whispered.

'Don't talk—' he admonished her, and went on to tell her of the tip-off that had led them at last to the Old Manse in Laragh.

'When I saw my daughter like that, I lost what little was left of my reason. When I held her and felt the fever and heard her scream with lingering terror, I would have killed—' He broke off and they were silent until she protested with a small gasp and he realized that his hand had closed on her upper arm and his fingers were biting into her flesh with the force of his memories.

'I'm sorry.' He relaxed his grip, and lifted the hand to touch her cheek. 'Then they told me about you.'

'Who?' she whispered.

'The Atlas Command.'

'Parker?'

'Yes, and Colin Noble.'

'What did they tell you?'

'They told me how your father brought you to Paris when you were a child. They told me that even then you were bright and pretty and special—' He began to recite it for her. ' – When your father was killed—' and she moved restlessly against his chest as he said it ' – you went to live with foster parents, all of them members of the party, and in the end you were so special that they sent somebody to take you back to Poland. Somebody who posed as your uncle—'

'I believed he was—' She nodded. ' – For ten years I believed it. He used to write to me—' She stopped herself with an effort, was silent a moment and then, ' – he was all I ever had after Papa.'

'You were selected to go to Odessa,' Peter went on, and felt her go very still in his arms, so he repeated it with the harshness unconcealed in his tone, ' – to the special school in Odessa.'

'You know about Odessa?' she whispered. 'Or you think you know – but nobody who has never been there could ever really know.'

'I know they taught you to—' He paused, imagining again a beautiful young girl in a special room overlooking the Black Sea, learning to use her body to trap and beguile a man, any man. ' – They taught you many things.' He could not make the accusation.

'Yes,' she murmured. 'Many, many things.'

'Like how to kill a man with your hands.'

'I think that subconsciously I could not bring myself to kill you, Peter. God knows you should not have survived. I loved you, even though I hated you for betraying me, I could not really do it—'

She sighed again, a broken gusty sound.

' – And when I thought that you were going to kill me – it was almost a relief. I was ready to accept that, against living on without the love that I thought I had found.'

'You talk too much.' He stopped her. 'You'll damage your throat further.' He touched her lips with his fingers, to silence her, and then went on. 'And at Odessa you became one of the chosen, one of the élite.'

'It was like entering the church, a beautiful mystic thing—' she whispered. 'I cannot explain it. I would have done everything or anything for the State, for what I knew was right for "Mother Russia".'

'All of this is true?' He marvelled that she made no effort to deny it.

'All of it,' she nodded painfully. 'I will never lie to you again, Peter. I swear it.'

'Then they sent you back to France – to Paris?' he asked, and she nodded.

'You did your job, even better than they had expected you to do it You were the best, the very best. No man could resist you.'

She did not answer, but she did not lower her eyes from his. It was not a defiance but merely a total acceptance of what he was saying.

'There were men. Rich and powerful men—' His voice was bitter now. He could not help himself. 'Many, many men Nobody knows how many, and from each of them you gathered harvest.'

'Poor Peter,' she whispered 'Have you tortured yourself with that?'

'It helped me to hate you,' he said simply.

'Yes, I understand that There is nothing that I can give you for your comfort – except this I never loved a man until I met you.'

She was keeping her word. There were no more lies nor deceptions now. He was certain of it.

'Then they decided that you could be used to take over control of Aaron Altmann and his Empire—'

'No,' she whispered, shaking her head 'I decided on Aaron. He had been the only one man who I had not been able to—' Her voice pinched out and she took a sip of the bourbon and let it trickle slowly down her throat before she went on. 'He fascinated me. I had never met a man like that before. So strong, such raw power.'

'All right,' Peter agreed. 'You might even have grown tired of the other role by then—'

'It's hard work being a courtesan—' She smiled for the first time since he had begun speaking, but it was a sad self-mocking smile.

'You went about it exactly the right way. First you made yourself indispensable to him. Already he was a sick man, beginning to need a crutch, somebody he could trust entirely. You gave him that—'

She said nothing, but memories passed across her eyes, changing the green shadows like sunlight through a deep still pool.

' – And when he trusted you there was nothing you could not supply to your masters. Your value had increased a hundredfold.'

He went on talking quietly while outside the day died in a fury of crimsons and royal purples, slowly altering the light in the cabin and dimming it down so that her face was all that existed in the soft gloom. A pale intense expression, listening quietly to the accusations, to the recitation of betrayals and deceits. Only occasionally she made a little gesture of denial, a shake of her head or the pressure of fingers on his arms. Sometimes she closed her eyes briefly as though she could not accept some particularly cruel memory, and once or twice an exclamation was wrung from her in that strained and tortured whisper.

'Oh God, Peter! It's true!'

He told her how she had gradually developed the taste for the power she was able to wield as Aaron Altmann's wife, and how that flourished as Aaron's strength declined. How she at last even opposed the Baron on some issues.

'Like that of supplying arms to the South African Government,' Peter said, and she nodded and made one of her rare comments.

'Yes. We argued. That was one of the few times we argued.' And she smiled softly, as though at a private memory that she could not share even with him.

He told her how the taste of power and the trappings of

power gradually eroded her commitment to her earlier political ideals, how her masters slowly realized they were losing their hold over her and of the pressures they attempted to apply to force her back into the fold. 'But you were too powerful now to respond to the usual pressures. You had even succeeded in penetrating Aaron's Mossad connections, and had that protection.'

'This is incredible!' she whispered. 'It's so close, so very close that it is the truth.' He waited for her to elaborate, but instead she motioned him to continue.

'When they threatened to expose you to the Baron as a communist agent, you had no choice but to get rid of him – and you did it in such a way that you not only got rid of the threat to your existence but you also achieved control of Altmann Industries, and to put the cherry on the top of the pie you got yourself twenty-five million in operating capital. You arranged the abduction and killing of Aaron Altmann, you paid yourself the twenty-five million and personally supervised its transfer, probably to a numbered account in Switzerland—'

'Oh God, Peter!' she whispered, and in the dark of the cabin her eyes were fathomless and huge as the empty cavities of a skull.

'Is it true?' Peter asked for confirmation for the first time

'It's too horrible. Go on please.'

'It worked so well that it opened up a new world of possibilities for you. Just about this time you truly became Caliph. The taking of Flight 070 was possibly not the first stroke after the kidnapping of Aaron Altmann – there may have been others Vienna and the OPEC ministers, the Red Brigade activities in Rome – but 070 was the first time you used the name Caliph. It worked, except for the dereliction of duty by a subordinate officer.' He indicated himself. 'That was all that stopped it – and that was how I attracted your attention originally.'

Now it was almost totally dark in the cabin and Magda

reached across and switched on the reading light beside them, adjusting the rheostat down to a soft golden glow. In its light she studied his face seriously as he went on.

' – By this time you were aware through your special sources, probably the Mossad connection and almost certainly through the French SID, that somebody was onto Caliph. That somebody turned out to be Kingston Parker and his Atlas organization, and I was the ideal person to firstly confirm that Parker was the hunter – and secondly, to assassinate him. I had the special training and talents for the job, I could get close to him without arousing his suspicions, and I needed only to be sufficiently motivated—'

'No,' she whispered, unable to take her eyes from his face.

'It holds together,' he said. 'All of it.' And she had no reply.

'When I received Melissa-Jane's finger, I was ready for anything—'

'I think I am going to be sick.'

'I'm sorry.' He gave her the glass and she drank the shot of dark liquor it contained, gagging a little on it. Then she sat for a few moments with her eyes closed and her hand on her bruised throat.

'All right?' he asked at last.

'Yes. All right now. Go on.'

'It worked perfectly – except for the tip-off to the hide-out in Ireland. But nobody could have foreseen that, not even Caliph.'

'But there was no proof!' she protested. 'It was all conjecture. No proof that I was Caliph.'

'There was,' he told her quietly. 'O'Shaughnessy, the head of the gang that kidnapped Melissa-Jane, made two telephone calls. They were traced to Rambouillet 47–87–47.'

She stared at him wordlessly.

'He was reporting to his master – to Caliph, you see.' And he waited for her reply. There was none, so after a minute of silence he went on to tell her the arrangements he had made for her execution – the sites he had chosen at Longchamp race course and in the Avenue Victor Hugo, and she shuddered as though she had felt the brush of the black angels' wings across her skin.

'I would have been there,' she admitted. 'You chose the two best sites. Yves has arranged a private showing for me on the sixth of next month. I would have gone to it.'

' – Then you saved me the trouble. You invited me here. I knew that it was an invitation to die, that you knew I had become aware, that I had learned you were Caliph. I saw it in your eyes during that meeting at Orly Airport, I saw it proven by the way you were suddenly avoiding me, the way you were giving me no opportunity to do the job I had to do.'

'Go on.'

'You had me searched when I landed at Tahiti-Faaa.'

She nodded.

'You had the grey wolves search my room again last night, and you set it up for today. I knew I had to strike first, and I did.'

'Yes,' she murmured. 'You did.' And rubbed her throat again.

He went to recharge the glasses from the concealed liquor cabinet behind the bulkhead, and came back to sit beside her.

She shifted slightly, moving inside the circle of his arm, and he held her in silence. The telling of it had exhausted him, and his body ached relentlessly, but he was glad it was said, somehow it was like lancing a malignant abscess – the release of poisons was a relief, and now the healing process could begin.

He could feel his own exhaustion echoed in the slim body that drooped against him, but he sensed that hers was deeper, she had taken too much already – and when he lifted her in his arms again she made no protest, and he carried her like a sleeping child through to the master cabin and laid her on the bunk.

He found pillows and a blanket in the locker below. He slid into the bunk with her, under the single blanket, and she fitted neatly into the curve of his body, pressing gently against him, her back against his chest, her hard round buttocks against the front of his thighs, and her head pillowed into the crook of his arm, while with his other arm he cuddled her close and his hand naturally cupped one of her breasts. They fell asleep like that, pressing closely, and when he rolled over she moved without waking, reversing their positions, moulding herself to his back and pressing her face into the nape of his neck, clasping him with one arm and with a leg thrown over his lower body as though to enfold him completely.

Once he woke and she was gone, and the strength of his alarm surprised him, a hundred new doubts and fears assailed him from the darkness, then he heard the liquid purr in the bowl of the heads and he relaxed. When she returned to the bunk, she had stripped off the terry towelling track suit and her naked body felt somehow very vulnerable and precious in his arms.

They woke together with sunlight pouring into the cabin through one porthole like stage lighting.

'My God – it must be noon.' She sat up, and tossed back the long mane of dark hair over her tanned bare shoulders – but when Peter tried to rise, he froze and groaned aloud.

'*Qu'a tu, chéri?*'

'I must have got caught in a concrete mixer,' he moaned. His bruises had stiffened during the night, torn muscle and strained sinews protested his slightest movement.

'There is only one cure for both of us,' she told him. 'It's in three parts.'

And she helped him off the bunk as though he was an

old man He exaggerated the extent of his injuries a little to make her chuckle. The chuckle was a little hoarse, but her voice was stronger and clearer and she favoured her own bruises only a little as she led him up onto the deck. Her powers of recuperation were those of a young and superbly fit thoroughbred animal

They swam from the diving platform over the Chris-craft's stern.

'It's working,' Peter admitted as the support of warm salt-water soothed his battered body. They swam side by side, both naked, slowly at first and then faster, changing the sedate breast-stroke for a hard overarm crawl, back as far as the reef, treading water there and gasping at the exertion.

'Better?' she panted with her hair floating around her like the tendrils of some beautiful water plant.

'Much better.'

'Race you back.'

They reached the Chris-craft together and clambered up into the cockpit, cascading water and laughing and panting, but when he reached for her, she allowed only a fleeting caress before pulling away.

'First Phase Two of the cure.'

She worked in the galley with only a floral apron around her waist which covered the dark bruises of her belly.

'I never thought an apron could be provocative before.'

'You are supposed to be doing the coffee,' she admonished him and gave him a lewd little bump and grind with her bare backside.

Her omelettes were thick and golden and fluffy, and they ate them in the early sunlight on the upper deck. The trade wind was sheep-dogging a flock of fluffy silver cloud across the heavens, and in the gaps the sky was a peculiar brilliant blue.

They ate with huge appetites, for the bright new morning seemed to have changed the mood of doom that had overpowered them the previous night. Neither of them wanted to break this mood, and they chattered inconsequential nonsense, and exclaimed at the beauty of the day and threw bread crusts to the seagulls, like two children on a picnic.

At last she came to sit in his lap, and made a show of taking his pulse.

'The patient is much improved,' she announced; 'is now probably strong enough for Phase Three of the cure.'

'Which is?' he asked.

'Peter *chéri*, even if you *are* English, you are not that dense.' And she wriggled her bottom in his lap.

They made love in the warm sunlight, on one of the foam mattresses, with the trade wind teasing their bodies like unseen fingers.

It began in banter and with low gurgles of laughter, little gasps of rediscovery, and murmurs of welcome and encouragement – then suddenly it changed, it became charged with almost unbearable intensity, a storm of emotion that sought to sweep all the ugliness and doubt. They were caught up in the raging torrent that carried them helplessly beyond mere physical response into an unknown dimension from which there seemed no way back, a total affirmation of their bodies and their minds that made all else seem inconsequential.

'I love you,' she cried at the very end, as though to deny all else that she had been forced to do. 'I have loved only you.' It was a cry torn from the very depths of her soul.

It took a long time for them to return from the far place to which they had been driven, to become two separate people again, but when they did somehow they both sensed that they would never again be completely separated; there had been a deeper more significant union than just that of their two bodies, and the knowledge sobered them and yet, at the same time, gave them both new strength and a deep elation that neither had to voice – it was there, and they both simply knew it.

They slid the big inflatable Avon S 650 dinghy over the stern, and went ashore, pulling the rubber craft above the high-water level and mooring it to one of the slanting palm boles.

Then they wandered inland, picking their way hand in hand between the seabird nests that had been crudely scraped in the earth. Half a dozen different species of birds were breeding together in one sprawling colony that covered most of the twenty-acre island. Their eggs varied from cool pale blue as big as that of a goose's, to others the size of a pullet's and speckled and spotted in lovely free-form designs. The chicks were either grotesquely ugly with bare parboiled bodies or were cute as Walt Disney animations. The entire island was pervaded by an endless susurration of thousands of wings and the uproar of squawking, screeching, feuding and mating birds.

Magda knew the zoological names of each species, its range and its habits, and its chances of survival or extinction in the changing eco-systems of the oceans.

Peter listened to her tolerantly, sensing that behind this chatter and studied gaiety she was steeling herself to answer the accusations that he had levelled at her.

At the far end of the island was a single massive takamaka tree, with dense green foliage spreading widely over the fluffy white sand. By now the sun was fiercely bright and the heat and humidity smothered them like a woollen blanket dipped in hot water.

They sought the shade of the takamaka gratefully, and sat close together on the sand staring out across the unruffled waters of the lagoon to the silhouette of the main island, five miles away. At this range and angle there was no sign of the buildings nor of the jetty, and Peter had an illusion of the primeval paradise with the two of them the first man and woman on a fresh and innocent earth.

Magda's next words dispelled that illusion entirely.

'Who ordered you to kill me, Peter? How was the

command given? I must know that before I tell you about myself.'

'Nobody,' he answered.

'Nobody? There was no message like the one you received ordering you to kill Parker?'

'No.'

'Parker himself or Colin Noble? They did not order you to do it – or suggest it?'

'Parker expressly ordered me not to do it. You were not to be touched – until you could be taken in jeopardy.'

'It was your own decision?' she insisted.

'It was my duty.'

'To avenge your daughter?'

He hesitated, would have qualified it, then nodded with total self-honesty. 'Yes, that was the most part of it, Melissa-Jane, but I saw it also as my duty to destroy anything evil enough to envisage the taking of 070, the abduction of Aaron Altmann and the mutilation of my daughter.'

'Caliph knows about us. Understands us better than we understand ourselves. I am not a coward, Peter, but now I am truly afraid.'

'Fear is the tool of his trade,' Peter agreed, and she moved slightly, inviting physical contact. He placed one arm about her bare brown shoulders and she leaned lightly against him

'All that you told me last night was the truth, only the inferences and conclusions were false. Papa's death, the lonely years with strangers as foster-parents – of that period my clearest memories are of lying awake at night and trying to muffle the sound of my weeping with a false blanket. The return to Poland, yes, that was right, and the Odessa school – all of that. I will tell you about Odessa one day, if you truly want to hear it – ?'

'I don't think I do,' he said.

'Perhaps you are wise; do you want to hear about the return to Paris?'

'Only what is necessary.'

'All right, Peter. There were men. That was what I had been selected and trained for. Yes, there were men—' She broke off, and reached up to take his face between her hands, turning it so she could look into his eyes. 'Does that make a difference between us, Peter?'

'I love you,' he replied firmly.

She stared into his eyes for a long time looking for evidence of deceit, and then when she found none, 'Yes. It is so. You really mean that.'

She sighed with relief and laid her head against his shoulder, speaking quietly with just that intriguing touch of accent and the occasional unusual turn of phrase.

'I did not like the men, either, Peter. I think that was why I chose Aaron Altmann. One man, yes I could still respect myself—' She shrugged lightly. 'I chose Aaron, and Moscow agreed. It was, as you said, delicate work. First I had to win his respect. He had never respected a woman before. I proved to him I was as good as any man, at any task he wished to set me. After I had his respect, all else followed—' She paused and chuckled softly. ' – Life plays naughty tricks. I found firstly that I liked him, then I grew to respect him also. He was a great ugly bull of a man, but the power . . . A huge raw power, like some cosmic force, became the centre of my existence.' She lifted her head to touch Peter's cheek with her lips in reassurance. 'No. Peter, I never came to love him. I never loved before you. But I stood in vast awe of him, like a member of a primitive tribe worships the lightning and the thunder. It was like that. He dominated my existence – more than a father, more than a teacher, as much as a god – but less, very much less than a lover. He was crude and strong. He did not make love, he could only rut and tup like the bull he was.'

She broke off and looked seriously at him. 'Do you understand that, Peter? Perhaps I explained it badly?'

'No,' he assured her. 'You explained it very well.'

'Physically he did not move me, his smell and the hairiness. He had hair on his shoulders and like a pelt down his back. His belly was bulging and hard as iron—' She shivered briefly. ' – But I had been trained to be able to ignore that. To switch off something in the front of my brain. Yet in all other ways he fascinated me. He goaded me to think forbidden thoughts, to open vaults of my mind that my training had securely locked. All right, he taught me about power and its trappings. You accused me of that, Peter, and I admit it. The flavour of power and money was to my taste. I like it. I like it very much indeed. Aaron introduced me to that. He showed me how to appreciate fine and beautiful things, for he was only physically a bull and he had a wonderful appreciation of the refinements of life – he made me come completely alive. Then he laughed at me. God, I can still hear the bellow of his laughter, and see that great hairy belly shaking with it.'

She paused to remember it, almost reverently, and then she chuckled her own husky little laugh.

'"My fine little communist lady,"' he mocked me. 'Yes, Peter, it was I who was deceived, he had known from the beginning who I was. He also knew about the school at Odessa. He had accepted me as a challenge, certainly he loved me – or his version of love, but he took me knowingly and corrupted my pure ideological convictions. Only then did I learn that all the information which I had been able to pass to Moscow had been carefully screened by Aaron. He doubled me, as I had been sent to double him. He was Mossad, but of course you know that. He was a Zionist, you know that also. And he made me realize that I was a Jewess, and what it meant to be that. He showed me every fatal flaw in the doctrine of Universal Communism, he convinced me of democracy and the Western Capitalist system and then he recruited me to Mossad—'

She stopped again, and shook her head vehemently.

' – To believe that I could have wished to destroy such a

one. That I could have ordered his abduction and mutilation – Towards the end, when he was getting weak, when the pain was very bad, that was the closest I ever came to loving him, the way a mother loves a child. He became pathetically dependent upon me; he used to say the only thing that could lull the pain was my touch. I used to sit for hours rubbing that hairy belly – feeling that awful thing growing bigger inside him each day, like a cauliflower or a grotesque foetus. He would not let them cut it. He hated them, "butchers" he called them. "Butchers with their knives and rubber tubes – "'

She broke off and Peter realized that her eyes were filled with tears. He hugged her a little more firmly and waited for her to recover.

'It must have been about this time that Caliph made contact with Aaron. Thinking back I can remember the time when he became suddenly terribly agitated. It made little sense to me then, but he held long diatribes about right-wing tyranny being indistinguishable from tyranny of the left. He never mentioned the name Caliph, I do not think Caliph had yet used that name – and I do believe that Aaron would eventually have told me of the contact in detail, if he had lived. It was the way he was, even with me, he could be as wary and subtle as he could be overpowering. He would have told me of Caliph – but Caliph saw to it that he did not.'

She pulled away from Peter's arms so she could again see his face.

'You must understand, *chéri*, that much of this I have earned only recently – in the last few weeks. Much of it I can only piece together like a jig puzzle – pardon, a jig-saw puzzle.' She corrected herself swiftly. 'But this is what must have happened. Caliph contacted Aaron with a proposition. It was a very simple proposition. He was invited to become a partner of Caliph. Aaron was to make a substantial financial contribution to Caliph's war-chest, and to place his privileged knowledge and lines of influence at Caliph's disposal. In return he would have a hand in engineering Caliph's brave new world It was a miscalculation on Caliph's part, perhaps the only mistake he has made up to now. He had misjudged Aaron Altmann. Aaron turned him down flat – but much more dangerously Caliph had made the mistake of revealing his identity to Aaron. I expect that he had to do that in an effort to convince Aaron. You see, Aaron was not a man who would indulge in a game of code-names and hidden identities. That much Caliph had divined correctly So he had to confront Aaron face to face, and when he discovered that Aaron would not join in a campaign of murder and extortion – no matter how laudable the ultimate ends – Caliph had no choice. He took Aaron, killed him after torturing him hideously for information that could have been useful, mainly information about his Mossad connection I imagine. Then he persuaded me to pay the ransom. He won two major tricks with a single card. He silenced Aaron, and he gained the twenty-five million for his war-chest.'

'How did you learn this? If only you had explained to me before—' Peter heard the bitterness in his own voice.

'I did not know it when we first met, *chéri*, please believe me. I will tell you how I learned it, but please be patient with me. Let me tell it as it happened.'

'I am sorry,' he said simply

'The first time I heard the name "Caliph" was the day I delivered the ransom. I told you about that, didn't I?'

'Yes '

'So we come now to your part. I heard of you for the first time with the Johannesburg hijacking of Flight 070 I thought that you might be the one to help me hunt down Caliph. I found out about you, Peter. I was even able to have a computer printout on you—' She paused, and there was that mischievous flash in her eye again. ' – I will admit to being very impressed with the formidable list of your ladies.'

Peter held up both hands in a gesture of surrender.

'Never again,' he pleaded. 'Not another word – agreed?'

'Agreed.' She laughed, and then, 'I'm hungry, and my throat is sore again with all this talking.'

They crossed the island again, with their bare feet baking on the sun-heated sand, and went back on board the Chris-craft.

The chef had stocked the refrigerator with a cornucopia of food, and Peter opened a bottle of Veuve Cliquot champagne.

'You've got expensive tastes,' he observed. 'I don't know if I can afford to keep you – on my salary.'

'I'm sure we could arrange a raise from your boss,' she assured him with the twinkle in her eyes. In tacit agreement they did not mention Caliph again until they had eaten.

' – There is one other thing you must understand, Peter. I am of Mossad, but I do not control them. They control me. It was the same with Aaron. Both of us were and are very valuable agents, possibly amongst the most valuable of all their networks, but I do not make decisions, nor am I able to have access to all their secrets.

'Mossad's single-minded goal is the safety and security of the state of Israel. It has no other reason for existence. I was certain that Aaron had made a full report to Mossad of Caliph's identity, that he had detailed the proposition that Caliph had proposed – and I suspect that Mossad had ordered Aaron to co-operate with Caliph—'

'Why?' Peter demanded sharply.

'I do not know for certain – but I can think of two reasons. Caliph must have been such a powerful and influential man that his support would have been valuable. Then again I suspect that Caliph had pro-Israeli leanings, or professed to have those leanings. Mossad finds allies where it can, and does not question their morals. I think they ordered Aaron to co-operate with Caliph – but—'

'But?' Peter prompted her.

'But you do not order a man like Aaron to go against his deepest convictions, and under that forbidding exterior Aaron Altmann was a man of great humanity. I think that the reason for his agitation was the conflict of duty and belief that he was forced to endure His instinct warned him to destroy Caliph, and his duty—'

She shrugged, and picked up her fluted champagne glass, twisting it between those long slim fingers and studying the pinpricks of bubbles as they rose slowly through the pale golden wine. When she spoke again she had changed direction disconcertingly.

'A thousand times I had tried to discover what was so different between you and me than with the other men I have known. Why none of them could move me – and yet with you it was almost instantaneous—' She looked up at him again as though she was still seeking the reason. ' – Of course, I knew so much about you. You had the qualities I admire in another human being, so I was disposed favourably – but there are other qualities you cannot detail on a computer printout nor capture in a photograph. There was something about you that made me—' She made a helpless gesture as she searched for the word. ' – You made me tingle.'

'That's a good word,' Peter smiled.

'And I had never tingled before. So I had to be very sure It was a new experience to want a man merely because he is gentle and strong and—' she chuckled, ' – just plain sexy You are sexy, you know that, Peter, but also you are something else—' She broke off 'No, I am not going to flatter you any more. I do not want you to get swollen ankles—' mixing the French idiom quaintly with the English, and this time not correcting herself. She went straight on. 'Caliph must have realized that I had recruited a dangerous ally. He made the attempt to kill you that night on the Rambouillet road—'

'They were after you,' Peter cut in.

'Who, Peter? Who was after me?'

'The Russians – by that time they knew you were a double agent.'

'Yes, they knew—' She cocked her head and narrowed her eyes. 'I had thought about it, of course, and there had been two previous attempts on me, but I do not think the attempt on the Rambouillet road was Russian.'

'All right, Caliph then, but after you – not me,' Peter suggested.

'Perhaps, but again I do not think so. My instinct tells me they had the right target. They were after you.'

'I would have to agree,' Peter said. 'I think I was followed when I left Paris that evening—' and he told her about the Citroën. ' – I think they knew that I was alone in the Maserati.'

'Then we accept it was Caliph,' she stated flatly.

' – or Mossad,' Peter murmured, and her eyes slowly widened, turning a darker thoughtful green as Peter went on.

'What if Mossad did not want an Atlas man getting close to their star agent, they didn't want you to have an ally in your hunt for Caliph? What if they just didn't want me cluttering up the carefully rehearsed scenario?'

'Peter, it's very deep water—'

' – and there are packs of sharks.'

'Let's leave that night on the Rambouillet road for the moment,' she suggested. 'It merely complicates the story I am trying to tell you.'

'All right,' Peter agreed. 'We can come back to it, if we have to.'

'The next significant move was the abduction of Melissa-Jane,' she said, and Peter's expression changed, becoming flat and stony.

'The choice of the victim was genius-inspired,' she said. 'But it required no special knowledge of you or your domestic arrangements. There was no secret that you had an only child, and it needed but a casual appraisal of your character to understand how powerful a lever she could be—' Magda dipped the tip of her finger into the champagne and then sucked it thoughtfully, pursing her lips and frowning slightly.

'You must understand that by this time I had faced the fact that I was in love with you. The gift was supposed to affirm that—' She flushed slightly under her honey tan, and it was appealing and child-like. He had never seen her blush before and it twisted something in his chest.

'The book,' he remembered. 'The Cornwallis Harris first edition.'

'My first love gift ever. I bought it when I finally admitted it to myself – but I was determined that I would not admit it to you. I am old-fashioned enough to believe the man must speak first.'

'I did.'

'God, I'll never forget it,' she said fervently, and they both thought of the savage confrontation the previous day which had ended incongruously in a declaration of love.

'I try to be unconventional,' he said, and she shook her head smiling.

'You succeed, *mon amour*, oh how you succeed.' Then she sobered again. 'I was in love with you. Your distress was mine. The child was a lovely girl, she had captivated me when we met – and on top of all that I felt deadly responsible for her plight. I had inveigled you into joining my hunt for Caliph, and because of that you had lost your daughter.'

He bowed his head slightly, remembering how he had believed that she had engineered it. She recognized the gesture.

'Yes, Peter. For me it was the cruellest stroke. That you

should believe it of me. There was nothing that I would not have done to give her back to you – and yet there seemed nothing that I could do. My contacts with French intelligence had nothing for me. They had no inkling of how or where the child was being held – and my control at Mossad was unaccountably evasive. Somehow I had the feeling that Mossad had the key to the kidnapping. If they were not directly involved they knew more than anybody else. I have already explained that I believed Aaron had given them the identity of Caliph. If that was so, then they must know something that could have helped you to recover your child – but from Paris I was powerless to gather that information. I had to go in person to Israel and confront my control there. It was the one chance that I could get them to co-operate. They might believe my value as an agent was worth enough to give me a lead to Melissa-Jane—'

'You threatened Mossad with resignation?' Peter asked wonderingly. 'You would have done that for me?'

'Oh, Peter, don't you understand? I loved you – and I had never been in love before. I would have done anything for you.'

'You make me feel humble,' he said.

She did not reply, but let the statement stand as though she were savouring it, then she sighed contentedly and went on. 'I left everything in Paris. I have an established routine for disappearing when it is necessary. Pierre took me to Rome in the Lear; from there I telephoned you but I could not tell you what I was going to do. Then I switched identity and took a commercial flight to Tel Aviv. My task in Israel was difficult, much more difficult than I had bargained for. It was five days before my control would see me. He is an old friend. No! perhaps not a friend, but we have known each other a long time. He is the deputy-director of Mossad. That is how highly they value my services, to give me such an important controller, but still it took five days before he would see me, and he was cold.

There was no help they could give me, he said. They knew nothing.' She chuckled. 'You have never seen me when I want something really badly, Peter. Ha! – What a battle. There is much I knew that would embarrass Mossad with her powerful allies of the West – with France and Great Britain and the U.S.A. – I threatened to hold a Press conference in New York. He became less cold, he told me that the security of the State took precedence over all personal feelings, and I said something very rude about the security of the State, and reminded him of some outstanding business which I would happily leave outstanding. He became warmer – but all this was taking time, days, many days, too many days. I was going crazy. I remembered how they had found Aaron's body, and I could not sleep at night for worrying about that lovely child. And you, oh Peter, you will never know how I prayed to a god that I was not too sure of. You will never know how I wanted to be with you to comfort you. I wanted so desperately just to hear your voice – but I could not break my cover from Tel Aviv I could not even telephone you, nor send you a letter—' She broke off. ' – I hoped you would not believe bad things of me You would not believe that I did not care. That I was not prepared to help you I could only hope that I would be able to bring you some information of value to prove it was not true – but I never dreamed that one day you would believe that it was I who had taken your daughter and tortured her.'

'I am sorry,' he said quietly.

'No, do not say you are sorry. We were both Caliph's playthings. There is no blame on you.' She laid her hand upon his arm and smiled at him. 'It was not you alone who believed bad things. For at last I had prevailed on my Mossad control to give me some little scraps of information. At first he denied completely that they had ever heard of Caliph, but I risked lying to him. I told him that Aaron had told me he had reported the Caliph contact He gave ground. Yes, he admitted. They knew of Caliph, but they did not know who he was. I hammered on, demanding to see my controller each day, driving him as mad as I was – until he threatened to have me deported even. But each time we met I wheedled and bullied a little more from him.

'At last he admitted, "All right, we know Caliph but he is very dangerous, very powerful – and he will become more powerful – God willing, he will become one of the most powerful men in the world, and he is a friend of Israel. Or rather we believe he is a friend of Israel."

'I bullied some more and he told me, "We have put an agent close to Caliph, very close to him, and we cannot jeopardize this agent. He is a valuable agent, very valuable but very vulnerable to Caliph. We cannot take the chance that Caliph could trace information back to him. We have to protect our man."

'Now I threatened, and he told me the agent's code-name to protect both of us should we ever have to make contact. The code-name is "CACTUS FLOWER".'

'That was all?' Peter asked, with evident disappointment.

'No, my control gave me another name. As a sop – and as a warning. The name they gave me was so close to Caliph as to be virtually the same. Again he warned me that he was giving me the name for my own protection.'

'What was it?' Peter demanded eagerly.

'Your name,' she said softly. 'Stride.'

Peter made an irritable gesture of dismissal. 'My name is nonsensical. Why would I kidnap and mutilate my own daughter – and Cactus Flower. He might as well have said, "Kentucky Fried Chicken". '

'Now it's my turn to say I'm sorry.'

Peter caught himself, realizing suddenly that he had been too quick to dismiss these scraps of information. He stood up and paced the deck of the Chris-craft with choppy, agitated steps, frowning heavily. 'Cactus Flower,' he repeated. 'Have you ever heard it before?'

'No,' she shook her head.

'Since then?'

'No,' again.

He searched his memory, trying for a sympathetic echo. There was none.

'All right.' He accepted that as having no immediate value. 'We'll just remember it for now. Let's come to my name – Peter Stride. What did you make of that?'

'It didn't mean anything then, except as a shock. Strangely enough I did not immediately think of you, but I thought of confusion between the kidnapper and the victim.'

'Stride?' he asked. 'Peter Stride? I don't understand.'

'No, well – Melissa-Jane is a Stride also.'

'Yes, of course. They didn't give you the name Peter Stride then?'

'No. Just Stride.'

'I see.' Peter stopped in mid-pace as an idea struck him – and stared out thoughtfully to where the ocean met a blue horizon.

'But they gave me your full name later,' she interrupted his thoughts.

'When?'

'After we received the news that Melissa-Jane had been rescued. Of course, I wanted to return to Paris immediately – to be with you. I was able to get onto a flight from Ben-Gurion Airport six hours after we heard the news. My heart was singing, Peter. Melissa-Jane was safe, and I was in love. I was going to be with you very soon. At the airport, while I was going through the security check before departure, the policewoman took me aside – to the security office. My control was waiting for me there. He had rushed out from Tel Aviv to catch me before I left for home, and he was very worried. They had just received an urgent message from Cactus Flower. General Peter Stride was now definitely Caliph-motivated, and would assassinate me at the first opportunity, he told me. And I laughed at him – but he was deadly serious. "My dear Baroness, Cactus Flower is a first-class man. You must take this warning seriously," he kept repeating.'

Magda shrugged. 'I still did not believe it, Peter. It was impossible. I loved you, and I knew you loved me – although perhaps you had not yet realized that yourself. It was crazy. But on the aircraft I had time to think. My control at Mossad has never been wrong before. Can you imagine my dilemma now – how dearly I wanted to be with you, and yet I was now terrified – not that you would kill me. That did not seem important – but that you would truly turn out to be Caliph. That was what really frightened me. You see, I had never loved a man before. I don't think I could have stood it.'

She was quiet for a while, remembering the pain and confusion, and then she shook her head so that the thick fall of dark shimmering hair rustled around her shoulders.

'Once I reached Paris, my first concern was to learn that you and Melissa-Jane were safe at Abbots Yew, and then I could begin to try and find out how much substance there was in Cactus Flower's warning – but until I could decide on how safe it was I could not take the chance of being alone with you. Every time you attempted to contact me, I had to deny you, and it felt as though some little part of me was dying.'

She reached across and took his hand now, opened the fingers and bowed her head to kiss the palm and then held it to her cheek as she went on.

'A hundred times I convinced myself that it could not be true, and I was on the point of going to you. Oh, Peter – finally I could take it no longer. I decided to meet you at Orly that day and find out one way or the other, end the terrible uncertainty. I had the grey wolves with me, as you remember, and they had been warned to expect trouble – I didn't tell them to watch you,' she explained quickly, as if trying to dispel any memory of disloyalty, 'but if you had tried to get at me they would have—' She broke off, and let his hand fall away from her cheek. 'The moment you walked into the private lounge at Orly, I saw it was true. I could sense it, there was an aura of death around you. It was the most frightening and devastating moment of my life, you looked like a different man – not the Peter Stride I knew – your whole face seemed to be altered and restructured by hatred and anger. I kissed you goodbye, because I knew we could never meet again.' Remembering it her face darkened with sadness, as though a cloud shadow had passed over them. 'I even thought that I had to protect myself by—' She gagged the words. ' – You were part of Caliph, you see, and it would have been the wise thing to do. I admit that I thought of it, Peter. Have you killed, before you could kill me – but it was only a thought and it did not go farther than that. Instead I went on with the business of living, work has always been an opiate for me. If I work hard enough I can forget anything – but this time it didn't turn out that way. I've said it before, but it explains so much that I will say it again. I had never been in love before, Peter, and I could not turn it off. It tormented me, and I cherished doubts – about Cactus Flower's warning and what I had seen so clearly in the lounge at Orly Airport. It couldn't be, it just couldn't be true – I loved you and you loved me, and you just couldn't be plotting to kill me. I almost convinced myself of that.'

She laughed curtly, but it had no humour in the sound, only the bitterness of disillusion.

'I came out here—' she made a gesture that embraced sea and sky and islands ' – to be away from the temptation of going to you. A sanctuary where I could recover from my wounds and begin to get over you. But it didn't work, Peter. It was worse here. I had more time to think, to torture myself with wild speculation and grotesque theories. There was only one way. Finally I recognized that. I would bring you out here and give you the chance to kill me.' She laughed again, and now there was the old husky warmth in it. 'It was the most crazy thing I have ever done in my life – but thank God, I did it.'

'We went right to the very brink,' Peter agreed.

'Peter, why didn't you ask me outright if I was Caliph?' she wanted to know.

'The same reason you didn't ask me outright if I was plotting to kill you.'

'Yes,' she agreed. 'We were just caught up in the web that Caliph had spun for us. I have only one more question, Peter *chéri*. If I was Caliph, do you truly believe that I would have been so stupid as to give my telephone number at Rambouillet to the man who kidnapped Melissa-Jane, and instruct him to ring me for a friendly chat whenever he felt like it?'

Peter looked startled, 'I thought—' he began, then stopped. ' – No, I didn't think. I wasn't thinking clearly at all. Of course, you wouldn't have done that – and yet, even the cleverest criminals make the most elementary mistakes.'

'Not those who have been trained at the Odessa school,' she reminded him, and seemed immediately to regret the words, for she went on quickly. 'So there is my side of the story, Peter. I may have left something out – if you can think of anything, then ask me, darling, and I'll try to fill in any missing pieces.'

And so they started once again at the very beginning, and went over the ground minutely, searching for anything they might have overlooked at the first telling of it, this time exhaustively re-examining each fact from every angle, both of them applying their trained minds to the full without being able to come up with more than they already had.

'One thing we must never let out of sight for a moment is the quality of the opposition.' Peter summed it up as the sun began lowering itself towards the western horizon, its majestic progress flanked by cohorts of cumulo-nimbus cloud rising into towering anvil heads over the scattered islands, like silent nuclear explosions.

'There are layers upon layers, reasons behind reasons, the kidnapping of Melissa-Jane was not merely to force me to assassinate Kingston Parker, but you as well – the proverbial two birds – with a third bird to follow. If I had succeeded I would have been hooked into Caliph for ever.'

'Where do you and I go from here, Peter?' she asked, tacitly transferring ultimate decision-making to him.

'How about home, right now,' he suggested. 'Unless you fancy another night out here.'

Peter found that his possessions had been discreetly moved from the guest bungalow to the owner's magnificent private quarters on the north tip of the island.

His toilet articles had been laid out in the mirrored master bathroom, which flanked that of the mistress. His clothing, all freshly cleaned and pressed, was in the master's dressing-room where there was one hundred and fifty-five feet of louvred hanging space – Peter paced it out and calculated it would take three hundred suits of clothing. There were specially designed swinging shelves for another three hundred shirts and racks for a hundred pairs of shoes although all were empty.

His light cotton suit looked as lonely as a single camel in the midst of the Sahara desert. His shoes had been burnished to a gloss that even his batman had never been able to achieve. Despite himself he searched the dressing-room swiftly for the signs of previous occupancy – and was ridiculously relieved to find none.

'I could learn to rough it like this,' he told his reflection in the mirror as he combed the damp, darkly curling locks off his forehead.

The sitting-room off the suite was on three levels, and had been decorated with cane furniture and luxuriant tropical plants growing in ancient Greek wine amphoras or in rockeries that were incorporated into the flowing design of the room. The creepers and huge glossy leaves of the plants toned in artistically with jungle-patterned curtaining and the dense growth of exotic plants beyond the tall picture windows – yet the room was cool and inviting, although the sound of air-conditioning was covered by the twinkle of a waterfall down the cunningly contrived rock face that comprised one curved wall of the room. Tropical fish floated gracefully in the clear pools into which the waterfall spilled, and the perfume of growing flowers pervaded the room, and their blooms glowed in the subdued lighting.

One of the little golden Polynesian girls brought a tray of four tall frosted glasses for Peter to choose from. They were all filled with fruit and he could smell the sweet warm odour of rum mingled with the fruit. He guessed they would be almost lethal and asked for a whisky, then relented with the girl's eyes flooded with disappointment.

'I make them myself,' she wailed.

'In that case—' He sipped while she waited anxiously.

'*Parfait*!' He exclaimed, and she giggled with gratification, and went off wriggling her bottom under the brief pareo like a happy puppy.

Magda came then in a chiffon dress so gossamer-light that it floated about her like a fine green sea mist, through which her limbs gleamed as the light caught them.

He felt the catch in his breathing as she came towards him, and he wondered if he would ever accustom himself to the impact of her beauty.

She took the glass from his hand and tasted it.

'Good,' she said, and handed it back. But when the girl brought the tray she refused with a smile.

They moved about the room, Magda on his arm as she pointed out the rarer plants and fishes.

'I built this wing after Aaron's death,' she told him, and he realized that she wanted him to know that it contained no memories of another man. It amused him that she should find that important – and then he remembered his own furtive search of the dressing-room for signs of a lover before him, and the amusement turned inward.

One wall of the private dining-room was a single sheet of armoured glass, beyond which the living jewels of coral fish drifted in subtly-lit sea caverns and the fronds of magnificent sea plants waved in gentle unseen currents.

Magda ordered the seating changed so they could be side by side in the low lovers' seat facing the aquarium.

'I do not like you to be far away any more,' she explained, and she picked special titbits from the serving dishes for his plate.

'This is a speciality of Les Neuf Poissons. You will eat it nowhere else in the world.' She selected small deep-sea crustaceans from a steaming creole sauce of spices and coconut cream and at the end of the meal she peeled chilled grapes from Australia with those delicate fingers, using the long shell-pink nails with the precision of a skilled surgeon to remove the pips and then placing them between his lips with thumb and forefinger.

'You spoil me,' he smiled.

'I never had a doll when I was a little girl,' she explained, smiling.

A circular stone staircase led to the beach fifty feet below the dining-room and they left their shoes on the bottom step and walked bare-footed on the smooth, damp sand, compacted as hard as cement by the receding tide. The moon was a few days past full, and its reflection drew a pathway of yellow light to the horizon.

'Caliph must be made to believe that he has succeeded,' Peter said abruptly, and she shivered against him.

'I wish we could forget Caliph for one night.'

'We cannot afford to forget him for a moment.'

'No, you are right. How do we make him believe that?'

'You have to die—' He felt her stiffen.

' – or at least appear to do so. It has to look as though I killed you.'

'Tell me,' she invited quietly.

'You told me that you have special arrangements for when you want to disappear.'

'Yes, I do.'

'How would you disappear from here if you had to do so?'

She thought for only a moment. 'Pierre would fly me to Bora-Bora. I have friends there. Good friends. I would take the island airline to Tahiti-Faaa on another passport – and then a scheduled airline in the same name to California or New Zealand.'

'You have other papers?' he demanded.

'Yes, of course.' She sounded so surprised by the question, that he expected her to ask ' – doesn't everybody?'

'Fine,' he said. 'And we'll arrange a suspicious accident here. A scuba diving accident, shark attack in deep water, no corpse.'

'What is the point of all this, Peter?'

'If you are dead – Caliph is not going to make another attempt to have you killed.'

'Good!' she agreed.

'So you stay officially dead until we flush Caliph out,' Peter told her, and it sounded like an order but she did not demur as he went on. 'And if I carry out Caliph's evident wishes by killing you, it's going to make me a very valuable asset. I will have proved myself, and so he will cherish me It will give me another chance to get close to him. At least it will give me a chance to check out a few wild hunches.'

'Don't let's make my death too convincing, my love. I

am a great favourite of the police on Tahiti,' she murmured. 'I'd hate to have you end up under the guillotine at Tuarruru.'

Peter woke before her and raised himself on one elbow over her to study her face, delighting to find new planes and angles to her high broad cheekbones, gloating in the velvety texture of her skin, so fine that the pores were indefinable from farther than a few inches. Then he transferred his attention to the curve of her eyelashes that interlocked into a thick dark palisade seeming to seal her eyelids perpetually in sleep – yet they sprang open suddenly, the huge black pools of her pupils shrinking rapidly as she focused, and for the first time he realized that the irises were not pure green but were flecked and shot through with gold and violet.

The surprise of finding him over her changed slowly to pleasure, and she stretched her arms out over her head and arched her back, the way a lazy panther does when it rouses itself. The satin sheet slid down to her waist and she prolonged the stretch a little longer than was necessary, a deliberate display of her body.

'Every other morning of my life that I woke without you there was wasted,' she murmured huskily, and raised her arms still at full stretch to him, folding them gracefully around his neck, still holding her back arched so that the prominent dark-red nipples brushed lightly against the crisp dark mat of curls that covered his own chest.

'Let's pretend this will last for ever,' she whispered, with her lips an inch from his, and her breath was rich as an overblown rose, heavy with the smell of vital woman and rising passion; then her lips spread softly, warmly against his and she sucked his tongue deeply into her mouth, with a low moan of wanting – and the hard slim body began to work against his, the hands breaking from his neck and hunting down his spine, long curved nails pricking and goading him just short of pain. His own arousal was so swift and so brutally hard that she moaned again, and the tension went out of her body, it seemed to soften and spread like a wax figure held too close to the flame, her eyelids trembling closed and her thighs falling apart.

'So strong—' she whispered, deep in her throat and he reared up over her, feeling supreme, invincible.

'Peter, Peter,' she cried. 'Oh yes like that. Please like that.' Both of them striving triumphantly for the moment of glory when each was able to lose self and become for a fleeting instant part of the godhead.

Long afterwards they lay side by side in the enormous bed, both of them stretched out flat upon their backs, not touching except for the fingers of one hand intertwined as their bodies had been.

'I will go away—' she whispered, ' – because I have to, but not now. Not yet.'

He did not reply, the effort was beyond him, and her own voice was languorous with a surfeit of pleasure.

'I will make a bargain with you. Give me three days more. Only three days, to be happy like this. For me it is the first time. I have never known this before, and it may be the last time—'

He tried to rouse himself to deny it, but she squeezed his fingers for silence and went on.

' – It may be the last,' she repeated. 'And I want to have it all. Three days, in which we do not mention Caliph, in which we do not think of the blood and striving and suffering out there. If you give me that I will do everything that you want me to do. Is it a bargain, Peter? Tell me we can have that.'

'Yes. We can have that.'

'Then tell me you love me again, I do not think I can hear you say it too often.'

He said it often during those magic days, and she had spoken the truth, each time he told her she accepted with as much joy as the last time, and always each seemed to be within touching distance of the other.

Even when tearing side by side across the warm flat waters of the lagoon, leaning back with straight arms on the tow lines, skis hissing angrily and carving fiercely sparkling wings of water from the surface as they wove back and forth in a *pas de deux* across the streaming, creaming water, laughing together in the wind and the engine roar of the Chris-craft, Hapiti the Polynesian boatman on the flying bridge looking back with a great white grin of sympathy for their joy.

Finning gently through mysterious blue and dappled depths, the only sound the wheezing suck and blow of their scuba valves and the soft clicking and the eternal echoing susurration that is the pulse beat of the ocean, holding hands as they sank down to the long abandoned hull of the Japanese aircraft carrier, now overgrown with a waving forest of sea growth and populated by a teeming fascinating multitude of beautiful and bizarre creatures.

Flying silently down the sheer steel cliff of the canted flight deck, which seemed to reach down into the very oceanic depths, so that there was the eerie fear of suddenly being deprived of support and falling down to where the surface light blued out in nothingness.

Pausing to peer through their glass face-plates into the still gaping wounds rent into the steel by aerial bombs and high explosive, and then entering through those cruel caverns cautiously as children into a haunted house and emerging victoriously with carrier nets of trophies, coins and cutlery, brass and porcelain.

Strolling on the secluded beaches of the outer islands, still hand in hand, naked in the sunlight.

Fishing the seething tide-race through the main channel at full spring tide, and shouting with excitement as the big golden amberjack came boiling up in the wake, bellies flashing like mirrors, to hit the dancing feather lures, and send the Penn reels screeching a wild protest, and the fibreglass rods nodding and kicking.

Out in the humbling silences of the unrestricted ocean, when even the smudge of the islands disappeared beyond the wave crests for minutes at a time, with only the creak and whisper of the rigging, the trembling pregnancy of the main sail, and the rustle as the twin hulls of the big Hobie cat knifed the tops off the swells.

Strolling the long curving beaches in the moonlight, searching for the heavenly bodies that so seldom show through the turbid skies of Europe – Orion the hunter and the Seven Sisters – exclaiming at the stranger constellations of this hemisphere governed by the great fixed cross in the southern heavens.

Each day beginning and ending in the special wonder and mystery of the circular bed, in loving that welded their bodies and their souls together each time more securely.

Then on the fourth day day Peter woke to find her gone, and for a moment experienced an appalling sensation of total loss.

When she came back to him he did not recognize her for a breath of time.

Then he realized that she had cut away the long dark tresses of her hair, cropped it down short so that it curled close against her skull, like the petals of a dark flower. It had the effect of making her seem even taller. Her neck like the stem of the flower, longer, and the curve of the throat accentuated so that it became delicate and swan-like.

She saw his expression, and explained in a matter-of-fact tone.

'I thought some change was necessary, if I am to leave under a new identity. It will grow again, if you want it that way.'

She seemed to have changed completely herself, the

languid amorous mood given way to the brisk business-like efficiency of before. While they ate a last breakfast of sweet yellow papaya and the juice of freshly squeezed limes she explained her intentions, as she went swiftly through the buff envelope that her secretary had silently laid beside her plate.

There was a red Israeli diplomatic passport in the envelope.

'I will be using the name Ruth Levy—' and she picked up the thick booklet of airline tickets, ' – and I have decided to go back to Jerusalem. I have a house there. It's not in my name, and I do not think anybody else outside of Mossad is aware of it. It will be an ideal base, close to my control at Mossad. I will try to give you what support I can, try to get further information to assist you in the hunt—'

She passed him a typed sheet of notepaper.

' – That is a telephone number at Mossad where you can get a message to me. Use the name Ruth Levy.'

He memorized the number while she went on talking, and then shredded the sheet of paper.

'I have modified the arrangements for my departure,' she told him. 'We will take the Chris-craft across to Bora-Bora. It's only a hundred miles. I will radio ahead. My friends will meet me off the beach after dark.'

They crept in through a narrow passage in the coral with all the lights on the Chris-craft doused, Magda's boatman using only what was left of the waning moon and his own intimate knowledge of the islands to take her in.

'I wanted Hapiti to see me go ashore alive,' she whispered quietly, leaning against Peter's chest to draw comfort from their last minutes together. 'I did not exaggerate the danger you might be in if the local people thought what we want Caliph to think. Hapiti will keep his mouth shut—' she assured him,' – and will back up your story of a shark attack, unless you order him to tell the truth.'

'You think of everything.'

'I have only just found you, monsieur,' she chuckled. 'I do not want to lose you yet. I have even decided to speak a word to the Chief of Police on Tahiti, when I pass through. He is an old friend. When you get back to Les Neuf Poissons, have my secretary radio Tahiti—'

She went on quietly, covering every detail of her arrangements, and he could find no omissions. She was interrupted by a soft hail from out of the darkness and Hapiti throttled the diesels back to idle. They drifted down closer to the loom of the island. A canoe bumped against the side, and Magda turned quickly in his arms, reaching up for his mouth with hers.

'Please be careful, Peter,' was all that she said, and then she broke away and stepped down into the canoe as Hapiti handed down her single valise. The canoe pushed away immediately, and was lost in the dark. There was nothing to wave at, and Peter liked it better that way, but still he stared back over the stern into the night as the Chris-craft groped blindly for the channel again.

There was a hollow feeling under his ribs, as though part of himself was missing; he tried to fill it with a memory of Magda that had amused him because it epitomized for him her quick and pragmatic mind.

' – When the news of your death hits the market, the bottom is going to drop out of Altmann stock.' He had realized this halfway through their final discussion that morning. 'I hadn't thought of that.' He was troubled by the complication.

'I had,' she smiled serenely. 'I estimate it will lose a hundred francs a share within the first week after the news breaks.'

'Doesn't that worry you?'

'Not really.' She gave that sudden wicked grin. 'I telexed a buying order to Zurich this morning. I expect to show a profit of not less than a hundred million francs when the stock bounces back.' Again the mischievous flash of green eyes. 'I do have to be recompensed for all this inconvenience, *tu ne penses pas?*'

And although he still smiled at the memory, the hollow place remained there inside him.

Pierre flew the Tahitian police out to Les Neuf Poissons in the Tri-Islander, and there followed two days of questions and statements. Nearly every member of the community wished to make a statement to the police, there had seldom been such entertainment and excitement available on the islands.

Nearly all of the statements were glowing eulogies to 'La Baronne' delivered to the accompaniment of lamentation and weeping. Only Hapiti had first-hand information and he made the most of this position of importance, embroidering and gilding the tale. He was even able to give a positive identification of the shark as a 'Dead White' – The English name startled Peter until he remembered that the movie *Jaws* was in the island's cassette video library and was undoubtedly the source of the big boatman's inspiration. Hapiti went on to describe its fangs as long and sharp as cane knives, and to give a gruesome imitation of the sound they made as they closed on 'La Baronne' – Peter would willingly have gagged him to prevent those flights of imagination, which were not supported by Peter's own statement, but the police sergeant was greatly impressed and encouraged Hapiti to further acts of creation with cries of astonishment.

On the last evening there was a funeral feast on the beach for Magda. It was a moving ritual, and Peter found himself curiously affected when the women of the island, swaying and wailing at the water's edge, cast wreaths of frangipani blooms onto the tide to be carried out beyond the reef.

Peter flew back to Tahiti-Faaa with the police the following morning, and they stayed with him, flanking him discreetly, on the drive to the headquarters of gendarmerie in the town. However, his interview with the Chief of Police was brief and courteous – clearly Magda had been there before him – and if there was no actual exchange of winks and nudges, the commissioner's handshake of farewell was firm and friendly.

'Any friend of La Baronne is a friend here.' And he used the present tense, then sent Peter back to the airport in an official car.

The UTA flight landed in California through that sulphurous eye-stinging layer of yellow air trapped between sea and mountains. Peter did not leave the airport, but after he had shaved and changed his shirt in the men's room he found a copy of the *Wall Street Journal* in the first-class Pan-Am Clipper lounge. It was dated the previous day, and the report of Magda Altmann's death was on Page Three. It was a full column, and Peter was surprised by the depth of the Altmann Industries involvement in the American financial scene. The complex of holdings was listed, followed by a résumé of Baron Aaron Altmann's career and that of his widow. The cause of death as given by the Tahitian police was 'Shark Attack' while scuba diving in the company of a friend – General Peter Stride – Peter was grimly satisfied that his name was mentioned. Caliph would read it, wherever he was, and draw the appropriate conclusion. Peter could expect something to happen now; he was not quite sure what, but he knew that he was being drawn closer to the centre like a fragment of iron to the magnet.

He managed to sleep for an hour, in one of the big armchairs, before the hostess roused him for the Pan-Am Polar flight to London's Heathrow.

He called Pat Stride, his sister-in-law, from Heathrow Airport. She was unaffectedly delighted to hear his voice.

' – Steven is in Spain, but I am expecting him home

tomorrow before lunch, that is if his meetings go the way he wants them. They want to build a thirty-six-hole golf course at San Istaban—' Steven's companies owned a complex of tourist hotels on the Spanish coast ' – and Steven had to go through the motions with the Spanish authorities. But, why don't you come down to Abbots Yew tonight? Alex and Priscilla are here, and there will be an amusing house party for the weekend—' He could hear the sudden calculating tone in Pat's voice as she began instinctively to run through the shortlist of potential mates for Peter.

After he had accepted and hung up, he dialled the Cambridge number and was relieved that Cynthia's husband, George Barrow, answered.

Give me a Bolshevik intellectual over a neurotic ex-wife any day, he thought as he greeted Melissa-Jane's stepfather warmly. Cynthia was at a meeting of the Faculty Wives Association, and Melissa-Jane was auditioning for a part in a production of Gilbert and Sullivan by the local drama society.

'How is she?' Peter wanted to know.

'I think she is well over it now, Peter. The hand is completely healed. She seems to have settled down—' They spoke for a few minutes more, then ran out of conversation The two women were all they had in common.

'Give Melissa-Jane my very best love,' Peter told him, and picked up a copy of *The Financial Times* from a newsstand on his way to the Avis desk. He hired a compact and while waiting for it to be delivered he searched swiftly through the newspaper for mention of Magda Altmann. It was on an inside page, clearly a follow-up article to a previous report of her death. There had been a severe reaction on the London and European stock exchanges – the hundred-franc drop in Altmann stock that Magda had anticipated had already been exceeded on the Bourse – and again there was a brief mention of his own name in a repetition of the circumstances of her death. He was satisfied with the publicity, and with Magda's judgement in buying back her own stock. Indeed it all seemed to be going a little too smoothly. He became aware of the fateful prickle of apprehension down his spine, his own personal barometer of impending danger.

As always Abbots Yew was like coming home, and Pat met him on the gravel of the front drive, kissed him with sisterly affection and linked her arm through his to lead him into the gracious old house.

'Steven will be delighted,' she promised him. 'I expect he will telephone this evening. He always does when he is away.'

There was a buff cable envelope propped on the bedside table of the guest room overlooking the stables that was always reserved for Peter. The message originated at Ben-Gurion Airport, Tel Aviv, and was a single word – the code he had arranged with Magda to let him know that she arrived safely and without complication. The message gave him a sharp pang of wanting, and he lay in a deep hot bath and thought about her, remembering small details of conversation and shared experience that suddenly were of inflated value.

While he towelled himself he regarded his image in the steamed mirror with a critical eye. He was lean and hard and burned dark as a desert Arab by the Pacific sun. He watched the play of muscle under the tanned skin as he moved, and he knew that he was as fit and as mentally prepared for action as he had ever been, glad that Magda was safely beyond the reach of Caliph's talons so that he could concentrate all his energies on what his instincts told him must be the final stage of the hunt.

He went through to his bedroom with the towel around his waist and stretched out on the bed to wait for the cocktail hour in Pat Stride's rigidly run household.

He wondered what made him so certain that this was

the lead which would carry him to Caliph, it seemed so slim a chance and yet the certainty was like a steel thread, and the steel was in his heart.

That made him pause. Once again he went carefully over the changes which had taken place within him since his first exposure to Caliph's malignant influence; the fatal miasma of corruption that seemed to spread around Caliph like the poisonous mists from some evil swamp seemed to have engulfed Peter entirely.

He thought again of his execution of the blonde girl at Johannesburg what seemed like a thousand years before, but with mild surprise realized was months not years ago.

He thought of how he had been prepared to kill both Kingston Parker and Magda Altmann – and realized that contact with violence was brutalizing, capable of eroding the principles and convictions which he had believed inviolate after almost forty years of having lived with them.

If this was so, then after Caliph – if he succeeded in destroying him – what was there after Caliph? Would he ever be the same man again? Had he advanced too far beyond the frontiers of social behaviour and conscience? Would he ever go back? he wondered. Then he thought about Magda Altmann and realized she was his hope for the future, after Caliph there would be Magda.

These doubts were weakening, he told himself. There must be no distractions now, for once again he was in the arena with the adversary. No distraction, no doubts – only total concentration on the conflict ahead.

He stood up from the bed and began to dress.

Steven was delighted to have Peter at Abbots Yew again, as Pat had predicted.

He also was tanned from the short stay in Spain, but he had again put on weight, only a few pounds, but it would soon be a serious problem, good food and drink were two of the occupational hazards of success: the most evident but not the most dangerous temptations that face a man who has money enough to buy whatever idly engages his fancy.

Peter watched him covertly durıng the lunch, studying the handsome head which was so very much like his own, the same broad brow and straight aristocratic nose, and yet was so different in small but significant details, and it was not only Steven's thick dark moustache.

All right, it's easy to be wise afterwards, Peter told himself, as he watched his twin brother. Seeing again the little marks, which only now seemed to have meaning. The narrower set of eyes, slightly too close together, so that even when he laughed that deep bluff guffaw of his they seemed still to retain a cold cruel light, the mouth that even in laughter was still too hard, too determined, the mouth of a man who would brook no check to his ambitions, no thwarting of his desires. Or am I imagining it now? Peter wondered. It was so easy to see what you looked for expectantly.

The conversation at lunch dwelt almost exclusively on the prospects for the flat-racing season which had opened at Doncaster the previous weekend, and Peter joined it knowledgeably; but as he chatted he was casting back along the years, to the incidents that might have troubled him more if he had not immediately submerged them under an instinctive and unquestioning loyalty to his twin brother.

There was Sandhurst when Steven had been sent down, and Peter had known unquestioningly that it was unjust. No Stride was capable of what Steven had been accused of, and he had not even had to discuss it with his brother. He had affirmed his loyalty with a handshake and a few embarrassed muttered words.

'Thank you, Peter. I'll never forget that,' Steven had told him fervently, meeting Peter's gaze with steady clear eye.

Since then Steven's rise had been meteoric through the post-war years in which it seemed almost impossible for even the most able man to amass a great fortune, a man had to have special talents and take terrible risks to achieve what Steven had.

Now sitting at his brother's board, eating roast saddle of lamb and the first crisp white asparagus shoots of the season flown in from the Continent, Peter was at last covering forbidden ground, examining loyalties which until then had been unquestioned. Yet they were straws scattered by the winds of time, possibly without significance. Peter transferred his thoughts to the present.

'Stride,' Magda's control at Mossad in Tel-Aviv had said. Just the two names: 'Cactus Flower' and 'Stride'. That was fact and not conjecture.

Down the length of the luncheon table Sir Steven Stride caught his brother's eye.

'Wine with you, my dear fellow.' Steven lifted the glass of claret in the old salute.

'Enchanted, I'm sure.' Peter gave the correct reply, a little ritual between them, a hangover from Sandhurst days, and Peter was surprised at the depth of his regret. Perhaps Caliph has not yet succeeded in corrupting me entirely, Peter thought, as he drank the toast.

After lunch there was another of their brotherly rituals. Steven signalled it with a jerk of the head and Peter nodded agreement. Peter's old army duffle coat was in the cupboard below the back staircase with his Wellingtons, and he and Steven changed into rough clothing sitting side by side on the monk's bench in the rear entrance hall as they had so often before.

Then Steven went through into the gunroom, took down

a Purdey Royal shotgun from the rack, and thrust a handful of cartridges in his coat pocket.

'Damned vixen has a litter of cubs somewhere in the bottoms, playing merry hell with the pheasant chicks—' he explained as Peter asked a silent question. 'It goes against the grain a bit to shoot a fox but I must put a stop to her – haven't had a chance at her yet—' and he led the way out of the back door through the orchard towards the stream.

It was almost a formal beating of the bounds, the leisurely circuit of the estate boundaries that the two brothers always made on Peter's first day at Abbots Yew, another old comfortable tradition which allowed them time to have each other's news and reaffirm the bond between them

They sauntered along the riverbank, side by side, moving into single file with Steven leading when the path narrowed and turned away from the stream and went up through the woods.

Steven was elated by the success of his visit to Spain, and he boasted of his achievements in obtaining another parcel of prime seafront property on which to build the new golf course and to extend the hotel by another five hundred rooms.

'Now's the time to buy. Mark my words, Peter – we are on the verge of another explosion.'

'The cut-back in oil price is going to help, I'd expect,' Peter agreed.

'That's not the half of it, old boy.' Steven turned to glance back over his shoulder and he winked knowingly at Peter. 'You can expect another five per cent cut in six months, take my word on it. The Arabs and the Shah have come to their senses.' Steven went on swiftly, picking out those types of industry which would benefit most dramatically from the reduction in crude prices, then selecting the leading companies in those sectors. ' – If you have a few pounds lying idle, that's where to put it.' Steven's whole personality seemed to change when he spoke like this of power and great wealth. Then he came out from behind the façade of the English country squire which he was usually at such pains to cultivate; the glitter in his eyes was now undisguised and his bushy moustache bristled like the whiskers of some big dangerous predator.

He was still talking quickly and persuasively as they left the woods and began to cross the open fields towards the ruins of the Roman camp on the crest of the low hills.

' – These people have still to be told what to do, you know. Those damned shop stewards up in Westminster may have thrown the Empire away, but we still have our responsibilities.' Steven changed the Purdey shotgun from one arm to the other, carrying it in the crook of the arm, the gun broken open and the shining brass caps of the Eley Kynoch cartridges showing in the breeches. ' – Government only by those fit to govern.' Steven enlarged on that for a few minutes.

Then suddenly Steven fell silent, almost as though he had suddenly decided that he had spoken too much, even to somebody as trusted as his own younger twin. Peter was silent also, trudging up the curve of the hill with his boots squelching in the soft damp earth. There was something completely unreal about the moment, walking over well-remembered ground in the beautiful mellow sunlight of an English spring afternoon with a man he had known from the day of his birth – and yet perhaps had never known at all.

It was not the first time he had heard Steven talk like this, and yet perhaps it was the first time he had ever listened. He shivered and Steven glanced at him.

'Cold?'

'Goose walked over my grave,' Peter explained, and Steven nodded as they clambered up the shallow earth bank that marked the perimeter of the Roman camp.

They stood on the lip under the branches of a lovely copper beech, resplendent in its new spring growth of russet.

Steven was breathing hard from the pull up the hill, that extra weight was already beginning to tell. There was a spot of high unhealthy colour in each cheek, and little blisters of sweat speckled his chin.

He closed the breech of the shotgun with a metallic clash, and leaned the weapon against the trunk of the copper beech as he struggled to regain his breath.

Peter moved across casually and propped his shoulder against the copper beech, but his thumbs were hooked into the lapels of the duffle coat, not thrust into pockets, and he was still in balance, weight slightly forward on the balls of his feet. Although he seemed to be entirely relaxed and at rest he was in fact coiled like a spring, poised on the brink of violent action – and the shotgun was within easy reach of his right hand.

He had seen that Steven had loaded with number four shot. At ten paces it would disembowel a man. The safety catch on the top of the pistol grip of the butt engaged automatically when the breech was opened and closed again, but the right thumb would instinctively slip the catch forward as the hand closed on the grip.

Steven took a silver cigarette case from the side pocket of his coat and tapped down a cigarette on the lid.

'Damned shame about Magda Altmann,' he said gruffly, not meeting Peter's eyes.

'Yes,' Peter agreed softly

'Glad they handled it in a civilized fashion. Could have made it awkward for you, you know.'

'I suppose they could have,' Peter agreed.

'What about your job at Narmco?'

'I don't know yet. I will not know until I get back to Brussels.'

'Well, my offer still stands, old boy. I could do with a bit of help. I really could. Somebody I could trust. You'd be doing me a favour.'

'Damned decent of you, Steven.'

'No, really, I mean it.' Steven lit the cigarette with a gold Dunhill lighter and inhaled with evident pleasure, and after a moment Peter asked him:

'I hope you were not in a heavy position in Altmann stock. I see it has taken an awful tumble.'

'Strange that.' Steven shook his head. 'Pulled out of Altmann's a few weeks ago, actually. Needed the money for San Istaban.'

'Lucky,' Peter murmured, or much more than luck. He wondered why Steven admitted the share transaction so readily. 'Of course,' he realized, 'it would have been very substantial and therefore easily traced.'

He studied his brother now, staring at him with a slight scowl of concentration. Was it possible? he asked himself. Could Steven really have masterminded something so complex, where ideology and self-interest and delusions of omnipotence seemed so inextricably snarled and entwined.

'What is it, old boy?' Steven asked, frowning slightly in sympathy.

'I was just thinking that the whole concept and execution has been incredible, Steven. I would never have suspected you were capable of it.'

'I'm sorry, Peter. I don't understand. What are you talking about?'

'Caliph,' Peter said softly.

It was there! Peter saw it instantly. The instant of utter stillness, like a startled jungle animal – but the flinch of the eyes, followed immediately by the effort of control.

The expression of Steven's face had not altered, the little frown of polite inquiry held perfectly, then turning slowly, deeper into puzzlement.

'I'm afraid you just lost me there, old chap.'

It was superbly done. Despite himself Peter was impressed. There were depths to his brother which he had never suspected – but that was his own omission. No matter which way you looked at it, it took an extraordinary ability to achieve what Steven had achieved in less than twenty years, against the most appalling odds. No matter how he had done it, it was the working of a particular type of genius.

He was capable of running Caliph, Peter accepted the fact at last – and immediately had a focal point for the corroding hatred he had carried within him for so long.

'Your only mistake so far, Steven, was to let Aaron Altmann know your name,' Peter went on quietly. 'I suspect you did not then know that he was a Mossad agent, and that your name would go straight onto the Israeli intelligence computer. Nobody, nothing, can ever wipe it from the memory rolls, Steven. You are known.'

Steven's eyes flickered down to the shotgun; it was instinctive, uncontrollable, the final confirmation if Peter needed one.

'No, Steven. That's not for you.' Peter shook his head. 'That's my work. You're fat and out of condition, and you have never had the training. You must stick to hiring others to do the actual killing. You wouldn't even get a hand on it.'

Steven's eyes darted back to his brother's face. Still the expression of his face had not altered.

'I think you've gone out of your head, old boy.'

Peter ignored it. 'You of all people should know that I am capable of killing anybody. You have conditioned me to that.'

'We are getting into an awful tangle now,' Steven protested. 'What on earth should you want to kill anybody for?'

'Steven, you are insulting both of us. I know. There is no point in going on with the act. We have to work out between us what we are going to do about it.'

He had phrased it carefully, offering the chance of

compromise. He saw the waver of doubt in Steven's eyes, the slight twist of his mouth, as he struggled to reach a decision.

' – But please do not underestimate the danger you are in, Steven.' As he spoke Peter produced an old worn pair of dark leather gloves from his pocket and began to pull them on. There was something infinitely menacing in that simple act, and again Steven's eyes were drawn irresistibly.

'Why are you doing that?' For the first time Steven's voice croaked slightly.

'I haven't yet touched the gun,' Peter explained reasonably. 'It has only your prints upon it.'

'Christ, you'd never get away with it, Peter.'

'Why, Steven? It is always dangerous to carry a loaded shotgun over muddy and uneven ground.'

'You couldn't do it, not in cold blood.' The edge of terror was in Steven's voice.

'Why not? You had no such qualms with Prince Hassied Abdel Hayek.'

'I am your brother – he was only a bloody wog—' Steven choked it off, staring now at Peter with stricken eyes, the expression of his face beginning at last to crack and crumble as he realized that he had made the fateful admission.

Peter reached for the shotgun without taking his eyes from his brother's.

'Wait!' Steven cried. 'Wait, Peter!'

'For what?'

'You've got to let me explain.'

'All right, go ahead.'

'You can't just say go ahead, like that. It's so complicated '

'All right, Steven. Let's start at the beginning – with Flight 070. Tell me why?'

'We had to do it, Peter. Don't you see? There is over four billions of British investment in that country, another three billions of American money. It's the major world producer of gold and uranium, chrome and a dozen other strategic minerals. My God, Peter. Those ham-handed oafs in control now are on a suicide course. We had to take it away from them, and put in a controllable government. If we don't do that the Reds will have it all within ten years – probably much less.'

'You had an alternative government chosen?'

'Of course,' Steven told him urgently, persuasively, watching the shotgun that Peter still held low across his hips. 'It was planned in every detail. It took two years.'

'All right.' Peter nodded. 'Tell me about the murder of Prince Hassied.'

'It wasn't murder, for God's sake, man, it was absolutely essential. It was a matter of survival. They were destroying Western civilization with their childlike irresponsibility. Drunk with power, they were no longer amenable to reason, like spoiled children in a sweet shop – we had to put a stop to it, or face a breakdown of the capitalist system. They have probably done irreparable damage to the prestige of the dollar, they have taken sterling hostage and hold it in daily jeopardy with the threat of withdrawing those astronomic balances from London. We had to bring them to their senses, and look how small a price. We can reduce the price of crude oil gradually to its 1970 level. We can restore sanity to the currencies of the Western world and secure real growth and prosperity for hundreds of millions of peoples – all at the cost of a single life.'

'And anyway, he was only a bloody wog. Wasn't he?' Peter agreed reasonably.

'Look here, Peter. I said that but I didn't mean it. You are being unreasonable.'

'I will try not to be,' Peter assured him mildly. 'Tell me where it goes from here. Who do you bring under control next – the British Trade Union movement, perhaps?'

And Steven stared at him wordlessly for a moment.

'Damn it, Peter. That was a hell of a guess. But could

you imagine if we had a five-year wage freeze, and no industrial action during that time. It's them or us, Peter. We could get back to being one of the major industrial powers of the Western world. Great Britain! We could be that again.'

'You are very convincing, Steven,' Peter acknowledged. 'There are only a few details that worry me a little.'

'What are they, Peter?'

'Why was it necessary to arrange the murder of Kingston Parker and Magda Altmann—'

Steven stared at him, his jaw unhinging slightly and the hard line of his mouth going slack with astonishment. 'No,' he shook his head. 'That's not so.'

' – and why was it necessary to kill Baron Altmann, and torture him to death?'

'That was not my doing – all right, it was done. And I knew it was done – but I had nothing to do with it, Peter. Not the murder at least. Oh God, all right I knew it had to be done, but—' His voice tailed off, and he stared helplessly at Peter.

'From the beginning again, Steven. Let's hear it all—' Peter spoke almost gently.

'I cannot, Peter. You don't understand what might happen, what will happen if I tell you—'

Peter slid the safety catch off the Purdey shotgun. The click of the mechanism was unnaturally loud in the silence, and Steven Stride started and stepped back a pace, blinking at his brother, fastening all his attention on Peter's eyes.

'God,' he whispered. 'You would do it too.'

'Tell me about Aaron Altmann.'

'Can I have another cigarette?'

Peter nodded and Steven lit it with hands that trembled very slightly.

'You have to understand how it worked, before I can explain.'

'Tell me how it worked,' Peter invited.

'I was recruited—'

'Steven, don't lie to me – you are Caliph.'

'No, God, no, Peter. You have it all wrong,' Steven cried. 'It's a chain. I am only a link in Caliph's chain. I am not Caliph.'

'You are a part of Caliph, then?'

'Only a link in the chain,' Steven repeated vehemently.

'Tell me,' Peter invited with a small movement of the shotgun barrel that drew Steven's eyes immediately.

'There is a man I have known a long time. We have worked together before. A man with greater wealth and influence than I have. It was not an immediate thing. It grew out of many discussions and conversations over a long time, years, in which we both voiced our concern with the way that power had shifted to blocks of persons unfit to wield it—'

'All right,' Peter nodded grimly. 'I understand your political and ideological sentiments. Leave them out of the account.'

'Very well,' Steven agreed. ' – Well, finally this man asked me if I would be prepared to join an association of Western world political and industrial leaders dedicated to restoring power to the hands of those fitted by training and upbringing to govern.'

'Who was this man?'

'Peter, I cannot tell you.'

'You have no choice,' Peter told him, and there was a long moment as they locked eyes and wills; then Steven sighed in capitulation.

'It was—' The name was that of a mining magnate who controlled most of the free world supply of nuclear fuel and gold and precious stones.

'So he is the one who would have been in control of the new South African government with which you intended replacing the present regime in that country, if the taking of 070 had succeeded?' Peter demanded, and Steven nodded wordlessly.

'All right,' Peter nodded. 'Go on.'

'He had been recruited as I was,' Steven explained. 'But I was never to know by whom. In my turn I was to recruit another desirable member – but I would be the only one who knew who that was. It was how the security of the chain was to be maintained. Each link would know only the one above and below him, the man who had recruited him and the one who he recruited in his turn—'

'Caliph?' Peter demanded. 'What about Caliph?'

'Nobody knows who he is.'

'Yet he must know who you are.'

'Yes, of course.'

'Then there must be some way for you to get a message to Caliph,' Peter insisted. 'For instance, when you recruit a new member, you must be able to pass on the information? When he wants something from you, he must be able to contact you.'

'Yes.'

'How?'

'Christ, Peter. It's more than my life is worth.'

'We'll come back to it,' said Peter impatiently. 'Go on, tell me about Aaron Altmann.'

'That was a disaster. I chose Aaron as the man I would recruit. He seemed exactly the kind of man we needed. I had known him for years. I knew he could be very tough when it was necessary. So I approached him. He seemed very eager at first, leading me on. Getting me to explain the way Caliph would work. I was delighted to have recruited such an important man. He intimated that he would contribute twenty-five million dollars to the funds of the association, so I passed a message to Caliph. I told him that I had almost succeeded in recruiting Baron Altmann—'

Steven stopped nervously, and dropped the stub of his

cigarette onto the damp turf, grinding it out under his heel.

'What happened then?' Peter demanded.

'Caliph responded immediately. I was ordered to break off all contact with Aaron Altmann at once. I realized I must have chosen a potentially dangerous person. You tell me now he was Mossad. I did not know that – but Caliph must have known it. I did as I was told and dropped Aaron like a hot chestnut – and four days later he was abducted. I had nothing to do with it, Peter. I swear to you. I liked the man immensely. I admired him—'

'Yet he was abducted and horribly tortured. You must have known that Caliph had done it, and that you were responsible?'

'Yes.' Steven said the word flatly, without evasion. Peter felt a small stir of admiration for that.

'They tortured him to find out if he had passed the information you had given him about Caliph to Mossad,' Peter insisted.

'Yes. I expect so. I do not know.'

'If the picture I have of Aaron Altmann was correct they received no information from him.'

'No. He was like that. They must have lost patience with him in the end – to do what they did to him. It was my first moment of disillusionment with Caliph,' Steven muttered sombrely.

They were both silent now, until Peter burst out angrily. 'My God, Steven, can't you see what a disgusting business you are mixed up in?' And Steven was mute. 'Couldn't you see it?' Peter insisted, the anger raw in his voice. 'Couldn't you realize it from the beginning?'

'Not at the beginning.' Steven shook his head miserably. 'It seemed a brilliant solution for all the diseases of the Western world – and then once I began it was like being on board a speeding express train. It was just impossible to get off again.'

'All right. So then you tried to have me assassinated on the Rambouillet road?'

'Good God, no.' Steven was truly appalled. 'You're my brother, good God—'

'Caliph did it to stop me getting close to Aaron's widow who was out to avenge him.'

'I didn't know a thing about it, I swear to you. If Caliph did it, he knew better than to let me in on it.' Steven was pleading now. 'You must believe that.'

Peter felt a softening of his resolve, but forced back the knowledge that this man was his brother, someone who had been very dear over a lifetime.

'What was your next operation for Caliph then?' He asked without allowing the softness to reach his voice.

'There wasn't—'

'Damn you, Steven, don't lie to me.' Peter's voice cracked like a whiplash. 'You knew about Prince Hassied Abdel Hayek!'

'All right. I arranged that. Caliph told me what to do and I did it.'

'Then you kidnapped Melissa-Jane and had her mutilated—'

'Oh God! No!' Steven's voice was a sob.

' – To force me to assassinate Kingston Parker—'

'No, Peter. No!'

' – And then to kill Magda Altmann—'

'Peter, I swear to you. Not Melissa-Jane. I love her like one of my own daughters. You must know that. I had no idea it was Caliph.'

Steven was pleading wildly now.

' – You have to believe me. I would never have allowed that to happen. That is too horrible.'

Peter watched him with a steely merciless glint of blue in his eyes, cold and cutting as the edge of the executioner's blade.

'I will do anything to prove to you I had nothing to do

with Melissa-Jane. Anything you say, Peter. I'll take any chance to prove it to you. I swear it to you.'

Steven Stride's dismay and sincerity were beyond question. His face was drained of all colour and his lips were marble white and trembling with the strength of his denial.

Peter handed the shotgun to his brother without a word. Startled, Steven held it for a moment at arm's length.

'You are in bad trouble, Steven,' Peter said quietly. He knew that from now on he needed Steven's unreserved and whole-hearted commitment. He could not be forced to do what he must do at the point of a shotgun.

Steven recognized the gesture, and slowly lowered the gun. With his thumb he pushed across the breech-locking mechanism, and the weapon hinged open. He pulled the cartridges from the double eyes of the breeches and dropped them into the pocket of his shooting jacket.

'Let's get down to the house,' Steven said, his voice still unsteady with the trauma of the last minutes. 'I need a stiff whisky—'

There was a log fire burning in the deep walk-in fireplace of Steven's study. The portals were magnificently carved altar surrounds from a sixteenth-century German church, salvaged from the ruins of World War II Allied bombing and purchased by Steven from a Spanish dealer, after having been smuggled out through Switzerland.

Opposite the fireplace, bow windows with leaded panes and ancient wavy glass looked out over the rose garden. The other two walls housed Steven's collection of rare books, each boxed in its individual leather-bound container and lettered in gold leaf. The shelves reached from floor to the high moulded ceiling. It was a passion that the brothers shared.

Steven stood now in the fireplace with his back to the flames, one hand clasped in the small of his back, hoisting up the skirts of his tweed jacket to warm his backside. In the other hand he held a deep crystal tumbler, still half filled with whisky, hardly diluted by the soda he had dashed into it from the syphon.

Steven still looked shaken and pale, and every few minutes he shivered uncontrollably, although the room was oppressively heated by the blazing fire and all the windows were closed tightly.

Peter sprawled in the brocade-upholstered Louis Quatorze chair across the room, his legs thrust out straight and crossed at the ankles, hands thrust deeply into his pockets, and his chin lowered on his chest in deep thought.

'How much was your contribution to Caliph's war chest?' Peter asked abruptly.

'I was not in the same class as Aaron Altmann,' Steven answered quietly. 'I pledged five millions in sterling over five years.'

'So we must imagine a network extending across all international boundaries. Powerful men in every country, each contributing enormous sums of money – and almost unlimited information and influence—'

Steven nodded and took another swallow of his dark-toned whisky.

' – There is no reason to believe that it was only one man in each country. There may be a dozen in England, another dozen in Western Germany, fifty in the United States—'

'It's possible,' Steven agreed.

'So that Caliph could very easily have arranged the kidnapping of Melissa-Jane through another of his chain in this country.'

'You must believe I had nothing to do with it, Peter.'

Peter dismissed this new protestation impatiently, and went on thinking out aloud.

'It is still possible that Caliph is a committee of the founder members – not one man at all.'

'I don't think so—' Steven hesitated. ' – I had a very strong impression that it all was one man. I do not think a committee would be capable of such swift and determined action.' He shook his head, trying to cast his mind back for the exact words which had formed his impressions. ' – You must remember that I have only discussed Caliph with one other person, the man who recruited me. However, you can be certain that we discussed it in depth and over an extended period. I was not about to put out five million on something that didn't satisfy me entirely. No, it was one man who would make the decision for all of us – but the decisions would be in the interest of all.'

'Yet there was no guarantee that any individual member of the chain would be informed of every decision?'

'No. Of course not. That would have been madness. Security was the key to success.'

'You could trust somebody you had never met, whose identity was hidden from you – you could trust him with vast sums of money, and the destiny of the world as we know it?'

Steven hesitated again as if seeking the right words. 'Caliph has an aura that seems to envelop all of us. The man who recruited me—' Steven seemed reluctant to repeat the name again, proof to Peter of the influence that Caliph exerted ' – is a man whose judgement I respect tremendously. He was convinced, and this helped to convince me.'

'What do you think now?' Peter asked abruptly. 'Are you still convinced?'

Steven drained the whisky glass, and then smoothed his moustache with a little nervous gesture.

'Come on, Steven,' Peter encouraged him.

'I still think Caliph had the right idea—' he said reluctantly. ' – The rules have changed, Peter. We were fighting for survival of the world as we know it. We were merely playing to the new morality—'

He crossed to the silver tray on the corner of his desk and refilled the whisky glass.

' – Up to now we have had one hand tied behind our backs, while the Reds and the extreme left and the members of the Third World have had both hands to fight with and a dagger in each one. All Caliph did was to take off our shackles.'

'What has made you change your mind then?' Peter asked.

'I'm not sure that I have changed my mind.' Steven turned back to face him. 'I still think it was the right idea—'

' – But?' Peter insisted.

Steven shrugged. 'The murder of Aaron Altmann, the mutilation of Melissa-Jane—' He hesitated. ' – Other acts of which I suspect Caliph was the originator. They were not for the common good. They were merely to protect Caliph's personal safety, or to satisfy what I am beginning to believe is vaunted and unbridled lust for power.' Steven shook his head again. 'I believed Caliph to be noble and dedicated – but there is no nobility in some of the things he has done. He has acted like a common criminal. He has acted for personal advantage and glorification. I believe in the concept of Caliph – but I know now we have chosen the wrong man. He has been corrupted by the power that we placed in his hands.'

Peter listened to him carefully, his head cocked to one side, his blue eyes clear and quietly searching.

'All right, Steven. So we discover that Caliph is not a deity – but a man with a man's petty greed and self-interest.'

'Yes, I suppose I do.' Steven's handsome florid face was heavy with regret. 'Caliph is not what I believed he might be.'

'Do you accept now that he is evil – truly evil?'

'Yes, I accept that.' Then, fiercely, 'But God, how I wish Caliph had been what I believed he was at the beginning.'

Peter could understand that and he nodded.

'It was what this crazy world of ours needed—' Steven went on bitterly. ' – We need somebody, a strong man to tell us what to do. I thought it was Caliph. I wanted it so badly to be him.'

'So now, do you accept that Caliph was not that man?'

'Yes,' said Steven simply. 'But if there was a man like that I would follow him again, unquestioningly.'

'You said you would do anything to prove to me that you had nothing to do with Melissa-Jane – will you help me to destroy Caliph?'

'Yes.' Steven did not hesitate.

'There will be great personal risk,' Peter pointed out, and now Steven met his eyes steadily.

'I know that. I know Caliph better than you.'

Peter found that his affection for his brother was now reinforced with admiration. Steven lacked very few of the manly virtues, he thought. He had strength and courage and brains, perhaps his major vice was that he had too much of each.

'What do you want me to do, Peter?'

'I want you to arrange a meeting with Caliph – face to face.'

'Impossible.' Steven dismissed it immediately.

'You said that you had means of getting a message to him?'

'Yes, but Caliph would never agree to a meeting.'

'Steven, what is the single – the only weakness that Caliph has shown so far?'

'He has shown no weakness.'

'Yes, he has,' Peter denied.

'What is it?'

'He is obsessed with protecting his personal identity and safety,' Peter pointed out. 'As soon as that is threatened, he immediately reverts to abduction and torture and murder.'

'That isn't a weakness—' Steven pointed out. 'It's a strength.'

'If you can get a message to him – that his identity is in jeopardy. That somebody, an enemy, has penetrated his security screen and has managed to get close to him,' Peter suggested, and Steven considered it long and carefully.

'He would react very strongly,' Steven agreed. 'But it would not take him very long to find out that I was lying. That would immediately discredit me, and as you said earlier I would be at grave risk for no good reason.'

'It isn't a lie,' Peter told him grimly. 'There is a Mossad agent close to Caliph. Very close to him.'

'How do you know that?' Steven asked sharply.

'I cannot tell you,' Peter said. 'But the information is iron-clad. I even know the agent's code-name. I give you my word that the information is genuine.'

'In that case—' Steven thought it out again ' – Caliph would probably already be suspicious and would be prepared to accept my warning. However, all he would do would be to ask me to give him the name – pass it to him along his usual communications channel. That would be it.'

'You would refuse to pass the information – except face to face. You will protest that the information is much too sensitive. You would protest that your personal safety was at stake. What would be his reaction?'

'I would expect him to put pressure on me to divulge the name—'

'If you resisted?'

'I suppose he would have to agree to a meeting. As you have pointed out, it is his major obsession. But, if he met me face to face, his identity would be revealed anyway.'

'Think, Steven. You know how his mind works.'

It took a few seconds, then Steven's expression changed, consternation twisting his lips as though he was in pain.

'Good God – of course. If I forced him to a face-to-face meeting, I would be highly unlikely to survive it.'

'Exactly,' Peter nodded. 'If we baited it with something absolutely irresistible, Caliph would have to agree to meet you – but he would make arrangements to have you silenced immediately, before you had a chance to pass on his identity to anyone else.'

'Hell, Peter, this is creepy. As you told me earlier today, I am fat and out of condition. I wouldn't be much of a match against Caliph.'

'Caliph would take that into consideration when deciding whether to meet you or not,' Peter agreed.

'It sounds like suicide,' Steven persisted.

'You just signed on to be tough,' Peter reminded him.

'Tough is one thing, stupid is another.'

'You would be in no danger until you delivered the message. Caliph would not dare dispose of you until you delivered your message,' Peter pointed out. 'And I give you my word that I will never call on you to go to an assignation with Caliph.'

'I can't ask for more than that, I suppose.' Steven threw up his hands. 'When do you want me to contact him?'

'How do you do it – the contact?'

'Advert in the Personal column,' Steven told him, and Peter grinned with reluctant admiration. Neat, efficient and entirely untraceable.

'Do it as soon as you can,' Peter instructed.

'Monday morning,' Steven nodded, and went on studying his brother with a peculiarly intent expression.

'What is it, Steven?'

'I was just thinking. If only Caliph had been somebody like you, Peter.'

'Me?' For the first time Peter was truly startled.

'The warrior king – utterly ruthless in the pursuit of the vision of justice and rightness and duty.'

'I am not like that.' Peter denied it.

'Yes, you are,' Steven said positively. 'You are the type of man that I hoped Caliph might be. The type of man we needed.'

Peter had to presume that Caliph was watching him. After his murder of Baroness Altmann, Caliph's interest would be intense. Peter had to act predictably.

He caught the early Monday flight back to Brussels, and before midday was at his desk in Narmco headquarters Here also he was the centre of much interest and power-play. Altmann Industries had lost its chief executive and there were strong undercurrents and court intrigues already afoot. Despite a number of subtle approaches Peter stayed aloof from the struggle.

On Tuesday evening Peter picked up the newspaper from the news-stand in the Hilton lobby. Steven's contact request was in the small-ads section.

> The children of Israel asked counsel of the Lord, saying, shall I go up again to battle? Judges. 20:23.

The quotation that Caliph had chosen seemed to epitomize his view of himself. He saw himself as godlike, set high above his fellow men.

Steven had explained to Peter that Caliph took up to forty-eight hours to answer.

Steven would wait each day after the appearance of the personal announcement at his desk in his office suite in Leadenhall Street, from noon until twenty minutes past the hour. He would have no visitors nor appointments for that time, and he would make certain that his direct unlisted telephone line was unengaged to receive the incoming contact.

There was no contact that Wednesday, but Steven had not expected one. On the Thursday Steven paced restlessly up and down the antique silk Kirman carpet as he waited for the call. He was already wearing the jacket of his suit, and his bowler and rolled umbrella were on the corner of the ornate French ormolu desk that squatted like some benign monster beneath the windows which looked across the street at Lloyds Exchange.

Steven Stride was afraid. He acknowledged the fact with direct self-honesty. Intrigue was part of his existence, had been for nearly all of his life – but always the game had been played to certain rules. He knew he was entering a new jungle, a savage wilderness where those few rules ceased entirely to exist. He was going in over his head; Peter had pointed out to him that this was not his way, and he knew Peter was right. Peter was right, and Steven was afraid as he had never been in his life. Yet he knew that he was going ahead with it. He had heard that it was the mark of true courage – to be able to meet and acknowledge fear, and yet control it sufficiently to be able to go ahead and do what duty dictated must be done.

He did not feel like a brave man.

The telephone rang once, too loud, too shrill – and every nerve in his body jumped taut and he found himself frozen, paralysed with fear in the centre of the beautiful and precious carpet.

The telephone rang again, the insistent double note sounded in his ears like the peal of doom, and he felt his bowels filled with the hot oily slime of fear, hardly to be contained.

The telephone rang the third time, and with an enormous effort he forced himself to make the three paces to his desk.

He lifted the telephone receiver, and heard the sharp chimes of the interference from the public telephone system.

'Stride,' he said. His voice was strained, high and almost shrill, and he heard the drop of the coin.

The voice terrified him. It was an electronic drone, inhuman, without gender, without the timbre of living emotion, without neither high nor low notes

'Aldgate and Leadenhall Street,' said the voice.

Steven repeated the rendezvous and immediately the connection was broken.

Steven dropped the receiver onto its cradle and snatched up his bowler and umbrella as he hurried to the door.

His secretary looked up at him and smiled expectantly She was a handsome grey-haired woman who had been with Steven for fifteen years.

'Sir?' She still called him that.

'I'm popping out for half an hour, May,' Steven told her. 'Look after the shop, there is a dear ' And he stepped into his private elevator and rode down swiftly to the underground garage where his Rolls was kept, together with the private vehicles of his senior executives.

In the elevator mirror he checked the exact angle of his bowler, a slightly raffish tilt over the right eye, and rearranged the bloom of the crimson carnation in the buttonhole of the dark blue Savile Row suit with its faint and elegant chalk stripe. It was important that he looked and acted entirely naturally during the next few minutes His staff would remark on any departure from the normal

In the garage he did not approach the dark-maroon Rolls-Royce which glowed in the subdued lighting like some precious gem. Instead he went towards the wicket gate in the steel roll-up garage door, and the doorman in his little glassed cubicle beside the door looked up from his football pools coupons, recognized the master and leaped to his feet.

'Afternoon, guv.'

'Good day, Harold. I won't be taking the car. Just stepping out for a few minutes.'

He stepped over the threshold of the gate, into the street and turned left, down towards the junction of Leadenhall Street and Aldgate. He walked fast, without seeming to hurry. Caliph spaced his intervals very tight, to make it difficult for the subject to pass a message to a surveillance unit. Steven knew he had only minutes to get from his office to the call box on the corner. Caliph seemed to know exactly how long it would take him.

The telephone in the red-framed and glass call box started to ring when he was still twenty paces away. Steven ran the distance.

'Stride,' he said, his voice slightly puffed with exertion, and immediately the coin dropped and the same electronic droning voice gave him the next contact point. It was the public call box at the High Street entrance to Aldgate tube station. Steven confirmed and the voice troubled him deeply, it sounded like that of a robot from some science fiction movie. It would not have been so bad if he had felt human contact.

The two receiving stations, neither of which was predictable, and the distances between them, had been carefully calculated to make it only just possible to reach them in time, to make it impossible for the call to be traced while the line was still open. Caliph or his agent was clearly moving from one call box to the next in another part of the city. Tracing them even a minute after he had left would be of no possible use in trying to establish identity.

The voice distorter that Caliph was using was a simple device no bigger than a small pocket calculator. Peter had told Steven that it could be purchased from a number of firms specializing in electronic surveillance, security and counter-measure equipment. It cost less than fifty dollars, and so altered the human voice – phasing out all sound outside the middle range – that even the most sophisticated recording device would not be able to lift a useable voice-print to compare with a computer bank memory. It would not even be able to determine whether the speaker was a man, a woman or a child.

Steven had an unusually clear path to the station, and found himself waiting outside the call box in the crowded entrance to the station while a young man in paint-speckled overalls, with long greasy blond hair, finished his conversation. Caliph's system allowed for prior use of the chosen public telephone, and as soon as the scruffy youth finished his leisurely chat, Steven pushed into the booth and made a show of consulting the directory.

The phone rang, and even though he was expecting it, Steven jumped with shock. He was perspiring now, with the walk and the tension, and his voice was ragged as he snatched the receiver.

'Stride,' he gulped.

The coin dropped and Caliph's impersonal tones chilled him again.

'Yes?'

'I have a message.'

'Yes?'

'There is danger for Caliph.'

'Yes?'

'A government intelligence agency has put an agent close to him, close enough to be extremely dangerous.'

'Say the source of your information.'

'My brother. General Peter Stride.' Peter had instructed him to tell the truth, as much as was possible.

'Say the government agency involved.'

'Negative. The information is too sensitive. I must have assurance that Caliph receives it personally.'

'Say the name or position of the enemy agent.'

'Negative. For the same reasons.'

Steven glanced at his gold Cartier tank watch with its black alligator strap. They had been speaking for fifteen seconds – he knew the contact would not last longer than thirty seconds. Caliph would not risk exposure beyond that time. He did not wait for the next question or instruction.

'I will pass the information only to Caliph, and I must be certain it is him, not one of his agents. I request a personal meeting.'

'That is not possible,' droned the inhuman voice.

'Then Caliph will be in great personal danger.' Steven found courage to say it.

'I repeat, say the name and position of enemy agent.'

Twenty-five seconds had passed.

'I say again, negative. You must arrange a face-to-face meeting for transfer of this information.'

A single droplet of sweat broke from the hairline of Steven's temple and ran down his cheek. He felt as though he were suffocating in the claustrophobic little telephone box.

'You will be contacted,' droned the voice and the line clicked dead.

Steven took the white silk handkerchief from his top pocket and dabbed at his face. Then he carefully rearranged the scrap of silk in his pocket, not folded into neat spikes but with a deliberately casual drape.

He squared his shoulders, lifted his chin and left the booth. Now for the first time he felt like a brave man. It was a feeling he relished, and he stepped out boldly swinging the rolled umbrella with a small flourish at each pace.

Peter had been within call of the telephone all that week, during the hours of involvement with the series of Narmco projects which he had put in train before his departure for Tahiti, and which all seemed to be maturing simultaneously. There were meetings that began in the morning and lasted until after dark, there were two separate day journeys, one to Oslo and another to Frankfurt, catching the early businessman's plane and back in the Narmco office before evening. Always he was within reach of a telephone and Steven Stride knew the number; even when he was in the NATO Officers Club gymnasium, sharpening his body to peak physical condition, or practising until after midnight in the underground pistol range until the 9-mm Cobra was an extension of his hands – either hand, left or right, equally capable of grouping the X circle at fifty metres, from any position, standing, kneeling or prone, always he was within reach of the telephone.

Peter felt like a prize fighter in training camp, concentrating all his attention on the preparations for the confrontation he knew lay ahead.

At last the weekend loomed, with the prospect of being boring and frustrating. He refused invitations to visit the country home of one of his Narmco colleagues, another to fly down to Paris for the Saturday racing – and he stayed alone in the Hilton suite, waiting for the call from Steven.

On Sunday morning he had all the papers sent up to his room, English and American and French – German which he could read better than he spoke, and even the Dutch and Italian papers which he could stumble through haltingly, missing every third word or so.

He went through them carefully, trying to find a hint of Caliph's activity. New abductions, hijackings or other acts which might give him a lead to some new Caliph-dominated pressures.

Italy was in a political uproar. The confusion so great that he could only guess at how much of it was from the left and how much from the right. There had been an assassination in Naples of five known members of the Terrorist Red Brigade, all five taken out neatly with a single grenade. The grenade type had been determined as standard NATO issue, and the execution had been in the kitchen of a Red

Brigade safe apartment in a slum area of the city. The police had no leads. It sounded like Caliph. There was no reason to believe that his 'chain' did not include prominent Italian businessmen. A millionaire Italian living in his own country had to be the earth's most endangered species after the blue whale, Peter thought wryly, and they might have called on Caliph to go on the offensive.

Peter finished the continental papers, and turned with relief to the English and American. It was a little before Sunday noon, and he wondered how he could live out the desolate hours until Monday morning. He was certain that there would be no reply to Steven's request for a meeting before then.

He started on the English-language newspapers, spinning them out to cover the blank time ahead.

The British Leyland Motor Company strike was in its fifteenth week – with no prospect of settlement. Now there was a case for Caliph, Peter smiled wryly, remembering his discussion with Steven. Knock a few heads together for their own good.

There was only one other item of interest in his morning's reading. The President of the United States had appointed a special negotiator in another attempt to find a solution to the Israeli occupation of the disputed territories in the Middle East. The man he had chosen was Dr Kingston Parker, who was described as a personal friend of the President and one of the senior members of his inner circle of advisors, a man well thought of by all parties in the dispute, and an ideal choice for the difficult job Again Peter found himself in agreement. Kingston Parker's energies and resources seemed bottomless.

Peter dropped the last paper and found himself facing a void of boredom that would extend through until the following day. There were three books he should read beside his bed, and the Hermes crocodile case was half-filled with

Narmco material, yet he knew that he would not be able to concentrate – not with the prospect of the confrontation with Caliph over-shadowing all else.

He went through into the mirrored bathroom of the suite, and found the package that he had purchased the previous day in the cosmetic section of Galéries Anspach, one of the city's largest departmental stores.

The wig was of good-quality human hair, not the obviously shiny nylon substitute. It was in his own natural colour, but much longer than Peter wore his hair. He arranged it carefully along his own hairline, and then set to work with a pair of scissors, trimming and tidying it. When he had it as close to his liking as possible, he began to tint the temples with 'Italian Boy' hair silvering.

It took him most of the afternoon, for he was in no hurry, and he was critical of his own work. Every few minutes he consulted the snapshot which Melissa-Jane had taken with her new Polaroid camera, Peter's Christmas present to her, at Abbots Yew on New Year's Day. It was a good likeness of both the Stride brothers, Peter and Steven, standing full face and smiling indulgently at Melissa-Jane's command to do so.

It highlighted the resemblances of the two brothers, and also pointed out their physical differences. The natural hair colouring was identical but Steven's was fashionably longer, curling on his collar at the back, and appreciably greyer at the temples and streaked at the front.

Steven's face was heavier, with the first trace of jowls, and his colour was higher, perhaps the first ruddy warnings of heart malfunction or merely the banner of good living in his cheeks. Yet with the wig on his head, Peter's own face seemed much fuller.

Next Peter shaped the moustache, trimming it down into the infantry officer model that Steven favoured. There had been a good selection of artificial moustaches to choose from in the cosmetic section, amongst a display of artificial eyelashes and eyebrows, but none had been exactly right. Peter had to work on it carefully with the scissors, and then tint it with a little silver.

When he fastened it in place with the special adhesive gum, the result was quite startling. The moustache filled out his face even further, and of course the eyes of the twins were almost exactly the same shape and colour. Their noses were both straight and bony. Peter's mouth was a little more generous, and did not have the same hard relentless line of lip – but the moustache concealed much of that.

Peter stood back and examined himself in the full-length mirror. He and Steven were within a quarter of an inch in height, they had the same breadth of shoulder. Steven was heavier in the gut, and his neck was thickening, giving him a thrusting bull-like set to his head and shoulders. Peter altered his stance slightly. It worked. He doubted that anybody who did not know both of them intimately would be able to detect the substitution. There was no reason to believe that Caliph or any of his closest lieutenants would have seen either Steven or Peter in the flesh.

He spent an hour practising Steven's gait, watching himself in the mirror, trying to capture the buoyant cockiness of Steven's movements, searching for little personal mannerisms, the way Steven stood with both hands clasped under the skirts of his jacket; the way he brushed his moustache with one finger, from the parting under his nose – left and right.

Clothing was not a serious problem. Both brothers had used the same tailor since Sandhurst days, and Steven's dress habits were invariable and inviolable. Peter's knew exactly what he would wear in any given situation.

Peter stripped off wig and moustache and repacked them carefully in their Galéries Anspach plastic packets, then buttoned them into one of the interior divisions of the Hermes case.

Next he removed the Cobra parabellum from another

division. It was still in the chamois leather holster, and he bounced the familiar weight of the weapon in the palm of his hand. Reluctantly he decided he could not take it with him. The meeting would almost certainly be in England. The contact that Steven had had on Thursday had clearly originated in London. He had to believe the next contact would be in that same city. He could not take the chance of walking through British customs with a deadly weapon on his person. If he was stopped, there would be publicity. It would instantly alert Caliph. He would be able to get another weapon from Thor Command once he was in England Colin Noble would supply him, just as soon as Peter explained the need, he was certain of that.

Peter went down and checked the Cobra pistol into the safe deposit box of the hotel reception office, and returned to his room to face the wearying and indefinite wait. It was one of a soldier's duties to which he had never entirely accustomed himself – he always hated the waiting

However, he settled down to read Robert Asprey's *War in the Shadows*, that definitive tome on the history and practice of guerrilla warfare down the ages. He managed to lose himself sufficiently to be mildly surprised when he glanced at his watch and saw it was after eight o'clock. He ordered an omelette to be sent up by room service, and ten seconds after he replaced the receiver, the telephone rang He thought it might be a query from the kitchen about his dinner order

'Yes, what is it?' he demanded irritably.

'Peter?'

'Steven?'

'He has agreed to a meeting.'

Peter felt his heart lunge wildly.

'When? Where?'

'I don't know. I have to fly to Orly tomorrow. There will be instructions for me at the airport.'

Caliph covering and backtracking. Peter should have

expected it. Desperately he cast his mind back to the layout of Orly Airport. He had to find a private place to meet Steven and make the change-over. He discarded swiftly the idea of meeting in one of the lounges or washrooms. That left one other location.

'What time will you be there?' Peter demanded.

'Cooks have got me onto the early flight. I'll be there at eleven fifteen.'

'I'll be there before you,' Peter told him. He knew the Sabena timetable by heart and all senior Narmco executives had special VIP cards which assured a seat on any flight.

'I will book a room at the Air Hotel on the fourth floor of Orly South terminal in your name,' he told Steven now. 'I'll wait in the lobby. Go directly to the reception desk and ask for your key. I will check behind you to make certain you are not followed. Do not acknowledge me in any way. Have you got that, Steven?'

'Yes.'

'Until tomorrow, then.'

Peter broke the connection, and went through into the bathroom He studied his own face in the mirror.

'Well, that takes care of getting a weapon from Thor.' Caliph had not set the meeting in England. It was clear now that Paris was only a staging point, and that in his usual careful fashion Caliph would move the subject on from there – perhaps through one or more staging points, to the final rendezvous.

The subject would go in unarmed, and unsupported – and Peter was certain that afterwards Caliph would take his usual pains to ensure that the subject would be unable to carry back a report of the meeting.

I am drawing two cards inside for a straight flush, and Caliph is the dealer from a pack that he has had plenty of time to prepare, Peter thought coldly, but at least the waiting was over. He began to pack his toilet articles into the waterproof Gucci bag.

Sir Steven Stride marched into the lobby of Orly South Air Hotel at five minutes past noon, and Peter smiled to himself in self-congratulation. Steven was wearing a blue double-breasted blazer, white shirt and cricket-club tie, above grey woollen slacks and black English handmade shoes – none of your fancy Italian footwear for Steven.

It was Steven's standard informal dress, and Peter had only been wrong about the tie – he had guessed that it would be an I Zingari pattern. Peter himself wore a double-breaster and grey slacks under his trench coat and his shoes were black Barkers.

Steven's eyes flickered around the lobby, passing over Peter sitting in a far corner with a copy of *Le Monde*, then Steven moved authoritively to the reception desk.

'My name is Stride, do you have a reservation for me?' Steven spoke slowly, in rich plummy tones, for very few of these damned people spoke English. The clerk checked swiftly, nodded, murmured a welcome and gave Steven the form and the key.

'Four One Six.' Steven checked the number loudly enough for Peter to hear. Peter had been watching the entrance carefully; fortunately there had been very few guests entering the lobby during the few minutes since Steven's arrival, and none of those could possibly have been Caliph surveillance. Of course, if this was a staging point, as Peter was certain it was, then Caliph would have no reason to put surveillance on Steven – not until he got much closer to the ultimate destination.

Steven moved to the elevator with a porter carrying his single small valise, and Peter drifted across and joined the small cluster of guests waiting at the elevators.

He rode up shoulder to shoulder with Steven in the crowded elevator, neither of them acknowledging the other's existence, and when Steven and the porter left at the fourth stage Peter rode on up three floors, walked the length of the corridor and back, then took the descending elevator to Steven's floor.

Steven had left the door to 416 off the catch, and Peter pushed it open and slipped in without knocking.

'My dear boy.' Steven was in his shirt sleeves. He had switched on the television, but now he turned down the sound volume and hurried to greet him with both affection and vast relief.

'No problems?' Peter asked.

'Like clockwork,' Steven told him. 'Would you like a drink? I got a bottle in the duty-free.'

While he hunted for glasses in the bathroom, Peter checked the room swiftly. A view down towards the square functional buildings of the market that had replaced the picturesque Les Halles in central Paris, matching curtains and covers on the twin beds, television and radio sets, between the beds, modern soulless furniture – it was a room, that was the most and the least that could be said for it

Steven carried in the glasses and handed one to Peter.

'Cheers!'

Peter tasted his whisky. It was too strong and the Parisian tap water tasted of chlorine. He put it aside.

'How is Caliph going to get instructions to you?'

'Got them already.' Steven went to his blazer, hanging over the back of the chair, and found a long white envelope in the inside pocket. 'This was left at the Air France Information Desk.'

Peter took the envelope and as he split the flap he sank onto one of the armchairs. There were three items in the envelope.

A first-class Air France airline ticket, a voucher for a chauffeur-driven limousine and a hotel reservation voucher.

The air ticket could have been purchased for cash at any Air France outlet or agency, the limousine and hotel bookings could have been made equally anonymously. There was no possibility of a trace back from any of these documents.

Peter opened the Air France ticket and read the destination. Something began to crawl against his skin, like the loathsome touch of body vermin. He closed the ticket and checked the two vouchers; now the sick feeling of betrayal and evil spread through his entire body, numbing his fingertips and coating the back of his tongue with a bitter metallic taste like copper salts.

The air ticket was for this evening's flight from Orly to Ben-Gurion Airport in Israel, the hired-car voucher was good for a single journey from there to Jerusalem, the hotel voucher was for a room in the King David Hotel in that ancient and holy city.

'What is it, Peter?'

'Nothing,' said Peter, only then aware that the sickness must have shown on his face. 'Jerusalem,' he went on. 'Caliph wants you in Jerusalem.'

There was one person in Jerusalem at that moment. Somebody who had been in his thoughts almost unceasingly since last he had embraced her in the darkness of Bora-Bora Island – so very long ago.

Caliph was in Jerusalem, and Magda Altmann was in Jerusalem – and the sickness was heavy in the pit of his stomach.

The deviousness of Caliph.

No, he told himself firmly. I have travelled that road already. It cannot be Magda.

The genius of Caliph, evil and effortless.

It is possible. He had to admit it then. With Caliph, anything is possible. Every time Caliph shook the dice box the numbers changed, different numbers, making different totals – but always completely plausible, always completely believable.

It was one of the basic proven theorems of his trade that

a man, any man, was blinded and deafened and rendered senseless by love. Peter was in love, and he knew it.

All right. So now I have to try and free my mind and think it all over again, as though I were not besotted.

'Peter, are you all right?' Steven demanded again, now with real concern. It was impossible to think with Steven hovering over him. He would have to put it aside.

'I am going to Jerusalem in your place,' Peter said.

'Come again, old boy?'

'We are changing places – you and I.'

'You won't get away with it.' Steven shook his head decidedly. 'Caliph will take you on the full toss.'

Peter picked up his Hermes case and went through into the bathroom. He worked quickly with the wig and artificial moustache and then called.

'Steven, come here.'

They stood side by side and stared at themselves in the mirror.

'Good God!' Steven grunted. Peter altered his stance slightly, conforming more closely to his brother.

'That's incredible. Never knew you were such a good-looking blighter,' Steven chuckled, and wagged his head wonderingly. Peter imitated the gesture perfectly.

'Damn it, Peter.' The chuckle dried on Steven's lips. 'That's enough. You're giving me the creeps.'

Peter pulled the wig off his head. 'It will work.'

'Yes,' Steven conceded. 'It will work – but how the hell did you know I would be wearing a blazer and greys?'

'Trick of the trade,' Peter told him. 'Don't worry about it. Let's go through the paperwork now.'

In the bedroom they laid out their personal documents in two piles, and went swiftly through them.

The passport photographs would pass readily enough.

'You have to shave your soup-strainer,' Peter told him, and Steven stroked his moustache with one finger, left and right – lingeringly, regretfully.

'Is that absolutely necessary? I'd feel like I was walking around in public with no trousers on.'

Peter took the slim gold ball-point from his inside pocket and a sheaf of hotel stationery from the drawer. He studied Steven's signature in the passport for a minute, and then dashed it off on the top sheet.

'No ' He shook his head, and tried again. It was like Steven's walk, cocky and confident, the 'T' was crossed with a flourishing sword stroke of the pen.

In sixty seconds he had it perfected.

'With that wig on your head you could walk into my bank any day and sign for the whole damned bundle,' Steven muttered uneasily. 'Then go home and climb into bed with Pat.'

'Now, *there* is an idea.' Peter looked thoughtful.

'Don't joke about it,' Steven pleaded.

'Who's joking?' Peter went through the credit cards, club membership cards, driver's licence and all the other clutter of civilized existence.

Steven's mastery of his brother's signature was not nearly as effective, but after twenty minutes' practice was just adequate for hotel registration purposes.

'Here is the address of a hotel on the left bank. Magnificent restaurant, and the management are very understanding if you should want to invite a young lady up to your room for a drink.'

'Perish the thought.' Steven looked smug at the prospect.

'It should only be for a few days, Steven. Just keep very low. Pay cash for everything. Keep clear of the George V or the Meurice, Le Doyen and Maxim's – all the places where they know you.'

They went carefully over the last details of the exchange of identity, while Steven shaved off the moustache and anointed the bare patch tenderly with Eau de Sauvage.

'You'd better move now,' Peter told him at last. 'Wear

this—' It was Peter's buff trenchcoat that would cover his blazer. ' – And let's change ties.'

Steven was ready, and he stood rather awkwardly by the door, in the tightly fitting trenchcoat.

'Steven, can I ask you a question?' Peter did not know why he had to know now, it had been buried so deeply for so long and yet at this moment it was deadly important to know.

'Of course, old boy.' Steven seemed to welcome the postponement of the moment of parting.

'Sandhurst.' Peter tried to keep the embarrassment out of his voice. 'I never asked you before – but you didn't do it, did you, Steven?'

Steven met his eyes calmly, steadily. 'No, Peter. I did not do it. My word on it.'

Peter took his brother's proffered right hand and squeezed it hard. It was ridiculous to feel so relieved.

'I'm glad, Steven.'

'Take care of yourself, old boy.'

'I will,' Peter nodded. 'But if anything happens,' Peter hesitated, ' – Melissa-Jane—'

'Don't worry. I'll take care of it.'

Why do Englishmen have such difficulty talking to each other, Peter wondered, let alone communicating affection and gratitude?

'Well, I'll be getting along then,' said Steven.

'Take a guard on your middle stump, and don't be caught in the slips,' Peter cautioned him with the old inanity.

'Count on it,' said Steven, and went out into the passage, closing the door behind him firmly, leaving his brother to think about Jerusalem.

Only the name had changed from Lod to Ben-Gurion – otherwise the Arrivals Hall was as Peter remembered it. One of the few airports on the globe which has sufficient luggage trolleys, so that the passengers do not have to fight for possession.

In the Arrivals Hall there was a young Israeli driver with the name:

Sir Steven Stride

printed in white chalk on a schoolboy's black slate.

The driver wore a navy-blue cap with a black patent-leather peak. It was his only item of uniform, otherwise he was dressed in sandals and a white cotton shirt. His English had the usual strong American turn to it, and his attitude was casual and friendly – he might be driving the limousine today, but tomorrow he could be at the controls of a Centurion tank, and he was as good a man as his passenger any day.

'Shalom, Shalom,' he greeted Peter. 'Is that all your luggage?'

'Yes.'

'*Beserder*. Let's go.' He did not offer to push Peter's trolley, but chatted amicably as he led him out to the limousine.

It was a stretched-out 240 D Mercedes Benz – almost brand new, lovingly polished – but somebody had painted a pair of squinting eyes on each side of the chrome three-pointed star on the boot of the vehicle.

They had hardly pulled out through the airport gates when one of the characteristic aromas of Israel filled the cab of the Mercedes – the smell of orange blossom from the citrus orchards that lined each side of the road.

For some reason the smell made Peter feel uneasy, a sensation of having missed something, of having neglected some vital aspect. He tried to think it all out again, from the beginning, but the driver kept up a running commentary as they pulled up the new double highway, over the hills through the pine forests towards Jerusalem, and the voice distracted him.

Peter wished he had kept the list that he had drawn up in the hotel room at Orly instead of destroying it. He tried to reconstruct it in his mind.

There were a dozen items on the plus side. The third was:

Magda told me about Cactus Flower. Would she have done so if she was Caliph?

And then directly opposite, in the 'minus' column:

If Magda is Caliph, then 'Cactus Flower' does not exist. It was an invention for some undisclosed reason.

This was the item that pricked him like a burr in a woollen sock. He kept coming back to it; there was a link missing from the logic of it and he tried to tease it loose. It was there just below the surface of his mind, and he knew instinctively that if he missed it the consequences would be dire.

The driver kept chatting, turning to glance back at him every few minutes with a cheerful demand for recognition.

'That's right, isn't it?'

Peter grunted. The man was irritating him – the missing item was there, just beginning to surface. He could see the shape of it. Why had the smell of orange blossom worried him? The smell of flowers? Cactus flower? There was something there, something missing from the list.

If Magda is not Caliph then— Was that it? He was not certain. ' – Will that be all right, then?' The driver was insisting again.

'I'm sorry – what was that?'

'I said, I had to drop a parcel off at my mother-in-law,' the driver explained again. 'It's from my wife.'

'Can't you do that on your way back?'

'I'm not going back tonight—' The driver grinned

winningly over his shoulder. ' – My mother-in-law lives right on our way. It won't take five minutes. I promised my wife I'd get it to her mother today.'

'Oh, very well then,' Peter snapped. There was something about the man he did not like, and he had lost track of the item that had been worrying him.

He felt as though he was in a chess game with a vastly superior opponent, and he had overlooked a castle on an open file, or a knight in a position to fork simultaneous check on his king and queen.

'We turn off here,' the driver explained, and swung off into a section of new apartment blocks, all of them built of the custard-yellow Jerusalem stone, row upon row of them, Israel's desperate attempt to house its new citizens. At this time of evening the streets were deserted, as families gathered for the evening meal.

The driver jinked through the maze of identical-seeming streets with garrulous confidence and then braked and parked in front of one of the square, boxlike, yellow buildings.

'Two minutes,' he promised, and jumped out of the Mercedes, scampered around to the rear and opened the boot. There was a scratching sound, a small bump and then the lid of the boot slammed and the driver came back into Peter's line of vision – carrying a brown paper parcel.

He grinned at Peter, with the ridiculous cap pushed onto the back of his head, mouthed another assurance through the closed window: 'Two minutes—' and went into the main door of the apartment.

Peter hoped he might be longer. The silence was precious. He closed his eyes, and concentrated.

If Magda is not Caliph then – then— There was the ticking sound of the engine cooling, or was it the dashboard clock? Peter thrust the sound to the back of his mind.

– then – then Cactus Flower exists. Yes, that was it!

Cactus Flower exists, and if he exists he is close enough to Caliph to know of Sir Steven Stride's threat to expose him—

Peter sat upright, rigid in his seat. He had believed that Steven Stride would be perfectly safe – until after the meeting with Caliph. That was the terrible mistake.

– Cactus Flower must stop Steven Stride reaching Caliph! Yes, of course. Christ, how had he not seen it before. Cactus Flower was Mossad, and Peter was sitting in a street of Jerusalem – Mossad's front yard – dressed as Steven Stride.

Christ! He felt the certainty of mortal danger Cactus Flower probably made the arrangements himself. If Magda Altmann is not Caliph, then I am walking right into Cactus Flower's sucker punch!

The damned clock kept ticking, a sound as nerve-racking as a leaky faucet.

I am in Cactus Flower's city – in Cactus Flower's limo—

The ticking. Oh God! It was not coming from the dashboard Peter turned his head. It was coming from *behind him*; from the boot which the driver had opened and in which he had moved something. Something that was now ticking away quietly.

Peter wrenched the door handle and hit the door with his shoulder, instinctively grabbing the Hermes case with his other hand.

They would have stripped out the metal partition between the boot and the back seat to allow the blast to cut through. There was probably only the leather upholstery between him and whatever was ticking. That was why he had heard it so clearly.

Time seemed to have slowed, so he was free to think it out as the seconds dropped as lingeringly as spilled honey.

Infernal machine, he thought. Why that ridiculously nineteenth-century term should occur to him now, he could not guess, a relic from the childhood days when he read *Boy's Own Paper*, perhaps.

He was out of the Mercedes now, almost losing his balance as his feet hit the unsurfaced and broken sidewalk.

It is probably plastic explosive with a clockwork timer on the detonator, he thought, as he started to run. What delay would they use? Thirty seconds? No, the driver had to get well away. He had said two minutes, said it twice –

The thoughts raced through his mind, but his legs seemed to be shackled, dragging against an enormous weight. Like trying to run waist deep in the sucking surf of a sandy beach.

– It will be two minutes, and he has been gone that long—

Ten paces ahead of him there was a low wall that had been built as a flower box around the apartment block. It was knee high, a double brick wall with the cavity filled with dry yellow earth and precariously sustaining the life of a few wizened oleander bushes.

Peter dived head first over the wall, breaking his fall with shoulder and forearm, and rolling back hard under the protection of the low wall.

Above his head were the large windows of the ground-floor apartments. Lying on his side, peering up at them, Peter saw the reflection of the parked Mercedes as though in a mirror.

He covered his ears with the palms of both hands. The Mercedes was only fifty feet away. He watched it in the glass, his body braced, his mouth wide open to absorb blast shock in his sinuses.

The Mercedes erupted. It seemed to open quite sedately, like one of those time-elapse movies of a rose blooming. The shining metal spread and distorted like grotesque black petals, and bright white flame shot through it – that was all Peter saw, for the row of apartment windows disappeared, blown away in a million glittering shards by the blast wave, leaving the windows gaping like the toothless mouths of old decrepit men, and at the same moment the blast smashed into Peter.

Even though it was muted by the thick wall of the flower box, it crushed him, seemed to drive in his ribs, and the air whooshed from his lungs. The fearsome din of the explosion clamoured in his head, filling his skull with little bright chips of rainbow light.

He thought he must have lost consciousness for a moment, then there was the patter of falling debris raining down around him and something struck him a painful blow in the small of his back. It spurred him.

He dragged himself to his feet, struggling to refill his empty lungs. He knew he had to get away before the security forces arrived, or he could expect intensive interrogation which would certainly disclose the fact that he was not Sir Steven.

He started to run. The street was still deserted, although he could hear the beginning of the uproar which must follow. The cries of anguish and of fear.

He reached the corner and stopped running. He walked quickly to the next alley behind an apartment block. There were no street lights and he paused in the shadows. By now a dozen figures shouting questions and conjecture were hurrying towards the smoke and dust of the explosion.

Peter recovered his breath and dusted down his blazer and slacks, waiting until the confusion and shouting were at their peak. Then he walked quietly away.

On the main road he joined a short queue at the bus stop. The bus dropped him off in the Jaffa Road.

He found a café opposite the bus stop and went through into the men's room. He was unmarked, but pale and strained; his hands still shook from the shock of the blast as he combed his hair.

He went back into the café, found a corner seat and ordered falafel and pitta bread with coffee.

He sat there for half an hour, considering his next move.

If Magda Altmann is not Caliph— he repeated the conundrum which he had solved just in time to save his life.

Magda Altmann is not Caliph! He knew it then with utter certainty. Cactus Flower had tried to stop Sir Steven Stride reaching Caliph with his denunciation. Therefore Magda had told him the truth. His relief flooded his body with a great warm glow – and his first instinct was to telephone her at the Mossad number she had given him. Then he saw the danger. Cactus Flower was Mossad. He dared not go near her – not yet.

What must he do then? And he knew the answer without having to search for it. He must do what he had come to do. He must find Caliph, and the only fragile thread he had to follow was the trail that Caliph had laid for him.

He left the café and found a taxi at the rank on the corner.

'King David Hotel,' Peter said, and sank back in the seat.

At least I know the danger of Cactus Flower now, he thought grimly. I won't walk into the next one blind.

Peter took one glance around the room that had been reserved for him. It was in the back of the hotel and across the road the tall bell tower of the Y.M.C.A. made a fine stance from which a sniper could command the two windows.

'I ordered a suite,' Peter snapped at the reception clerk who had led him up.

'I'm sorry, Sir Steven.' The man was immediately flustered. 'There must have been a mistake.'

Another glance around the room and Peter had noted half a dozen sites at which Cactus Flower might have laid another explosive charge to back up the one that had failed in the back of the Mercedes. He would prefer to spend a night in a pit full of cobras rather than accept the quarters that Cactus Flower had prepared for him.

Peter stepped back into the passage and fixed the clerk with his most imperious gaze. The man scampered and returned within five minutes – looking mightily relieved.

'We have one of our best suites for you.'

Number 122 commanded a magnificent view across the valley to the Jaffa Gate in the wall of the Old City, and in the centre of this vista towered the Church of the Last Supper.

The gardens of the hotel were lush with lawns and tall graceful palms, children shrieked gleefully around the swimming pool while a cool light breeze broke the heat.

The suite abutted onto the long open terrace, and the moment he was alone, Peter lowered the heavy roller shutters across the terrace door. Cactus Flower could too easily send a man in that way. Then Peter stepped out onto the private balcony.

On the tall stone battlements of the French Consulate adjoining the gardens they were lowering the Tricolour against the flaming backdrop of the sunset. Peter watched it for a moment – then concentrated again on the security of the suite.

There was possible access from the room next door, an easy step across from window to balcony. Peter hesitated – then decided to leave the balcony unshuttered. He could not bring himself to accept the claustrophobic effect of a completely shuttered room.

Instead he drew the curtains and ordered a large whisky and soda from room service. He needed it. It had been a long hard day.

Then he stripped off tie and shirt, wig and moustache and washed away some of the tensions. He was towelling himself when there was a tap on the door.

'Damned quick service,' he muttered, and clapped the wig on his head and stepped into the lounge, just as a key rattled in the lock and the door swung open. Peter lifted the towel and pretended to be still drying his face to cover the lack of moustache on his lip.

'Come in,' he gruffed through the towel, and then froze in the doorway, and a vice seemed to close around his heart and restrict his breathing.

She wore a man's open-neck shirt, with patch pockets on the breasts, and khaki combat breeches hugged her narrow hips. The long legs were thrust into soft-soled canvas boots. Yet she carried herself with the same unforced chic as if she had been dressed in the height of Parisian fashion

'Sir Steven.' She closed the door swiftly behind her, and Peter saw her palm the slim metal pick with which she had turned the lock. 'I'm Magda Altmann, we have met before I have come to warn you that you are in very grave danger.'

The abundant short curls formed a dark halo around her head, and her eyes were huge and green with concern.

'You must immediately leave this country. I have my private executive jet aircraft at an airfield near here—'

Peter lowered the towel enough to allow himself to speak.

'Why are you telling me this?' he interrupted her brusquely. 'And why should I believe you?'

He saw the quick roses of anger bloom in her cheeks.

'You are dabbling in things you do not understand.'

'Why should you want to warn me?' Peter insisted.

'Because—' she hesitated and then went on sharply, ' – because you are Peter Stride's brother. For that reason and no other I would not want you killed.'

Peter tossed the towel back into the bathroom and with the same movement pulled off the wig and dropped it onto the chair beside him.

'Peter!' Astonishment riveted her and she stared at him, the colour that anger had painted in her cheeks fled and her eyes turned a deep luminous green. He had forgotten once again how beautiful she was.

'Well, don't just stand there,' he said, and she ran to him on those long, graceful legs and flung her arms around his neck.

They strained together silently, neither of them found words necessary for many minutes. Then she broke away.

'Peter, darling – I cannot stay long. I took a terrible chance coming here at all. They are watching the hotel and the girls on the switchboard are Mossad. That is why I could not telephone—'

'Tell me everything you can,' he ordered.

'All right, but hold me, *chéri*. I do not wish to waste a minute of this little time we have together.'

She hid in the bathroom when the waiter brought the whisky, then joined Peter on the couch.

'Cactus Flower reported to control that Steven had requested a meeting with Caliph, and that he intended to denounce him. That was all I knew until yesterday – but I could build on that. First of all I was amazed that Steven was the subject of the first Cactus Flower report and not you, Peter—' She caressed the smooth hard brown muscle of his chest as she spoke. ' – It had never occured to me, even when we discussed the fact that the report mentioned no Christian name.'

'It didn't occur to me either, not until I'd already left Les Neuf Poissons.'

'Then, of course, I guessed that you had taxed Steven with it, and told him the source of your information. It would have been a crazy thing to do – not your usual style, at all. But I thought that being your brother—' She trailed off.

'That is exactly what I did—'

'Peter, we could still talk if we were on the bed,' she murmured. 'I have been without you for so long.'

Her bare skin felt like hot satin, and they lay entwined with the hard smooth plain of her belly pressed to his. Her mouth was against his ear.

' – Steven's request for a meeting went directly to Caliph through a channel other than Cactus Flower. He had no chance to head it off—'

'Who is Cactus Flower, have you found that out?'

'No.' She shook her head. 'I still do not know.' And she raked her long fingernails lightly down across his belly.

'If you do that – I cannot think clearly,' he protested.

'I am sorry.' She brought her hand up to his cheek. 'Anyway, Caliph instructed Cactus Flower to arrange the meeting with Steven. I did not know what arrangements were being made – until I saw Sir Steven's name on the immigration lists this evening. I was not particularly looking for his name, but as soon as I saw it I guessed what was happening. I guessed that Cactus Flower had enticed him here to make his interception easier. It took me three hours to find where Sir Steven would be staying.'

They were both silent now, and she lowered her face and pressed it into the soft of his neck, sighing with happiness.

'Oh God, Peter. How I missed you.'

'Listen, my darling. You must tell me everything else you have.' Peter lifted her chin tenderly so he could see her face and her eyes came back into focus.

'Did you know that there was to be an assassination attempt on Steven?'

'No – but it was the logical step for Mossad to protect Cactus Flower.'

'What else?'

'Nothing.'

'You don't know if actual arrangements have been made for a meeting between Caliph and Steven?'

'No, I don't know,' she admitted.

'You still have no indication at all of Caliph's identity?'

'No, none at all.'

They were silent again, but now she propped herself on one elbow and watched his face as he spoke.

'Cactus Flower would have to make the arrangements for the meeting as Caliph instructed. He would not be able to take the chance of faking it – not with Caliph.'

Magda nodded in silent agreement.

'Therefore we have to believe that at this moment Caliph is close, very close.'

'Yes.' She nodded again, but reluctantly.

'That means that I have to go on impersonating Steven.'

'Peter, no. They will kill you.'

'They have already tried—' Peter told her grimly, and quietly outlined the destruction of the Mercedes. She touched the bruise in the small of his back where he had been struck by flying debris from the explosion.

'They won't let you get close to Caliph.'

'They may have no choice,' Peter told her. 'Caliph is so concerned for his own safety – he is going to insist on the meeting.'

'They will try and kill you again,' she implored him.

'Perhaps, but I'm betting the meeting with Caliph is arranged to take place very soon. They won't have much opportunity to set up another elaborate trap like the Mercedes, and I'll be expecting it – I've got to go ahead with it, Magda.'

'Oh, Peter—' But he touched her lips, silencing the protest, and he was thinking aloud again.

'Let's suppose Mossad knew that I was not Steven Stride, that my real purpose was not to denounce Cactus Flower? What difference would that make to the thinking at Mossad?'

She considered that. 'I'm not certain.'

'If they knew it was Peter Stride impersonating Steven Stride,' he insisted, 'would that make them curious enough to let the meeting go ahead?'

'Peter, are you suggesting I turn in a report to my control at Mossad – ?'

'Would you do that?'

'Sweet merciful God,' she whispered. 'I could be signing your death warrant, Peter my darling.'

' – or you could be saving my life.'

'I don't know.' She sat up erect in the bed and ran the fingers of both hands through the short dark curls, the lamplight glowed on her skin with a pale, smooth opalescence and the small fine breasts changed shape as she moved her arms. 'Oh, Peter, I don't know.'

'It could be our only chance to ever get close to Caliph,' he insisted, and the lovely face was racked with indecision.

'Caliph believes I have killed you, he believes that I have transmitted a warning to him through my brother. He will have his guard as low as ever it will be. We will never have a chance again like this.'

'I am so afraid for you, Peter. I am so afraid for myself without you—' She did not finish it, but pulled up her long naked legs and hugged her knees to her breasts. It was a defensive foetal position.

'Will you do it?' he asked gently.

'You want me to tell my control your real identity, to tell him that I believe your real purpose is not to denounce Cactus Flower – but some other unknown—'

'That is right.'

She turned her head and looked at him.

'I will do it in exchange for your promise,' she decided.

'What is that?'

'If I judge from my control at Mossad that you are still in danger, and that they still intend intercepting you before you reach Caliph – then I want your promise that you will abandon the attempt. That you will immediately go to where the Lear is waiting and that you will allow Pierre to fly you out of here to a safe place.'

'You will be honest with me?' he asked. 'You will judge Mossad's reaction fairly – and even if there is a half-decent chance of me reaching Caliph you will allow me to take that chance?'

She nodded, but he went on grimly, making certain of it.

'Swear it to me!'

'I would not try to prevent you – just as long as there is a chance of success.'

'Swear it to me, Magda.'

'On my love for you, I swear it,' she said quietly, and he relaxed slightly.

'And I in turn swear to you that if there is no chance of meeting Caliph – I will leave on the Lear.'

She turned against his chest, wrapping both her arms around his neck.

'Make love to me, Peter. Now! Quickly! I have to have that at least.'

As she dressed she went over the arrangements for communicating.

'I cannot come through the switchboard here – I explained why,' she told him as she laced the canvas boots 'You must stay here, in this room where I can reach you If there is danger I will send someone to you. It will be somebody I trust. He will say simply. "Magda sent me," and you must go with him. He will take you to Pierre and the Lear jet.'

She stood up and belted the khaki breeches around her narrow waist, crossing to the mirror to comb out the dark damp tangle of her curls.

'If you hear nothing from me it will mean that I judge there is still a chance of reaching Caliph—' Then she paused and her expression altered. ' – Are you armed, Peter?' She was watching him in the mirror as she worked with her hair. He shook his head.

'I could get a weapon to you – a knife, a pistol?'

And again he shook his head. 'They will search me before I am allowed near Caliph. If they find a weapon—' He did not have to finish it.

'You are right,' she agreed.

She turned back to him from the mirror, buttoning the shirt over the nipples of her breasts, which were still swollen and dark rosy red from their loving.

'It will all happen very quickly now, Peter. One way or the other it will be over by tomorrow night. I have a feeling here—' She touched herself between the small breasts that pushed out the cotton of her shirt. 'Now kiss me. I have stayed too long already – for the safety of both of us.'

Peter slept very little after Magda left him, even though he was very tired. A dozen times he started awake during the night with every nerve strung tightly, rigid and sweating in his bed.

He was up before first light, and ordered one of those strange Israeli breakfasts of salads and hard-boiled eggs with pale green centres to be sent up to his room.

Then he settled down once more to wait.

He waited the morning out, and when there had been no message from Magda by noon, the certainty increased that Mossad had decided not to prevent the meeting with Caliph. If there had been any doubt in Magda's mind she would have sent for him. He had a light lunch sent up to the room.

The flat bright glare of noon gradually mellowed into warm butter-yellow, the shadows crept out timidly from the foot of the palm trees in the garden as the sun wheeled across a sky of clear high aching blue, and still Peter waited.

When there was an hour left of daylight, the telephone rang again. It startled him, but he reached for it quickly.

'Good evening, Sir Steven. Your driver is here to fetch you,' said the girl at the reception desk.

'Thank you. Please tell him I will be down directly,' said Peter.

He was fully dressed, had been ready all that day to move immediately. He needed only to place the crocodile skin case in the cupboard and lock it, then he left the room and strode down the corridor to the elevators

He had no way of knowing if he was going to meet Caliph, or if he was about to be spirited out of Israel in Magda's Lear jet.

'Your limousine is waiting outside,' the pretty girl at the desk told him. 'Have a nice evening.'

'I hope so,' Peter agreed. 'Thank you.'

The car was a small Japanese compact, and the driver was a woman, plump and grey-haired with a friendly, ugly face like Golda Meir, Peter thought.

He let himself into the back seat, and waited expectantly for the message, 'Magda sent me.'

Instead, the woman bade him 'Shalom Shalom' politely, started the engine, switched on the headlights and drove serenely out of the hotel grounds.

They swept sedately around the outer walls of the old city in the gathering dusk, and dropped down in the valley of Kidron. Glancing back Peter saw the elegant new buildings of the Jewish quarter rising above the tops of the walls.

When last he had been in Jerusalem that area had been a deserted ruin, deliberately devastated by the Arabs.

The resurrection of that holy quarter of Judaism seemed to epitomize the spirit of these extraordinary people, Peter thought.

It was a good conversational opening, and he remarked on the new development to his driver.

She replied in Hebrew, clearly denying the ability to speak English. Peter tried her in French with the same result

The lady has been ordered to keep her mouth tight shut, he decided.

The night came down upon them as they skirted the lower slopes of the Mount of Olives, and left the last straggling buildings of the Arab settlements. The lady driver settled down to a comfortable speed, and the road was almost deserted. It dropped gently down through a dark shallow valley, with the crests of a desolate desert landscape humped up on each side of the wide metalled road.

The sky was empty of cloud or haze, and the stars were brighter white and clearer, as the last of the day faded from the western sky behind them.

The road had been well sign-posted, ever since they had left the city. Their direction was eastward towards the Jordan, the Dead Sea and Jericho – and twenty-five minutes after leaving the King David, Peter glimpsed in the headlights the signpost on the right-hand side of the road, declaring in English, Arabic and Hebrew that they were now descending below sea level into the valley of the Dead Sea.

Once again Peter attempted to engage the driver in conversation, but her reply was monosyllabic. Anyway, Peter decided, there was nothing she would be able to tell him. The car was from a hire company. There was a plastic nameplate fastened onto the dashboard giving the company's name, address and hire rates. All she would know was their final destination – and he would know that soon enough himself.

Peter made no further attempt to speak to her, but remained completely alert; without detectable movement he performed the pre-jump paratrooper exercises, pitting muscle against muscle so that his body would not stiffen with long inactivity but would be tuned to explode from stillness into instant violent action.

Ahead of them the warning signals of the crossroads caught the headlights, and the driver slowed and signalled the left turn. As the headlights caught the signpost, Peter saw that they had taken the Jericho road, turning away from the Dead Sea, and heading up the valley of the Jordan towards Galilee in the north.

Now the bull's horns of the new moon rose slowly over the harsh mountain peaks across the valley, and gave enough light to pick out small features in the dry blasted desert around them.

Again the driver slowed, this time for the town of Jericho itself, the oldest site of human communal habitation on this earth – for six thousand years men had lived here and their wastes had raised a mountainous tell hundreds of feet above the desert floor. Archaeologists had already excavated the collapsed walls that Joshua had brought crashing down with a blast of his ram's horns.

'A hell of a trick.' Peter grinned in the darkness. 'Better than the nuke bomb.'

Just before they reached the tell, the driver swung off the main road. She took the narrow secondary road between the clustered buildings – souvenir stalls, Arab cafés, antique dealers – and slowed for the twisting uneven surface.

They ground up onto higher dry hills in low gear, and at the crest the driver turned again onto a dirt track. Now fine talcum dust filled the interior and Peter sneezed once at the tickle of it.

Half a mile along the track a noticeboard stood on trestle legs, blocking the right of way.

'Military Zone,' it proclaimed. 'No access beyond this point.'

The driver had to pull out onto the rocky verge to avoid the notice, and there were no sentries to enforce the printed order.

Quite suddenly Peter became aware of the great black cliff face that rose sheer into the starry night ahead of them – blotting out half the sky.

Something stirred in Peter's memory – the high cliffs above Jericho, looking out across the valley of the Dead Sea; of course, he remembered then – this was the scene of the temptation of Christ. How did Matthew record it? Peter cast for the exact quotation:

> Again, the devil taketh him up into an exceeding high mountain, and sheweth him all the kingdoms of the world, and the glory of them –

Had Caliph deliberately chosen this place for its mystical association, was it all part of the quasi-religious image that Caliph had of himself?

> He shall give his angels charge concerning thee: and in their hands they shall bear thee up –

Did Caliph truly see himself as the heir to ultimate power over all the kingdoms of the world – that power that the ancient chroniclers had referred to as 'The Sixth Order of Angels'?

Peter felt his spirits quail in the face of such monumental madness, such immense and menacing vision, compared to which he felt insignificant and ineffectual. Fear fell over him like a gladiator's net, enmeshing his resolve, weakening him. He struggled with it silently, fighting himself clear of its mesh before it could render him helpless in Caliph's all-embracing power.

The driver stopped abruptly, turned in the seat and switched on the cab light. She studied him for a moment.

Was there a touch of pity in her old and ugly face, Peter wondered?

'Here,' she said gently.

Peter drew his wallet from the inner pocket of his blazer.

'No,' she shook her head. 'No, you owe nothing.'

'*Toda raba.*' Peter thanked her in his fragmentary Hebrew, and opened the side door.

The desert air was still and cold, and there was the sagey smell of the low thorny scrub.

'Shalom,' said the woman through the open window; then she swung the vehicle in a tight turn. The headlights swept the grove of date palms ahead of them, and then turned back towards the open desert. Slowly the small car pitched and wove along the track in the direction from which they had come.

Peter turned his back on it, allowing his eyes to become accustomed to the muted light of the yellow horned moon and the whiter light of the fat desert stars.

After a few minutes he picked his way carefully into the palm grove. There was the smell of smoke from a dung fire, and the fine blue mist of smoke hung amongst the trees.

Somewhere in the grove he heard a goat bleat plaintively, and then the high thin wail of a child – there must be a Bedouin encampment in the oasis. He moved towards it, and came abruptly into an opening surrounded by the palms. The earth had been churned by the hooves of many beasts, and Peter stumbled slightly in the loose footing and then caught his balance.

In the centre of the opening was the stone parapet which guarded a deep fresh-water well. There was a primitive windlass set above the parapet and another dark object which Peter could not immediately identify, dark and shapeless, crouching upon the parapet.

He went towards it cautiously, and felt his heart tumble within him as it moved.

It was a human figure, in some long voluminous robe

that swept the sandy earth, so that it seemed to float towards him in the gloom.

The figure stopped five paces from him, and he saw that the head was covered by a monk's cowl of the same dark woollen cloth, so that the face was in a forbidding black hole beneath the cowl.

'Who are you?' Peter demanded, and his voice rasped in his own ears. The monk did not reply, but shook one hand free of the wide sleeve and beckoned to him to follow, then turned and glided away into the palm grove.

Peter went after him, and within a hundred yards was stepping out hard to keep the monk in sight. His light city shoes were not made for this heavy going, loose sand with scattered outcrops of shattered rock.

They left the palm grove and directly ahead of them, less than a quarter of a mile away, the cliff fell from the sky like a vast cascade of black stone.

The monk led him along a rough but well-used footpath, and though Peter tried to narrow the distance between them, he found that he would have to break into a trot to do so – for although the monk appeared to be a broad and heavy man beneath the billowing robe, yet he moved lithely and lightly.

They reached the cliff, and the path zig-zagged up it, at such a gradient that they had to lean forward into it. The surface was loose with shale and dry earth – becoming progressively steeper. Then underfoot the path was paved, the worn steps of solid rock.

On one hand the drop away into the valley was deeper always and the sheer cliff on the other seemed to lean out as though to press him over the edge.

Always the monk was ahead of him, tireless and quick, his feet silent on the worn steps, and there was no sound of labouring breath. Peter realized that a man of that stamina and bulk must be immensely powerful. He did not move as you might expect a man of God and prayer to move. There was the awareness and balance of a fighting man about him, the unconscious pride and force of the warrior. With Caliph nothing was ever as it seemed, he thought.

The higher they climbed, so the moonlit panorama below them became more magnificent, a soaring vista of desert and mountain with the great shield of the Dead Sea a brilliant beaten silver beneath the stars.

– All the kingdoms of the world, and the glory of them, Peter thought.

They had not paused to rest once on the climb. How high was it, Peter wondered – a thousand feet, fifteen hundred perhaps? His own breathing was deep and steady, he was not yet fully extended and the light sweat that dewed his forehead cooled in the night air.

Something nudged his memory, and he sniffed at the faintly perfumed aroma on the air. It was not steady, but he had caught it faintly once or twice during the climb.

Peter was plagued by the non-smoker's acute sense of smell; perfumes and odours always had special significance for him – and this smell was important, but he could not quite place it now. It nagged at him, but then it was lost in a host of other more powerful odours – the smell of human beings in community.

The smell of cooking smoke, of food and the underlying sickly taint of rotting garbage and primitive sewage disposal.

Somewhere long ago he had seen photographs of the ancient monastery built into the top of these spectacular cliffs, the caves and subterranean chambers honeycombed the crest of the rock face, and walls of hewn rock had been built above them by men dead these thousand years.

Yet the memory of that faint perfumed aroma lingered with Peter, as they climbed the last hundred feet of that terrifying drop and came out suddenly against the stone tower and thick fortification, into which was set a heavy timber door twelve feet high and studded with iron bolts.

At their approach the door swung open. There was a

narrow stone passageway ahead of them lit by a single storm lantern in a niche at the corner of the passageway.

As Peter stepped through the gate, two other figures closed on each side of him out of the darkness and he moved instinctively to defend himself, but checked the movement and stood quiescent with his hand half raised as they searched him with painstaking expertise for a weapon.

Both these men were dressed in single-piece combat suits, and they wore canvas paratrooper boots. Their heads were covered by coarse woollen scarves wound over mouth and nose so only their eyes showed. Each of them carried the ubiquitous Uzi sub-machine guns, loaded and cocked and slung on shoulder straps.

At last they stood back satisfied, and the monk led Peter on through a maze of narrow passages. Somewhere there was the sound of monks at their devotions, the harsh chanting of the Greek Orthodox service. The sound of it, and the smoky cedarwood aroma of burning incense, became stronger, until the monk led Peter into a cavernous, dimly lit church nave hewn from the living rock of the cliff.

In the gloom the old Greek monks sat like long embalmed mummies in their tall dark wooden pews. Their time-worn faces masked by the great black bushes of their beards. Only their eyes glittered, alive as the jewels and precious metals that gilded the ancient religious icons on the stone walls.

The reek of incense was overpowering, and the hoarse chant of the office missed not a single beat as Peter and the robed monk passed swiftly amongst them.

In the impenetrable shadows at the rear of the church, the monk seemed abruptly to disappear, but when Peter reached the spot he discovered that one of the carved pews had been swung aside to reveal a dark secret opening in the rock.

Peter went into it cautiously It was totally dark – but his feet found shallow stone steps, and he climbed a twisting stairway through the rock – counting the steps to five hundred, each step approximately six inches high.

Abruptly he stepped out into the cool desert night again. He was in a paved open courtyard, with the brilliant panoply of the stars overhead, the cliff rising straight ahead and a low stone parapet protecting the sheer drop into the valley behind him.

Peter realized that this must be one of the remotest and most easily defensible rendezvous that Caliph could have chosen – and there were more guards here.

Again they came forward, two of them, and searched him once again even more thoroughly than at the monastery gate.

While they worked Peter looked around him swiftly. The level courtyard was perched like an eagle's eyrie on the brink of the precipice, the parapet wall was five feet high Across the courtyard were the oblong entrances to caves carved into the cliff face. They would probably be the retreats of the monks seeking solitude.

There were other men in the courtyard, wearing the same uniform with heads hidden by the Arab shawl headgear. Two of them were setting out flashlight beacons in the shape of a pyramid.

Peter realized they were beacons for an aircraft. – Not an aircraft. A helicopter was the only vehicle which would be able to get into this precarious perch on the side of the precipice.

All right then, the beacons would serve to direct a helicopter down into the level paved courtyard.

One of the armed guards ended his body search by checking the buckle of Peter's belt, tugging it experimentally to make certain it was not the handle of a concealed blade.

He stood back and motioned Peter forward. Across the courtyard the big monk waited patiently at the entrance to one of the stone cells that opened onto the courtyard.

Peter stooped through the low entrance. The cell was dimly lit by a stinking kerosene lamp set in a stone niche above the narrow cot. There was a crude wooden table against one wall, a plain crucifix above it and no other ornamentation.

Hewn from the rock wall was a ledge which acted as a shelf for a dozen heavy battered leather-bound books and a few basic eating utensils. It was also a primitive seat.

The monk motioned him towards it, but himself remained standing by the entrance to the cell with his hands thrust into the wide sleeves of his cassock, his face turned away and still masked completely by the deep hood.

There was utter silence from the courtyard beyond the doorway, but it was an electric waiting silence.

Suddenly Peter was aware of the perfumed aroma again, here in the crude stone cell, and then with a small tingling shock he recognized it. The smell came from the monk.

He knew instantly who the big man in the monk's cowl was, and the knowledge confused him utterly, for long stricken moments.

Then like the click of a well-oiled lock slipping home it all came together. He knew – oh God – he knew at last.

The aroma he had recognized was the faint trace of the perfumed smoke of expensive Dutch cheroots, and he stared fixedly at the big hooded monk.

Now there was a sound on the air, a faint flutter like moth's wings against the glass of the lantern, and the monk cocked his head slightly, listening intently.

Peter was balancing distances and times and odds in his head.

The monk, the five armed men in the courtyard, the approaching helicopter –

The monk was the most dangerous factor. Now that Peter knew who he was, he knew also that he was one of the most highly trained fighting men against whom he could ever match himself.

The five men in the yard – Peter blinked with sudden realization. *They would not be there any longer* It was as simple as that. Caliph would never allow himself to be seen by any but his most trusted lieutenants, and by those about to die. The monk would have sent them away. They would be waiting close by, but it would take them time to get back into action.

There were only the monk and Caliph. For he knew that the dinning of rotor and engine was bringing Caliph in to the rendezvous. The helicopter sounded as though it were already directly overhead. The monk's attention was on it. Peter could see how he held his head under the cowl, he was off-guard for the first time.

Peter heard the sound of the spinning rotors change as the pilot altered pitch for the vertical descent into the tiny courtyard. The cell was lit through the doorway by the reflection of the helicopter's landing lights beating down into the courtyard with a relentless white glare.

Dust began to swirl from the down-draught of the rotors, it smoked in pale wisps into the cell and the monk moved.

He stepped to the doorway, the empty dark hole in the cowl which was his face turned briefly away from Peter as he glanced out through the entrance of the cell.

It was the moment for which Peter had waited, his whole body was charged, like the S in an adder's neck before it strikes. At the instant that the monk turned his head away, Peter launched himself across the cell.

He had ten feet to go, and the thunder of the helicopter's engines covered all sound – yet still some instinct of the fighting man warned the huge monk, and he spun into the arc of Peter's attack. The head under the cowl dropped defensively, so that Peter had to change his stroke. He could no longer go for the kill at the neck, and he chose the right shoulder for a crippling blow. His hand was stiff as a headman's blade and it slogged into the monk's shoulder between the neck and the humerus joint of the upper arm.

Peter heard the collar bone break with a sharp brittle crack, high above even the roar of the helicopter's engines.

With his left hand Peter caught the monk's crippled arm at the elbow and yanked it up savagely, driving the one edge of shattered bone against the other so it grated harshly, twisting it so the bone shards were razor cutting edges in their own living flesh – and the monk screamed, doubling from the waist to try and relieve the intolerable agony in his shoulder.

Shock had paralysed him, the big powerful body went slack in Peter's grasp.

Peter used all his weight and the impetus of his rush to drive the monk's head into the doorjamb of the cell; skull met stone with a solid clunk and the big man dropped face-down to the paved floor.

Peter rolled him swiftly and pulled up the skirts of the cassock. Under it the man wore paratrooper boots and the blue full-length overalls of Thor Command. On his webbing belt was the blue steel and polished walnut butt of the Browning Hi-power .45 pistol in its quick-release holster. Peter sprang it from its steel retaining clamp and cocked the pistol with a sweep of the left hand. It would be loaded with Velex explosives.

The woollen folds of the cowl had fallen back from Colin Noble's head, the wide generous mouth now hanging open slackly, the burned-toffee eyes glazed with concussion, the big crooked prize-fighter's nose – all the well-remembered features, once so dearly cherished in comradeship.

Blood was streaming from Colin's thick curling hairline, running down his forehead and under his ear – but he was still conscious.

Peter put the muzzle of the Browning against the bridge of his nose The Velex bullet would cut the top off his skull. Peter had lost his wig in those desperate seconds, and he saw recognition spark in Colin's stunned eyes.

'Peter! No!' croaked Colin desperately. ' – I'm Cactus Flower!'

The shock of it hit Peter solidly, and he released the pressure on the Browning's trigger. It held him for only a moment and then he turned and ducked through the low doorway leaving Colin sprawling on the stone floor of the cell.

The helicopter had settled into the courtyard. It was a five-seater Bell Jet Ranger, painted in the blue and gold colours of Thor Command – and on its side was the Thor emblem and the words:

THOR COMMUNICATIONS

There was a pilot still at the controls, and one other man who had already left the cabin of the machine and was coming towards the entrance of the cell.

Even though he was doubled over to avoid the swirling rotor blades, there was no mistaking the tall powerful frame. The high wind of the rotors tumbled the thick greying leonine curls about the noble head, and the landing lights lit him starkly like the central character in some Shakespearian tragedy – a towering presence that transcended his mere physical stature.

Kingston Parker straightened as he came out from under the swinging rotor, and for an earth-stopping instant of time he stared at Peter across the stone-paved courtyard. Without the wig he recognized Peter instantly.

Kingston Parker stood for that instant like an old lion brought to bay.

'Caliph!' Peter called harshly, and the last doubt was gone as Kingston Parker whirled, incredibly swiftly for such a big man. He had almost reached the cabin door of the Jet Ranger before Peter had the Browning up.

The first shot hit Parker in the back, and flung him

forward through the open door, but the gun had thrown high and right. It was not a killing shot, Peter knew it, and now the helicopter was rising swiftly, turning on its own axis, rising out over the edge of the precipice.

Peter ran twenty feet and jumped to the parapet of the hewn stone wall. The Jet Ranger soared above him, its belly white and bloated like that of a man-eating shark, the landing lights blazing down, half dazzling Peter. It swung out over the edge of the cliff.

Peter took the Browning double-handed, shooting directly upwards, judging the exact position of the fuel tank in the rear of the fuselage, where it joined the long stalk-like tail – and he pumped the big heavy explosive shells out of the gun, the recoil pounding down his outflung arms and jolting into his shoulders.

He saw the Velex bullets biting into the thin metal skin of the underbelly, the tiny wink of each bullet as it burst, but still the machine reared away above him – and he had been counting his shots. The Browning was almost empty.

Seven, eight – then suddenly the sky above him filled with flame, and the great whooshing concussion of air jarred the stone under his feet.

The Jet Ranger turned over on her back, a bright bouquet of flame, the engine howling its death cry, and it toppled beyond the edge of the precipice and plunged, burning savagely, into the dark void below where Peter stood.

Peter began to turn back towards the courtyard, and he saw the armed men pouring in through the stone gateway.

They were Thor men, picked fighting men, men he had trained himself. There was one bullet left in the Browning. He knew he was not going to make it – but he made a try for the entrance to the stairway, his only escape route.

He ran along the top of the stone wall like a tightrope artist, and he snapped the single remaining bullet at the running men to distract them.

The crackle of passing shot dinned in his head, and he

'Thank you,' she whispered. 'Thank you for coming back to me, my darling.'

Then there was the room at La Pierre Bénite, with its high gilded ceilings and the view through the tall sash windows across the terraced lawns down to the lake. The trees along the edge of the water were in full leaf, and the very air seemed charged with spring and the promise of new life. Magda had filled the room with banks of flowers, and she was with him during most of each day.

'What happened when you walked back into the boardroom at Altmann Industries?' was one of the first questions he asked her.

'Consternation, *chéri*.' She chuckled, that husky little laugh of hers. 'They had already divided the spoils.'

The visitor came when Peter had been at La Pierre Bénite for eight days, and was able to sit in one of the brocaded chairs by the window.

Magda was standing beside Peter's chair, ready to protect him from over-exertion – physically or emotionally.

Colin Noble came into the room like a sheepish St Bernard dog. His right arm was strapped and carried in a sling across his chest. He touched it with his good hand.

'If I'd known it was you – and not Sir Steven – I'd never have turned my back on you,' he told Peter, and grinned placatingly.

Peter had stiffened, his face had transformed into a white rigid mask. Magda laid her hand upon his shoulder.

'Gently, Peter,' she whispered.

'Tell me one thing,' Peter hissed. 'Did you arrange the kidnapping of Melissa-Jane?'

Colin shook his head. 'My word on it. Parker used one of his other agents. I did not know it was going to happen.'

Peter stared at him, hard and unforgiving.

'Only after we had recovered Melissa-Jane, only then I knew that Caliph had planned it. If I had known – I would never have let it happen. Caliph must have known that. That is why he did not make me do it.' Colin was speaking quickly, urgently.

'What was Parker's object?' Peter's voice was still a vicious hiss.

'He had three separate objects. Firstly, to convince you that he was not Caliph. That's why his first order was to have you kill Parker himself. Of course, you never would have got near him. Then you were allowed to recover your daughter. It was Caliph himself who gave us O'Shaughnessy's name and where to find him. Then you were turned onto Magda Altmann—' Colin glanced at her apologetically. ' – Once you had killed her, you would have been bound to Caliph by guilt.'

'When did you learn this?' Peter demanded.

'The day after we found Melissa-Jane. By then there was nothing I could do that would not expose me as Cactus Flower – all I could do was to pass a warning to Magda through Mossad.'

'It's true, Peter,' said Magda quietly.

Slowly the rigidity went out of Peter's shoulders.

'When did Caliph recruit you as his Chief Lieutenant?' he asked, his voice also had altered, softened.

'As soon as I took over Thor Command from you. He was never certain of you, Peter, that was why he opposed your appointment to head of Thor – and why he jumped at the first chance to have you fired. That was why he tried to have you killed on the Rambouillet road. Only after the attempt failed did he realize your potential value to him.'

'Are the other Atlas unit commanders Caliph's lieutenants – Tanner at Mercury Command, Peterson at Diana?'

'All three of us. Yes!' Colin nodded, and there was a long silence.

'What else do you want to know, Peter?' Colin asked softly. 'Are there any other questions?'

'Not now.' Peter shook his head wearily. 'There will be many others later.'

Colin looked up at Magda Altmann inquiringly. 'Is he strong enough yet?' he asked. 'Can I tell him the rest of it?'

She hesitated a moment. 'Yes,' she decided. 'Tell him now.'

'Atlas was to be the secret dagger in the sleeve of Western civilization – a civilization which had emasculated itself and abased itself before its enemies. For once we would be able to meet naked violence and piracy with raw force Atlas is a chain of powerful men of many nations banded together, and Caliph was to be its executive chief. Atlas is the only agency which transcends all national boundaries, and has as its object the survival of Western society as we know it. Atlas still exists, its structure is complete – only Caliph is dead. He died in a most unfortunate air accident over the Jordan valley – but Atlas still exists. It has to go on, once that part which Caliph has perverted is rooted out. It is our hope for the future in a world gone mad.'

Peter had never heard him speak so articulately, so persuasively.

'You know, of course, Peter, that you were the original choice to command Atlas. However, the wrong man superseded you – although nobody could know he was the wrong man at that time. Kingston Parker seemed to have all the qualities needed for the task – but there were hidden defects which only became apparent much later.' Colin began enumerating them, holding up the fingers of his uninjured arm.

'Firstly, he lacked physical courage. He became obsessed with his own physical safety – grossly abusing his powers to protect himself.

'Secondly, he was a man of unsuspected and overbearing ambition, with an ungoverned lust for raw power. Atlas swiftly became the vehicle to carry him to glory. His first goal was the Presidency of the United States. He was using Atlas to destroy his political opponents. Had he succeeded in achieving the presidency, no man can tell what his next goal would have been.'

Colin dropped his hand and balled it into a fist.

'The decision to allow you to reach the rendezvous with Kingston Parker on the cliffs above Jericho was made by more than one man – in more than one country.'

Colin grinned again, boyishly, disarmingly.

'I did not even know it was you. I believed it was Steven Stride, right up until the moment I turned my back on you!'

'Tell him,' said Magda quietly, 'Get it over with, Colin. He is still very weak.'

'Yes,' Colin agreed. 'I'll do it now. Yesterday at noon, your appointment to succeed Doctor Kingston Parker as head of Atlas Command was secretly confirmed.'

For Peter it was as though a door had at last opened, a door so long closed and locked, but through it now he could see his destiny stretching out ahead of him; clearly he could see it for the first time.

'You are the man best suited by nature and by training to fill the void which Kingston Parker has left.'

Even through the weakness of his abused body, Peter could feel a deep well of strength and determination within himself which he had never before suspected. It was as though it had been reserved expressly for this time, for this task.

'Will you accept the command of Atlas?' Colin asked. 'What answer must I take back with me?'

Magda's long fingers tightened on his shoulder, and they waited while he made his decision. It came almost immediately. There was no alternative open to him, Peter knew that – it was his destiny

'Yes,' he said clearly. 'Tell them I accept the responsibility.'

It was a solemn moment, nobody smiled nor spoke for long seconds, and then:

'Caliph is dead,' Magda whispered. 'Long live Caliph.'

Peter Stride raised his head to look at her, but his voice when he replied was so cold that it seemed to frost upon his lips.

'Never,' he said, 'call me that again, ever.'

Magda made a small gesture of acquiescence, of total accord, then she stooped to kiss him on the mouth.